Adorning the Florida coastline stands Poinciana, the fabulous mansion of the Logan family. Inside its regal walls a volcano of intrigue and violent emotion has begun to erupt, and not one of the Logans is safe.

Especially not Sharon Hollis Logan, the lovely young bride of the patriarchal Ross Logan. For reasons unknown to Sharon, Ross seems to be hated by Gretchen, his daughter from a previous marriage, by her ne'er-do-well husband, Vasily, and by Ross's crazed mother, Allegra—and all their hostility is readily transferred to Sharon. But as she tries to find out why, Sharon uncovers a devastating secret about her own relationship with her husband—a secret that, in the end, will test the limits of her courage as well as her ability to love....

PHYLLIS A. WHITNEY

Poinciana

FAWCETT CREST • NEW YORK

POINCIANA

This book contains the complete text of the original hardcover edition.

Published by Fawcett Crest Books, a unit of CBS Publications, the Consumer Publishing Division of CBS Inc., by arrangement with Doubleday & Company, Inc.

ISBN: 0-449-24447-4

Alternate Selection of the Literary Guild
Selection of the Doubleday Book Club

Printed in the United States of America

First Fawcett Crest printing: November 1981

10 9 8 7 6 5 4 3 2 1

For PATRICIA MYRER, who has from the beginning held the hands of every one of my heroines through all their tribulations.

With love and gratitude

With special thanks to my sister- and brother-in-law, Mabel and Lloyd Houvenagle, for making my life so much more pleasant, and for driving me around Florida.

My thanks as well to Leone King; to Helen McKinney of the Library, Society of the Four Arts; and to Elyse Strickland of the Doubleday Bookshop, all of whom helped me with my Palm Beach background.

Chapter

1

Outside the long windows of the library, a Florida March was mild, almost balmy. Sunset light touched fine book bindings, turning polished mahogany rosy, but I sat well away from the windows, huddled in a wing chair and hidden by the deepest shadow I could find.

Though the door was closed upon sounds beyond, I heard someone calling, "Sharon? Sharon, where are you?" I shut out the summons. On a table nearby, the tape recorder played, and I listened only to the singing voice.

I had run frantically from the turmoil in the rest of the house—that turmoil when family and friends gather to console one another and dine hungrily on whatever fare is provided for body and emotions. At Poinciana any feast was sure to be sumptuous, and I had needed to give few orders. The household had been

beautifully run before Ross Logan had ever brought
home a new young wife, and it could run smoothly
without me.

The voice on the tape sang poignantly of "purple
shadows and blue champagne ...." and I steeled myself
against the sound. It was that appealing, throaty quality of voice that could only be Ysobel Hollis whispering
of heartbreak and loss. Heartbreak—when she had
been the happiest woman I had ever known! My
mother. The shivering inside me began again as I remembered. Yet it was not Ysobel who had died two
days ago.

I had come here as Ross Logan's wife, believing that
the very real problems of my life were being solved. I
hadn't known then what it meant to be afraid.

Any death in a household such as this one meant an
astonishing stir in the presses of the world. What plat-
itudes and banalities had been given out—because the
truth was too dangerous to reveal. All the family were
on guard now, even against one another. Jarrett
Nichols, Ross's powerful right hand, stood behind
the story that must be told. None of us were to be inter-
viewed, and the fortress of the house protected everyone
in it. Except me.

Within the house, this had not been protection
enough. Their eyes accused me. Without words, they
were saying, *You are to blame for what happened.*

The taped voice whispered on, and I heard its husky
yearning—*I keep a blue rendezvous ...* I had endless
reasons to find that song disturbing, but I made myself
listen, made myself remember every detail.

For the sake of my own sanity, I needed to remember,
to retrace, to understand exactly what I was doing here
at Poinciana, how I had come to this moment in this
room. Death brings its own sense of unreality, and I
had three deaths to assimilate. Ysobel and Ian—my
mother and father—and now this new and dreadful
one.

Everything had begun—such a little while ago!—on

that afternoon in Belfast in Northern Ireland. My mother, her beautiful, funny face alight, had been singing to children brought to the concert hall from an orphanage. My father was in the wings as always, since Ysobel was something of his creation, as well as the focus of his life. Hers was the magic and the talent, but his had been the imagination to recognize, and to present her to her audiences as she needed to be presented. That day I had been sitting near the outside end of the third row, with children all around me. I'd been watching the children's bright faces as they listened, entranced, to the singing of Ysobel Hollis. She wasn't giving them the sad songs of loss and pain that her adult audiences doted on. These children had enough of that in their lives, so she brought them gaiety and hope and life—something she could do equally well. And I was listening, though not as thoroughly entranced as the children.

We were completely different, Ysobel and I. She had been born in New Orleans, I in San Francisco. The outward differences, as I'd always accepted, were not in my favor. She was small and pert, and her black hair fluffed in curls around her face. I was tall and my hair was blond and straight like my father's. I usually drew it back in a coil on the nape of my neck, emphasizing the difference. My father used to tell me I was beautiful, that I had "good bones." I laughed at his words, never believing. I'd have liked a saucy, upturned nose like Ysobel's and dark eyes that could flash with light, instead of blue eyes that Ross had told me were like quiet seas. *I* knew that my seas were never quiet, but I didn't want the world to suspect, and I wore a careful guise that came to suit me like a well-designed gown.

Father adored Ysobel, of course, and he was dramatic enough in his own right. Ian Hollis, Scottish-American, ex-actor. Though sometimes I wasn't so sure it was "ex." He managed Ysobel's fortunes, handled her publicity, built her into the world-famous musical comedy star she became. He was the impresario personified.

I supposed they loved me, when they thought about
it, and had time. But it was necessary to leave me in
whatever schools were available, from New York to
London to Geneva. Never for a long enough time to put
down roots and make lasting friends, but enough to
give me a background of experience few other children
had. Always in a new place there was the whispering
behind my back, the eager curiosity because I was the
daughter of Ysobel Hollis. Because of this, I was always
engaged in a struggle to be *me*. Until recently, a secret
struggle that I never let the world suspect.

When I grew up, I could travel everywhere with
them, and that was both exciting and smothering. I
didn't mind being useful. Mother said I could dress her
faster and more skillfully for her performances than
anyone else, and she loved to have me do her hair.
Little else was required of me—certainly not to attend
many parties with them, or be present at press interviews. I could understand that a growing daughter
might draw attention from Ysobel Hollis in an unde-
sirable way. As a reward for not being demanding or
too conspicuous, I was allowed to go my own way much
of the time. Strangely, for a young woman, my fantasy
life had to do with museums.

I loved to wander echoing marble halls, until even
the guards came to recognize and smile at me. I could
imagine myself the elegant doyenne of a mansion housing some fabulous collection about which I was wholly
knowledgeable. The Oriental wings drew me especially, and I developed an affinity for Japanese art and
culture. China was too big for me to grasp, but Japan
was more compact, for all its complexity, and I began
to learn about it. Someday I would visit those islands,
even though Ysobel had had no desire to travel to the
Far East. On my twentieth birthday, when Father
asked me what I wanted most, I told him I would love
to own a set of Oriental jade, and he took me to Gump's
in San Francisco, where I chose a pendant of heavenly
clear green, with a gold dragon coiled about it. There

were tiny gold and jade earrings to match, and while my father sighed over the cost, he could give generously on occasion. Ysobel never bothered about money, and she didn't mind. She was never the type for jade.

How foolish and how terribly young I'd been. Perhaps "arrested" was the word! But ready for a terrible awakening.

On that afternoon in Belfast, there was no warning of danger. Ysobel was laughing one moment, singing her heart out, and in the next she was gone in a flash of light and shattering sound.

It was as though the seats around me exploded and I was thrown outward against the wall of the theater. When I opened my eyes the stage was aflame, the wings burning, and there were shouts and screams everywhere. Pain stabbed through my arm, and there seemed to be blood streaming down my face. My brain had given up working properly. There was no way I could reach the stage, and I knew only that I must get as many children as possible out the side door of the hall.

I grabbed and pulled, shouted myself hoarse, and somehow managed to bundle a few of them through the door, starting an exodus, so that others followed. Fright and agony were screaming inside me, yet I went on doggedly, bringing a number of us out to the sidewalk.

I don't know what happened after that. I was told later that I'd collapsed. When I opened my eyes again it was to find that I had been in the hospital for two days. The sister at my bedside hushed and soothed me, refused to answer questions.

Then Ross Logan came. What Ross Logan ordered, people provided. A private room for me, the best of doctors, and Ross himself there at all hours. He had been my parents' great friend for many years and I remembered him from my childhood as an always impressive figure. In London he had heard the shocking news, knew that I was alone, and had come at once by plane. As always, he was possessed of an enormous vitality. Phones around him were never still, and he could talk with equal authority to Washington or Tokyo, London or Bonn.

He sat at my bedside, his athlete's body erect and youthful, because at nearly sixty he still kept himself in top condition. He sounded like the American he was, exuberant most of the time, and always handsome and dynamic—his hair barely touched with gray, an intensity brimming in dark eyes and tightening the corners of his mouth. As I was soon to recognize, he exuded power. I, who had never felt so weak, could begin to learn and trust a little.

It was Ross who told me they were both gone. Ysobel and Ian. They had been killed at once and hadn't suffered, he assured me. I, their daughter, had helped to save a great many children from the fire that had followed the bombing, and was something of a heroine. It was a comfort to me when Ross took over all the dreadful funeral arrangements, requiring nothing of me but agreement. However, the most comforting release he brought me was his own grief. He had loved my parents, he told me, and felt it no shame to weep— so we cried together, and my healing began. I didn't understand until later why he cried, or how angry such tears could be. My own, as well as his.

When I had recovered enough physically, my damaged arm in a sling, he carried me off to his town house in London. His housekeeper, a sensible older woman, took me in charge, and again I need take no action, make no decisions. Ross went away to his business meetings, flew to New York and back again. When he was in London he took me everywhere. To the best plays and restaurants, on a flying visit to friends in Scotland in his own plane. I began to see as never before what a figure of power and importance he represented wherever he went. The press was apt to follow him, and they even took an interest in me, as they would in any woman to whom he paid attention. That I was also Ysobel Hollis's daughter, with a tragedy behind me, whetted their appetite for sensation. Ross handled them skillfully, and escaped them when he could. He seemed to inspire an almost awed respect on every hand, and I began to feel a little giddy in such high-powered company. Giddy, but not very real.

As far as my own affairs went, I was still in a state of shock and unable to plan for myself. I couldn't believe I would never see my parents again, and I was glad for any distraction possible.

My future stretched ahead blank, empty, a question mark. Ysobel and Ian Hollis had been bountiful spenders. I had my mother's few jewels and that was about all. There were astonishing debts. Her income from recordings soon went to pay those off. I had been trained for nothing practical, but must now somehow find myself a job. Perhaps as a model? I was told I might do well enough at modeling. What people called my poise would get me by, with no one ever guessing that it was an outer casing I wore that made me seem cool and confident and remote—with no hint of the disturbing emotions that might be surging underneath. I wanted *not* to be theatrical, not to be like Ysobel—whom I could never emulate anyway—and not to be like my father, who sometimes played at charades. So who was I?

There weren't any permanent men in my life, only casual friends. I'd learned when I was thirteen not to bring young males around my mother. She couldn't resist captivating them. I didn't blame her, but perhaps I grew a little cynical about men before I was old enough to have one of my own. Later on, I suppose I put men off. They didn't know how to smash through the protective glass that encased me, and I hadn't met the man who could coax me outside. They thought I was cold, when sometimes I felt as though I were burning up in futile anger.

"So you're Ysobel Hollis's daughter?" they'd ask, and we would talk admiringly about *her,* while *I* went into hiding and seethed.

My relationship with Ross was something new. I

began to relax a little in response to his enormous charm, his skill with a woman, his tenderness. That he was fifty-six to my twenty-five was only reassuring. A younger man might have stirred up my uncertainties, my resentments, while Ross offered strength and dependability, as well as a total concern with me. A concern such as no one else had ever given me.

He had been married twice before. Helen, his first wife, had died. His second, Brett Inness (as she called herself now), he had divorced. An impossible woman, he said. There was one daughter by this second marriage, and he appeared to love her dearly. Yet when he talked about her, I found myself unexpectedly wary. I knew about fathers who loved their daughters, but were too busy to pay them much attention. Without ever having met her, I began to harbor a secret sympathy for Gretchen Logan.

"She's a difficult girl, Sharon," Ross told me. "Unruly. And too sexual too young. At twenty, she's already had an affair or two and seems quite willing to throw herself away on any man who shows an interest in her. Right now, she's running around with a man named Vasily Karl. He's some sort of Balkan fellow—Rumanian, Bulgarian? Maybe a dash of Hungarian or Russian—who is obviously after her money. I'm trying to put a stop to it, but she's not likely to listen."

I could grieve for him about his daughter, even while I instinctively sympathized with her. By way of advice I offered nothing, but I was a good listener, and Ross liked to talk. Especially about his family.

His father, Charles Maynard Logan, had made his own great fortune and had been the founder of Meridian Oil, as well as establishing the Logan banks. He'd known as well how to spend and how to collect. Among other things, he had collected the midwestern beauty who became Ross's mother, and who gained her own fame as Allegra Logan. Allegra had taken to Florida with enthusiasm, perhaps in reaction to Minnesota cold, coming to the island of Palm Beach in the twen-

ties, and setting her mark upon it. It was there she had
built her fantasy house, Poinciana, flinging down the
challenge to Marjorie Merriweather Post, a lady who
had a few fantasies of her own. Ross smiled a bit ruefully as he spoke of his mother.

"She must have driven her architects crazy, stealing
from Mizner and anyone else whose houses appealed
to her, so that she built a hodgepodge so spectacular
that it made its own name and importance, and no one
dared to laugh."

I gathered that both his parents were gone now,
though he wouldn't talk about their death. Ross had
kept Allegra's creation, and Poinciana was clearly his
favorite place on earth, though he owned several houses
elsewhere. It was to Poinciana that he brought his
father's collection of art and antiques, and it was there
he chose to make his headquarters for at least part of
each year. Let New York and London and Washington
come to *him*.

During those days of our getting acquainted in London, while I convalesced, I began to recognize Ross's
growing interest in me, and I could hardly believe in
what was happening. For the first time in my life I
could fall in love without being fearful of Ysobel. Ross
was vitally exciting and virile, and he aroused feelings
in me that had never been stirred before. The hidden
cynicism I had developed as a protective coating for my
emotions was melting away. The inner turmoil was
dying.

When he brought me a stunning ring of diamonds
and sapphires and put it on my finger, I knew all my
problems were over. Ross would rescue me, protect me,
love me forever. I needn't ever be adrift and lost again,
and *I* would have someone to love.

As he talked to me about his growing up in Poinciana, I began to glimpse its magnificence in my mind,
and the thought of it revived old fancies. I had visited
splendid houses often enough with my parents, and I
had as well all those museum hours behind me. Ross

told me frankly that one of the things that impressed him about me was my background of sophistication and my surprising knowledge of Oriental art. I could accept the latter, but I wasn't sure about that word "sophistication." Disguise was my specialty. Nor was I sure that I could cope with either the legend or reality of Poinciana—though something in me wanted terribly to try.

The house, Ross told me, contained not only the treasures collected by Charles Maynard Logan and his wife Allegra, but Ross's own celebrated Oriental prints, lacquers, ceramics, and Japanese netsuke. The idea of the Oriental collection excited me. All those exquisite pieces of cloisonné and Satsuma, to say nothing of the prints and the miniature world of netsuke art, about which I knew very little at that time, since such collections were rare. My imagination was fired. All my life I'd viewed, but never been able to touch, to hold, to relish. Now all the old dreams were about to come true.

Before I knew it, Ross was making plans. We would be married quietly outside of London to avoid the press, and then we would honeymoon in Japan. I was nearly speechless with delight. I knew that he had been stationed in Japan under MacArthur long ago, and had fallen in love with the country and its people. Later he had been American Consul in Kyoto for a time. He had always been interested in things Oriental, and his wealth and power had made him useful to his government. He could have been an ambassador, had he wished, but he was no career diplomat. The oil business was still the main focus of his life. He was less interested in the banking aspects, but it was possible to make friends in Japan who would further business interests later. That I should match this passion of his for Japanese art made me one woman in a million in his eyes—or so he assured me.

Now and then I would catch him studying me with a look of appreciative delight, yet no hint of warning touched me. No one had ever appreciated *me* before, so how could I not respond? How could I possibly suspect what lay hidden so terribly in the background?

We could stay in Kyoto as long as we liked, since Ross was thinking of early retirement, and there were many executives in charge of Logan interests. He had already stepped down as chairman of the board of Meridian Oil. And the great Logan trusts and foundations, the philanthropies, were in the hands of others, though under the advisorship of a man named Jarrett Nichols, Ross's principal aide and consultant. He had taken Jarrett on some years ago as a young lawyer and molded him into his most valuable assistant and executive. I would meet him when we returned to Poinciana, where he had his headquarters at present, awaiting Ross's return.

There, Ross said, was where we would live. Perhaps even in the summer, if I could face it. He'd always hated his mother's habit of flitting around from season to season, living in different houses. His daughter Gretchen was there now, and it was the house he had grown up in and most wanted me to love. I would be the one to restore it from shabbiness to new beauty. I would understand Poinciana and what Allegra Logan had built. He already knew that about me. What he wanted most of all for himself when our honeymoon was over was to return to Florida and write the book on Japanese netsuke that he had long been planning, and on which he'd done too little work.

I still felt dazed and unable to resist the avalanche that was sweeping me along. What he expected of me in Florida, I would not think about now. A line had been held out to rescue me, and all I could do was cling to it for my very life. If at times I found Ross a little moody, if some communications from the States caused him to be preoccupied at times, I made nothing of this. The oil business was, to say the least, in a state of unrest, and this must cause him considerable worry.

Nevertheless, Ross decided to put all business mat-

ters away from him for now, and this time he would
travel with no entourage. He sent the young man who
was his personal secretary off on a long holiday, and
told Jarrett Nichols by phone to handle all mail and
messages at that end, unless something very important
came up. I was delighted at the prospect of traveling
unencumbered and having my husband all to myself.

Our wedding was quiet, with only a few of Ross's
friends present, and the press for once evaded. There
was no one whom I especially wanted to invite. Before
I quite knew what was happening we were on our way
to Kyoto. Long plane flights were a familiar enough
experience for me, but to travel on Ross's private jet
was something new and exhilarating. Every luxury
was at our disposal, and I became increasingly aware
of the strange world of the super-wealthy that I had
married into.

At the airport outside Tokyo we were besieged by
reporters, but welcoming government officials were on
hand to take us through. We went by one of Japan's
crack trains to Kyoto, and stepped into a quieter and
older world. I could understand very quickly why Ross
had wanted to bring me here.

The Miyako Hotel was set on a hillside with mountains all around, and I loved it at once, as I loved the
temples and gardens, the narrow streets of the older
part of the city that had once been a capital, and which
had never been destroyed by war. The reality of Japan
was even more fascinating than all my reading had led
me to expect. Teahouses and Japanese food were both
attractive under Ross's tutelage, and not a cloud
marred my happiness.

One day in a curio shop, Ross held up a lovely ivory
figurine and said it was like me—exquisite. He bought
it for me, and told me that we would both grace Poinciana on our return. For just an instant, standing beside
my husband in that dark little shop with its unfamiliar,
not unpleasant scent—was it camphorwood or sandal-
wood?—a question flashed through me. What was I

doing here? I was no ivory figurine. Nothing so perfect as that. What did Ross really know about *me?* But reality was dangerous. Reality was a theater in flames and screaming children and the terrible pain of loss. I put it away from me quickly.

Only sometimes when Ross made love to me there was a return of uneasiness. In this one aspect I could only feel that I disappointed him. Inexperienced as I was, I knew only a passive, submissive role, expecting him to teach me, feeling very little myself. He sensed my concern and was gentle with me. Wait until we reached Poinciana, he said. Everything would be better there. I didn't understand, and I wondered uncertainly why it should be different in Florida.

Unexpectedly, I didn't always have Ross to myself during our honeymoon. There were certain Japanese businessmen who came quietly—almost secretly—to consult with him at the hotel. On these occasions I was sent off in a car contributed for my pleasure, to sightsee, or wander in temple gardens. The first time this happened, I asked questions, wanting to share all that interested my husband. But Ross had been curt and preoccupied, and I began to realize that there were some interests he didn't want to share with me. I knew without rancor that this would be a fact of marriage that I must accept.

Then something shattering happened in Kyoto, cutting our visit short. A long-distance call came from Jarrett Nichols, and I was with Ross in our suite at the hotel when he picked up the phone. I saw the dark flush of anger rise in his expressive face.

"We'll come home at once," he told Jarrett. "I'll cable arrangements as soon as they're made." When he hung up, he turned to me, more shaken than I'd ever seen him.

"Gretchen has married Vasily Karl," he said. "Totally against my wishes. And they've moved into Poinciana."

I wondered to myself how he could expect anything

else, considering that he was so seldom with his daughter, but I said nothing, watching his anger in alarm. I had never seen him in a rage before, and it was frightening. When he stamped out of the hotel and went walking alone in the streets of the city, I went into the garden beyond the glass walls of the dining room and sat trying to be quiet and calm, watching goldfish dart about in a small pond.

Again I found myself thinking about Gretchen. After all, her father had given her no warning of *his* marriage to me. He was foisting an unknown stepmother upon her with no preparation. A stepmother only a few years older than Gretchen herself. He had never even told me how his daughter felt about Brett, her mother. Now I couldn't help wondering if Gretchen's sudden marriage was a deliberate slap in the face for a father she might both love and resent.

I knew what that feeling could be like. Love for one's parents could very well be mixed with a flavoring of resentment. I had been raised to recognize that Ysobel's career was all-important in our lives. Yet sometimes I'd thought rebelliously that she and Ian might have come for a birthday, wherever they'd left me, or even have brought me to them. Christmas at school, with Ysobel and Ian across a continent, could be utterly lonely, even though they phoned and sent me wonderful gifts. As I sat waiting for Ross's return, I began to hope that I could win Gretchen's liking, let her know that I could understand, that perhaps we weren't too far apart and might be friends. I longed suddenly, unexpectedly, for a friend, and knew with disturbing clarity that true friendship was something I would never find with Ross. A man didn't make friends with an ivory figure on a shelf. Certainly not a forceful, vibrant man like Ross.

We were to have stayed in Japan through cherry blossom time, but when Ross returned to the hotel he was the man of action again. All had been arranged. We were going to Tokyo tomorrow, flying home the day after. First, however, we would make one more visit here in Kyoto.

We took a taxi to a small Japanese house off a side street and enclosed by a high bamboo fence. There were dwarf pines and the usual fishpond in the garden, with a little red lacquered bridge arched across it.

A bowing Japanese woman wearing a kimono led us to stone steps, where we could sit and remove our shoes. Then we followed her into the house, through sliding paper shoji, padding across springy straw tatami, climbing polished stairs to a room that opened upon a narrow wooden gallery overlooking the garden and nearby rooftops of gray tile. An old man with a fringe of white hair rose from his cushion to greet us. He was dressed in the old-fashioned way in a fine silk kimono of charcoal gray, with a small white crest on each sleeve.

He bowed deeply, then gave his hand to Ross Logan in a warm clasp of friendship, and I knew there was respect between these two. I was presented to Gentaro Sato with a formality that emphasized this respect. Cushions were brought for our comfort and I sat cross-legged, unable to fold my knees under me for long, as Japanese women did. A low tray-table was brought in by the woman, set with a flowered teapot that had a curved bamboo handle, and accompanying small, handleless cups. She poured our tea and offered a plate of bean paste cakes shaped like four-petaled flowers of pink, green, and white.

I looked for the alcove I'd read about, with its single treasured vase and flower, the hanging kakemono, and other spare ornaments of art. But in this room something different was evident. On shelves here and there were displayed tiny carved objects, some with cords threaded through them. These were netsuke. I'd seen them occasionally in museums here and there.

"Sato-san is a sculptor who makes fine netsuke," Ross told me. "Not for sale to the public as a rule, but

to satisfy his own creative talent and preserve an old
art form that is being lost."

Mr. Sato rose, went to a shelf and made a selection,
returning to hand me a tiny wood carving. "For you,"
he said.

I thanked him warmly, and turned the beautiful little thing about in my fingers. It was no more than an
inch and a half wide—a carving of a mother frog with
a baby frog clinging to her back, one foot set carelessly
over its mother's eye. There was humor and great delicacy in the carving, and the detail in so small an object
was amazing. The eyes of both frogs were inlaid in shell
and black coral.

"Netsuke aren't popular in Japan any more," Ross
said. "When men used to wear the kimono, they tucked
pouches into the obi band around their waists, with the
netsuke on a cord with a sliding bead, hanging outside
to anchor the pouch."

As I listened, I had no idea that these little objects
were to become so important in my life—and so disturbing. But I realized that the art had fired Ross's
imagination, and he was ready to go on talking about
them.

Unfortunately, the creation of so utilitarian an art
had not been properly valued in the past, and the carv-
ers were often neglected and unappreciated. Even the
museums of Japan had been negligent about collecting
them, so that it had been the foreigner who had delighted in this miniature art, and taken most of them
out of the country into private ownership. Ross himself
had a fine collection at Poinciana, which he was eager
to show me.

When I commented on the charm of the little frogs
Mr. Sato had given me, he motioned gently toward the
garden, where there were undoubtedly real frogs in the
fishpond.

"My teachers," he said, and I looked about at the
carvings with new eyes. Some were pure fantasy, or

based on myth or legend, but even those were glimpses of life and nature as one man perceived them.

Apparently Gentaro Sato now sold some of his own modern work to a few respected collectors, but he also kept an eye out for such ancient netsuke as surfaced from time to time around Japan. He harbored a slight bitterness against his country for not having placed sufficient value upon such artists and their work in the past. Ross had promised him that someday his own private collection would be given back to the government of Japan, to form a nucleus of netsuke art.

When his business with Gentaro Sato was concluded, and a neat wooden box had been packed with several carvings Ross had chosen, we returned to the hotel and prepared for our journey home.

All that evening, Ross continued remote and preoccupied. Once I tried to talk to him about Gretchen, but he closed me out with a coldness I hadn't seen in him before. It was as though he said, "Keep your place. Don't touch my real life," and I found myself alone again. Alone and bewildered. It was his very directness that I'd most admired, and now he seemed coolly evasive.

That night I put on a kimono of golden chrysanthemums that Ross had given me, and that he'd been delighted to see me wear. But when I went to him he looked at me as though I were suddenly a stranger, and turned away. Later, I lay on my side of the bed, finding that I was still shut out, and that for the first time since our wedding there were no loving arms to hold me. I told myself that his strangeness was not due to me, or anything I had done. Undoubtedly the news about Gretchen had upset him, and he would come back to me in time.

Nevertheless, I lay awake for a long while that night. Once during those hours when he became aware that I wasn't sleeping, he touched me lightly and repeated those strange words he'd spoken before: "It will be better when we reach Poinciana," and again I asked myself: *Why?*

From Tokyo we flew to New York for a brief business stopover—a trip many hours long, even by private jet. Ross was still preoccupied and distant. This time we couldn't avoid the press and we were besieged with questions that Ross handled skillfully out of long experience. He spoke for me and I said very few words and smiled a lot. We stayed overnight at the Pierre Hotel, rather than open up the New York apartment, and the next day we continued on the short flight to Florida. It was midafternoon when we reached the West Palm Beach airport.

There I had my first glimpse of the elegant Rolls that was only one of the cars that would be at our disposal at Poinciana. Albert, the Logan chauffeur, met us, attended to our baggage, and answered Ross's rather testy questions as to why neither Jarrett Nichols nor Gretchen had come to meet us.

It seemed to me that Albert, after his first smile of greeting, was edgy and uncomfortable.

"Miss Gretchen had an accident this morning, Mr. Logan," he said. "I understand it was nothing serious. She—uh—fell on the stairs coming down from the belvedere. Mr. Nichols thought he should stay at the house until you arrived."

Ross was anything but satisfied. "Gretchen is as surefooted as a goat, so what happened? Where was this new husband of hers?"

Albert busied himself putting our bags in the trunk of the car. "Sir, he seems to have gone out. I'm sure Mr. Nichols will explain."

Albert was past middle age and belonged to an older era, his behavior impeccable and correct. Ross had told me that he had been with the family for a long time, and I suspected that he knew very well what had happened to Gretchen, but he would say nothing at this time. Especially not in front of me.

Ross helped me into the luxurious back seat and

plumped himself down beside me. I had looked forward
to having him show me Florida, but Albert's news had
disgruntled my husband, and I watched the passing
landscape in silence, continuing to feel a little lost.

This was one state I had missed in my travels with
Ysobel and Ian, and I found it different from any place
I'd known. The country seemed to be made up of palm
trees and sand, and a land as flat as the ocean we had
flown over, its rises marked only by condominiums.

At least I had done my homework on Palm Beach,
and I knew that the Intracoastal Waterway flowed into
Lake Worth, which bordered most of Palm Beach on
the west. The island was only thirteen miles long, and
a mere three quarters of a mile at its widest. Beyond,
to the east, lay the ocean.

We crossed at a bridge near the Bird Sanctuary and
drove along South Ocean Boulevard. On our right, as
the road dipped near it, ran a continuous stretch of
beach, and I had glimpses of whitecaps out on the water.
Large houses, most of them dating back to the twenties
or earlier, came up on our left, and I saw the trademark
of red-tiled roofs that belonged to the Spanish revival
that architect Addison Mizner had created here. Most
of the houses were of stucco or stone, since wood rotted
easily in the salt air, and they were painted pink or
cream, or a dazzling white. Between the houses and the
ocean a natural sand dune rose in protection, and sea
grape grew rampant everywhere, its big tough leaves
a dirty rust color at this time of the year. Inland they
were greener.

The houses faced the ocean behind walls and hedges,
though only Poinciana and one or two others occupied
property that ran through from ocean to lake. Behind
most of these ocean houses were streets and other
houses that fronted on Lake Worth. Those that faced
the ocean had marvelous views of the Atlantic from
their upper windows, but their residents had to cross
the boulevard to reach their private beaches.

Everywhere, palm trees grew tall—the stately royal

palms as well as slender coconut palms that leaned away from the prevailing wind.

"Here we are," Ross said, and my heart jumped. I hadn't lost my sense of uneasiness about coming to Poinciana.

A high wall of coquina rock, with bright hibiscus growing against it, ran along on our left until it reached wide gates with pillars of the same coral rock on either side. Once these gates must have been fashioned of wrought iron, but now they were modern steel, and were electrified. At a beep from Albert's horn, they swung open away from us, and a man came out of the gatehouse and touched his cap to Ross Logan. We drove in, following a curved way that led between well-trimmed ficus trees, and I had my first unimpeded view of the house.

Allegra Logan's fantasy had indeed been just that. Poinciana was built of rosy stone brought from the Spanish Pyrenees, and decorated with roofs of red tile. This was not Spanish architecture, however, nor, in fact, any sort of identifiable architecture. It jutted here, and indented itself there, in a rapturously experimental way, inviting amazement, inciting in me an eagerness to explore. Commanding the entire rambling structure was a high, curiously domed cupola, with windows and a tiny balcony all around. This must be the belvedere, on whose stairs Gretchen had fallen. What a view there must be up there, I thought, and planned to climb it as soon as I could. Off to the right, beyond the house, I could glimpse smaller cottages, with their own red-tiled roofs. The grounds, Ross had told me, occupied some thirty acres, and the house was rooted sturdily into an ancient reef of coral, hurricane-proof.

As we neared the porte cochere, he slipped an arm about my shoulders, and I turned to him eagerly. Ever since we'd left the airport I had felt alone and increasingly anxious.

"Welcome to Poinciana, darling," he said. "I want

you to be happy here. I had always hoped that Ysobel would visit this house someday, but there never seemed to be time in her busy life. So I'm glad her daughter has come to us."

It was a strange welcome, and I could have wished that the emphasis had been less on my mother. Nevertheless, I turned to him eagerly, relieved by this thawing of a remoteness that had seemed to shut him away from me.

Albert drew the Rolls up before an arched entrance, the huge, carved front door set well back for weather protection—an impressive door of heavy Florida cypress, with brass ornamentation. It opened as we mounted the few steps, and I knew that my life at Poinciana was about to begin.

Chapter

2

A woman stood framed in the open doorway. She was tall and rather heavily built, and wore a trim gray skirt topped by a white blouse. Her hair was even blonder than my own and had been coiffed into a complex of coils pinned neatly and securely on top of her head.

This, of course, was Mrs. Broderick. Helga Broderick, who had come here from Norway as a young girl in Allegra's day, later marrying an American, Tom Broderick. Tom had once been in charge of everything outside the house, but he had died a few years ago, and Mrs. Broderick was a widow. All this I knew from Ross's previous briefing. He had also warned me that she was never to be considered a servant, even if I'd been likely to use that term. She was an administrator, and one spoke of the "staff" in referring to employees. Allegra Logan had been nothing if not democratic, for all that she lived like an aristocrat.

Ross shook hands with Mrs. Broderick warmly and introduced me.

"Welcome to Poinciana, Mrs. Logan," Mrs. Broderick said, but her handclasp offered no warmth and her pale blue eyes dismissed me quickly. Obviously I wasn't up to exclusive Palm Beach standards, and for a moment I felt subtly diminished. I could never live up to Allegra's measurements, I was sure, but something in me stiffened. I mustn't think like that. Perhaps Mrs. Broderick would need to live up to mine.

"Mr. Nichols will be right down," she said to Ross, stepping back from the doorway. "He is with Miss Gretchen. There has been an unfortunate accident—though nothing serious."

"Albert told me," Ross said. "I'll go up at once. I want to know what happened."

Mrs. Broderick bowed her head in compliance. "Miss Gretchen—that is, Mrs. Karl—and her husband have moved into the south wing," she added.

Ross nodded, his mouth tightening, and motioned me in ahead of him. Albert had already vanished around to the rear with an armload of bags. I stepped into the entry hall and forgot everything else as its stunning impact struck me.

It was an utterly beautiful and formal room done entirely in red and white, and not as large as might have been expected in such a house.

The walls were covered with tapestried silk the color of Chinese lacquer, the square of floor was white marble, lightly veined, and a suspended white stairway rose on the left, carried upward by wrought-iron balusters and rail. The lacy iron curved across the back of the hall at half-level, without visible support, and then turned toward the front, the treads vanishing as they reached the upper floor. The underside of the stairs gleamed white as they performed their act of magical balance.

Straight ahead at the half-level, white columns framed the red of a wall that held portraits, except for one conspicuously blank in the center. Beneath the floating stairs, more columns framed a door at the back, guarded on each side by marble busts on tall pedestals. Where the stairs began, a pot of Sèvres porcelain held a glowing rhododendron.

I must have been standing open-mouthed, for Ross put an arm about me, laughing. "Allegra used to watch for just that reaction the first time any guest stepped into her house. That stairway is still famous in architectural circles."

"It's *so* beautiful," I said. "It takes my breath away. Yet for all its formality the room seems almost modern. Perhaps a classic modern."

Ross approved my words. "My mother could do things like that. She had the imagination to fly ahead into new worlds at times. She didn't want marble staircases and the ballroom-sized entry hall that Flagler chose for his home, so she created this out of clouds and made someone build it for her."

"I already admire her tremendously," I said.

In some strange way, he seemed to withdraw a little from the warmth in my words, and went on more coolly. "The empty space up there above the stairs used to hold a portrait that Sargent painted of Allegra. It's at the Metropolitan in New York now. Perhaps we'll replace it with one of you."

"Oh, no!" I said too hastily, and he laughed again. I hadn't earned the right to be up there, and I wondered uncomfortably if other wives had hung there too, and been in turn removed. But that wasn't fair. I tried to cover my haste. "I'm going to love everything about this house."

"Don't be too sure yet," he said in the same cool tone. "It's a difficult house to know. But come along. I want you to meet Gretchen before we settle into our rooms."

I wasn't sure this was wise, under the circumstances, but I knew better by now than to object to anything that Ross proposed. We mounted the beautiful white stairs and I touched wrought iron lightly. The handsome foyer hardly prepared me for the drab and rather shabby hallway that stretched across the wide front of the house. Once its carpet had been rich with glowing color, but now it was faded and threadbare. Here and there a Louis Quinze chair or console interrupted the emptiness, and the flowered wallpaper was peeling in one corner.

"So much neglect, as you can see," Ross said. "Some of the house has been kept up, but Allegra would hate what has happened to the rest. Poinciana needs you, Sharon."

That pleased me more than anything. I wanted to be needed, and I meant to live up to what was expected of me. Somehow.

The curious architecture of the house became evident as we followed the hall. Other corridors turned off at odd angles, and unexpected flights of steps led up or down. At the end of the hall, double doors of mahogany had been closed across the far apartment. Near the doors a tall, red-haired man in jeans and a blue pullover stood beside a table talking on a telephone. He gave Ross a salute of finger to temple, glanced at me with appraising gray eyes, and went on speaking in a low, assured voice.

Ross didn't knock, but opened the far doors that gave upon a formal parlor, and crossed it to a door that stood ajar upon a darkened bedroom. Here he tapped a warning of our presence.

"Gretchen?" he said. "Gretchen, I'm home. I missed you at the airport. What's all this about a fall downstairs?"

"Go away!" said Ross's daughter.

The words made no impression on her father. He pushed the door wide and drew me with him into the bedroom. It was high-ceilinged, with two tall windows across the front. Draperies of some light, neutral material had been drawn across to shut out sunlight and leave the room in shadow. I could barely make out the double bed with its rumpled covering, and a dark head just visible on the pillow, Bits of clothing had been strewn around the room and I stepped over a scuffed sneaker.

Ross advanced upon the bed, leaving me to stand hesitantly near the door. "None of that now! Sit up and let me have a look at you. I want you to meet Sharon."

The girl under the covers groaned deeply and flung a sheet over her head.

"Open the draperies, please," Ross said to me. I wanted to escape, but there seemed nothing to do but obey, permitting bright Florida sunlight to flood the room.

Gretchen bounced indignantly and tried to burrow further under the covers. To my astonishment her father reached out and grasped the bedclothes, pulling them down, and when Gretchen would have turned over to hide her face in a pillow, he pinned her shoulders with both hands so that she had to look up at him.

Gretchen Karl was developing a very colorful black eye.

"So!" he said, as she went limp under his hands. "That creep hit you, didn't he? No fall downstairs did that."

"Oh, Daddy!" Gretchen wailed, and held out her arms. Ross sat on the side of the bed and enveloped her in an angry hug.

I slipped quietly back to the hall, postponing any introduction, and found the man at the telephone just hanging up.

"Hello," he said, and held out his hand. "I'm Jarrett Nichols, Mrs. Logan. It's too bad this had to happen right when Ross was coming home."

When I'd shaken his hand and murmured some agreement, I could find nothing more to say, and I stood in uncomfortable silence, waiting for someone to tell me what to do next. What had happened to that poise I was so noted for?

"Anyway," he went on, "it's a good thing you're here, both of you. I don't believe in feuds."

"I didn't know there was one," I said hesitantly.

He seemed to concentrate on me for the first time since that initial cool look in my direction, and I stood my ground and studied him back, starting at the top of his tousled red head. Somehow, I had expected that the man in whom Ross put so much trust would be older—and different. More polished in appearance perhaps, and not so informally dressed. The gray eyes I'd already noted were emphasized by scraggly red brows, his nose had a slight bend in it that was not unattractive, and his chin had a fighter's look. Above it, the mouth was unexpectedly tender in a face so strong— though I had a feeling that this man smiled very little. I felt wary with him at once. Like Mrs. Broderick, he was ready to weigh me and find me wanting.

"Mm," he said, finishing his own appraisal. "You don't look much like Ysobel Hollis."

"Did you know my mother?" I asked directly.

"Not really. I met her a few times. And of course I saw her on stage. What happened in Belfast has hit everyone who admired her. I'm sorry about all that horror you've had to go through."

He sounded sorry enough, but my distrust remained, and I was glad of that glass case I could close around me, concealing what I felt. I had always backed away from talk about my mother, however admiring. And now I did so more than ever. Ysobel was in the past and it was safer for me if she stayed that way.

"You've come as a surprise to this house," he went on bluntly. "You might as well be aware of that."

"Marrying Ross was a surprise to me, too," I admitted.

His look continued to measure, but told me nothing of his conclusions. "Never mind. It's done and you're here. I suppose we'll all get used to one another."

Again, a strange welcome. I wished Ross would come and rescue me from this outspoken man.

"What do you think of the house?" he asked when the silence grew between us.

"I haven't seen much of it yet. The foyer downstairs took my breath away. I'm eager to learn more about Allegra Logan. Did you know her?"

"A remarkable lady," he said, but there seemed an odd inflection in his voice, as though he held back when it came to any discussion of Ross's mother.

Again there was silence, and Jarrett Nichols went a bit impatiently to the door of Gretchen's suite and looked in. Ross beckoned to him from the bedroom, and he left me with apparent relief. It was obvious that he did not approve of Ross's marriage and that all he could offer me was cool courtesy. Never mind—I could play that game, too!

Just talking to him, I had begun to feel geared for resistance. How often in the past I had lived in a state of quiet combat. Even inside a glass case, one could be quietly stubborn. This wasn't what I wanted now, but I had to find my own way to acceptance and respect, and I'd had more practice at this sort of resistance than Ross dreamed. I mustn't bristle, but I wouldn't be put down either.

At that moment Mrs. Broderick reappeared around a far corner and came toward me. "Would you like me to show you to your room, Mrs. Logan?"

I glanced toward the open door of Gretchen's suite and saw that Ross and Jarrett were already deep in discussion. It occurred to me wryly that I hadn't been formally dismissed by Ross as yet, but it was time to make a choice.

"Thank you," I told the housekeeper, and followed her down the hall.

She led the way along a secondary corridor past a flight of circular steps that ran upward.

"That's the way to the rooms in the belvedere," she told me. "Mr. Logan's mother had a sitting room up there at the top, and her nap room, as she called it, was just below. We've prepared a room for you next to Mr. Logan's, down this corridor, though of course you may want to make changes if you are going to live here."

I knew very well the customs of the rich. In Ross's case there was a house in East Hampton and in Virginia, and the apartments in New York and London, but he had spoken as though he might not make the usual seasonal exodus. He never minded hot weather, he'd told me, and had thrived on it as a boy, just as his mother did.

The wing we were now in seemed to extend at a right angle from the back of the house toward the lake. At the end of the corridor were two open doors, and Mrs. Broderick gestured toward the one on the left.

"This is the Ivory Room. Mr. Logan's room is on the right, with a connecting door between." She stepped back to let me enter ahead of her.

The room was indeed ivory. Pale and beautifully elegant—a silken room with hardly a touch of color except for light yellow draperies and a golden pillow on the chaise longue. A perfect room for a woman who lived in a glass case, I thought, and wondered why I felt depressed.

"Your bath is over there," Mrs. Broderick said, her feet whispering across the champagne carpet. "The dressing room adjoins it and I see that Albert has brought up your bags. I'll send one of the maids to unpack for you, Mrs. Logan."

I told her that I preferred to unpack for myself, and she indicated the bell, in case I wanted to summon assistance.

"Or you can always reach me on the house connection," she added. "Just dial three."

I looked into the bathroom and found it enormous, with mirrors and gilded fixtures, and a great deal of old marble, including the huge sunken tub. The gold rug would be furry and soft, shielding one's feet from the marble floor.

In this suite there was no shabbiness and I wondered if Brett, Ross's second wife, had done it over for herself.

"How large is the staff at Poinciana?" I asked, moving back to the bedroom.

"We're somewhat shorthanded these days. There are only eight of the indoor help at present. Not including kitchen and laundry, of course. I want to consult with Mr. Logan about hiring more when he has time. Though help is difficult to find these days, and in any case Mr. Logan doesn't like a house cluttered with people. The maids are supposed to keep out of his sight as much as possible. So you'll need to ring if you want anyone. Of course, old Mrs. Logan had at least seventeen servants in the house when she was in residence here." Apparently Mrs. Broderick didn't mind the word "servant" if it wasn't applied to her.

The fact that she hadn't considered consulting with me about the hiring didn't disturb me. I had no feeling that I was in any way mistress of Poinciana as yet, but merely a stranger, visiting.

Looking about at all this ivory perfection, however, I felt an urge to muss up the pillows, rumple the well-dressed bed, set the furniture askew.

"This wasn't Allegra Logan's bedroom, was it?" I asked.

Mrs. Broderick permitted herself a faint smile, and the intricate coils of her blond hair dipped slightly in my direction. "No, this wasn't one of Mrs. Logan's rooms. She preferred richer colors. That is, in the old days. Her rooms have been shut off for a long time. We don't use them any more. There's no need, with so many other rooms available and empty. Mr. Logan has done very little entertaining here for many years." She hesitated. "Though of course that may change now."

If there was a question in her voice, I didn't know the answer, and I remained silent.

"Old Mrs. Logan designed and furnished the entire house originally," Mrs. Broderick went on, a hint of pride coming into her voice. "Though I worked for her only in her later years, I know what wonderful taste she had. She knew all about the antiques and fine paintings her husband had collected, and often she brought in experts to advise her. Until—" She broke off and I had the same sense of something suppressed that I'd had with Jarrett Nichols.

"What happened to her?" I asked, trying to sound casual. I was beginning to feel increasingly interested in the woman who had built this house. In some ways she seemed more alive to me than those I had met within its walls.

Mrs. Broderick's expression reproved me for my question. "Perhaps Mr. Logan will be better able to tell you about that. If there is nothing else you wish, Mrs. Logan, will you excuse me? Word that you were coming was rather sudden, and there has been much to do to get ready. Dinner will be served at eight, but Mr. Logan usually likes cocktails downstairs around seven-thirty."

When she'd gone, I stood for a moment lost in thoughts of Allegra. There always seemed to be a sense of hesitation when her name came up, as though something of importance was being held back. I had been ready to admire her as the creator of Poinciana. In her role as mother, I wasn't so sure. Talented and dramatic mothers could often leave something lacking where their children were concerned, but this had not seemed to be the case with Ross's mother. After all, she had done a spectacularly good job with him. Hadn't she? Anyway, I had other things to think about now.

I stopped pretending to be sure and in command of all I surveyed.

Across the room were arched doors that opened to the outside. I stepped through them eagerly and found myself on a wide upper loggia floored in terra cotta tiles. Moorish arches framed the view of the lake and ran along past a series of rooms, mine being one of them. Tiled steps led down to a pebbled courtyard, where tropical trees grew against the walls of the house, and bougainvillea clambered to the roof. Beyond, a wide lawn sloped toward the lake, its lush green dotted with coconut and royal palms. Strange to think that in the beginning there had been no palm trees in

Palm Beach. They had all been imported when the island was built up from its sandbar state.

In the distance, from the other side of the house, I could hear the ocean murmuring, rushing up on a beach, but on this side the lake lay calm and blue-gold in warming sunlight. Out on its waters a sailboat moved under power toward one of the bridges, and on the far side rose the buildings of that busy commercial city that was West Palm Beach.

As I knew, Palm Beach itself had been the invention of Henry Flagler, Rockefeller's partner in Standard Oil. He had seen the possibilities for an exclusive resort, and had run a railroad down to make the island accessible. It had been reclaimed from its wilderness of sand and shell and scrub growth into very much what it was now. Then he had built West Palm Beach across Lake Worth, to house, as he said, those who would serve the wealthy on the island of Palm Beach. West Palm Beach had thrived and spread and continued to marvel at the fantasies of the rich islanders whom it often served.

I turned against the rail of the balcony and looked about at what I could see of the house. It rambled away in all directions without apparent plan—which made it all the more interesting, though, as Ross had said, Allegra must have driven her architects mad in its building. Dominating all else, rose the tower that I'd heard referred to as the belvedere. There were windows and a balcony up there beneath the curiously domed roof that would command a splendid view in all directions. I liked to think of that room as belonging to Allegra, and I was already calling it Allegra's Tower in my mind.

At the far end of this pleasant arched loggia, with its long chairs intended for sunning, a small door of carved cypress had been set into a rounded bulge of wall—obviously not the door to a bedroom. I went to it and turned the brass knob. Circular walls closed around me as I stepped inside, and I felt along the edge of the door for a light switch. When I touched it a ship's lantern that hung from the ceiling came on, lighting a narrow flight of stairs curving away at my feet.

I smiled, remembering a secret staircase in a castle I had visited with Ysobel and Ian in Portugal. Clearly Allegra had loved her little surprises. Holding to the rail, I descended the flight and tried the knob of another closed door. Nothing seemed to be locked, and it opened easily. Once again I caught my breath in astonishment, as I'd done when I first entered Poinciana.

The room was enormous, its shadowy length cut into by long beams of sunlight from the tall windows at one end, turning it into a golden room, bathed in yellow light. Truly a golden room, I thought, for unless I was mistaken, the coffered ceiling was done in gold leaf, and so were panels along the end wall. No furniture occupied the center of the great room with its gleaming parquet floor, but there was a recessed dais for an orchestra, and little French chairs of tarnished gilt and frayed satin stood in place all the way around the walls, like guests waiting for the music to begin.

I wished I could have seen Allegra dancing here! What beautiful gowns she must have worn. Perhaps some of them were still hanging in the closets of her unused rooms. She must have been a great beauty in her time, and in that vanished era such parties must have been given regularly here as were never seen today.

Feeling like Cinderella wandering in a deserted palace, I walked across the room, peopling it in my mind with waltzing couples. No—not the waltz! Those were the Scott Fitzgerald days, so they'd have been dancing the fox-trot, and perhaps those who were young and daring would have Charlestoned madly across the parquet floor. More than ever, I wanted to see a picture of Allegra, wanted to know more about what she had been like.

A sound surprised me into turning and I saw that a door nearby had opened and a man stood staring at me. I recognized the uniform and cap of a guard, and after an instant of startled exchange, he touched a finger to his cap.

"Sorry, Mrs. Logan," he said, and the door closed quietly as he disappeared.

Ross hadn't mentioned guards, but I supposed they would be necessary at Poinciana, where several valuable collections were housed. For the first time, I had a sense of walls, not only holding out the world, but imprisoning those who lived here as well.

I shook off the fancy impatiently. Certainly I could come and go as I pleased and the walls had nothing to do with me. But now I had better find my way back to the other part of the house. Across the ballroom were wide double doors, arched and gilded, but I would explore where they went another time. I ran up the stairs and through the cypress door to stand at the loggia rail again. Someone shouted below me, and as I watched, a boy of about ten came running into sight, with a small nondescript brown dog at his heels. He slid to a halt on the grass as he saw me, while the dog leaped around him.

"Hello," I called down. "My name is Sharon Logan. What's yours?"

He didn't answer me directly, though his curly red hair hinted at his identity. He simply stared at me for a long, unblinking moment before he spoke.

"So you're the new one?" he said.

He was like his father, blunt. "And you must be Jarrett Nichols's son? Do you have a name?"

"Sure. It's Keith," he informed me. "Keith Nichols. Gretchen said you were coming."

And she hadn't said it flatteringly, I suspected. "Do you live here?" I asked.

"Of course. All the time. My father stays here when he's not in New York or Washington or someplace. We live over there in Palmetto Cottage. That's the one closest to the lake." He waved an arm, but from my balcony the cottage was out of sight around the next wing of the house.

"What a wonderful place to grow up in," I said.

He nodded, and as his look moved to the right and left of me, I sensed in this boy a certain proprietorship about the house.

"Anything you want to know about Poinciana, you can just ask me," he said. "I know things *they* don't know. Things *she* told me."

"You mean Mrs. Logan?"

"Of course." Gray eyes that were like his father's seemed suddenly bright with mystery. "Come on, Brewster!" he shouted, and boy and dog went racing toward the lake.

Brewster? Whose whimsy was that? He had spoken of his father and himself living at the cottage, with no word about a mother. And what was all that about some mysterious knowledge concerning the house? Well, the Nichols family was not my affair. There was too much else to occupy me now.

I turned back to my ivory room and began to unpack, while water ran in the marble tub. I hadn't recovered from jet lag, and a hot soaking would be pleasant. But first I went to the door of the adjoining bedroom and tapped on the panel. There was no answer and I opened it, feeling almost surreptitious.

The room matched my own for size, but there was nothing of feminine elegance here. The big bed was covered by a woven hemp-colored spread, and the window draperies were of the same natural weave—suitable for warm weather. An easy chair of red leather sat near the inevitable fireplace—that could also be needed in Florida—and above the mantel hung a colorful hunting scene, with red coats on horses that were dashing for a fence. An open cabinet revealed a record player and stereo set, making me wonder what Ross's tastes were in music. There was still so much to learn about my husband, but now, with an oddly guilty sense of spying, I closed the door and went to take my bath.

Later, dressed in a silk tunic and trousers of pale coral, I sat at the rosewood dressing table and brushed my hair, wound its coil at the back of my neck, and tucked in a tortoiseshell comb. Then I opened the fawn leather jewel case that had belonged to Ysobel and took out the jade my father had given me. In the padded ring tray were emerald earrings that were Ross's gift, but for tonight I chose the jade. The golden chain that suspended the dragon pendant held jade beads at intervals along its strand, and when I put it over my head the green glowed with life against the pale coral of my tunic. When I'd fastened the matching earrings in ears that Ysobel had long ago caused me to have pierced, I was ready.

There was an instant, looking in the mirror, when I had the feeling that all this luxury was playacting. Make-believe. Out there somewhere was a real world where women worked for a living, and no one had eight indoor servants, let alone seventeen, or a house with a hundred rooms.

Ah well, I would playact for a while longer. Never in my life had there been enough money to do anything I wished. Ysobel might spend as she pleased, but I had never been permitted more than a small allowance. Everything was bought *for* me that I might want. So now I might as well enjoy and try to become accustomed. Nevertheless, it still seemed unreal, and sooner or later I would have to come down to earth and find something useful and interesting to do. Goodness only knew what, since apparently I was not expected to run the house or get a job.

Earrings secured, I searched the jewel case for the tissue-wrapped netsuke of frogs that Gentara Sato had given me in Kyoto. Once more I admired the intricate delicacy of the carving, and especially its subtle humor. If a frog mother could wear an expression that spoke for all maternal tolerance, this little frog wore it. Obviously, she was fatuously satisfied to have her heedless child put his foot in her eye.

There were holes for the cord, so perhaps I could have it made into a pendant. I really liked it much better than the ivory figurine Ross had given me, and which was still locked away in a trunk.

A light tap sounded at the door. I set down the frog carving and turned about on the dressing table bench to call, "Come in."

A curly head of dark hair popped around the edge of the door, and a pair of bright green eyes regarded me speculatively. Then a dimple appeared in one cheek, and a small, rather pert woman pranced in. She was probably thirty-eight or forty, but her manner seemed more youthful.

"Pranced" was the word. She moved rather like a pony, and she skittered around the room without the slightest by-your-leave, looking all around before she came opposite my bench, where she stopped to smile at my astonishment.

"Hello," she said. "I'm Myra Ritter." The accent was slightly Germanic. "And of course you are the new Mrs. Logan. Ysobel Hollis's daughter. Mm."

That considering "Mm" was already familiar to me. "I know I don't look like her," I said dryly.

Myra's smile broadened. "I wasn't going to say that. I thought you might be feeling a bit oppressed and that a friendly face would help. Do I look friendly?"

I recognized that she wasn't being impertinent, or rudely familiar. She was clearly an original and it was evident that neither Poinciana nor its occupants impressed her to a point of subservient respect.

I had to smile. "Thank you. You've given me a name for yourself, but I still don't have an identity to go with it."

"Sorry! The room rather stunned me. Though I should be used to the house by now. I'm Mr. Nichols's assistant. That sounds better than secretary, doesn't it? I was just leaving and thought I would look in on you first. There's been quite a stir about your coming, as you can probably guess. I've only worked here a few months myself, so I know what it's like to spend your first days at Poinciana. At least I can get away at night. I don't think I'd stay if the pay wasn't so good!"

By any of the "proper" social standards that I had been quietly resisting most of my life, what she was doing was entirely outrageous. But she was being human, and I immediately liked her for it. Also, Myra Ritter, as I would come to know, had the ability to fly to the heart of a problem, discarding the extraneous. There was a shrewdness in her, seasoned by an enormous curiosity that she hadn't the slightest interest in stifling.

"Thank you for coming," I said. "Everything is strange and quite wonderful, but I don't really believe in any of it yet. Won't you sit down?"

She dropped into a chair and crossed a pretty pair of legs. She was young enough in years, yet older in intuitive wisdom, and she possessed a rather intense vitality.

"Money is always real," she observed. "A very practical matter when one doesn't have much of it. Though I find I can adapt to all this quite easily. But then, as I say, I can go home to my little apartment every night."

"Tell me about yourself," I said.

She pursed her lips thoughtfully. "I was born in Vienna, but my parents brought me here when I was very young. I've been to school in Switzerland. I've worked at all sorts of jobs, here and there. Both in America and abroad. There was a marriage that broke up. Not a lot to tell, really."

We chatted for a moment about schools in Switzerland, though mine were different from hers. I wondered if she might inform me about other members of the household. There was so much I needed to know.

"What is Mr. Nichols like to work for?" I asked.

"Considerate. Most of the time. He works very hard and he suppresses his suffering. Sometimes I think Americans can be as inhibited as the English. And the men of course are worse."

I had no idea what she meant by the word "suffering."

She went on without my asking, quite ready to gossip. I suppose I should have stopped her, but I didn't. "Perhaps you don't know? His wife died in an auto accident two or three years ago. There was some question about what really happened—whether it was suicide on her part. He's a very good father to his son but the loss has been hard on both of them."

I felt both shocked and sorry. "How dreadful," I said, and wondered why Ross had never mentioned the tragedy. "I'm still ignorant about a great deal," I went on. "I know some of the things that Mr. Nichols does for my husband, but just what do they encompass?"

She cocked her dark head on one side, grinning impishly. "I might quote one of the Mellons and say that Jarrett Nichols hires *presidents* of companies. Perhaps that's not it exactly, but he does keep on eye on all those Logan Foundations, among other things."

The picture of enormous power was coming clearer, but I turned from it with a conscious effort. "This house is what fascinates me. All the care Allegra Logan must have given to building and furnishing it!"

Myra nodded. "Yes—a fabulous lady. I've been reading about her in books from Poinciana's library. She must have been very dramatic and willful when she was young, and always given to getting her own way with all her husbands. There were three of them, as you probably know. The first two she couldn't stand and threw out. But I gather she was faithful to Charlie Logan all his life. There are several books in the library downstairs with whole chapters on Allegra Logan. Everything she did was news. And she's the one who started a lot of the philanthropies Mr. Logan keeps up, and which Mr. Nichols helps to administrate. It's his job to check new causes they might invest in. Tons of requests come in every year. Of course it's all wonderful for tax saving, and of course makes Meridian Oil look soundly virtuous."

Clearly, respect for the Logan empires was not uppermost in Myra Ritter's mind, and I didn't especially care.

"This is the first time I've met Mr. Logan," she went on, "though of course I've talked to him by long-distance on any number of occasions, taking messages for my boss."

Apparently, she had sat still long enough, and now she jumped up. I was to learn that Myra never made smooth, easy movements. She jumped and darted nervously, and now she skittered toward the door.

"Just wanted to say hello. I'll run along now. Don't let Gretchen put you down." Again there was that intuitive leap to an understanding not altogether welcome, so that I felt unmasked.

She waved her fingers and disappeared through the door, closing it briskly behind her. For a moment I sat staring at its panel, not entirely comfortable at having been seen through so easily. It was as though with Myra Ritter my protective glass casing didn't exist. She had seen straight into the uneasy truths that hid at my very core. Uncertainty and self-doubt had seemed visible at a glance to this odd little woman.

I turned back to my mirror and used my lipstick brush. So Gretchen was sure to be a problem. I wished I had asked Myra about Vasily Karl, the "Balkan" husband. It would be more useful to know about him than to study Allegra Logan's life in the library downstairs—much as the idea appealed to me. Had he really given his wife a black eye? And if he had, what would Ross do—throw him out?

These were questions that would eventually answer themselves. Now that I was dressed, there was still time before cocktails, so I might as well move about the house, learn to find my way through its maze. I stepped into the corridor and met Ross coming from the stairs. He hurried to put his arms around me, then held me away.

"Beautiful, Sharon! That coral silk becomes you. You

do have an elegance your mother never had. You make me very proud, you know."

What my mother had had was love. Love pouring out to her from every audience she faced, love cradling her from her friends, and most of all, Ian's enveloping love. Mine too. At least I had been eager to give it whenever she had time to accept the giving. But such a thought came close to something I'd never had the courage to face fully, and I moved away from it now, pleased that Ross had compared me with Ysobel and found her wanting. Ross was one man whom Ysobel would never have been able to manage.

He had returned to me fully, and when he kissed me I felt again the marvelous warmth of his protection. All my uncertainties could go into hiding, and I need only drift with Ross's arms around me and be forever safe. I thrust back the small inner voice that asked if this was all I wanted of life—just to be safe?

"Where are you off to?" he asked.

"I thought I might wander about the house for a little while. Get acquainted with it. I've already found the ballroom. Do you mind?"

"Of course not. It's your home now. I'll give you a proper guided tour tomorrow, but you can explore in the meantime. I'll shower and change, and then join you downstairs. Have fun."

His second light kiss sent me on my way, and I knew this wasn't the time to ask about Gretchen.

Much of the upstairs floor, as I discovered in my roaming, was shut off and unused. Allegra had obviously done a great deal of entertaining in her day, and there must have been times when every room was full. But now bedroom after bedroom closed its door upon whatever life remained in the house. All were beautifully, tastefully furnished, though a little frayed and worn. Often they had their own sitting rooms, and fine paintings hung on their walls. Allegra must have liked the French moderns, and it was surprising to find a Cézanne sketch or a Renoir watercolor tucked away

casually in a sitting room where no one came any more.
The art collection downstairs was undoubtedly fabulous.

Once Mrs. Broderick heard me opening and closing
doors, and came out of her own room to ask if she could
help me. I thanked her and went on in the face of what
I sensed as disapproval. To her I was still an intruder,
but she would have to get used to me.

Looking out a window, I discovered for myself the
servants' wing, set on a lower level from the main floor,
and apart from the house by a roofed passageway.

Of course the tower drew me. I wanted to see it when
I was alone, and not with anyone who would instruct
and inform. Information could come later. Right now
I wanted to sense Allegra as she must once have been.
If old houses were haunted by ghosts, then Allegra's
must surely walk these halls, and perhaps had already
begun to haunt me, filling my imagination, leading me
in a direction in which I felt compelled to go.

I found my way to the iron treads that circled up to
a third-floor level in the tower, and climbed, clinging
to the rail. The steps opened from a landing into a room
where all the shutters were closed and little light penetrated. There was a musty odor, a slight dampness,
and what furniture remained had been shrouded in
white covers.

The stairs led me upward, and I climbed to the top
level, where window shutters stood open, and a breeze
blew in from the sea. At one side a door opened onto
a tiny, circling balcony, and I went through it to stand
high above the red-tiled roofs of the house. It was like
being at the top of a lighthouse, and I loved the mild
wind on my face, the view of ocean breakers rolling in
upon a narrow strip of beach. I could see the swimming
pool down there, and the tennis court. But the room
itself interested me even more, and I returned to examine it.

Here no shrouding had been done. Comfortable rattan furniture covered with bright chintzes invited one.

Across one corner was set a small desk and chair. Allegra had perhaps come to this tower room to free her mind when it was troubled, to feel close to the shaggy tops of the palm trees outside, and to view sky, sea, and lake, as they were visible from every window.

This, however, was not an unused room. An open portfolio of photographs lay on the desk, and tacked on the brief space of wall between windows were double photos in black and white. Both were pictures of Ross, and I went to stand before them, my interest caught.

Each was an action shot in which Ross had been moving toward the camera. In one he was striding free, his arms swinging, athletic and handsome, as I had so often seen him, his head up and eyes alight with characteristic vitality. He seemed to move with force and purpose and that eagerness for life that I loved in him, since it was the force that had brought me back to life.

The other photograph was in startling contrast, and it disturbed me deeply. Again Ross moved toward the camera, but now his arms were bent at the elbow, fists clenched, as if he were running. Late sun threw shadows slanting across his face, giving it a look of dark fury. I had never noticed that faintly diabolic slant of his brows before, or the way deep lines could etch his mouth, giving it a sinister look. Yet in this picture too he was driven by some vital force, so that he charged at the camera angrily, as though he meant to destroy it.

The contrast between the two shots was startling and unsettling. In the one picture, he moved into sunlight with confidence and courage, and you knew he was a man who could do anything he chose. In the other, he charged like a bull and the force that drove him was destructive—an ancient, dangerous force that grew out of some terrible frustration and despair. Only a despairing man could be as angry as that.

"What do you think?" said a light voice behind me. "Which one do *you* think he is like?"

I whirled about and knew that the small, sturdy

young woman in tight jeans and plaid shirt must be Gretchen Karl. If no other clue was given me, the spreading purples of the bruise about one eye would have been enough.

Chapter

3

"Hello," I said. "I'm Sharon. I hope I'm not intruding up here. The tower drew me, and your father said I might explore."

Her expression reminded me of the dark look worn by the man in the second photograph, with no smile, no brightening of the dark eyes that stared at me. She was examining me carefully, rudely, detail by detail from head to toe, and I stood quite still, meeting her searching look.

Then she said coldly, "You'll be just fine for his collection." Her meaning was clearly insulting.

I tried to ignore her manner, studying the picture again, searching for something to say.

"You haven't replied to my question," she went on. "What do you think of those photos?"

"I only know the man on the right," I told her quietly.

"I've never seen the other one." Or had I, briefly, that last night in Kyoto?

"He tried to smash my camera on the day that was taken." Her lips twisted wryly. "I grabbed it and ran—so I saved the picture."

"What was it that made him so angry?"

Her eyes flashed with the indignation of memory, and she moved her head so that black hair, cut in the thick, swirling bob that Sassoon had stamped upon the country, flew out, and then fell back, with every strand in place.

"He was angry with my mother—and so with me for defending her. It's a wonder he didn't kill her one of those times before they were divorced. You have something to look forward to if you haven't seen him angry yet. My father can be a very destructive man."

She was throwing out one challenge after another. Antagonism toward me seethed in her voice, in her contemptuous look. Yet I wanted to make some tentative gesture toward her that might lessen this hostility. I glanced down at the open portfolio of photographs on the desk.

"You're very good," I said. "Do you do this professionally?"

"I don't do anything professionally." But her tone softened just a little and she seemed to relent. "The library asked me about exhibiting some of my work, and I've been wondering whether to let them."

"It's a wonderful idea. Have you picked out the pictures you might use?"

"I couldn't make up my mind."

"May I look at them?"

For an instant, I thought she might refuse, but she shrugged instead and flung herself into a rattan chair, legs outstretched, toes upturned in dirty sneakers. I was uncomfortably aware of my silk tunic and trousers and Saint Laurent perfume. I had a feeling that she disapproved thoroughly of everything about me.

Trying to move as quietly as though I were in the

company of a wild animal cub, I went behind the desk
and sat down. One by one, I turned over the large glossy
prints, now and then setting one aside, aware of her
watchfulness that was still guarded and suspicious.

The photographs were good. Very good. "You've a
special gift for seeing," I said. "The lighting is exactly
right and your subjects come to life. But a photographer
has to see quickly and choose the perfect instant—
which you've done. These pictures are never static."

"I hate studio portraits," she admitted.

"They'd be easier to do than this. It takes tremendous
skill to catch someone in motion at the one precise
moment." I was speaking the truth, but if I'd thought
to win her with it, I'd failed.

"What the hell do you know about it?" she challenged.

"Very little. I know more about painting. Mostly
from visiting museums when my parents parked me
somewhere while they traveled."

I could sense her thinking about that, but I said
nothing more, turning the pictures again. One photograph stopped me. It was of a young woman standing
against a strange, many-trunked tree, looking up at a
boy of five or six stretched upon a massive branch above
her head. I had met an older version of the boy—Keith
Nichols.

Gretchen came out of her chair to see which picture
had caught my attention. "That's Pamela Nichols, Jarrett's wife. Was. She's dead."

I looked more closely at the slim figure in Bermudas,
her dark hair thick about her shoulders, her small,
rather humorous face tilted to look up at her son.

"She doesn't look unstable," I said. "Myra Ritter told
me there was some concern about possible suicide."

With a quick, violent movement that startled me,
Gretchen reached for the print and ripped it in two,
tossing the pieces on the floor. Then she closed the
portfolio with a slap.

"That's enough! I'll pick the ones I might show myself. If I show any."

For an instant I considered trying to talk to her about the really good prints I had pulled out, but I knew this wasn't the time. I rose and came around the desk, moving slowly toward the stairs.

"This is a charming room," I said. "Was it your grandmother's?"

Her voice changed. It was a voice that could show lively color and resonance, or could be as light and wispy as air. Now she sounded wistful.

"Yes, it was Gran's. I haven't changed a stick of it since the days when she used to come here." She went around the desk and dropped into the chair I had left, suddenly forlorn. "I miss my grandmother. She was the only one around here who knew how to be kind. She would tell me what to do—if only she could!"

To my dismay, tears spilled over as I watched, and rolled down her cheeks. She wept openly, like a child, and I wanted to comfort her, but dared not make a move, certain of rejection if I did. Instead, I turned my back and went to look out one of the windows, my eyes following the driveway that wound between ficus trees toward the front gate. What did Ross really know about his daughter? I wondered. Had he any idea that she was as lonely as this, that she still longed for her dead grandmother? How little parents really knew about their children.

I spoke softly. "Your father was disappointed when you didn't meet him at the airport today."

She raised her head and stared at me with tear-blinded eyes. "I hate airports!"

I agreed. "Airports are for saying goodbye. I hate them too."

For just an instant there was a hint of understanding between us. Then her rejection of me surged back.

"Why did you have to come here? You'll be sorry! He makes everyone sorry!"

I edged toward the stairs. There was nothing more

I could say to her now. Just as I reached the top step, however, a man came rushing up, brushed past me and threw himself across the room, to kneel and envelop Gretchen impetuously in his arms.

"My darling! How I've hurt you! Will you ever forgive me?" It was all theatrical and more than a little startling, but Gretchen's face lighted and she leaned into his arms for comfort.

"It was my fault, Vasily," she told him, her wet cheek against his. "What could you do with a wildcat coming at you? You're the one who must forgive me."

Embarrassed by this outpouring, I turned away. I had found that retreat was the only solution when raw emotion reached out to engulf me. That was what throbbed in this room—raw, ungovernable emotion. Fury, despair, anguish, love, were all a part of it, and it was more than I wanted to face. I'd started down the stairs when Vasily Karl left his young wife and came to grasp my hand and draw me back to the room, speaking with his precise, foreign-born English.

"No—don't go, please. You are Sharon, yes? This is all very unfortunate, but we are glad to have you here. I was a devotee of your mother's. I saw her many times in London, Paris, Rome. My heart goes out to you in your loss."

I kept my head down, shrinking from being pulled into this vortex. "Thank you. I must go downstairs now and find Ross."

He continued to hold my hand, restraining me, so that I really had to look at him for the first time—and I received a shock. Somewhere, perhaps a long time ago, I had seen this man, and recognition seemed to carry with it a sense of unpleasantness, even of fear.

He was not someone to be easily forgotten. Probably in his mid-thirties, he was rather thin, with blond, waving hair and a face that just missed being too good-looking. It was his eyes, most of all, that gave me a sense of remembering. They were very dark in contrast to his light hair, and with a slightly Oriental tilt. A short white scar lifted the edge of his right eyebrow, giving him a permanent expression of cynical surprise.

"You are very lovely," he said. "Mr. Logan is to be congratulated."

I ignored this. "I've seen you somewhere before, haven't I? Surely we've met somewhere?"

The hand that held mine gently, yet with such strength, was long, with slender, sensitive fingers, and it tightened slightly on mine. He bent his head to kiss my hand in a gesture that was natural to him, and then looked at me with an amused, almost sleepy expression.

"Had I ever met you, Mrs. Logan, I would remember," he said.

I withdrew my hand firmly, further embarrassed, and this time he let me go. Without looking back as I went down the circling stairs, I knew that he watched my flight, and that perhaps he was not altogether amused. I *had* seen him somewhere before, and not under happy circumstances. That much I knew, though memory eluded me. The answer would probably return when I wasn't searching for it. Now all I wanted was to put the tower room behind me.

Outbursts of theatrical emotion were not unfamilar in my life. Both my father and mother had lived at a top vibrancy of feeling, and in self-defense I had learned to insulate myself. I was glad that most of the time Ross was the cool businessman, who would never let himself go in an emotional tantrum. I had seen him angry, but even then it was a sternly controlled anger that got him whatever he wanted. Certainly I had never seen the dark, destructive side that Gretchen had caught in her photo. At least I didn't want to think I had.

Now I searched for the floating stairway that had brought me up from the foyer, and when I found it I followed its descent past red walls and white pillars, until I reached the marble floor below. The double doors beneath the stairs were open, and I could see a fire burning across a vast room. Ross stood beside a scrolled black marble mantelpiece, glass in hand, waiting for me, and I was struck again by his distinguished good looks.

In relief at the sight of his calm presence, and aware of soft and soothing colors, I crossed the gray-green carpet to a chair of rose brocade drawn beside the fire. Candles had been lighted in delicate girandoles that reflected their gleam from the walls, and here and there a lamp shed further subdued light on the elaborate and exquisite room. Pale draperies of rose damask were pulled across windows closed against the chill of evening. From one large wall a large classic mirror framed in thin gilt gave back the scene, increasing the room's depth and width still more, and adding a further glow of rose and gold.

With a sense of luxury, I sank into the chair, accepting the glass Ross brought me, and let all thoughts of what had happened in the tower room flow away from me.

"I wish we could have the house to ourselves," Ross said. "Perhaps that time will come. At least we can have our own rooms. Tomorrow you must look through the house and see if you find something that suits you better. I've been using my present bedroom for years whenever I came here for visits. But now I'm going to stay and work on my book, so we might as well settle in."

"The book on netsuke?"

"Of course. I've been working on it off and on for some time, and Gretchen's been doing the color photographs for it. Tomorrow I'll show you my collection, and perhaps you can help me with it."

There was unexpected fervor in his words, as though this was something he cared about with a passion that I'd not seen in him before. I had an odd sense of revelation—but of what? It was as though some basic emotion had surfaced in Ross that was new to me, and I wondered why it made me slightly uneasy. But he was waiting for my response, and I gave it hurriedly.

"I'd love to help, if I can. And of course I'm eager to see your collection."

He was pleased with me, and that very fact warmed and reassured me. I sipped my drink, sitting quietly before the fire, and for the first time in a long while I began to feel entirely at peace. As though, at last, I had come home. Ysobel would have been astonished, and perhaps Ian too. They had always seen me as an adjunct to themselves. Someone not quite grown up as yet. Someone for whom marriage lay in the distant future— if ever. Ysobel had sometimes been openly doubtful about my appeal for men. Too cool and chaste, she'd said, teasing me, and had never suspected the small, angry flame that had leapt inside me at her words.

Now I was mistress of this stunningly beautiful home, and I could have anything I wished, do anything I wanted. Though it might take a little time to convince myself of that. Most of all, I had a husband who loved and needed me, and I would never again doubt my own appeal for a man.

"You're looking pensive," Ross said. "What are you thinking about?"

I had no words to tell him. I had never learned how to express what I was feeling, and I was afraid of being laughed at for the turbulent emotions that could boil up inside me. So now I withdrew into being matter-of-fact.

"There's so much to consider. So much that is new. So much to learn." It was time now to tell him. "I've met Gretchen and Vasily," I said.

The sense of peace was shattered in an instant. Ross came to my chair with a quick movement that set his drink tilting to the rim of the glass.

"He's had the gall to come back? I hope Gretchen has told him where to get off. If she hasn't I'll see him myself and do it for her!"

"When I left them they were in each other's arms

and she was telling him that it was all her fault. It sounded as though she may have instigated their quarrel."

"Nonsense—a little thing like that! There's something vicious about that fellow. He actually struck her! Of course he only married her for her money, and the sooner she wakes up, the better."

I wondered if I should tell him of my sense of recognition when I'd met Vasily Karl, but with nothing definite to recall, it was too nebulous to talk about. Besides, my sympathy was really with Gretchen and I had to make some mild protest against his words.

"Perhaps Gretchen needs someone of her own in her life." After all, *I* knew what that yearning could be like.

"There are plenty of men in America. She could have her pick."

"Perhaps he *is* her pick. She looked very happy in his arms."

"I won't have it! I won't have my daughter exploited. He'll wind up breaking her heart."

Though I knew I shouldn't, I went on. "Why don't you wait and see? Isn't her happiness worth it?"

His expression was colder than I'd ever seen, and I wondered with a faint twinge of disloyalty if he was capable of considering Gretchen's happiness. This was a man who possessed a power that I was only beginning to understand. Presidents listened, financial empires trembled at Ross Logan's edicts. What he commanded must be done. I had begun to recognize this in small ways as we traveled together, and I saw it in the attentions and services that were paid him, and paid me because I was with him. But could a man who had found his way to such a position learn to accept defeat in anything? Was that what made him strong—refusing ever to be defeated? If so, there might be a painful time ahead for Gretchen and Vasily, and I wondered if his daughter could be equally strong in order to fight him. Her rage was very great. I had already seen that. But had she the iron in her to best him?

Ross sipped his drink and looked at me again, his gaze softening. "I'm sorry, darling. I don't want anything to spoil our first night together at Poinciana."

I was a little like Gretchen, I thought with unexpected clarity. When Ross looked at me the way Vasily looked at her, I melted. I wanted so terribly to be loved, cared for, protected, and I didn't want to live with my guard up all the time.

Shortly before dinner was announced, Jarrett Nichols came into the room, greeted me with distant courtesy, and accepted a scotch and soda from Ross. Again I was conscious of his striking red hair, and of the strength this man too seemed to exude. Though it was a different strength from Ross's. Not so much a power that commanded outward events, but something inner that could be relied upon by others. This was undoubtedly why Ross depended on him, trusted him implicitly. And because of this I wished he might look at me with less antagonism.

Jarrett, as became clear quickly enough, was here at Ross's invitation. I gathered that he usually dined with his son in their cottage when he was at Poinciana, but tonight there were more business affairs to discuss.

A butler, whom I hadn't seen before, came to announce dinner, and we went down an inner hallway to a pair of open doors. On the threshold I stopped to view a room that was a perfect picture in itself.

"Allegra again?" I said.

Ross smiled. "My mother believed that any room worth doing must be seen like a painting on first sight."

A painting it was, done in glowing pink and silver gray. The walls were of pale gray satin, the Directoire chairs, about an oval table, upholstered in deep pink moiré. Mantelpiece and ceiling were a cloudy gray, and a shining Waterford chandelier hung above the table, glass tapers alight. A centerpiece of luscious pink rhododendron graced a cloth of heirloom lace.

Ross's hand guided me to my chair opposite his at

the long end of the oval. Places were set for only three and Jarrett sat between us.

"This is the family dining room," Ross told me. "There's a larger, more formal room for grander affairs. In Allegra's day it was used frequently, but this was one of her favorite rooms. Brett had these chairs done over, but the rest is just as it was in my mother's time, and the colors have never been changed."

I sipped white wine and thought again of Allegra Logan. She must sometimes have been a little bizarre and ostentatious, yet capable of creating this room of delicate beauty. A lady of contrasts and great imagination. Once more I saluted her and hoped humbly that her spirit would bear with me.

"How old would Allegra be now if she had lived?" I asked.

Ross glanced at Jarrett before he answered—a look I didn't understand. "Ninety-two," he said. "She was thirty-six when I was born. There were two other children ahead of me who died. A girl and a boy."

I was aware of Jarrett, staring at his plate in a fixed way, and remembered his previous withdrawal at the mention of Allegra's name. There was something here that I didn't understand.

I began to spoon my cream of parsley soup, and it was Jarrett who finally turned the conversation to me by asking how I had liked Japan.

I told him of our visit to Mr. Sato in Kyoto, and about the gift the old man had made me of the mother-and-child frog netsuke.

"Perhaps I can have it made into a pendant," I said. "It's so beautiful and I would love to wear it."

Ross looked shocked. "Of course you will do nothing of the kind. That is a valuable collector's item. Tomorrow you can bring it to the netsuke room and we'll find a proper spot for it."

For just an instant I wanted to protest that the carving had been given to me, that he had no right to order what I should do with it. But I wanted no quarrel, and he was probably right, so I said nothing, though I was aware of Jarrett's frank look upon me. A look that might be derisive. My intense awareness of this blunt red-haired man made me uncomfortable. What did it matter if he didn't like me? I turned away quickly.

For the rest of the meal, Ross talked mostly with Jarrett, and though my attention wandered now and then, I became aware of a certain tension growing between the two men.

"I'm out of all that," Ross was saying. "I haven't been on the board of Meridian for more than a year."

"You're still the major stockholder and you vote. Your influence isn't likely to be overlooked. You know very well that new explorations for oil are vital. Ours should be moving ahead a lot faster. You need to urge this on personally."

"You worry too much," Ross told him, and gave his attention to the steak that had been perfectly broiled with mushrooms.

Yet even while Ross ate his dinner with obvious relish, I grew aware of a certain choler that had arisen in him. A flush had mottled his face at Jarrett's words, and I wondered at its cause. Jarrett himself seemed coolly controlled, betraying nothing, and he let that particular topic go and turned to less irksome matters. I wished I might ask questions, learn more about my husband's empire, but I knew that I lacked the knowledge to ask with intelligence, and that probably both these intimidating power figures would regard any words of mine as frivolous and ignorant. If I wanted to learn, I would have to go about it in more indirect ways.

We finished the meal with a sherbet, and I became increasingly aware that I would not be needed in this house for the planning of meals. Not that living in hotels and schools had prepared me for a kitchen. But sometimes I had the whimsical wish that I might be turned loose with a cookbook and assorted pots and pans, just to see what adventures might await me in that unfamiliar world. At Poinciana it was likely to stay unfamiliar. Of those who worked here, no one but Mrs. Broderick had paid me the slightest attention, and I was quite aware that her acceptance of me had been laced with polite disapproval. I had yet to earn my wings.

After dinner, Jarrett returned to his cottage, and Ross went up to my room to fetch me a shawl. We walked outside, and the sound of traffic seemed far away beyond the coquina rock walls that guarded Poinciana. Nearby sounds were only the rattle of the wind in palm fronds and the rushing of waves onto a beach. What a perfect jewel of a world! An antique if not archaic jewel, really, to be thus removed from everything that was ugly and painful and threatening. All those things that had hurt me so deeply could never touch Poinciana.

I walked with my arm through Ross's, safe in my imaginary sphere, able to believe for a little while that clocks could be turned back, and that a life like this was still possible.

Lights burned in the windows of several cottages and I waved a hand in their direction. "Who lives down there?"

"Some are empty. They were guest cottages in Allegra's day. Jarrett and Keith and their housekeeper occupy the largest. A few of the staff who've been with us a long while live down there if they have families. Let's go this way. I want to show you something."

We walked around the front of the house and toward the boulevard, where Palm Beach traffic went by. Ross led me to a locked gate, which he opened, and we went down several steps to a stone passageway that led under the road. Allegra had seen to everything, including a private way to the beach.

The echoing stone tunnel was damp, but it was free of debris and had obviously been swept. I could feel the rush of the wind through the arched openings as we approached the ocean. Another short flight of steps, another gate, and we were out on the sand. Off to our right were the tennis court and swimming pool. I smiled to myself, remembering what someone had told me about Palm Beach: "Nobody who is anybody swims in the ocean." But *I* would.

The beach ran the length of the island—not very wide, and bordered by sea grape on the land side. We went to the water's edge, where the sand was packed damp and firm, and walked together, my hand in Ross's. Though the beaches along here were private, no one could be barred from walking the sand, but no one was out tonight. Beyond the sea walls and the road, the great houses, their windows alight, seemed remote and of another world. The world of the rich and the favored that I didn't really belong to.

Appropriately, a huge Florida moon hung over the water, and I smiled to myself, thinking of Ysobel's *Moon Songs* in a long-ago album, remembering that I'd thought them sentimental, when she herself was not. Tonight I could dare to be sentimental myself. The scene about us was so beautifully, unbelievably romantic, and I knew when Ross slipped an arm about me as we followed the strip of sand that he was feeling it too. Under his breath he began to hum an old song that Ysobel had helped to popularize—"Blue Champagne." I might have wished that he had chosen some other tune, but I would not let thoughts of Ysobel trouble me now.

Perhaps anticipation is one of the essential parts of lovemaking. To be close and to know what lies ahead, so that excitement begins to build in a warm awareness of what is to come. How lucky I was to have been chosen by a man like Ross. A man who knew every tender, arousing touch of love, who knew what a woman wanted. Especially a woman who had known so little about love until now.

When he bent his head to kiss me, my mouth responded and I felt the tiny pulse awaken in my lips.

"Let's go up to the house," he said, and we turned

together and walked quickly across the sand, eager now, hurrying back through the tunnel.

High in Allegra's Tower, a light burned, but I turned my eyes away from it. I didn't want to wonder who was up there. I didn't want to think of Gretchen and Vasily, but only of Ross and me. Tonight there would be no repetition of that strange rejection I'd experienced on our last night in Japan. Tonight we were ready for each other. Perhaps more than we'd ever been before. I remembered that he had told me everything would be better at Poinciana, and I was beginning to understand what he meant.

Up the lovely front staircase we floated, and at the door of my room he let me go. "Come when you're ready," he said, and went through the next door.

Even though eager haste befuddled my fingers, I undressed tidily. Living in schools taught one not to drop clothes heedlessly about. When I'd put on a gown of sheerest chiffon, I sat at the dressing table to remove my jade earrings. For just an instant, my eyes rested on the frog netsuke, and a feeling I didn't want to entertain ran through me. He had no right... But I wouldn't think of that now. For this whole entrancing night I would think only of Ross and of how much I loved him, how much he loved me.

As I moved barefoot toward the closed door to his room, I heard the sound of instrumental music starting—the same tune he had hummed earlier down on the beach. How lovely, how perfect! How well Ross understood that a woman needed the romantic. I adored that beautiful sentimental tune, and I no longer minded his choice. I knew it would make just the right background for our expression of feeling for each other.

I had reached the door, my hand on the knob, when the singing voice began—and I froze. That was Ysobel in her old recording, and for a moment I couldn't move. The idea of music was beautiful, but not my mother's voice singing to us at a time like this. *I keep a blue rendezvous...* It was all wrong, jarring. Wrong for some instinctive feeling in me that perhaps went back to my childhood. Perhaps a confusion about sex and love—and what one's mother mustn't know. A confusion about my own feelings toward Ysobel.

Quickly I opened the door and went into the room. I meant to go straight to the stereo and turn it off, but I never reached the machine. Ross was there, waiting for me.

"Come here," he said. "Come here, my darling," and there was something in his voice that I had never heard before. In one terrible, rending realization, I understood. And there was nothing I could do. Short of utter rejection, there was nothing at all I could do.

I heard the note of undisguised sexual feeling that could throb in Ysobel's tones, and knew that it held and stirred my husband as I had never been able to. Stirred him because *she* was in his mind.

I went to him slowly, unable to help myself, and he held me in his arms as he had always done, yet with a difference. That I had stiffened in something like horror seemed to matter not at all. For him, I wasn't there as myself. He held another woman, from another time, and made love to her with a passion I had never felt in him before. A passion tinged with a strange hint of anger, though he had never been rough with me, as he was now. And all the while Ysobel's velvety voice cradled us in its warmth. A warmth that was totally false. Though this was a bitter thought that I had never accepted fully until this moment, when it helped to make what I had believed was Ross's love for me equally false. I lay beside him while tears wet my cheeks. He never knew. He had fallen into a deep, satisfying sleep, after pouring out his love for Ysobel through Ysobel's daughter.

Chapter

4

Ross had always awakened early, and I was adjusting to the same pattern. I heard him rise and go into his bath, and I got out of bed hastily and fled to my room. There must be no repetition of last night, and I was glad that he had spent himself, as a younger man might not have done.

Under my shower I tried to wash myself clean of memory. An impossible wish. What had happened had completely shattered me. For most of the night I had lain awake with my thoughts churning. The escape from the past, from Ysobel herself, that Ross had offered me, had been no escape at all. If I believed in what had just happened, then all my newfound confidence as a woman must be denied. As always, I was nothing—Ysobel everything.

But morning light could bring a remembered courage, a lessening of night terrors. A slow, deep anger began to grow in me—against them both. Against Ross and Ysobel. If this was what Ross wanted in me as a wife, he must be shown how wrong he was, no matter how furious that might make him. I recalled the photographs Gretchen had taken of her father. I had seen in it a man who could charge furiously, like a bull, and I shivered.

Moving automatically now, I dressed in cream-colored slacks and a silky shirt of pale amber, braided my hair into a thick strand down my back, and was nearly ready when Ross tapped on my door and opened it. I sat stiff and frozen on the dressing table bench, watching him indirectly in the mirror, steeling myself against whatever might come. He seemed no different than on any other morning in our brief married life, except that he was at home now and ready to return to his own busy and ordered existence. For the first time since last night, a faint uncertainty stirred in me, and I grasped at the fragile straw. Was it possible that I hadn't really understood? Oh, if only that could be true!

He kissed me with affection, and if I held back a little, he appeared not to notice as he linked my arm through his when we went down to breakfast. I found that I could still play my old game of concealment. If others were false and not to be trusted, I could be like that too. It was a game that sickened me, because it had never been what I'd wanted in life. In marrying Ross, I had believed myself free of Ysobel, free of all pretense. This morning, however, pride was everything, and all that mattered was for me to hide the remnants of my shattered fantasy. What had happened must never happen again, but in the meantime I must play the role required of me as the new mistress of Poinciana.

The breakfast room was still another, smaller room done with green bamboo wallpaper, and accented in tones of lemon. Ross seated me at a small table set with woven place mats, and rang for the same man who had served us last night. I found I wasn't especially hungry, and I settled for papaya, toast, and coffee.

Glass doors opened on a pebbled courtyard and looked out toward the lake. The water seemed as calm as it had been yesterday, with only a tiny breeze to rustle the palms. It was good to engage myself with the physical details of my surroundings and put last night far, far away. Putting something out of my mind, pretending it hadn't happened, was an ability I'd developed over the years when I'd felt hurt and lonely. It was nearly always possible to enjoy the small pleasures of the present and not allow what stood outside the circle of the immediate hour to threaten me. Postpone the hour of reckoning, and the evil thereof!

Listening to Ross and watching him, I could almost convince myself that my interpretation of last night was wrong. I was Sharon to him again, and he condescended to me just a little, as he often did, and I didn't especially mind. How could he not, with the difference in our ages, so that sometimes he must look on me as very young indeed, and in need of educating and directing. Besides, I admired him in so many ways—for the ease of his bearing, his brilliance and knowledge, for his natural authority.

"I want to show you the netsuke collection first of all this morning," he told me. "You must have something to occupy your time, and I think I may be able to involve you in this work—if you're willing."

I brightened a little. I was more than willing to make any sort of plan that would keep me busy. One of the things I'd been dreading was too much idle time. I wanted to develop a purpose, a direction—something to engage my full and enthusiastic attention. When I'd been with Ysobel and Ian, there had always been so much to do that life progressed at a breathless pace. Perhaps I hadn't been using *me* fully then, but now that they were gone, I seemed to be drifting and becalmed.

On the other hand, I knew all about the wives of

wealthy men, who engaged fervently in work for charity, for one cause or another. All laudable enough as far as it went, but not for me. I wanted something that would use whatever talents and abilities I might have.

After breakfast, Ross needed to confer with Jarrett Nichols for a half hour or so, and I said I'd go for a walk.

"Just stay away from the cottages," he directed. "We like to give them privacy, as we enjoy ours."

I was glad enough to get off by myself for a little while. Ross's company still left me uneasy this morning, though more and more I was trying to be reasonable about last night. The sick conclusion I'd jumped to must be wrong. It had to be. If it were true, the consequences to me would be more devastating than I knew how to face.

Outdoors, I gulped deep breaths of salty, invigorating air as I walked along. I stayed away from the beach this morning, since it would remind me of last night. Besides, there were other parts of the grounds that I wanted to explore.

Most of the plantings seemed old and well established, so Allegra must have had a hand in them, as she had in all else about Poinciana. Best of all I liked the great spreading tree that Ross had pointed out to me as a poinciana. Flowers came before the foliage, and I could see pink buds starting along graceful gray branches. Before long it would glow with red blossoms, its other name being the flame tree.

Paths of ground shell wound along and I followed them at random. Rounding a bed of tall Spanish flag, I found that my circling path had taken me after all in the direction of the cottages. I stopped to look toward them for a moment before turning back. Most were painted a clean white, with red-tiled roofs for contrast, and they were not set too close together. One, in particular, was remote from the others, and unlike the rest, its color was pale pink. Shutters had been the style in the day when these structures were built, and all the shutters on the pink cottage were closed, so perhaps it was unoccupied.

I wondered who had lived in this rather special little house that was set apart from the others. Palmetto, where Jarrett and his son lived, was closest to the house, while this was the farthest one of all. In the distance I could hear the sound of a riding mower being driven by one of the yardmen, but around the cottages no one moved. Probably the occupants were all busy with their duties by this time. Then, as I watched, the door of the pink cottage opened and a woman came out, to start along the shell path toward me.

Sheltered as I was by the flower bed, I hadn't been seen, and I stood my ground, watching her. She was an arresting figure, moving with an authority and assurance that would make her notable anywhere. Though she was well into middle age, her hair was carefully brown, and she had pulled it into a knob on top of her head in a style that was fashionable, but not especially flattering. Though I suspected that wouldn't matter to this particular woman. Her very wearing of the style gave it a certain elegance. Her well-cut jacket, vest, and trousers were of a deep lime color. She was anything but the jeans type.

As she came closer, she glanced in my direction, saw me, but did not slow her steps. Once, she must have been a strikingly beautiful woman, and she was still handsome, with eyes of an odd, dark violet, strongly carved features, and a skin that had suffered from too much sun.

"Good morning," I said as she came closer. "I'm Sharon—"

"I know who you are," she said with a touch of hauteur. "Good morning." And she walked straight past me without troubling to introduce herself.

I watched in surprise as she strode off with a long, free swing that took her rapidly away from the direction of the house. In a few moments she disappeared around a grove of live oak, and didn't come into view again. What lay over in that area, I had no idea, but there was no time to explore. I suspected that this woman was not one of Ross's employees. Her air of authority was too evident; even her manner of dressing wouldn't have been suitable for someone coming to work around a house or office. My curiosity was thoroughly aroused and I would have to find out who she was. But not right now. A glance at my watch told me I'd better get back to meet Ross.

On the way, Keith Nichols crossed my path, schoolbooks under one arm, red hair slicked neatly down.

"Hello," I said. "Where do you go to school, and how do you get there?"

He grinned at me in friendly fashion, his red hair shining in the sun. "Albert takes me when he's not busy. There's always somebody around to drive me. I go to Palm Beach Day School."

Perhaps Keith Nichols might give me an answer to what had been puzzling me.

"Can you tell me who lives in the pink cottage that is farthest from the others?" I asked as he fell into step beside me.

"That's Coral Cottage," he said, but his eyes evaded mine. "*She* stays there. But I'm not supposed to talk about her. Not ever. Mr. Logan says so." He broke away from me and ran off toward the huge garage that housed the cars of Poinciana.

I walked on thoughtfully, and let myself in a side door. Another mystery! Poinciana seemed full of them. Now, more than ever, I wanted to learn the identity of that remarkable-looking woman. Yet at the same time I smiled and said to myself, "Mrs. Bluebeard, be careful." For some reason—perhaps because of Keith's words—I knew I wasn't going to ask Ross who she was.

The room in which Ross kept his netsuke collection had been his mother's morning room. It was a more intimate room than some, but still large enough so that shelves and cabinets didn't seem to crowd it. Again, it was on the lake side, with long French doors that opened upon a little patio surrounded by potted plants. The desk at which Allegra had once worked on her plans for each day was now Ross's, and manuscript papers were stacked upon it, presided over by a portable typewriter.

But what caught my attention, what drew me most were the rows of shelves with their marvelous display of Japanese Satsuma and cloisonné, ivory and lacquer. I stood open-mouthed until Ross came to me, pleased at my reaction.

"Yes, there are some remarkable pieces here. And I found every one of them myself. The rest of the house belongs to my parents, but these things are mine."

I'd not heard such pride in his voice before, and I understood something new about Ross that gave me an unexpected feeling of tenderness. Both Allegra and Charles Maynard Logan must have been overpowering figures, and Ross had grown up in their shadow. So of course he would prize especially something he had created, brought together out of his own knowledge and taste. Some of my resistance toward him began to fade.

He had brought a stack of mail from his office to sort through, and he set the pile down on the desk. There were several invitations, and the office phones had already been ringing with calls from old friends, and with requests for interviews with both of us. But Ross was postponing all that for the moment, and letting Jarrett, with Myra's assistance, handle anything that seemed urgent. Ross's own secretary wasn't due back from his holiday for several weeks, and Ross seemed to enjoy the freedom of being without him. Now his collection could have his full attention, and he wanted me to learn all about it.

"First," he told me, "I'd like you to familiarize yourself with the netsuke pieces. There are over three hundred items on those shelves at the far end of the room, and they've never been properly catalogued. Perhaps that's one job you can do for me, if you'd like. Of course, I have records of purchase of everything in the collection, but they should be numbered and identified in one journal. My manuscript is a narrative account and will cover some of them. I'll want you to read what I've written and look carefully at Gretchen's photographs."

All of which I was happy and eager to do. At Ross's direction I started at the far end of the room, where shelves covered the wall from waist height up, with cabinet doors below. Ross sat at the desk and began to work on his papers.

Fatefully—because I didn't know then the role she would play in all our lives—the first netsuke I picked up was carved of pale pink coral, and represented a tiny mermaid, sleeping sweetly with her hands clasped under one cheek, and her tail curled up to shield her body. Again, there was the light touch of humor, of whimsy, lending reality to the fantasy. The mermaid was so exquisitely rendered in every tiniest detail that it seemed as though she might open her eyes at any moment and look up at me.

"How beautiful!" I said. "She's absolutely exquisite!"

"They're all exquisite," Ross agreed, sounding faintly impatient at my interruption. However, he did look at the tiny object on my palm and his tone changed. "Oh— the Sleeping Mermaid. That was my mother's favorite of the entire collection. Sometimes she used to carry it up to the tower with her. For a 'visit,' she used to say— so the mermaid could see her home in the ocean. Of course, I never approved of any of the collection's being taken out of this room. We can't have them scattered about the house. They're always here to be admired and enjoyed, but let's keep them here."

I hadn't proposed keeping them anywhere else, except for my frogs, but I was glad that Allegra had been capable of her own little conceit about the mermaid.

As I went on along the shelves, pausing to pick up a piece now and then, I came upon one that caught my interest especially. It was hardly more than two inches long—the crouching figure of a man in a pointed straw hat and grass cape, with every blade of straw visible in the carving. His head was turned so that he looked backward watchfully, his large eyes rolled, his mouth sly. Again I was enchanted.

Ross saw my face and relented to come and stand beside me.

"Oh, all right. I'd better introduce you—or at least make a start. They won't mean much to you otherwise. That little fellow is probably a ronin disguised as a farmer. You can just glimpse the sword hidden beneath his body. Do you know about the ronin?"

I remembered them from my reading and nodded. A ronin was a masterless samurai turned robber, and this one was undoubtedly waiting to ambush some helpless passerby.

"He was carved from a whale tooth," Ross pointed out. "Unsigned, as so many of the netsuke are, unfortunately, because, as you know, so humble an art was thought not worth signing."

He pointed out others among his favorites. A Lion Dancer in a gold lacquer kimono, no more than an inch and a half in height—a No dancer wearing the mask for the lion dance. This one was signed with characters that Ross translated as the Koma Bunsai. Next Ross pointed out a snail carved of wood, with the shell and soft part of the body clearly distinguished by the texture of the carving. The body actually looked damp and shiny, in contrast to the shell.

I was particularly taken by the Fox Priest—a taller figure than most, being nearly four inches. The pointed fox head and feet contrasted with human hands and the body of a man dressed in a flowing kimono. Often the figures illustrated some legend, and these, Ross said, I must learn from books he would give me to read.

He had just picked up a tiny temple dog when Jarrett Nichols looked in the door.

"Good morning. Ross, there's a Japanese friend of yours on the phone from New York, if you'd like to talk to him. A Mr. Yakata."

"I'll take the call in my office," Ross said, and went out of the room.

Jarrett looked around. "So he's breaking you in?"

Again I seemed to hear a hint of derision in his words, and I bristled inwardly. "There's so much to see that I hardly know where to begin. Ross wants me to learn about the collection so that I can help catalogue it."

"That should keep you busy."

I didn't like his tone, and I changed the subject. "I want to learn about Allegra too. She *was* Poinciana and her mark is on everything in the house. Are there any pictures of her when she was young?"

Jarrett opened a cabinet door beneath a netsuke shelf. "Those are Allegra Logan's scrapbooks. She kept them faithfully over the years." He pulled out a fat, leather-bound volume and laid it on the desk, turning its pages. "There you are. That's a color photo of the famous Sargent portrait that hangs in the Metropolitan."

The period was early in the century and she wore an evening dress of summery blue, cut with a round neck that showed her beautiful throat. No jewels were needed to add to such shining beauty. Though perhaps not beauty in a conventional sense. Not prettiness. One became aware of an overpowering strength of personality that attracted and held. She wore her dark hair puffed over her forehead and there was an eagerness for life in the eyes that looked out at the world. Her chin still wore the soft curves of a very young woman, and there was a certain willfulness about the mouth that hinted of a lady accustomed to having her own way. The only ornament in the painting was the rose she held in her hand.

"Did you know her?" I asked.

"Not until she was in her late seventies. She was the one who picked me out of law school and told Ross he could use me. A marvelous lady—always."

"She interests me even more than the netsuke," I

confessed. "Everything she was is stamped somewhere in this house, and I want to learn about her, about what she was like and what she wanted. Ross feels that some restoring should be done, but I hope he'll keep the house the way she planned it."

Jarrett's look softened a little. "Good for you. I was afraid you'd want to bring everything up to date."

"Of course not! I wish I could have known her—Allegra Logan."

"You'd better get acquainted with the netsuke first," Jarrett said curtly.

"Oh, I shall. It's an exciting art. And of course it must be recorded, preserved. But I've already studied Japanese art a bit and I'm used to it. It's not alive—not any more."

"And you think Poinciana is?"

I warmed to the subject. "Of course! After all, it's the creation of a woman who is still close to us in time. Lives have been lived here. People have died and been born and suffered and laughed—as it is with any old house."

"It belongs to the past, nevertheless," Jarrett said. "A museum piece, and I hope it will be cared for as such."

"I'm not so sure of that. From the little I've seen, the present is shaking its walls right now. But I expect they've withstood storms before this."

He knew what I meant. "Yes—Gretchen and Vasily. Sometimes Gretchen reminds me of her grandmother. The way she digs in and won't be budged, once she has an idea between her teeth. Of course, that's Ross too. You'll need to understand that."

The faint resentment toward this man that I had felt before rose in me again. He had no right to tell *me* about my husband. As though I were a stranger whom he needed to instruct. He presumed far too much.

Again I changed topics with an abruptness that I hoped would show him my displeasure. "This morning when I went for a walk, I saw a woman coming from the direction of the pink cottage that is farthest away. Quite a striking woman. Perhaps in her fifties. With her hair in a knot on top of her head, and very well dressed. I tried to introduce myself, but she barely acknowledged me and hurried off right away. Rather rudely, I thought. Do you know who she could have been?"

Jarrett sighed. "I'm afraid I do. That must have been Brett Inness, Gretchen's mother. I haven't told Ross yet, since he has enough problems on his hands with Vasily. Brett has been around regularly, and Gretchen has given her a key to the north gate so she can come and go as she pleases. The guards have been told not to interfere with her. If Ross stops this, there will be an explosion from Gretchen. But he must be told. He won't want her around."

I felt decidedly upset. I hadn't expected a former wife of Ross's to have such easy access to Poinciana—especially when this was a woman he seemed to detest.

"I've talked to your son a couple of times, and I liked him very much. This morning he told me that the woman I saw lives in the pink cottage. He called it Coral Cottage."

Jarrett's answer was firm. "You must have misunderstood him. Of course she doesn't *live* there. She must have been visiting, that's all."

I let the matter go, and sat down on the floor before the shelf of scrapbooks, with the one he'd opened for me on my lap.

Jarrett said, "I'll see you later," and went out of the room.

Relieved to be alone, I began to turn the pages. There were numerous news clippings of elaborate affairs held at Poinciana, and I found I could pick Allegra out of any group in which she had been photographed. Even as styles changed, she had kept that puff of hair above her forehead—her own distinctive hairdo—and she was always the most imposing woman around, for all that she hadn't been very tall. Seen alone, she looked tall because of the proud way she held her head, her shoulders, and I could well imagine that she had made a formidable impression.

One page showed the Logan yacht, in which she had been sailing the Mediterranean, visiting the Isle of Rhodes. There was a delightful picture of her in the ruins of Lindos, where I had been long ago with Ysobel and Ian on one of those rare times when they had taken me with them on a holiday. Allegra looked almost Grecian herself in her flowing scarves. Of course the yacht, bought for her by Charlie Logan, had been called *Allegra*.

So engrossed was I in these accounts of Ross's mother that I didn't hear his return.

"I thought you'd be going through the netsuke," he said. "Not mooning over dead history."

He bent to take the scrapbook from my knees and returned it to its place on the shelf. Once more, a hint of resentment sparked in me, but I managed to suppress it.

"I asked Jarrett Nichols if there was a picture of your mother I could see," I explained as Ross pulled me up. "That's why he showed me these scrapbooks. I want to read them all eventually. If I'm to know her house, I must know her. Will you show me the house now?"

For some reason he was not entirely pleased with my interest in Allegra's scrapbooks, and I wished I could ask him why openly. But I had already learned to tread with caution around Ross's sensibilities, and I recognized that the subject of his mother was one he wanted to drop. Showing me Poinciana was different, however. He put an arm around me as we started on our tour.

The downstairs rooms were extensive. Hundreds of people could have been lost in them. There were drawing rooms and small parlors, a wing of offices, a huge library with thousands of books on the shelves—a place I would return to again and again, I knew. Shabbiness was evident in those rooms that went unused today, but I could glimpse what they had once been. On every hand were antiques of a value that could hardly be estimated, and I felt a small thrill over fulfilling my dream of my own private museum to learn about and study.

The formal dining room was enormous, with high-backed chairs down each side of a long, shining table, bare now of place settings. No concession to Florida climate had been made here, and there were no flowered fabrics, no warm-weather lightness. From elaborate plaster rosettes hung two chandeliers, their shining pear drops of rock crystal. As Ross touched a switch their reflection gleamed from the long table. Against light green damask walls hung family portraits.

The place of honor above the mantel was held by a handsome portrait of Charles Maynard Logan, and I went to stand before it. He had chosen to be pictured sitting at his desk, with a globe on a stand nearby—symbol of far-flung Logan interests. I could make out the lands of the Middle East, from which Meridian Oil had made its billions. He wore the sober clothes of a businessman, with the wider collar and foulard tie of another day. His hair had been gray when the portrait was painted and it was not a young man who looked down at me, but a man of great assurance and strength.

I wondered what he would have thought of his son's new marriage. Would he have disapproved of Ross's taking so young a wife? I thought I saw a glint of humor in the eyes of Allegra's husband, as though it amused him to find himself sitting for his portrait.

Making a sudden comparison that disturbed me, I realized that humor was a trait Ross seemed to lack.

"I think your father must have enjoyed a good joke," I said.

"He did. Too often and sometimes inappropriately," Ross told me. "My mother was forever trying to hush him when he got out of hand."

"Couldn't she laugh too?"

"Oh, she laughed all right—but mostly at her own jokes."

I ventured on delicate ground. "I've never heard you tell a joke, Ross. In fact, I don't think you laugh a great deal."

"Perhaps I find very little to laugh about. But aren't we getting too serious about humor?"

His arm around me tightened, and I felt again a twinge of apprehension. As the day wore on, the hours would move relentlessly toward night. It was easy to assure myself that I would never allow last night to be repeated. But how could I stop it when the time came? I hadn't stopped it last night. If what I'd believed then was true, what was I to do? There seemed a sudden void at the very pit of my being. Perhaps I wasn't facing the truth because I didn't dare to.

I moved from his touch to walk beneath other portraits on a side wall, and Ross introduced me to them, one by one—aunts and uncles, the young brother and sister who had died. But oddly, no grandfathers or grandmothers. The heritage of wealth that led to portraits must have begun wholly with Ross's father. There was, however, a fine painting of Ross himself.

He had chosen to stand with his back to a window, through which Poinciana's belvedere could be glimpsed. On the other side of the window in the painting stood a handsome vitrine, its glass cabinet on high spindly legs. It was probably of walnut, with fruitwood marquetry, all meticulously painted in by the artist. The inlaid motifs had obviously been inspired by Japanese art, and the glass shelves held tiny netsuke. I stood before the picture, fascinated by its detail.

"This is hardly a standard portrait," I said. "Much more interesting, though some of the focus is taken away from the central figure."

"Not really. Like that globe in my father's portrait, the details here show *my* interests." He seemed pleased that I liked the painting. "You can't tell much about a man's life from most of these portraits."

I went on, looking for the one picture I didn't see. "Isn't there one of Allegra?"

"She never liked to be painted. The Sargent was the only one she would ever sit still for, and that was when she was young. She knew the value of being painted by an artist like Sargent, but she was too active and vigorous a woman to give up time to a lot of foolish sittings. So she preferred to have photographs taken. How many times I've seen her bustling about this room, giving orders for some enormous dinner party. And then presiding in style—her own inimitable style—for a great occasion."

"You must have given a few dinner parties in this room yourself?"

His mouth seemed to tighten. "Too many. That's over now, thank God. I hated it. Come along and I'll start you on the art collections. There's something in the gallery I want to show you. A surprise I've been saving."

As I went with him, I was still puzzling over his remark about too many dinner parties. Had the life Ross inherited been far more of a burden than I had guessed? Again I felt a touch of sympathy for the imposing, complex man I had married.

As we followed another branching corridor, I tried to speak of pleasanter things, and told him of my admiration for Gretchen's photographs that I'd seen in the tower room. Again he seemed pleased.

"I saw the double shots she did of you," I told him.

"Ah yes—my dual nature. Which one do you think I am?"

Perhaps this wasn't a pleasant topic, after all. The question was casually asked, never doubting my answer, and I should have replied quickly. But the right words wouldn't come, and my hesitation lasted a moment too long.

His eyebrows went up a little. "So you're not sure?" he said, yet, strangely, he sounded almost pleased.

I looked into a face that seemed more saturnine than

I'd realized, and saw that his silver-flecked eyebrows really did have an upward twist.

"She caught your eyebrows very well," I said.

His laughter rang out along the corridor. "There! You see, I can laugh. As a matter of fact, I felt rather flattered by that picture. I would say that fellow was a very forceful man."

Like his father? There had been unquestioned strength in Charles Maynard Logan's face. One couldn't doubt that he had been a powerful force in his day. I had taken it for granted that Ross possessed much of the same quality, yet now I sensed his need for reinforcement—as though he himself might doubt that very fact. Somehow a disquieting thought.

"There was one thing that happened when I was in the tower that I don't understand," I went on. "I was looking through a portfolio of Gretchen's pictures when I came across one she took of Jarrett Nichols's wife and son. I was interested in it, but Gretchen snatched it out of my hand and tore it up. Why?"

"Come along," Ross said, his hand firm on my elbow. "We'll never be through with the house at this rate. And I want to get back to work."

For once I didn't let him overrule me, but pulled back. "No! Please, Ross. I'm tired of mysteries. I've been running into blockades that you've set up against me ever since we arrived at Poinciana. Topics that seem to be forbidden. I've even thought of Bluebeard's wife!" I managed a smile. "Don't you think that when I ask a question it should be answered?"

The saturnine look was back—that dark look of Gretchen's picture. For a moment I thought he might stride angrily away from me. Instead, he made an effort and returned my smile.

"Sometimes you provoke me a little, Sharon. There's a time and a place for your questions. I don't much like it when they come popping out of nowhere. We'll talk about Pamela Nichols some other day."

I couldn't accept either his tone or his words, but I

had to be satisfied for now, and we went on toward the gallery wing. Allegra, he told me, had built it especially to hold Charles Logan's collection of paintings, and she had added many finds of her own. Wealth was to spend, and there were no limitations in Allegra's day.

Again there were generous double doors, and when Ross opened them we stepped through into a long, narrow room that stretched toward the lake at the southwest end of the house. I remembered noting it earlier when I'd explored the grounds. The Italian influence was in evidence here, with marble floor and arches, and a high, ornate ceiling. But the lighting of the pictures was excellent, and nothing was lost in distorting shadow.

As we came in, a guard left his chair near the doors, saluting Ross with finger to cap before he disappeared behind us, clearly obeying the edict that those who served around the house were to remain invisible.

I saw at once that it would take months of returning to this room before I could appreciate all of its treasures. The first look was bewildering. I was more accustomed to the carefully spaced displays of museums. Here, every inch of wall space had been covered with framed pictures. There were Cézannes and Renoirs that I had never seen in reproductions. Several Gauguins occupied a corner, and there were two Van Goghs.

"My mother bought all of those," Ross said. "Dad leaned more toward Turners and Constables, as you can see."

As he spoke, I caught a faint movement from the corner of my eye. A door at the far end of the room seemed to be open just a crack—as though someone might be standing there listening. Ross didn't notice, and as we moved on I decided to ignore whatever I had seen.

"Did your parents collect any of the American artists?" I asked.

"Of course. You'll find Mary Cassatt, Bellows, Eakins, even a lesser Whistler. And with his interest in landscape my father was attracted to the Hudson River school, with all those mountains and rather rigid outdoor scenes."

As we moved on, I paused in delight before a Breughel—a charming winter scene of white snow and black tree trunks, with little figures of dogs and men, and a distant pond dotted with skaters.

"How on earth do you protect all this?" I asked.

"There's an excellent alarm system, and a special inner room for the most valuable paintings. Here is the door. I've turned off the alarm for the moment."

The same door that had been left ajar was closed, but when we went through there was no one there. No other exit from the room seemed evident, so I must have been mistaken.

This extension of miniature gallery was less ornate and lighted entirely by ceiling fixtures along the top of each wall. I gasped at what I saw. Rubens, Vermeer, Tintoretto! A Study of a Spanish town done in brooding tones of green and black. El Greco! Just to walk among such paintings outside of a museum sent shivers up my spine. Yet somehow, so private and protected a collection seemed a sad fate for work that deserved to be seen by hundreds of thousands.

"Shouldn't these be in a museum?" I asked.

"Some have been given away, when the tax savings were right. But my father liked the idea of owning them, and so did Mother."

"Do you feel that way too? About owning?"

"Of course. I can spend hours here whenever I please. I enjoy what I possess. I suppose I'll eventually will them to one of the museums that are always begging for them."

The way he spoke of possessing made me uneasy again. I was beginning to find certain aspects of Poinciana more unsettling than I'd expected, and I remembered too what Gretchen had said about my fitting into her father's collections. Rebellion was stirring in me, but I mustn't let it out. Not yet.

"My mother was a great accumulator," Ross went on. "She had her own wealth to spend as she pleased, but she had a good business sense too. She knew that what she bought would increase in value. There are antiques in some of those rooms we walked through that are priceless."

I turned from the magnificent paintings, feeling invisible walls moving in around me. Suddenly I wanted to escape from this private, self-absorbed world.

"Mrs. Broderick told me that your mother's rooms have been kept as they used to be," I said. "May I see them?"

"If you wish. But first there's that surprise I have for you. Come over here."

A small half-circle of alcove had been built into one end of the room. I had thought it empty at first glance, but now I saw that curtains of azure blue velvet hung across the space. Ross stepped to one side and drew on the cords of a pulley. The curtains parted to show the portrait hidden behind them. I gasped as Ysobel Hollis smiled down at me from a background of more blue curtains. My mother was younger in the painting than I remembered her, but it was so lifelike, so real, that if I reached out I would surely touch flesh and blood. My own flesh and blood. She was wearing a favorite primrose yellow dress, her short curly hair black in contrast, her face pert and smiling.

Ross's arm came about me and for a moment I leaned against him weakly, then drew away. "Do you remember when that portrait was painted?" he asked.

I did indeed. It had been done a number of years ago, and its painting had become something of a joke in our family. Some "secret" admirer of my mother's had commissioned it. It was to be his if my mother would pose and accept a fabulous sum as a gift for the children's hospital she was sponsoring. We were in London at the time and a notable English portrait painter had been engaged to paint her. When the portrait was done, Ysobel had liked it so much that she had been reluctant to part with it. The artist had caught not only her verve and vitality, but a lovely generosity that looked out of the canvas, saying the same things she always told her audiences with her eyes and voice: "I love you. Come to me."

I stared dry-eyed at the portrait, remembering something strange my father had said in a soft undertone that first time he had viewed the finished portrait: "Things are not always what they seem."

Only now was I beginning to understand a little what he had meant. Now, if I looked long enough at Ysobel's face, I might discover truths that I had long kept hidden from myself. Truths that I was perhaps not yet ready to face. In any case, what did they matter now? Only Ross mattered to me at this instant, and the terrible inference of the portrait. He too had seemed to be what he was not.

Tears came at last, not only because the portrait had opened wounds, but also because it was Ross Logan who had commissioned the painting. Now I must confront what I had been trying all morning to deny: *Last night had been real.*

He was clearly dismayed by my tears. "Darling, you mustn't cry over this. I thought you would be pleased."

He tilted my head to kiss my lips and I kept my eyes closed because I didn't want to know whether he looked at the portrait while he kissed me.

When he gave me a handkerchief, I dried my eyes, trying hard once more to save my pride. "I'm sorry. It was just—just the shock of seeing that portrait again. Everything came back so sharply."

"Of course. I understand," he said, and I knew that he didn't understand at all.

When I turned to escape this small space that had begun to stifle me, he put a hand on my arm.

"Wait, Sharon. I want to show you another whimsy of Allegra's. Look here."

He pulled back a portion of the curtain behind Yso-

.bel's portrait to reveal a door. It opened away from us into a passage that moved into darkness.

"Where does it go?" I asked.

"It opens into an annex at one end of the ballroom. Allegra always liked to have her escape routes handy."

"Escape from what?"

"Bores. People she disliked or didn't want to see at that moment. When she chose, she could disappear with the expertise of a magician."

Now I understood that something I had noted earlier would have been possible. "Ross, when we were in the big gallery, I noticed that the door to this room was ajar. Or thought I did. But when I looked again it had closed. Do you suppose someone could have been here, and gone away down the passage? Isn't it dangerous to leave this entrance to the gallery unprotected?"

"Oh, it's not unprotected," he said. "The door at the far end of the passage is kept bolted from this side. And the alarm system works there too."

"Is it bolted now?"

He touched a switch that lighted the passageway, and went to the door at the far end. The bolt was open. He closed it impatiently and came back to me. "Of course, others in the house have access to these rooms. But this door is supposed to be kept locked at all times. I'll speak to the guard about it. Then if you want to see Allegra's rooms, I'll take you to them."

When he'd spoken in imperious anger to the man he addressed as "Steve," he led the way out of the long gallery, and up one of those unexpected flights of stairs that Allegra had caused to be placed around turning corridors.

At the top I was startled by the sudden appearance of Keith Nichols. The boy had been nowhere in sight, and then without warning he was there, staring at us, equally startled. I wondered if he had been the watcher who had opened and closed the doors downstairs. Since this was Saturday, he had no school.

Ross regarded him sternly. "I thought all this was going to stop. Were you down in the gallery just now?"

"Yes, sir, I was." Keith tilted his head of red hair, looking up at Ross, undaunted. "I lost Brewster, and I think he's hiding in the house. Mrs. Broderick said he wasn't to come inside, so I'm trying to find him."

"That had better be the truth," Ross said.

"Yes, sir!" Keith grinned at us impishly and seemed to disappear through the wall.

"Where on earth did he go?" I asked in astonishment.

"Never mind. That wall is a *trompe l'oeil* touch that hides a real door. Keith grew up at Poinciana and he knows every trick that Allegra built into it. She used to show him her secrets herself."

"What an imagination she had," I said. "I'm glad Keith can enjoy it while he's young." I listened to my own words and felt far removed from them. Only that portrait of Ysobel was real, and must eventually be confronted.

"I don't want him to have the run of the house unsupervised," Ross went on. "But most of all I don't want you to become obsessed with Allegra. Don't build her into some romantic conception in your mind. This house and most of what is in it was her vocation. She was very good at what she really cared about. But the extravagances she indulged are done and gone. Her reign is over. This is another day. *Your* day. Remember that."

My day—or Ysobel's?

Again we followed a shabby upper corridor into a wing that jutted out at the opposite end from Gretchen's suite. Ross opened the double doors with a key.

"This was my mother's favorite room in her later years," Ross said. "It's a bit different from what you've seen downstairs."

It was indeed. I found myself on the threshold of an airy, uncrowded space, with wide windows that looked out toward the ocean. The muted reds of a Turkish rug contrasted with pale walls, and a long couch of plump cushions was oyster gray. Over a chaste, uncarved mantel of white marble hung a painting of angular design in shades of blue.

"Picasso!" I cried. "A marvelous one too."

An open door opposite the sea window led us into a wide room with more windows on the far side. Allegra's bedroom casements offered a view of the lake, while at the end glass doors opened on a balcony overlooking walks and flower beds that led in the direction of the cottages.

The room itself surprised me, even more than her quiet sitting room. That Allegra Logan's bedroom should have been as austere as a cell was unexpected. The walls and ceiling were a soft, cool white, and there was a rug of palest pewter. The only color to be found blossomed in tiny yellow buds on the borders of two bedspreads. The beds were of brass and quite narrow. This was a time when Allegra would have slept alone. On a bed table were a few books, as she might have left them, but no pictures hung upon the plain white walls. It was a room in which you could close your eyes and rest.

"It's astonishing," I said. "With everything so elaborate downstairs, that she would want her own rooms—"

"She was nearly eighty when she moved in here. She'd begun to reject her old life. She began to retreat. There are two beds only because she would sometimes invite Gretchen to stay with her for the night. Something Gretchen always loved."

I could easily understand why. A lonely little girl with a fabulous grandmother might very well come visiting here whenever she was permitted.

"Did she die in this room?" I asked. "I hope she did, and not in a hospital."

Ross made a queer, choking sound, and then cleared his throat. "Come here," he said, and there was a rough note in his voice, as though I had somehow angered him.

He took my arm and walked me firmly to the French

doors, opened them and stepped through to the balcony, drawing me with him.

"I haven't wanted to tell you," he said. "I wanted you to get used to the house first, and learn to be happy here before we brought in tragedy. But now, with this infatuation for Allegra developing, I think you'll have to be told. Look out there. That farthest cottage—do you see it?"

I followed his pointing finger and saw that the cottage he indicated was the pink one that young Keith had called "Coral." It was the cottage from which Brett Inness had emerged this morning.

"Yes," I said. "I see it." Dread had started somewhere inside me. I wanted to keep my fantasy of Allegra Logan secure, and I sensed that it was about to be destroyed forever.

"I never told you that she was dead," Ross said. "You leaped to that conclusion yourself. Unfortunately, my mother is still alive. She lives in that cottage with her nurse, Miss Cox. She is ninety-two and has to be taken care of and watched constantly."

"Is she ill?" I asked sadly.

"She's mad," Ross told me. "Mad as any hatter. Before long I'm going to send her away to a good place where she will be cared for properly. I've avoided this because of the publicity it'll bring. But I'm afraid the time has come. We lack the facilities to care for her here. I'm only sorry this wasn't done before you came. But now you have it—the skeleton in my closet."

I felt a shock of loss, as though someone I'd known and loved had met with disaster. Yet at the same time I experienced a disturbing chill. In Ross's words there had been no real mourning for his mother, for the woman she had once been. No pity for what she had become. His concern seemed to be with the avoidance of unfavorable publicity, and with the expediency of removing her from Poinciana. *Her* Poinciana. If she had lucid moments, what did she feel about that?

"I would still like to see her," I said. "Will you take me to her cottage sometime?"

"No! Absolutely not. Leave her alone. She won't understand who you are, and it would only upset you. Now, my dear, let's get back to the netsuke and go to work."

I stood for a moment longer looking out toward Coral Cottage, stirred by pity. No matter what Allegra had become, she had been all that I imagined in her youth, and even into old age. There was a new longing in me to reach out to her. A longing I must conceal from Ross. What he didn't know about me, what I had hardly admitted to myself, was that my life with Ysobel and Ian had taught me to dissemble and move quietly toward goals that were my own. I had one now.

Something drew me irresistibly to Coral Cottage.

Chapter

5

After a quiet lunch, at which I found I wasn't hungry, we returned to the netsuke room, and I began the task of identifying various items in Ross's collection. It was difficult to postpone an examination of all the other treasures of lacquer and cloisonné and ivory, to say nothing of the files of Japanese prints. But I must please Ross and work on the netsuke first as he wished. They were certainly fascinating in themselves.

He gave me a thick folder of vouchers to use as reference, many of them written in awkward Japanese-English. These indicated what Ross had paid for each, and gave dates and other descriptions that would guide me. He also handed me an envelope of glossy prints—the photographs Gretchen had taken as illustrations for his book.

Those netsuke that were brightly colored had been placed against backgrounds of mossy green, or a soft, hollyhock red, while the black-and-white pictures were done against textureless neutral backgrounds. All had been skillfully lighted and photographed. These would be useful in helping me to identify the pieces, and were also small works of art in themselves.

"How very good she is," I said, turning them over one by one.

Ross shrugged. "Some of them will need to be done over."

I felt impatient with his lack of appreciation, but I said nothing. Giving my attention to the vouchers, I began to sort them into piles that represented signed and unsigned netsuke. Then I began the long task of matching each item to its corresponding voucher. Once I had found an item and identified it, I placed it on a shelf I had cleared, and entered it in the journal Ross had given me. After each entry I left a space for Ross to set down those details that I couldn't know. At his suggestion I used a simple numbering system.

I was glad to have something painstaking to do with my mind and my hands. Glad to be able to hold off my growing confusion, my fears. I wasn't always successful. Once I simply stopped what I was doing for a little while and sat with my eyes closed, trying to find a calm place to go to inside me. Instead, there was only a churning of questions. I must find a way to talk to Ross—talk about *us*. Talk about a marriage in which Ysobel Hollis could play no role. But the thought of such a confrontation frightened me. It was the sort of thing I had fled from all my life. It was so much easier to step inside my glass case and close the door upon anything that might shatter me.

Around three that afternoon, Ross told me he had an appointment in town and would be away for a couple of hours. I needn't feel that I must be tied to this room if there was anything I wished to do. I was progressing well with the netsuke and they could wait.

I was in the middle of a search for an ebony carp done by Kiyoshi, and I said I would find it before I stopped. Perhaps then I would do something else. So much awaited me throughout the house. So much to distract me, and keep me from thinking.

Shortly after Ross left, Myra Ritter came into the room carrying a tray with cups, a steaming pot, and some English tea biscuits. I hadn't seen her since last evening, and she grinned at me cheerfully, her wide green eyes alive with interest, her dark, curly hair fluffed about her face.

"I've instituted the custom of having tea since I've come to work at Poinciana," she said. "I understand that Mrs. Logan always used to serve tea in the afternoon. I thought you might join me. Here—I'll find a place."

She set the tray down on a corner of Ross's desk, opened a small folding table, and waved me toward a chair. Her ability to enjoy life was evident again, and so was the faintly sly look that took amusement from everything around her. Today she wore a blue jump suit that suited her small, unbulging person. It also suggested that Jarrett Nichols's informality of dress spilled over to those who worked for him.

While she poured tea, I went on with my search for the elusive carp, sounding my frustration aloud.

"I've been over every single netsuke three times, and I can't find anything that answers to the description," I said. "Do you know if Mr. Logan keeps any of his collection somewhere else?"

She shook her head. "I wouldn't know. It's not my territory."

"This is the second netsuke I haven't been able to find," I said. "The other is a coiled dragon done in cherry wood. I didn't want to bother Mr. Logan about this, but now I might as well give up until he gets back."

Myra's brew had a jasmine fragrance, and I hadn't tasted such frosted biscuits since my last stay in London. It was pleasant to sit with this sprightly little woman and chat about the unimportant. I needed distraction from my own thoughts.

"My boss is off having a conference somewhere," she told me. "I've finished my work until he gets back, so we can take our time. You've been on a Poinciana tour, I understand."

I was to learn that almost anything one did in this house was immediately reported on the grapevine.

"Yes. I've been through the downstairs rooms, and to see the gallery of paintings." I left that subject quickly, lest I find myself talking about Ysobel's portrait. "The rooms that interested me especially were Allegra Logan's. They're such a contrast with what she did in decorating the rest of the house. Almost without color. Comfortable, but utterly plain. Have you seen them?"

"I've hardly been invited on a tour," Myra said wryly. "About your missing netsuke—one thing occurs to me. Do you suppose the old lady could have taken them?"

So she knew about Coral Cottage and Allegra Logan's present state? But then, everyone at Poinciana must know.

"What do you mean?" I asked.

Small shoulders moved in an expressive shrug. "I've heard that this collection has a special fascination for her."

"I thought her fondness was for just one piece," I said, and went to the shelves I had not yet listed. The Sleeping Mermaid was in the same place it had occupied this morning. "Besides, how could she come to the house? I understand she has a nurse."

"Who can't stay awake all the time, watching her. Mrs. Logan doesn't always swallow her sleeping pills, and she likes to run away every chance she gets. I understand that Mr. Logan is considering taking her to some more suitable place."

I was growing curious about the grapevine. "How do you know all this?"

"Mr. Nichols was talking with Mr. Logan about it just a little while ago." She sipped her tea complacently. "Why not go down to Coral Cottage and find out for yourself? Not that you'll get any answers easily. It's hard to talk to her. I've tried."

I was surprised. "You have?"

"Oh, I probably wasn't supposed to, but I feel sorry for the poor old thing. Sometimes when I bake at home, I take her coffee cake or raisin bread. I expect the nurse eats them, but Mrs. Logan nibbles, and sometimes she's glad to see me."

My own resolve began to rise. Why shouldn't I do as Myra suggested, and do it now? Ross wouldn't like it, and I might be seeding his wrath, but the spirit of rebellion was growing in me. No matter what she had become—perhaps all the more because of it—I admired Allegra and I wanted to see her and tell her so.

"Perhaps I will go down there," I said to Myra. "Though I'm sure the two pieces will turn up in some place I don't know about."

We finished our tea, and when I'd thanked her, Myra picked up the tray in her usual quick way, and went to the door, where she paused.

"Are you all right, Mrs. Logan?"

I stared at her in surprise. "Of course I'm all right. Why shouldn't I be?" But even as I spoke I heard the edge in my voice.

She lowered long lashes demurely and went away, leaving me even more uneasy than I'd been before. Did what I was feeling show that much?

I put my cataloguing aside, but before I left the room I ran quickly through Gretchen's photographs. When I came upon those of the carp and dragon I knew they were nowhere on the shelves. These I hadn't seen before.

Without further delay, I found my way out of the house, and as I followed a shell path in the direction of the cottages, I had a sense of windows watching me. The invisible "staff" had lives and curiosities of their own, undoubtedly—like Myra Ritter. And they would be curious about me. Perhaps they would even report my movements to Ross. Well, let them! The time had come to be myself, if I was not to be forever smothered. There were matters to be resolved between Ross and me, and one of them had to be my freedom of movement.

The afternoon was pleasantly warm, and buds on the poinciana were beginning to open, so that spreading gray branches were dotted with color. Along a wall that hid a service center for the house, a row of ficus trees had been planted—one of the variations of fig. Allowed to grow untrimmed, a species of these could turn into the exotic banyan trees that dripped aerial tendrils to root in the ground and form myriad trunks. Trimmed and shaped as these were, they became beautifully formal.

Ahead of me, Coral Cottage drowsed in the sun, its shutters open now to receive the light that would be less welcome later in the year. No one moved around the cottage, as I approached from the rear, but I heard voices drifting out through an open window. Probably nurse and patient talking. But then I heard another voice—a man's tones—and hesitated. I would rather visit the cottage when Allegra and Miss Cox were alone. However, since I had come this far, I would at least walk around it.

As I turned a corner of the small pink stucco house, I stopped in surprise. A bench had been placed on the side nearest the lake, and Vasily Karl lounged there, staring out at the water, a cigarette in his fingers. He got up with alacrity at my appearance, stamping out the cigarette in the grass. I was aware again of his good looks. His fair hair shone in the sun, and his teeth flashed as he smiled. I was aware too of the small scar that lifted one eyebrow and gave me a sense of familiarity.

"Good afternoon," he greeted me. "If you've come to call on old Mrs. Logan, this might not be the best time. There is, it seems, a certain controversy."

His glance indicated the window behind him, and I could hear voices again. Gretchen's, for one. And the man sounded like Jarrett Nichols. I hesitated between flight and curiosity, staring openly at Vasily.

"I'm sure I've met you somewhere," I repeated.

"I would remember you," he said, as he had before. "But if you have really come to call on Mrs. Logan, perhaps I can help you."

He put an assured hand on my elbow and turned me in the direction of the cottage's front door. Somehow, I was certain that he knew very well where we had met, and perhaps eventually I too would remember. I went with him, no longer caring whether I intruded or not. Who could tell but what Allegra might need someone on her side. That I was already there, I knew.

Vasily pulled open the screen door and waved me ahead. "You have a visitor," he told the three in the room.

Jarrett and the nurse stared at me, and Gretchen's already stormy look turned upon me, the bruise about one eye slightly subdued by makeup. Allegra Logan herself was not present.

"Go away," Gretchen said rudely. "You aren't wanted here."

When I would have retreated, Vasily stopped me, and I saw the look in his dark eyes that so contrasted with his fair hair. He was enjoying this, I thought uneasily. It was quite possible that Vasily Karl was a man who liked to stir up fireworks.

"Now, now, darling," he said to his wife. "Didn't they teach you more politeness in all those schools you went to? I would say that Mrs. Logan has every right to be here, if she pleases."

I broke in before Gretchen could respond. "I just wanted to meet Allegra. Ross took me around the house this morning, and I—I wanted to tell her—" I hated myself for dissembling.

Jarrett, who had been silent, seemed to make up his mind. "Come in and sit down, Mrs. Logan. Perhaps it's just as well if you're in on this conference."

"So she can tattle to my father?" Gretchen snapped. "So she can fight me on his side?"

"I suspect," Jarrett said shrewdly, "that Mrs. Logan isn't one to take sides."

The quiet words stung. Why should he think that about me? I had exchanged only a few words with him since my arrival, yet whenever we were in the same room a spark of antagonism seemed to flame between us.

"Oh, all right!" Gretchen said crossly.

"That's my good girl," Vasily approved.

I sat stiffly in the chair Jarrett indicated, and looked around. It was clear that Allegra Logan had done no decorating here. The room had been made comfortable enough with white wicker furniture and grass green rugs. The pictures on the walls were undistinguished, and it was as impersonal as a hotel room. Two doors led off from it, and both were closed.

The nurse—"Coxie," as Gretchen called her—was introduced to me by Jarrett Nichols. She was probably in her mid-fifties, with determinedly curled brown hair, and a short white uniform that showed too much of a sturdy pair of legs. If it were necessary, she would be capable of restraining her patient physically. At the moment a worried frown creased her forehead and she kept pressing her lips together, as though the talk had upset her. When I sat down she gave me a look of sharp appraisal, and then didn't glance at me again.

"Perhaps I'd better explain what this is all about," Jarrett said. "First, though, may I ask if Ross knows that you're here?"

I felt myself flushing. "I came on my own. I asked if I could meet Allegra Logan. I didn't know she was still alive until this morning. But he told me to stay away from her cottage. So I came."

Jarrett looked faintly surprised, which pleased me in a contrary way. Gretchen merely grunted. Vasily was smiling again, enjoying himself.

"If Ross doesn't wish it, perhaps it wasn't very wise of you to come," Jarrett said.

I didn't want to discuss my small rebellion with any of them. In fact, I hadn't really analyzed my own motives, though I'd given myself excuses for coming.

"I'm here," I said curtly, and he accepted that with a nod of his red head.

"To explain," he went on, "Ross feels that his mother can no longer be cared for suitably here. He has several people looking into good nursing homes that take only a few privileged patients, and where she would be treated well."

"If they send her away, she'll die," Gretchen said flatly.

"She will do that before long in any case," Vasily reminded her.

"The point is," Jarrett said, "that Mrs. Logan puts herself into unnecessarily dangerous positions. She has become cunning about escaping from Miss Cox, who certainly can't stay awake all night to watch her. Ross is reluctant to bring in another special nurse. After all, Coxie has been with the family for years and isn't given to talking outside."

The nurse ducked her head in quick agreement.

Jarrett continued, speaking directly to Gretchen now. "Last week your grandmother nearly slipped into the lake on one of her midnight ramblings. If I hadn't been sleepless and out there myself, she might have fallen in and drowned."

"She can be watched better right here," Gretchen protested. "Dad's got to be made to understand that."

I surprised myself by speaking. "Are *you* in favor of putting her away?" I asked Jarrett.

"I don't like your phrasing," he said. "I'm neither in favor of, nor against it. I'm trying to find a reasonable solution."

"He's in favor of," Gretchen said. "And I'm against. I won't have this done to Gran. She hasn't earned such treatment from us. And I know my mother will help on this." She threw me a quick, defiant look.

"I don't think there is anything Brett can do," Jarrett said.

"But there's plenty *you* could do. My father listens to you."

I thought of the missing netsuke that Allegra might have taken, but said nothing. I wanted to add no further coals to this kindling fire.

"Does Mrs. Logan herself know about this?" I asked. "Why isn't she present at this conference?"

The white cap on Coxie's head moved from side to side in denial. "She's altogether out of it most of the time, poor lady."

"Then why," Vasily asked, "does it matter where she is? Perhaps it would be more interesting for her with people around, things she might do?"

Gretchen's small, sturdy person seemed to take on a look of disapproval. "Gran *is* Poinciana. Take it away from her and she'll know, all right. She'll just stop breathing. Jarrett, you've got to make my father see!"

Jarrett walked to a window to stare out at slanting coco palms, and Gretchen turned to me.

"What do *you* think? Even though you've only been here so short a time, you must have an opinion. Where do you stand?"

I couldn't decide how to answer her. "I'm not sure. How can I be, when I've never even seen Allegra Logan?"

"Then why not see her?" Jarrett turned from the window and went to open the nearest door. "Come here," he said to me.

I was beginning to wish I'd never come. I'd been seeking a fantasy. I had wanted to find, somehow, a hint of the Allegra who had created Poinciana. I didn't want to see the wreckage age had made of her. But there was no escape now. He beckoned me, and I walked to the door of the adjoining bedroom and looked in.

A small, frail woman in a dark green robe sat in a

rocker beside a window. She didn't look around as Jarrett spoke to her, and I could see only a coil of white hair piled on her head—much as she'd worn it in younger photographs. From the back, she looked shrunken and fragile as a doll. I closed my eyes.

"Please don't disturb her," I said, and knew that I sounded angry. I was angry. Angry at life for destroying a legend, for ending like this. Ysobel would always be young and beautiful, but perhaps Allegra Logan had lived too long.

The woman heard my voice and turned her head. "Oh, you've brought me a visitor?"

Jarrett drew me into the room. "Mrs. Logan, this is Sharon, Ross's new wife. You remember—he told you that he had married again. She admires Poinciana and wants to meet you."

There was a certain elegance of bearing about her as she sat waiting for my approach. An air of authority in the way she held her head, and in the entirely calm look she turned upon me. I had been wrong—she was still beautiful. Neither the lines of age nor the falling away of flesh could destroy good bone structure and the fine carving of temple and cheek and chin. The hand she held out to me bore the stigmata of age, but there was grace in her gesture, and the welcome of a woman who had spent a great many years in the role of accomplished hostess.

I went to her and took her hand, holding it in mine like a small bird. Then it tightened in a grasp that still carried strength behind it, as though she sensed support in me and clung to it.

"Mr. Nichols is right about how I feel toward Poinciana," I said. "Ross has been showing me through the house, and it's so beautiful. So much that was creative and imaginative has gone into it. I've wanted very much to meet you."

Thin lips moved in a faint smile. "I'm glad you approve, since you're going to live there. Ross might have brought you himself to meet me. I hope you will be as

happy in our house as I have been. What did Jarrett
say your name is?"

"Sharon," I told her. "I was Sharon Hollis before I
married Ross."

"Sharon Hollis. How very strange. I thought your
name was Brett." She shook her head in gentle confusion and sighed. "You must come to see me again. I
want to know all about you."

"I will come," I promised. Then I spoke softly to Jarrett. "Is there a way out? I don't want to go back through
the other room."

He led me to a door that opened upon an entryway
at the back of the cottage, and came with me when I
left. By the time we were in warm sunshine again, my
anger was ready for release.

"Why can't she live in her own house, her own rooms?
Why can't she be among all the things that belong to
her? She doesn't deserve to be banished like this!"

He must have known that I was close to angry tears,
but he walked beside me without comment. When we
were well away from the cottage, he paused beside a
huge banyan tree that I recognized from one of Gretchen's
photographs, studying me thoughtfully. I was intensely
aware of his long, solemn face beneath red hair that
blew untidily in the breeze, of gray eyes that were cool,
and a mouth that could be unexpectedly tender. A man
of power. One to be feared if he set himself against me.

"You had better ask Ross your questions," he said.

I didn't try to hide my indignation. "Everyone puts
me off! Ross said his mother was completely mad, that
she had to be restrained. But it's only old age she suffers
from. She's gentle and helpless."

"Not gentle. She was never that. And probably not
as helpless as you might think."

"She only seems confused. So why must she stay in
that horrid little place? Why can't she be brought back
to the house? Perhaps something can be arranged."

"You'd better ask Ross," he said, and turned away
from me.

I caught his arm, surprising both of us. "No! Oh, I will ask him—believe me, I will! But I want you to tell me too. I want everyone at Poinciana who knows her to tell me why she has to live like a prisoner. What harm can it do if she wants to wander about a house that she built and will always belong to?"

He was watching me, and his eyes were no longer cool. "You *are* a surprise! Ross isn't going to like this, you know. He doesn't care for anyone to disobey his orders, and he doesn't like explosive women."

I faltered, caught up in my own astonishment at the way I'd behaved. "I'm sorry. I didn't mean to get angry. I don't usually. I—" I floundered to a stop and found tissues in a pocket to wipe my sudden tears. This was the second time I'd wept today. Once for Ysobel, once for Allegra Logan. And perhaps both times for myself. What was happening to me? Where were my disguises? Had I already shattered my crystal case?

"Let's walk down to the water," Jarrett said. "I'd better tell you a few things."

I walked beside him toward the lake. On the way my toe kicked something that I thought was a croquet ball, but when I stopped to look down, I found it was a half-grown coconut. Perhaps because it gave me time to delay, I picked it up. The shell had no shaggy coat, but was smooth in texture and slightly tapering at one end. I carried it with me and moved on, never guessing that someone besides Jarrett was watching me even then.

"A souvenir," I said. "I'll take it back to my room."

"If you want to. But it will rot, you know, and the ants will come."

At least I carried it with me to the bench beside the lake, where I sat down. Jarrett stood beside me, with one foot on the low stone wall that held the water from the land.

"How long has Mrs. Logan lived in that cottage?" I asked.

"Several years. I've lost track. She's accustomed to

it now. And some of the time she doesn't really know where she is, so it can't matter to her all that much."

"I think it does," I said, beginning to heat up again. "I agree with Gretchen. Somewhere in her mind she knows."

Jarrett sat down beside me. "Don't go overboard, Sharon." It was the first time he hadn't called me "Mrs. Logan," and I felt reproved, as though I'd been a child. "It may be that Ross is right and she would be happier among others close to her own age. And in a place that offered more to interest her, take her attention. She's being bored to death now."

"She wouldn't be bored at the house among her own things. Tell me why she was put there?"

He was watching a sailboat skim along the lake, its course smooth as a flying bird's. For a moment I thought he would once more sidestep my question. Then he spoke quietly, evenly, without emotion.

"She tried to kill Ross one night, and she very nearly succeeded."

I could only stare at him. "That little, frail woman? A man in Ross's superb condition?"

"A gun can be effective, no matter what hand holds it. He still carries the scar of the wound on his upper arm."

I had seen the scar and asked about it, but Ross had brushed aside my question.

"But why?" I pleaded. "Why would she do a thing like that?"

"Perhaps because she isn't always in her right mind. Isn't that a good enough answer? Isn't that a good enough reason for her being moved to the cottage? Of course, no weapons are ever left unlocked any more, though Ross keeps a gun in his desk and one in his bedroom upstairs."

"Why guns?"

He repeated his usual refrain. "Ask Ross. Anyway, there have been other times when Allegra escaped Coxie and came to the house. Though I don't think she has ever again wanted to kill him. Allegra always cared a great deal about her son."

We sat in silence for a little while, and Jarrett stared across Lake Worth at the skyline of West Palm Beach. His profile had a cold, carved look. He often seemed a stone man, I thought. Yet not always. I knew so little about him, about what he did for Ross Logan, and why he served him with such deep loyalty. If that was what it was. It was difficult to be sure of anything with a man like Jarrett Nichols.

He stood up abruptly. "I must get back to the house."

"Thank you for telling me," I said.

He nodded remotely and strode off among the coco palms. From another part of the grounds a small figure came running. Jarrett stopped and waited until his son reached him and they walked on together. There seemed a difference in the man as he turned his interest upon the boy—certainly a loosening of tension around his shoulders, a bending of that stiff neck. How would he behave toward a woman he liked? I wondered. That he disliked and distrusted me had been clear from the first, so I would probably never know.

Soon Ross would be coming home, and I must tell him what I had done, what I now knew about his mother. And I must tell him as well about the two missing netsuke. Later on, there was still the night to be faced. None of these thoughts raised my spirits, and I too was staring fixedly at the shimmering pane of water that reached to the city on the opposite shore, when I heard someone beside me and looked up at Gretchen Karl.

She dropped onto the far end of the bench and I glanced around to see Vasily walking toward the house alone.

"Well?" Gretchen challenged. "Now that you've seen my grandmother, do you think she should be sent off to some horrible institution?"

"I don't think your father will pick a horrible place, do you?"

"You were talking to Jarrett. Did he tell you what happened? What Gran tried to do?"

"Yes, he told me. But not the reason."

"I was the reason. And my mother. The hideous things he has tried to do to my mother! I hope someone pays him back sometime. I really do!"

In a gesture that I wasn't aware of until after I'd made it, I crossed my arms and hugged myself—as if in protection from all the ugly things that were being hurled at me in too brief a space of time.

Gretchen snorted in wry amusement. "After a while you'll start rocking yourself the way my grandmother sometimes does. The way they do in madhouses. I'm tempted to often enough myself. Or was until I met Vasily. Poinciana is a place to drive anyone mad. Because of my father. Only because of my father!"

She jumped up and started off toward the house, then stopped and turned around. I was still watching her in dismay.

"Will you come with me to town tomorrow? Just tell Dad you have to shop on the Avenue and we'll go in for lunch. Can you do that?"

Her about-face was surprising, but I would accept anything that might bring me closer to Ross's daughter. "Of course," I said. That Gretchen left me bewildered didn't matter. She was one of the more important problems to be faced at Poinciana. Much as I wanted to help Allegra, her life was mainly behind her, while Gretchen's lay ahead—equally threatened by Ross. He had already shown how much he detested Vasily, and I suspected that it was only a matter of time before he used his power to interfere with his daughter's marriage.

I was not ready to look closely yet at my own relationship to Ross. I was still holding that time away, but if I could make friends with his daughter, I wanted to try.

The afternoon was nearly gone, and after a time I started reluctantly back to the house. The bald coconut I'd picked up stayed behind me on the bench.

Mrs. Broderick must have seen me from a window, for she came to meet me. "Mr. Logan has telephoned," she said. "He will not be home for dinner, Mrs. Logan. He has been detained."

I thought with distaste of sitting alone in the dining room. "May I have a tray brought to my room, Mrs. Broderick? Not a full dinner. And perhaps earlier than the usual dinner hour?"

"Of course, Mrs. Logan." She gave me a regal bow of convoluted blond coils and went away.

I walked around one end of the house to enter the beautiful red and white foyer, and my footsteps echoed on marble. Somehow a lonely sound. More than ever I began to feel the emptiness of Poinciana. It was as though no one lived within its walls. Now and then I glimpsed a maid or a workman, but they were like shadows, fleeing from my approach.

I went slowly up the beautiful floating staircase and down branching corridors to my room. There I closed the long shutters and lay on the bed. As long as I was awake, I would be aware of time ticking along toward the hour I dreaded. It was better to lose myself in sleep than try to solve all the problems I had stumbled into that were churning through my mind. I shut my eyes and tried not to see Allegra Logan's face. Or Gretchen's. Tried not to remember the portrait of Ysobel. I wanted to see only darkness and emptiness. I had not yet begun what was to become a struggle for my very life.

Chapter

6

A tap on my door brought me awake, and I sat up on the bed. A young maid in a gray and white uniform came in, carrying a tray.

"Mrs. Broderick said you would like something to eat early, madam."

"Thank you. You can put the tray on that table near the window, and I'll open the shutters."

But she was well trained and wouldn't allow that. Quickly and efficiently, she managed tray, table, and shutters. Then drew up a chair for me.

"Will there be anything else, madam?"

"Yes," I said. "Tell me your name."

She was a pretty young thing, brown-haired, with dark, intelligent eyes. "Susan," she told me.

I wasn't content with that. A whole person had a last name. "What is the rest of it?"

She hesitated, eyes downcast. "It is Broderick."

"Mrs. Broderick's daughter?" Somehow I was surprised.

She agreed and was silent, waiting for dismissal.

"Do you like working here?" I asked.

"Of course, madam. It's a beautiful house."

"But what else are you going to do with your life?"

She relaxed a little, and suddenly her brown eyes were faintly impish and the polite smile turned into a grin. "I'm only here part-time—to help out with extras for college. I'm interested in archaeology."

"You play the role of maid very well." I smiled at her. "Can't you sit down and talk to me?"

"My mother would kill me. But thanks, just the same, Mrs. Logan. Madam." She ducked me a slightly exaggerated curtsy and slipped out of the room.

Surprise, surprise, I thought, and wondered how Mrs. Broderick felt about her Susan going into archaeology. I hadn't imagined Mrs. Broderick in the role of mother.

My supper was delectable. A mushroom omelette, delicately brown, corn muffins with sweet butter, a tossed salad and a choice of dressings, with a slice of papaya for dessert. The coffee steamed hot in a silver container, the china wore a scattering of pink buds, and the heavy silverware was cool to my touch. Across the linen napkin lay a red hibiscus blossom. I tucked the flower into my hair and proceeded to enjoy every mouthful of food. From outdoors, the distant sound of waves rushing upon a beach was endless and soothing. I was beginning to feel a great deal better. And more hopeful. A foolish optimism.

When I was through, I rang for the tray to be taken away, but this time a more stolid young woman appeared and I didn't try to talk to her. Determinedly, I thrust all problems away and sat at an elegant drop-leaf desk to write a letter to an acquaintance in London. Stationery and pens had been provided and I saw that the paper wore the tiny emblem of a flowering poinciana tree. I gave myself to a rapturous description of the house and my new life that was just beginning here. It wasn't hard to whip up enthusiasm when I thought only of pleasant things.

By the time the letter was finished—written as much to me as to my casual friend—the moon had risen. It would be pleasant to walk outdoors again. Alone.

I drew a light stole around my shoulders and left by the loggia stairs that took me directly outside. The moon was still low and huge, its reflection glimmering in the lake as I turned away from the ocean to walk among leaning palm trees. No one was about. There were lights in Gretchen's apartment, but no sounds, so perhaps she and her husband had gone out. Some of the cottages were lighted, but I could see no glow at the windows of Coral Cottage, so perhaps Allegra and Coxie retired early. Palmetto Cottage was a magnet, drawing me toward its bright windows, but I turned away. There was nothing for me there. Jarrett's abrasive qualities would only destroy the healing peace that I was seeking.

Once I thought I saw something move a little distance away, but when I stopped to watch, all the shadows cast by house and trees were still. The staff of Poinciana continued to guard its invisibility by night, though I could hear muted voices from the servants' quarters.

In the mild evening, my thoughts were quiet as I wandered about the grounds. I had found my way back to my own quiet inner enclosure, and I didn't want to come out again. I had no sense that these would be my last peaceful moments for a long while.

When I had walked long enough, I returned to the house and used a door I hadn't come upon before. It opened into the ballroom, where only moonlight filtered through arched windows, illumining the vast expanse. I crossed the floor lightly, as though I danced to some ghostly whisper of music, and found my way to the same curving stairs I had explored yesterday, and which led to the loggia outside my room.

The narrow tiled steps were dark and I couldn't find the switch at the bottom. It didn't matter. There was a faint patch of light where they turned upward at the top, which meant that the door must be open around the curve. I knew my way and started up, my hand on the rail.

There was no time for me to be startled, no time to draw back against the wall. The rush down the stairs came so rapidly, the hands that reached out were upon me so unexpectedly, that I had no chance to tighten my grasp on the rail. Ugly whispered words carried the same vicious intent as the push against my chest. My hand was torn from the rail and I went pitching backward into space. I turned as I fell and struck my shoulder and the side of my head, stunning myself.

When I opened my eyes, my head was throbbing, and the tiles were cold under my body. As I lay there, the frightening whispered words that had come with the attack seemed to buzz in my ears. "Go! Go away or you'll be sorry!" Had I heard them or dreamed them in my daze?

No guard seemed to be about to help me, and I had a feeling that no scream would be heard in other parts of this enormous house. Gradually I pushed myself to a sitting position, and then stood up. At once dizziness assailed me, but my head cleared a little as I leaned against the wall, trying to collect myself.

These stairs were still the quickest way up to my room, and my assailant had rushed past me, running the other way. I pulled my body up one careful step at a time, until I could breathe fresh air on the loggia outside my room. I had left a lamp burning, and the French doors were open. Quickly I went inside and closed them, sliding the bolt.

Someone had to be told what had happened, but first I went into the bathroom and splashed cold water on my face. A gingerly exploration of my head showed a rising lump, but no bleeding. I went out into the hall.

Standing there, still feeling dizzy, was like looking

down a hotel corridor, except that in a hotel I would know there were people behind the closed doors. Here there was no one. At least I knew the way to Mrs. Broderick's room, but when I went to tap on her door, there was no answer. Since I was ignorant of the workings of the house, I had no idea where to find her.

As long as I was able to act, I could hold off the fright that waited to engulf me. So now I would try Gretchen. Perhaps she and her husband had come home by this time. Again I followed what seemed an endless corridor to Gretchen's suite. Before I reached it, however, the doors opened and Myra Ritter came through.

She saw at once that something was wrong. "You look faint. What has happened?" she asked.

"I—I had a fall."

For all her skittishness, Myra could take charge capably when she had to. "Come down to the office, where I can telephone. When you've collected yourself, you can tell me what happened, and if you need a doctor. Mrs. Karl has gone out. I've just checked. Why didn't you ring for help?"

"I never thought of it," I confessed wryly.

"I know. All these conveniences take some getting used to."

I was feeling shakier by the moment, and willing enough to give myself into comforting hands. We went downstairs to the section of offices, which I hadn't seen before. Myra's desk occupied a pleasant space with an outside window. The two main offices opened on either hand, and she led me into Ross's elegant room, with its Chinese rug of sapphire blue, its great mahogany desk and black leather chairs. There was a leather sofa as well, and she helped me to it.

"Now then, tell me what happened."

I told her of the thrusting hands that had come so suddenly out of the dark, and of my fall backwards. I said nothing about that whisper I thought I'd heard.

"Luckily, it was only a few steps, but I banged my head on the tiles, and it's still throbbing."

She felt the scalp under my hair. "There's a good-sized lump rising. Would you like to see a doctor?"

"No. I'll be all right. But the guards should be alerted, shouldn't they? Someone should be searching. Though I'm afraid it's already too late."

"I'll call Mr. Nichols." She went to the phone on Ross's desk and spoke to Jarrett, then hung up and rang the gatehouse.

It was all out of my hands now, and I stretched out on the leather couch and closed my eyes.

"It's lucky I was here," Myra said as she came back to me. "Mr. Nichols had some urgent letters, so they sent in some dinner and I worked right through. He was coming back this evening, anyway. I took a letter for Mrs. Karl too, but when I went to her room with it just now, her husband said she was out."

I closed my eyes again and waited for Jarrett to come. He brought one of the guards with him, and I answered questions as best I could. No, I hadn't seen anyone clearly. Just a dark shape rushing down the stairs to push me. Yes, I thought the push had been deliberate. But I didn't say why. I wasn't ready to face that yet.

A call was put through to Ross in town, and I could hear the crackle of his anger over the line as Jarrett held the receiver. He would come home at once, Jarrett told us.

The phone was busy after that, with reports from various parts of the house and grounds. Apparently nothing unusual had been noted by guards or staff. They were still talking on the phones when Ross arrived in a black fury. He considered the attack upon me to be an attack upon him, and he spoke to those around him with a barely controlled anger. Myra skittered back to her outer desk to escape the storm, while Jarrett heard him out implacably. No answers were to be found tonight, but the grounds would be thoroughly searched again by daylight for any clue to an intruder.

I wished that Ross would stop giving orders and just come to sit beside me and hold me. I wanted to be protected, comforted, told that I couldn't possibly have been so viciously threatened.

During the discussion, Vasily was summoned from his rooms and came to lounge in the doorway of Ross's office, watching us all with his usual air of sardonic amusement. It was a look that further infuriated Ross. But being angry with Vasily was like fighting with fog. He never stayed quite where one expected him to, always moving away from any direct confrontation. He was, I was beginning to realize, on everyone's side— and on no one's. He'd been reading a spy novel, he said, and hadn't stirred out of his room all evening. So he had heard and seen nothing. Gretchen was off visiting friends, and he hadn't cared to go. But she would know nothing either.

"All right—go back to your damn book," Ross told him.

Vasily said gently, "Perhaps someone should pay attention to the young lady and her hurts."

Jarrett threw me a startled look that carried a certain guilt, but it wasn't for him to apologize.

"I will take care of my wife," Ross told Vasily.

When he had gone, Ross came and sat beside me solicitously. "I'm sorry that this should have happened. Tomorrow we will get you to a doctor if you wish, but now I'll take you to your room, darling."

I thanked Myra, and went with him a little stiffly, feeling sorry for myself. Vasily was right. Everyone had been so concerned with capturing the enemy within the walls that very little attention had been paid to me, the victim. My injury and fright seemed of little importance to anyone but me. "Sniff-sniff," I thought, and halted this course of self-pity.

In my room, I told Ross that I could get to bed by myself, and to my relief he made no effort to help me.

"I'll come back when you're in bed," he told me. "I've a couple more phone calls I want to make."

Through the closed door I could hear him on the telephone, his voice still grim. I undressed quickly, and when he returned in response to my call, he sat on the side of the bed and held my hands.

"What if it wasn't an outsider?" I asked. "What if it was someone inside this house?"

"That's nonsense. We've had break-ins once or twice before, in spite of security. We can't live in a fortress. You just happened to be in the wrong place at the wrong time."

I bristled a little. "There's something you ought to know. I'm sure that what happened was deliberate and intended for me, because whoever pushed me whispered something like 'Go away, or you'll be sorry.' "

"Why haven't you told me this before?"

I wasn't entirely sure why I had held back. Perhaps because I'd feared his disbelief. "It all happened so quickly. I'm not certain—"

"Of course you aren't, darling. All sorts of frightening thoughts must have gone through your head. But don't you think you're imagining this whisper?"

There had been some uncertainty in me, but now I began to feel stubbornly sure. I *had* heard those words, and they'd been intended for me. But I knew that no matter what I said, I wouldn't be able to convince Ross.

"Go to sleep now, darling," he told me. "We'll talk again in the morning."

He kissed me lightly on the cheek and went away, and I watched him disappear into his room, feeling a strange mixture of relief and resentment. I wanted to be believed. But for one more night at least, all the problems that tormented me could be postponed. I needn't tell him about my visit to Coral Cottage. And I needn't listen in dread for the sound of Ysobel's voice in that recording of "Blue Champagne." At the moment I was too tired and sore—and frightened—to be anything but a coward.

It wasn't very late and with the lamp off I could see the moonlit sky over the lake. Ross had checked the loggia doors that I'd locked, and opened only the windows at the side of my room. I could hear the sound of

the ocean—a pleasant lullaby. With Ross in the next
room, I was not afraid. My picture of him as strong and
invincible persisted, and I could at least trust him with
my physical safety. If, otherwise, it proved that I had
fallen in love with a man who lived only in my imagination, I wasn't sure what I would do about that.

I left a lamp burning when I went to sleep.

It was two-thirty in the morning by my watch when
I came suddenly wide awake. Sleep was gone for good,
and turning in bed meant once more giving in to the
terrors of my own thoughts. I should have brought
something to read from the library, but the idea of
venturing through a dark house in search of a book
was more than I could face.

Restlessly, I sat up in bed. As my attention drifted
idly about the room, I saw something unfamiliar on my
dressing table—a lumpish something. I got out of bed
and crossed the room to see what it was.

Resting upon my hand mirror lay the smooth brown-
ish sphere of a coconut, such as the one I'd picked up
on the lawn. For an instant I felt pleased. Someone
must have noticed my interest in the coconuts and
brought me one—my souvenir.

Then I saw the nastiness. I saw with disgust the
oozing mass at one end, aswarm with ants that fed upon
it. Ants that crawled across my mirror, over my comb
and brush, carrying morsels of decay among my intimate possessions. Sickened, I understood. This was no
gift. Nor was it some child's prank. This was something
far more unnerving, more disquieting—faintly obscene. This was to remind me that the whispered warning on the stairway had been real—and intended for
me.

How long this had lain here I didn't know. I had
undressed in the bathroom and I hadn't sat down at
the dressing table before I went to bed. But at some
time this infested object had been placed here—clearly
to make me uncomfortable, to put further pressure

upon me to leave Poinciana. I could almost hear that whisper again: *Go away!* Well—I wouldn't go.

Sudden, absolute fury shook me. I picked up the coconut, catching an odor of decay as I did so. Scattering ants, I carried it to the loggia door, unbolted it, and strode into the wind in my nightgown. With all my strength I hurled the thing from me into the yard, and then slapped crawling ants from my arms. I was so angry I was trembling.

I had had enough. Enough! Poinciana had given me nothing but pain and fright and humiliation since I'd stepped beneath its roof, but I would take no more.

This was the moment when I began to fight for my own sanity. I had no idea what I must oppose, or whom. Perhaps all of them. Good enough! I would not be intimidated by malicious tricks. Not even in the matter of getting myself something to read. If I wanted a book, I would go downstairs and get one. Now.

I pulled on my robe defiantly, thrust my feet into slippers, taking no care to be quiet. Ross always slept heavily and I could hear his breathing in the next room. At least my head was no longer throbbing as I let myself boldly into the corridor, where wall lights had been left burning.

I was still too angry to be cautious, but the very hour gave me protection. Who would expect a victim like me to be up and about in these empty corridors? I was through being a victim. From now on, let the enemy beware!

By the time I reached the lower floor, I was ready for anything, armored by my own outrage. But nothing threatened me. Only when I turned a corner in the lower hall and saw a streak of light that fell through an open door, did I make some effort to get myself in hand.

That was the door to the Japanese collection room, and clearly someone was up ahead of me. Perhaps the very person who had removed the missing netsuke. Perhaps the same person who had met me on the stairs, and put the coconut in my room. Fine! An open confrontation might do both of us good.

Nevertheless, I moved more quietly as I edged along the wall. I would look cautiously into the room and see who was there, before I burst in with accusations. Without making a sound, I reached the door and peered around the jamb.

At the desk that had once been hers, nibbling thoughtfully on a pencil, sat Allegra Logan. She had changed into slacks and a brown pullover, and she was talking to herself in a light whisper.

"The John Pillsburys, of course. And Mrs. William Randolph Hearst. The Vanderbilts and the Huttons. Mrs. Post, if she's home at Mar-a-Lago."

The white head, with its still regal neck, bent over a sheet of paper on which she was setting down names, a tiny smile of satisfaction curving her lips. This was not my enemy, and some of my anger began to fade. I stepped into the room and she looked up, imperious and questioning.

"Who are you?"

"I'm Sharon Logan," I said gently. "Do you remember meeting me this afternoon at the cottage?"

"I've never seen you before. I don't know anyone named Sharon. Where is Brett? Where is Gretchen?"

I tried to reassure her. "I'll go and tell Ross you are here. I know he'll want to see you."

"No! I don't care to see him. He's behaved very badly lately. He's trying to get rid of me...." Her look changed, sharpened into recognition, as though she'd remembered who I was. "Don't trust him," she went on. "There's something you ought to know. Something I must show you. Only I've lost it. I came here tonight to look for it, but I can't remember where I've put it." The mists seemed to close in again, and her lined face crumpled with the effort of thought. "I'm sorry. I can't always remember clearly these days. But he's trying to do something I don't like, and if you stay here he'll hurt you. The way he did *her*."

I wondered how I could call the cottage. Perhaps I could phone Mrs. Broderick's room and she would let the nurse know, so she could come and get her patient. But when I went to the desk to pick up the phone, Allegra tapped my hand sharply with her pencil.

"Leave that alone. I know what you're going to do. But I have work to finish here. After all, the party is only two weeks away, and I haven't sent out all the invitations yet. It's so difficult these days trying to do everything without a social secretary. I can't think why Ross sent Madge away."

I drew a chair close to the desk and sat down. "Ross showed me around Poinciana this morning, Mrs. Logan, and I've never seen a more beautiful, more fascinating house. It must have taken you years to finish it."

She relaxed perceptibly and put down her pencil. "It was never finished. After Charlie died I lost interest. Oh, there was plenty of work for me to do, but I could never care about it as much as I did before. He was so proud of everything I built here. He was proud of me. The only one of my husbands who wasn't afraid of me! I wish Ross were more like him."

"I saw your husband's portrait in the dining room yesterday. He must have been a very strong and forceful man."

"He was. The only man I ever knew who was stronger than I was. At least in those days. It's different now. I don't know how to fight Ross. He was never all that strong, really. Only obsessed. But he knew how to put strong people around him. Only now—now...oh, never mind. Gretchen won't let it happen. She has promised me."

Allegra broke off and stared at me with bright, sharp eyes. "I'm sorry. I have so much trouble with my memory these days. I can remember perfectly things that happened long ago, but I can be confused about today. Old age is a dreadful nuisance, my dear. You'll have to tell me who you are again."

"I'm Sharon Logan, Ross's new wife. You remember that he was divorced from Brett?"

"Yes, of course. Though Brett still comes to see me. And I can remember Helen very well. The first one. Poor little Helen. So beautiful and so inadequate. She was the most determinedly unhappy young woman I've ever known."

"Helen was Ross's first wife? The one who died?"

She nodded. "Sick all the time. Hypochondria. Frightened to death of him. It never pays to be afraid of Ross. Brett never was—which is one of the reasons he divorced her. But now Brett comes to see me oftener than Ross does. Sharon? A pretty name, though not one that was popular in my day. Are you in love with him, Sharon?"

"That's why I married him," I said. "Has he told you anything about me?"

She thought for a moment and then drew the right answer from the tumbled files in her brain. "Of course! You're the daughter of that singer, aren't you?"

"Yes. Ysobel Hollis."

"The only woman Ross ever lost. Of course, he never forgave her for that. I remember how angry he was when she turned him down for that enterprising fellow she married."

I spoke quickly. "I don't think that's quite right. Ross was always my parents' friend. I remember his visits from the time when I was small."

"Oh, I'm sure he would visit. Ingratiate himself. Because he never gave up on anything he wanted. Though there was a difference between him and his father. My Charlie worked hard for everything he had. He was a brilliant man and he could handle being important and wealthy. He could even handle me! But everything was *given* to Ross. Too much power too early. He's been clever enough to hire men around him as executives and advisers. What he wants, he takes, and he never forgives anyone who thwarts him. Like Jarrett Nichols, who is a treasure. I found him, you know. But to thwart Ross is to make him a lesser man than his father. Such people he destroys. Remember that. Oh, I could tell you about the lives he has destroyed!"

I stood up, not daring to hear any more, dreading corroboration of what I had begun to believe last night. This was the one thing for which I couldn't fight—Ross's love.

"You really must return to the cottage now, Mrs. Logan. I'll call Ross and he will take you back to your bed. It's nearly three in the morning, you know."

She fluttered a glance at a wrist that was free of any watch, and shook her head despairingly. "I'm sorry. I do get so confused about time. It goes by so quickly." The names she had jotted on paper caught her attention, and astonishment came into her eyes. "Did I write these? Just now? But they belong to years and years ago! These people are dead. I'm the only one who is still here—outliving my time, outliving my life."

There was anguish in the look she turned upon me, and she did not resist as I raised her gently from her chair. I wasn't sure how to manage this, since she opposed my phoning for help. The easiest solution would be to walk her across the grounds myself. Perhaps a guard could be found to escort us.

Before we reached the door, however, I heard running feet, and Gretchen burst into the room, her expensively cut dark hair as tidy as though it had just been brushed, while everything else about her was thrown together—slacks, a cardigan, under which a pajama top showed, sneakers on her bare feet. The bruise about her eye had grown in discoloration without makeup, and somehow increased her look of dishevelment. She rushed to her grandmother, pushing me aside.

"Oh, darling! You promised me you wouldn't run away again. Coxie just phoned, and she was frantic. I thought you might be here, writing notes for the day. You must come back to the cottage with me now, Gran.

If Dad finds you here, he'll be angrier than ever—and
that will only hurt you." She whirled suddenly on me.
"Don't you tell him—you hear? It's hard enough to stop
what he's trying to do, and this will only make it worse.
They feed her drugs that confuse her, and can even
make her hallucinate. Then he takes advantage."

"Stop chattering!" The command came with complete
authority, and for an instant I glimpsed the woman
Allegra Logan had once been. "*I* don't matter now," she
went on. "I've lived my life and it's been a good one.
But you matter, Gretchen, and so does this new young
wife Ross has brought home. He's angry about your
marriage, Gretchen, and he'll break it up if he can. And
this young woman he'll use in unspeakable ways." She
looked at me sadly as her vision clouded and the moment of sharp intelligence dimmed.

Like a chastened child, she stood up with her granddaughter's arm about her. "I know I shouldn't be here.
I just came to get this. At least I *think* that's why I
came."

She reached one birdlike hand to the desk and picked
up a small object that I hadn't noticed until now. It was
the little pink coral netsuke—the Sleeping Mermaid.

"No, darling," Gretchen took it from her and handed
it to me. "Put it back, Sharon—wherever it goes."

"But Ross gave it to me!" Allegra wailed. "He said
it was always to be mine."

"He never keeps his word," Gretchen said harshly.
"Put it back, Sharon. He'll have a fit if he finds it
missing."

I spoke for the first time since Gretchen had rushed
into the room. "Mrs. Logan, do you suppose you could
have picked up any of the other netsuke the last time
you came to this room?"

She looked about vaguely, confused again, and I
knew she would not remember. But I had caught
Gretchen's attention.

"What do you mean? Are there others missing?"

"I'm not sure if they're really missing. There are two

I haven't been able to find. I expect they'll turn up somewhere. Do you suppose you could look among your grandmother's things at the cottage?"

"Gran wouldn't take them. It's only the mermaid she wants. Come along, darling. I'm going to get you back to bed."

"Perhaps I could call a guard—?" I began.

"No, of course not. Why should I bother with a guard?"

"Didn't Vasily tell you what happened to me earlier?"

Gretchen and Allegra had reached the door, and Gretchen turned for a backward glance. "Oh, that! But no one will be after me. You're the one who's getting all the backs up, you know. You're the only one who would get pushed downstairs. Unless it was my father."

I wanted to ask what she meant, and why I should be anyone's target, but she was moving briskly down the hall, with Allegra trotting along beside her, content to be in her granddaughter's charge.

Feeling too limp to move, I sat in the chair Allegra had left, staring at the pitiful list of names she had jotted down. I must destroy this paper, so there would be no evidence that she had been here in these early-morning hours.

Absently I tore the slip into bits as I sat on, considering Gretchen's words. There were only two possible reasons behind that push on the stairs. One would be Gretchen's—that I was deliberately the target. The other was that I had been about to discover someone who shouldn't be there, and who had to silence me and escape. Which of these choices might be the right one, I couldn't tell. Surely there was no reason why *I* should be a target, yet there was the matter of that coconut, placed so maliciously where I would find it strewing decay. And the whisper that had been directed at me.

Was the reason behind this torment simply the fact that I had married Ross Logan?

I put the ugly thought away from me and considered again the missing netsuke.

In spite of what Gretchen had said, perhaps Allegra in her confused state might have picked them up on one of these nocturnal visits, when she escaped from Miss Cox. Suddenly I considered something else. If she could get away to roam about the house, could she have been on the stairs earlier in the evening, coming in from outdoors and mistaking me for some imagined enemy? She wasn't feeble, by any means, for all her frailty, and it wouldn't take much of a shove to throw someone off balance on those narrow, turning stairs.

I would have liked to believe this because it was a fairly innocent explanation. But I didn't. It was possible, but not probable. As I sat there in the stillness of early morning, with the house hushed around me, and my first anger gone, fear began to rise, coursing through me, so that my heart thudded, and I felt chilled to my fingertips. I dropped the torn bits of paper in a wastebasket and walked out of the room.

This time it took courage to follow the dim halls, find my way upstairs, and let myself into my room, the books I'd gone down for forgotten. I went first to my dressing table, but the ants that had crawled there had dispersed, cheated of their source of food. Before I got into bed I listened at Ross's door and heard his breathing. Luckily he hadn't wakened. I slipped between cold sheets and lay on my back, all my concerns rushing through my mind in a confusion as great as Allegra's.

"Mad as a hatter," Ross had said about his mother. But Gretchen had spoken of the drugs she was given. There were certainly times when she was perfectly lucid and aware of the present—not in the least mad. I wondered if he had tried to have her certified and had failed. Clearly she had become an embarrassment to him in her present state, and if he had once held any love for his mother, it must be gone.

Anger began to stir in me again, but this time it was a quieter, stronger, more reasoned emotion. Tomorrow, somehow, the struggle must begin. It must begin with *me*.

Chapter

7

After a breakfast that Ross sent up to my room, I felt somewhat better. My head was reasonably clear, though I had discovered new bruises, and my shoulder was sore. The quieter anger, with which I'd fallen asleep, had not abated, but this morning I knew I must move with care. I mustn't flail out blindly against whatever threatened me.

Ross came into my room as I finished dressing, and we sat outside, where morning shadows darkened the arches of the loggia. He kissed me with tender affection, and I felt again the aura of protection he could place around me. I had only to relax and do exactly as I wished and nothing dreadful could happen to me. For a moment I didn't want to remember his mother's words. I didn't want to remember that portrait of Ysobel, or her voice singing as he made love to her daughter. I wanted to forget hands in the dark, that whisper, and the obscenity of a coconut on my dressing table.

I remembered everything.

While I was asleep, Gretchen had slipped a note under my door, reminding me that she still hoped to take me into town for a late lunch and some shopping on Worth Avenue. The note was typed on her personal stationery with her name and "Poinciana" engraved at the top of heavy cream paper. She hadn't signed it, but had drawn at the bottom of the sheet a smiling face with upcurved mouth, round eyes, and three hairs, coming out of the top of the head.

I showed it to Ross and he chuckled. "Typical. Gretchen's handwriting is illegible, so she always types. And when it's family or friends, her signature is one of those faces. Smiling, or sad, or with a zigzag for anger. I'm really pleased. This means she's making friends with you. You can be a good influence on her, I know."

Which probably meant that I was to influence her in a direction he might want her to go. Anyway, I wasn't convinced that the invitation was a friendly gesture. Gretchen's motives were likely to be devious, from what little I'd seen of her.

Ross assured me that a further search had been made of the grounds this morning, but no trace of last night's intruder had been found.

I asked the same question that I'd asked before. "What if it was someone inside the house?"

Again there was quick dismissal of the notion. "Nonsense! There's no one in the house who would want to hurt you. In any case, the security men are on the alert now. I've put one hell of a scare into them. It won't happen again."

I considered bringing up the matter of the coconut, but that was minor compared with everything else that Ross must be told this morning, and it could wait. I plunged into an account of my visit to Coral Cottage, and he sat listening, his expression forbiddingly dark, and once, when he would have interrupted, I hurried on, my inner anger sustaining me.

"Ross, I can't live here as a semi-prisoner. I hate this atmosphere of secrets around me, and of motives I don't understand. Can't we bring everything into the open? I'd like to know more about your mother."

I could see that my plea was useless. Even as I spoke, his mouth had tightened in displeasure. "I do not choose to discuss the problem of my mother. It's not something you can deal with intelligently when you have so little to go on."

"Jarrett told me about the attack she made on you a few years ago. But isn't it possible that she's better now, so she could be brought back to her own rooms? You can have her constantly watched."

He was already dismissing the suggestion. "I prefer not to be murdered in my own bed."

I wanted to ask the question I had been silent about when I talked to Jarrett. I wanted to ask why Ross's mother had made such an attack, but I held back words that might further anger him and asked another question.

"Why do you need to keep guns about?"

"Don't be naïve," he told me with biting scorn. "Anyone in my position faces constant danger from the crazies out there."

I supposed I must accept that. But I couldn't leave the subject of Allegra without another try.

"I'd like to visit your mother now and then," I went on. "I'm sure there are times when she could talk to me about the days when she lived in Poinciana and I would enjoy listening."

Ross left his chair and walked across the tiles to stand for a moment at the rail. When he turned about he was smiling. He had made his decision not to be angry. This time.

"Life with you isn't going to be dull, Sharon. You are full of surprises."

"I'm not that figurine you said I was in Kyoto," I reminded him.

"I'm beginning to see that. And I rather like it—providing you don't carry these notions too far."

I hurried to a subject less personal, though I suspected that it might upset him a lot more.

"After you left yesterday, I went on with my work in the netsuke collection. It's coming along well, but there are two items that I haven't been able to locate. The vouchers for them are there, and so are Gretchen's photographs. One is the carving of a carp done in ebony, and the other a dragon carved in cherry wood. I've gone over every netsuke several times, and I can't find either of them."

Ross was on his feet before I finished. "Come downstairs with me, and we'll have a look together. Perhaps you just haven't recognized them."

I doubted that was the case, and when Ross himself had gone over the shelves piece by piece, he could only come to the same conclusion. Two netsuke were missing. After that, phones began to ring around the house. Jarret was summoned and Myra Ritter came with him, steno book in hand. Gretchen and Vasily were found and brought in. Mrs. Broderick was instructed about questioning the staff.

"If necessary," Ross told us as we assembled in the room, "I'll call in the police. But I hope it won't come to that. If the missing netsuke are returned to this room at once, I will ask no more questions. These are not toys. Such pieces are irreplaceable. I've collected them over the years at great trouble and expense. We'll wait a few days and institute a search. That's all for now."

Vasily put a proprietary arm about Gretchen, with a sardonic look for Ross. Myra ducked out of the room in Jarrett's wake, and Mrs. Broderick bustled off to confront the household staff.

Gretchen nodded to me. "If you're ready, we can go into town now." For once she was wearing a dress instead of jeans, and I wondered at her insistence upon this trip.

"Would you like me to stay home?" I asked Ross.

"Of course not. Run along, you two."

Gretchen came with me when I went upstairs to change, as though she was afraid I might have second thoughts about this luncheon date.

"Do you really think anyone in the house would dare to touch your father's netsuke collection?" I asked her when we reached my room.

"Who knows? The staff has been with us for years. And there aren't many of the rest of us to choose from, are there? Besides, what would any of *us* want with the netsuke?"

That seemed true enough. Gretchen was wealthy in her own name, and the money a few such objects would bring could hardly be an incentive. Not even if it ran to thousands of dollars.

She went out on the loggia to wait for me, and I put on a white dress flowered in pale blue, and changed to open-toed shoes. When I sat before the dressing table mirror, I discovered a lone ant wandering over my comb, and I brushed it away in disgust, considering whether I should tell Gretchen about what I'd found here last night. Better not. Better to play everything by ear for the moment until I knew my true direction. Anger could wait, and perhaps be strengthened by the very delay. The intent against me—which others were discounting—was too serious and alarming for me to dismiss. Nor could I be sure that Gretchen wasn't behind what had happened.

When I rejoined her, we went down to the front door, where a car was waiting for us. She got in behind the wheel and I sat beside her, still puzzled by her manner, which seemed to alternate between antagonism and an effort to be friendly that I didn't really trust. Right now some secret purpose seemed to be pushing her, and the very fact made me watchful and alert.

In her red Jag we drove along South Ocean Boulevard past impressive houses. She pointed out the Addison Mizner touch of red-tiled Spanish roofs visible amidst tropical growth. We cut across the island on Royal Palm Way, where handsome, big-boled palms marched down a wide strip of grass that divided the street. No Palm Beach street that ran east and west could be very long, because of the water boundary each way. Our destination, Gretchen said, was Worth Avenue, and we turned off to reach it.

Among the magical shopping streets of the world, Worth stood near the top, though it was only a few blocks long. Rimming its sidewalks were the most famous of shops, where elegance and wealth were almost commonplace. Here were offered jewels and perfume, clothes by the great designers, to say nothing of fabulous art works. On this island where the Gulf Stream flowed nearest the shore, thus moderating temperatures the year round, there existed what some had called the American Riviera. The rich and famous played and rested in Palm Beach, and celebrities abounded. Worth had been called the "Mink Mile."

At the end of the First World War, Addison Mizner had appeared to put the mark of his own architectural whimsy upon the island that Flagler had developed, giving Palm Beach its Spanish-Moorish-Mediterranean character. He had lived in Spain and South America and California. He had borrowed, and he had also created out of his own imagination. It was he who designed Worth Avenue, with its Spanish façades, and charming arcades. As an architect, he had sometimes been more imaginative than practical, and odd "mistakes" sometimes turned up in his houses.

His own apartment, Gretchen pointed out, had been up there under the red-tiled tower that dominated the street.

We drove past Bentleys and Rolls-Royces, Cadillacs and Mercedes-Benz cars that were a common sight at the curbs of this famous street, and found a place to park. Palm trees grew along the way, and there were

plants everywhere, in tubs, or thriving lushly in court-
yards. Bougainvillea climbed the walls and spilled over
balconies, and the scarlet of hibiscus could be glimpsed
everywhere.

In some ways the street reminded me of the French
Quarter of New Orleans, and as we walked along I was
treated to glimpses of fountains, tiled walks, archways,
and arcades.

Gretchen drew me past an inner fountain to stop
before a Gucci window. She seemed to move in a leisurely way, yet I had the feeling that she was merely
marking time as we approached some event that lay
ahead. It wasn't likely that she had invited me out for
the pleasure of my company. Something was going to
happen—eventually—and when it did, I suspected that
I would not like it.

Out again on the street, she stopped for purchases
in a shop with shining mirrors and a gleaming marble
floor, where the saleswoman knew her and greeted her
by name.

I bought nothing. How could I need for anything with
all that Ross had given me from the stores of London
and Tokyo and Kyoto? Yet all the while as I followed
Gretchen, I felt as though I floated in a sea of unreality.
This was a world of such expensive artifice that it had
little to do with the realities of living.

It wasn't that I couldn't respond to luxury with my
senses, or that I couldn't enjoy this sort of artificial
beauty. I had lived very close to this world for a good
part of my life. I had seen such shopwindows in New
York, London, Paris, Rome, but I had never really belonged to this fantasy world, and I couldn't belong to
it now.

As we left the last shop, Gretchen said, "You look
a bit dazed. What are you thinking about?"

"I'm not quite sure. I love to look in the windows, to
go into the shops, watch the people. But I feel as though
I were attending a not very real play."

"I know what you mean!" There was a sudden passion in Gretchen's words that startled me. "I grew up with all this, and sometimes I hate it. Sometimes I hate everything about the Logan money, and all my father's power. Sometimes I hate everything about Poinciana except Gran. And Gran is being sent away because he is afraid of her. She was always the *real* one. Even though she could make unreal things happen, she kept in touch with life. My father has never had that touch. That's why he employs men like Jarrett Nichols, who are real. That's why I married Vasily Karl—because he's real."

That surprised me still more. We were walking back to her car, and I could think of no response to make.

When we got in and she drove away from the curb, Gretchen gave me a smiling look that challenged whatever I was thinking. "A fortune hunter can be very real, you know. Oh, don't feel embarrassed. I know exactly why he married me, and I know why I married him. We understand each other, and we have something very good going between us. But I've made you uncomfortable, haven't I? Because you aren't used to talking about things as they really are. Are you, Mrs. Ross Logan?"

"I don't think you know very much about me," I said. "Are you judging me?"

"Of course. Why shouldn't I? Don't we all judge everyone else? It just surprised me a little that you would even recognize that all of this is make-believe. Of course, we compromise and satisfy our egos. Jarrett Nichols too—though he's closer to the real world than the rest of us."

"I wish I could be as sure as you are," I said. "I don't know where the boundaries are any more. Perhaps you've escaped to some extent through your camera."

She said nothing to that, and we drove a block or two in silence before Gretchen parked the car again and glanced at her watch. "I've made a reservation at the Brazilian Court, so come along."

We walked through a large open court where tables

were shaded by bright umbrellas, and went up a few
steps to an enclosed pavilion. Here again Gretchen was
recognized and we were seated by a window. I noted a
third place setting, and Gretchen cocked an eyebrow
at me.

"I've invited someone to join us. Someone you really
ought to know. But we needn't wait. We can decide
about lunch right away."

So this was the event we had been moving toward.
I studied the menu, while my uneasiness grew. When
I looked up and saw Brett Inness coming toward us
across the room, I knew my fears were justified.

"She doesn't know you're to be here either," Gretchen
whispered, grinning.

I was furious with her for her presumption, but there
was nothing to do but face it out now.

Her mother wore a sleeveless blue linen frock, ele-
gantly simple, with a strand of white coral beads at her
throat. Gretchen commented first on her dress.

"I do like that. It's your own design, isn't it?" And
then to me, "My mother is a marvelous dress designer.
She has her own shop here in town. Sharon, I'd like
you to meet Brett Inness. And Brett, this is Ross's new
wife, Sharon. I thought you two ought to know each
other."

Long experience in dealing with the unexpected
around Ysobel came to my aid, and I managed to be
polite and a little remote. Brett was clearly as annoyed
with her daughter as I, but she acknowledged the introduction and sat down opposite me.

"Outrageous," she said to Gretchen, and then looked
at me. "I suppose we'll have to make the best of it."

"I'm sorry that I didn't know who you were when I
saw you on the grounds the other day," I said.

"I thought it just as well if you didn't. I'm trying not
to annoy Ross, since I want to be able to visit Allegra
on occasion."

"He can't forbid you the grounds," Gretchen said.

"If he tries, there will be a bang-up fight between us. So he'll pretend not to know."

My attention was on Brett at that moment, and my first impression of a woman of will and authority was growing. She still wore her hair in the brown knob on top of her head, and perhaps it was right for her angular style. Florida sun had not spared her skin, and I noted the lines, the weathering. Now I could see her odd, violet eyes more closely, and I was aware of their chill regard. She showed no warmth, even toward her daughter, and in spite of Gretchen's outrageous behavior, my sympathy for her grew. I knew about mothers.

When we'd ordered, Gretchen looked from one to the other of us, serious now, and no longer impish.

"I didn't do this just to upset you both. There isn't any reason why you should be friends. Or even acquaintances."

Her mother broke in. "Oh, I don't know—we may have a lot in common. Though perhaps Mrs.—ah—Logan hasn't worn that name long enough yet to be aware of this."

Anger would not serve me now, or resentment. I retreated into my glass case, where no words could reach me, and smiled politely, distantly, saying nothing. Neither of them could possibly touch me. That was the thought I must hold on to.

Gretchen continued. "I brought you both here to talk about Allegra. To help me plan a battle—a war, if necessary. You're already on her side, Brett, though I think it's only because you like to oppose Ross. And I can tell that the Allegra legend has gotten through to Sharon, so perhaps she'll help us too. Then we can work on this together."

My self-imposed retreat wasn't working too well, I discovered. In spite of myself, I was becoming involved, and wondering about Gretchen. Ostensibly, she was fighting a battle for her grandmother, but I suspected that whether she knew it or not, this was only part of a larger war with her father. And there my sympathies

were engaged, even more than for Allegra. Gretchen's
life still lay ahead of her.

"How can you stop your father if he's made up his
mind?" I asked.

"That's what we have to figure out. My father isn't
an easy man to stop. But the way each of you feels
should help. You're a softy, Sharon. You'd like to help
Gran because you're tenderhearted. Oh, don't look at
me like that. You hide behind that front you wear, but
the softness still shows. That's the reason Dad married
you. One of the reasons. He likes people close to him
that he can hurt. Don't I know!"

"Stop it, Gretchen," her mother said, her voice low.
"You used to have a few manners."

Oddly enough, Gretchen subsided. "Well, what can
we use for a lever with my father?" she asked, faintly
sullen. "It's not only Gran, you know. He's after Vasily,
too."

Someone was also after me, but this wasn't the time
to point that out.

The waitress brought our orders and we said little
until she went away. I had nothing practical to offer,
and I felt increasingly uncomfortable in the presence
of these two. Brett watched me obliquely, and Gretchen
was obviously hoping to make me squirm. I wasn't sure
how fond she was of her mother, but I was still the
interloper on territory that Gretchen had no wish to
share. If Ross liked to hurt people, perhaps his daughter
shared something of that trait as well.

When the waitress had gone, she put her question
again. "Any suggestions to offer?"

I looked out the open windows at bright umbrellas
in the courtyard and at people dining cheerfully at
small tables. I tasted my shrimp-stuffed avocado, but
I had no appetite.

Brett said, "There is always *l'affaire* Pamela Nichols.
A touch of blackmail can be useful at times. Ross has
gotten away with too much for too many years."

I found it hard to swallow my food. "What about Pamela Nichols?"

"Shut up," Gretchen told her mother, as if for the first time she regretted her plan. "You don't have a thing to go on."

"But Allegra does," Brett said sweetly. She was enjoying her pompano almandine with an appetite neither Gretchen nor I had. "She knows *something*. She's hinted as much to me. Don't underestimate your grandmother when she's lucid, Gretchen. Why else do you think Ross wants to put her away, except that she has something on him when it comes to Pam?"

My attention was caught. I remembered Gretchen's burst of temper that day in the belvedere when she'd snatched the picture of Jarrett's wife and son from me and torn it up. And I remembered Ross's evasion when I'd mentioned the incident to him.

Gretchen glowered at her mother for a moment, and I knew this was a topic she was unwilling to face.

"Pay no attention," she told me. "I can tell you the real reason why my father wants to send Gran away. And it's not this nonsense Brett is trying to foist on you."

I was silent, waiting. Brett waited too, but with a gleam in those violet eyes.

"Of course, Dad is the main stockholder in Meridian Oil, but Gran holds the next-largest block of stock. Not that she does anything about it these days. Jarrett makes a big thing of consulting with her, and she votes her proxies as he and Dad think best. But if my father could have her declared incompetent, then everything of hers would pass into his hands, and he'd feel a lot surer of total control."

"That's only part of it," Brett said.

"If this is true, why hasn't he taken the step of sending her away before?" I asked. "She seems to have lapses of memory at times that would give him cause."

"I'll tell you why," Brett said. "He's afraid of her— that's why. When she is thinking clearly, she can be dangerous to him. So he's afraid to bring in anyone else she can talk to openly. He probably feels that it's also risky to send her away. But at least in the company of other loonies, no one is likely to pay much attention to what she says. Now that you're here, Sharon, he hasn't been able to keep you apart. She might talk to you at any time and let a few tigers out of the bag."

"What tigers are *in* the bag?" I asked.

Gretchen answered me curtly. "I only want to see my father persuaded. I don't want to damage him."

"Our goals aren't exactly the same, are they?" Brett said. "But since you've called this little meeting and asked for suggestions, I've made one. Poor, foolish Pam might still be useful."

There was more than a hint of venom in Brett's cultivated tones, and I retreated again, saying nothing more, not wanting to hear, willing myself not to participate. I didn't know what they were talking about, and I didn't want to know. To know might, on top of everything else, be more than I could bear. Nevertheless, I listened carefully to every word.

Gretchen had cut her mother off sharply. "Pam has nothing to do with us now. We've got to decide what action to take in the present." She buttered a roll, scowling.

"You've always been clumsy, darling," her mother said sweetly. "Impetuous. You thought that bringing Sharon and me together would be entertaining. But somehow it's you who usually winds up in deep water. Nothing ever turns out right for you, does it?"

"I don't want anything to eat," I said. "I'd rather not stay and listen to this."

"You'll stay." Gretchen's hand was on my arm, and I couldn't rise without a struggle.

"You'd better not oppose her," Brett said to me. "My daughter has a dreadful temper. Like her father. Being so unsure of themselves basically, they keep trying to prove something. And they fly into rages when they're opposed." Her angular face with its strong features seemed bright with a malice that equaled Gretchen's.

I made no further attempt to rise. Once more, it seemed to me that Gretchen needed help, even more than Allegra did. My sympathy for her had its roots in the past, in my own girlhood, and it continued even in the face of her behavior toward me.

She released her hold on my arm and gave it a little pat, ignoring her mother's words. "That's better, Sharon. Everyone's been giving in to me ever since I was three— just because I could make such awful scenes. People who are well brought up have a terrible handicap. They've been taught that the greatest sin of all is to be bad-mannered. So they're at the mercy of people like me—who just don't care. But to get back to our problem. I won't stand by and see Gran railroaded. She's not all that crazy, and maybe she's the only person I've ever loved. Or who's ever loved me."

"You aren't always lovable, darling," Brett said. "What about Jarrett Nichols. Won't he help you?"

"I've already talked to him. He's not sufficiently *against* her being sent away. He even thinks it might help her. But I know what would happen. She'd be put away in some posh place where the horrors of rich families are kept hidden from the world. Gran doesn't belong with the horrors, but she could become one of them if she's put in that sort of big happy family!"

I told them about speaking to Ross. "I asked him to bring Allegra back to her own rooms in the house. I still think that could be done."

"What did he say?" Gretchen seemed surprised.

"He doesn't want her in the house. Because of what happened. I've been told about her attack on your father. He feels she's not responsible."

"She only did what a lot of people might like to do," Brett said with quiet venom. "I still think we should consider Jarrett. Ross is a little afraid of him. You know that, Gretchen. So what happened to Pamela might still be useful now. After all, she was Jarrett's wife."

"What are you proposing to do?" Gretchen demanded.

"Oh, *you* would have to do it. Just drop a hint or two, raise some doubts in Ross's mind. Hint at something you might want to talk to Jarrett about if your father doesn't see things your way about Allegra. Nothing too heavy."

"You really can be poisonous," Gretchen said. "How could I possibly do that? He would wind up hating me."

"Of course, that's your biggest problem," Brett said. "You brag about not caring, but you do. You've always wanted to be loved, and you never knew how to be lovable."

I hated what Brett was doing. Hated her mockery and her willingness to hurt her daughter. I could forgive Gretchen's attempts to be outrageous better than I could her mother's deliberate cruelty. I had to say something—anything.

"Don't put yourself down," I told Brett, and was pleased to see her startled look. "You've raised a very talented and clever daughter. I can't blame her for the way she feels about me—an outsider coming in without warning. I hope I can live that down in time. If there's anything I can do to help your grandmother, Gretchen, I'd like to. But I don't have any other ideas."

Gretchen was watching me as though I puzzled her, for all that she'd been so quick to judge my character.

"Perhaps you'll be the one to find the way," she admitted grudgingly. "This isn't only the matter of keeping Gran at Poinciana, you know. It's your freedom too that's involved, and mine. Our happiness. If there is such a thing as happiness. Gran can help us as well as herself. Power against power."

Before I could pursue this, she looked toward the glass doors, and her face brightened. When I glanced around, I saw Vasily Karl coming up the steps of the pavilion.

"Here comes more support," Gretchen said. "I asked him to join us."

He moved with a graceful, jaunty air, and I realized for the first time that he was a rather small man. His slenderness, the high sweep of blond hair, and his erect carriage gave an illusion of height that I recognized now as only an illusion.

He greeted Gretchen with a kiss on the cheek, bent over Brett's hand, and gave me his most charming smile. "How fortunate to be meeting three such lovely ladies," he said.

"No games," Gretchen told him. "We're into a serious discussion about my grandmother, Vasily. Will you sit down and have lunch?"

Someone pulled out the fourth chair for him, but he waved the menu aside. "When you're ready for dessert I'll join you. The library exhibit is going well, dear. I've been consulting about the hanging of your photos."

I hadn't realized that Gretchen's proposed exhibit was this far along.

"Vasily used to have his own art gallery in London," she explained. "That's where I met him."

I had wondered what Vasily Karl had done in the past, and I suspected that he'd held a few other jobs as well. Once more I found myself staring at the little scar that raised one eyebrow. It hypnotized me with that sense of having seen it before. Perhaps in London?

Despite his smiles and compliments, and the looks he cast upon each of us in turn, I sensed that all was not entirely well with Gretchen's husband. He was not lazily at ease, as I'd seen him before.

"What's wrong, Vasily?" Gretchen asked. "Something has upset you."

He shrugged eloquently. "It's nothing, darling. One of your father's whims. He's having me investigated. A full-scale detective job. It was to be expected, of course."

Gretchen flushed angrily, her face mottling, the bruise about her eye becoming more vivid. "Brussels?"

"No, no, of course not. All that was cleared up long

ago. There is nothing he can do. It just upsets me to
know that I am so little trusted."

I had a feeling that Vasily Karl was quite accustomed to being little trusted, but Gretchen said, "Don't
worry—I'll talk to him."

"That will help a lot," Brett said.

"Never mind." Vasily patted his wife's arm. "Let's
not discuss unpleasant matters now. What will Sharon
think of her new family?"

At times he watched me and I saw that he had a
curious way of stroking the scarred eyebrow as though
to erase the mark. My feeling of recognition became
stronger. Yet I be couldn't be sure. It was too dim a
memory—if it was even that. Something to do with my
mother?

"Of course it's typical of Ross to take such action,"
Brett said. "He will get rid of you if he can, Vasily, and
he'll stop at nothing. So I hope you have a spotless
past."

Gretchen spoke grimly. "My father has to be stopped.
Sharon, you're the only one who has his ear right now.
Maybe he'll listen to you. You've got to persuade him
not to send Gran away, and to cut out this nonsense
over Vasily."

Brett was shaking her head. "Don't put any heavier
load on Sharon than she's able to carry. She has her
own problems. You're the one, Gretchen. You or Jarrett. You're the only ones he's ever been afraid of."

What did she know of my problems? I wondered.
What could she know—and how?

Gretchen's expressive mouth had twisted in anguish.
"I don't want any of this! I don't want to struggle and
fight and throw tantrums. I only want to be left in
peace!"

"Then why did you move back into Poinciana?" Brett
asked. "Never mind—don't try to think up an answer.
Peace would bore you as quickly as it bores Ross. You
started out a fighter back in your playpen, and you're
still one. Thank God I'm on the outside now, and I

prefer to stay there. I've told you what you can do to help, but I expect you'll play everything by ear as you always do, Gretchen. Now let's order dessert and end this impossible luncheon."

Menus were brought and the other three ordered. I wanted nothing but coffee, and a chance to escape as quickly as possible.

Nevertheless, having all three of them here together was more of a temptation than I could resist. I wanted to watch their reactions, and I told them quietly about finding a rotting coconut on my dressing table last night.

There was a moment's silence while they all stared at me.

Vasily spoke first. "How very shocking! And how extremely vindictive!"

"Disgusting," Brett said, wrinkling her sharp nose. "Sharon, have you been getting up on the wrong side of the servants?"

"I've hardly spoken to any of them," I told her.

I was watching Gretchen, who had picked up her napkin and was creasing it thoughtfully.

"Have you any ideas?" I asked her.

My question broke through her concentration and she shook her head vigorously, setting her short hair aswirl. "No, of course not. What a silly trick!"

I let the matter go, and Vasily, with his usual skill, turned the talk to safer subjects. The hanging of Gretchen's best photographs interested him, and she listened to his words, his suggestions, in almost pitiful agreement. What a strange, prickly girl she was— wanting so much the very things she seemed to have little talent for winning. Puzzling too. I had a feeling that she knew something about that coconut. She was even capable of playing such a trick herself. It would be futile, however, to press her, and I found myself thinking of Brett's odd references to Jarrett's late wife, Pamela Nichols.

Direct questions, I was sure, would never provide

the answers I wanted, but this was something I must pursue when I had the chance. Perhaps with Gretchen—who had torn up Pam's picture so angrily.

When Gretchen and I returned to Poinciana, Vasily came with us, filled with good spirits that I suspected were artificial. His presence kept me from asking any more questions then, and I left them at the door.

When I reached my room, I went out on the loggia, where I could refresh myself with a view of the lake, and try to recover from what had been a disturbing experience. On a blanket, down near the edge of the water, Susan Broderick, my part-time maid, was seated cross-legged, her books around her. I ran down the outside steps and across the lawn.

"May I join you?" I asked as she looked up.

She shook her head despairingly. "If you sit down, I'll have to stand up. In fact, I suppose I should stand up anyway. Mother is a great one for the proper behavior of her housemaids. We're not supposed to fraternize."

"You're off duty," I said, and dropped down on a corner of the blanket, my hand out to keep her from rising. "I'll talk to her. I just want to relax for a few minutes. I've been doing Worth Avenue with Gretchen and having lunch with her husband and her mother, and I'm feeling a bit limp."

Susan bent her head so that a wing of dark hair fell across her face, hiding her expression.

"I grew up with Gretchen," she said after a moment. "There weren't any restrictions on us as kids. Old Mrs. Logan was very proper on the surface, but she was human, and she was always interested in the problems of those who worked for her. She even set up a trust to put me through college, you know."

I picked up one of the books from beside her. "Is archaeology the subject that really interests you most?"

"Yes, it does. Last summer I went on a dig out in Arizona. It's what I'd really like to do. When I'm through with school, maybe I can get a job with an expedition. I'd like to go to any of the Middle East countries, where so much history is buried. Though there's also a lot of it buried right here at home that's never been dug up."

"What does your mother think?"

Susan wrinkled her nose. "She hates me to get dirty. Dirt is the enemy. And that I should want to go out and dig in it offends her. What about you? What do you want to do?"

It was a strange question, but from this young woman perhaps a natural one. Unlike the others, she didn't take it for granted that being Mrs. Ross Logan was the whole of my existence.

"Right now I'm trying to learn about my husband's netsuke collection," I told her. "It's never been properly catalogued, and I'm trying to correct that."

"I heard about the ones that are missing. We've all been questioned. Though I can't imagine any of the staff touching anything at Poinciana. They've all been here a long time and they're quite loyal. This has upset everyone a lot. Mother's in a real tizzy. But it's even more important that you were pushed down those stairs last night. I hope you weren't badly hurt."

"Just a few bruises. Susan, is there any talk about who might have done that to me?"

She looked away, out across the lake. "There's always talk. Gossip. But it's only speculation."

"Would you be willing to tell me?"

"If I believed in it, I would. As it happens, I don't."

"Gretchen?"

There was no answer, and I couldn't expect one. She had been Gretchen's friend when they were small. I asked another question.

"Susan, did you know Pamela Nichols?"

"Of course." She relaxed a little, as though this was a safer topic. "I wasn't working here then, though I lived at Poinciana with my mother. In a way, we were friends. I can still cry when I think of her terrible death."

"What happened exactly?"

"They say her brakes must have failed. She always drove too fast. There was a truck—and she couldn't stop in time. She must have died at once."

I could feel the sickness and hurt along the nerves of my own body. I hadn't known Pam, but I knew Jarrett, who had lost his wife so terribly.

"What was she like?" I asked.

Susan began to stack her books. "My mother would say that it isn't proper for me to talk about her." Blue eyes looked up at me ingenuously. "But I will, anyhow. Pam was always happy and laughing. Except that she was a little afraid of her husband. It's strange, really. She was the one with a good family and inherited money, while Mr. Nichols was someone Allegra Logan had pulled out of the slums. But he was the one who grew and became really important, while she could never keep up with him. I think he loved her, but she didn't have much confidence in herself, and he was too busy to build her up in the way she needed." Susan broke off, suddenly aghast. "I'm talking too much! I should never be telling you these things."

I had listened in some astonishment. "You're a psychologist too!"

The long fall of hair swept across her face again. "Just because I like to dig up shards and bones, doesn't mean I'm not interested in live people. Growing up at Poinciana was always like living in the first row of a play. Old Mrs. Logan liked to talk to me sometimes. She wanted me to stretch my mind, and she'd make me tell her about the people I saw and listened to. Tell her what I thought of them. She was a great one for figuring out human nature. So some of what I've just said about Pamela came from her. Mr. Nichols wanted all those things his wife had stood for naturally. I suppose she was the unreachable that he finally reached for."

I was glad that this girl had been one of Allegra's protégées. But the remarks Brett Inness had made at our lunch table still puzzled me. How could anything about Pamela be used against Ross?

Susan Broderick gathered up her books and rose to her feet. "I have to go in now. It's time to get back to work."

I helped her fold the blanket and watched her run across the lawn toward the house, dodging palm trees. For a while I sat on the wall beside the lake and stared at rippling water. Everything that had been said at lunch today came indirectly back to Ross—to his influence upon all our lives. A fierce anger began to rise in me against him. I was beginning to see what his mother had meant—about the lives he'd destroyed. I couldn't know about the past, but I could see what was happening right now. All around him human beings were being used and manipulated. Allegra and Gretchen. Brett, who was still filled with bitterness. Me. Perhaps even Jarrett Nichols, though I wasn't sure about him. Almost without my being aware of it, I had begun to trust in Jarrett's strength and good judgment.

"Mrs. Logan! Mrs. Logan!" The voice had an excited ring. I turned to see the nurse, Coxie, coming from the direction of Coral Cottage, and I left the wall to hurry toward her.

"Please," she said as we came together, "will you come inside the cottage with me? I want to show you something. I've phoned the house, but I couldn't reach Mr. Logan."

"Is anything wrong?" I asked.

"No, no! That is, not exactly. I just want to show you."

At the door of the cottage she put a finger to her lips. "Mrs. Logan is asleep, and sometimes she sleeps very lightly, so we'll try not to wake her."

She led the way through the small living room and into the bedroom, where Allegra lay on her side, looking tiny and withered beneath the afghan tossed over her. Her eyes were closed and lashes that were still long, but very white, lay upon her cheeks. She looked rather like a child, lying there.

Coxie went to the dressing table and opened a drawer. "Look!" she whispered. "Just look in there."

I looked and saw the two netsuke nestled together beside a box of face powder. The small ebony carp and the cherry-wood dragon! I picked up the carp and examined the intricacy of a carving in which every fish scale was represented in meticulous detail. I was playing for time, dismayed that these should be found in Allegra's possession. When Ross knew, it would make everything that much worse for her, and I didn't suppose he could be kept from knowing.

"How do you suppose they got here?" I asked.

"Why—she brought them, of course. She's done that before, you know, with that mermaid she says belongs to her. But she's never touched anything else until now."

I found that my anger hadn't died away. What if she hadn't touched these either? With everyone alerted, warned, wouldn't it be clever of the real thief to place them here, where Allegra would be blamed?

"Have you been out of the cottage today?" I asked.

"Yes, of course. I always take her for a walk in the early morning. She likes to go down to the lake and watch the boats go by."

Like a child, I thought, and winced. "So anyone could have come into the cottage while you were out?"

"I suppose so, Mrs. Logan. The doors can't be seen from the water. There's never been any point in locking up down here in the cottage. But I don't see—"

"It's all right," I assured her. "It's not your fault. No one could watch her every minute."

She bristled a little, a frown on her broad face. "I do the best I can. Mr. Logan doesn't want anyone but me to take care of her."

Because he paid her well not to talk, no matter what Allegra said to her?

"I understand." I pulled some tissue from a box on

the dressing table and wrapped each netsuke carefully. "I'll take these back to the house and explain. I know everyone will be relieved to find them."

"Thank you, Mrs. Logan."

She looked relieved herself over not having to face Ross's possible ire.

As I started back, I wondered what I could do under these circumstances to protect Allegra. And myself, if I hid the truth. Perhaps Jarrett Nichols could help us both. Perhaps this was the time when I could talk to him, whether he approved of me or not.

Chapter

8

I found Jarrett in his office seated behind a desk equally as large as Ross's, and a great deal more untidy. When I spoke to Myra, she motioned me into Jarrett's office, glancing curiously at the small parcels in my hand.

He rose as I appeared and I went to sit in a green leather chair beside his desk. Today his red hair had been combed into some semblance of order, and he wore tan slacks and a pullover. Gray eyes that always made me uneasy—as though he could see past any dissembling—watched as I unwrapped the carp and the dragon and placed them before him.

"These are the netsuke that were missing?" he asked.

"Yes. Miss Cox found them in Mrs. Logan's dressing table drawer."

"That's unfortunate. It's terrible that she's had to

deteriorate in this way. I wish something could be done to help her, Sharon."

I hesitated before I went on. "I suppose we have to tell Ross where they were found?"

His manner seemed slightly less brusque with me than before. "I can understand how you feel. You've become fond of Allegra, haven't you?"

"It's not only Allegra. It's Gretchen too. We're all involved. What if Allegra didn't take these in the first place?"

He looked mildly startled. "What do you mean?"

"After they were discovered missing, perhaps the real thief became nervous and put them in the cottage so everyone would think Mrs. Logan had taken them?"

"An interesting theory, but unlikely. According to your idea, who would you pick for the thief?"

"No one. I haven't anything to go on except a feeling that Allegra never touched anything but the mermaid she believed was hers. Even Miss Cox said she was only interested in the mermaid."

"I suppose you can suggest this to Ross." He sounded doubtful.

I must have sighed, because once more he was studying me disconcertingly. "How are *you*? Have you recovered from your fall?"

I sat up straight in my chair. "Don't you see? Something is happening in this house! And I don't think Allegra has anything to do with it. Sometimes... sometimes I feel I'm being watched. And I know there was real vindictiveness behind that push on the stairs when I fell. And do you remember when I picked up a coconut from the lawn and you said it would rot if I tried to keep it? Well, someone carried one into my room that was in worse condition, crawling with ants, and left it on my dressing table."

If I'd shocked him in the least, he showed nothing. He was the perfect lawyer, playing it cool, and my anger began to include him.

"Have you told Ross?" he asked.

"No! I don't want to. He'd just call another meeting and dress everyone down." I lost my last trace of patience. "Don't be so smug and blind! There's some sort of dreadful purpose behind what's happening! Only I haven't a clue as to what it can be. Or even what the source is. That's the awful part. And we're all going to suffer if it isn't stopped."

He didn't take offense at my anger, but shook his head at me. "You mustn't get so excited. You mustn't let foolish tricks upset you like this. Or frighten you."

"I'm not frightened! Not any more. I'm just mad clear through. I feel outraged and—and furious!"

His guard had slipped a little and he was at least betraying astonishment. "And to think I believed that you were the unruffled type."

"I used to be. I liked being that way. Poinciana has done something strange to me, and I'm not enjoying it. I've never lived in a place so thick with secrets."

"Secrets?"

It was useless to try to explain. Jarrett Nichols was a realist. How could I explain feelings which were still nebulous? I could hardly reveal anything so personal as the eerie playing of "Blue Champagne" on my first night in this house, or tell him of the way I felt when I saw my mother's portrait in the gallery, admired in secret by my own husband. And there were those other secrets Gretchen and Brett and Allegra were all harboring—some of them concerning Jarrett's own wife.

"That push on the stairs was real," I said sharply. "Yet no one seems to know what lies behind it. If I can't walk around the house safely in broad daylight—" I broke off, remembering what Susan had said about the brakes of Pam Nichols's car. Others had not been safe either. For the first time I questioned that "accident."

Myra came scurrying through the adjoining door, halting her rush at Jarrett's desk. "Mr. Logan in coming up the driveway in his car. If he starts upstairs, shall I ask him to come in here first?"

"Yes, do that," Jarrett said.

She bounced off with her light walk, as though she moved on rubber. I imagined she couldn't help hearing every word we'd spoken, and I wondered what scraps of information she might have about Poinciana that might be useful to me if I found the right questions to ask her. At least her interruption had helped me to relax a little.

"How was your morning on Worth Avenue?" he asked.

"It didn't make me comfortable," I told him. "It's hard to believe in all that money. Somehow such a lavish display of wealth seems almost—obscene."

His smile was wry. "What's this—reverse snobbery? As Mrs. Ross Logan, you'd better be aware that money is very real. Though I don't suppose you have even a beginning notion of the tremendous good Ross does with his money. All the philanthropies, the trusts and foundations—have you any idea of what they do for thousands upon thousands of people?"

"Of course I do," I protested. "Oh, I don't know all the details. But what has that to do with high fashion and priceless gems, exotic perfume, and custom-made cars?"

"Well, well, well! What have we here—a proletarian at Poinciana? You mean you don't care for any of those things?"

I was growing indignant. "My mother and father had them to some extent. But they came as a reward for years of hard work and sometimes doing without. Perhaps it's just as well that Allegra Logan can't run Poinciana the way she used to. It's too—too—"

"Decadent?" He was laughing at me.

"Where do *you* fit in?" I challenged.

He sobered at once. "Perhaps the channeling I do is useful. Isn't that possible?"

I suspected that he did a great deal more than "channeling." I remembered the few facts I'd been told about Jarrett Nichols—the way Allegra had picked him out and put him in Ross's charge. Of his marrying a woman who had by inheritance all the things he'd never had. Yet I felt that the basic man had never changed. Money had not used him, as it had used Ross. In some instinctive way I believed this, and I quieted a little.

"You undoubtedly do a great deal of good yourself in Ross's world," I said, and knew how lame the words sounded. Even when I stopped being angry with him, there seemed no way to get through to Jarrett, much as I might want his help.

I was relieved to hear Ross's voice in the outer office at that moment, so that I could end this disquieting discussion. Yet I dreaded what was to come and wished I could sweep the two netsuke into a drawer. I did not move, and when Ross reached us the first things he saw were the small carp and dragon lying on Jarrett's desk. He bent to kiss me on the cheek and I looked up at him as he stood beside my chair, with one hand resting lightly, possessively, on my shoulder. For just a moment I was intensely aware of the two men. Ross, vital and dynamic, as he always seemed, quick of temper and explosive, as he could be. Jarrett, all quiet control over whatever fires raged within. Often sardonic, always strong. He would be able to stand quite still at the center of a storm and he would probably master it, I thought. In the same instant I wondered if a real hurricane would blow Ross away, and winced at my own disloyalty.

Ross was already speaking. "Where did you find them?" he asked us, picking up the netsuke.

"Mrs. Logan found them," Jarrett said, and Ross looked down at me.

"They were in a dressing table drawer in Coral Cottage," I told him. "Miss Cox discovered them and called me because she couldn't reach you. I brought them here."

"Did you talk to my mother about them? Not that it would have done any good."

"She was sleeping. I didn't want to disturb her."

"She'd never remember taking them anyway. I'm glad to have them back, but this means I'll need to make a decision all the more quickly. I was in town this morning talking to an old friend who has an aunt in a fine home in upstate New York. When we've had a look at the place, I'll take Mother there."

"New York?" I cried. "Upstate—in the winter? When she's used to Florida?"

"There are heated houses," he said mildly. "She won't be abandoned in a snowdrift. And, after all, she grew up in Minnesota."

I gave up trying to contain myself. "I think it's a terrible thing to do! I think it's disgraceful, when you have all these empty rooms, where she could be happy and live out her life in a familiar and loved place—with nurses to care for her constantly."

His expression darkened as I spoke, and I saw the anger in his eyes. He moved away from me and placed a sheet of paper on Jarrett's desk.

"I'd like you to talk to the woman in charge of this place, Jarrett. Draw up a list of practical questions to ask. And then make an appointment for me to go there."

As they discussed Ross's plan, I became aware of Myra in the doorway, wiggling her fingers at me and making faces. But before I could understand her signaling, Gretchen was in the room. Myra hurried back to her desk and Gretchen faced her father.

"What's this about a home? Dad, you can't send Gran away! I won't let you!"

Ross held the netsuke out to her. "These were found in your grandmother's dressing table drawer. She's become totally irresponsible, Gretchen, and she can't be controlled any longer at Poinciana."

"You're not going to do it!" Gretchen's look was as dark as her father's and they glowered at each other.

"*You* are going to stop me?" Ross demanded.

"If I can." Gretchen whirled and walked out of the room, her rage with her father almost sizzling.

"I'll take care of this," Jarrett said quietly, picking up the sheet of paper.

I gave him a look filled with scorn. Of course! He would always do whatever Ross Logan required. That was why he was behind that desk. My brief vision of strength and solidity had vanished. I couldn't stand either of them any longer, and I couldn't stand this house. I jumped up and ran through the outer office, where Myra stared in wry amusement, and went out the front door to the driveway.

Immediately a man in uniform appeared from the gatehouse and came toward me. "You'd like a car, Mrs. Logan?"

"Yes, please. And someone to drive me."

Albert, the chauffeur who had met us on arrival, was still putting the Rolls away, and at the gateman's signal he turned it around and drove back to the porte cochere.

When he held the car door open for me and asked where I wished to go, I told him to take me to some peaceful spot where I could get out and just walk around.

He knew exactly the place, Albert assured me, and we went north along South Ocean Boulevard in the direction of town. We drove through Palm Beach streets until Albert drew up to the curb before a great Gothic church near the lake.

"Bethesda-by-the-Sea," he told me. "The gardens are very beautiful, Mrs. Logan."

It was the open-air solace of the gardens I sought, rather than the shadowy nave of the church itself. I walked through a long stone arcade to find a courtyard where palm trees slanted up through paving stones that had been set around each bole, and where bougainvillea climbed the walls. My steps echoing on stone flags told me I was alone. Through an archway I saw the graceful gray branches of a poinciana tree, where blossoms were turning to flame. Another archway and stone steps with fanciful stone abutments led me to a higher garden of patterned flower beds in contrasts of red and green. A bench invited me, and I sat down and raised my face to the constant Florida sun, letting its healing warmth pour over me from a limitless blue sky.

All I wanted was to quiet my thoughts, my emotions. When Ross Logan had come into my life at its lowest ebb, taking away my load of problems, helping to assuage my grief, I had wanted the peace he'd seemed to offer more than anything else. With his arms around me, I had felt safe and able to breathe again. Some of the soreness of memory began to abate, and I could love a man for the first time. I had been grateful for his love and his rescue of me in my need. Yet in the short time I had been at Poinciana, all the good feelings of safety and peace had been shattered, and my world turned upside down in more frightful turmoil than ever. A turmoil that was part of a fearful present. I could no longer be an observer on the sidelines. I had been plunged into the tumultuous heart of whatever was happening. Perhaps I was really coming to life for the first time. The movement of blood through frozen limbs is always painful.

From the corner of my eye I was aware of movement in another part of this formal garden. Without turning my head, I was aware that a man walked alone beyond the flower beds. I didn't look at him, and he kept to himself. We would respect each other's solitude.

But the small distraction had disturbed the peace I was seeking. Everything crowded in upon me, centered upon fears that I knew were justified, even though others discounted them. Gretchen, Allegra, and I were all tied together now, but because of my presence, some unseen enemy had moved—where perhaps there had been no need to move at all before. And an enemy who is faceless is the most terrifying of all.

True, it was Ross who wanted to send his mother away, but I'd begun to sense some other ominous movement behind the scenes, and it frightened me not to know the hand that moved us as if we were chess pieces.

Which one played the powerful role of Queen, and was the disguise worn by male or female? I'd been unable to tell about the sex of whoever had pushed me down the stairs.

I sat with my head bowed in my hands, only to become suddenly aware that the man who shared this solitude had come close to my bench and was watching me. With a sense of shock, I looked up into the face of Vasily Karl.

Chapter

9

Again the sharp sense of recognition assailed me, and with it came memory. The last time I had seen that face it had worn a beard, thick and blond and slightly curly.

"I knew you'd remember," Vasily said. "I knew we had better talk when I could find you alone. So when I saw you rush out of the house a little while ago and drive off in the Rolls, I followed you. I'm sorry to disturb your contemplation in this beautiful spot, but it is necessary, don't you think? You were only thirteen, I believe, but you remember now, don't you?"

Yes, I remembered. It had been in Amsterdam. How I'd loved that museum filled with Vandykes. Ysobel wouldn't look at them in spite of my pleading. She was upset because a handsome emerald necklace that had been given her by a Spanish nobleman had been stolen. I couldn't remember the necklace as well as I did the

Vandykes because it had been sold later for a tidy sum
when Ysobel and Ian had found themselves in debt.

"Emeralds," I said. "The necklace, I mean. And a few
diamonds sprinkled in. I never understood what happened, but I was in the room when the police brought
you to see Ysobel. I remember that I was fascinated by
your beard and your eyes, and that scar over one eyebrow."

I didn't tell him that I'd also been terribly frightened
that day. There had been something about the young
man who was brought to see my mother that I didn't
like. Perhaps a child could sense more deeply beneath
the surface than an adult did. I hadn't liked him, and
I was afraid that he meant to hurt my mother.

Vasily sat beside me, studying me with those slightly
tilted eyes that I remembered. "A distant Mongol an-
cestor must have furnished the eyes," he said. "The scar
was made by a knife. Together, they make disguises
difficult. What else do you remember?"

"I'm not sure of the details. Was it you who took the
necklace?"

He laughed softly and his amusement seemed genuine. "No—my career has usually operated well inside
the law. But I was living at the time with an uncle who
was, I believe, an excellent fence. I happened to have
seen the necklace in his shop. So when I read about it
in the papers, I decided to go to the police. After all, I
had been charmed by your mother in a recent performance and I couldn't bear to see her unhappy. My uncle
was a rascal anyway, and we were never very good
friends after that. But your mother was generous in
the reward she gave me and best of all in her kindness."

He made it all sound so innocent, so light and amusing. Yet I had been afraid.

"Yes," I said, "I do remember. I was there in the
room when you put the necklace into her hands."

"And I remember you. A small girl with very big
eyes and already with a beauty far greater in promise
than your mother's would ever be. I wished at the time

that I could have brought you chocolates or a nosegay. But I gave you neither, and now I am in your hands."

"Why do you think that? I don't know anything about you, except that you brought back something which my mother valued."

"Mr. Logan is bent on investigating my life. And not all of it bears investigation. He will not be pleased if he goes back to Amsterdam. In those days I had another name."

"Then you must have been in trouble with the law?"

"But never caught. There is a difference, I think."

"Does Gretchen know about any of this?"

"She knows all there is to know. Or almost all. I must throw myself on your mercy. If you will give me your silence about ever having seen me in Amsterdam—give it for just a little while—perhaps you will be doing Gretchen a favor. She needs our help, wouldn't you say?"

He had a winning charm of his own, and besides, I had no wish to see Ross destroy whatever happiness Gretchen had found. I mustn't rely too much on the instinctive fear of that child in Amsterdam.

"There's no reason for me to say anything about my mother's necklace, or about meeting you in Amsterdam," I told him.

"Thank you." He took my hand. "I'll leave you to your solitude now. My car is on another street, since I thought it wiser not to have Albert see me come into the gardens."

He bent his blond head and kissed my hand, but when he stood up to leave, I stopped him.

"There's one other thing. Do you know that the two netsuke—the ones that were missing—have been found among Mrs. Logan's things at her cottage?"

"I had not heard that," he said gravely. There was a slight lift to that already raised eyebrow and I wondered if he spoke the truth. Certainly I had the feeling that I had given him something slightly disturbing to think about as he bowed again and turned away. Intrigue was his medium, however, and I suspected that he would come through his troubles, whatever they were.

Watching him cross the grass, go down the few steps, and walk off toward the arcade, I continued to wonder about him. Wondered about Amsterdam, and about what had led Gretchen to marry him. Again I remembered my father's words—"Things are not always what they seem." She must have met a great many charming, fortune-hungry men. So why Vasily? Never mind—this wasn't the main problem that faced me. That, as always, was my husband, Ross Logan. How would I ever find the truth behind his façade? To this puzzle, my father had given me no key.

When I returned to the car, Albert was leaning against the hood, smoking a cigarette. He put it out when he saw me and sprang to open the door.

"Thank you," I said. "This was a perfect place to bring me. I'll want to come back another time and go inside the church. But now I'll go back to Poinciana."

"You look a little better, Mrs. Logan," he told me, and got behind the wheel. He was a kind man, and very loyal to Allegra's son and the old regime.

"Of course, you were here in Allegra Logan's time?" I said as he started the car.

"Yes indeed, Mrs. Logan. I've driven her all around this area many times."

"How can I help her, Albert?" I wanted to add, *How can I help myself and help Gretchen?* But I wouldn't shock him like that. I could tell by the stiffening of his shoulders that I'd startled him as it was.

He turned the car around before he spoke. "Mrs. Charles Logan has always been devoted to Poinciana, Mrs. Logan. If there is something she could help with around the house—?"

"Yes. That's what I think too. But what?"

He thought for a moment as we drove through pleasant tropical streets. "There are those paintings she used to collect, Mrs. Logan. Is there anything you could consult her about that concerns them?"

"Perhaps there is. A very good idea. Thank you, Albert."

We were silent for the rest of the short drive home. When I left the car at the front door, I walked down a long corridor to the gallery wing and opened its door cautiously, half fearing to hear the alarms go off. But the security guard was inside, snoozing in his chair, and he sprang to attention as I entered.

"I don't know the rules," I told him. "When is the alarm usually set?"

"It's on for the door behind the curtain right now," he told me. "But during the day there is always a man on duty at this end of the gallery."

"I'd like to walk through again," I said, "but I won't open the far door."

He touched his cap, and I started along the marble aisle of marvelous paintings. Albert's suggestion might be a good one. Perhaps Allegra could be consulted about the rather haphazard hanging. But to answer that was not my purpose now, and I went on down the long gallery to the second, smaller room, where the real treasures were kept. I knew what drew me like a magnet.

I hadn't wanted to return to this spot. I'd run from it before—because of Ross. But now I wanted to see Ysobel's portrait for myself. There was a need in me to face the truth about my mother. The truth, not only about her, but about *me*.

The curtained recess reminded me of a shrine, and again I hated it fiercely that Ross should have hung her picture like this—in a secret place that only he would come to. If her portrait had been hung where everyone could see it, that would have seemed more normal, and it would have pleased Ysobel. I was sure she would have hated being hidden away like this.

An audience for this rendezvous was the last thing I wanted, and I was glad to be out of sight of the guard when I reached the curtain pulleys.

I put my hand on cords that would open the curtain, hesitating, wondering if I could ever forgive her. Ever forgive myself for hating her as much as I loved her. Now, before I looked into her face again, I must accept that truth, accept the opposing feelings that warred in me and accept them without guilt. None of that lovely generosity Ysobel had directed toward the world had ever been for me. I need not feel guilty. *I* had been the lonely one, watching their happiness together from a distance.

Once, at a time when I was too young to handle bitter reality, she had explained it all to me. She'd done it jokingly, but I had known what she said for the terrible truth it was—that she had never wanted a child. Though if she'd had to have one, a son would have been more acceptable. A son could have been properly adoring, and would never have made her seem old. A daughter could grow up to be a rival. Not that she ever intended that to happen. By the time I was grown, I'd been reduced to a position of useful attendant. She often forgot to introduce me to new friends, and kept me away from the press.

I'd withdrawn into my protective case and tried to feel nothing. It was the only way to live, and I was not actively unhappy or sorry for myself. Resources of my own began to develop. Besides, when I had really wanted something, I had learned how to fight her quietly until she gave in. But now, here at Poinciana, it had all begun to spill out. I could stand before her portrait and for the first time accept the ugly truths. Only then could I send them away from me. Somehow I must forgive her in order to forgive myself. She had never been able to be anything but what she was—a tinsel woman who *had* to be loved, but who had never learned how to love back. I was better off than she, because I had found out that I could love. I had even loved Ysobel in a hungry sort of way. And I had hated her— always concealing both emotions from myself because it hurt too much to indulge them.

Reasoning was no use now, however. I couldn't rid myself of old angers so easily. With a sudden, compulsive movement, I pulled the cords. The blue velvet curtains parted, and the shock of surprise stunned me. I was keyed to face Ysobel, but the space on the wall where the portrait had hung was empty. For several moments I stared blankly at blue curtains. Then I ran back through the small room and down the long gallery to where the guard waited for me.

"My mother's picture is gone," I said. "Do you know what has happened to it?"

He stood up hurriedly. "No, Mrs. Logan. I didn't know it had been removed."

He came with me through the rooms to the recess and looked in some dismay at the empty wall. "Mr. Logan must have given some order that I don't know about. I should have been told. I'm responsible for the security of these galleries."

Steps echoed loudly down the long marble room, and I turned to see Gretchen hurrying toward us. She had changed to her usual shabby jeans, and wore a blouse with a button missing. She moved with an accustomed, purposeful vigor, though sometimes I wondered if she really knew what that purpose was.

When she stopped beside me, her words were almost accusing.

"So here you are! I've been looking for you, Sharon. Susan Broderick told me she'd seen you coming this way."

"My mother's portrait is gone," I said. "It was here only yesterday, when Ross showed it to me."

Gretchen nodded to the guard. "It's all right, Steve. My father took the picture down himself. I saw him this morning when he was carrying it upstairs."

"But why?" I asked, my sense of surprise increasing. "Why did he move it?"

Gretchen looked at me soberly, and for once without mockery. "Maybe we'd better talk. We'll go out the rear way, Steve. You can put the alarm back on when we're out."

She opened a small panel behind blue curtains. Inside was a gray metal box. Gretchen turned the alarm key and led the way through Allegra's "secret" door that Ross had showed me.

"I know the very place for a quiet, intimate conversation," she said, the mockery creeping back. "Come along."

By the time we had made a turn or two, I was lost again, but this was the home that Gretchen had grown up in, and when she opened a pair of double doors I saw that we were in one of the vast drawing rooms that I'd visited on my tour with Ross.

The outer shutters were closed and the great room was dim. Gretchen touched a switch and two priceless chandeliers of rock crystal flashed into light. This was what Allegra had called the French Drawing Room. She had furnished it with gilded Louis XVI chairs upholstered in the pictorial designs of Gobelin tapestry. The wall vitrines on either side of a gold and white marble mantelpiece were filled with Sèvres porcelain that picked up the color motifs of chairs and Savonnerie rug. Upon a cabinet inlaid with mother-of-pearl stood a gilded ormolu clock, its hands stilled at some forgotten hour. Pink Fabergé Easter eggs rested on their own stands on either side of the clock.

"When she was young, Gran turned her rooms into museums," Gretchen said. "You'd never know the same lady furnished the austere suite she took for herself after Grandfather Charlie died."

She went to a window and pulled heavy cords to open the draperies that hung from ceiling to floor. Then she opened the glass and set shutters ajar to let in air and filtered light. When she'd turned off the chandeliers, she led the way to a place by the open windows.

"Gran always arranged little islands for conversation in these big rooms, so this is as good a spot as any. No one will disturb us here."

We sat in tapestried chairs beside a table inlaid with more mother-of-pearl. A collection of millefiore glass paperweights graced its surface. I still felt a reverence for everything around me, but I had no time for appreciation now.

"Why do you think your father moved the picture?" I asked.

"You haven't found out the truth about him yet, have you? You're still infatuated with his position and money and power. All that tremendous effect he makes wherever he goes!"

I was shaking my head before she finished. "No! Those things have never impressed me in the way you mean. Except, perhaps, to make me feel safe."

"Then why did you marry him?"

Somehow it was easy to say the words in this dim and shadowy room that belonged to the past. "He was kind to me. He rescued me and loved me, and I loved him."

"A very pretty picture. But that you believe it only means you haven't discovered that my father is a very sick man. He's powerful and can't be touched, but he's a whole lot sicker, I sometimes feel, than Gran ever was. That's why he's taken the picture upstairs. Because he has an obsession with Ysobel Hollis. He's had it for years. It's one of the things that drove my mother away. It will be a whole lot worse for you because you're *her* daughter."

I could feel the rush of blood to my face, feel the trembling start inside me. She was telling me a truth I had already known, but I'd wanted neither to believe nor to accept it.

When I started to rise, she put out her hand to stop me. "Wait. Vasily told me about finding you in the Bethesda-by-the-Sea gardens this afternoon. He told me what you said about not giving him away to my father. At least I can thank you for that. I know I've resented you. I've wished you'd hate it here and go away. Maybe I still do. But I think you really do want to help with Gran, and it could be you're the only one who can get through to my father. So don't take it too hard about the picture. He can't help himself. Be careful you don't destroy what you care about most."

I already felt that what I'd cared about in Ross Logan was disintegrating because it was based on something that existed only in my mind. I was growing very tired of people who couldn't help themselves—myself included. Somewhere along the way we all had to be responsible for our own actions. But I could say none of this to Ross's daughter, no matter how she might criticize her father herself.

She seemed not to notice my silence. "You must have missed the big battle between Dad and Jarrett today," she went on. "Or have you heard about that?"

I couldn't care a great deal right now, though this would have startled me at another time. "What do you mean?"

"Jarrett seldom loses his temper. Sometimes he has too much control, so that he explodes when he lets go. I was too far away to hear anything but the shouting. I'll have to pump Myra when I get a chance. Jarrett rushed off in a rage just as I reached the office, but I don't think Dad would ever fire him. He couldn't operate without him. Dad was all right—just sputtering mad. It was something about Meridian Oil, I think. About some Japanese businessmen who want to come to see him. He wouldn't talk to me except about Vasily, so I left too and came looking for you."

My mind was still upon what Ross had done with my mother's portrait—my *fear* of what he had done with it—and I listened without much comprehension. I wanted no more of Gretchen's company at the moment, and I left my chair slowly, carefully, as though something were wrong with my balance. It was just that trembling feeling again. I thanked her politely, though I wasn't sure what for, and I didn't hurry until I was out of the room.

In the corridor, I wandered blindly for a few moments

before I got my bearings and found a back way that
took me upstairs. Once I knew where I was, I fled down
the hall and into my room. There I started through an
automatic routine, not allowing my eyes to stray toward Ross's closed door. Postponing. Because I was
afraid of what I would find when I opened that door.
I'd thought that nothing could become much worse between Ross and me, but I already knew better.

When I'd taken off the coral earrings I was wearing,
I pulled my jewel box toward me to put them away.
Ysobel's jewel box. It seemed only partially closed, and
when I lifted the lid I saw why. A packet of envelopes
had been stuffed into the top tray just under the lid.
They were nothing I had placed there and I picked them
up with a sense of fatality.

At first glance I saw that the top envelope was addressed to Ysobel in San Francisco, where she had
taken her last show. By this time I knew the handwriting very well—the letter was from Ross. Quickly
I ran through a dozen or so envelopes—all addressed
to Ysobel in various parts of the country and the world,
all in the same handwriting.

I had no intention of reading them, but I had to be
sure. I opened the top envelope and took out the letter
on stiff Poinciana stationery, turning quickly to the
last page, where Ross's name had been signed, "lovingly." My eyes scanned the page, and the words of love
leaped out at me. Someone with vindictive intent had
placed this collection of love letters that Ross had written to my mother here in Ysobel's jewel box for me to
find. One more thing I had to know. Quickly I ran
through the postmarks. Most of them were old letters,
a few bore dates of more recent years, but there was
nothing in the immediate past.

How they had come back to this house, I had no idea,
unless Ysobel herself had returned them to him. Which
was likely, of course. In that case, someone in this house
had taken them from wherever he'd put them, and left

them here for me to see—intending to hurt me as deeply as possible.

With fingers that fumbled in their haste, I started to fold the letter I'd opened, in order to replace it in its envelope, when a name on the page caught my eye— "Brett." I read the paragraph. Ross had written rather chattily about the weapon he could hold over Brett's head if she ever became a threat to him. Apparently Gretchen's mother had gone deeply into debt in order to open the exclusive shop where her designs were sold. Unknown to Brett, it was Ross who held the note for the loan she had taken, and if he chose he could call it in at any time. If he did this before she was ready, he could very well ruin her. A sense of malevolence, of a cruelty he might enjoy, marked his choice of words, and I felt further sickened.

If someone else had found these letters—Gretchen?— then it was possible that Brett knew very well the dangerous position she might be in, if she had not yet paid up the loan. I wondered what threat she might hold over Ross that had resulted in an impasse.

I stuffed the letter quickly back in its envelope and sat for a moment with the packet in my hand. When I glanced at my own reflection in the mirror, I saw how wide and staring my eyes were, and how pale I looked. There could be no more postponement. I thrust the pack of letters into a lower drawer of my dressing table and placed a box of tissues over them. Later I would decide what to do with them, but now there was the matter I had come here to face.

I got up and went to the closed door of Ross's room. When I tapped there was no answer, so I opened the door and looked in. A hunting scene that had hung over the fireplace was gone, and the portrait of Ysobel Hollis had been put in its place. I crossed the room and stood before the picture, looking up into eyes that had always laughed, as if at a joyous secret, and at lips that smiled for her audience. Any audience. This must be my own private moment of truth.

The secret had been that Ysobel had looked forever in a mirror, and that anything or anyone who came between herself and her flattering self-image was likely to be treated with subtle, smiling cruelty. My father had known well enough, but he had loved her and he had learned how to play the game that would hold her to him. He only took my side when we were alone. At times I'd felt a great impatience with him, yet I could understand his predicament more clearly now. Now I was out of my protective case, and at least I could thank Ysobel and Ross for that. I would never go back.

It was going to hurt a lot out here in the open, I thought fiercely—but here I would stay. Ross's hanging of her portrait in his room erased the last of my doubts. This time I would not wince away from the confrontation that lay ahead. Nor was I in any mood to forgive Ysobel now.

Filled with a new, quiet determination, I returned to the pale champagne colors of my room and lay across the bed. I had no need to will myself into the escape of nothingness now. My mind was clear and I was deeply weary. Sleep carried me restfully into late afternoon, when I awoke to the touch of Ross's hand on my arm, and opened my eyes to see him standing beside my bed.

Chapter

10

Ross was wearing the blue tie-silk dressing gown I'd bought as a gift for him in London, and he smelled pleasantly of soap and shaving lotion. He sat beside me on the bed, leaning over to nuzzle his face into my neck.

"You've had a good sleep," he said. "You're warm and soft and relaxed—the way you should be. Darling, I want to show something."

He scooped me up easily in his arms and carried me through the open door into his room. When he laid me on the bed, I could look up at Ysobel's picture over the mantel and I stared at it fixedly.

"Aren't you pleased?" he said. "I thought you wouldn't want her hidden away in a museum. Besides, she must see how happy we are, my darling. Don't move now. Close your eyes and wait a moment."

I knew what was going to happen as he reached for the switch on the stereo set. The recording began near the end of a phrase, and I heard the huskiness of her voice—"...memories of blue champagne..."

"No!" I cried and sat up on the bed. "Don't play that! Don't ever play it again!"

"Of course I'll play it." His voice was low, gentle, but it brushed aside my objections. "It's the one perfect tune for *our* lovemaking. Her voice, her song. And let her watch—*let* her!"

I pushed against him, rolling to the far side of the bed. "No! I won't let you do this! I won't let you make love to her through me."

He pulled me back to him and all gentleness was gone. "Is that what you think? That I'd make love to her through you? Don't you know how much I hated her, detested her? But I want her here now—here in this room so she can see that I've beaten her. That I've married her daughter."

The singing voice went on beside us, disembodied and terribly wrong, when there was nothing of flesh and blood behind it. What he was telling me was even worse than the sickness I'd suspected. Ysobel was the only woman who had ever refused him, denied him, sent him away, so now he must try to punish her through me, by making love to me.

"Let's get you out of all these clothes," he whispered against my cheek.

Only humiliation could result in a physical struggle against him. There was a better way.

"What a fool you are!" I said softly. "What fools we've both been. Can't you see that Ysobel has won? We are her discards—both of us!"

He let me go and sat up beside me with a curious blankness in his eyes. I slid off the bed and stood up.

"Get out of my room!" he said, his tone ominously low. "Get out of my sight!" The threat in his voice was terrifying.

I rushed into the hall, and it didn't matter where I ran. I only needed, as he said, to get out of his sight.

I had made him a *nothing,* and that was the one thing Ross Logan could never endure to be.

It was all over—everything I'd trusted in so mistakenly, everything I'd hoped for so stupidly and innocently in this marriage. There were tears on my cheeks and sobs were catching my breath as I ran down the nearest stairs, stumbling, clinging to the rail to keep from falling, hoping that I would meet no one until I could find a place to hide. Because I was afraid of myself—of falling apart in some disastrous breakdown of the sort I'd been close to after that fire in Belfast. I no longer had any inner place of concealment to run to—and no confidence in my ability to face what lay outside.

Because I was hurtling blindly, I ran directly into Jarrett Nichols as he came out of the offices into my path. By this time I was weeping wildly in reaction, and he shook me hard, shook me back into my senses, so that I gulped for air and went limp in his hands.

"Come in here," he said, and drew me into his office, thrust me into a chair. Myra had gone for the day, and he closed the door to the outer office and came back to sit on a corner of the desk beside me. "Would you like a drink? Do you want to talk?"

I shook my head and wept into my hands. How could I ever tell anyone, when what had happened was so painful, so shameful? Only Gretchen would have understood, yet in her way she loved her father, and I could never talk to her, never talk to anyone.

I'd been wrong about the office being empty, however. In my distress, I hadn't seen the quiet figure in a corner of the room. When I heard movement, I took my hands from my face in surprise. Allegra Logan left her chair and came to touch me gently on the shoulder. She was wearing slacks and a sweater again—her costume when she went roving from the cottage.

"What has my son done this time?" she asked. Her eyes were bright in her lined face, and they were perfectly sane and aware.

I only shook my head.

"Jarrett, get her a glass of something. It will help her to relax. She's obviously had a shock. My son has always been a vulnerable man, and that makes him dangerous."

Jarrett brought me a small glass of brandy and put it in my hand. Then he pulled a chair for Allegra close to mine, and seated her in it.

"This house still needs me," Allegra said. "He's going to spoil Gretchen's life, and he's trying to destroy this poor young thing. I'm needed here, but I haven't the strength any more to do what ought to be done. Besides, he means to send me away—and how am I to fight that?"

If in the past Jarrett had wavered in what he thought might be best for Allegra Logan, he now made up his mind. "No one is going to send you away. I'll do my best to prevent that."

I managed to sip brandy, letting its warmth flow through me, relaxing a little, watching them both.

Allegra looked up at Jarrett. "I had one weapon, if only I could have used it. He doesn't know it exists, or that I lost it somehow when they moved me out of the house. Perhaps I put it away somewhere carefully. Only I can't remember where. Of course, it's all in my head, as well, and that's what he's afraid of. But having it in my head isn't strong enough to use against him now."

She had caught Jarrett's attention. "What are you talking about, Mrs. Logan?"

"Nothing I have any intention of telling you," she said calmly. "You don't need this, as I do. You already have the power. You're the one person he won't dare to go against if you make up your mind to oppose him. Though I'm not sure you'll really go that far. You've protected him for too long."

"I stopped protecting him today," Jarrett said bitterly. "We had the worst row this afternoon that I've ever had with him. And I was the one who walked out. We've trained him for too long to believe in his own fantasies."

"Of being a great man? Yes. I don't know how you've stayed with him for so long. Or perhaps I do. You've put the money in the right places. Without you as his conscience, he'd never have cared."

"This afternoon he lost the last of his conscience," Jarrett said.

"But he's no longer on the board, is he? He's been letting the reins go, turning to other things?"

"Ostensibly. Outwardly—to give himself protection. But the board chairman is still in his pocket. Ross never lets go of what he wants." He glanced at me in sudden embarrassment and apology.

"It's all right," I said. "I must try to understand."

Allegra closed her eyes wearily. Then she opened them and looked at me.

"What about you, child? If you love him, that's important too. God knows, I've loved the wrong men at times. But you're not another Brett. We all know what she wanted of marriage. But whatever Ross has done, he will get over it if you give him time."

"*I* won't get over it," I told her. "Not after what has happened." My voice broke again, and suddenly the words came pouring out—words I'd thought I couldn't speak. "He hung Ysobel's portrait in his room. That painting of my mother that he commissioned years ago. And he played a song of hers—with *her* voice singing! He's still in love with her!"

But I couldn't tell them the rest, and I broke off as Jarrett started pacing around the room. Allegra leaned forward to touch my hand with thin, dry fingers.

"You must be very careful now. He can never bear to be thwarted—my son. He came to see me earlier today. Because of the two netsuke he says I took from his collection and hid in my room. Of course I didn't, but this is why I gave Coxie the slip and came here to talk to Jarrett. I tried to persuade Ross that I would never have taken them. I never much liked that collection, except for my little mermaid. It's become too much of an obsession with him—as though this book he wants to write will give him the distinction he's never really been able to grasp in other ways. But he wouldn't believe me. He doesn't want to believe me."

Jarrett paused before her chair to take her hands in his. "If I'm to help you, I have to be sure of what I'm doing. I'm going to say something now that it may be hard for you to hear. Do you remember the time when you fired a shot at Ross? That time when he moved you out of the house? Can you remember why?"

"Certainly I remember! It was just after your wife's death. I shot at him because I knew he would never be convicted of anything he did, and he would just go on destroying people. Good people. He had to be stopped. I gave him his life, so perhaps it was my duty to take it away. Unfortunately, I wasn't a very good shot. Perhaps at the last moment I didn't really mean to be. Charlie would have been ashamed of such terrible aim. But it was more than that. There was a *special* reason why I shot him...only...only..." Her voice faltered to a halt as her strength faded.

Jarrett was at her side at once. "That's enough now. Never mind the reason. Let me take you back to your room at the cottage."

She rallied a little, however, and reached a hand toward me. "I meant what I said. If you want to leave him, then you must do it quickly, before he can guess what you intend. You must be very careful of his anger."

I already knew this and I nodded mutely. I had seen that look in Ross's eyes, and I'd fled from it instinctively. But while she could still talk, I needed to know whatever she could tell me.

"You said a little while ago that Ross was vulnerable. What did you mean?"

"If Charlie had lost every bit of money he made, it wouldn't have mattered. He'd have been perfectly sure that he had the brains and gumption and character to do it all over again. But Ross is a second-generation *heir*. He didn't earn it himself out of a business that he'd built and loved. I suppose some heirs do fine, but Ross knows he'll never be much on his own without money to back him. So all he can think about is getting more and more, without really having any good reason for needing it."

"Right now," Jarrett said, "he's trying to prove what he can do on his own, and he's stepping into deep and dangerous waters. The trouble is that a great many more innocent lives hang in the balance than his."

Allegra bowed her head in agreement. "He's frightened to death of losing anything that belongs to him. He couldn't stand it when he almost won Ysobel Hollis, and then she turned him down for your father, Sharon. That's what he can never take—ridicule, defeat. Our defeats make most of us tough. Not Ross. Now he is trying to undo all this by strking out in some new direction. He has never understood that he's vulnerable. That's what makes him so dangerous."

She had talked for too long, and she sank wearily back in her chair. I saw that her hands were trembling.

"We'll go to the cottage now," Jarrett said. "Do you think you can ride with me in the golf cart?"

"Of course. If you'll boost me into it. I just came to find out where you stand, Jarrett. At least I know that you'll try to help me—even if you fail."

"I will try," he said. "I'll talk to Ross. Will you come with us, Sharon? You're still looking rocky. I don't want to leave you here alone."

The phone rang on Jarrett's desk and he picked it up.

"That will be Coxie," Allegra said, and it was. Jarrett reassured the nurse, and we went into the outer office. Myra Ritter, busy at her desk, looked up at us innocently.

"I thought you'd gone home," Jarrett said.

"I did leave, but then I remembered something I hadn't finished, so I came back. I didn't want to disturb you."

"We're taking Mrs. Logan down to the cottage," Jarrett told her. "If anyone asks, you haven't seen her."

"Of course I haven't, Mr. Nichols." I suspected that she was on our side and would say nothing to Ross if the matter came up.

Outside, the golf cart that was often used for quick transport around the grounds waited for us at a side door. But before she got in, Allegra looked sadly up at the house. "It's too quiet and empty these days. Palm Beach used to be so full of parties. Everyone gave parties and there was always some charity ball coming up. We did some good while we had all that expensive fun."

"It's still going on," Jarrett said. "You can go to three parties a day on the island when the season is on. If you wanted to. This little stretch of land holds more ball gowns and jewels and magnums of champagne than most of the population of America ever sees in a lifetime."

If she heard the sting in his words, she paid no attention, and her face, for all its myriad lines, looked dreamy with an illusion of youth.

"But they were never like the parties *I* gave. Rajahs and maharanis came to Poinciana in those days. Kings and princes and all kinds of presidents. Of countries and of businesses. If we got bored with what was happening on land, I took them all off on the *Allegra* and we would sail to the Bahamas, or the Greek isles—or anywhere our fancy chose."

She stood transfixed beside the car, her thoughts in the past.

"Let me help you." Jarrett spoke gently.

"Wait." She turned to me. "You must bring it all back. You must make it come to life again—my beautiful house. With all my chandeliers lighted, and all the crystal and silver shining. Guests will come, you know, the minute you whistle—because you're a Logan and this is Poinciana."

Already she had forgotten that I might be leaving Ross.

"I'm not sure I want all that," I told her.

For a moment her eyes looked directly into mine. "No, I suppose you won't want it. You've much better sense. In the end, of course, I didn't want it either. When Charlie died and Brett gave the parties, I never went. I moved into those lovely, peaceful gray rooms. I had time to read books then, and listen to music. Not music played just for dancing. All right, Jarrett, take me back to the cottage. It's antiseptic and ugly. But I'm used to it now. I don't even see what's around me most of the time, and I can still look out the windows and walk outside."

He lifted her into the front seat, and I climbed into the back, facing the other way. Which is why I had a full view of the house as we drove off across the lawn. Ross had come through his mother's rooms and was standing on her small balcony looking out this way, watching us go, his face expressionless. In bright sunshine I felt chilled and more than a little frightened.

"He's watching us," I warned. "Just standing there on a balcony watching us."

"Let him," Jarrett said.

But I couldn't shrug off that chilling emptiness on Ross's face. I must get away quickly, while there was still time.

When we reached the cottage, Jarrett took Allegra inside, and I saw that she faltered now as she moved, and that her mind had lost its moments of clarity and taken her far back into the past.

Jarrett returned to the cart, where I waited. "Are you all right now?"

"I'm not sure. I'm not sure of anything, except that I must leave."

"You'd better *be* sure, because Ross will be very sure of everything. But you need to be sure because you've thought it all through, not because you're running away scared."

I wanted to trust him, to listen, to lean on a strength that I felt was real and to be counted on. But I'd been

learning the hard way not to trust, and I must lean on
no one but myself.

"I'm angry now, but I'm frightened too," I told him.
"I have to go away. Perhaps I can move into town for
a while. Just to have time to think. Alone."

"Don't act in too much of a hurry. It's better not to
antagonize him, if you can help it. Besides, have you
considered that you may be needed here more than you
believe? Allegra knew she was needed at Poinciana,
but she's too old to cope now, and she realizes that. So
perhaps it's your turn. You've made a start with
Gretchen. She and Allegra both need you here."

"Need me! Allegra had forgotten me by the time we
reached the cottage. And Gretchen doesn't like me."

"If you think those things, you're blinder than I believed. Isn't it possible that you could be good for Ross
as well, if you stay and see this through? Have you ever
considered that he might be running scared too?"

My indignation surged. "Allegra, who knows him
best of all, thought I should go. She believes he's dangerous. Besides, just a little while ago in your office
you were critical of Ross. You didn't sound sympathetic
toward him then."

"That doesn't mean I'm going to walk out. I can be
critical of him, and sorry for him at the same time.
Allegra spoke the truth. He *is* vulnerable. More so than
you know."

I hardly listened. "Allegra knows something," I
mused. "Something in particular that might be used
against Ross."

"That's probably all in her imagination. And no
matter if it were true, I wouldn't want to see it used.
A great many issues are involved here—complex issues."

"But I have to save myself. I can't stay here and be
destroyed."

"I think you're stronger than you've let yourself discover. And if you leave, he'll come after you. You have
to realize that. You have to recognize the fact that

you're surrounded by the enormous power of one of the
most omnipotent men in the world. In a sense, I'm in
the same position you are. But I'll stay because greater
issues *are* involved. I'll stay and compromise, in spite
of my mixed feelings about Ross Logan."

"I don't know if I can compromise. Or if I should."

"You're a woman. Win him. Win him over Ysobel!"

I stared angrily at Jarrett—at the blowing red hair,
into eyes that watched me coolly, at a mouth that seldom smiled. I resented him utterly. Resented most of
all what he had just said to me. Words that were an
affront and that I couldn't accept.

We'd reached the house and the cart came to a stop.
"I can't think of larger issues," I told him. "I can only
think about getting away."

"Gretchen is frightened too. And so is Allegra. So
think about yourself, but think about them too."

I didn't want to listen to any more. I jumped down
from the cart without waiting for Jarrett's help, and
ran toward the nearest door.

Susan Broderick stood in the doorway, waiting for
me. She was in uniform again, and playing the proper
maid.

"Mrs. Logan, Mr. Logan would like you to come to
the library as soon as possible, please."

Alarm ran through me, but I managed to thank her
and went into the shadowy coolness of the house. By
this time I knew my way to the library, and I moved
reluctantly down the hall, feeling totally unprepared
for an immediate interview with my husband.

At the doorway I hesitated, looking into the big,
slightly gloomy room. Ross sat at a long refectory table
at the far end. The only light came from a Tiffany lamp
on the table. Behind him a Coromandel screen of lacquered black and gold formed a luminous backdrop.
When he saw me he left his chair to come toward me
quickly, and it was clear that all the earlier rage had
gone out of him. But my own emotions couldn't shift

so quickly, and though my immediate alarm lessened, I moved toward him stiffly.

"Sharon darling, we must talk," he said. "We haven't understood each other at all, have we?"

"I understood that you wanted me out of your sight. I was just going upstairs to pack and move into town. Perhaps I can stay at the Breakers for a while."

He put an arm around me and walked me to the leather couch, where he sat beside me. "I'm sorry I lost my temper. You'll have to get used to that at times. When I'm angry, everything pours out and I may say things I'm sorry for later. Listen to me, darling. The portrait of your mother will be taken down. And I'll put away that recording. Ysobel Hollis has nothing to do with us."

"I think she has everything to do with us. I realize now that I'm only here because I'm her daughter."

He put a hand against my face in the tender way I'd loved, and drew me close to him. "You're wrong to think that. Perhaps I did have my own foolish fantasy of revenge, but it's been played out now. It's over with— done. You are my young love, who has brought me more happiness than I've ever known. And I think you've loved me too."

All the old charm and tenderness were working and I felt his appeal. Yet a part of my mind stood away, distrusting and unaffected. I didn't believe anything he was saying, and I moved so that I could sit apart, so that his hands couldn't weave their caressing spell.

"I don't know," I said.

"You don't know what?"

I faltered in my uncertainty. "I mean I'm not sure of anything right now. Cruelty frightens me."

"Cruelty? Oh, come now, Sharon. I'm hardly a cruel man. Am I being cruel now?"

"I don't know," I repeated. "I really don't know. Not only because of what has happened between us, but also because of what you're doing to your mother and to Gretchen."

He stood up against the rich golds of the Coromandel screen, impatient with me again. "Don't you think that I must be allowed to judge what is best for my mother?"

"I can't help feeling the way I do," I said. "I believe your judgment is wrong on this. I had a chance to talk with Allegra today. She can be perfectly normal and sensible. Quite wise, really. What happened that one time shouldn't be held against her. If she came back to live in her own rooms, she might improve."

I sensed a sudden wariness in him. "She might also improve if she were placed in the care of a resident expert in mental illness."

"She would only be put on drugs and she could become really senile then. Why not give her a chance here first? You could always send her away later. Is this too much to ask?"

I knew we were playing a game. If Ross had reason to fear the knowledge Allegra possessed, the issue was not where he sent her, but how he stopped her from talking. As with Brett, in that mention in the letters. I wondered if Brett knew the same thing Allegra claimed to know.

"I'll think about it," he said. "But now let's talk about Gretchen and Vasily. There is a great deal about her husband that she doesn't know. For instance, that he was married for a couple of years to an actress named Elberta Sheldon. In London. Oh, they were divorced, all right. The records show that, but it's a little matter he hasn't told Gretchen about. I know, because I asked her this afternoon. He's an adventurer of the worst sort. He was still married to this woman when he met Gretchen, but he got out of his marriage pretty quickly when better prospects came into view."

"I think Gretchen looks at him realistically, whatever he's done," I said, feeling that nothing I learned about Vasily would surprise me.

"She's a baby! He got out of Brussels just ahead of the law and changed his name. If he's sent back there he'll be arrested and tried, and probably put in prison.

So I have him where I want him. I talked to him an hour ago and gave him a choice. He will either leave Gretchen at once, or I will have him sent back to Belgium. Gretchen will have to accept this and let him go."

For a moment I could only stare at Ross in dismay. "She'll hate you forever if you do this. Can't you see the effect on Gretchen? She knows about Brussels. Vasily has told her everything."

"He's an expert liar. I won't have you defending him."

"I'm only trying to keep you from injuring your daughter. And yourself, too, because I think you do love her. Ross, if Vasily is really no good, then let her find it out for herself. If you give her time, perhaps she'll be ready to leave him on her own. But if you do what you're planning, you'll lose her for good."

"I must be the judge of that."

There was nothing more to be said. "I'll go and pack," I told him. "I don't want to spend another night in this house."

At once he dropped to the couch beside me. "Now you're the one who is acting hastily. Most of the time you are a very mature young woman, and you try to think things through sensibly. So don't rush off in haste and regret it later."

He didn't understand anything about me, I thought. He had no idea of the way I'd been shattered, damaged as a woman, from the moment I had realized that it was Ysobel he was making love to, not me. He really believed that a few denials and apologies would now make everything all right. If I hadn't been so thoroughly spent by my own emotions, I might have stood my ground and opposed him further. But I couldn't fight him any longer right now.

"I'll stay for tonight," I said. "Perhaps I can think more clearly in the morning."

"Good." He was pleased over what he must regard

as the winning of a disagreement. He seemed to have
no idea of how deep this went with me.

I stood up and he rose to hold me for a moment and
kiss me warmly. "That's my girl. Let me take you out
for dinner tonight. Let's get away from Poinciana and
recapture what we had in Kyoto. It's still there, you
know. Let it surface again."

I was already shaking my head before he had finished. "No, Ross, please. I want to spend some time
alone. Let me have that before we talk again."

He let me go reluctantly and I went upstairs to my
room. Susan Broderick was there, turning down my
bed for the night. I told her I had a slight headache and
would have supper here—something light. She was at
once concerned and kind.

"I'll bring a tray up for you myself," she promised.

I undressed and drew on a long robe. Then I went
out on the loggia to look at a sky that was taking on
hints of sunset vermilion. As I stood there a flock of
flamingos sailed past and as I watched the flight of
exotic birds some of the tension went out of me.

Ross had been right, and so had Jarrett, even though
I'd resented his words. I couldn't dismiss everything
lightly, but I would wait and think about it, allow what
had happened to fall into some sort of perspective.

When I heard sounds in my room, I returned, to find
that not Susan, but her mother, had brought up my
tray.

"Mr. Logan asked me to look in on you and see if
there is anything you wish," Mrs. Broderick told me.
"He's concerned that you aren't feeling well, Mrs. Logan."

I sensed a disapproval behind her words that she
couldn't entirely hide.

"I'll be fine," I said. "Thank you for bringing me a
tray."

She sat it upon a table she pulled near the loggia
doors, where I could sit and watch the sunset.

When I'd finished my light meal I went outside by

the loggia steps and crossed the lawn to sit on the wall beside the lake. My thoughts had quieted to some extent, but I was only holding away the time of decision, of taking a stand. Nothing could ever be the same again between Ross and me. The simple element of trust was gone, and no matter what he claimed, I would doubt him from now on.

What Jarrett had said about my usefulness here seemed unreal. Even if there was anything I could do for Gretchen or Allegra, I would be of little use to anyone until I could mend myself.

As I sat there on the wall, Brewster, Keith's dog, came trotting over to examine my presence. Jarrett's son followed him and sat beside me, his legs dangling toward the water. They were undemanding company. The boy told me that Brewster had been named for a gardener at Poinciana, whom Keith had liked.

"I want to be an air pilot when I grow up," he went on. "I want to go everywhere. Like you. Dad told me you've lived in all sorts of countries. What was it like?"

So simple a question, and one so difficult to answer. What would seem strange and different to this young boy had been everyday to me. Alps on the horizon were commonplace, and so was the sight of Big Ben across the Thames. I knew the Paris Métro well, and I had once stayed in a castle on the Rhine.

I tried to tell him a little about all this, tried to make it amusing. As I related a funny story about a concierge in Paris, I heard myself laugh, and realized that it was not only Ross who had lacked a sense of humor lately.

Boy and dog were good for me. Before the afterglow was gone from the sky, they walked me back to the steps and then ran off toward their cottage. I felt more relaxed than I had all day.

Inside, I bolted the loggia doors, locked my hall door, and got ready for bed. All the while, those letters to Ysobel seemed to burn in my consciousness—their physical presence in this room a further threat to me.

Not because Ross had written them, but because secret malice had brought them to me.

There was no key to Ross's room and nothing I could do about that. I was enormously tired, physically and emotionally. In the morning perhaps I could face what had to be faced.

Fortunately, sleep came easily that night, in spite of the early hour, and at first I slept soundly. There were dreams and in the hours after midnight they grew disturbing. But they were gone in a flash when I awoke to a dreadful sound of disaster.

An alarm bell was ringing wildly, clamoring all through the house. I sat up against my pillow, stiff with fright, and listened to that horrible, shattering sound that seemed never to end. A glance at my watch told me that it was two-fifteen in the morning. I rolled out of bed and pulled on my robe, ran through the door into Ross's room. It was empty and his bed had not been slept in.

Chapter

11

I ran into the empty corridor and rushed toward the nearest stairs. In this vast house a dozen people must be moving about, summoned by the clamor, yet corridors and rooms seemed ominously empty. As though only I could hear that terrible, shrilling alarm.

It was coming, I realized, from the direction of the art gallery at the other end of the house. When I reached the lower hall, I saw light from the offices cutting through an open door, and I ran past Myra's desk into Ross's office. He was there, and so was Jarrett Nichols, but if either of them heard that terrible ringing, they gave no sign.

Ross, fully dressed, lay slumped across his desk, while Jarrett, in a terry robe, stood beside him, a sheet of notepaper in his hand. He stared at me as I came into the room, and I had never seen him look so desperately grim.

"I just found him." As he spoke, Jarrett thrust the sheet of paper beneath an engagement book on Ross's desk. "Sharon, I'm afraid he's gone. I'm going to try mouth-to-mouth. Help me get him out of that chair."

Together we managed to lower Ross to the floor. I was too numb and unbelieving to do anything but what I was told. Jarrett scribbled a number on a pad and handed it to me.

"Call this doctor," he ordered, and knelt beside Ross's prostrate body.

I hardly knew what I was doing as I dialed the number. And all the while the hideous clamor of the alarm bell seemed to go on and on. Then, just as a sleepy voice answered on the line, the sound stopped with an abruptness that left the silence ringing.

Since I was using Ross Logan's name, there was no question but that the doctor would come as soon as he could get here. I set the phone down just as Jarrett looked up at me.

"It's no use," he said. "He's gone." He rose and went to Ross's desk, where papers lay scattered.

Still numb with shock, I knelt beside my husband and touched his shoulder, half expecting him to respond to me. His expression was contorted, as though he had died in a moment of great distress. Only a short while ago I had loved this man, depended upon him, and trusted him. Yet during the last days, even the last hours, all that had gone out of me, and kneeling here beside him, I could feel nothing. It was only numbness, of course. Feeling would come later—a sense of loss and sorrow.

Jarrett had begun to gather and stack the papers across which Ross had fallen. "Before the police come," he said.

I echoed the word dully. "Police?"

"He died unattended. The doctor will report this."

"Then should you touch his desk? Won't the police want everything left as it was?"

He paid no attention, but took an empty folder from a drawer, thrust the stack of papers into it.

"Remember," he said, "you know nothing about these."

I came to life a little. "I don't understand. Why are you putting Ross's papers away?"

"It's only for the time being. I can't explain everything now, Sharon. It's too complicated. I'll tell you later."

"Tell me now. Tell me what happened to Ross."

Without answering, Jarrett went to the phone, and a moment later he was talking to the police. Next he telephoned the gatehouse and spoke to the guard who was posted there. When he'd questioned him about the alarm, he explained that Mr. Logan had had an accident.

"Why did the alarm go off?" I asked when he hung up.

"They don't seem to know. Sit down, Sharon—you're looking shaky."

He was clearly shaken himself, for all his control, and when I didn't move he picked up the folder of papers and carried it into his own office.

Almost without thought, I went to the desk and drew out the sheet I'd seen Jarrett slip beneath Ross's engagement book. Something was wrong here, and I had to know what it was. I could tell as I folded it into the pocket of my robe that the note was on Poinciana notepaper. There was no time to examine it, however, before Jarrett was back.

"Gretchen must be told," he said. "This shouldn't be done by phone, but I can't send you, Sharon."

"I'll go," I said. "I can manage."

There was no need. Even as I spoke, Gretchen burst into the office, still in pajamas, a gown clutched about her.

"What's happening?" she demanded. "The alarm woke me and I went down to the gallery. But no one was there, so I turned it off and came along here."

"It's your father, Gretchen," Jarrett said.

She looked at him, and then at me, saw the direction of my eyes, and came around the desk. Her cry was one of true anguish as she dropped to the floor and tried to rouse him, calling to him, pleading for him to answer.

Jarrett raised her gently and took her to a chair. "You have to face this, Gretchen. We've called Dr. Lorrimer, and the police as well. And I've notified the gatehouse. They don't know who set off the alarm. Guards are searching the grounds now. Shall I phone your rooms for Vasily to come?"

Gretchen stared at him blankly, emotion draining out of her. "Vasily's not there. He must not have come to bed at all last night." She broke off, trying to get herself in hand. "Tell me what happened."

I still wanted to know that myself, and I sat down beside Gretchen.

"Your father called me on the phone just a short time ago and asked me to come here at once," Jarrett said. "He told me it couldn't wait until morning. So I came as fast as I could—and found him slumped across his desk. I'd barely stepped into the office when the alarm started. Sharon heard the ringing and came. She called the doctor, while I tried to revive him. I don't know what happened, Gretchen. He may have felt a heart attack coming on when he phoned me. He was upset about something."

Gretchen started to speak, and he stopped her.

"Before anyone comes—is there anything you know about this?"

A strange question to ask, I thought, as I saw her bristle.

"What should I know? You're the one who upset him badly with that row you had. You and—and *her*. He's had nothing but pain and disappointment from Sharon!"

That hadn't been the way she had talked to me about her father in the library. But now she was growing excited.

"He's had too much from both of you! And I'm going to tell the doctor that. Believe me, I am!"

Jarrett answered her quietly. "You'll need to get yourself in hand, Gretchen, before anyone comes. You know as well as I do how explosive anything that's said here now can be. It won't help if you fly off with wild charges. What we need to know is the truth. If there is something you know about this, you'd better tell us now. About what shocked him and brought on this attack."

She shrank into her chair, her anger evaporating. "I don't know anything about it. How should I?"

I wondered uneasily about Jarrett's insistent probing. Was she trying to protect Vasily in some way by accusing us? Her husband—who had every reason to quarrel with Ross—would be in the clear if we were to blame. Now, at least, the detectives would be called off from their investigation of Vasily, and he would no longer be held to a grim bargain by Ross Logan.

Jarrett went to the coffee maker in a corner of the office and brought us each a cup of hot coffee. I warmed my hands around the china cup, wondering if the chill would ever go out of me. Nothing would ever be the same again. Not for me, not for Gretchen, or even for Jarrett. Allegra would be saved from the fate that had awaited her. Strange that Ross's death should bring hope to so many people. But I couldn't deal with that now. I couldn't even assimilate the fact that he was dead. At any moment he would surely open his eyes and take up his life as the strong, dynamic man we had all known. It was he who should be giving orders in this crisis, not any of us.

The sheet of notepaper seemed to burn in my pocket, but I dared not take it out and examine it, though I had a strong feeling that it would tell me something— something that ought to be known, and which Jarrett had instinctively tried to hide.

As though the intensity of my thoughts touched him, he set down his cup and went casually to Ross's desk, where he moved the engagement book an inch or two. I saw him freeze for an instant. Then he looked directly at me. I stared back, willing myself not to let my eyes falter, while unspoken accusations leapt between us.

Gretchen suddenly began to cry. She wept like a child—wildly and with abandon, and I wished that I could cry in the same way. During the last few days I had seemed to weep easily and often. Yet now, when there was terrible cause, no tears came.

Jarrett let her cry. He left the desk to stand before me. "Give it to me," he said softly. "It doesn't concern you."

Once more, I managed to meet his eyes. "I will not," I told him.

The gray, shaken look was still upon him. "Be careful of the damage you may do," he told me. "It will be better for everyone if you burn that note without reading it."

Were these Ross's last words that burned in my pocket? What damning things might he have written? But I didn't know yet what I would do with the note— except that I couldn't do as Jarrett asked. It was time for the terrible secrets that had haunted this house to come into the open. That one thing I knew.

"I wonder why Mrs. Broderick isn't here?" I asked. "She should have heard the alarm, like the rest of us."

Gretchen looked up woefully. "She left last evening with Susan to visit a sister in Boca Raton. She told me they would come home today."

For the first time I missed the presence of Ross's efficient housekeeper. But at least others of the staff were about, including the reliable Albert, who had chauffeured me only yesterday afternoon. He came in, bringing with him the doctor—a slightly stooped, elderly man, with an air of authority. Ross would have had his personal physician for a long time, and he would be the best.

Dr. Lorrimer began his examination at once, and a few moments later the local police arrived. In charge

was Lieutenant Hillis, a quiet, youngish man, with
sandy hair that had begun to thin. He was clearly re-
spectful of these august surroundings, yet hardly awed
by them. I sensed a strength in him that would probably
get results without any barking of orders.

He explained that it would be necessary to ask a few
questions of those present. Dr. Lorrimer informed him
with an air of complete assurance that the cause of
death was heart failure, making his findings very clear.
Undoubtedly he was aware that no questions must be
left hanging for police or press to pick up. His patient
had had heart difficulties for years, he pointed out. He
had been warned repeatedly that he must avoid disturbing emotions, avoid any overtaxing of his strength.
Apparently he had driven himself hard last night,
working past midnight without rest. The expected pen-
alty had at last been exacted. All this was news to me.
Not once had Ross mentioned any trouble with his
heart.

Gretchen had stopped crying and sat curled up in
her chair, her legs under her, and I knew she listened
intently to every word. As we all did. Because of so
many guilty secrets? I wondered. I was sure that Jarrett
and Gretchen did not believe that Ross's death had
come about so simply as Dr. Lorrimer claimed, though
not one of us was going to dispute his words. In spite
of her threat that she would blame Jarrett and me for
upsetting her father, Gretchen said nothing now.

Lieutenant Hillis informed us of what would happen.
An autopsy would be performed, after which the body
would be released to the family.

Jarrett nodded. "It's better that no questions about
Mr. Logan's death be left unanswered. May Mrs. Karl
and Mrs. Logan go back to bed? I'll stay as long as you
need me."

The lieutenant agreed readily. There would be time
later in the day for more questions, if they seemed
necessary.

Dr. Lorrimer had been watching Gretchen, and he

spoke to her gently. "I'll see you up to your room now
and give you something to help you sleep. You mustn't
stay alone at this time. Where is your husband?"

Before she could answer, the telephone rang shrilly
and Jarrett picked it up. His reply was curt. "Don't let
anyone past the gates. Tell them I'll come out and make
a statement shortly."

The press, of course, I thought. The media! This
would be no quiet, private death. The news line of the
world would hum furiously for days, weeks, and we
would be given no peace unless Jarrett set up the bar-
ricades.

Before the doctor could repeat his question about
Gretchen's husband, Vasily himself appeared in the
doorway, pausing a moment to take us all in before he
went to his wife. He looked properly grave and regretful, and had apparently heard what had happened.
However, I was beginning to know him a little by this
time, and I suspected that he could barely conceal the
mood of elation surging up inside him. It was there in
the very spring of his step, in the brightness of his eyes.
Vasily would always think first of himself.

"Darling," he said. "This is all too terrible. I came
as soon as I heard."

She sprang from her chair and let herself be folded
into his arms. I noticed that she didn't demand to know
where he had been.

"Good," Dr. Lorrimer said. "I'll go with you to your
bedroom and give her something to help her sleep. You
must stay with her now, Mr. Karl." Then he turned
to me. "Are you all right, Mrs. Logan? Would you
like—?"

I reassured him quickly. "I have a prescription I can
take if I need it." After all, I had been through two
deaths recently. I was well prepared, wasn't I?

He gave me a slightly doubtful look, as though he
feared some delayed reaction in me, and I spoke again
quietly.

"I really am all right." It was strange how calm I

could manage to be, and a little frightening. Had I lost all ability to feel?

Gretchen glanced at me with eyes that were faintly accusing before she allowed Vasily and the doctor to help her from the room. More than anything else, I was aware of Jarrett's stillness as he watched them go—a stillness that covered whatever he was thinking.

No one asked aloud the question that must have been in Gretchen's mind, as well as in Jarrett's and mine. Where had Vasily been, and how had he heard what had happened? Apparently, since everything seemed clear cut and settled about Ross's death, this was not a question that Lieutenant Hillis had any need to ask.

But even as it stirred in the silence of our minds, Vasily came back to us through Myra's empty office.

"I should have explained," he said quickly. "I have been in Allegra Logan's company all evening. When I went to see her earlier, I found her very much upset. So I stayed until the nurse got her to sleep. It must have been nearly two in the morning, and afterwards I dozed in her living room for a while, lest she waken and be upset again. I heard the alarm go off, of course, and I was awake when one of the guards came to tell us what had happened. I instructed Miss Cox to say nothing to Allegra until a member of the family could tell her. Then I came straight to the house."

He looked from Jarrett to me as though his words carried some barely hidden triumph, and then hurried after his wife and the doctor. No one said anything.

The medical examiner and further police entourage were arriving, and Jarrett came over to me.

"You needn't stay for any of this. Let me take you up to your room."

The last thing I wanted was to be alone with Jarrett Nichols. Not until I knew the contents of that note. He looked quite capable of taking it from me by force if he chose.

I jumped to my feet with a suddenness that caused

Lieutenant Hillis to stare at me. "I just want to be by myself!" I cried. "I know the way to my room!"

I ran into the hall, and heard Jarrett coming after me. One of the guards had posted himself near the door to the offices, and I rushed up to him.

"Please take me upstairs. Mr. Nichols has to stay with the police, and—and I feel a little dizzy."

He was the man called Steve, who was usually posted in the gallery. He showed quick concern. "Of course, Mrs. Logan. I'll get her upstairs all right, Mr. Nichols. And I'll call one of the maids to come and stay with her. Everyone's up by now."

Jarrett nodded grimly and went back to Ross's office. I clung gratefully to Steve's arm, discovering that I really did feel uncertain about where I put my feet. On the way I thought of one question to ask.

"Were you in the gallery when the alarm went off?"

"Yes, Mrs. Logan. This was my night to be on duty. When it rang, I ran through the gallery and out the far door. I didn't even stop to turn off the alarm, because searching at once was more important. But I couldn't find anyone."

When we reached my room, I refused to let him call a maid, thanked him, and sent him away.

Safely inside, I went through the now familiar ritual of checking and locking my doors. After a moment of hesitation, I went through Ross's room and locked his door to the corridor as well. Ysobel watched me, smiling warmly from her place on the wall. Before I returned to my room, I stood for a moment looking up at her.

"I don't know who has won, or who has lost," I told her.

Back in my room, with the connecting door closed, I dropped onto the chaise longue and stretched out. The lamp beside me gave light for reading, and there was just one thing I must do at this moment.

I unfolded the notepaper I had thrust into my pocket and saw that it had been typed, and then signed with one of Gretchen's curious little signature faces. This one displayed zigzagged teeth—the sign, Ross had told me, that indicated displeasure or bad news. There were only a few lines.

> Dad:
> If you send Vasily away, I will
> tell Jarrett what I know about
> you and Pam.

That was all, but it had clearly been enough. Ross must have read the note and reacted with a heart attack that had killed him. Yet he had first summoned Jarrett, and perhaps we would never know why. He had been working alone over papers that Jarrett had not wanted the police to see. Had he actually meant to show Jarrett the note from Gretchen and perhaps discount it? Or had he felt the attack coming on, called for help, and then been overcome before Jarrett could get there? He must have fallen across his desk with the note from Gretchen close at hand, and Jarrett had found it.

No wonder he had looked so shaken when I'd walked in. No wonder he had thrust the note out of sight, meaning to retrieve it later, and had been so deeply disturbed to discover that I had taken it from its hiding place. Now I remembered with more understanding that moment in the belvedere when Gretchen had torn up a picture of Pam. If she knew something about her father and Jarrett's wife, then Pam must have been a sore subject with her, and when I praised the picture, she had reacted by tearing it up.

This note, certainly, was something that must be kept private at all costs, so Jarrett needn't worry about what I would do with it. Somehow, the typed words gave me no sense of shock concerning Ross. There had been previous hints now and then about Pam, though I'd never paid much attention to them. I had no doubt that Ross would have gone after any woman who appealed to him, regardless of whether she was the wife of a man he needed and trusted above all others.

A man he dared not lose?

That was the point, wasn't it? That Jarrett must not know? Yet how could he not have known? He was anything but obtuse, anything but trusting and simple, and he had grown up the hard way, subjected to the harshness of life at an early age. Even more important now were Gretchen's actions. Surely she must guess that her note had brought on her father's heart attack—which would account for Jarrett's earnest questioning of her, and also for her defensive accusations against Jarrett and me. She might have been stirring up a smoke screen.

A sudden knocking brought me up from the chaise longue in dismay. The knock sounded again, and I had to respond.

"Who is it?"

"It's Jarrett," he said. "I must talk to you, Sharon."

I couldn't face him now. Not with this knowledge about his wife so newly in my hands. "No," I said. "Not any more tonight. I'll talk with you in the morning. You needn't worry—I won't do anything. You can have the note back then."

"I'm sorry," he insisted, "but it's necessary for us to talk. Not only about Gretchen's note. In the morning everything will explode around here. I've made a statement, shut off the phones, but tomorrow the world will move in on us. We have to talk together *now*. You are Mrs. Ross Logan. You have responsibilities."

I pulled my robe more closely about me, feeling not only the chill of this Florida night, but the coldness inside me, the coldness of fears that were all too ready to possess me. I took several deep breaths to steady myself and went to unlock the door.

Jarrett came into the room, looking even more weary and grim. But not beaten. At least he would be here for all of us to depend upon. And as Ross had trusted him, so must I. Until I had good reason not to. I gestured him toward a chair and went back to the chaise longue, drawing a crocheted throw over me. I felt utterly, achingly tired, yet far from ready to sleep.

He ignored the easy chair I'd motioned him toward, and pulled a straight desk chair around, to sit astride of it, his arms resting on its back as he faced me.

"I've read Gretchen's note," I said. "I can't blame her for trying to save Vasily by accusing us. But she must know now that her note is what shocked her father into a heart attack. That will be a heavy load for her to carry."

"I didn't come here to talk about that. Except to ask you to burn the note."

I shook my head listlessly. "Not yet. Perhaps I'll give it back to Gretchen."

"To punish her?"

I wasn't sure about that. I wasn't sure about anything.

He looked at me long and steadily, and I was reminded somehow of a boxer who was still in the ring. Perhaps it was his slightly crooked nose, that might once have been broken when he was young, that made me think of a pugilist—and that stubborn chin.

"What I want to talk about," he went on, "concerns the papers Ross was working on, and which I put into a folder and locked in a drawer in my own office. You were concerned that I seemed to be concealing something. I am. And I want your promise to say nothing about this."

"How can I give you a promise when I don't understand what I'm promising?"

"That's why I'm here now. To explain a little. It's very complex, both in the ramifications and in the reasons that lie behind what Ross was trying to do. He wanted to keep me from finding out, because he knew I'd oppose him. But he couldn't get away with that. It was Yakata, the man who came here from Tokyo to see him, and whom Ross went to meet in Palm Beach yesterday, who gave things away. I began to suspect, so

I searched for the evidence. Because what he intended has to be stopped without any publicity."

"What do you mean?"

"It was nothing illegal, but certainly something that would let down the best interests of the United States. Japan needs oil. So do we. Ross would have seen to it that millions of barrels needed here would go into the hands of an element in Japan that would profit from it mightily. So would Meridian Oil. Not the government of Japan, but a few sleazy businessmen there who are interested only in profit."

"But there'd have been an enormous scandal when it came out. And it would have to come out, wouldn't it?"

"I don't know. Not for a while. I'd have kept it quiet if I could."

I had enough strength left for indignation. "To protect Ross?"

"No. I told you it was a complex matter. If the stock of Meridian Oil plunged, it would mean not only catastrophe for the charitable foundations—not all of which are self-sustaining—and a collapse of all the good they do, but disaster for millions of stockholders as well."

"Stockholders!" I put scorn into the words.

"Don't be stupid, Sharon. Stockholders aren't only corporations, some of which might go under with disastrous results. They are also people—*individuals*—who have invested their money, trusted in the integrity of Meridian Oil. There are times when the truth can cause more havoc than it mends."

As might have happened if Jarrett had faced the truth about his wife and Ross Logan? I wondered.

"Perhaps there are times when the truth ought to come first," I said grimly.

"I wish I knew how to make that simple choice, Sharon." There seemed no sarcasm in his words, but only weariness and a deep sorrow.

"Ross must have known that he had a great deal to lose if this came out," I said.

"He was ready to gamble. He fooled himself into thinking he could handle anything that happened and ride it through. That he was powerful enough to do as he pleased."

"And wasn't he?"

"That was his delusion. Allegra could tell you. She understood. Oh, not about this deal, but about what he was trying to prove. It was always the same thing. He wanted to show that he was as powerful and clever a man in his own right as Charles Maynard Logan had ever been."

"But—but that's childish," I protested. "Ross *was* a great man."

"Deep-seated motives often go back to the child in us. Any psychiatrist can tell you that. A great many of the world's problems come straight from the childish self-delusions of men in power. You've only to look at history. You've only to listen to the screaming of today's headlines. The madness, the ferocity, the crying out for vengeance. By men. This is the way that wars are started. The child in such men can be enormously dangerous."

"What will happen now?"

"None of this will come out, if we choose to keep it quiet. It hasn't gone far enough yet. Yakata and his pals must be told that the deal is off. They have no legitimate hold on Meridian, and I can take care of this myself. It's not something that's been brought up before the board. Ross was acting in a completely clandestine way. By the time anyone could have tried to stop him, the whole thing would have been too far along to be halted without an even bigger scandal. That's why he was trying to keep it from me. That's why he was working late hours to accomplish what he needed to do before I could take any action to oppose him."

"He was trying to prove something to you, too." I didn't put it as a question. I was beginning to understand just a little the love-hate relationship that must have existed on both sides between Ross Logan and Jarrett Nichols. Ross would have needed him desperately in all sorts of ways, yet how bitterly he must have resented such a needing. Jarrett was no ordinary aide-de-camp. All too often he must have been the brain behind whatever was accomplished, and that was the weight Ross had been trying so recklessly to escape. His growing compulsion to prove himself—evident in his life with me too—had begun to verge on the unbalanced.

"Perhaps he was stopped just in time," I said, and felt chilled by the sound of my own words. As though Ross had been *deliberately* stopped. I went on quickly, veering away from implications I didn't want to make. "I mean for his own sake, as well as everyone else's. What might have happened if he'd lived could have been worse than anything he dreamed of. Or are we being callous? About Ross's death, and about something called truth?"

Jarrett shook his head. "Only realistic. It's tragic to have to recognize how many people will be saved by what has happened to Ross."

Myself among them, I thought, and winced at the silent admission. There was a great deal I was going to have to examine inside myself in the coming weeks.

"You can count on me," I said at last, and my voice was empty of emotion.

Jarrett didn't leave at once. Instead, he sat staring at me with so searching a look that I closed my eyes. I didn't want him to see all those things that I wasn't yet ready to face in myself.

"You'll be all right," he said with strange conviction, and started for the door.

The ringing of the telephone stopped him. I got up to answer it, and found that my legs were no longer shaky.

It was the nurse, Miss Cox, on the line. "I've been trying to reach Mr. Nichols. But no one seems to know where he is, so I'm calling you. Mrs. Logan is awake and she's listening to the radio, as she sometimes does at night when she can't sleep. News programs. I'm afraid..."

I broke in. "Mr. Nichols is here now. We'll come right down and talk to her. I don't think we should disturb Mrs. Karl. Try to distract her until we get there."

"Allegra?" Jarrett asked as I hung up.

"Yes. She's awake, and Coxie is afraid of what she may hear on the radio."

"I'll take care of it," Jarrett said. "You needn't come."

I was already getting a coat from the closet, flinging it on over my robe and gown, thrusting my feet into shoes. "I can't sleep anyway, and perhaps I can help."

Some of the tension seemed to leave him and he smiled wryly as he held out a hand. "Thank God Ross married *you,*" he said.

I wasn't sure whether I could agree to this sentiment, but I took his hand, accepting his strength, and let him pull me along as we hurried through the house. Outside, the golf cart stood beside the door, and I climbed into the seat beside Jarrett. The sound of its starting seemed to shatter the night, and a guard came running toward us. Jarrett waved to the man, and we went off toward Coral Cottage, shortcutting across the lawn. The cart had been equipped with head lamps, and there was no difficulty about finding our way in the dark.

Coxie came to the cottage door, a vast relief on her face. "You're just in time! I couldn't keep her away from the radio any longer."

We went into the bedroom together, to find that Allegra was sitting up, dwarfed by the huge pillows around her, her face looking almost young and eager in the softened light. She greeted us with lucidity, and I sighed in relief. It would be too hard to get through to her if she were living in the past again.

She reached out with a thin, still graceful hand and switched off the radio. "You've taken your time about getting here," she said. "Ross is dead, and I've been waiting for someone to come and tell me what happened."

I could hear the catch in Jarrett's breath. "We didn't want you to hear it that way. We hoped you'd sleep straight through the night. The moment we knew you were awake, we came."

"Thank you. Though I thought it might be Gretchen. But I expect she's having a bad time right now. His dying will make everything easier for her, but she loved him a great deal. I suppose I loved him too. Once. At least, I loved the little boy and young man he used to be. I haven't loved the man he became for a long while."

For just an instant I felt an unfamiliar sympathy for Ross. Then I remembered what he'd been doing to Allegra, and I pulled a chair close to her bed.

Surprisingly, she reached out to pat my hand and then looked up at Jarrett.

"I wish you had been my son. You'd have been worthy of Charlie. Tell me whatever you can."

Jarrett explained that Ross had had a heart attack, and that there were police formalities, which would soon be over. Then the funeral could be arranged for.

"Keep it private," Allegra said.

Jarrett agreed. "Of course. As far as we can. That will suit you, won't it, Sharon?"

I could only nod, remembering that it had been Ross who had taken the details of that other terrible funeral out of my hands. Now others would help me again, but I would be expected to make decisions. Or would I? Gretchen must be consulted tomorrow. Today. It was really her wishes and Allegra's that must be considered. I didn't even know if I had any wishes.

We stayed with her for a little while until she grew weary and let us go. Then we returned to the cart.

"She's a marvel," Jarrett said. "That was a lot easier than I ever expected. I might have known that she can still come to grips with reality when she has to. And when she's not being drugged."

We rode back toward the house, where lights still

burned aplenty. As we passed the spreading shadow of
the great banyan tree, a slimmer shadow detached itself and came toward us. Jarrett braked the car, and
in its lights Brett Inness emerged. She wore slacks and
a jacket, and for once her hair was not wound in a knot
on top of her head, but hung to her shoulders, caught
back by a clasp.

Jarrett switched off the motor. "Hello, Brett. You've
heard what has happened?"

"Yes." In the bright shock of intense light all color
seemed to have been washed from her face. "There was
a news broadcast that I heard because I couldn't sleep."

How few of us seemed to have slept through this
night.

"How did you get in?" Jarrett asked.

She seemed to draw herself up with a touch of that
hauteur she could assume so well, and she ignored me
completely. "Why shouldn't I come? He was my husband once, and Gretchen's father. It's possible that she
may need me now."

"I merely asked *how* you got in," Jarrett said.
"Guards have been placed at every entrance—even the
beach tunnel."

"Of course. But I do have a key, and the guards were
given orders by Gretchen long ago to let me in whenever I pleased to come. You know I've visited Allegra
often."

Jarrett nodded, but I sensed his suspicion toward
this woman and her motives. "Why tonight? Gretchen
will have been sedated by now. What can you do?"

She seemed suddenly forlorn and lonely, standing
there, and I remembered that all this had belonged to
her, as Ross's wife. And she was still, as she'd said,
Gretchen's mother.

I spoke for the first time. "You may want to be with
Gretchen in the morning. You're welcome to spend the
rest of the night at Poinciana. Can we take you up to
the house?"

"Thank you," she said with dignity. "I'll walk. I can certainly find my way."

Jarrett gave me a long look, but he had nothing more to say, and we went on toward the house. I was aware of a lightening of the sky out over the Atlantic. Dawn was not far away. When we stopped, Jarrett came around to help me down from the cart, and he still looked quizzical and a little surprised.

"What will happen to me now?" I asked, the momentary authority I'd assumed with Brett already dissolving. "Where will I go? I don't know where I belong any more."

"That will be up to you, won't it?" Jarrett said. "You took charge quite capably just now. So of course that's what you'll continue to do."

I shook my head wearily as we went in through a side door. "I'm not in charge of anything."

"Of course you are. You're mistress of Poinciana now. Ross left it all to you. I've seen his will."

Once more, my knees betrayed me, and Jarrett steadied me with his arm. His words had shocked me, and I couldn't absorb their full meaning at once. This was something I'd never thought about at all. Ross *was* Poinciana.

Jarrett helped me up the stairs to my room and came in for a moment to make sure I'd be all right. The sometimes hard, life-weathered look was gone from his face, and his eyes were kind.

"When you came here," he said, "I took it for granted that you'd married what Ross Logan stood for, and all that he could give you. I know I was hard on you in my judgment. Now I can understand better that you were frightened and needed to be looked after."

I let Jarrett help me off with my coat. "I know what you thought. You never troubled to hide it."

"I'm sorry. But I think you'll manage now, though it won't be easy. Get to bed, Sharon. You're tired enough to sleep. I'm almost that tired myself. Don't think about anything. It can all wait until much later today."

He let himself out the door, and I felt grateful to him, as I'd never felt before. Grateful for his talking to me so honestly. Grateful because he had let me glimpse his own torment and moments of not being sure. He would help me if he could. And I would need all the help I could get. There were those in this house who had hated me—and now that might be even worse.

Soon the sun would be up, but I must sleep now and do as Jarrett had said—think about nothing.

At once as my head touched the pillow, I thought of Ross, and felt a pang of loss for something I'd never really had. And something of sorrow for him, too, because all that he'd been, the good and the bad, had come so suddenly to an end.

I thought curiously as well of Brett Inness. How long had she been on Poinciana grounds? Had she come here, perhaps, before Ross had died? And I thought of Gretchen's note. For the first time, I questioned it. Had she really written it? Was it even possible that someone else had copied her simple method of note writing? Perhaps someone who wanted to hide behind Gretchen might have done that very thing. But such suppositions were beyond me now.

When sleep caught me, I went out completely, and I heard nothing at all for a good many hours into the new day.

Chapter

12

It was all over. The ceremonies, the eulogy, the funeral, the visiting relatives—a few of them still in the house. Ross's "close" friends had been there—though I think he had been close to very few. For a "private" affair, it had seemed distastefully large to me. The press members who had been allowed to attend had been issued only the most carefully worded statements.

This hardly stopped the media from clamoring for more details concerning Ross's death, and as often happens in such cases, unpleasant rumors and speculation began to circulate, appearing in the sleazier journals. Everything was brought to me, on Jarrett's orders, though I read little of what was printed.

Allegra had appeared for some of the ritual, a proud and fragile lady, who could not be wholly grief-stricken over the death of her son, yet put up a very good front. Coxie hovered in attendance, watching her charge, but

Allegra, free of "pills," performed admirably and with great self-possession. Whenever she was present, Jarrett kept watchfully close.

There had been a lavish buffet luncheon afterwards, which had been a strain for me to endure. It all seemed a sham to me, a ritual to be observed, though the signs of true grief, of deep regret for Ross's passing were few. I resented this more for Gretchen's sake than for my own. Of those who thronged the house, her mourning was the most genuine, even though in her, too, it must have been laced with relief.

Vasily stayed by her side every moment, making an effort to be properly solemn for the occasion, but now and then allowing elation to break through to the surface and gleam in his eyes.

Jarrett kept his distance where I was concerned. Those early-morning hours of revelation between us had slipped into a hazy past, and we'd spoken impersonally whenever we met. I had no idea what he was thinking and I wasn't sure now of what his function was, or mine, or exactly what our relationship should be. There was an unspoken understanding that he would go on as before for the time being, and that at the appropriate moment we would talk and sort a few things out.

By the time I could escape from the social part of the day, it was nearly evening, and I had come here to the gloom of the library, where sunset light touched the windows. I had come here to try to put some sense into the confusion and disorder of my thoughts.

Beside me, the tape recorder played "Blue Champagne," and Ysobel's voice filled the empty cavern of the room. I played this song of hers deliberately, allowing my emotions free rein. I had gone back every step of the way, trying to understand, trying to find answers. My life had lost its simplicity even before Ross's death, and with the making of his will he had plunged me into complications that I had no idea how to handle.

If only he had left Poinciana to Gretchen, instead of

to me. Perhaps he would have done so, if she hadn't married Vasily. This was her punishment—Ross still reaching out to hurt her from his grave. He had left Gretchen even more wealthy than she was, Jarrett told me—something she cared little about—but he had not given her what she wanted most: Poinciana. Nor had he left her his shares in Meridian Oil. Those, as well as a sizable fortune, came into my hands. Everything, of course, wisely invested, giving me an income that was big enough to support the estate, and do anything I wished besides—even after the enormous inheritance taxes. It all seemed completely unreal and beyond my comprehension.

There was only one stipulation. Poinciana was to be mine for as long as I chose to live here and care for it. Otherwise, it would go to Gretchen. Or it would go to her if she outlived me. My first impulse was to walk away from the burden, and I told Jarrett so. He had said, "Wait. Don't do anything hasty. If it goes to Gretchen now, it also goes to Vasily Karl. *Her* will leaves everything to him—in defiance of her father, of course. I see no reason why she might change this, now that Ross is gone. Vasily will see to that."

Other reasons were developing to keep me from walking away. There was still the question of the note, purportedly from Gretchen, but which anyone could have forged—and which had surely been the cause of Ross's heart attack. I had not yet confronted Gretchen with the existence of that note, but I must do so soon. It would be difficult to talk to her, because she was blaming me quite vocally for Ross's death. Though not to the police. I was the one who had so wickedly shocked and upset her father, she kept pointing out. By this time, she was brushing past the earlier quarrel with Jarrett that she'd included in her first accusations. *I* was the one, and she was ready to tell this to all who would listen. I'd felt a little sorry for bewildered friends and distant relatives, who were not yet sure of my position in the house, and reluctant to offend Gretchen by befriending me.

The sound of Ysobel's voice on the tape broke into my thoughts insistently, and I knew that one unhappy problem, at least, had been ended. I would never again be made love to because I was Ysobel Hollis's daughter. The need to leave Ross was gone. He had escaped from us all, and from his own torments that he had tried to conceal.

Already Brett Inness came and went about the house as she pleased, and I could only regret my earlier generosity. Gretchen had told her about the will, and she too resented the leaving of Poinciana to Ross's present wife. She and Gretchen had clearly allied themselves against me.

The gossip columns were not ignoring us. The hint had appeared of some serious quarrel between Ross and me shortly before his death, and I could guess that Brett was its possible source. Such columns would be only too ready to pounce upon anything connected with Ross Logan. Fortunately, there were those in powerful places who had stepped in to play down rumors that might affect the stability of Meridian Oil, though no one cared very much what I might be feeling.

Except for Jarrett. He saw what was happening. "You can put Gretchen and Vasily out of the house, if you like," he told me curtly. "It's up to you. There's nothing that says Gretchen and her husband are entitled to live here. And you don't have to take Brett's presence at all."

Put Gretchen out of her own home? Forbid her the comfort of seeing her mother in her own surroundings? I wasn't tough enough for that, but I must certainly have a talk with Gretchen as soon as she could be persuaded to listen to me. I wanted to know whether she had really written the note Jarrett had found in Ross's possession at the time of his death. If she had, it might account for her desperate effort at self-delusion by placing the blame elsewhere.

The song on the tape came to an end, and the recorder turned itself off. The big room, with its Coromandel screen darkened now in the gloom, seemed more forbidding than ever. Once this library had been the courtroom to which Ross brought those who displeased him, and from which he issued his judgments and punishments. I had stood for arraignment here. Now it was only an empty shell of a room, yet I had chosen it to flee to in order to judge myself.

Behind me, someone opened the door and tiptoed in. "Mrs. Logan? Are you here?" The voice was Myra Ritter's.

"I'm here," I said, and she came to stand before me.

For once she was formally dressed in a dark frock, suitable for the occasion, though I'd seen plenty of floral prints at both church and cemetery. Myra had heard the radio early the morning of Ross's death, and she had wasted no time in coming to Poinciana and making herself useful. If I sometimes had the faint impression that she was part of the audience at a dramatic and entertaining play for which she had a box seat, I could forgive her that. So what if she was interested and involved with all that happened at Poinciana, when she had no great life of her own? This was a vicarious thrill for her, and I suspected that her one regret was that she hadn't been present when it had happened.

She had run errands, given advice, whether asked for or not, answered hundreds of telephone calls with skill and diplomacy, and served us all tea when our spirits faltered. Even Mrs. Broderick, shocked almost to the point of tears—but not quite—had found her useful.

Now Myra dropped into a chair opposite mine and kicked off her high-heeled shoes, sighing with relief. "Back to flats tomorrow," she said. "How are you feeling? Is there anything I can get you?"

"Nothing," I said. "Thank you for all you've done, Myra. I just wanted to escape from everyone for a little while. Are the guests thinning out by this time?"

"Mostly. They've been asking for you to pay their courtesies before leaving, but you're supposed to collapse in private grief now, so that lets you off the hook. Though I'm not sure how many in this house have done any grieving. I mean besides you and Mrs. Karl, of course."

She lay back in her chair and wiggled her toes, sighing again with pleasure.

There was no need to answer her, and pretty soon she would go away. Or else she would come around to the real purpose behind this visit.

"I found out something pretty shocking today," she said at last.

I thought I was past all surprises, and I said nothing. Gossip was not something I wanted to encourage in Jarrett's secretary. Though it was hard to discourage in the face of her open enjoyment in other people's affairs.

"Did you know that Brett Inness isn't Mrs. Karl's real mother?" she asked.

That brought me up in my chair. "I don't know what you're talking about."

"Mrs. Karl was having a row with her mother this afternoon after the funeral. Mr. Karl and I were there and we stepped out of the room because it was getting embarrassing. He was upset, and that's when he told me."

"He told you *what?*"

She shrugged. "He can get pretty emotional and Russian at times, and he blurted out that Mrs. Karl isn't Miss Inness's natural daughter. I wasn't to tell anyone—and of course I won't. The newspapers would love this."

"So why are you telling me?"

Again the shrug. My question didn't seem to disturb her. "You're family. Maybe I'd like to keep my job here. Maybe I can be useful at times, and it's not Mrs. Karl now who can get me fired."

At least she was direct and down-to-earth. I sus-

pected that she was quite ready to tell me more of
whatever she had picked up, but I didn't want it to
come from her. What she had revealed might furnish
a strong clue to Gretchen's behavior, and I would need
to think about it.

"Mr. Karl was right," I said. "There are things that
shouldn't be talked about. It's more important now than
ever, since almost anything can be blown out of proportion."

Reluctantly, she wiggled her toes for a last time and
put on her pumps. "You can count on me. If the time
comes when you need a social secretary, you might
consider me," she said, and slipped out of the room as
quietly as she had entered.

After a moment I roused myself to follow. I didn't
know what to do with the information that had been
given me, except to bleed a little for Gretchen. An
adoptive mother could be as loved and loving as a natural one, if she behaved like a mother. But I wondered
if Brett ever had.

Upstairs, I stood before the long mirror that hung
on my bathroom door. "What am I to do?" I asked the
woman in the glass. She had no more idea of the answer
than I did, and she looked as helpless and ineffectual
as I felt.

With an effort, I straightened my shoulders. I could
remember that strengthening moment only a few days
ago when I had made a stand against the things that
beset me. But now I knew less than ever what to struggle against, or what I really wanted—except to get
away from Poinciana. Everything here threatened me,
and if there had been animosity toward me before, it
must be a hundredfold greater now. With Gretchen as
the source?

Aimlessly, I went outside to stand at one of the
arches of the loggia. In the fading light, Jarrett Nichols
walked among leaning palm trees. As he approached
the house, he raised his head to see me standing there
above him. At once he came to the foot of the steps.

"May I come up?"

"I don't mind," I said. The words sounded ungracious, but I seemed to have no desires left in one direction or another.

He climbed the steps and drew up a chair for me, then dropped into one beside it.

"You carried it off very well today," he told me.

"No—I only sleepwalked. I didn't know what I was doing half the time."

"Then your performance deserves all the more credit. You're tired now. A night's sleep will help."

He was tired again too. I could hear it in his voice. Much more strain and responsibility had rested on him than on the rest of us, and I wished I knew how to thank him properly. But, for all his sympathetic words, something in him that seemed forbidding held me off.

There were a hundred questions I needed to ask, but this wasn't the time and I had no heart for them, any more than he was likely to have heart for the answers. Anyway, there was just one question everything boiled down to: *What am I to do?* I had asked it of him before, and it was still too futile to be repeated. I thought dully of Myra and her disturbing news.

"I've just learned that Brett Inness isn't Gretchen's real mother," I said.

Jarrett was silent for a moment, looking no more or less somber than before. "Who told you that?"

"Your secretary. Vasily apparently spilled this out to Myra at a time when he was upset because Brett and Gretchen were quarreling. She could hardly wait to come and tell me, though I don't think she was being malicious about it."

"I'll speak to Myra. That was pretty idiotic of Vasily."

"Have you always known?"

"Not until I'd been with Ross for a couple of years. It's hardly common knowledge."

"Why hasn't it come out?"

"That's a long story. I suppose you might as well know—though I'm not sure it serves any good purpose now. I understand that Gretchen's real mother was a young woman who worked here. A girl whom Ross took a fancy to while he was married to Brett. Neither of his wives had given him a child, and he wanted a son. So when he knew the girl was going to have a baby, he made secret arrangements. Brett had no choice. He sent her away, and then brought her back with the child when the time was right. Unfortunately for him, it was a daughter. Brett had to accept her, while the real mother was sent to some distant state with a sizable payoff if she would never return. She hasn't been heard from since. Allegra knew, but no one else until I was told."

"Has Gretchen always known?"

Jarrett shook his head. "I think she should have been told early, so that she could grow up with the facts. But she was fifteen when Brett lost her temper one day and told her the truth—rather scornfully. She couldn't even offer Gretchen the solace of having been deliberately chosen, as most adopted children are. And it was never enough that Ross was her real father. I suppose Gretchen had spent her childhood trying to win Brett's affection, never understanding why she was rejected. Oddly enough, after she knew, Gretchen and Brett became better friends, and they could plot together against Ross when it suited them."

When it came to rejection by a mother, I had more in common with Ross's daughter than I'd dreamed, I thought wearily. Even though I'd been the child of both my parents, Ysobel and Brett had felt alike about their daughters. Yet while this might have given us a basis for some understanding at least—by willing Poinciana to me, Ross had made Gretchen my mortal enemy. I turned away from so painful a subject.

"How is Allegra?" I asked.

"She's magnificent. It's good to see her taking a stand with Coxie and telling *her* what to do for a change. Just the same, she's frailer than she believes, and all this has been a strain for her."

"Tomorrow I'll find out whether she wants to move back into the house."

He brightened a little as he stood up. "I'd hoped you would do that. You'll be here to look out for her now. I suppose I should offer you my formal resignation in the next few days."

My alarm was complete and so shattering that it astonished me. He smiled as he put out a steadying hand.

"Hey—don't look like that! Your ship isn't sinking. Of course I want to stay. I *need* to stay. But I had to give you the chance to make a choice."

"There isn't any choice. I'm the one who has to think about leaving."

His hand tightened on my arm and he pulled me up from my chair almost roughly. "Not yet, Sharon. There's a lot you need to do before you go running away."

He could still make me angry. There was at least that much emotion left in me. I pulled away from his hand, no longer shaky.

"*I* will decide what *I* want to do," I said.

"That's the spirit! It's time you started telling a few of us off. Sleep well—tomorrow is a day of battle."

He grinned at me wickedly and went down the steps to the lawn. I was still feeling outraged, but my anger died as I watched him walk off toward his cottage. There was that new weariness in the set of his shoulders, in the slowness of movements that were usually brisk and assured.

These last days must have been terrible for him. I thought of the note that linked the wife he'd loved with the man he had served so long and loyally. How had he lived with this ambivalence toward Ross and kept his sanity? Jarrett was never a man to be pitied, yet there was a welling up in me of sorrow for him as I went back to my room. A sorrow I could do nothing about, because he, of all people, would accept sympathy from no one.

I didn't want to go to bed. Sleep was something far away, for all my weariness. I longed for some distraction to occupy my too active mind. As I sat there, I could not control the pictures that insisted on unrolling. Sharpest of all was my memory of Ross slumped across his desk, with all the vitality that had been so much a part of him gone forever. I could weep for him now. Weep for him, not as my husband, but as a man who had suffered and been struck down in a moment of shock and anger. In a sense, he had been destroyed by a few typed words on paper. All of this, however, was more than I could face right now.

In the end, I was left with just one thought in my mind—one phrase that played itself over and over. The words Jarrett had spoken before he left.

Tomorrow is a day of battle.

Since when must I become a warrior? Since when must I stand and fight? Yet I knew that tomorrow this would have to be done, and that sooner or later, I had better put on my armor.

Chapter

13

The battle began early in the morning, when Gretchen sent for me right after breakfast.

She waited in the Japanese room, and Vasily was with her. The moment I went through the door I knew by her look and manner that she considered herself the rightful mistress of Poinciana. A few mere facts of law would change nothing in the mind of Ross's daughter. Her purpose was clear and uncomplicated—to drive me out. Once all the workings of the law had been performed and the will probated, the house would revert to her if I decided to move away. I couldn't help but feel that this would be a greater justice than Ross had done in leaving it to me.

Except for Vasily. He was still the question mark that Jarrett had raised. Was I willing to have it all wind up in his hands? As Gretchen's husband, his influence would be very strong. While I had no wish to

see him parted from his wife, as Ross had been so determined to have happen, there were still uncertainties
that troubled me. His past was a little too checkered,
to say the least. It might be easier for me to turn Poinciana over to Gretchen and leave at once, but I still had
an obligation to Ross, and perhaps even to Gretchen
herself, that I couldn't sidestep. Even though Gretchen
wanted me gone, and would do what she could to make
life at Poinciana uncomfortable for me, I must stay for
now. Later, perhaps I could let her have it, and get
away.

When I walked in, Vasily was standing at a tall
window, where morning sun streamed in to light his
fair hair. Gretchen sat at the desk that had been Allegra's, tapping irritably on its surface with a pencil.

"Good morning," I said, including them both.

Vasily sprang to fetch me a chair, placing it on the
other side of the desk from his wife.

"You look more rested," he said. "You've slept well?"

That didn't bear talking about, and I gave my attention to Gretchen. She scowled at me with no greeting.

"What have you done with my father's manuscript?"
she demanded, going straight into her attack.

Such a challenge was the last thing I expected. "I
don't know what you're talking about."

"Of course you do. He always kept everything right
here in this desk. The manuscript and the photographs
I did for his book were always here, and they're not
now. Neither are Dad's receipts and vouchers that he
kept on every item he purchased for the collection. Only
the record book that you started is here. So what have
you done with the rest?"

Her small face, with its pointed chin, and its frame
of dark hair, looked more pugnacious than ever this
morning, and I didn't know how to deal with her attack.
I hadn't thought about the netsuke since Ross's death.

"I haven't been in this room for days," I told her.

"I haven't even thought about the collection, or about Ross's manuscript."

"Of course you're lying," she said. "Why?"

Vasily made a small, placating sound, but she waved him aside.

"I'm not very good at lying," I said evenly. "Surely these things will turn up. Your father must have put them somewhere else himself. In one of his safes, perhaps?"

She ran both hands through the mop of short, straight hair. "Don't talk nonsense! I've already searched and they're not anywhere. They make a big package, along with the pages he'd done and my glossy prints. So they should be found easily. But why would you want to hide them?"

"I haven't hidden anything. If you want me to help you look, I will."

Perhaps something in my face, in my tone of voice, began to get through to her, and for the first time she looked faintly shaken in her conviction.

"Then why are these things gone? Who would take them?"

I could only shake my head. The whole thing seemed unimportant in the face of all else that was wrong at the moment.

"Why is it so urgent to find the manuscript right now?" I asked.

"It's urgent because I want to work on it. It's something I can do for my father. It's the only thing I can do for him. I could have done the cataloguing. I know all about his collection. I've worked with him, making those photographs, and he's told me about every item in this room. Now the book must be finished and published under his name, as he wished."

I could recognize and understand her intense need to be close to her father and preserve his work. In a sense, she could keep him alive by throwing herself into this project. In a situation where nothing could be done, she could find consolation in performing a task closely connected with her father. While I was still in London, I had helped to instigate the publishing of a new collection of Ysobel's songs—that would have pleased both her and Ian—and Ross had thrown himself into helping me. I realized now that we'd been doing exactly what Gretchen was trying to do now. And I would help her all I could, if only she would let me.

"This is a fine idea," I said. "Of course it should be carried out, and you're the one to do it. Perhaps we can look through his office and his bedroom and see if we can find where he put the package."

"I've looked," she said.

This was a dead end for the moment, and I let it go. I had come downstairs armed with something else that must now be dealt with.

"I've been wanting to talk to you," I went on. "There was one item that was held back from the police after Ross's death. It's something that might have so upset your father that it could have brought on his attack. Jarrett felt that it should not be given out because of all the ramifications."

I placed before her the note typed on Poinciana stationery and signed with one of the little faces she had adopted as her signature.

She read the few lines, and a flush came into her face. "You'd better explain," she said.

"I thought you might be able to explain. Jarrett found this in your father's possession when he reached his office that night in response to Ross's call and found him dead."

Vasily had come to stand behind Gretchen's chair, and he read the note over her shoulder. "What is this? What does it mean?"

"I think," I told them carefully, "it means that someone was threatening him. Perhaps with blackmail, or for vengeance. Perhaps to frighten him into taking some action, or not taking some action. Someone knew, or pretended to know, something that would have caused the loss of Jarrett's services if he was told."

Gretchen stared at the sheet of paper. "This was typed on my machine. I can recognize that crooked *w*. And someone has copied the silly way I sometimes sign my notes. But I didn't write this. I would never have threatened my father—no matter what I suspected."

"Not even if it could have stopped him from sending Vasily away?"

I half expected outrage at my words, but she answered me openly. "I might have tried. I meant to try. But not this way. Besides, it's foolish. Dad wouldn't have been afraid of anything like this. Jarrett already knew about Pam and my father. I think he was trying to decide what to do at the time Pam died in the car accident. Afterwards, it didn't matter enough any more, when there were so many big issues to keep him here." Gretchen looked at Vasily. "What do you think?"

He didn't touch the sheet of paper, but he leaned forward to read the words again. "Your mother?" he said to Gretchen.

"Maybe. I'll show it to her."

"I'd rather do that myself," I said, and picked the note up to slip it into the handbag I'd brought downstairs with me.

Gretchen made no effort to stop me. "Why would Brett try anything like that?" She was still speaking to Vasily. "It's too silly. Too weak."

"Perhaps not," he said. "Brett was here on the grounds that night. She was here in the house."

I caught him up on that. "When? At what time?" This was the question I should have asked Brett myself, when Jarrett and I came upon her that night.

Vasily shrugged delicately and returned to stand beside the window. Either he didn't know, or he didn't mean to say.

"There's no reason why my mother would do this," Gretchen said to me. "Dad paid her a lot of alimony. He even loaned her money to start her shop. Indirectly, that is. She didn't know for a while that it came from him. Anyway, he would never have given her a cent more for anything—let alone blackmail."

"On the day before your father died," I said, "I found some letters that had been left on my dressing table. In one of them—"

"Oh, so you read them? I thought you would."

"Was it you who put them there?"

"Of course. Vasily didn't want me to. He thought I was being too mean to you and—"

Her husband broke in. "I felt that you were really on our side, Sharon. I saw no reason to try to hurt you."

"But I *wanted* to hurt you!" Gretchen cried. "And that was a good way, wasn't it? All those drippy letters Dad wrote to Ysobel Hollis!" She turned back to me. "I wasn't sure you'd read them, but I hoped you'd see that he never loved *you*."

"I didn't read them." Somehow I managed to speak quietly. "I only read a snatch here and there, to see what they were. But when I came to one that mentioned Brett's name, I did read that part. Ross wrote my mother that he held some sort of weapon over Brett's head. In case she became a threat to him. Apparently you didn't read the letters yourself."

"Of course not—except to see what they were. But Brett knew about them. He was writing to Ysobel even while they were married. She knew that Ysobel used to send them back to him, and that he kept them in his bedroom safe. So one time when he was away, she took them. She said they might be useful sometime. Anyway, I thought it a good idea to give them to you now."

"Then your mother would have known that Ross might call in that note he held any time he chose?"

"Of course she knew that. She found out quickly enough, but she never tried to do anything about it. What could she do, except hope that he wouldn't call it in before she was ready?"

I didn't speak aloud the thought in my mind—that Brett Inness might have come to see Ross in those early-

morning hours in order to threaten him. Yet if, as
Gretchen believed, this note hardly made a strong
enough threat, then this theory was probably wrong.
I let it go for now.

"There's something else I've wanted to consult you
about," I said. "Do you think your grandmother would
like to be moved back into her own rooms at Poinciana?
Do you think we should ask her?"

Gretchen's face could take on the look of a small,
impudent monkey when she grinned. "Of course she
would. I've already thought about that and discussed
it with Brett. It isn't up to you. She's _my_ grandmother."

I had been properly snubbed, and I could feel a flush
rise in my cheeks. Gretchen was right. It wasn't up to
me to make arrangements of this sort, even though I
was supposed to be the owner of Poinciana. Yet it was
important to my own sense of justice that I make the
effort first.

Vasily turned from the window. "My wife has only
been _thinking_ of doing this. I believe it would be a fine
thing if you two could act together in this matter. Allegra knows that Poinciana has been left to you,
Sharon, and not to my wife. There are certain courtesies
that should be considered, and it would be more reassuring to her if you approached her together."

To my astonishment, Gretchen threw her husband
a wildly angry look, burst into tears, and ran out of the
room. He made no effort to follow her, but took her
place across the desk from me.

"You must forgive my wife. Her father's will has
hurt her deeply. She is feeling very bitter against you
at the moment. I hope this will pass. You will not send
her away from Poinciana?"

"Of course not," I said. "This is her home. Much more
than it can ever be mine."

"Then perhaps you will not choose to go on living
here, now that your husband is dead?"

Somehow, I thought, I was being maneuvered with

these soft, apparently kindly words, and I stiffened a little. "I'm not sure what I will do."

He smiled at me, and if it hadn't been for that faintly lifted eyebrow, I might have been inclined to trust him more than I wanted to. He was a surprisingly compelling man, but that scar reminded me of too many things.

"Last week," I said, "Ross told me that Gretchen knows about your former marriage."

"Of course." He remained unabashed. "Oh, perhaps I should have told her sooner than I did. But my wife has a temper, and I wanted to make her happy first. Then I knew she wouldn't care so much about the past. Now she understands that my previous marriage had already ended before I met her. When her father brought it up, it only made her angry with him, and anger is an ugly emotion. Don't you agree, Sharon?"

As I stared at him helplessly, he reached across the desk to touch my hand. "There has been too much anger and ugliness under this roof. I hope we may all live together amicably now. I suggest that you speak with Gretchen when she is calm again. Persuade her to let you accompany her when Allegra Logan is invited to return to this house. This would be a good thing for all of you."

I could almost believe in his effort toward peace-making. Almost, but not quite. Because Vasily Karl's motives were never clear, and I was never exactly sure what he was after. He had a talent for being on everybody's side. Whether I would do as he asked, I didn't know, and I drew my hand from beneath his, resisting the charming way in which I was being manipulated.

Instead of answering, I asked another question. "What do you think about my husband's manuscript and Gretchen's photographs disappearing?"

He seemed to consider my words solemnly, closing his eyes as though he consulted some inner muse. When he opened them he wore a quizzical look.

"If I were you, I would check very carefully to see

whether any of the netsuke collection should prove to be missing. Now, if you will excuse me, I shall go and look for my wife. By this time she will be feeling regretful over her outburst. She loses her temper quickly, but fortunately, she also recovers just as quickly."

He stood up, gave me his quick little formal bow, and went out the door. I sat where I was, thinking about his words. That was very good advice—to check the netsuke collection to see if any items were missing. Except for one thing. Without the manuscript, the photographs, the invoices, nothing could be checked. Or at least only that portion of the collection that I had already catalogued could be tallied. Which, of course, could be the reason why these things had disappeared— the reason Vasily was pointing out to me. I found the thought disturbing, and I didn't want to accept it.

Nevertheless, I went to the shelves of tiny carvings and stood looking at them, trying to remember. But I hadn't gone far enough with my listing. I had examined with care only those I had listed for Ross.

Last time there had been a hullabaloo about two missing netsuke, but they had turned up in Allegra's possession. A thought that gave me no comfort now, because Allegra herself had probably not put them there. The netsuke thief was still operating, and Ross was no longer here to know what had been taken.

Idly, I picked up a carved brown ball, hardly bigger than a marble. A tiny rat was cunningly curled around itself in the wood. Every detail was perfect—ears, lacquered black eyes, sharp teeth and claws, a broad tail held amusingly in one paw. One hind foot was scratching an ear. When I turned the piece over, I could see the characters of the sculptor's name etched on the bottom beside the curving tail. Strange to think that this small item might be worth several thousand dollars. Such a sum would mean little to Gretchen, but it might represent a fortune to someone who needed money, and could see it multiply in such tiny, easily taken objects. Where would one dispose of such things?

Who would have the sophistication and knowledgeable background to find a market for them?

I wondered, too, how large an allowance Vasily was given. Had he amusements, indulgences that were expensive and of which Gretchen might not be fully aware? Or might want to discourage? How disarmingly innocent he would seem in suggesting to me what would become obvious soon anyway—that some of the netsuke could be missing.

But I didn't want to think this. I didn't want to believe that Vasily would steal from Poinciana. To some extent, he had won me.

I put the carving aside and picked up Allegra's favorite, the Sleeping Mermaid. Perhaps this could be given to her now, as Ross had given it long ago, and on second thought had taken it back. It might please her to own it, and this was a small thing I could do for her. But not yet. It didn't belong to me yet, and I mustn't tamper with the collection until it was really mine.

How still the house seemed with all the commotion of the last few days quieted. How empty of everything except its memories. Strange how strongly I could feel Ross's presence in this room. I could see him clearly at the desk where he had worked, almost hear his voice admonishing me. An odd little quiver went through me, and I recognized in distress that it was once more a feeling of relief. But how could one feel relief over a death? This was a totally unacceptable emotion.

"Mrs. Logan?" a voice reached me, and I turned to find Mrs. Broderick in the doorway, looking more worried than I had ever seen her.

"Has something happened?" I asked.

"I've been looking for Mrs. Karl. She would know what to do. No one has told me—we weren't prepared—

"I'm sorry," I said. "I don't understand. Perhaps I can help?"

A look which doubted that flicked across her face.

To Mrs. Broderick too, Gretchen was the real mistress of Poinciana.

"Mrs. Allegra is moving in upstairs," she continued reluctantly. "But her rooms aren't ready. I was not told this would be happening. When I tried to object—"

I broke in, smiling. "But that's wonderful! She's taken things into her own hands at last. Mrs. Karl and I were thinking of arranging for this, but she's a whole move ahead of us."

"Mrs. Allegra is not the same person she used to be," Mrs. Broderick said, thoroughly disapproving. "Mr. Logan would not have allowed this to happen."

"*I* will allow it," I said, keeping my tone pleasant. "Let's go upstairs and see what we can do to make her comfortable."

The emotions that crossed Mrs. Broderick's usually passive face made me smile again. I could read them so clearly: *That I had no right to give orders in this house. That Ross Logan's wishes were still to be obeyed. That if anyone made changes, it should be Gretchen Karl.*

"Come along, please," I said. "We'll need you to see to the new arrangements."

There was nothing else for her to do, and she followed me upstairs, stiffly forbidding and displeased, but not yet in open rebellion. I felt astonished that I had been able to give an order and have it obeyed. That she was still trying to tell me something, and that I wasn't listening, didn't come home to me until later.

Chapter

14

When we reached the upper hall, Mrs. Broderick tried to speak to me again. "Mrs. Logan, there is something you should know—"

Unfortunately, I still didn't listen. I had the bit between my teeth, and short of open rebellion, I knew now that she would do as I said. Which gave me a heady feeling. I was delighted that Allegra had taken action herself and returned to the home where she belonged.

Aware that I was paying no attention to her, Mrs. Broderick gave up and opened the suite's bedroom door, stepping aside, every inch of her exuding disapproval.

I burst into the bedroom, eager to show my pleasure—and stopped in surprise, barely across the sill. Brett Inness was unpacking a suitcase on the bed, and behind me Mrs. Broderick made a further clucking sound of disparagement. She would have told me, if I'd given her a chance.

Brett glanced around in mild surprise at my abrupt entrance. She looked as elegant as ever, in a light pullover and pants of saffron silk. There were gold bangles on her bare, tanned arms, and a gold skewer thrust through the knot on top of her head.

"Hello," she said. "I decided that no more time should be wasted, and that I would do as Gretchen wishes. So I've brought Allegra back to her own home."

I could find no words of response. Near a window, Allegra sat in her own small rocker, still dressed in robe and slippers, looking bewildered and ill at ease. Her inner disturbance was evident in the trembling of her lips.

I went to her and took her hands in mine. "Are we rushing you too much? I meant to come down to your cottage this morning and ask if you would like to move into these rooms again."

"Of course she wants to move into them!" Brett said. "Don't you, darling? Look now—I'm putting your toilet things in the bathroom, where you can find them. Coxie is packing everything else for you at the cottage. I've sent Albert to bring up your suitcases. You needn't lift a finger."

Allegra's bewilderment hurt me. "Tell me," I said, ignoring Brett, "what do you really want to do?"

"I—I'm not sure," she managed. "Brett and Gretchen want me to do this, I know. But I'd gotten used to the cottage. I could get outside so easily down there. Now there are stairs."

"You must stay exactly where you wish to stay," I told her. "I think we've all been in too much of a hurry to have you do what we believed you'd want. It's time we asked you."

"I'm tired right now," she said. "Perhaps I could lie down on one of those beds for a little while?"

"Of course. Let me help you."

"I'll get her into bed," Brett said. "I'm used to this."

She turned down one of the spreads with its yellow sprinkling of buds, and came to help Allegra out of her robe. In a moment the old lady was snug beneath a light quilt, her eyes closing with weariness. Brett put a finger to her lips and nodded toward the adjoining parlor. I went in ahead of her, and she left the bedroom door ajar, dropping onto the long oyster-colored sofa before an empty fireplace. Mrs. Broderick followed us.

"You can go, Broderick," Brett said. "You can fuss about the rooms later."

"Yes, madam." Mrs. Broderick had long been accustomed to taking orders from Brett Inness, and she went out the door, her back still stiff, but with less open disapproval than she'd shown me.

"She's going to be hard to handle with Ross gone," Brett said cheerfully. "You'll never manage her. But I expect Gretchen will take her down a notch or two. Broderick's been spoiled because Ross has been here so little and she's become rather a tyrant in the house."

I said nothing. Both outrage and alarm were warring inside me. Outrage at the audacity of this woman, and alarm because I was beginning to doubt whether I could handle any of what was happening.

"I'm glad of this opportunity," Brett said. "We need to talk. I think you're probably right that we've rushed poor Allegra into a move she wasn't prepared for. The old like what they're accustomed to, and we should have thought of that. Of course she must come back to the house. But we haven't been altogether sensitive to her wishes."

I wanted to say, *"You* haven't been sensitive," but not speaking at all seemed the best defensive weapon I could use. I hadn't seen Brett since the funeral—to which she'd come with the air of belonging, even returning to the house with Gretchen afterwards. And she had been much more at home with family and friends than I could be, since I was the suspect stranger who had probably married Ross for his money.

"There's something I've wanted to ask you," she went on, undisturbed by my silence. "Have you decided yet whether you will move out of Poinciana? I'm sure this can't be the pleasantest place in the world for you now, and it would seem wise to leave."

In the face of such arrogance, I found my voice. "Since it's going to belong to me, I expect I will stay." That might not be true, but I had no intention of raising her hopes, or Gretchen's. Not until a number of things had been cleared up could I make a decision about Poinciana.

"Oh, dear!" I heard the mock distress in her voice. "Gretchen has been so sure that you won't want to stay."

"I don't want to. But I have a few obligations. To Ross, first of all. He wanted me here. I'm not sure of his reasons, but I expect I'll learn about them."

"The only reason is because he was angry with Gretchen and made impulsive changes in his will. Given time, he'd have come to his senses."

"You mean as soon as he got rid of Vasily?"

"Oh, Gretchen would have got around him on that. Ross really adored her, you know. However, there's something else I've wanted to consult you about. My daughter can be obstinate at times. Her current attitude is to pretend that you don't exist, no matter what Ross's will may say. She needs to accept reality more gracefully."

Brett paused to take a cigarette from her bag, lighting it with an initialed gold cylinder. Her every move was one of calm and graceful assurance. Or, as I had thought before—arrogance. She was far more suited to being mistress of Poinciana than either Gretchen or I, and I resented her with all my heart, knowing that Ross's wishes would be on my side in this at least. Nevertheless, I felt ineffectual in the face of such poise and self-confidence. I'd once been able to assume just such a manner of aplomb, but with me it had always been a screen, hiding the uncertainty that lurked underneath. With Brett, it was the real thing, grown from years of nurturing, and it intimidated me more than a little, much as I wanted to stand up to her.

When she had taken a puff or two, she went on, still unconcerned by my rigid silence. "Gretchen has invited me to live here again. My apartment in town has become rather much to keep up when I must give my time to my work. Also she rather depends on me in a number of ways. Vasily is charming and loving, but his advice isn't always wise. I hope you will have no objection. I can be of some help to my daughter."

I made a slight movement of indecision, but before I could speak, she went on quickly. For the first time I wondered if her self-confidence, too, might be partly bluff. Was everyone fooling everyone else?

"Gretchen, of course, had no business issuing such an invitation to me. You and I both know that, but I hope you'll forgive her." Brett's smile suggested that she and I were women of the world, and could solve our differences amicably. "I can only do this with your permission, naturally. My rooms would be in Gretchen's wing of the house, and she'll want, in any case, to open up one of the downstairs rooms for our dining. Your path and mine would hardly need to cross, and you would have all the solitary time you wish in which to decide what you'd really like to do with your life. The world is your oyster now." A slight acerbity crept into the last words, belying the cordiality.

I reminded myself that the world was no longer Brett Inness's oyster, and that she wouldn't be human if resentments against me didn't go deep. I remembered Ross's letter to Ysobel concerning the note he held for Brett, and which he'd hinted he might use against her. I thought, too, of how she must have come to hate him. Had she hated him enough to forge a letter from her daughter in order to shock him into taking some move that she wanted him to take? Such as returning her note?

She was waiting for my answer, batting away cigarette smoke with a gesture not entirely controlled. There were perhaps chinks in an armor I'd thought altogether attack-proof.

"I don't know if this would work out well," I said a bit stiffly. "I'd like to discuss it with Gretchen first. Of course, she may decide that *she* wants to live elsewhere."

"You'd better not count on that." The slightly acid smile appeared again. "Anyway, there's no need for hostility between us, is there? We're not likely to be chums, but we can behave in a civilized manner."

Implying that if I gave her a negative answer, I was hardly civilized? How badly did she need money? I wondered, and thought of the letter again, folded in my bag. I took it out and handed it to her.

She read the words with no show of emotion and gave it back. "You mean this was sent to Ross?"

"I don't know how it came to him, but it must have been one of the last things he read before he died. Gretchen says she didn't write it and never would have tried to hurt him that way."

"It does seem rather pointless, doesn't it? Something that happened more than two years ago. Whoever wrote it must have been naïve to think it could upset Ross at this late date. The fact of his affair with Pam Nichols would come as a surprise to no one. Not even Jarrett, I'm sure. And there are always those around whose job it is to protect the reputation of a man like Ross Logan."

She seemed entirely open and casual, unimpressed by the note, yet I sensed an inner stiffening. As though something that she kept from the surface disturbed her. Perhaps even frightened her. Why I received this sudden flash of insight, I didn't know, but something—for just an instant—told me that Brett Inness might indeed be far less calm and assured than she was pretending to be.

In the face of this sudden strong awareness, my own assurance began to revive. "Did you see Ross the night he died?" I asked.

Her hand with the cigarette moved nervously. "See him? Why should I see him? When I came to Poinciana

I always tried to avoid running into Ross. I'd hardly be likely to seek him out."

There was no way in which I could put pressure upon her to tell the truth—if she wasn't telling it—and this unpleasant interview had continued long enough. I went to the bedroom door and looked in. Allegra lay sleeping peacefully. Perhaps this bed would seem familiar to her when she awakened, and she would have a feeling of belonging again in Poinciana. If she decided to remain at the house, I would talk to Jarrett about having a stair seat installed that could take her up and down stairs easily.

Brett stood up as I returned to the room. "I must run. There's so much I need to do now. My shop has been neglected and I haven't worked at my designing board for days. Thank you, Sharon, for being so generous and understanding."

I had been neither, and I merely nodded. We left Allegra's suite together, to find Albert coming along the hall carrying a suitcase in each hand. Miss Cox trotted after him, her plump face tinged with pink in an effort to keep up. She didn't look in the least pleased with this move, which would probably interfere with her own authority, but she gave us each a careful smile, clearly uncertain as to where the source of real power lay.

I stopped to speak to her. "Mrs. Logan is asleep. She was very tired. When she wakes up, tell her we can solve the stair problem for her so she can get outside when she wishes."

The nurse nodded, directed a questioning look at Brett, and followed Albert down the hall. Brett hurried away from me, presumably to look for Gretchen. I would not be surprised if she moved into the house immediately, whether I granted permission or not. And without an ugly confrontation, there didn't seem to be much I could do about it.

I went on toward the branching corridor that led to my room, no longer certain of anything. That nothing was what it seemed to be was a recurring theme in this house, and I hated the confusion and uncertainty. I wanted only to believe and trust, yet such simple virtues seemed to have disappeared from my life.

Beside me, the wall appeared to move, and Keith Nichols popped out of the very woodwork. We stared at each other in surprise, as we had done that other time when I'd been with Ross and *trompe l'oeil* had deceived me.

"Hello," I said. "One of these days you must introduce me to some of Allegra's secret passages."

The apprehension in his eyes faded. "You mean you don't care if I come inside the house sometimes?"

"It's all right," I said, "if your father approves, and providing you don't touch anything you're not supposed to."

"Like the netsuke? I wouldn't do that. Not ever."

"Why did you think of the netsuke?"

"I don't know. I guess somebody said there were some more missing. Only Mrs. Allegra doesn't take them. I know she doesn't, because she's told me not to. They're awfully valuable, aren't they?"

"I believe they are. Is there someone you're looking for now?"

"Her. Mrs. Allegra. Albert said they'd moved her up to the house, and I wanted to visit her and see if she's all right."

His young face looked up at me with such open candor that I felt a certain relief. Keith, at least, could be taken exactly as he was—a small boy with an attachment for an old lady that was refreshing.

"She's asleep now," I said. "But perhaps you can come back later and talk to her. Only you can use the stairs nearest her room and not startle people by coming out of the wall."

"I was in there looking for something. Something Mrs. Allegra wants me to find. Only she doesn't remember exactly what it is, or where she put it. She thinks that she hid it somewhere in the house a long time ago. She said it was important. I was looking the other day too, when Mr. Logan brought you into the art gallery."

"You mean it was you who watched us through the door at the far end that day?"

"Sure. I know how to turn off the alarm. And I didn't let him catch me that time. But I didn't find anything there either."

I let the matter go. "Come back later," I repeated. "I know Mrs. Logan will like to see you. And will you do something for me when you come, Keith? Will you try to find out whether she really wants to stay here in this house, as Gretchen thinks she should?"

"She'll want to," Keith said with confidence. "After she moves things around in her head, she'll want to. She's always telling me about how wonderful the house is, and about those rooms she fixed for herself when she got pretty old."

I put a hand on his shoulder. "Thank you, Keith. You've just said something more sensible than anything the rest of us have come up with. I may want to use you as a counselor again sometime."

"Or a detective? There are a lot of mysteries around here, aren't there?"

"Indeed there are."

"Like how that alarm went off the night Mr. Logan had a heart attack?"

I answered carefully, suppressing any eagerness that might stop him. "Do you know anything about that?"

He looked pleased with himself. "That's not really a mystery, is it? Because Miss Inness turned it on. Didn't you know about that?"

I could only stare at him in astonishment. "Keith, why do you believe she turned it on?"

He wasn't ready to tell me that, however, and his gaze shifted to a point far down the hall. "Oh, I guess I just knew," he said, and ran off toward the stairs.

What was it I'd been thinking? That Keith, at least, was exactly the small boy he seemed? Ingenuous and

believable? Only now it appeared that he had his secrets too. This would bear looking into, when I found
a way to do it. Why would Brett, of all people, have
turned on the alarm?

When I reached my room, the phone was ringing,
and I picked it up, to hear Jarrett's voice.

"Are you all right?" he asked.

"I'm fine. But I have a lot of things to tell you."

"I thought you might. Would you care to come down
to our cottage tonight and have dinner with Keith and
me? We dine early, so six-thirty would be fine."

"I'd love to," I said, and when I put down the phone
I felt better than I had all morning. Perhaps Jarrett
Nichols was the one person in this house to whom I
could talk openly. But what was I to do with my day
that would be useful until it was time for dinner?

The answer came readily. I could look for Ross's
missing manuscript and the photographs Gretchen had
taken for his book. The obvious place to start was in
his office, even though Gretchen claimed to have
searched it thoroughly.

I went downstairs and found Myra working at her
desk. Ross's door was closed, but Jarrett's office stood
open and empty.

Myra caught the direction of my look. "Mr. Nichols
has just gone out." Again she had discarded her casual
slacks for a neat cotton dress—perhaps still being re-
spectful to a proper atmosphere of mourning? Her smile
was one of sympathy. "You look tired, Mrs. Logan."

I went directly to my purpose. "Mrs. Karl hasn't been
able to find the manuscript my husband was working
on, and I thought I might look through his office. It
isn't locked, is it?"

"Nothing's locked except the safe." She left her desk
and went to open the door for me. "Mrs. Karl was here
earlier, but she wasn't able to find that manuscript
herself."

"Then I probably won't find it either."

As she stepped aside, I went past her with a sense

of apprehension and stood looking around the big,
handsome room. Nothing had changed about its impressive air of luxury, from black leather chairs and
walnut desk to the Chinese carpet, bordered by polished
parquetry. The last time I had stepped into Ross's office
had been on that terrible night when I'd found him
slumped across his desk, with Jarrett beside him. The
memory was vivid in my mind, and I could almost hear
the shrilling of that dreadful alarm.

Myra was still at my elbow. "I don't know if it's any
help, Mrs. Logan, but on the same day that it happened,
Mr. Logan brought his manuscript and those photos
Mrs. Karl took, into his office and was working on them
here. So perhaps he never put them back where he
usually kept them."

"Did you tell Mrs. Karl that?"

"She didn't give me much chance," Myra said ruefully. "And probably it's no help anyway, since I don't
know where he put them after that."

I hardly knew where to begin my search. The obvious
starting place was Ross's desk, but I was sure it had
been gone through carefully by this time, and not only
by Gretchen. In any case, I was reluctant to touch Ross's
desk at all. Memory was too vivid.

"Do you mind if I speak out of turn?" Myra asked.

"You don't usually wait for permission," I said, and
she grinned.

"We're in the same boat, in a way, aren't we? Oh,
I know you're the top lady of all this now, and I'm
hardly a speck on the horizon. Just the same, we're
both outsiders, aren't we? And I don't know what to do
now, any more than you do."

As usual, she had penetrated through all the subterfuge. Perhaps it would be more useful to talk with
Myra Ritter than to start what was sure to be a futile
search.

"Why don't you sit down," she said, "and I'll fix us
some coffee."

I sat in one of the big leather chairs and let her

minister to me, feeling oddly grateful. She remembered that I took my coffee black, and when she'd put a mug in my hands, she pulled another chair around and curled herself up in it, rather like a small cat.

"I suppose the main thing we have to remember," she said, "is not to let them railroad us into doing what we don't want to do."

"I don't feel that I'm being railroaded," I said. "I'm making my own choices, such as they are."

"That's what you think. But aren't you letting them make you stay at Poinciana, when all you want, really, is to get away?"

"How can you possibly think that?"

"Because it makes sense. I can put myself in your place. And if I were there, I'd get out so fast you wouldn't see me for smoke."

I sipped coffee and smiled at her. "That is what I want, and you're perfectly right. But it's not what I can do. There are responsibilities."

"For instance?" She was openly curious.

"My husband's will. He wanted me to stay here. He must have thought that it would be best for Poinciana in the long run."

"It's only a house."

"Nevertheless, it should be preserved. Perhaps turned into a museum, or a trust eventually. That is, if Mrs. Karl and her husband should decide not to live here. Or when Allegra Logan dies."

"So you'll hang on and be miserable here, when all that would probably come about anyway?"

I couldn't confide my uneasiness concerning Vasily Karl. I couldn't talk to her about the note that had been sent to Ross. I couldn't say, "Perhaps someone frightened my husband to death and I want to know who and why."

"I can understand," she said. "I know it must be hard to decide. I feel the same way. I mean, Mr. Nichols isn't going to stay here after everything's settled. His work is in New York and Washington. He only came here regularly because Mr. Logan insisted. But it's not very convenient to run everything from Florida. So I expect he'll take his little boy and leave before long."

The sinking feeling at the pit of my stomach was not wholly unexpected. I had felt this way when Jarrett spoke of resigning. The very thought of Poinciana without Jarrett Nichols here to depend upon gave me a shivery feeling, as though I'd suddenly stepped into a cold wind.

"Of course, I suppose you're his boss now," Myra went on, watching me shrewdly. "I suppose you could order him to stay, if you want."

"I couldn't do that."

She sighed. "I didn't think you would, but I had to find out. You see, what he does affects me. Oh, I think he'd take me along. I've worked for him pretty well. I like it here in Florida. I like my little apartment, and I don't want to leave. I suppose I can get another job here, but it won't be the same. I've enjoyed working for Mr. Nichols. Being at Poinciana has been like living in a play. So you see I have a dilemma too. Though it's not on the same level as yours."

I remembered her mentioning earlier that I might need a social secretary. But that time hadn't come as yet, and I wasn't prepared to make a decision now.

"Anyway," I said, "I expect everything will run along as usual for a while. At least until the will is probated."

I'd finished my coffee, and she got up to take my empty mug. "I suppose that's true. Then there will be the litigation while Mrs. Karl tries to get Poinciana back."

Such a thought appalled me. The last thing I wanted was to be embroiled in an unpleasant contesting of Ross's will.

"Surely that won't happen," I said.

"Maybe not. Especially if you wind up leaving. They'll try to get you out between them—Mrs. Karl and her mother. And I think if you're smart and like your freedom, you'll go."

I might want to go, but I didn't mean to be forced out by Gretchen and Brett Inness. Where did Vasily stand in all this? I wondered. What did he really want? But I knew I couldn't count on anything Vasily Karl said, even if I asked him straight out.

"I'm not sure what I'll do," I told Myra. "Except that now I had better see if I can find my husband's manuscript. Can you think of any place where she might not have searched?"

Myra considered. "Only the locked safe. She wasn't able to look into that because Mr. Nichols wasn't here to give her the combination. You could ask him about that."

It seemed the logical place, and perhaps if Jarrett had been through it, he hadn't recognized the manuscript package for what it was.

"You're probably right," I said. "There's not much point in searching where Mrs. Karl has already looked. I'll get Mr. Nichols to open the safe for me later."

I thanked her and went into the long corridor. At the far end, one of the maids scuttled out of sight, still restrained by the rules of invisibility Ross had laid down. Mrs. Broderick would probably see to it that they were adhered to, and would allow no slackening.

Were the things I was doing merely a marking of time because I hadn't come to grips with a real purpose for my life? Was I keeping busy with mere intrigue, while larger issues escaped me?

But even if this were true, I couldn't deal with anything larger now. Keeping busy at *something* was all I could manage. So a visit to the tower rooms next would be as good to do as anything else.

Not because I expected to find any answers there, but because those rooms might tell me something further about Gretchen, and perhaps about Allegra herself. I hadn't been up to the belvedere since my first uncomfortable encounter there with Gretchen and Vasily.

Once more I climbed the circular iron stairs, holding

on to the curving rail. The steps were wedge-shaped and difficult, and I wondered that Allegra had wanted to use these rooms for herself. However, she had been agile and athletic enough, even into her fifties and sixties. The clippings I'd seen had told me that.

The lower room that she had called her "nap" room was one I hadn't explored, and I stepped off the stairs and stood looking about its square expanse. Blinds were closed, the furniture still shrouded. Again, as in the room above, there were windows all around, though more wall space had been allowed here. There was no outside balcony at this level.

As my eyes became accustomed to the shuttered light, I saw that an elegant French armoire had been placed across one corner. I remembered the time when I'd stood in the ballroom downstairs and wondered if any of Allegra's gowns from her earlier days had been preserved. Perhaps this was one place to look.

Double doors pulled outward as I turned the handles, swinging wide to emit an odor of mothballs and faded sachet. The big armoire was hung solid with covered dresses. The plastic protection they wore belonged to a later day than the dresses themselves, and I could see them through the transparency. How beautiful they were—all ball gowns, apparently, and of every imaginable style. Nothing must ever have been given away that she had worn to a party. I lifted a hanger from the rack and held up a long, slim frock of midnight blue satin, trimmed with crystal bugle beads. It rustled softly, as if stirring from a long sleep. Its décolletage was low, front and back, and there was a tiny train that she must have picked up by its wrist cord when she was dancing. How Allegra must have glittered as she moved, holding every eye.

I heard my own sigh as I replaced the dress among its sisters. Strange that these things should remain in all their perfection, while the woman who had worn them aged and faded. Another time, I would come here to examine every gown in the armoire. Perhaps I would even ask Allegra about their stories. "A long time ago" was a time she would remember more easily than yesterday.

I closed the doors softly, so as not to disturb old ghosts, and climbed the stairs to the top of the tower.

There seemed little change in this upper room since the last time I had seen it. If Gretchen still used it for her studio, however, there was no evidence, though the two contrasting photos of Ross still hung on the wall near the desk. I felt a pang as I studied them again.

How sure—how almost sure—I'd been on that innocent day when I'd first seen them that Ross's true character was revealed in the dynamic picture in which he moved toward the camera with a confident smile, exuding the power and vibrant spirit I had known him to possess. Now, I could look at the second picture and remember all too well that the darker side of him had existed too, and perhaps been in ascendancy here at Poinciana. That far more dangerous side. Yet in the end the danger had ricocheted back to him.

A clang of metal from the stairs startled me. Someone had stepped onto the iron wedges and was coming up. An instinctive reluctance to be found here sent me to the balcony door. I pulled it open and stepped into the wind, closing it after me. I wasn't sure why I'd moved so swiftly and fearfully, except that I had once been pushed down a flight of stairs, and that nothing since then had caused me to feel safe and secure in this house. I wanted to know who climbed those stairs before I made my presence known.

The climber paused at the floor below, but only for a moment, and then came on to the upper room. I moved around the narrow wooden balcony that followed the square turns of the tower, and found a window where I could watch around the edge, with a minimum likelihood of being seen.

Vasily Karl's fair head emerged from the stair opening, and he stepped into the studio room and stood looking about. Looking for what? Had Gretchen sent

him here on a search for her father's manuscript? But
surely Ross would never have brought it to the belvedere.

As I watched Vasily standing there, studying the
room, I still thought that some search must be in his
mind. But his next move showed clearly that he knew
what he was looking for, and where it was hidden. He
went to a wicker chair and lifted out the chintz-covered
cushion. Reaching beneath it for something, he found
whatever it was and dropped it quickly into his jacket
pocket. In a moment he would be gone again, down the
stairs.

Vasily didn't frighten me. Though perhaps he should
have. I ran around the balcony, not bothering to be
quiet, so that he heard me coming and turned to stare
at the door as I entered the tower room.

"Hello, Vasily," I said.

For once I had taken him by surprise. Accustomed
as he must have been to difficult situations in which
he had lived by his wits and clever deceptions, he was
able to think of nothing to say or do in the face of my
sudden appearance. Only after a long pause did he recover and smile at me brightly.

"Are you up here admiring the view, Sharon?"

"I'm not sure why I'm here," I said. "ESP, perhaps.
Something pulled me to the tower. And I was right,
wasn't I? I had reason to come here."

His shrug was as easy and comfortable as though he
had not been taken by surprise a moment before. "Oh,
well. I suppose it doesn't really matter now. I told
Gretchen that her idea was foolish, and that you would
have to know sooner or later."

He went to the desk and opened a bottom drawer.
From it he drew a large red folder and placed it on top
of the desk. I knew what it was without the slightest
doubt.

"How did Ross's manuscript come to be here?" I
asked.

Again the careless shrug. "Let's not go into that. Isn't it enough that it has been recovered?"

"Does Gretchen know it was here?"

"Of course. She put it in that drawer herself."

"In order to make a stir? In order to upset me?"

"Sit down for a moment," he said, suddenly grave as he motioned me into the chair where the cushion had been replaced. "It will be just as well not to confront my wife with this, Sharon. Sometimes her moods aren't altogether rational, and it's not wise to disturb her unnecessarily. This is a difficult time for her, as it must be for you. I've been wanting to assure you that I will do everything possible to persuade Gretchen to leave Poinciana. I would like to travel abroad with her. There are so many places in Europe that we could see together, and I hope to convince her that this would be a good thing to do right now. It would also help to heal her loss."

"You mean you'll try to persuade her to give up Poinciana?"

"Not exactly. She needn't live in the house to fight this will, if that becomes her desire. Neither does she need to outwait you here. I suspect that you may find that you don't want to live in this mausoleum of a place alone. Everyone will be leaving, you know. And will you enjoy being its custodian all alone? Especially during the summer. This isn't a house that can be air-conditioned, except for a few rooms."

"Allegra and Charles Logan sometimes spent their summers here without air conditioning."

"I don't want to argue with you. I shall try to persuade Gretchen that if we all leave, and that will include Brett and Allegra—whatever must be done about her—then some of the servants will give notice, and you will find that you have no wish to stay here, no matter what selfish thing Ross may have asked of you."

He seemed strangely eager to convince me, and he had grown less mockingly assured. There was almost an urgency of need in him to persuade me.

"It isn't just that you want me out so that Gretchen will inherit Poinciana, is it?" I asked.

His usually easy manner evaporated. I had never seen him so grave. "No, it is not. For your own sake, Sharon, you are better away."

"But why, Vasily? Tell me why?"

"There have already been attempts to injure and torment you. Isn't that enough reason? Do you believe in primitive force, Sharon?"

This was a surprising turn. "I'm not sure what you mean."

"I'm not being esoteric. I have come to believe that there are contrasting natures in all of us. One is the primitive side that we learn to suppress as children, and it must be kept suppressed, or it can become a primitive force for destruction. As happens in some people."

I glanced at Gretchen's photograph of Ross. "My father used to say it in a different way—that things are seldom what they seem."

"Exactly. Have you felt this force in yourself at times, Sharon?"

"I don't think so." There had been occasions when I was with Ross...but I had hardly turned primitive.

"I have felt this in myself," he went on, "and sometimes it has frightened me."

That was what I had begun to sense in Vasily—that he was frightened—and the very fact alarmed me.

"I'd like to leave this house right now," I told him. "But there are certain things I must know first, and I mean to stay and find them out."

"Don't stay," he pleaded. "Don't try to find out." He hesitated and then went on, still deeply in earnest. "There are times in a life when one may be caught in a net of one's own weaving. The strands are there to hold you, and there is no way to cut yourself free. So move now, Sharon. Get away before the deadly strands tighten."

As he was caught in his marriage to Gretchen? I

wondered. But all this about primitive forces and deadly strands grew a little too melodramatic. Vasily was skilled to perfection in building the sensational, and I must not be convinced by his efforts. I began to relax a little.

When he picked up the manuscript and turned toward the stairs, I held out my hand. "I'll take that folder, please."

He gave it to me, though I sensed his reluctance. There was a new eagerness in him to escape my company, and I could easily guess why. He had said all he wished to say, and he didn't want me to pick up on something he wanted to conceal. I picked up on it.

"What was it you retrieved from this chair?" I asked him.

His stiff smile seemed to warn me that I was going too far. "Let's say that is my own small secret. You must not push too far, Sharon. You are still young and somewhat heedless—as I used to be. Now I count safety as a virtue in itself, and I value it greatly. I recommend that you do the same. You have lost your powerful protector, and you must remember that."

I watched as he gave me a mocking salute and disappeared down the turning stairs. There had been absolutely nothing I could do or say in the face of his veiled warnings. If I'd demanded to see what he had taken from the chair and dropped into his pocket, he might either have laughed at me, or become angry. For the first time it occurred to me that I would not like to see Vasily Karl angry. Not that he had seemed in the least enraged. He had been more fearful than angry, and the knowledge that something was frightening him was rather terrifying in itself. He might deal in melodrama, but I couldn't dismiss what he said because of that.

The folder was in my hands, and I opened it and looked inside. The pages Ross had finished were there, as were the photographs and invoices. Had Gretchen really been the one to bring these things to the tower room? I couldn't be sure that Vasily had told me the truth about anything he had said. His reluctance to have me mention this meeting to his wife seemed to suggest that he had not told me the entire truth.

At least, with the manuscript in hand again, I knew what I must do before anything else happened. I must go downstairs immediately and check every item on the netsuke shelves against the records I held in my hands.

Chapter

15

I worked meticulously, systematically, and I was now familiar enough with many of the individual netsuke so that I could find them to check against the records. Two that were missing showed up quickly. Vasily had been right in his first wry suggestion that these records might have been hidden so that subsequent thefts would not be discovered. But surely Gretchen—oh, the very thought was ridiculous.

The missing items this time were a carp with a baby turtle in its mouth—in itself an amusing reversal of nature, since snapping turtles were more likely to bother the fish—and a Daruma, who was described as reading and chuckling over an erotic "pillow book" when he should have been doing his religious meditations. Both items were signed and were valuable in themselves. But only to the extent of a few thousand dollars.

Either or both would have been small enough to hide beneath the cushion of a chair, and later slipped into a jacket pocket if Vasily had wanted to carry them away.

Yet I could hardly accuse Vasily of the theft, or even be sure that the netsuke, like the manuscript, had been hidden in the tower room. It would seem a good place for such concealment, since Gretchen never allowed the maids to come up there to clean, and apparently she had seen little of those rooms herself in recent days.

But who was the thief? Perhaps this was just another trick of Gretchen's to give her an excuse to keep me off balance. Or it could be that Vasily was stealing for his own profit. Gretchen, being her father's daughter, might very well be keeping him on a short leash. The strands of that net he had mentioned?

A deep, unreasoned conviction was growing in me that some missing element existed in all this. If I could uncover the one connecting link, everything else would fall into place and be tied together—from Ross's death, to the alarm-setting, to the hiding of the manuscript. Even to the fact that two valuable netsuke were missing. Also, as Vasily had reminded me, there were those hands that had pushed me down a flight of stairs—an intent that might have killed me. To say nothing of the harmless, yet utterly disturbing trick with a rotting coconut. All were connected, and I must somehow learn in what way.

Earlier, I'd wondered if I had been simply busying myself with intrigue to avoid meeting larger issues head on. Now I was growing certain that everything was part of that larger issue that still escaped me, and with which I must eventually come face to face. When I knew the answer to this and this, then the dark human motives, the primitive force that Vasily had spoken of, would be revealed. Only then would I see clearly where danger lay, and I could only pray that my knowledge wouldn't come too late. That was the awful part—

not knowing the face of my enemy, or from what direction the next attack might come.

In the meantime, I had better keep busy if I wasn't to be shaken into flight. One problem now was how to protect the netsuke collection from further raids. But even if they were removed from their shelves and locked away, there was still the rest of Poinciana—an enormous collection of far more valuable items, many of them small enough to be easily pilfered. When the will was settled, perhaps I could return the netsuke collection to Japan as Ross had mentioned doing. But there was little I could do now about all these treasures except to try to be as watchful as possible.

A certain rebellion and resentment began to stir in me. This was a dreadful way to live! To be constantly in fear that valuable possessions would be stolen was to be owned by those possessions—and that was not for me. The house should be turned into a museum, and be supported and guarded as such, however much of Ross's wealth this might cost. Once I had thought nothing could be more marvelous than to live in such a place—my own private museum. I didn't think so any longer. There were treasures here and they should be seen, appreciated, not kept selfishly private as Ross had wanted to keep them. He had wanted me to stay here, to restore, to give myself to Poinciana. And that was something I had no intention of doing.

Nevertheless, until the house and its property were clearly in my hands, there was little I could do. It might even be that the pilfering lay within the family, and that would be very hard to deal with.

One thing I knew. For the moment, I'd had enough of Poinciana and all it contained. Except for the funeral, I hadn't been outside the gate for days. Perhaps I could even think more clearly if I got away for a while. Tonight at dinner I could pour everything out into Jarrett's sensible ears, but I didn't know where he was right now.

I went upstairs and changed into something suitable

for town. When I was ready in beige linen and brown pumps, with a touch of coral at neck and ears, I went downstairs and asked for the car and Albert.

I was told that Mrs. Karl had already taken the Rolls, with Albert to drive her, and had gone into town to view her exhibit of pictures in the library. Would I care to drive myself? There was, of course, a choice of cars.

There was no reason why I shouldn't drive myself. I accepted a white Ferrari that Vasily sometimes used. It would do as well as any, and perhaps it would be an advantage to catch Gretchen away from the house. I too would visit the exhibit at the library.

I had overlooked what it was like to be a Logan at this time. As I drove through the gate, photographers and reporters swarmed upon me, hurling questions, snapping their camera shutters. I had seen such assaults on television news programs, but this was the real thing. Away from the protection of the house, I had to roll up my windows, and try to drive without running anyone down.

For days I had scarcely looked at the newspapers, and I hadn't realized what I should have taken for granted—that the world was fascinated by Ross Logan, his death, his family, and that repercussions would take a long while to die down.

Until this moment, no one had been able to get near me. Now I was uncomfortably aware that cars were following me into town and that I would be surrounded again the moment I left the Ferrari. Better to join them than fight them! When I came to a place where I could stop on the narrow boulevard without blocking traffic, I pulled off and waited. A car squealed behind me, and a woman got out and came running up to the window of my car. She was young and eager, and I rolled it down and smiled at her.

"Would you like to act as my guide?" I asked. "I'm going into town to see Mrs. Karl's exhibit of photographs. If you mean to follow me anyway, you might as well go on ahead and show me where the library is."

She agreed cheerfully. "Sure. If you'll answer some questions for me at the other end."

"I'll try," I promised.

She grinned in the direction of two other cars that had slowed behind us, and got into her battered Chevy. When she drove around me, touching her horn, I followed, and the rest of the entourage fell in behind.

Oddly enough, away from Poinciana, I didn't mind so much. These people were doing their job, and after all I was one of the reading public who had followed with interest what happened to the world's celebrated. Except that I couldn't see myself existing in that category, even after my marriage to Ross Logan.

We drove into the center of Palm Beach to Four Arts Plaza, and parked. My guide whipped out of her car and came to slip into the front seat of mine.

Strangely, I felt more relaxed than I had in days, as, notebook and pencil in hand, she began her questions. I tried to keep my wits about me, and remember what everything would sound like in print.

For the most part, her questions were straightforward enough. What were my plans? Would I stay on in Poinciana, or leave and allow Mr. Logan's daughter to inherit? (So news of the will was common property?) How did I feel to be one of the world's wealthiest women? What would I do with my time?

I asked a question or two of my own. My inquisitioner's name was Meg, and she worked for the woman's page of a Florida paper.

It was my own feelings about what was happening to me that most interested her. In most cases I had to answer with an I-don't-know. I really hadn't thought about being wealthy. I hadn't had time to get used to it. I hadn't thought about a lot of things, apparently.

How did I feel about my husband's daughter? I told her cautiously that we hadn't had time to become well acquainted, but that I admired her work in photogra-

phy, and was interested in seeing her exhibit at the
library. No, of course there was no antagonism between
us. Already I was discovering that one lied glibly to the
press. Not until I asked to be let off from any further
questions did she put the one that most upset me.

"How do you feel about the rumors that your husband's death was not due to a heart attack?"

After the first shock, I tried to answer carefully. "I
haven't heard any such rumors. You have only to check
with his doctor."

"Oh, we have. But there seem to be unanswered
questions about just what brought on the heart attack."

I mananged to keep myself in hand. "I was *there,*
and there is nothing more to know."

The girl beside me recognized that her interview was
at an end.

"You'll enjoy the library," she said. "An interesting
building. It's not a public library, you know. Local residents support it. Don't you love those bronze jaguars
on either side of the steps?"

"I'll go in now," I said.

"Thanks a lot for letting me talk with you," she told
me, and returned to her Chevy. I could hope that she
would be reasonably kind in whatever she wrote.

There were more reporters waiting, having followed
me here, but I hurried through and went up the wide
steps between the two prowling animals. I had a quick
glimpse of a white stone building—Quattrocento Italian in style—and then I was through the arches of the
red-tiled portico.

The interior was cool after bright sunlight, and I
stopped to look up at the stunning portrait that hung
over the desk. It was a painting of a seated woman, her
white hair partly hidden by black lace, her eyes of arresting intensity. A remarkable face.

The librarian behind the desk greeted me as I came
in. "Good morning, Mrs. Logan. If you're looking for
Mrs. Karl, she's already here."

I supposed that my picture must have appeared in

papers across the country, and I had to get used to being recognized.

"Thank you," I said. "I've come to see her photographs."

"They've been hung upstairs in the children's room, where we have more wall space," she said, and directed me.

I took the elevator up and found the big room with its bright book jackets, low tables and small chairs. It was empty when I walked in, except for Gretchen, who stood looking up at a matted photograph she had taken of her husband.

The photo seemed extremely posed, yet, knowing Vasily, I suspected that she had caught him quite off guard. He fell naturally into poses. In the black-and-white full-length, he leaned against the trunk of a coco palm on the grounds of Poinciana. A familiar glimpse of the belvedere identified the setting. His blond head rested against the trunk, his arms were folded, and one foot crossed over the other. The collar of his white shirt was open at the throat to reveal a gold coin he wore on a chain—a gift from Gretchen. He seemed completely relaxed and unaware of any camera nearby, his expression one I'd seen before—the look of a man who accepted life as it came, and was entertained by it. The face of a romantic, an adventurer. *The Thief of Baghdad*, I thought to myself. That was where Vasily belonged— in the *Arabian Nights*. But this was a dangerous look for a modern man to wear.

"You've caught him very well," I said softly to Gretchen.

She whirled to stare at me, quick anger rising in her eyes.

"Please," I said. "A truce. I only want to talk with you. We're really on the same side, but you never give us a chance to find this out."

From beneath the fall of short hair, her look was one of hostility. She said, "We can't talk here. But come along, and we'll find a place."

- She led the way to a narrow room with a table and chairs placed near an end window. Books lined the shelves, and Gretchen waved a casual hand at them as we entered.

"This was the personal collection of the architectural books that belonged to Addison Mizner. He's the man who gave Palm Beach its Spanish-Mediterranean look." She sat down at the table. "Okay. What do you want to talk about?"

"I have the netsuke manuscript," I said, sitting opposite her.

Her look of surprise seemed real. "Where did you find it?"

"Oddly enough, it was in the upper room of the belvedere, in a drawer of your grandmother's desk. I thought you might have put it there."

"Of course I didn't!" Again her outrage seemed sincere, but before she could further vent her indignation, I went on.

"I took it down to the Japanese room and started checking. I haven't finished, but I've found two netsuke missing. I suppose that's why these records were hidden. So there would be a delay in our discovering a theft."

Her first angry flush had died away, leaving her pale. So much for Vasily's veracity in telling me that it was Gretchen who had hidden the manuscript.

"How did you happen to look in the belvedere?" she asked.

"You'd looked everywhere else," I said. "Though I didn't really go up there for the purpose of searching for the manuscript. I stopped to look at an armoire full of Allegra's gowns, and then I went upstairs and—and found the folder with Ross's papers and your photos." I would keep Vasily out of it for now.

Gretchen was silent, still pale. And frightened? Yet with a different fear from that I'd sensed in her husband. He had been afraid of something or someone. There had been an awareness, a direction about his fear that I had sensed distinctly. Perhaps a fear of his wife. Gretchen was afraid without knowing why. Or perhaps she was afraid *to* know why.

"How much do you trust your mother?" I asked bluntly. I wanted to ask how well she could trust Vasily, but I didn't dare.

For once, she took no offense. "I can trust her as long as her interest coincides with mine." An old bitterness sounded in the words.

"I'm not making accusations," I said, "but I can't help wondering. Just this morning Jarrett's son, Keith, told me that it was Brett who set off the alarm that night."

This time I hadn't surprised her. She reached across the small table and grasped me tightly by the wrist. "Don't think whatever it is you're thinking. Brett's okay."

So she knew. So it was true. "I'm not able to conclude much of anything," I told her. "That's the trouble. Perhaps none of it matters now anyway. These things aren't what is real—old grudges, suspicions. It's our lives *now* that matter. What I am going to do, and whether you're happy in your life. Are you, Gretchen?"

"Of course I'm happy! Except for what's happened to my father, more than I've ever been. Vasily wants us to go on a trip through Europe, until after things are settled. I think perhaps I will. There's so much he wants to show me over there, and we need to get away from Poinciana for a while. Until it can belong to us. As it will, Sharon. As it has to!"

"Of course it has to," I agreed. "That's what I'd like you to understand. I don't want any part of it. Your father was angry with you when he changed his will. But he would probably have changed it back if there'd been time. I only wish he had."

She was staring at me again, in disbelief. "But I thought—"

"You didn't think, Gretchen. You only made accusations and jumped to false conclusions. I can under-

stand that you never wanted your father to marry me.
I know my coming couldn't have been more unwelcome.
But that's over now. I don't want Poinciana for myself.
But I'd like to see it preserved and protected, as your
grandmother and your father would wish. So I'll stay
for now. Especially if you're going away. Later you can
decide what you want to do, and how you mean to take
over. Besides, with Allegra back in the house, someone
has to stay around."

"Allegra? Back in the house? But how—"

"Your mother brought her there. Brett moved her
upstairs with most of her things this morning, and she
went to bed in her old room. But I'm not sure she's
happy about the move. Brett said you wanted it, and
so did she, and I think she acted out of good intent.
Only it was too fast for your grandmother to realize
what was happening. It must have been a shock to be
suddenly uprooted like that."

"Brett!" Again Gretchen put bitterness into her
voice. "She never even consulted me."

This was the moment for attack. There was something I could probably settle now. "I'd rather not have
your mother stay in the house," I said. "She has told
me she plans to move in."

I could sense the quick rising of resistance to me that
was second nature to Gretchen, and I hurried on.

"I don't believe you want her there either. It's not
necessary to spite me any more."

She made a sudden switch to a new attack of her
own. "Did you ever really love my father, Sharon?"

Reasonable words were hard to find, and I answered
with an indirection. "Do you remember those two photographs you took of him—the ones that I saw in the
tower room? I was in love with the man in one of those
pictures. I could never have loved the other one, but I
didn't know he existed until I came to Poinciana. Which
one was real? Perhaps I was only in love with a man
I imagined. Perhaps Ross and I were both cheated. I
wonder if women always marry imaginary heroes."

"I didn't! I know everything about Vasily. The bad things and the good, and I know how much I love him." She spoke the words defiantly, as though she slapped some sort of challenge down between us.

"Could he have taken the netsuke that are missing?" I asked.

"Of course he could have. It would be very like him. But I don't know whether he did or not. I'll find out. Is that all you wanted to talk about?"

"For now," I said. The feeling of depression and helplessness was returning. Perhaps I had wanted more from a meeting with Gretchen than was possible. Not information, not answers, but a lessening of the strain between us. And there I'd failed.

She went to shelves that lined one side of the room and took down a volume, riffling through its pages. "Maurice Fatio. He was the architect who designed this building, and he had a hand in Poinciana too. Though Grandmother Allegra went through a score of architects trying to incorporate her own ideas. That's why it's such a hodgepodge."

But it wasn't architects that concerned her now. "I still can't believe he's gone," she said as she returned the book to its place. "I still think of things I want to tell my father, share with him. Even argue with him about. At first I was just numb. But now feeling is beginning to come back, and I don't know how I can bear it."

"I know," I said. "I keep expecting him to come through a door at any moment. It's always that way for a while, I suppose. I still feel as though I ought to write my parents a letter, and I still wait for one from them. Perhaps it's a sense of unreality that helps us to get through until we can handle what has happened."

"Too many deaths," Gretchen said. "You've suffered too many deaths, haven't you, Sharon? Just the same— for me—there's a kind of relief as well. I don't have to fight him any longer. I don't have to worry about that terrible bargain he made with Vasily. Which doesn't

mean that I don't miss him at every turn. It's strange
how mixed up emotions can be." She broke off and
stared at me. "Do you ever feel relief, Sharon?"

The tone of her voice had changed to one of challenge,
and I knew she would never allow me what she felt
herself. Whatever I said now, she would deride.

Without answering, I picked up my handbag and
started for the door.

"Sharon?" she said more gently, and I turned to see
that she looked almost contrite. "Listen—I know a little
courtyard off Worth, where we can sit at a small table
outdoors and have sandwiches and coffee. Will you
come with me? I don't want to be alone right now."

Surprised as I was, I didn't hesitate. "I'd like that,"
I said.

We went downstairs together, and out the door between the guardian jaguars—to be greeted by the clicking of cameras. The throng had grown.

"Smile at them," Gretchen said between her teeth.

Albert came quickly from the Rolls to assist us, but
Gretchen told him she would come with me and he
could take the big car home. We were followed to the
Ferrari, but Gretchen took it all in her stride and put
on a good face. She got behind the wheel as her right,
and I gave her the key.

"You might as well grin and bear it," she told me as
we drove off. "Anybody with the Logan name is news
all the time. But more so than ever now. You and I,
especially. Just look at them cheerfully, or you'll find
scowling pictures of yourself plastered across every
newspaper you pick up."

"All I can manage is to look blank," I said. "I can't
get used to any of this. It was never as bad with Ysobel."

"Then you'd better toughen up," she told me.

When we reached Worth Avenue she found a space
between a Lincoln Continental and a pickup truck—
the latter a sign of democracy moving in. We followed
an arcade to a sunny courtyard, where umbrellas
shaded small round tables.

Once an enterprising photographer popped in to snap a picture before he was banished by a waitress, but for the most part our lunch together was a green oasis in the dry and lonely desert in which I seemed to be lost. There was a relaxing of defenses at last, almost an approach to friendliness between us for a little while. I was to remember this hour we spent together—Ross's daughter and I. I was to remember it later in the face of all the dreadful things that were to come.

During the meal we talked at first about neither Ross nor Vasily. Gretchen spoke of her grandmother as she remembered her from the past. She told me some of the stories about her that had taken on the quality of legend. Once when Allegra was young and given to laughing at the proprieties, she had ridden a horse rudely among the tables of the Coconut Grove at the august Royal Poinciana Hotel.

"It really was a coconut grove and outdoors then," Gretchen said. "So it wasn't like riding under a roof. I wish I could have seen her. She used to tell me about the Royal Poinciana. Flagler built it way back in the 1890's, and he painted it lemon yellow, the way he did everything. It was the largest wooden building in the world, and the grandest of the grand hotels. But then people began to build what they called 'cottages' in Palm Beach. The Royal Poinciana was damaged in a hurricane, and finally torn down in 1936. All ancient history."

"At least Palm Beach still has the Breakers."

"Yes, and it's pretty grand. It burned down on three occasions, but every time it rose from the ashes, so that it has become a landmark, with those big white towers on the ocean. The Breakers was Flagler's baby too, in the beginning. One of these days I must take you to Whitehall. That was his home, you know. It's a beautiful museum now, with the rooms all intact."

How pleasant it was to be peaceful, to talk about ordinary things, to rest emotionally. I think Gretchen felt it too and that these moments were as welcome to her as they were to me.

The sense of peace lasted all the way back to Poinciana, and that was the end of it. Susan Broderick, home from her morning classes, waited for us as we came in.

"Mother told me to watch for you. There's a problem with Mrs. Allegra. She seems to be going berserk in the art gallery, and you'd better go there at once. Mr. Nichols is away and can't be reached. As usual, Coxie doesn't know what to do."

Gretchen and I looked at each other, and then started for the gallery at a run.

Chapter

16

Allegra was dressed once more in her running-away costume of brown slacks and pullover, her white hair braided out of the way and tied with a pert velvet ribbon. When we came in she was standing in the center of the long gallery, her arms set akimbo, hands on hips. Coxie and Steve, the guard, were both remonstrating with her.

"I want to know where those two pictures are!" Her voice managed to be indignant and still ladylike at the same time. This was not the Allegra who would ride a horse impudently through the Coconut Grove. Instead of flying in the face of authority, she was authority itself.

Gretchen ran down the room to fling her arms about her grandmother. "I'm so glad to have you home!" she cried. "Even if Brett shouldn't have done this when I wasn't there to help."

Allegra released herself gently from her grand-daughter's embrace, eyeing me over Gretchen's shoulder. It was to me she spoke.

"You're my son's wife, so you're in charge now, and you must answer my question. There are two paintings missing that always hung on that wall."

I looked up at the wall she indicated, and saw no empty spaces.

"I'm sorry," I said. "I don't know the collection well as yet. Will you please explain?"

"There were two Lautrecs that always hung right there. I didn't like Ross's arrangement, but I got used to it, and I know every painting on these walls. Now he seems to have hung a couple of unimportant Hudson River schools there. Why? What has happened to the Lautrecs? They are valuable."

Gretchen flung up her hands. "Oh, Gran! There's no use asking Sharon. What does she know? Dad moved things around whenever the notion struck him. You've been away for a long time, and he might have done anything at all with those paintings. There are a lot put away in storage, you know."

I was staring at the wall. "Wait! I think I do remember one of those pictures. I noticed it especially because it wasn't the Moulin Rouge sort of thing that Lautrec made so popular. It was an oil of a carriage drawn by a single horse, with a driver on the high seat, wearing a top hat. A lovely picture."

"That's it!" Allegra tapped me smartly on the arm in approval. "That was one of them. So you must have seen it on this wall recently."

"I believe I did. It could even have been here on the day Ross died."

"I knew it, I knew it! There's been a theft. Two Lautrecs are missing!"

Gretchen gave me a look of reproach. "Gran, we don't know that. Dad moved the portrait of Ysobel Hollis that last day. He might have moved others as well."

Allegra looked at me brightly. "*You* don't think so, do you?"

I didn't think so, but Gretchen was shaking her head at me in warning.

"I can't be absolutely sure," I said.

Allegra seemed to wilt a little, suddenly a very old lady. "I'm tired. Take me upstairs," she said to Gretchen. "*If* I can climb those stairs."

She climbed them between Gretchen and me, with Coxie trailing after us, and on the way Gretchen whispered sharply in my ear. "Just let it alone," she warned me.

Mrs. Broderick had taken the opportunity to get two of her maids into Allegra's rooms, and they were being tidied and dusted. Gretchen shooed them out of the bedroom, kissed her grandmother lovingly, and turned her over to the nurse. "I'll come visit you later, Gran."

We went into the corridor together. "Do you think those paintings have been put somewhere else?" I asked.

"I think they've been stolen," she said. "Just as the netsuke have been stolen. But I don't want Gran worried about this. I'll see what I can do about it."

She went off looking grim and tense, and I wondered if Vasily was in for a bad time. If he'd taken these things, he deserved it. Perhaps it would be easier for everyone if she took him off to Europe for a while. Yet somehow I was glad to have them both in the house. I hated to think of these echoing halls with so many of the family gone. It would be especially lonely at night, when the servants all vanished to their own quarters. But I mustn't start frightening myself.

When I stepped into my room it seemed more alien than ever. I must move out of it soon. Perhaps to a smaller bedroom, with a sitting room. In some strange way, I could feel Brett's presence here, and I was always aware that she had planned and furnished its pale elegance for herself. Besides, I didn't want to stay here, with Ross's room and all its unhappy memories right next door. And there was still the portrait of Ysobel Hollis to be dealt with. It must be hung somewhere else—or put away.

But I didn't want to decide anything now. All I needed to do was mark time until I could see Jarrett this evening. Always, through this strange morning, the thought of him had been warm at the back of my mind. I would talk to him tonight, tell him everything of my day, and of fears that he would help me to dismiss.

Something inside me said, "Wait, wait! You've been wrong before. You mustn't trust so easily. You mustn't care so easily." But I wanted to trust. I wanted to care. I didn't want to live by that cynical rule of my father's— that things were seldom what they seemed. There had been an unexpected warming in me toward Jarrett and I *wanted* to turn to him.

Once more, the outdoors drew me, and I went down the gracefully curving stairs to the yard. I'd hardly stepped out of the house since Ross's death, except for the funeral and my trip to town just now. I needed to push walls away from me, to breathe clear, salty air blowing in from the Atlantic.

The afternoon was warm and sunny—a real taste of Florida. I would go down and walk on the beach, I thought. It was time I faced those sands again, and banished memories that hurt me. But as I turned in the direction of the water, I saw with delight the flame tree—the flamboyant—the poinciana! It had burst into full bloom with every spreading branch ablaze with glorious fire. I stopped to drink in its beauty. All over southern Florida, these trees would be flaming now. Allegra must have seen to the planting of this one, since she'd honored the name for her own Poinciana. For how many seasons had Ross watched this blooming? Yet now he would never see it again, and the realization brought sadness with it. I walked on slowly.

As usual, there were two or three men at work on the grounds, tending the mowing, the watering, the flower beds, ready to pounce on any weed that showed itself. I stopped beside a man who was inserting something through a funnel into the trunk of a coconut palm and asked what he was doing.

He shook his head gloomily. "All over Palm Beach the coco palms are dying of a disease. The town is having them all injected, but I'm not sure it's doing much good."

These palms were plentiful at Poinciana. From every upstairs window one looked out upon their shaggy heads and slim, leaning trunks. In the days when there had always been visitors at the house, I'd been told that these trees were kept free of coconut clusters, lest they fall upon the heads of innocent guests.

I found my way to the tiled tunnel through which Ross had taken me on our way to the beach. Overhead, traffic was zooming past, while I walked on echoing stone. When I came out upon the sand at the far end, I saw the bathhouse and swimming pool Allegra had built, but it was the ocean that drew me.

Today the wind was strong and whitecaps rolled in, curling a froth of lace onto the sand. The ocean's voice roared in the sound of the waves, and where the beach was wet and firm I followed the edge of the water as it reached my feet. Sea grape grew against the wall that protected the boulevard, rusty brown from salt winds, with spiky branches as thick as my arm, and big tough leaves. In the summer I would come down here and swim. *If* I were still here in the summer.

I'd been afraid of being haunted by the memory of that night of a Florida moon when I'd walked here with Ross. Strangely, however, that was beginning to seem another lifetime away, another man I had walked with. A man I had lost because of the stranger he had turned into. I couldn't mourn for the stranger. Gretchen was right. We must both admit to a sense of relief some of the time.

I walked on, looking up at the roofs of large houses that fronted on the water across the boulevard, and when I began to tire I turned back toward the tunnel

again. But as I went down the steps to its sunken floor,
I heard echoing voices. At once I drew myself close to
the wall, where I wouldn't be silhouetted against the
light, not wanting to meet anyone now.

As my eyes became accustomed to the dim mustiness
of the tunnel, I made out the two people standing together at the far end. There was an air of secrecy, perhaps of conspiracy, about them, and I knew instinctively that they had come here separately to a private
meeting. One was Vasily Karl, the other Brett Inness.

The clattering echoes of their own voices must have
warned them, for they began to speak more quietly,
and I couldn't make out the words. Crouching against
the wall, I didn't hesitate to listen, to strain to pick up
any phrase I could catch.

Once I heard Brett's words, "She knows..." and then
her voice was lowered. The clamminess of unreasoned
fear dampened my arms. Ever since I'd come to Poinciana, I had sensed secrets that were hidden beneath
our everyday lives. I'd tried to speak of this to Ross,
and he'd shrugged it aside. Perhaps that very shrug-
ging off had been fatal for him. Perhaps what he had
chosen to ignore so arrogantly had in the long run killed
him. The troubling question returned to me.

Why had Brett turned on the alarm system?

A voice was raised again—Vasily's voice: "...stop
this."

"Hush," Brett said. "You have no other choice."

I began to wonder how visible I might be if they
really looked this way. But I was afraid to move, lest
the slightest sound betray my presence. There was
something terribly wrong at Poinciana. Something—
evil. Yet I wasn't sure against whom it might be directed. There seemed only two choices—Gretchen and
me. And I was the likely one. *She knows,* Brett had
said. I could only think she meant me. But *what* did I
know? And why should it matter when I'd already made
it clear to everyone that I meant to leave Poinciana to
Gretchen as soon as it was possible for me to get away?

Or was there a more far-reaching plot against me? If something happened to me, then *everything* would revert to Gretchen. That would mean investments, the controlling shares of Meridian Oil stock, property in other towns—I really had no idea of all that Ross had left me. I only knew that it had not been a gift of love, but one of revenge and punishment against his daughter.

The murmuring voices had stopped. There was movement now at the other end of the tunnel, and I saw Brett's elegant figure stand briefly against the sunlight of the arched opening. Then she disappeared up the steps to the yard. After a moment Vasily followed, moving to the left, approaching the house from another direction.

I returned to the sand, where children were playing with a beach ball. Out over the water a flock of brown pelicans caught my eye. They were spectacular birds, diving accurately into the water from a great height to capture fish in their huge yellow beaks.

When I'd watched long enough, I returned and dared to go cautiously through the tunnel. Even then, I didn't step immediately into the sunlight, but clung to the wall as I climbed the steps and looked carefully around the grounds.

Except for a gardener, no one was in sight, and I stepped onto the grass and started toward the right wing of the house. If anyone saw me approaching, it might be thought that I'd come from somewhere else than the tunnel.

"Good afternoon, Sharon," said a voice behind me.

I whirled in alarm, to see Vasily Karl leaning against the coquina rock wall that ran along the edge of the boulevard. Beyond him cars whipped past. I was totally unable to speak. He smiled at me easily, but I sensed watchfulness in his eyes, and suspicion.

"Don't look so astonished, Sharon," he said. "Did you think you were being clever by waiting a while before you came back through the tunnel? Of course I saw you all along, standing there, listening. Though I think Brett did not. When she left, I decided to sit here and wait for the rabbit to come out of the hole."

I made a desperate effort to collect myself. "Much good it did me," I told him. "I couldn't hear a word either of you was saying."

"I quite believe you," he said cheerfully. "When I saw you come into the tunnel, I took care to keep my voice down, and I persuaded Brett of the need for quiet. So now you have another mystery, don't you? This strange meeting between Gretchen's mother and her husband. Whatever can they be up to?"

"Would you like to tell me?" I asked.

"Good! I like a lady who can bluff when she is frightened. You are frightened, aren't you, Sharon? And with good reason. It would be very wise at this time to turn everyone out of Poinciana, including Allegra, and close it up for a while. Then take yourself far away from Palm Beach. Where you will be safe."

"Safe from what?"

"You wouldn't even begin to guess," he said. "Just take my word and leave."

"Is that what you're really advising?"

"Advising, yes. But I think you will refuse to go. You are just stubborn enough to refuse to give in to your fears. Isn't that so, Sharon?"

"I don't want to talk to you!"

I moved away from him across the grass. The lawn seemed to go on forever, but I didn't stop or look back until I was safely inside the house. Then I paused beside a window from which I could see the ocean and the entrance to the tunnel under the boulevard. Vasily was nowhere in sight.

My first thought was of Jarrett. He was the only one I could turn to and I hurried to his office. He still hadn't returned, but Myra took one look at my face and said, "Sit down, Mrs. Logan."

She went through her usual ministering of refreshments—her cure for everything—and for once was discreet enough to ask no questions. After a while I stopped shaking.

"Tomorrow," I said, "I'm going to move out of my room upstairs. It's too big for me now."

"And too lonely," she observed wisely. "*I* wouldn't want to rattle around in that empty wing all alone. Especially not if I had a feeling that there were those in the house who didn't mean me any good."

I stared at her. "Why do you say that?"

"It's obvious, isn't it? Mrs. Karl has hated your marriage from the beginning. She can't be happy about you now."

But it wasn't Gretchen I feared, though I couldn't tell Myra that.

"Anyway, moving would be fun, wouldn't it?" she went on. "I mean, to have all the rooms there are in this house to choose from? To be able to furnish your own apartment any way you wish?"

"I don't suppose I'll bother," I said. "I doubt I'll be here long enough."

She sighed, and I could see the wheels going around in her head. Obviously, she thought me foolish not to take every advantage I could of being Mrs. Ross Logan. I couldn't tell her that Mrs. Ross Logan was someone I didn't want to be.

"There's one thing I'd like to ask you," I went on. "Do you happen to know whether Mr. Logan removed any pictures from the gallery on the day before he died?"

She thought about that for a moment. "There was the portrait of your mother. He brought it to his office in the afternoon, and I wondered if he was going to hang it there."

That would have been like him, I thought. But he had a better idea.

"That's not the one I mean. Mrs. Logan thinks there are a couple of Toulouse-Lautrec paintings that are missing. And I believe I've seen one of them hanging in the gallery since I came."

She thought about that solemnly, and then hopped up from her chair and scooted toward Ross's office, flinging words back at me.

"I don't know for sure," she said. "I mean I don't know what pictures they were, but I believe he brought some things from the gallery here either that last day or the day before. Let's look."

I followed her and watched as she opened a deep cabinet, gesturing for me to look inside. I could see the edges of frames standing on their sides, and I drew one of them out. It was an oil on wood of coach and horse, the driver sitting up in front, with his whip and top hat. I pulled it out in delighted relief and reached in to pull out the second picture—the portrait of a lady in a garden. Another Lautrec.

"That's wonderful!" I cried. "Now I can put Mrs. Logan's mind at rest. But I wonder why my husband brought these here?"

Myra managed to look both wise and arch at the same time, while she said nothing.

"Stop playing games," I told her impatiently. "Even if you're only speculating, I'd like to know what you're thinking."

She bent to close the cabinet, and then looked at me with a half-smile that was both appealing and apologetic. "I really do like you, Mrs. Logan. You don't look down your nose at the help, and you've tried to be kind to my friend."

"Your friend?"

"The old lady. Mrs. Logan. I understand she's back in the house again. Just the same, I don't want to stick out my neck with things I'm not really sure of at all. And I don't want to hurt you."

"I can stand being hurt," I said. "And I expect you're perfectly sure about a lot of what goes on at Poinciana."

She was still hesitant. "But this is pretty crazy—really far out. Do you suppose rich men ever steal from themselves?"

I went to the big leather armchair opposite Ross's

desk, remembering that it was in this chair I'd sat that
night when I'd run away from him and come here with
Jarrett. The last night.

"Maybe you'd better explain," I said.

She was airy about her reply, still being cautious.
"The rich don't always keep a lot of cash in their pockets. Isn't it true that sometimes they have to liquidate
funds in order to pay big debts? So couldn't a rich man
who owned a great many valuable possessions put some
of them—well, in hock, so to speak, in order to raise
money if he needed it?"

I had never thought of such a thing. If Ross had
needed cash, I was sure that Jarrett could have raised
it for him in a moment. Millions. We had never been
short while we traveled, though now that I thought
about it, most of the time we'd managed on lavish
credit. One thing I knew. Not for a moment must I
openly accept such an idea from Myra Ritter. I owed
it to Ross not to give her fertile imagination anything
to build on. Besides, even if it could possibly be true,
it had all been brought to a halt now. It didn't matter.
The paintings had been found.

I shook my head emphatically. "Mr. Logan would
never have touched his netsuke collection, or his precious paintings. So I'm afraid that idea is out. Anyway,
thank you for the coffee, Myra."

I left her and started up the stairs that led to the
wing where Allegra had her rooms, but I couldn't put
her words from my mind. Certainly Ross's anger over
the first two missing netsuke had seemed real. And he
had seemed convinced that his mother might have
taken them. Yet I knew too that he would have been
perfectly capable of putting up a smoke screen to serve
his own ends. Perhaps there were funds he didn't want
to touch. Or he might not have wanted to ask Jarrett
when so many vast interests were involved. The rich
were different, as Scott Fitzgerald said.

The netsuke, no, but about the paintings I was less
sure. Ross hadn't collected those himself, even though

he had enjoyed owning them. In any case, I was too close to all of this to judge what Ross might or might not have done. Myra, the outsider, might well have cut through to an unpleasant truth.

Jarrett would know. Increasingly, this was becoming my refrain. Tonight at dinner I would be able to talk to Jarrett. But now I could at least set Allegra's mind at rest about the Lautrecs, and if she was awake, I would tell her now. I must also let Gretchen know— and soon.

Allegra was no longer in bed when I reached her rooms. She had installed herself at the desk in her parlor and was making notes with a pencil. I hoped she wasn't back in the past planning another ball.

Coxie sat knitting in a chair by a window, and both of them looked up when I appeared at the door.

"Good," Allegra said. "I wanted to talk to you. I want you to tell Coxie to throw out all those pills and things she keeps pushing at me."

"The doctor—" Coxie began.

"Let me know the next time he comes," I said. "Mrs. Karl and I would like to speak with him."

"Then there's the matter of those missing paintings," she went on, making a check beside an item on her list.

"That's what I came to tell you about, Mrs. Logan," I said quickly. "Both the Lautrecs have been found. Ross had put them away in his office for some reason."

"In his office?" Her look sharpened. "I wonder what he was planning? Anyway, I'm glad you found them."

When I'd made sure there was nothing else she wanted at the moment, I left her and followed the corridor, looking for rooms I might move into. If I chose this wing, I would be close to Allegra and her nurse as well, and not off in lonely, isolated grandeur. I would also be at the opposite end of the house from Gretchen and Vasily, which would suit me very well.

I selected a room that opened toward the lake and would make a pleasant sitting room. Next door would serve as my bedroom, and the changes in furniture would be simple enough for my temporary purposes. I would have a phone connected, and move in here tomorrow. Mrs. Broderick could manage all this, I was sure.

I found the housekeeper supervising the cleaning of a suite in Gretchen's wing. She explained with barely concealed satisfaction that these rooms were to be for Miss Inness, who was moving into them later this afternoon.

So Gretchen had paid no attention to my request. Or else Brett had overruled her. This was not something I could settle with Mrs. Broderick. I explained about the change I wanted to make in my own living quarters.

"I'll wait until tomorrow to move," I said. "That should give you time to make a few changes. I'll show you the rooms I've chosen whenever you're free."

Mrs. Broderick inclined her head. "As you wish, Mrs. Logan," she said, and I knew that she guessed the reasons for my moving and was scornful of such weakness. Since Ross's death, she had become even more of a fortress of authority, as though the uncertainty of all our lives at the moment must not be allowed to touch the running of Poinciana.

I made a small effort to placate her. "We must have a talk before long. I know very well that you are the one who keeps the house running smoothly."

"Thank you, Mrs. Logan," she said, but I knew I was still the stranger, of whom she disapproved.

The rest of the afternoon I spent in the Japanese room checking through the remainder of the netsuke. No more seemed to be missing, and when I'd examined them, briefly, I was able to give my attention to the ivory carvings, the cloisonné and Satsuma that I'd wanted to learn about ever since I'd come to the house. My old excitement over such treasures had weakened, however, and I knew I was only waiting for the hour when I could go to Jarrett's cottage.

In the late afternoon, I showered and dressed carefully. The coming visit might not be altogether easy and enjoyable. There was too much that was unpleasant that I had to tell Jarrett—even to the question Myra Ritter had raised about Ross and the paintings. Thus my dressing was, in a sense, like putting on armor for the evening.

I wore my lime green silk from Hong Kong, and added no jewelry, except for the rings Ross had given me. In a sense, my rings were the symbol of my right to be in this house. I was still Mrs. Ross Logan, whether I liked it or not, and their presence on my hand prevented me from tossing everything over and running for my life. Which was what Vasily had suggested that I ought to do, and which was what I really wanted to do. Yet I must stay. For a while.

Somewhere in all those frantic years with Ysobel and Ian, a sense of duty to others had somehow been inculcated in me. Perhaps a stodgy, old-fashioned principle, but it was still there, operating in me, and I had to obey its edicts. Once Ian had told me that I was the one responsible member of the family, and I recalled that I'd laughed at his words.

An unexpected flash of memory swept through me. There had been a night in San Francisco...I had been waiting when Ysobel returned to her dressing room. Something had shaken her confidence during her performance, and she, who was determined to remain forever young, had felt suddenly old. Ian had been out front checking on the house, and we were alone.

"I'm losing it," she said bleakly. "Something's slipping away, and I can't stop its going. They weren't responding out there tonight. And if they don't respond, I'm not anything."

I couldn't bear to see her in such a mood, and I had given myself to reassuring her. Just before she went on again she came to put her arms about me, and her cheek against mine. I could still remember the scent of her stage makeup, and her special perfume.

"Thank you for being my friend," she said, and went

out to where the applause that greeted her sounded as enthusiastic as ever.

I had sat down before her dressing table and looked at myself in the mirror in astonishment. I touched the cheek hers had touched, and felt a comfort I'd never known before. Her *friend*, she had said. And if she had lived, perhaps that was what we might have been eventually—friends.

Now, looking into another mirror in another time, something seemed to melt the coldness inside me. In the past I had allowed harsh words, perhaps carelessly spoken, to freeze me, so that I could never see Ysobel as vulnerable and human too. I'd been absorbed in my own self-pity.

The poignancy of loss was intense at that moment, and yet there was a healing too, a beginning of true comfort for me. I went downstairs with a new courage lifting my steps.

The grounds were empty as I followed the shell path to Jarrett's cottage. Keith saw me coming and ran to open the screen door, with Brewster at his heels.

"Dad's in the kitchen," he told me, smiling and excited. "He's making lasagne, and he makes it better than anybody. Mrs. Simmons had to go home to see a sick daughter, so we're on our own tonight. I'm fixing the salad."

He ran off, with the dog after him, and while I hesitated, Jarrett called from the kitchen. "Sit down, Sharon, and I'll be with you in a moment."

I sat down and looked around. The cottage had been charmingly furnished with old, well-worn pieces that suited its character. A few throw rugs were scattered across polished floors, and the sofa wore cheerful chintz. Part of the wide room had been separated into a dining area, from which steps led up to an outside deck. A plain oak table was set with woven place mats and old silver.

Jarrett came out of the kitchen with a spatula in hand. "Hello, Sharon." His red hair was in his eyes, and from beneath it his look approved of me. "We're nearly ready. So come and bring things in."

I began to relax as I carried salad bowls and a basket of bread sticks to the table. From where Jarrett seated me I could look out toward the fiery poinciana tree and see beyond it the belvedere that rose above the roofs of the big house. I wished I need never go back under that roof again.

The lasagne was perfection, as Keith had promised, and for dessert there were sweet Florida melons. No long silences troubled us while we ate, though the talk was of the inconsequential. Brewster had had his own dinner, and he lay watching us with bright doggy interest. I could almost believe that life was normal, and that the threats of Poinciana had ceased to exist. Tonight I was seeing a Jarrett that I'd never glimpsed before. An easier, more contented, simpler man. Which only meant that I'd not even begun to understand his complexity.

When we'd eaten, I helped to put dishes in the washer, and it seemed pleasant to be doing those small domestic chores that had never been a part of my nomad's life.

When Keith had taken his bicycle and Brewster and gone off to visit a friend, Jarrett led me up inside stairs to the raised deck he had built along one side of the cottage. We stretched out in long teak chairs to watch the sun go down over the lake, and I hadn't felt so peaceful in months.

"Is this the way you always live?" I asked him.

"When I'm in Florida. Pam and I had a home in Maryland, but I've let that go. I'm not sure where we'll live when you close Poinciana—or do whatever you decide to do with it. Perhaps Gretchen and Vasily will stay, if you leave it to them. But my work is up North. If I'm to continue, that is."

Again the certainty of Jarrett's leaving was a fact, and I closed my eyes, not wanting to think about it. For this little while there had been no antagonism between us, and he had treated me with a solicitousness that seemed almost tender.

But the sense of peace, the deceptive atmosphere of normal living could not last.

"You'd better tell me," he said. "I could see the strain in your face when you came in. Has it been a bad day?"

Slowly, groping for words at first, I told him everything. About the missing netsuke and the uncomfortable meeting with Gretchen. About our lunching together, and my surprise glimpse of Vasily and Brett in the tunnel. About Vasily's words to me afterwards, and especially of his coming to the tower and retrieving Ross's manuscript. I spoke too of the missing Lautrecs, and of how they were discovered in Ross's office. Finally I told him what his son had said about Brett Inness turning on the alarm. This last didn't surprise him.

"Yes, I know. Keith told me the next day. He was up late that night and he's always loved to roam the grounds after dark. He was near the house, down at the art gallery, and when the alarm went off and he saw Brett come running out of the house, he was sure she'd turned it on. But what was happening scared him, and he came straight to the cottage and sneaked back to bed. Of course, he wasn't supposed to be out in the first place."

"What do you make of this?"

"Nothing—yet."

"But you didn't bring it up with the police?"

He smiled at me ruefully. "There's an old Logan rule dating back to Allegra's time. We protect the family. I'll talk to Brett when I have a chance."

Once more, I disliked the concealment that always seemed part of the very atmosphere of Poinciana.

"I don't believe she left that 'Gretchen' note for Ross, if that's what you're thinking," he said. "Brett would take stronger action than that."

I was considering this when Jarrett surprised me by reaching out to take my hand. The gesture seemed to happen quite simply, and the touch of his fingers quieted me, easing my turbulent thoughts so that a sense of contentment filled me. His touch asked for nothing and offered nothing. Only friendship. Yet something in me knew that if I wanted it, this might very well be a beginning. If only I could trust again as easily as I had done with Ross. Instead, I thought of women who built those imaginary heroes they fell in love with, and I was wary. After a moment I slipped my hand away. It was myself I distrusted, more than Jarrett.

I went on to tell him what Myra Ritter had said about the possibility of a rich man stealing from himself. Jarrett seemed neither surprised nor outraged, as I'd half hoped he might be.

"I don't know that this is what happened," he said. "But it's not impossible. Ross enjoyed the little games he sometimes played. Power games, meant to fool those around him and subject them to his will. There's no telling now what he might have been up to. I'm glad the Lautrecs have been found. Perhaps the netsuke will also turn up."

"Why did you work for him?" I asked. "Why did you go on working for him?"

"I suppose the trap closes. One gets caught. Getting out becomes hopelessly complicated. If I'd left, a number of projects that I believe are important would have been abandoned. Ross was never a philanthropist at heart. It was my job to make it seem that he was one. But I've already told you this."

"You must have hated him."

"Not always. Not entirely. There were times when I was sorry for him."

"Sorry for Ross Logan?"

"He wasn't a happy man. He was caught in the trap too. A trap set up in the beginning by Charles and Allegra, and baited with all the things they expected of him."

At that moment there was no compassion in me for Ross. "But how could you *not* hate him, when—?" I broke off because the thought of his wife could not be spoken.

"Sometimes I suppose I did," he agreed.

A voice spoke out of the darkness that had gathered around the deck. "And when you did, you could have killed him. Is that not so?"

The voice was Vasily's, and there was both mockery and challenge in the words.

Jarrett left his chair to move to the rail, and I sensed a barely controlled violence in him. "You have some reason for a remark like that?"

"Not I," Vasily said cheerfully. "Gretchen. It's her latest theory. Will you permit me to come up and join you? I thought it might be well for you to know what she is saying, and what she plans."

He didn't wait for Jarrett to answer, but came up the outside steps and leaned against the rail beside him. "Good evening, Sharon. Have you been thinking over the things we discussed this afternoon?"

"Sit down," Jarrett said. "You'd better tell us what's on your mind." He had already suppressed his first instinct to anger.

Instead of taking a chair, Vasily perched on the broad rail, swinging his legs. "My wife has, I believe at Brett's prompting, decided that you and Sharon caused the shock that resulted in her father's death. She has been claiming that all along, as you know. But now she means to give an interview to this effect. I've tried to dissuade her. Give me credit for that, at least. But when Gretchen goes on an emotional binge, I know of no way to stop her."

Jarrett swore softly under his breath. "Nor does anyone else. I'll try to talk to her, but that might be only a red flag. Thanks for coming to tell me. Incidentally, why did you?"

In the reflection of light from the windows behind me, I could see Vasily's face, see that for once he looked a little anxious.

"Let's call it self-preservation," he said. "I lack the

talent for destruction that Gretchen has. What she cannot win, she destroys. That she herself may be ruined in the process never seems to stop her."

I broke in. "But she can't have any possible basis for claiming such a thing. Oh, I know she's thrown out wild accusations, but I didn't think she took them seriously herself. I had lunch with her today, and she seemed almost friendly. Why should she do this now?"

Vasily moved his hands in an eloquent gesture that was thoroughly European. "She has been bróoding. You were both there immediately after her father's death. Perhaps you were even there before he died?"

I knew that *I* had not been, but for the first time I wondered if Jarrett could have reached the office while Ross was still alive. By his own admission, he too was capable of subterfuge. I hated my own mistrust, and I had to answer Vasily.

"That's nonsense! Anyway, why would Gretchen do this? I've already told her she can have Poinciana. What more does she want?"

"Brett has convinced her that you will never give it up. Tomorrow she will act. She's planning to call a press conference in the early afternoon. I myself think this is unwise, and I would like to see her stopped. Among other things, she will claim that there have been thefts at Poinciana, and that one of you may be filching valuable items to sell outside. Items that ought to belong to her."

"She's absolutely mad!" I cried.

"She may very well be," Jarrett agreed. "I'd better go talk to her now, and see if I can coax her back to reason. I'm sorry to end the evening this way, Sharon. Would you like to come back to the house with me? Do you want to talk to Gretchen?"

"I'll go back," I said. "But I've had enough of talking to Gretchen for one day." What I didn't want was to be left alone with Vasily, who was making me increasingly uneasy.

"Remember," Vasily said, "you didn't see me. It wouldn't do for Gretchen to know that I came down here." He faded away into the darkness of the grounds, out of which he'd come.

. All the lovely evening had been spoiled, and I felt hopeless again as I walked beside Jarrett toward the house.

He put an arm around me as we came near. "There's nothing to worry about. Gretchen can't back up her wild claims. People in the media will see through her, and I'll call a conference of my own if necessary. Though news of conflict at Poinciana won't do us any good."

"Why would Brett urge her into this?"

"Because she is a vindictive woman. Because she's still trying to punish Ross for all he did to her. She has some grounds for feeling the way she does, you know. But she has always managed to keep her influence with Gretchen. Love can be a very strange and mixed-up thing between mother and daughter, as well as can all the other kinds."

How well I knew that. "I doubt that Brett ever loved Gretchen."

"That's probably true. It's Gretchen, unfortunately, who grew up wanting Brett's affection and approval as she never wanted anything else, especially since she wasn't her natural child. She didn't have to work so hard with her father."

"In spite of everything, I feel sorry for Gretchen," I said. "She has so much going for her, and she doesn't use it."

When we reached a side door, Jarrett put his hand on my arm. "Take it easy, Sharon. Things will work out. Don't try to solve everything inside your head all at once. I'll phone you later, after I've talked to Gretchen. Will you be in your room?"

I said I would wait for his call, and went upstairs. Even when I was away from him, I could still feel the touch of his hand and see the kindness in his eyes.

The corridor that led to my room seemed emptier than ever as I hurried along, and I closed my door quickly, locking it. I wondered now why I had been willing to spend one more night in this room.

Chapter

17

When I was ready for bed, I sat propped against my pillows, reading one of the many books about early Palm Beach that I'd found in the library. Mainly, however, I was waiting for my phone to ring.

Nearly two hours passed and I'd dropped my book and fallen into a doze when the shrilling woke me.

Jarrett's voice sounded calm and reassuring. "I've done what I could. Fortunately, I caught Gretchen alone, without Brett, and in her way she's been fond of me since she was a little girl. So at least she listened. Part of the time she argued furiously, but I don't think she believes a word of her own accusations. She wants to make trouble for you. Brett has managed to instill that purpose in her, though I think something else is operating too. It's almost as though she may be covering something up with this outburst. Something that frightens her. I'm not sure what."

"But if it's me she wants to hurt, why is she accusing you too?"

"I'm tarred by the same brush, apparently. We were both in the office soon after Ross died. So she wants to claim that we were there before he died."

"Will she really call that news conference?"

"I'm not sure. She can change so fast. Are you all right, Sharon? If you're worried about staying at the house, Mrs. Simmons's room is empty and you can spend the night here at the cottage, if you'd be more comfortable."

For an instant, I wanted to accept his invitation joyfully. Instead, I held back. It would not be wise. There would be gossip and there were dangers at the cottage too. I mustn't move into that until I was sure. I had moved too soon with Ross, and I couldn't entirely trust myself. Besides, my own fears of this house were something I needed to overcome. I would be safe enough in this room for one more night. It had been Ross I had been afraid of here.

When I'd thanked Jarrett and hung up, I went to check the locks again, both in my own room and in Ross's. I hated to go in there and when I went through the door I didn't turn on the light. I didn't want Ysobel to watch me from her place on the wall. Moonlight showed me my way, and I made certain that the door to the hallway was locked.

Then I took a mild sleeping pill and went to bed.

Somewhere around midnight the music began in my dreams. The music and the singing. I could hear the words clearly: "... purple shadows and blue champagne..."

I threw aside the covers and sat up in bed with cold sweat breaking out all over my body. My throat felt constricted by fear. In the remaining moonlight I could see that the door between my room and Ross's was open, and Ysobel's disembodied voice drifted through with a clarity that sent shivering fingers down my spine. The room beyond the doorway was as dark as my own, and shadowy—but the voice sang on and I didn't know what hand had set the tape running.

In my muddled, still half-conscious state, I thought first of Ross. If he could come back, this was just the sort of trick he would relish. I shook myself awake and slipped out of bed. That singing had to be stopped. If it went on, I might lose all self-control. I might cower here in terror forever if I didn't stop it. I might even start to scream.

Again I found my way, stumbling. I couldn't remember where the light switch was—probably by the door to the hall, so I eased around the edge of the bed, discovered a floor lamp, and turned it on. The room was empty. I fumbled my way to the record player and flipped the switch. Ysobel's voice slurred in the middle of a phrase, and I dropped onto the side of the bed and covered my face with my hands.

A cool breeze touched my shoulders, chilling me further, and I looked around to see that the door to the loggia was ajar. That door I must have forgotten to lock, and someone was out there in the darkness, watching me. I felt sure of it.

Shivering, I stood up, meaning to pull the spread from the bed and wrap it about me. But when I grasped a corner to turn it back, something rattled in the center of the spread. I paused to stare at the two tiny objects nestled there, clicking against each other. The Daruma and the carp with the turtle in its mouth—the two missing netsuke.

Moving automatically, I picked them up and placed them on a corner of the bed table. Then I went back to pull the spread free, and wrapped it about me. That felt a little better. When I'd picked up the netsuke again, I moved toward the open door to the loggia. I knew very well who was out there, and now I'd begun to tremble with rage as well as with the cold.

"You'd better come in," I said.

A small, square hand appeared to push the glass doors wider, and Gretchen slipped through the opening.

She was dressed in a long blue robe, with the collar turned up, and she was grinning her monkey grin that had little mirth in it.

"I've been watching you," she said. "I really frightened you, didn't I?"

My anger rose. "How could you possibly do a thing so cruel?" I demanded.

"It wasn't hard. I've grown up with two very good teachers—my father and Brett. I'm a prize, graduate pupil."

"Where did you get these?" I held out the netsuke.

"I have my ways," she said, and I knew she would never tell me.

My own urge to do violence surprised me. I wanted to slap her, shake her, punish her, but I knew that *my* control was the one thing I must not lose.

She was watching my face almost gleefully, as though she knew very well the emotions she aroused in me. "After all, I brought the netsuke back to you, didn't I? Why not give me credit for that?"

There was no possible answer. Not when she had deliberately turned on the recording of Ysobel's song, and waited outside in the dark to see what I would do. In spite of myself, my eyes were drawn to the portrait, and my mother's gaze seemed directed at me. In the shadowy room, where only one lamp burned, the generous warmth that she'd always given her audiences flowed out to me. If only she could have looked at me like that in life.

I turned again to Gretchen. "You'd better go now. You've done enough."

But she too was staring at the portrait. "Did you love her very much?" she asked softly.

The words surprised me. Even Gretchen's sudden changes of mood spoke of her unbalanced state. It was not for the first time that I wondered if everything that was unpleasant which had happened to me since I came to Poinciana had stemmed from just two sources—Ross and his daughter.

"I don't think this is the time for philosophical discussion," I said. "I'm going back to bed." I held up the netsuke. "I'll sleep with these under my pillow for the rest of the night."

She paid no attention, and her voice stopped me as I reached the door. "Just tell me the answer. Did you love your mother very much?"

"You've asked the wrong question," I said.

"I suppose I have." Her eyes didn't move from Ysobel's face. "I should have asked whether she loved you. Do you dare to tell me the answer to that, Sharon?"

I was very still as anger slipped away, leaving a strange pity behind it. I knew why she had asked me such a question. She had asked it because for all her life she had longed to be loved by Brett, just as I had longed to be loved by Ysobel Hollis. In this one thing we were sisters, Ross's daughter and I.

"I loved her a great deal," I said gently. "At least I did when I was small. And I wanted more than anything else to have her love me."

"I know," Gretchen said. "I understand that very well."

As had happened between us at odd moments in the past, enmity fell away, and we were kin. I reached out from under the spread I'd wrapped around me and took her hand.

"Come in here," I said, and led her into the room that was still mine, away from Ysobel's watchful eyes and Ross's invisible presence. I pushed her down upon the chaise longue and pulled the throw over her. Then I stretched out on my bed, propping myself on one elbow.

"Have you ever tried to find your real mother?" I asked.

Her eyes were closed, and I saw a tear coursing down her cheek. "No! I've never wanted to. Not when she sold me to my father. I don't really care who she is. I've never gotten over wanting Brett to love me as if I were really her daughter. Fathers are important. But it's mothers we're closest to in the beginning. Or want to be closest to. Until we find someone outside to love us. I have that now in Vasily. And Brett and I are friends, in a way. I still want to please her, make her like me. Though I can see her more clearly now."

"Is that why you're planning a press conference tomorrow? Because she wants you to?"

She opened her eyes wide and stared at me. "How did you know that?"

I repeated her own words, faintly mocking. "I have my ways."

"Vasily," she said. "Of course."

I didn't give him away. "No—it was Jarrett. He phoned me tonight after he'd talked to you."

"Oh?" I heard the note of relief in her voice. "I suppose I thought it was Vasily because he can never be trusted any farther than I can see him. Yet I know he loves me. I *do* know that!"

I said nothing, hoping this wasn't a whistling in the dark for her.

"I wish I could tell you something," she went on, "but I can't trust you either."

Again I was silent. Later, I would wish I had urged her to confide in me, but I missed the chance with my silence.

"Just the same," she mused, "I'm lucky to have Vasily. I'm luckier than you are, Sharon. Because my father never really cared about you, did he? He only cared about Ysobel Hollis."

The cruel intent was back, and I lay silent on the bed, already regretting the impulse that had caused me to bring her into this room.

"There!" she said. "You see—I've done it again! Vasily says I use my tongue like a sword. But it's only because I speak my mind. I don't pussyfoot. I don't really mean—"

"You didn't mean to open the door to my room and set that recorder playing? You didn't wait deliberately for me to come?"

She sat up, somehow looking young and defenseless—which she certainly was not.

"Nobody's ever stopped me from doing the first thing that came into my head. Except maybe Grandmother Allegra. Everybody else let me go my own way. I guess my father was disciplined a lot by his parents when he was a boy, so he wouldn't do that to me. And Brett never cared, unless I bothered *her*. At least you've learned something about self-control, haven't you, Sharon? You've behaved admirably."

"I don't know if that's what you'd call it. In the end I suppose we all have ourselves to blame, whatever we do."

"I know. Take responsibility for our own acts! That's what Gran is always preaching. But she never does it herself. None of us looks at ourselves as we really are, do we? Never mind. I'll go now." She walked to the door and stood for a moment, hesitating. "I can't tell you I'm sorry, because I'm not. I enjoyed what I was doing. I really did. And that's pretty sick, isn't it?"

I said nothing and she scowled at me.

"My father should never have left you Poinciana," she said, and went out the door, pulling it shut after her.

I got up to lock it again. Then I went into Ross's room, where the lamp still burned, and this time I locked both doors. But I didn't turn off the light. I didn't want to think of darkness pulsing in that empty room. Back in my own bed, I thrust the two netsuke under my pillow and lay on my back with my eyes closed, all emotion draining from me, all sleep hopelessly far away. Limbo.

I must have slept eventually—heavily, deeply—for it was mid-morning when I opened my eyes to hear rain at all my windows. In the next room the lamp still burned, and memory returned sickly. The two netsuke were still beneath my pillow when I reached for them, but I closed my eyes, listening to the rain, remembering

mornings when I'd been eager to rise and start my day
because so much that was lovely and exciting awaited
me. For a little while Ross had given me that. And I
could almost believe that he had enjoyed giving it. If
we could have stayed away from Poinciana...

Better to make plans, I thought. Today I would
change my rooms. I would visit Allegra. I would make
lists of things that must be done. The thought brought
a smile. List-making was something I'd learned in self-
defense when I traveled with Ysobel. My mother had
been cheerfully heedless, depending on others to see
that she arrived where she was supposed to be at the
right time, that she didn't overspend her allowance,
that she dressed herself in the right assortment of
clothes. She must always be on stage, and others must
help to get her there. After which she performed beautifully on her own.

A flash of memory slanted through my thoughts, to
bring back another moment I'd had with Ysobel on that
tour that ended in San Francisco. Before we'd flown to
Ireland for that last performance. She had come into
the wings after taking numerous bows, and the applause was still ringing with all the love her audiences
held for her. She pushed through those who waited in
the wings, and came to where I stood alone, watching
her. I could remember the way she put a finger to her
forehead, rubbing as though a headache were starting,
and she'd looked at me in a puzzled way.

"I'm only real when I'm out there," she said. "What's
going to happen when they don't want me any more?"

In that instant I'd felt older than Ysobel, and I'd put
a comforting arm about her. "They'll always want you,"
I said.

At once she had laughed and pushed me away and
was herself again. But I had glimpsed again her vulnerability, and love for her had welled up in me,
stronger than old resentments.

Had Gretchen given me something last night, in
spite of malicious intent? She'd said, "None of us looks

at ourselves as we really are." It was time now to look, whether I liked it or not. Look and stop blaming.

Not something easy to do.

When I'd showered and dressed in slacks and a light pullover, I stood at the loggia door and watched rain slant across the tiles and stream down the drains. The palm trees looked wet, their trunks glistening dark, and the lake was a murky froth. Good! I was tired of everlasting sunshine. Rain suited my mood.

Susan brought my breakfast tray, since it was once more a Saturday and she was on duty. I was grateful for her unobtrusive presence as she set the tray down, drew up a chair for me, poured coffee—and waited.

"What's happening around the house?" I asked.

"I don't know really. Everything is spooky quiet, except that Mr. Nichols is working in his office, and has Miss Ritter in for the day so he can dictate. And my mother's turning out the rooms you want to move into, though I'm afraid she doesn't approve."

"This room belonged to Brett Inness."

"Yes, and Mother was devoted to her. She's upset because you don't want to stay in a room she thinks is absolute perfection."

I glanced about at pale elegance. "It's not for me. I like things cozier."

"Anyway, you shouldn't stay here."

"I agree. But why do you say that?"

"It's just a feeling. As though everyone in this house is plotting against everyone else. It's creepy."

"Including me?"

"Maybe you're not plotting enough," she said, and went quietly away.

I ate my breakfast in a thoughtful mood, wondering about the hint of warning in her words. Fine! I would plot. I would make lists, I would take action. I sat at my desk and wrote. It was easy enough to make lists. I was an expert.

When I was done I read through what I had written— all the earnest duties that I could begin to perform about the house—and found it utterly boring. I didn't want to live my life by the clock any more, or by making lists. And I didn't want to *plot*. There were things to be done, and I would do them. I tore up the list.

First, a visit to Allegra. I must tell her about my move into her wing.

I found her propped up in bed with her eyes closed, and Brett in a chair beside her, reading aloud about a certain Mrs. Pollifax, who was apparently an adventurous lady after Allegra's own heart.

The reading stopped as I appeared in the doorway, and Allegra opened her eyes. "Today I want to go up to my rooms in the tower," she said to no one in particular.

Brett closed the book. "Darling, those stairs would be hard for you. I've always hated them myself."

"Nonsense! Everyone used to complain about them. Because they are steep and make people dizzy. They are very easy stairs, really. You just put one foot after another very carefully and pull yourself up by the iron rail. I never had any trouble."

"But, darling, you're not as strong as you were then," Brett reminded her.

I had said nothing, and no one greeted me. Now Allegra gave me a rather wicked look, and lowered one eyelid in a wink that made the years fall away. I had a feeling that she would need to be watched very carefully today or she might indeed try to climb those stairs to the belvedere.

"There's something you wanted?" Brett asked, making it clear that I intruded, and that she had no intention of recognizing me as mistress of Poinciana.

I went closer to the bed, speaking to Allegra. "I wanted you to know that I'm moving into this wing today, Mrs. Logan. I don't want to stay off there by myself. Besides, if I'm closer to you, you can tell me more about the house."

Her nod was lively, pleased. "Come visit me any time."

I didn't wait to see how Brett took this exchange, but returned to the corridor, skirted a bed that had been moved out of what was to be my sitting room, and found my way downstairs to the office wing.

Myra apparently didn't mind working overtime on Saturday, and she was at her desk typing briskly. She looked up and shook her head. "If you're looking for Mr. Nichols, you can't go in right now, Mrs. Logan. He has an appointment with a man who has just arrived from New York."

I'd wanted to see Jarrett to tell him about Gretchen's visit the night before, but that could wait. Moving idly, I went toward Ross's door, and Myra stopped me again.

"Better not," she said. "Mrs. Karl is in there and I think she's having a bang-up fight with her husband. We'll probably have to get a new coffee set. She was throwing the crockery around." Clearly Myra was enjoying the whole scene.

Voices could be heard from beyond the heavy door, but no words came through. It was an awkward moment to have Brett follow me downstairs and walk in just as Ross's door flew open and Gretchen came storming out. She saw us both, and stopped for a moment, wildly angry.

"Vasily is threatening to divorce me!" she cried. "Him! I'll show him! I'm going to change my will as soon as I can!"

Brett put out a hand to stop her daughter, but Gretchen brushed blindly past. We followed her to the door and looked out. Halfway down the hall, she pulled open the door that led to the tower stairs, and I heard her clattering up the circular treads on her way to the upper rooms. Vasily came out of Ross's office, looking oddly helpless and white-faced.

"Those damned netsuke!" he said. "I gave them back to her, but she wasn't satisfied. She's gone a little crazy."

"You did have the two missing ones, then?" I asked,

surprised that he would admit it. "You had them that time in the tower?"

"Yes, yes—what does it matter? I returned them to her, didn't I? So why must she ask so many questions? Why did she have to go searching among her father's papers?"

"Searching for what?"

He was recovering himself and growing calmer. "My wife has decided to check up on me—as her father was doing. Instead of taking my word, she has decided to find out everything he thought he had uncovered about me."

I became aware of Myra, listening eagerly as usual.

"Let's not talk here," I said. "Come across the hall."

He was too excited to pay attention. "I've taken enough from her! I told her to divorce me and have done with it! I tried to make everything clear to her when we married—but it wasn't enough. So I will move out now!"

If Vasily walked out on Gretchen, she would lose everything she most valued—no matter what she was saying now in anger. Even if Vasily had taken the netsuke, it didn't matter in the face of his wife's unstable condition. I dreaded to think what might happen to her if he left her at this time.

"Just wait a while," I said. "You know she'll cool off when she stops to think."

He seemed to see me for the first time, and a faint smile returned to erase the anger. "You are a good person, Sharon, and you are also very naïve," he said, and went toward the door. He didn't speak to Brett, but she blocked his way.

"Sharon's right," Brett told him. "Give Gretchen time to come out of it. Maybe I can talk to her. She's gone up to the belvedere now. That's always been her refuge, just the way it used to be Allegra's. When she comes down, she'll feel better. So don't go running out on her, Vasily. After all, you've got a lot to lose if you do."

I watched them both intently, and I saw the strange look of understanding that passed between them. It was a look that made me think of their meeting in the beach tunnel, when I'd surprised them.

Vasily was already shaking his head. "It's too late. This time it's too late. I've had more than I can take—and perhaps she has too. So let her do her worst."

Brett started to speak, but he brushed past us both and disappeared down the hall. She looked after him soberly and I wondered what dark thoughts she was thinking. As always, she seemed an enigma. But I had no wish to stay and discuss what had happened with her, so I left the office and found my way outside to where a sheltered courtyard offered protection from the rain.

Wrought-iron chairs were grouped around a table, and I pulled one out, and sat down beneath the overhang. This little court was another of the curious indentations that Allegra had built into the house. Because of them, all the upstairs rooms had windows that opened upon the outdoors. Near where I sat, a strange twisted tree that Ross had called a gumbo-limbo shook its wet leaves as a breeze stirred them. I lifted my head, breathing the fresh scent of the rain.

The scene in the office had shaken me badly. Gretchen seemed intent upon destroying her own happiness. Or had Ross been right from the beginning, and had all possibility for happiness ended on the day when she'd married Vasily Karl? Strangely, there were times when I almost liked him. I didn't trust him, and I thought it might be characteristic if he had taken the netsuke. Yet there was something oddly likable about him—even while he was following his own devious bent. In a way, I could understand how he had captivated Gretchen. I could also imagine him doing quite dastardly things in a most charming and disarming way. As though to say, "You see—I know it is wrong, but obviously I cannot help myself."

I remembered his saying that I should close Poin-

ciana up while the will was being settled, and go away.
Probably that would not negate my ownership. Certainly Ross hadn't meant that I couldn't take a trip or
a vacation, or stir out of the house. As long as I was in
residence legally, I could go away and come back. If
there really was a divorce—though I couldn't see
Gretchen letting it go that far, unless she had driven
Vasily away for good this time—then it would be safe
to let Gretchen inherit Poinciana. But if they made up
again, Vasily might receive all of it should anything
happen to Gretchen. Ross hadn't wanted that, and I
didn't believe it was wise myself. Not unless the time
came when I could be more sure of him. If he had taken
the netsuke to sell, this hardly improved my opinion
of him.

Besides, this wouldn't have been the first time.
Again I wondered about the Lautrec paintings. Had it
really been Ross who had removed them?

No, even though I might like Vasily at times, I didn't
trust him for a moment.

Beyond the dry nook where I sat, rain sounded on
the tiles of the courtyard, and I listened to its soothing
rhythm. Always, I felt more peaceful when I was outside the house. How long I sat there, I don't know, but
suddenly the morning was pierced by a thin, high
scream. A chilling sound of terror, followed almost at
once by a shattering crash. I came to my feet, tense and
listening. The morning was still except for the rain.

I ran out upon wet grass, to where I could look back
at the house. The scream had come from the direction
of the tower, and I stood for a moment staring up at
the circling windows of the belvedere, and at the balcony that ran around the top. Nothing moved, and all
the windows I could see were closed.

Running again, I rounded the end of a wing, and
came out on the other side of the tower. Now I could
see the glass door that gave onto the gallery. It stood
open, and a portion of the rail had broken through,

with a piece hanging down. My throat closed with fear as I rushed across the grass.

Gretchen lay face down upon the paving stones at the base of the tower—lay in the one place where the tower stood away from the house, with no tiled roofs below. There had been nothing to break her fall.

She lay still, chillingly still, with rain beating around and over her, her arms outflung. Before I could reach her, others came running. One or two men first, and then a frightened maid. Jarrett was next, rushing out a nearby door, and it was Jarrett who knelt beside her.

In that dreadful suspended moment, while we stood around them, waiting, I was intensely aware of unimportant details. One of the girls, already soaked by the rain, was crying in choked sobs. The loose bit of balcony rail flapped in the wind, and the poinciana tree shed its bright petals as rain beat them into the earth. One of Gretchen's hands was curled about some small object that she must have clutched at the moment of her fall.

Jarrett looked up and spoke to one of the men. "Call for an ambulance. Hurry!"

He saw me among the others and shook his head, his face grim. "There's only a feather of pulse. Get me something to cover her with." A servant went back to the house.

As he touched her sad, broken body, something tiny rolled from her hand, and I bent to catch it. I felt a compulsion to stop for an instant to look up at the tower. It seemed to me that something moved up there. Not at the balcony level, but in the room below. It was no more than a flash, an impression at a window. Then I rushed inside and began to call for Vasily or Brett—or for someone to go and find them. From the direction of the boulevard came the screaming of an ambulance siren.

I opened my wet hand and stared at the tiny object

that I had caught from Gretchen's fingers as she opened them. It was a netsuke—the small carving of the Sleeping Mermaid that was Allegra's favorite of all the collection.

Chapter

18

When the others drove to the hospital, following the ambulance, Jarrett asked me not to come.

"There's nothing you can do," he said. "Stay at Poinciana and hold things together. Be with Allegra if she needs you."

I told no one about the little mermaid. Its presence frightened me. When I was alone I took it out and examined it carefully. It was just as I remembered—a mermaid sweetly asleep in pale pink coral, her tail curled neatly around her body—but it told me nothing. Or everything? Had Allegra indeed gone to her tower rooms? And if she had—? I put the puzzle away from me. Allegra had loved her granddaughter dearly. As she had once loved her son?

For the rest of that gloomy day, while I awaited word from the hospital, I did what I could. Though my clothes were still damp, I put off changing them, and talked to Mrs. Broderick. Badly shaken as she was, she called the staff together and informed them of what had happened.

Since Jarrett no longer needed her, Myra went home in an upset state, muttering that the house was accursed.

Then, when I'd put it off long enough, I climbed the stairs to talk to Allegra, uncertain as to whether I should explain at once what had happened, or if it might be better to wait for certainty later. Mostly, I tried to keep myself from thinking, from believing, from facing what had happened. More than anything else, I was afraid to question the presence of the mermaid in Gretchen's hand.

The door to Allegra's bedroom was open and I went in, to find that her bed was tousled and Allegra gone. Coxie sat placidly knitting in the next room. Nothing of what had happened had touched that remote wing, where sounds from the rest of the house were inaudible and the tower far away.

"Mrs. Logan is asleep," Coxie said as I looked in at her.

"She's not asleep. She's not there at all," I told her.

The nurse took the news calmly. "Well, don't worry. She likes to wander around the house when the spirit moves her. Do you want me to search for her?"

"I'll do it myself," I told her, and hurried off.

I knew where I would look first, reluctant as I was to go there. I remembered what Allegra had said about climbing to the tower. With all my heart, I hoped she had not been there when Gretchen fell, but I had to make sure those rooms were empty, and that nothing had happened to Allegra.

Along the corridor that led to the belvedere, I met Susan and saw that she was crying. "My mother's just phoned the hospital and talked to Mr. Nichols. He says there's very little hope."

I patted her shoulder and went on toward the tower stairs.

After the first sick shock of Gretchen's terrible fall, I had seemed to exist in a suspended state, where nothing about me had reality. There were duties that must be performed, and I would do them. My mind seemed to tick off what was necessary. It wasn't possible to face the fact that Gretchen might at this very moment be breathing out her young life. Numbness was a blessing. I could act without thinking or feeling.

As I climbed the iron treads I remembered Allegra's words—that the stairs were easy enough to mount. One set one's feet carefully on the wedged steps and clung to the rail. I went round and round to the top and stood looking about me. The little studio room seemed undisturbed. The two pictures of Ross hung in their usual place on the wall, and I was glad he couldn't know what had happened to his daughter.

Rain slanted through the open glass door and I went to look outside. The loose piece of railing still flapped in the wind, and there was an opening wide enough for anyone to fall through. Reality hit me like a blow to the pit of my stomach. Gretchen had stood exactly here. Had the rail broken when she leaned on it—or had she thrown herself against it, meaning to break through?

Yet she had screamed as she fell.

How awful, how terrible, to experience those seconds of falling—to be alive, with the ground rising—and then not to be. I felt so ill that I had to go inside and sit down for a little while. I must return to that safe state of being numb and not thinking. I mustn't let my imagination go. Yet the fearful record was ready to play itself over and over in my mind. I prayed a little—but without hope. Even though I had only glimpsed her face, I knew.

How different deaths could be. My mother's and father's—too horrible to be borne. Ross's had been shocking and sudden. But none of them had been terrible in the same way as this. Ross had lived a long, full life, and death could never destroy what he'd had and what he'd been. My parents had lived happily and

successfully for many years. But Gretchen's life was
still beginning. And she had been unhappy for so much
of it. All those pages of years might never be written
for her now, and I couldn't bear to think about that. Or
of the fact that I hadn't tried hard enough to befriend
her. This was familiar too—the blame one took upon
oneself when someone close died.

Nevertheless, I held back my tears, afraid to let them
come. If I cried now, I would be crying for too much
recent loss, for too much pain, and I might not be able
to stop. I must still find Allegra.

Returning to the stairs, I circled them to the room
below and looked into it. One glance was enough to
shock me. I walked into the small square area where
Allegra had liked to rest, and looked about. The armoire where her ball gowns were kept was open, and
dress after dress had been taken out and spread across
shrouded chairs and over the couch, where Allegra had
once napped. The room was a froth of satin and lace
and rainbow colors strewn everywhere. No damage had
been done to any of them, as far as I could see. It was
as though they had been laid out for display. Perhaps
in order to make a choice?

Now, with dread, I knew the answer to the faint
movement I'd seen at a window of the tower. Allegra
herself had been here, looking at her old gowns, perhaps savoring memories connected with each one, living her old life again. She must have brought the mermaid here, to give her once more a glimpse of her home,
the sea, as she used to say. Gretchen must have found
her grandmother here and taken the mermaid from
her. After that—what? I wasn't sure I wanted to know.
I was afraid to know.

I was certain of only one thing. I must find Allegra
at once, and these gowns suggested where I might look.

I ran outside through the rain to the closed door of
those stairs I had first explored, and which led down
from the loggia to the ballroom. This was a place I
hadn't cared to visit again, but now I ran down curving

tiled steps in the gloom, and opened the door at the bottom. Brilliance dazzled me.

All the chandeliers were lit, and she was there—beautiful, resplendent in chiffon the color of primroses, her white hair pinned carelessly on top of her head, her arms raised as she danced with an imaginary partner. The dance, obviously, was an old-fashioned waltz, and she moved to an echo of music I couldn't hear, swaying gracefully as she turned—forever young and untouched by the years that stretched behind her, as they might never do now for her granddaughter.

Though she must have seen my approach, she gave no sign of recognition, her eyes raised dreamily to a partner only she could see, her beautiful, lined face filled with love. Of course. She was dancing again with her Charlie.

I knew myself for the intruder I was. What was I to do—rush up and say, "No, no, you mustn't wear yourself out like this"? Was I to cry out that calamity had once more fallen on Poinciana, and this was no time for dancing? Or ask if she had seen Gretchen in the tower? Of course I did none of these. I went to sit on one of the small gilt chairs that edged the room. I sat very still and watched and thought of nothing but the present moment.

So beautifully did she dance that I could almost see her partner, almost hear the lilting three-quarter pulse of the music. In my imagination I could people the room with couples moving beneath great chandeliers that set gold leaf shining across the coffered ceiling. All this she had created out of her own will and imagination, and I would not stop Allegra Logan from dancing.

She stopped herself eventually, and came smiling to sit beside me. "Isn't it a lovely party?" she said.

"It's the most beautiful party I've ever seen," I told her, "and you're the most beautiful hostess."

She smiled at me benignly. "Thank you, my dear. I'm sorry, but I'm not sure of your name. There are so many..."

My heart did a turn as I realized that this wasn't make-believe for her. She had slipped entirely back into another world, and lost all touch with the present one.

"I'm Sharon Logan," I said. "I'm Ross's new wife."

Once more that puzzled her. "But Ross's new wife is named Brett." Her hands fluttered lightly, uncertainly, and I took them in mine.

"It's time to come home," I said gently. "This is another day. Ross and Brett have been divorced for years. And of course you—you do remember Gretchen?"

"Gretchen? I don't know anyone named Gretchen. Really, this is becoming a foolish conversation. Will you please find Charles for me? Our guests are beginning to leave, and we must be together to bid them good night."

I almost envied her. She had slipped into the past more completely than I had ever seen her do—a past in which there was far less pain than the present. There seemed no way in which I could call her back. I held her hands more tightly, frightened for her because she was living in a happier time, and the return to today would be all the more terrible. Yet I couldn't leave her in the place to which she had gone, lest she never return.

"Allegra, please come back," I said again. "Of course you remember Gretchen, your granddaughter. You must have seen her this afternoon in the tower rooms."

"No, no, stop it! I don't like to play games like this." She drew her hands from mine and looked eagerly about the room. "I can't think where Charlie can have gone. He was here only a moment ago."

How could I tell her? How could I tell her that Charlie was long dead, and Ross more recently, and that now Gretchen might very well be dying?

"Let me help you upstairs," I said.

She was growing bewildered, and her mind was still far away. She allowed me to raise her to her feet, and we walked out and stood for a moment in the center of

that vast parquet floor. I looked from arch to arch of
the doorways, wondering how to get her quickly back
to the main part of the house.

"I want to take you up to your rooms," I said gently.
"Miss Cox will be waiting for you."

That only drew a blank. "Miss Cox?"

"You do remember the rooms, don't you? Your beautiful silver-gray rooms that you enjoyed so much?"

"My gray rooms? Yes, I think so." Her bewilderment
was growing, but she made an effort to recover her air
of authority. "Of course—my gray rooms! I'd like to
show them to you. Come along—this is the simplest
way out."

She led me down the great ballroom, not toward one
of the doors, but to a panel in the wall. She touched it
lightly and it swiveled in. Without faltering, she
reached for a switch that lighted a narrow interior passageway which ran back toward equally narrow steps.
She was laughing a little now.

"Charlie used to worry about me. He said I would
get lost in my own house and never be found if I kept
using my secret routes. Come along, dear. Don't drag
your feet."

I wondered who she thought I was by this time, but
I went with her, feeling claustrophobic. The panel had
closed behind us at a touch of her hand, and the passageway smelled of musty dampness and mice. There
were probably all sorts of insects too, this being Florida.
Allegra picked up her chiffon skirts, not letting them
brush against the walls or floor, and moved lightly
ahead of me. Not walking like an old lady now, but like
the young, strong woman she had once been. So much
for what our minds could do for us! Believing herself
young, she walked with the lightness of youth, and
climbed the stairs without faltering. I followed her,
hating the tight walls that seemed to press in upon us,
the airlessness, and the horrid sense that if anything
happened we really could be lost in here, as Charlie
had said—and never be found.

At the top, the passage came to an end and Allegra reached out to push another panel. Again the wall swiveled and I saw that this was where Keith had popped out at Ross and me that time. She waited courteously for me to step through, and then touched another switch that turned off lights that were strung all the way from the ballroom. The panel pushed shut behind her, and there was only a *trompe l'oeil* doorway painted on the wall.

Only then did she falter and grow uncertain. Youth crumbled away in an instant, and she seemed to age before my eyes. Yet the change brought only bewilderment with it, and no recognition of the passing years, or of my identity.

"We'll go to your rooms now," I said gently. "You'll want to rest. You must be tired from dancing."

She tossed her head and careless hairpins went flying. "Of course I'm not tired! I never got tired the way the others did—not even when I danced the whole night through." She broke off and looked at me piteously. "No—you're right. I am tired. Why is that?"

I put an arm about her and drew her along the corridor. After a few steps she resisted me, and clutched at her breast in a sudden frightening gesture, so that I wondered if her valiant heart had at last betrayed her.

But she wasn't clutching at her heart. She slipped a hand into her low-cut bodice and drew out something small and oblong, like a flat box.

"I forgot about this," she said. "I don't know what to do with it."

She held the box out to me, and I saw that it was a cassette tape. Uncertainly, I took it from her. "What is it? What do you want me to do with it?"

"I finally found the tape!" she cried, suddenly excited, and I heard the triumph in her voice. "I've been trying to remember what I did with it. I used to come to the house from the cottage to search for it sometimes, and today I found it—right there in a corner of the armoire, under my ball gowns."

With surprising ease she had slipped from past to present, and was with me in reality again. The small flat case seemed to have a life of its own in my hands, and I knew that I was afraid of whatever it contained.

"Help me," she said, and clung to my arm as she had not before. "I want to sit down. My—my knees feel very strange."

We went along the corridor to her own gray and crimson parlor. Even with the dark rain at the windows and the ocean stormy beyond, the Turkish rug glowed with its muted colors.

At the sight of Allegra in her primrose chiffon, Coxie dropped her knitting and jumped to her feet.

"Oh, dear! Oh, dear!" she cried. "What have you gotten into now? Where have you been?"

"Never mind," I told her sharply. "Mrs. Logan wants to sit here and rest a little."

"I'll put her to bed at once! Come along now, dearie. Coxie will help you."

"No!" I said, and led Allegra to an armchair, lowered her into it. Then I faced the nurse. "Just go away for a while."

Clearly, I'd outraged her, and she drew herself up to her bulky height. "I don't take orders from anyone but—"

"You're forgetting," I said. "You take orders from me. So go downstairs and talk to someone. Find Mrs. Broderick. Something has happened that you should know about. But don't come back here for at least an hour."

For a moment she looked shocked and a little frightened. Then she ducked her head and almost ran from the room. Allegra sat very straight, with her bright dress fluffed around her, looking incongruous now, her unrestrained locks coming down about her face.

"Good for you!" she cried. "I'm glad you told her off— whoever you are. I don't know when that woman came into my life—I can't remember. But she's a dreadful nuisance."

When she leaned back and closed her eyes, I was afraid she would slip away too deeply into the past again. Pulling a hassock close to her chair, I sat down and touched her hand.

"This tape, Mrs. Logan—tell me what it is." Strange, I could call her Allegra when she was in the past, but not in the present.

"I don't know," she said without opening her eyes. "I've never listened to it. I've never wanted to know what it contains."

"But where did you get it? Why did you hide it?"

Her time sequences might be confused, with lapses of memory bewildering her, but a thread of sense ran through her words.

"Pam Nichols gave it to me only the other day. She said I mustn't show it to anyone unless something happened to her. But of course nothing will happen to her—will it?"

I could almost lose myself in Allegra's mixed time periods. "I—I don't know," I said. "What else did she tell you when she gave it to you? Try to remember, please."

Her effort was clear in her face. "She told me that—that someone was trying to kill her. She told me that she had put all her suspicions down on tape, so that if anything happened, the guilty person would be accused."

"And then what? Try to remember."

She turned her head from side to side in anguish. "I don't know. I was sick for a long while afterwards. I'd put the tape away, and when I was well again I couldn't remember where it was. I tried to get that little boy, Keith, to help me find it, because he knows all the hiding places in the house. But he never could. Of course, he didn't think of looking among my dresses up in the tower."

"You still don't know what's on it?"

"No. Pam asked me not to play it unless—unless—
I don't remember. And then when I was well again, I
couldn't find it."

"Have you told anyone else about its existence?"

"Yes—I think so." The fogs were slipping away a
little now. "I told Gretchen. And I think I talked to
Brett about it. And perhaps to others. Ross was married
to her when Pam was in that accident, you know. She
did die, didn't she? But no one ever found the tape—
until I did myself—today!"

"Do you want to hear what it says?" I asked.

There was a long silence while she considered painfully. "No, I don't think so. He's my son. I don't want
to know. Because if I know I might have to do something about it." Her look was suddenly wise, perhaps
a little crafty. "That's too often the way, isn't it? We
have a choice and we do nothing. And then suddenly
it's too late. Afterwards, we don't dare admit what we
haven't done."

"What do you want me to do with the tape now?" I
asked.

This time she didn't hesitate. "I think you must play
it. I think you must know whatever there is to know.
You're Ross's wife, aren't you? I remember now. You
need to know how dangerous he can be. You need to
know, for your own protection. But you mustn't tell *me*.
I'm too old to bear any more. Ross was always an impossible boy. We hoped for so much for him. We gave
him so much."

Everything except understanding, I thought with
sudden clarity, seeing for the first time a lonely small
boy lost in the grandeurs of Poinciana, fearful that he
could never live up to all this, yet driven for all his life
into trying—in no matter how unscrupulous a way—
because he couldn't believe in himself. This would be
something that Allegra could never understand. Her
generation had not been given to much self-awareness.
That was difficult enough for a far more psychologically

oriented age to come by. We could only make beginnings out of ignorance.

She spoke to me again. "The tape is yours now. Your responsibility."

I wasn't sure this was a responsibility I wanted to accept, but the small, frail woman in the chair sat up straighter than ever and fixed me sternly with eyes that were quite clear. She was Allegra Logan, and hers was the authority that ruled this house.

"You have no choice. I had a choice. For a long while I had a choice, but I did nothing. Then when I knew that Ross meant to put me away in some terrible place, so that no one would listen to anything I said, I decided. I told Brett and Gretchen they must find the tape and stop Ross from what he meant to do. I'm sure they searched and searched, but neither of them found it. So now *you* have no choice. Take it away and listen to what it says. Listen to it right now!"

I sat on the edge of the hassock, with the cassette in my hands, and knew I would have to obey. But first there was something else I must ask, something that I'd postponed out of my own fears. I must face it now.

"Will you tell me, Mrs. Logan—when you were in the tower room today, did you see Gretchen there? Did you talk to her?" I took the little mermaid from my raincoat pocket and held it out to her. "What do you know about this?"

Before my eyes, she seemed to crumple in upon herself, shaking her head from side to side. "No, no! I didn't see anything! Where is Gretchen? I want Gretchen to come to me right away!"

Either she had seen nothing, or she had blocked out whatever had happened in the tower. Blocked it out then and there, so that she could journey into the past and dance in her ballroom again. I knew I could urge her no further now.

"Let me help you out of that dress," I said. "I'll find a robe for you, and—"

Once more she stiffened, recovering. "Go right now!"

she ordered. "Before anything happens to stop you. I'm perfectly comfortable here, and after a while Coxie will come and see to me. She irritates me, and sometimes I fight her. But I'm used to her, and she does look after me."

"All right," I said. I kissed her cheek, and she reached out to pat my arm vaguely, again not quite sure who I was.

There were several tape recorders around the house, and one was in the library. So that was where I would go.

On my way downstairs, I met Coxie hurrying up, and knew by her face that she had been told about Gretchen. She hadn't waited out her hour.

"This will kill Mrs. Logan!" she cried. "She can't take any more, poor old thing."

"She's not a poor old thing," I said, "and she's probably tough enough to outlive us both. But don't *you* try to tell her."

The nurse fled from me up the stairs, intent on succoring her charge. I knew by now, however, that Allegra had her own means of escaping from whatever might disturb and injure her, and I could almost envy her that facility.

For me, the library was filled with memories, and Ysobel's recording was still in the machine. I took it out and replaced it with the first side of the unlabeled tape that Allegra had given me. Outside, the storm was growing stronger, slashing against window panes, bending the palm trees, banging a shutter somewhere in the house. The air seemed close inside, yet I felt cold and a little ill. Allegra's voice still commanded me. *Play it now.* I reached out and pressed the lever.

The voice was clear and sweet and filled with sorrow. I listened with all my being.

"Someday, Jarrett, you will hear these words I'm recording. And so will others. Because all the family must know. I watch you now, and I suffer for both of us. I know that you know, and I can see how hopelessly you are trapped. As I am trapped. You're angry with him—with Ross—and you're sorry for me because you know how foolish I've been. I think the time will come when you'll leave Ross because this is more than any man can bear. But it mustn't come to that. You will surely find a way to stop him.

"I know how much depends on you. There are all those people out there who will be damaged if you leave Ross. Because *he* doesn't care. None of what you're doing means anything to him. I've heard the callous way he talks. I know how indifferent he is. Yet he needs you to keep him in power, and he depends on you, much as he hates this very thing. You're the man he would like to be—perhaps that's his tragedy—and he can never forgive you for being what he isn't. So you are bound together, despising each other—and trapped. The thing I am most afraid of is violence. From either one of you."

"How did it happen? I mean between me and Ross. You have a right to know, and yet I'm not sure that I can tell you. It happened—that's all. Perhaps it was his revenge against you. But that's not what this tape is about. It's not what I'm trying to tell you now. I've loved him and hated him, and I have never stopped loving and admiring you—but in a different, healthier way. Let it go. As you'll have to let me go. But you must not let Ross get away with everything.

"He's grown tired of me, as he grows tired of anything that comes within his grasp. He always thinks he has to reach further. And perhaps Allegra is to blame for that. I know that part of my appeal for him lay in spiting you, but he has become like a drug for me, and I don't know how to go on living without him. So—foolishly—I've tried to threaten him. When he said he wouldn't meet me again, I told him I would go to you—inform you of everything. He laughed at me—but with that look in his eyes that told me he wasn't laughing inside.

"I think—I *know*—that he means to be rid of me,

stop me from talking. Somehow he will make it look like an accident, but I want you to know that it won't be one. Perhaps I could prevent this. Perhaps I could find a way to make him really afraid. But I shan't try. I don't want to go on living like this. I don't want *you* to go on living in this terrible way. So—I will let it happen, whatever it is. And I will not go to you as I threatened. My greatest sorrow is that I must leave Keith. But you will be a better father to him than I have been a mother. And someday you'll find another woman to mother him. Just make him understand always how much I loved him.

"Yesterday I saw Ross in the garage when Albert and the others were gone. He was working on my car. I went away and said nothing. Very soon I will drive out again—and then who knows? It will be best for all of us if it happens. For me and for you. And Ross will at last be exposed for what he is, because when you hear this tape you will have to act against him. It would be foolish to say I'm sorry. That would only be weak and useless. But I wish you had never gone to work for Ross Logan.

"Try not to hate me. You are the finest man I've ever known. I will put this tape in Allegra's hands to give to you if anything happens to me.

"This is Pam—signing off."

The tape recorder clicked to a stop, and I sat for a long while in the dim library. All about me on the shelves were a storing of words. Millions of words, ready to come to life whenever anyone opened a book. But only Pam Nichols's words echoed terribly through my mind with all their ramifications—their power to affect the lives of those who lived after her.

The evil I had sensed in this house had stemmed from Ross. Rather than see the man he depended upon turn against him, he had destroyed Jarrett's wife. First, he had satisfied his own need for power by seducing her, to spite the man he envied, but he could not risk

Jarrett's permanent loss, so he had rid himself of the danger she had threatened. Brett had been wise to get away. Perhaps I would have escaped eventually myself. Allegra knew her son. What she had never seen was the hand she had taken in forming him. Not that she could be blamed either. This wasn't a game of find-the-blame. Everyone was guilty—including those of us alive now. Allegra must have guessed. Ross had destroyed her too. Even though she had never played the tape herself, she had known, and when Pam died, she had become ill with the knowing, never again to be her old self.

What was I to do? What was the right thing, the wise thing, to do? Jarrett had every right to hear this tape. Yet how dreadful it would be for him to listen to Pam's voice, and learn all these things now, when he had at last begun to heal a little, and when Ross was gone and no longer could be held answerable. Jarrett had the right to hear it and Pam had the right to be heard. But I would wait a little while. I mustn't rush foolishly into damaging him further.

"May I come in?" a voice asked from the doorway.

I looked around in something of a daze, to see Brett Inness, bright in a frock printed with flame-colored blossoms. Poinciana blossoms? At once the present swept back.

"Gretchen?" I said with the painful question in my voice.

She walked into the room, turning on a lamp as she came down its length. She looked no less elegant than usual, and the gold bangles on her arms glittered in the light. When she reached my chair, she stood quite still, staring at me, her face devoid of emotion.

"Gretchen is gone," she said. "From the first there was no hope. The fall smashed her too badly. She was never conscious again, and she didn't suffer."

Even though I'd feared and expected this, my breath caught, and I leaned back, closing my eyes. Brett pulled over another chair and sat beside me.

"I went up to see Allegra just now. She will care most about this, you know. Her one grandchild—her only hope for immortality."

Words which might have carried sympathy were only scornful, and I shrank away from her. At once she sensed my rejection.

"You can't expect me to mourn as a mother would," she said. "I think you know the truth—that I never had a child of my own. I took Gretchen because she was forced upon me. The child of one of Ross's infidelities. How could *I* love her?"

I ached for Gretchen. "She needed your love."

"Need? Don't we all need? But I didn't have it to give. Though perhaps I made it up to her a little in recent years, when we became reasonably good friends."

They'd become friends because Brett wanted the power, the influence that close association with Gretchen could give her. Perhaps even the means of revenging herself upon Ross.

"Have you told Allegra?" I asked.

"No. She's slipping in and out of her fog. Coxie didn't know what to do, so I suggested that she say nothing for now. Though Allegra can sense things sometimes that the rest of us don't even know are happening. So she's uneasy now. She told me she'd found Pam's tape that she's been searching for all this time, and that she gave it to you to play. I thought you might come directly here." She glanced at the recorder beside me. "You've listened to it?"

I left my chair and removed the tape from the machine, slipped it into the case, and started from the room. "Yes, I've listened to it."

She came after me, caught me by the arm. "Wait! There are things we need to talk about, you and I. Sit down for a minute. Don't worry—I won't ask you to let me listen to it. I've been pretty sure all along what that tape contained. Ross managed Pam's death, didn't he? He fixed that car?"

Near the door were two massive Spanish chairs, and

I sat down on a cracked leather seat. I had better listen to anything she had to say, whether I liked her or not.

She took the opposite chair. "I'm sure you're all mixed up with feelings of loyalty toward your dear departed husband. Or had you already come to hate him as much as I did?"

I held to my silence. I would listen, but I wouldn't talk. I would tell her nothing.

"He deserved what came to him," she said, and I heard the anger in her voice. "I'm glad I was able to have a hand in his punishment."

In spite of myself, she had surprised me into words. "What are you talking about?"

"You might as well know. There's nothing that can be done to me now, and I'm sure you won't open things up with the police again. Or the press. I was there that night. I was with Ross when he died. Oh, don't look so shocked. Gretchen was the only one in this house who had mourned him at all, and even her feelings were mixed—because of Vasily. At least you can take some satisfaction in knowing that poor, silly Pam has been avenged. And so have the rest of us."

"You'd better explain."

"All right, I will. As long as Gretchen was alive, I meant to keep this to myself. Now it doesn't matter. I knew he was working late and alone that night. So I went to see him. He was planning to call in that note of mine he held—out of sheer spite. So I decided to fabricate a little. Every now and then Allegra has talked about the tape she'd misplaced. From bits and pieces I knew Pam had given it to her, and I couldn't guess why. So I told Ross that the tape existed and that it would incriminate him in Pam's death. I told him I would use it if he acted against me—and that perhaps I might use it anyway."

"And he had a heart attack?"

"Exactly. It all went better than I'd hoped. So you see it wasn't that silly note signed with one of Gretchen's little faces that set him off. That must have been one of Vasily's futile efforts. That young man can be pretty juvenile at times. It was what I told Ross about the tape and how I meant to use it that did it. Perhaps he'd have tried to attack me physically right then, he was so angry. But instead he turned purple and fell over on his desk. I knew he was dead and there was nothing to be done. Of course, I didn't want to rush out screaming and admit to my own presence in his office, but neither did I want him to lie there unattended. I have some sensibilities. And of course I didn't know then that he'd already phoned Jarrett."

Her words had left me stunned. "So you set off the alarm to waken the house and cause someone to come and find him?"

"That's right. I turned it on at the far end .of the gallery, where the guard couldn't see me. And before he could get there, I went down to Allegra's cottage and stayed there for the rest of the night. Keith saw me coming out of the house right after the alarm went off, and he may have guessed that I'd turned it on, but he didn't give me away."

So much was being explained. Yet I knew that it was as she said and none of this would be told against her now. Of what use would it be?

"It must have been cozy at the cottage, with Vasily hiding out there too," I said.

She smiled vaguely.

"Why have you told me this now?" I asked.

"Because you have Pam's tape. Because Ross has already been punished for what he did, and there's nothing further you can do by letting anyone else hear it."

"I haven't decided about that. Why are you interested in seeing it kept quiet?"

"If it should become public, there would be a huge scandal. And when one scandal comes out, others follow. The ripple effects could be devastating."

"To whom?"

"To the entire Logan empire, of course. I suggest

that you destroy this tape as quickly as you can. Otherwise, we may all be damaged."

"Jarrett has a right to hear it. And Pam has a right to be heard. Jarrett wouldn't use it in any way that might hurt Keith."

"Ah? I see. I had an idea the wind was blowing that way. You and Jarrett—well! Lovely possibilities for both of you there."

I'd endured enough, and this time when I stood up, I walked out the door. Nevertheless, she came with me, so I asked one more question.

"How is Vasily taking his wife's death?"

For the first time, Brett seemed puzzled. "I'm not sure. He rushed away from the hospital looking wild-eyed, and left all the complications in Jarrett's lap."

"Complications?"

"The police, of course. There'll still be all the questioning to go through again, before they decide it was suicide. I suggest that you say nothing to anyone about Allegra being in the tower today. Oh, of course she admitted it to me just now. But an insane grandmother who was present when her granddaughter fell to her death would give the media a field day. To say nothing of poor Allegra being driven further out of her head with questioning. Best to say nothing at all, Sharon my dear—just in case it wasn't suicide, after all."

She went her way then, bangles jingling, wafting behind her a trace of Givenchy perfume. I had always believed that every human being had some redeeming traits. Now I wondered in Brett's case. But I really knew nothing about her, knew nothing of what had formed her into the way she was. In any case, I could hardly feel generous toward her.

Chapter

19

Brett had been right in her forecasting. With Gretchen's death, all the police inquiries opened up again, and we were once more in a state of siege from the outside world, which was clamoring to know what had really happened at Poinciana. Even the small, unimportant interview I'd given the day I saw Gretchen at the library was blown out of all sensible proportion, with implications that had little to do with reality.

The official conclusion was one I didn't believe in, even though my own testimony seemed to support it. Unfortunately, there were too many witnesses to the last quarrel between Gretchen and her husband, and this couldn't be evaded. Brett and Myra and I had all heard Vasily angrily threatening divorce, and everyone knew how impulsive and emotional Gretchen could be. No one could claim that she had been in a calm and rational state when she rushed off to her grandmother's tower and climbed those stairs for the last time.

At least nothing ever came out to hint that Allegra Logan had been in the tower that day. Allegra herself still didn't seem to know exactly what had happened while she was taking out her gowns and Gretchen must have rushed past her on the stairs. It was Mrs. Broderick who saw to putting the gowns away before the police came.

I had told Jarrett of finding the mermaid netsuke, and we'd agreed that nothing could be gained by discussing this with anyone. Whatever had happened, Allegra must not be brought into this.

It was Jarrett, finally, who told Allegra of Gretchen's death. I was with him when he sat beside her in the silver-gray parlor and held her hands gently. Perhaps some of his own strength flowed into her frail person, for she took it better than he might have expected. In fact, she took it so calmly that I wondered if she already knew that Gretchen was dead. What *had* she seen in the tower? Perhaps we would never know, and perhaps it was better that way.

This time, Allegra did not come to the funeral. We all thought it would be too great a strain, and she herself escaped the day in her own happy manner, slipping back to a time when her husband and her son were with her at Poinciana, and there was not yet a Gretchen to think about.

When the funeral was over, she seemed to know, and came back to us quite sensibly, and to our surprise was even able to talk a little about what had happened.

"Gretchen would never have committed suicide," she insisted. "She was much too self-centered a girl. I can imagine her being violent against someone else, but never toward herself. She was like her father in that. Self-preservation came first. The harm she sometimes did herself could be serious and damaging, but that was because she never thought one minute ahead. To kill herself, however—no!"

I leaned toward Allegra and spoke to her quietly. "Mrs. Logan, was anyone else in the tower that day? Did anyone go up there to join Gretchen?"

She drew away from me at once, and I was to learn that any pressure of questions about that time in the tower was sure to send her into one of her "fogs." As quickly as though she closed a door, she shut out reality and escaped from any probing. When this happened, there was no calling her back until she chose to come of her own free will. Gretchen's death was something terrible for her to live with consciously for very long, and when she went into her retreat she might talk about her granddaughter happily, as though she were alive.

Strangely enough, in the days that had followed the funeral, Allegra never once asked what I had done with Pam's tape, and I didn't remind her of it. The tape seemed to matter less, when so much else that was agonizing in the present crushed in upon us.

When we left Allegra that day she had spoken of suicide being impossible for Gretchen, Jarrett and I went down the hall and sat in my cozy living room. I had unpacked a few things of my own that I'd brought with me to Poinciana and never used until now. It was good to have my own books and a few pictures and ornaments that I'd collected around me. For the first time, I could feel reasonably at home—even though I knew the feeling wasn't permanent. I couldn't stay here forever now.

"I like this room," Jarrett said, settling himself into an armchair that had belonged to my father, and which Ian had insisted on carting with him wherever he went.

"Do you think Allegra is right?" I asked. "Could it have been an accident?"

"She didn't say that, did she? She only insisted that it wasn't suicide. The railing was firm enough, as the police found out. Only if Gretchen had flung herself against it deliberately could she have broken through."

We didn't speak further of the third possibility that

was in both our minds. After all, the evil at Poinciana had died with Ross, and no one would have tried to kill Gretchen. Surely no one would have?

Jarrett left his chair and came to sit beside me on the sofa. "You're not taking care of yourself, Sharon. You've been losing weight and you're growing frown lines between your eyes."

I liked his concern. I wanted it. Gradually in these weeks, as I watched him taking on most of an impossible burden, I began to know myself a little. And to know him. Everything between us was too fresh and recent for expression, and we were both learning caution. Or perhaps I was. He already knew. Nevertheless, he showed me in small ways that he was watching over me when he could, and I tried to let him know that I was grateful.

Because of our closeness at that moment, I could at last do what I had been postponing, and which I knew must be done. I had no right to keep Pam's tape from him because of the pain I would feel over his pain. I went to the drawer where I'd put it and took out the cassette. Just beneath it was a folded sheet of Poinciana notepaper, and I took that out as well, not thinking much about it, because I was intent upon the explanation I must give Jarrett of how I'd come by the tape.

He listened without emotion except for a tightening of the muscles around his mouth. When I put the case into his hand, he closed his fingers about it reluctantly, and I knew that he sensed what lay ahead.

"Perhaps you'll destroy it without listening to it," I said. "I only wish I could have thrown it away myself. I've given up trying to decide what's wise, or right or wrong. This was meant for you and you must have it."

He sat very still with the cassette in his hands, and I longed to say something that would comfort him. Only I could find nothing comforting to say in this bleak moment.

For the first time I really looked at the sheet of

notepaper I still held, and then I sat down abruptly in the nearest chair, completely horrified.

This note was very much like the one that had purported to be from Gretchen—the note that had been on Ross's desk when he died, signed with one of Gretchen's signature faces. This time the face was grinning and the words were different:

> Be careful, Sharon. Don't be as foolish
> as I was. Stay away from high places.

Words from Gretchen—when Gretchen was dead?

My hand shook as I gave it to Jarrett. "Now we know the first note was never written by Gretchen."

Jarrett scowled, reading it, and shook his head wearily. "Perhaps this is the time to move you out of Poinciana."

"How can I go? There's too much that I'm responsible for."

"I know," he said. "At least when you're in here, lock your door."

He slipped the cassette into a pocket and stood up. I wanted to touch him, feel his physical presence, but I knew this was not the time. First he must listen to Pam's tape and fight his own demons, find his own peace. There were depths of emotion in Jarrett that frightened me a little when I glimpsed them. I remembered what Gretchen had said one time—that he held too much in. A release might come in words, if only we could talk, but at that moment we were poles apart, and Ross and Pam stood between us.

In the coming days he seemed unchanged. He was always grave, and now he became more seriously busy and more remote than ever. If there was a deepening of the lines in his face, I could very well guess the cause, but there was no opening for me to say anything. Not once did he mention the tape, or admit that he had listened to Pam's words. I bled a little, knowing his pain and unable to offer him comfort.

I wanted to tear up the note I'd found and burn the pieces, but I kept it in the drawer where I'd discovered it. Now and then I took it out and read it again, willing the words to tell me something that would betray the writer. But the grinning little face mocked me, hiding its identity, and I knew that evil was still alive at Poinciana.

Then one day, quite unexpectedly, Jarrett took me away from the house. We gave reporters the slip by running off in a boat across Lake Worth to a place where a friend had a car waiting for us. On the mainland side, we drove south, and I was aware of Florida blooming lushly all around us. There were even more blossoms and flowering vines and shrubs than before in a riot of tropical growth. Jacaranda, breathtakingly blue, azaleas of all shades, bougainvillea more colorful than ever.

In Boynton Beach we had lunch at Bernard's, a building of white stucco and red tiles that was a Mizner creation. In the dining room I sat in a wicker chair that spread behind me like a great open fan, and looked out through surrounding glass upon a jungle garden, gone wild with undergrowth and twisted banyan trees.

I felt almost happy to be away from the house and alone with Jarrett, and because he had wanted to bring me here. Yet at the same time I was uneasy. I could never be sure of what lay behind anything Jarrett did. For the moment he seemed almost relaxed and I began to relax a little too, postponing the time of reckoning that might lie ahead.

The wild tangle beyond our table had once been the famous Rainbow Tropical Gardens, he told me, where rare palms and plants had been gathered for visitors to enjoy. Gretchen had said once that she would bring me here "sometime."

Sometime! There was never enough time. It could be too late so quickly. I looked into what had once been an orderly garden and shivered at its dark, mysterious depths.

Jarrett reached across the table, and I put my hand in his. For the living there was still time. Time to take hold, to keep the days from being wasted. His warm clasp told me what I wanted to know. Perhaps Jarrett too was aware of hours speeding away with our lives.

We went outside then and followed a curving white wall roofed in red tiles. At a place where an arched wooden gate with great iron hinges opened into the wild garden, we went through. The days were growing hotter now, but here in this tangle of uncontrolled underbrush and plant life, a shadowy coolness welcomed us. We were in a quiet and secret place, and we sat together upon a fallen log.

"We've needed to talk," he said. "But Poinciana constrains me, and I haven't known how to begin. I don't really know now. I wanted to get you away from the house and have a little time with you first. Something pleasant to remember. Sharon, I've listened to Pam's tape."

I put out my hand. "You needn't talk unless you want to. I can understand."

He went on. "In these last days I've been thinking a great deal about truth—whatever that is. Sometimes it seems a hopeless abstract, impossible to grasp and hold on to. Maybe meaning something different to everyone who looks at it. Perhaps even dangerous to touch. Yet somehow one has to try. The lie can be even more damaging."

He paused as if waiting for some response from me. I had little to offer that was comforting, but I tried.

"My father used to tell me again and again that nothing is as it seems," I said. "I don't think he believed in truth as something in itself. It was always the lies of others that he thought about and feared, and he tried to make me distrustful. But I've never wanted to live that way. I want something I can believe in, even if I have to get hurt by believing."

"You're finding your own way, and it's a good way, Sharon. My trouble is that I've lost myself in a jungle as wild as this little counterpart where we're sitting. I know now that it wasn't good enough to believe in a kind of truth, if I couldn't live it. Oh, I had a dozen noble excuses. I've given you some of them. The good of the many! That always sounds laudable. But it can mean the beginning of the lies. If I hadn't gone down that road of deceiving myself as well as everyone else, Pam might be alive today. The good of the many might have been taken care of if I'd stood up to Ross and told him off. And I might have saved Pam. My own confusion doesn't excuse me."

Again there was that waiting pause, and I spoke into it, smiling faintly in memory. "Once when I went to school for a little while in Chicago, I had a teacher—an older man who was a devotee of H. L. Mencken. He had a favorite quotation that I liked so much that I memorized it. And I can still quote.

"'I believe that it is better to tell the truth than a lie. I believe it is better to be free than a slave. And I believe it is better to know than be ignorant.'"

I was relieved to see Jarrett smile too. "Yes, I know that one, and I've always liked it. Truth can be a pretty hazardous commodity, but it doesn't breed the same kind of dangers that the lies breed. It *is* better to know. I'm glad you didn't follow your kinder instincts and hold that tape back from me, Sharon."

"I wanted to," I said.

He put an arm about me, and for a little while no more words needed between us. They could wait until Jarrett had come through his own dark passageway.

We returned to our borrowed car and I felt closer to him on the drive back to the boat than ever before. The return trip across the lake was companionable, and I think his anguish had lessened a little because of talking it out. We crossed the lawn together, and then Jarrett turned in the direction of his office, while I went into the inner court where I'd sat in the rain that terrible day.

The table and two chairs were occupied. Allegra and Myra sat in the shade, finishing plates of cheesecake. Allegra smiled at me vaguely, and I knew this wasn't one of her better days.

"There's enough for you, Mrs. Logan," Myra said. "I made it myself last night. But now I see Mr. Nichols is back, so I'd better scoot before he misses me."

She jumped up and gave me a quick little nod, beckoning me to the nearest doorway.

"She's way out of it, poor lady," Myra said when we were alone. "Miss Inness was just here trying to find out if Mrs. Logan saw anything in the tower that day. Imagine tormenting her like that! That woman ought to stay away from her."

Myra waved her arms indignantly and rushed off in her abrupt way. I returned to the courtyard and sat down at the table. Allegra looked at me with a modicum of the rational in her eyes, and I wondered if she sometimes dissembled, to serve her own purposes.

"Brett just came to say goodbye," she told me. "Of course, with Gretchen gone, she feels she must move out of Poinciana. I said I didn't think you'd mind if she stayed, but she didn't agree with me."

"I'm afraid she's right," I admitted. "It will be more comfortable with her gone. And now there's really no need for her to stay. Did she try to ask you anything else when she was here?"

Allegra looked unhappy, confused. "All that about the tower, you mean? I don't know what she was getting at. I told her about taking out my beautiful gowns and dressing up. That's all I can remember. Except that I danced in the ballroom, and you found me there."

Her bright eyes were candid, guileless. I couldn't believe she was dissembling. A door had closed firmly somewhere in her mind, and if there was more she had no wish to remember it. The very fact was a relief. If ever she remembered something more, she might be in very real danger.

"I'd better tell Brett goodbye," I said. "Will you be all right if I leave you here?"

"Of course. I'll finish this delicious cheesecake. Coxie will come for me after a while, since she knows where I am."

I went upstairs to the wing that Gretchen and Vasily had occupied, and into which Brett had moved. It was not that I ever wanted to see her again, but that there were some untied threads left dangling that I still wanted to pick up.

The door to her room stood open, and I looked in to find her packing.

"Hello," she said. "Come in, do. I was about to go look you up. I've decided to return to the apartment over my shop in town. Everyone's leaving the house, I gather. You're going to have a big place to rattle around in alone. Do you mind if I come to see Allegra occasionally, while she's still here?"

"Of course not. But what do you mean—everyone's leaving?"

"Vasily too. Hadn't you heard?" She paused in packing her toilet case and regarded me thoughtfully. "Perhaps there are a few more things you ought to know. I don't suppose anyone else will tell you—if anyone even knows. You remember that bang-up argument Vasily and Gretchen were having that last day?"

I nodded.

"I know what it was about. In fact, I knew the cause earlier. I met Vasily one day down by the beach. He wanted to talk to me without being seen. He wanted to urge my silence. I told him what he had to do—that he had no other choice. But he wouldn't listen. Or perhaps he didn't know how to handle this himself. I tried to tell him that I thought Gretchen knew and that he'd better talk to her, reassure her, if he could. Before it was too late. I told him that again the night Ross died, and Vasily and I found ourselves camping out in Allegra's cottage, not trusting each other. I expect you've noticed his state of mind lately. He was scared then, and I think he still is."

I had noticed that he seemed to be under some strain, but I had set his distraught condition down to his grief over Gretchen's death. Though he had seemed more devastated than I might have expected him to be.

"What was it that he should have told her?"

Brett gave up her efforts at packing and dropped into a chair. "His big problem is that his ex-wife has turned up over in West Palm Beach, and he's been seeing her there. I suspect there's still some sort of attachment between them. Gretchen guessed that he was seeing another woman, only he never told her who it was. She might have understood better if he had. Instead he admitted it to me."

I remembered that time when Gretchen had come to Ross's room. There had been a moment when I thought she was about to tell me something, and then had held back. Was this the unhappy secret she'd been carrying? I could feel all the more angry with Vasily now.

"Why should Vasily tell you?" I asked.

"I think he couldn't handle it himself, and I suppose in a way I was in a neutral camp. He's turned to me on other occasions when he felt the world was closing in."

This was quite possible, I thought. Brett was intelligent and worldly wise, and she had few scruples that would make Vasily uneasy.

"Is this matter of the ex-wife one of the things Ross tracked down?" I asked.

"He knew about the wife, of course. She called herself Elberta Sheldon when she was an actress in London. But I don't know if she was here when Ross was alive. Anyway, Gretchen started to go through her father's files to find out about this."

"Will Vasily go back to his first wife now?"

"Maybe you'd better ask him," she said, and got up to close her last suitcase with an air of finality. "I'll be

leaving now, just as soon as Albert comes for my bags.
You don't mind if he drives me into town? Then he can
help me at the other end. I'll send for my car later."

We didn't shake hands. There was a strange moment
when we looked at each other across the room. A moment in which there was a certain wary appraisal, each
of the other. Then I acted on an impulse and took from
my handbag the little mermaid netsuke that Gretchen
had been holding when she fell from the tower.

"You remember this?" I said.

She recognized it at once. "Yes, of course. Allegra's
favorite. The one she was always picking up because
she said it was hers."

"Gretchen had it in her hand when she fell from the
tower," I said.

Color seemed to drain from Brett's face and she sat
down suddenly on the edge of the bed. "Then Gretchen
did see Allegra that day in the belvedere! Allegra must
have stolen the mermaid again, and then Gretchen took
it from her. So Allegra knew very well that Gretchen
was there and that she'd climbed to the upper room."

"Does it matter now?" I asked.

Brett answered me almost absently, and with indirection. "I remember Allegra the way she used to be
when I first came to this house. She was the only one
who was really kind to me. She knew all about Ross
and she knew what he would do to me. She was more
like a mother to me than my own mother ever was. In
the end, she was the only one I could care about in this
terrible place. And she was fond of me too. So of course
it matters!" Brett gave me a suddenly baleful look. "I
wouldn't want to see any further unhappiness come to
Allegra."

"No one but Jarrett knows about the mermaid," I
said. "And he thought it best not to mention it."

She nodded in a way that dismissed me, and I went
off, leaving her to finish with her suitcases.

From the hallway I could hear sounds coming from
Gretchen's rooms, where Vasily too was preparing to

leave. I went to the door of the parlor and looked in. He had set open bags around the room and was carrying out clothes from the bedroom to stuff into them. Through the open door I could see the bed piled with the suits and coats that Gretchen must have bought for him. Standing there silently, waiting to be noticed, I could see how wild and agitated he looked. Not at all the easy, confident man I had first seen in this house.

"You're leaving?" I asked after a moment.

He started and looked around at me, then made an effort to recover himself. "Ah—Sharon. I would have come to tell you, of course. It is necessary to get away from this house with all its terrible memories. I can't stay here another night."

"Where are you going?" I asked.

"France, perhaps. Paris. Perhaps the Greek isles." He almost smiled. "Strange to think that I can now go wherever I wish, do as I please. Now that it's too late."

"You'll be taking your former wife with you?"

That really startled him. "Who told you that?"

"I've just been talking to Brett," I said.

He seemed to relax a little, as though this somehow reassured him. "Brett, of course. But that lady doesn't 'know as much as she thinks she does. I tried to persuade her of that the time when we met in the tunnel and you discovered us so inopportunely."

"But your ex-wife *is* in West Palm Beach?"

"If you must know—yes. I am hoping to get out of the country before she knows I am gone. She hasn't been making my life easy. So I hope you will not send out any spies. Though, now that Gretchen is gone, there isn't much she can do."

I went on conversationally, wondering if I was on the track of something. "Gretchen admitted to me once that you'd probably married her for her money. Not hard to guess. Was that true?"

He didn't seem to mind my frankness. "In a way, yes. But there was more to it than that. Gretchen was a—a very special person. She—needed what I had to give her. With her there was something—something—oh, God!" He flung himself into a chair and buried his face in his hands. "If only she could have believed in herself a little more! If only she had not tried to punish and torment me for what I could never help!"

"I think," I said, "that you mustn't leave Poinciana right away, Vasily. In fact, if you try to leave, I will ask Jarrett to have you stopped. You must stay here a little while longer."

There was something like terror in the look he gave me. "No, no, Sharon! Don't ask this of me."

"We need your help," I went on. "If you should leave now we might never know who was in the tower with Gretchen before she died. I don't think it was an accident, Vasily. I believe that Gretchen was pushed through that railing to fall to her death. Just as I was pushed on the stairs that time by the same person."

Vasily had grown up in a culture that was not afraid of tears and emotion, and now he was weeping helplessly.

For a moment longer I stood staring at him. At any moment he would look up and see what was in my face. I had said too much, and I couldn't stay here a moment longer. Everything was beginning to fall into place now.

"Just don't leave the house yet, Vasily," I said softly, and went away from him, hurrying toward the stairs, hurrying to Jarrett's office.

Myra was at her desk typing, making up for lost time. She looked up in surprise as I rushed past her and through the open door to confront Jarrett.

"I know what happened to Gretchen!" I cried. "She was threatening to change her will because Vasily had been seeing his former wife in West Palm Beach. He wouldn't have divorced her, but she might've divorced him. So he must've followed Gretchen up to the tower. He must have fought with her there. Maybe he never meant to have it happen, but it was Vasily who threw her against the railing so that she fell through to her death."

"Whoa!" Jarrett said. "Wait—calm down a bit, Sharon."

I wouldn't be stopped. "There's no time to be calm! He's getting ready to leave right now. He's planning to leave the country! He's going to get away if we don't stop him."

"This is all supposition, Sharon. Even if you're right, we can't rush in and act on a conclusion you're jumping to."

That stopped me for only an instant. "Never mind that! Allegra knows. She knows very well who went up to the tower with Gretchen, and she's trying to shut the whole thing away so she won't have to face it. We must get her to talk. Now!"

Jarrett shook his head at me sadly. "You're going off half cocked. If you tackle Allegra in that state, you'll probably shock her into hiding forever. Wait until you cool down, Sharon."

All my life I had been trained to be calm and cool and let nothing disturb me. Now all the bars were down, and I was out and free. Cool judicial thinking would let Vasily get away. If Jarrett wouldn't help me, I would have to do this myself.

Again I ran past an astonished Myra and down those endless corridors, up the stairs, and into Allegra's suite. Coxie was putting her to bed when I flew through the door.

"I want to talk to her," I told the nurse. "Just leave us alone for a little while."

Reluctantly, Coxie left and I turned to the bed. Allegra watched me with sudden alarm in her eyes, and I brought my voice down, forcing myself to speak quietly.

"You must help us now," I said. "For Gretchen's sake, you must help us."

I could almost see the curtains come down as she

retreated, escaping once more from what she dared not face.

I reached for one frail hand. "Please, Allegra. Don't go away from me now. I know what happened in the tower. I know Vasily went up there and fought with his wife. You saw it all, didn't you? You know what happened. You mustn't run away from it any longer, no matter how much Gretchen's death hurts you. Help us, Allegra!"

She stared at me with a total lack of comprehension. Jarrett was right. In my need for haste, I had frightened her into retreat. Though I knew it was hopeless, I stayed a little while longer, trying to talk to her, struggling to break through those protective barriers she had raised. But it was no use, and I knew it. In the end I gave up and returned to the hall.

I was on my way to my room when Vasily appeared around a far corner and came walking toward me. I didn't like the strange look in his eyes.

"You've been talking to Allegra?" he said. "So what has she told you?"

I shook my head, trying to hide my sudden fear. "Nothing. She doesn't remember anything."

He still looked frightened, and in a man as unstable as Vasily, that was dangerous. Yet he spoke to me quietly enough.

"Sharon, you don't understand. There is nothing you can do now. I want to go away quietly, while there is still time. You must permit me that."

He took another step toward me, his eyes very bright, and I backed away, flat against the corridor wall. At that moment, from somewhere downstairs, I could hear Myra calling me. I knew Jarrett had sent her after me, and blessed him for it. Vasily turned, momentarily distracted, and I felt the panel move behind me. I stepped backward as it swiveled, and I let it close upon darkness. With a frantic hand I fumbled for the switch that would light my way of escape to the ballroom.

Lights came on down the long passageway, and I

moved toward the stairs, trying to make no sound behind this secret wall, uncertain of whether Vasily knew that the passage existed. I'd reached the top of the hidden stairway when I heard the panel in the corridor behind me open again, and when I turned to look, I knew I had lost. Vasily stepped in and swung the door closed behind him.

I gave up trying to be quiet, and shouted for Myra, praying that she would know about this way to the ballroom and that she would hear me. The rickety railing broke under my hand as I stumbled down the stairs. I recovered my footing and ran for the turn in the passageway, while walls seemed to press in upon me.

But clearly, Vasily knew the passage well, and he was coming after me. I heard nothing from Myra. Perhaps she had gone for help. Or more likely, she hadn't heard my cry at all. It took only seconds for Vasily to reach me, and I felt his wiry strength as he swung me around. "No, no, Sharon! You must not run from me. I would never hurt you."

I knew better than to believe him. I knew everything now.

"It was you all along!" I cried. "You thought I was a danger because you were afraid I would recognize you, give you away. That I'd spoil your plans to get your hands on Gretchen's money, and then go back to your first wife. You wanted to frighten me away from Poinciana, didn't you?"

"No, no! No one meant to push you on the stairs. You were there at the wrong moment. It became necessary."

It was all becoming horribly clear. "You were behind that child's trick with the coconut! And the two notes! The one left for Ross and the one I found in my room! It was you, Vasily! Gretchen suspected, didn't she? And tried to protect you."

"No, no—I never thought—"

"You've been cruel—utterly cruel! How did you kill Gretchen?"

He caught me by the shoulders, shaking me hard. "Stop it, Sharon!"

I squirmed desperately in his grasp and managed to break his hold. Blindly, I ran toward the ballroom and the way out. But the door was so far away—so far! And he was coming after me again with a wild strength moving him.

Then at the far end the concealed door opened and a shadow filled the slit. Rescue was coming, after all! I cried out, and ran toward the opening. It closed again, and in the wall lighting I could see Myra coming toward me.

"Help me!" I called to her. "Help me to get out!"

"I don't think so," she said. "It's all right, Vasily. We've got her cornered now. I think you'd better tell her everything."

Behind me, Vasily made a strange choking sound. I stood where I was, stunned with disbelief. What had Myra to do with anything?

"Oh, so you don't want to tell her?" she ran on, sounding almost pleased. "Then perhaps I had better do it for you."

I could see her clearly down the passageway, and there was a change in her that was astonishing. Her very look, her manner was different. She was a woman far more arresting than the Myra I knew.

She spoke with a self-assurance I'd never seen in her before. "I'm his wife, Sharon. I'm his *real* wife. Oh, we were officially divorced, of course, because we worked out this fine plan between us. Gretchen used to come into Vasily's gallery in London as a customer, and he had only to play up to her, win her—marry her! Then when enough of the money was in his hands, he would get a divorce and he and I would be together again with everything we'd never had before."

"Don't, Myra," Vasily said.

I'd had it right, and I'd had it all wrong.

She ran on again, paying no attention. "I rather liked you, Sharon. We had good visits together, didn't we?

It was too bad about that time on the stairs. But I was afraid of what you might do to our plan. You were beginning to remember who Vasily was. So I tried to warn you to go away. I didn't mean to hurt you, and I made it up to you afterwards, didn't I? Though I was laughing inside over the way you trusted me. Nothing more would have happened to you, if you hadn't turned into a real threat with all your poking and snooping. I used to watch you, Sharon—so many times when you never knew I was about. Why didn't you understand when I left that coconut for you, and that note? Of course I left the one for Ross, hoping it would make him change his mind about Vasily. And it gave me the idea for the one to you. Why didn't you get out while you could?"

The whole chilling picture of someone completely amoral was coming clear. This was the most dangerous kind of evil—never to recognize the truth about oneself. Vasily had understood and suffered over his own villainy. But Myra had played without conscience the role of a friendly, well-meaning woman—all the while appallingly bent upon her own venal purposes. I had seen only the character an actress had developed, mannerisms, attitudes, and all. Perhaps the best role Elberta Sheldon had ever played.

"Let her go," Vasily said. "You know I never intended any of this."

"Yes—you were always the weak one. You'd have let Gretchen get away with changing her will, divorcing you, fixing it so that in the end we'd have nothing. You found the netsuke under the cushion in the tower, where I hid them, and you made me return them both times. And the Lautrec paintings, when I could have sold them through people I know. Though at least you tried to protect me by hiding those manuscript pages, so what was missing couldn't be checked. I was pleased about that."

There was anger and grief in Vasily's voice. "You've lost, Myra! You must give up now."

"Because you thought you'd fallen in love with your temporary wife? Don't be foolish! I knew you would always come back to me. You had to come back, didn't you?"

"No! I told you it was over when you played that idiotic prank and got yourself a job as Jarrett's secretary. I told you you couldn't work in this house!"

"But I did, didn't I? I fooled them all! What fun I had playing that character. Though in a way, she *is* part of me. And you kept coming to see me over in town."

"To persuade you to leave. To keep you from any more scheming acts. I wasn't playing your game any more."

"It's not a game you could stop playing, Vasily. Yet only today you've tried to run away—without letting me know. How very foolish of you! Now you've brought us to this. We can't let Sharon go. You see that, don't you? Look what I have here."

She was holding something up, and Vasily cried out with a despair that shook me even more.

"It's Sharon's own husband's gun," Myra pointed out. "That nice little automatic he kept in his desk. How appropriate if Sharon commits suicide with it because she is grieving so for her beloved husband—and mother and father. It's all been too much for her. You can see that. But it must be done very convincingly, Vasily."

He moved then. I felt myself thrust against the wall as he plunged toward the woman who had been his wife. They were struggling together down near the ballroom entrance when the gun went off. Its cracking echoes seemed to reverberate forever in that narrow passageway. And then there was only a terrible silence.

Until the sobbing began.

Following the shot by moments came a distant shouting and the clatter of running feet. Everything resounded through the thin walls of Allegra's secret passage, until the door opened once more at the ballroom end, and this time it was Jarrett who came through.

"Sharon?" he called. "Sharon, are you there?"

I moved toward him with a greater relief than I'd ever felt in my life. Slipping past Vasily and Myra, not sure which one of them sobbed, I flung myself into Jarrett's arms. For a moment he held me, making sure I was unharmed. But others were crowding the narrow doorway now, and he set me aside, moving past me toward the place where Vasily crouched, holding Myra in his arms. Now I knew that it was he who wept, and I could see that Myra was bleeding.

Chapter

20

The immediate excitement is over. I can sit beside Jarrett on his deck above the lake and talk with him almost calmly. Myra has been taken to a hospital, where she will recover from the flesh wound inflicted when Vasily struggled with her for Ross's gun. The police have been questioning them, and the whole miserable story is out.

There can be no escaping the horror ahead that will keep everything painfully public for a long while. Myra will be tried for Gretchen's murder, but Jarrett believes that Vasily, for all his original intent, has done nothing legally criminal, and he certainly saved my life. All along he had been trying to stop his former wife from carrying out the plan she had launched them into. They were two adventurers, and perhaps that was her greatest appeal for him. Yet I think Gretchen was not wholly cheated by Vasily in their marriage.

Brett had managed to leave the house before everything exploded. She and Gretchen had been coming close to the truth, but neither had suspected that Vasily's former wife, Myra Ritter Karl, alias the actress Elberta Sheldon, had installed herself so impudently right under their noses at Poinciana.

When Jarrett had left for the hospital, along with the police, I had gone upstairs to see Allegra. She had heard the shot and it had brought her out of bed in trembling fright. I helped Coxie to quiet her, and then we sat together in her little gray and red parlor, while I told her everything. And at last she talked to me.

The sound waves of that shot shattering their way through Poinciana seemed to have broken through her defenses. That she had seen her granddaughter fall from the tower had nearly destroyed her sanity. Perhaps would have, if she hadn't been able to retreat into her own refuge. She had known Gretchen was in the tower, because her granddaughter had stopped to see what she was doing, had discovered that she had the Sleeping Mermaid again, and had taken it for safekeeping.

Yet Allegra had never known who was in the tower with Gretchen that day. She had been engrossed in examining her lovely gowns, lost in her memories, her fantasies, and she hadn't seen Myra climb the stairs. However, she had been standing near a window, holding a dress up to the light, when Gretchen had fallen past the glass. She had heard her scream, heard the crash of her fall—and the shock and horror had been too much for her to bear. She had fled into the past, dressing herself in a favorite gown and going by way of her secret passage to dance in the ballroom—where I had found her.

After that, she had drifted in and out, between past and present. Whenever the present came too close and threatened her with terror and collapse, she ran from it, saving herself. But she could have told us nothing useful anyway.

A few tumultuous days have passed, and now for this little while we can sit on the deck outside Jarrett's cottage, watching the brilliance of a Florida sunset. The poinciana tree is green now with plumy leafage, and I feel a deep sorrow because Gretchen will never see it again. Or Ross.

Jarrett and I are making our plans quietly, because we know now that there is never enough time. We will be married as soon as possible. When we can leave Poinciana, we will take Keith and Allegra with us to some suburb of New York or Washington, where we can find a smaller house, and live the sort of lives that will better suit us all.

Though I know we will return. Allegra must have her say about what will be done with Poinciana. She too wants it to be shared with those who come to visit in the future. Perhaps as Flagler's beautiful Whitehall is being shared.

But for now—for this little while—I am content to sit beside Jarrett, my hand warm in his, while Keith and Brewster play on the lawn nearby, rolling coconuts. I am content to experience these last peaceful moments at Poinciana.

We can never forget what has happened here, but there are good new memories to be made, and so much lies ahead for all of us.

CURRENT CREST BESTSELLERS

"And in chute number four, we have Sam McPhee,"
said the announcer over the PA system.

The world stopped turning.

Applause erupted from the bleachers. Michelle stood at the rail and gripped the rungs hard. She prayed she heard wrong. But she knew she hadn't. Oh, God. *Sam.*

Michelle looked at the chute at the end of the arena, and there he was. From a distance, he resembled any cowboy on a quarter horse. Yet she knew him. Knew the tilt of his head, the set of his shoulders, the fringe of sandy hair touching his collar. Sam appeared leaner, stronger, and quicker than ever. He retained that unique grace of movement she recalled so well. The years had hardly left a mark on him.

Michelle stared, spellbound, unable to move. He still had that slightly crooked grin that had once made her heart melt . . .

ALSO BY SUSAN WIGGS

Passing Through Paradise

The You
I Never Knew

Susan Wiggs

GRAND CENTRAL
PUBLISHING

NEW YORK   BOSTON

This book is a work of fiction. Names, characters, places, and incidents are the product of the author's imagination or are used fictitiously. Any resemblance to actual events, locales, or persons, living or dead, is coincidental.

Copyright © 2001 by Susan Wiggs
All rights reserved. Except as permitted under the U.S. Copyright Act of 1976, no part of this publication may be reproduced, distributed, or transmitted in any form or by any means, or stored in a database or retrieval system, without the prior written permission of the publisher.

Grand Central Publishing
Hachette Book Group
237 Park Avenue
New York, NY 10017
Visit our website at www.HachetteBookGroup.com

Grand Central Publishing is a division of Hachette Book Group, Inc. The Grand Central Publishing name and logo is a trademark of Hachette Book Group, Inc.

The publisher is not responsible for websites (or their content) that are not owned by the publisher.

Printed in the United States of America

First Printing: January 2001
First Special Price Edition: July 2008
Reissued: March 2011

10 9 8 7 6 5 4 3 2 1

To the women of my tribe:

my grandmother Marie
my mother Lou
my sister Lori
my daughter Elizabeth
who understand the necessary labors of loving

"Most of us become parents long before
we have stopped being children."

—Mignon McLaughlin,
   The Second Neurotic's Notebook (1966)

Acknowledgments

Writing a book is a joyous act, but it's also a lonely one. The support, advice, and fellowship of professional advisors and friends anchor, motivate, and inform me, and for this I'm deeply grateful. In particular, to Robert Gottlieb and Marcy Posner of the William Morris Agency for pushing me off in a new direction, to Joyce, Christina, Betty, Barb, and Alice for reading the manuscript with open minds and blood-red pencils, to Kristin, Jill, and Debbie for moral support, to my gifted editor, Claire Zion, who held up the mirror that transformed this work, and to Sara Schwager for careful copyediting, to Sandra Brashen, M.D., Leslie Townsend, Peggy Moreland and Curtiss Ann Matlock for technical advice, and most particularly to Donna Roberts, who gave her father the gift of life and generously shared her story.

Saturday

Chapter 1

After seventeen years, Michelle Turner was going back. Back to a past she didn't want to remember, to the father she barely knew, to the town where she grew up too fast, fell in love too hard, and wound up pregnant and alone.

During the long drive from Seattle to Montana, she rehearsed—under her breath so Cody wouldn't hear—what she would say when she got there.

"Hello, Daddy." Funny how she still thought of him as Daddy, even though he'd never been much more than a picture on the wall or sometimes a face on the TV screen late at night when his old movies played. "Sorry I didn't come sooner..." Sorry... sorry... sorry. All those regrets. So many of them.

Sorry wouldn't do. Gavin Slade—her father had kept

his professional name after retiring—knew damned well what had kept her away so long.

She flexed her hands on the steering wheel of the Range Rover and glanced over her shoulder at her son in the backseat. Cody was lost in the space between the headphones of his Discman. Maybe I'm the one who's lost, she thought. Here she was, thirty-five years old and the mother of a teenager, and the thought of facing her father made her feel like a kid again. Defensive. Powerless. Inadequate.

The Washington landscape roared by as she drove eastward, heading toward a place where she'd find no welcome. She and Cody had left their waterfront town house before dawn. The lights had still been shining in the steel skeleton of Seattle's Space Needle. By sunup, the Cascade Range had given way to rounded hills and scrubby flatland, then finally to high plateaus, a bare and colorless midwinter moonscape, a neutral zone.

She saw nothing out her window to interest the eye, nor to offend it.

Long ago, she used to be an artist, painting in savage color with emotions that spilled unrestrained over the canvas, dripping off the sides, because her feelings could not be confined to a finite space. But somewhere along the way she had reined in those mad and glorious impulses, as if a thief had come in the night and stolen the dreams inside her and she hadn't noticed they were gone until too late.

All that remained of the wild soul of her younger days was a cold, mechanical talent and a photographic eye. Airbrush and mousepad had replaced paint and canvas.

Her subjects had changed, too. She used to create art with passion and purity, whether it be a horse on her father's ranch or an abstract scramble of feelings. Inspiration used to govern her hand, and something far more powerful ignited her spirit. Once seen or imagined, the work rushed from her, generated by a force as strong as the need to breathe.

Now subjects came assigned to her by memo from the ad agency where she was up for full partner. She used a computer to design and animate dancing toilet brushes, talking dentures, or an army of weed-killer bags marching toward a forest of weeds.

Tugging her mind away from thoughts of work, she clicked on the wipers to bat away a few stray snow flurries. The day wore on. Spokane passed in a whisk of warehouses and industrial smokestacks. The interstate arrowed cleanly across the panhandle of Idaho. Between empty stretches of highway lay glaring commercial strip centers, tractor barns and silos, wood-frame houses huddled shoulder to shoulder against the elements. Deeper accumulations of snow formed crusty heaps on the side of the road. East of Coeur d'Alene, the landscape yielded to endless stretches of nothingness.

The monotony of the drive, and her purpose for racing across three states, caused an almost painful tectonic shift in her thoughts. Memories drifted toward dangerous places. Against her will, images from the past turned the barren snowscape to brilliant summer.

She saw herself as she was at eighteen. A little breathless at everything life had to offer. A little scared, but mostly happy and secure in her world. She finished high school with honors she didn't care about, a raw talent she didn't appreciate yet, and no sense of impending disaster. Her mother's cosmetic surgery was supposed to be routine. No one even considered the possibility that Sharon Turner would die from the complications.

In a shockingly short span of time, Michelle had found

herself alone and motherless—suddenly in need of the father she barely knew. She had expected him to hustle her off to college and breathe a sigh of relief when she was gone, but instead he'd surprised her. He had invited her to take a year off before college and spend the time with him in Montana. A year to grieve for her mother and to learn who her father was.

In that one brief season she experienced the events that were to shape her life: She learned what it was to be a motherless daughter. She fell in love. She became a painter. Not necessarily in that order. Everything sort of happened simultaneously. Even now, the years-old bittersweet ache rose as fresh as yesterday. It shouldn't still hurt, but it did, even though he was gone, long gone, from her life.

Except for the daily reminder he had left her.

She glanced into the rearview mirror again. Cody, who was sixteen and impossible, hadn't moved from his long-bodied position in the backseat. A tinny beat of heavy-metal music escaped from his headphones. He stared out at the endless swags of electrical lines strung along poles that bordered the highway. When a green-and-white sign welcomed them to Montana, his only reaction was to blink and shift position.

A billboard with a nauseating cartoon cowboy invited them to "Stop N Eat" in one mile.

"You hungry?" She raised her voice so he would hear.

He stuffed a wad of Fritos into his mouth. "Nope," he said around a mouthful of food. The roadside café, lit up by neon wagon wheels, disappeared in a smear of artificial light.

Just for a flash, she saw him as a toddler, cramming Cheerios into his cheeks like a baby squirrel. It seemed like only yesterday that he was her Cody-boy in Oshkosh overalls, with milk dribbling from his chin. That child was gone from her life now, she realized with a lurch of regret in her chest. He had slipped away when she wasn't looking. He'd vanished as swiftly and irretrievably as if he had wandered off at an airport, never to be found. In his place was this cynical, smart, exasperating stranger who seemed determined to push every button she had.

His sheer physical beauty then, as now, took her breath away. Only back then, she could tell him how adorable he was to her.

Now she could tell him nothing.

Cody had begged to stay in Seattle while she made this trip alone. He claimed he'd be fine, staying by himself at the town house. As if Michelle would consent to that.

Cody had even suggested that Brad could look after him.

Right. Brad couldn't handle Cody. Or wouldn't. And she was in no position to expect that level of support from Brad, their relationship notwithstanding. Her entire life was on hold until she dealt with her father.

A semi swung out and passed her, blasting its air horn. No speed limit in Montana, she recalled, and here she'd been dutifully doing sixty-five.

Life had trained her well for duty.

Defiantly, she pressed the accelerator. Sixty-five, seventy, seventy-five. She reveled in the speed, in the hum of the Rover's tires on cold bare pavement. Everything passed in a wavy smudge—streaks of cottonwood groves, shale rock ridges, coulees and brushy creeks, the blur of avalanche fence traversing the high meadows. The wind blew a dusting of snow along the highway. The snakelike motion and the subtle flickers of muted color were oddly exhilarating, and for a while she simply emptied her mind and drove.

The landscape lifted, a subtle change at first, but before long they would reach the high country of serrated crags, endless valleys, hanging alpine lakes. A chill of anticipation prickled her skin. Before long they would be at Blue Rock Ranch.

At Missoula, they turned northward, passing a giant statue of a Hereford bull at a combination tourist shop, café, and gas station.

"We're not in Kansas anymore," she murmured to Cody, but he didn't hear.

The Wild West kitsch was a sign that they had entered a different zone entirely, a land where the cowboy myth revolved around the solemn rites of rope and leather, where a sense of place and tall, endless skies surrounded and seduced her. Some said Montana was an empty land, but that wasn't quite right. It was just that the space was so vast it expanded the soul. She felt herself being drawn toward an encounter she had resisted for years. She tensed, unable to enjoy the beauty because this landscape held too many reminders of her past.

Highway 83 took them along the final leg of the journey. Against the brooding afternoon sky rose the peaks of the Swan and Mission Mountains. Shadows flickered in and out of coulees and valleys, creating a palette of sage and ocher and mysterious, restful earth tones that had no name.

"Cody, look!" She pointed out the side window. A huge herd of elk, winter migrants from the high country, grazed on the scrub-covered hills.

He stared at the milling herd, then yawned.

Well, what did she expect? "Gee whiz, Mommy" from a sixteen-year-old?

But oh, she wanted to share this with him, this sense of wonder inspired by the wild animals, the deep conifer forests and staggering snow-clad mountain peaks. A jewel-like chain of lakes bordered the highway. She wanted to tell him the lakes were formed as flood depressions in glacial moraines, filled when giant chunks of ice melted in each depression.

She wondered if that was what happened to people: When loss created a void that stayed empty too long, did the space fill up with ice?

They reached the turnoff for Crystal City, and the road began to climb in a series of sharp twists up into the mountains. Glacial violence made this harsh, craggy landscape as resistant to invasion as any man-made fortress. It took a special skill to breach it.

She hadn't driven in snow in ages, and the Range Rover fishtailed a little.

"Nice move, Mom," Cody observed from the backseat.

She gave silent thanks for the Rover's four-wheel drive. The tires gripped the sand-sprinkled snow. Forced to a Sunday-drive crawl, she saw everything with crystalline clarity. Open rangeland and broad meadows flowing past. A ring of mountains surrounding the valley like the walls of a mythical stronghold. Every tortuous inch of this road was familiar to her, so familiar that it made her eyes ache.

The valley slumbered in midwinter splendor, as if the entire landscape was holding its breath, waiting for the far-distant springtime.

She read the names on every rural mailbox they passed—Smith, Dodd, Gyenes, Bell, Jacobs. Most people who settled in the area seemed to stay forever. Each farm lay in perfect repose, a picture waiting to be painted: a white house with dark green shutters, a wisp of smoke twisting from the chimney, windowpanes glowing at the first touch of twilight.

There was a time when this sight had pierced her in a tender spot. She had painted this very scene long ago. Her brush had given life to the hillocks of untouched snow, to the luminous pink of the sunset, and to the fading sky behind alpine firs with their shoulders draped in white and icicles dripping from their branches. On a poorly prepared canvas with second-rate paints, she managed to convey a sense of soaring wonder at the world around her. It was a good painting. Better than good. But young. Impossibly, naively young as she had never been since the day she left this town in anguish and disgrace.

She wondered what had become of that painting. A part of her insisted that it was important to know. Creating that picture had been a defining act for her. It had opened a window into her future and sent her dreams off in a direction that would bring her joy and heartbreak for the rest of her life.

She peeked at Cody to see his reaction to their arrival. He stared out the window, his hands playing the air drums in his lap. His narrowed eyes were filled with nothing but indifference. She shouldn't be surprised. Indifference and contempt were the only emotions he exhibited these days.

A fading Rotary Club sign marked the city limits.

I'm back now, really and truly back. She knew it was just her imagination, but she heard a rush of wind as she felt herself going forward . . . into the past.

Across the Lions Club sign stretched a banner announcing the WINTER ROUNDUP—MARCH 2–3.

Great. That meant she wouldn't find her father at home. As the leading rodeo stock contractor in the state, he was bound to be at the arena. She punched his number into her cell phone—Lord, did *any*one but her father keep the same number for twenty-five years?

"Blue Rock." A young voice, not her father's, answered. One of his personal assistants, she supposed.

"Is Gavin in? This is . . . his daughter, Michelle Turner."

A pause. "I'm sorry, he's out for the evening. He was expecting you tomorrow, ma'am."

"Is he at the arena?" she asked.

"Yes, ma'am."

She supposed she could go to his place, sit, and wait for him, but she was too edgy to put the meeting off any longer. The entire town would witness their reunion. Would anyone remember her, and what had happened that year? Would heads shake and tongues wag? Would they look at her son and exchange knowing glances?

The next road sign posted a greeting from the Calvary Lutheran Church: YOU'RE ENTERING GOD'S COUNTRY.

"I'll find him there, then." She hung up the phone.

Main Street stretched before her, cold and straight as the barrel of a rifle. She passed the saddlery with its false log façade, Ray's Quik Chek, the Northern Lights Feed Store and Café, the Christian Science Reading Room, LaNelle's Quilt and Fabric Shoppe, a bank, and a picket-fronted bar that hadn't been there seventeen years ago. Blue-and-white signs pointed out the turns to the county hospital and the library.

On the other side of town was a flat-roofed restaurant hunched atop a knoll and surrounded by eighteen-wheelers with their running lights on—the Truxtop Café. She winced, recalling the last time she had set foot in that place.

Crystal City was a part of Michelle Turner, no matter how hard she tried to forget that fact.

Every once in a while she used to fantasize about coming back, but in her mind it was always a triumphant return. Not like this. Not with her heart frozen, her world in disarray, and her purpose to save the life of the father she hadn't seen in seventeen years.

Chapter 2

S am McPhee stared out the window at the ripples of snow on the hills behind his house. Though it was a familiar sight, he lingered there, watching as the last light of day rode the broken-backed mountains. The sight was a restful thing for a man to hold in his chest. In his youth, he'd carried the image with him no matter where he went, from Calgary to Cozumel, and when the time came to figure out where home was, he didn't need to look any farther than these hills.

He adjusted his hat and flexed his fingers into a pair of gloves. He straightened up and hitched back his hip, stomping his foot down into the boot, a characteristic gesture caught dozens of times by rodeo photographers.

Sam was a hard-bitten man, a loner who depended on no one, but sometimes the loneliness howled through him. Sometimes he wished he had someone to share these moments with, someone he could take by the hand, and say, "Look up at the hills tonight. Look at all those colors." After such a long time on his own, it shouldn't matter. But every once in a while, in the empty hover of time between evening and twilight, it did.

He flicked off most of the lights in the house, leaving one burning on the porch.

His boots crunching on the frozen drive, he went out to finish loading his trailer: saddle, tack, rope, blankets, Yellow Arrow liniment, an extra pair of gloves. These things were sacred to him and he handled them with the reverence and care of a priest performing the rites of consecration. They were the trappings of something so much a part of him that he couldn't even really think of it as a sport. Rodeo. His second love.

The sharp cold air needled his lungs as he crossed the yard to the bunkhouse, a squat log dwelling the former owners had remodeled into a guesthouse. Sam's partner in the horse ranch lived there now. He pounded on the door, then opened it. "Hey, Edward, you about ready?"

"Coming, coming. Hold your horses."

"My horses are already trailered, no thanks to you, pal."

"Yeah, well, I was busy," Edward called from the back bedroom.

"Did Diego get those stables done?" Sam closed the door behind him to keep in the heat from the woodstove.

"Diego took off. Got a job in a restaurant up at Big Mountain."

"Damn. That's the second stable hand we've lost this month."

"What you need is a slave," Edward called.

"Last time I checked, it was against the law to keep slaves."

"In this society," Edward said, "we call them kids."

"Yeah, well, I don't happen to have any handy." Sam didn't let himself dwell on it. "I guess I'll call Earl Meecham, see if one of his boys'll work after school each day."

Edward Bliss came out into the timber-ceilinged hall, a stack of folded blankets in his arms. Sam's partner was five-foot-two, half Salish Indian, and one hundred percent hell-raiser.

"What's with the blankets?" Sam asked.

"Ruby Lightning wove them. Asked me to put them out at the bake sale table tonight."

They climbed into the old Dodge truck, shivering against the chilled vinyl seats. The engine coughed in protest, then turned over with a flatulent blast of exhaust. Sam put it in gear and eased down the gravel drive. A thread of fiery orange sunset stitched across the peaks of the Mission Range. Foothills shadowed the lower pastures in shades of purple. The landscape looked bleak and cold, beautiful in a way few could admire.

He followed the dark rein of the road, glancing in the side mirrors to check the trailer. Rio and Zeus were probably dozing. The big quarter horses were used to the routine of loading up, driving, then waiting in the holding pen for a lightning ride that, in the old days, used to determine whether or not Sam got to eat that week.

"So what's Ruby up to lately?" he asked.

Edward took out a stick of Juicy Fruit, offering Sam the pack. "You ought to call her up and ask her."

Sam folded the gum in half twice and put it in his mouth. "Maybe I will. She doing all right?"

"You could ask her that, too."

An English teacher at the local high school, Ruby Lightning was also a single mom and an activist in the

Kootenai tribal government. She was scrubbed, earthy, and available, living in a frame house just a quarter mile down the road. They'd had some good times in the past, shared a few laughs, and could have shared more if he'd been so inclined.

Sam had simply stopped calling her. He wasn't proud of the way he drifted in and out of relationships. He'd tried marriage once and discovered it was a bad fit—like boots that were too tight. He didn't need a shrink to explain the parallels between his failed romances and his lousy childhood.

"How's that daughter of hers?" Sam wondered aloud.

"Molly's in the barrel-racing competition for sixteen-and-under."

"No kidding." It seemed only yesterday that he'd met little Molly Lightning, a dark-eyed waif, completely devoted to an old Welsh pony Ruby had bartered from Sam. Now Molly was nearly grown, slim and lithe as a bull-hide whip, probably leaving the halls of Crystal City High littered with broken hearts. Christ, where did the years go?

Like the best horses Sam had known, the girl had fire and heart. She also had, he recalled, a great mom.

Yeah, maybe he would give Ruby a call.

"How much does she want for those blankets?" he asked. Ruby was an expert weaver, using Montana-grown wool and traditional patterns and totems in her designs.

"Fifty bucks apiece," Edward said. "You want one?"

Sam grinned as he turned into the arena parking lot. "If I win the purse tonight, I'll buy them all."

"So you think you and old Rio'll win, eh, cowboy?" A gold tooth flashed in Edward's grin.

"Hey, we *always* win." It was a lie, and both he and Edward knew it. But there had been a time when Sam truly did rule the roping competitions. One winning ride used to net him $22,000, sometimes more. Most cowboys spent their winnings on silver-studded saddles and fancy rigs. Sam had used his for a different purpose altogether, a purpose that set him apart from other rodeo stars and made him something of an oddity in the circuit.

After he became a national champion, the trade sheets had a field day with him, focusing on the unorthodox choices he'd made. They'd documented his dazzling style, his natural grace in the sport. They'd published his hefty earnings. Plastered his face on calendars. For several seasons he'd been the golden boy of the circuit, the cowboy with a career plan.

What the reporters hadn't documented was the god-awful loneliness. The grinding tedium. The aches and bruises so deep they made him feel older than rock itself. It was a solitary life, traveling from show to show in a beat-up truck hauling a horse trailer, chasing down trashy, roped-out steers. But the prospect of another ride, another purse, had sustained him through the roughest times of his life.

"Nice rig," Edward said, as Sam drove past a white Ford 350 dually with a pristine white Cattleman trailer at least thirty-six feet long. Gleaming in the floodlights, the thing looked like a giant suppository.

On its side, in perfect custom commercial script, was a familiar logo in indigo paint: BLUE ROCK RANCH.

"Gavin Slade must've bought himself another new toy," Sam said. He used to resent everything Slade had and everything he was. But that was a long time ago.

Lately the whole town had been gossiping about Gavin in concerned undertones. Throwing his money away on expensive rigs wouldn't fix what was wrong. But it sure as hell wasn't Sam's place to tell Gavin that.

Edward spotted a cluster of women at the doorway

of the concession hall. "So hurry up and park already. I got people to see."

Despite his bantam-rooster stature, Edward Bliss was a ladies' man. He wrenched the rearview mirror toward himself, took off his Stetson, and checked his hair. He worked at flirting as seriously as he worked the ranch.

Sam yanked the mirror back and angled the truck toward his usual parking spot at the north end of the arena. "Damn," he said, cranking down the window and spitting out his gum.

"What is it?" asked Edward.

Sam glared at a late-model silver Range Rover with Washington plates. "Some idiot's parked in my spot."

Chapter 3

*T*his is totally bogus, Mom," Cody said through chattering teeth as they walked toward the main building of the arena. "I can't believe you're making me come to a Wild West show."

"It's not a Wild West show. It's a rodeo."

"I can't believe you're making me come anywhere near—shit!" Cody stopped walking and looked down.

"Horseshit, to be precise. Wipe your foot in the snow."

He got the worst of it off, grumbling the whole time. Somehow, it was impossible for Cody to be cool when he was scraping manure off his hundred-dollar Doc Martens.

"Can't we just go to his place and wait for him?" Cody demanded. "You said he had a guesthouse."

"Guesthouses—plural. My father never does anything part way." Blue Rock Ranch was the epitome of contemporary Western living: several thousand pristine acres complete with streams, ponds, and a compound of houses and barns that resembled a small, elegant village in a story-book setting. Some years back, *Architectural Digest* did a spread on the main house. And Michelle's father—never one to shun the public that validated his existence—made the most of it.

She had come across the article by accident. She'd been sitting at her drafting table at work one day, paging through magazines and looking at the ads to see what the competition was cooking up. Unsuspecting, she turned a page and found herself staring at a perfect shot of Blue Rock Ranch in high summer when avalanche lilies blanketed the hills and the grass was so green it hurt the eyes. The ensuing pages displayed room after perfect room. She recognized the window seat where she used to read and sketch, the rustic porch where she'd sat in the Stickley glider, spinning dreams she was absolutely certain would come true.

"So what say we go hang out in one of his 'plural' guesthouses?" Cody inspected the bottom of his shoe.

"No. We're here, and we're going to find my father."

"What's he doing out anyway? I thought he was sick."

"He's sick, all right, but not bedridden. His condition—"

"Jeez, it's cold." Cody stamped his feet on the straw-covered snow. "I guess if we're going in, let's go." He hunched his shoulders and headed for the main entrance. He never wanted to talk about her father's illness, never wanted to hear the details of what had to be done. He had a teenager's abiding horror of things medical and refused to consider his own mortality or that of anyone he knew.

Michelle bought tickets from a smiling girl with crooked teeth and loftily teased hair. "Right through there, ma'am." The girl gestured, displaying a lavishly fringed polyester sleeve.

"Don't say a word," Michelle warned Cody as they pushed through the turnstile. But the sarcastic look on his face said it all.

They found themselves amid a crowd of men in sheepskin-lined denim jackets and women in tight jeans with the creases ironed in blade-sharp. Michelle took a moment to inspect her son. Out of place would be putting it mildly. Torn black jeans with thick chains inexplicably draped from the pockets. A leather jacket studded with rivets along every seam. His hair was oddly colored—white sidewalls around his ears to show off a row of stainless-steel earrings, a long ponytail over the top and hanging down his back. The ends were still slightly green from when he'd dyed it for a Phish concert last summer.

Ah, but that face. Sullen, yes, but still so beautiful. *What happened to you, my precious boy?*

She resisted the urge to tell him to straighten his shoulders. Part of his determined coolness involved a studied slouch that gave his body the shape of a question mark.

Stand tall, like your father did.

Her stomach constricted nervously as they walked along the front of the bleachers in search of Gavin Slade. She'd see him soon. Good grief, what would they say to each other?

Their last face-to-face conversation had not been pleasant.

"I'm pregnant, Daddy."

Gavin had gone all stony-eyed. Then he'd said: "I'm not surprised. Your mother was careless, too."

"My *father* was careless," she'd shot back.

That same day, she'd left Blue Rock Ranch, vowing

never to return. But here she was, years later, her nerves strung taut with anticipation.

Heat blew into the arena through long tubes connected to generators. The smells of horse and leather and popcorn filled the air with poignant reminders of the past. Michelle couldn't help but notice the spot where she used to sit in the bleachers and watch the cowboys putting quarter horses through their paces. And there, in the middle of the arena, was the place where she'd lost her heart to a horse called Dooley.

She remembered the feel of the spirited animal beneath her as she learned the heart-tightening, dangerous joys of barrel racing. An experienced dressage rider, Michelle thought she knew how to handle a horse. But Dooley wasn't just any horse. He was a quarter horse bred for athletic ability, agility, and quickness, with Thoroughbred blood for extra speed and an explosive disposition. He took the turns around the barrels, expertly pivoting on one back leg. She still remembered the exhilaration of the flat-out run, the check at full speed, the turn 180 degrees around the barrel in a dizzying cloverleaf pattern. Across the years, she still could hear a voice calling encouragement, calling to the Michelle she used to be.

You're doing great for a city girl. Let him have his head. I think he likes you. . . .

Willing away the reminiscence, she watched a slim girl in black and turquoise ride into the ring on a piebald mare. Horse and rider flowed like water as they chased the cans. The girl, her shining black braid slapping as rhythmically as her quirt, wore a look of intense, exultant concentration on her face as she exited the course and the crowd applauded. The PA system blared an impressive time—17.5 seconds.

Ah, that smile, Michelle thought, studying the girl. Had she ever been that young? That happy?

Cody was watching the girl, too, and for once the expression on his face wasn't so snide. Even her urban animal of a son couldn't resist an event that featured beautifully dressed girls, powerful and good-looking horses, and fast action. Then he caught his mother studying him, and his rapt expression faded. "Well?" he asked. "You going to go find him or what?"

They passed the Chamber of Commerce table. She spotted a familiar face, and it gave her a start. Earl Meecham, owner of the Truxtop Café, was handing out flyers or coupons of some sort. He hadn't changed much— a little more paunch, maybe, a little more jowl. Shadowed by a ten-gallon Resistol hat, his grin reached from ear to ear.

Briefly, Meecham's eyes met Michelle's, but she could tell he didn't recognize her. She was a lot different from the girl with the long blond ponytail and the stars in her eyes.

Turning up the collar of her jacket, she moved toward the bleachers near the judges' booth. There, standing with one Lucchese boot propped on a hitch rail, a printed program clutched in his fist, was her father.

Instant panic set in. She had the urge to flee, to hide. *I can't do this.* Not here, not now. Yet at the heart of the panic lay something far more powerful. Love or hate or maybe a wrenching combination of the two. Resolve. *Duty.* She shoved the panic away.

Cody must have sensed her tension, because he stopped walking and followed the direction of her gaze. "That's him, isn't it?" His voice was bland, bored.

"Yes, that's him." The noise of the crowd and the

milling calves and horses fell away as she studied her father.

Gavin Slade. Thirty years ago he had been the hottest ticket in Hollywood, building a career on a body of tense, gritty Westerns and hard-edged police dramas. His rugged good looks had graced fan magazines and tabloids from *Life* to the *National Enquirer*. He was still good-looking, his face chiseled and lean, his air of command still evident, his magnetic charm still powerful.

At the height of his fame he had left Hollywood, migrating to Montana before it became fashionable to do so. He had discovered Crystal City during a location shoot and spent years building Blue Rock Ranch, becoming a rodeo stock contractor with an international reputation. Some of his bucking stock was better known than the champions who rode them. The people in the town lionized him. They considered him one of their own because he predated all the other California transplants. She'd never really known why he'd moved or what he hoped to find in Montana. Was he running away from the Hollywood rat race or was he running away from Michelle and her mother?

"He doesn't look sick," Cody observed, trying to appear casual but sounding relieved instead.

Gavin was a little too thin, perhaps, and maybe a yellowish cast haunted his complexion and the whites of his eyes, but Michelle allowed that the coloring might be from the arena lights. She took off her Gore-Tex gloves and stuck them in her pockets. Despite the midwinter cold, sweat dampened her palms. She wiped them on her jeans. "Let's go tell him we're here."

A short, bandy-legged cowboy carrying a stack of woven blankets jostled her as he passed, but she barely noticed. When she was a few feet away from her father, he glanced up. She didn't know this man well enough to read his expression. After all, she'd only spent half a year of her life with him. He'd always been a stranger to her. A stranger she called "Daddy."

"Michelle, honey." His trademark thousand-watt smile lit up his face, showing off his perfect teeth. "Come and give your old man a hug."

His arms went around her. She closed her eyes and inhaled. Clean laundry, breath mints, expensive aftershave. A strong embrace that enclosed her entirely. She told herself that it shouldn't feel this good. It shouldn't feel this right. He was a stranger. But when she drew back and looked up, tears swam across her eyes.

"Hi, Daddy."

"I didn't think you'd show up until tomorrow."

"We got an early start. The roads weren't bad, so we drove straight on through." She stepped back, blinking fast, refusing to shed the tears. "This is Cody."

Gavin's smile froze. She held her breath, hoping he'd look past the leather and chains, praying he'd see through the rebellious attitude. But Gavin had missed the wonder years with Cody, just as he had missed them with Michelle. He never knew the radiant joy of a toddler's face on Christmas morning, the triumphant exuberance of a nine-year-old who had just caught his first fish, the perfect tenderness of a boy holding a newly hatched duckling in his cupped hands, or his shy pride as he delivered breakfast in bed on Mother's Day.

Gavin saw only what stood before him now. His mouth took on the brittle edges of a false grin as he said, "Well, now. How do, youngster?" He stuck out his hand.

Cody took it briefly, then let go. "Okay."

Michelle found herself wishing she'd coached him for

this moment. Not that he would have listened, but shouldn't she have instructed him to be a little less sullen?

Awkwardness hung like a bad smell in the air. A dogie bawled in the pen outside. Michelle tried to will away her disappointment. What did she expect, that they'd fall into each other's arms just because one was her father, the other her son? That was something that might have happened in one of Gavin's old movies, not in real life.

She cleared her throat. "I knew we'd find you here."

"Wouldn't miss it, honey. Wouldn't miss it." He was the reason a town this size even had a rodeo. He needed a place to work his stock, and the arena had been built with civic funds—but with Gavin Slade in mind. He focused on the refreshment stand. "Can I get you two something to drink?"

"I think I'll go look around some." Cody jammed his hands into his pockets. His already sagging jeans lowered a notch. Michelle hoped her father didn't notice the *South Park* boxers that showed above the waistband.

"All right." She had promised herself she wouldn't try to force her father and son to get along. "Be back here in a half hour." As a reflex, she almost told him to stay out of trouble. She bit back the words. He generally took her warnings as invitations to step out of line. Watching him saunter away, she said, "I think he's a little tired and cranky from the long drive."

"How about you?" Gavin asked. "Can I get you something—coffee? A beer?"

"I'm fine."

He touched her shoulder. "Michelle. I feel stupid saying thank you for coming. How the hell can I thank you?"

She felt the color rise in her face. "Don't even try. I'm here. I'm going to help." She was filled with an impulse to milk this occasion, to bask in his gratitude. She was clearly the martyr here. She could use this to stitch together their tattered relationship.

But the impulse faded. That wasn't her purpose here.

"Help? Is that what you call it?"

"What would you call it, Daddy?"

"Hell, I don't know." He took off his hat and scratched his head. His hair was as thick and abundant as ever—but it had turned snow-white.

She hadn't pictured him white-haired. When she had reached him by phone, hearing his voice for the first time in seventeen years, she had envisioned the young, vital man he'd been during her eighteenth summer.

"I never meant for you to find out about my condition, Michelle," he said. The gravelly waver in his voice worried her. "And I sure as hell never meant for you to come riding to the rescue."

"This is one time you don't get to call all the shots, Dad." Out of the blue, a trust agreement had arrived in November. She'd been at work, fiddling on the computer with some coffee-bean graphics when a courier delivered a thick envelope bearing the logo of Blue Rock Ranch. She had nearly dropped the package in her surprise. Then she'd shuttered the blinds of her office, sat down at her desk, and opened the package. There was no cover letter, just little Post-it arrows indicating where to sign.

It had taken Michelle a few stunned moments to figure out what was going on. After nearly seventeen years of silence, her father was putting a staggering fortune in trust for her son.

She had broken a nail pecking in the phone number given on the trust agreement. The law firm in Missoula would tell her nothing, so she refused to sign the agreement.

That was when her father had called. He'd caught her

at home, loading the dishwasher and wondering why Brad hadn't phoned to tell her he'd miss dinner. The sound of her father's voice had banished her annoyance at Brad.

"Michelle, I've been sick."

She had closed her eyes and let out her breath. "What's the matter?"

"Damnedest thing. They call it end-stage renal failure."

"Kidney failure?"

"Yep. I had a spell of strep and ignored it, let it go on too long. There's a rare complication called glomerulonephritis—that's what developed. So far the tabloids haven't picked up on it, but the buzzards are circling."

The hated tabloids. They had made her childhood, as the daughter of a matinee idol, a nightmare. "So what's going to happen?"

Long hesitation. "I've started dialysis."

"Is there a cure?"

"Well, sort of."

"What's that supposed to mean, sort of?"

"My specialist in Missoula says I need a transplant."

"A kidney transplant." Comprehension burst over Michelle in a blaze so bright that she flinched. "From a living donor, right?"

"No. I'm on a waiting list for a cadaver."

Hearing the words, Michelle had the distinct sensation of stepping off a cliff. The knowledge of what she had to do came swiftly, pushing up through her like a geyser—unstoppable, filled with its own energy. She backed herself against the kitchen wall, sliding down it while the phone cord pulled to its limit. She knew she could stretch this strange moment out, make him talk to her, force him to ask, to beg, maybe. But instead, she shut her eyes and plunged right in.

"You don't have to wait for someone to die. I'll do it, Daddy," she practically whispered. "I'll give you a—" *Oh, Jesus.* "—a kidney."

"Michelle?" Gavin Slade's movie-idol voice beckoned her back to the present. "If you're tired from the drive, we can leave right now."

"No, let's stay. I'm too wired to relax just yet." She had gone through nine weeks of multiple preliminary screening exams at Swedish Hospital in Seattle: blood tests, chest X rays, detailed urinalysis, sonograms and MRIs. Against enormous odds, five out of six antigens matched. Physiologically, she was a near perfect donor for Gavin. Because her father's health was otherwise excellent, he made the ideal recipient.

He sent her a look she couldn't read. "We've got a lot to talk about."

At least he acknowledged it. At least he acknowledged that he'd broken seventeen years of silence only because he needed one of her kidneys.

Michelle stared at the arena ring where the barrels were being removed. She was determined to keep her face neutral. *I will not be angry at him,* she told herself, as she had told herself ever since learning of his condition. Anger had no place in this matter.

"So you remember how to get up to Blue Rock?" he asked.

"I could do that in my sleep, Dad. I might even let Cody drive. He got his license last summer, and he's been bugging me all day."

Gavin nodded to a passing couple, but they didn't stop to chat. The barrel racing had ended, and it was time for team roping. People took rodeo seriously in Crystal City, and there wasn't a lot of socializing going on. That would come after, when winners and losers alike headed out to the Grizzly Bar, a local honky-tonk, for drinking and dancing.

"So your boyfriend decided not to come?" Gavin asked.

"He's snowed under at work." She tucked her chin into the collar of her jacket. "His name's Brad, and he's more than a boyfriend. We've been together three years."

"Getting married?"

Her cheeks filled with color yet again. *Marriage.* That would force her and Brad to define their relationship. "We're in no hurry."

"Well, I'd like to meet him. So he's a pharmacist?"

"He's part owner in a big pharmacy franchise. He's helped me a lot—understanding your illness and what's going on with this transplant. At one time he was thinking of becoming a doctor—a surgeon—but pharmacy suits him better."

At least, that was what he always said. Michelle realized, with a start, that she really didn't understand what lay in Brad's heart. Odd. She usually thought of the two of them as knowing each other so well.

An announcement crackled over the PA system, and Gavin perked up. "Michelle, I have to go over to the chutes. I've got some new saddle broncs I'm testing. You want to come?"

"No, thanks. I was just going to see what Cody's up to."

"You do that." Gavin started to walk away, then turned back. "Michelle?"

"Yeah?"

"It feels good to have you home."

"Ditto, Dad." She forced the words out. Everything felt strange, dreamlike, with the shadows of a nightmare hovering at the edges. It was just nerves, Michelle told herself. If all went well, she'd be back in Seattle in a few weeks. "See you up at the house later."

Michelle had no trouble spotting Cody in the bleachers at the far end of the arena. Having never been to a rodeo before, he probably didn't realize it wasn't the best place to view the action.

She opened her mouth to call out, then stopped herself. She saw exactly why Cody had parked himself there. The barrel racer—the one in black and turquoise—sat a few rows over, sipping a Dr Pepper and talking to the girl with the teased hair and fringed shirt. They appeared completely unaware of Cody, but then, he appeared completely unaware of them. And Michelle knew damned well he was burning up with awareness.

Good, she thought. Maybe he'd finally get over his obsession with Claudia Teller, his girlfriend since the start of the school year. Claudia was a beautiful pale predator who never met Michelle's eyes and who answered her admittedly chirpy questions with monosyllables. Claudia had introduced Cody to cigarettes and Zima, and probably to things Michelle hadn't found out about yet. There was no creature quite so intoxicating as a provocative teenage girl. And no creature quite so malleable as a teenage boy on hormone overload. A girl like Claudia could make Eagle Scouts steal from their grandmothers. She wore makeup with the brand name Urban Decay. She had bottle red hair and kohl-deepened eyes, and she was as seductive as Spanish fly on Cody's defenseless adolescent libido. The most popular girl in the school, she wielded her power over him with casual ruthlessness.

Since Cody had taken up with Claudia, Michelle felt herself losing her maternal hold on him. Her son was a stranger. When he lied to her, she didn't know what to do.

Maybe the sojourn in Montana was a test period, Michelle thought. Could she win her son back, or was he already lost to her?

The barrel racer didn't look quite so predatory. Perhaps he'd see her in school. Against his will, Cody was going to have to attend Crystal City High during their stay in Montana because his grades had been terrible lately. He despised the idea, but his grade-level advisor had laid down the law. Attend school in Montana or repeat the term.

Michelle wandered off, pausing at the baked goods table to admire a plush wool Salish blanket. Handwoven in rich earth tones, the design touched a chord in her. She thought of Joseph Rain, the master painter she had once studied with. His work had held echoes of these ancient motifs. On impulse, she went out to the car to get her checkbook. There was no cold quite so piercing as the cold of a Montana winter night. The new snow was powdery and light beneath her boots. The Swan River was almost frozen over. Only a miserly trickle down the middle remained, though in spring it would transform itself into a roaring gush of white water.

When she returned to the arena, Cody had moved down one bench closer to the girls. The calf roping had started, bawling dogies and lightning-quick horses kicking up dirt as the cowboys flew at them. The chase lasted no more than a few seconds, but there was a peculiar drama in the frantic flight of the calf, the moment the rope drew taut, the cowboy vaulting from his saddle to bind the feet, the flagger's arm streaking up to mark the moment.

". . . and in chute number four, we have Sam McPhee," said the announcer over the PA system.

The world stopped turning.

"Ladies and gentlemen, please put your hands together for Sam McPhee. . . ."

Time, breath, heartbeat, everything seemed to stop.

Applause erupted from the bleachers. She stood at the rail and gripped the rungs hard.

Sam McPhee. Sam is here.

Michelle prayed she'd heard wrong. But she knew she hadn't. Oh, God. *Sam.*

"Six-time national champion Sam McPhee retired from the circuit in 1992, but we're lucky to have his local talent here in Crystal City. . . ." The announcer droned on, enumerating accomplishments that didn't surprise Michelle one bit. The only thing Sam McPhee hadn't done right was stick around.

After a few moments, she remembered to breathe again. She looked at the chute at the end of the arena, and there he was. From a distance he resembled any cowboy about to rope a calf. Battered hat jammed on his head, the brim angled down, piggin string clamped between his teeth, coiled rope clenched in his fist.

Yet she knew him. Knew the tilt of his head, the set of his shoulders, the fringe of sandy hair touching his collar. She couldn't help herself. She moved along the rail to get a closer look.

Sam nodded briefly, almost imperceptibly, at the guy in charge of the chutes. The calf lunged out. Sam followed on a glossy-hided, athletic quarter horse. He roped and dispatched the calf with a speed that drew gasps of admiration from the crowd. Admiration for a six-time national champion.

Michelle stared, spellbound, unable to move, a fly caught in a pool of honey. Sam appeared leaner, stronger, and quicker than ever. He retained that unique grace of movement she recalled so well. More than brute strength, it was an aura of raw ability coupled with arrogant confidence. He waved to the crowd. Everyone knew he'd made the winning time. Everyone knew he was the champion.

Sam had it in spades—the star power and magnetism of a true pro. She got a good look at him as he led his horse, showman-style, along the rail. The years had hardly left a mark on him. He still filled a pair of jeans like a Levi's poster boy. He still had that slightly crooked grin that had once made her heart melt. Accepting the accolades, he still had that funny, enchanting "aw-shucks" manner about him.

And he was still caught up in the shallow thrills of the rodeo, she reminded herself with a superior sniff as a leggy brunette handed him a trophy, accompanying it with a kiss.

Was it the rodeo that had seduced him away from her? That had made him disappear overnight? She had never seen him again. Until now.

"That was kind of cool, wasn't it?" Cody came up behind her.

"What, the calf roping?" Good God, thought Michelle. Panic beat so hard in her chest it felt like a heart attack. Cody didn't know. She never thought she would have to tell him. *Good God.*

"Yeah, the calf roping, whatever." He watched the handlers, done up like clowns, shooing dogies into pens. "It was pretty cool."

Was it genetic? Michelle wondered. "I thought you were into wholesome pursuits like slam dancing and body piercing."

"How about driving, Mom? Can I drive from here to your father's place?"

Michelle nodded, thinking irrationally that if she gave in, she wouldn't have to deal with the other. "All right. You can drive."

For a few moments longer, he watched Sam with interest. And why not? The tall cowboy, with his easy smile and smooth way with the ladies, was sure to appeal to a boy's imagination.

Her heart chilled, aching in her chest. Sam was here. Sam and Cody were both here. And they didn't know about each other.

Chapter 4

I t felt damned good to win. Winning always gave Sam a rush. Cheap thrills. They never lasted long, but they were easier to come by than the real thing.

"Nice ride." Edward Bliss fell in step with Sam while he walked Rio to cool out the big horse. "You done good, pardner." Beyond the paddock, some of the rigs were getting ready to leave, diesel engines idling.

"I guess I'll be buying all of Ruby's blankets." Sam led Rio in a wide circle. Steam rose from the quarter horse's body and plumed from his nostrils.

"You're too late. I just sold the last one. To a pretty blond lady I didn't recognize." Edward handed him a bottle of water.

"I assume you introduced yourself." Sam took a swig from the bottle.

"Nope. She was in a hurry. Had some whiny long-haired kid with her who kept saying it was his turn to drive."

"When you're a kid, it's *always* your turn to drive." Sam finished the water. Out in the parking lot, the sound of gunning engines roared. "So, you got a hot date?"

"Does a coyote have fleas?" Edward gestured at a plump, dark-haired woman in denims and a chinook jacket. She waved to him. "Pearl, from the bank. We're going up to Polson to have a few beers. Want to come?"

Sam grinned, thinking about the suggestion Loretta Sweeney had whispered in his ear when she'd given him the winner's trophy and check. "I've had a better offer."

Edward read his mind. "Loretta's a slut."

"That's what I like about her."

Edward took off. Sam bent to put on Rio's boots—he always put boots on the horses so they wouldn't damage their hooves in the trailer—when the whir of a spinning tire made the horse shy.

"Damn it." Sam dodged an iron-shod hoof.

A second later, he heard the unmistakable metal-on-metal crunch of two vehicles meeting. Rio grunted and flattened his ears. Looping the horse's lead around a rail, Sam went to see what the problem was.

"Shit," he said. "Shit, shit, shit."

The yuppie Range Rover from Washington had backed into his trailer. Its bumper was hooked into the rear, brake lights casting an eerie red glow over the dirty, churned-up snow. As Sam stalked across the parking lot, the yuppie gunned it again. With a wrenching sound of metal, the bumper unhooked. The Rover lurched forward.

Sam put two fingers to his lips and pierced the air with a loud whistle. "Hold on there!" he yelled, breaking into a run.

A few people stopped, shaking their heads when they

saw the damage. The driver's side door of the Rover opened and out jumped a slender teenage boy.

Great, thought Sam, eyeing the studded jacket and sleek ponytail. An underage driver to boot. He could see someone in the passenger seat of the Range Rover. The kid's date, maybe?

"Guess you had a little trouble backing up there," he said, keeping calm with an effort.

The kid tossed him an insolent glance. Light glinted off a small silver nose hoop. "Guess so. Sorry about your trailer. Insurance'll cover it."

The boy's nonchalance grated on Sam. Hell, he looked too young to have a license. A learner's permit—possibly.

When Sam thought of the time and expense repairs would take, he got more pissed. From the corner of his eye, he could see the boy's passenger rooting around in the glove compartment.

"Yeah, insurance'll cover it," Sam said, "but only after I fight with them for about six months. Tell you what— this looks like a few hundred dollars' worth of damage. You could come out to my place and work it off."

"Work it—"

"You know, work. Like with a shovel and a ton of horseshit." Sam dug in his pocket for a card with the ranch name and address on it. He held it out. "You show up to-morrow, and you can get started on the stables."

The kid didn't take the card. "Hey, I'm not from around here—"

"I never would have guessed," Sam snapped. "Look, you be there or—"

"He'll be there," said a soft voice behind Sam.

He froze, feeling a jab of premonition. *That voice.* He knew that voice. It was something the heart remembered long after the mind forgot.

He made himself turn slowly to face her. Awareness exploded over him, but there was only silence, and the smell of snow and exhaust, and a vague notion of folks walking to their cars in the parking lot. Each moment seemed endless, drawn out, excruciating. Denial reared in his chest, but he couldn't refute what his eyes were seeing.

"Michelle?"

"Hey, Sam." She had that same low, sweet voice and wide, fragile eyes, the same soft blond hair, cropped short now but curling in the same breezy way around a face he'd never forgotten.

The boy blew on his hands to warm them. "You guys know each other?"

"Reckon we do," said Sam, his gaze never leaving Michelle. Holy Christ, *Michelle Turner*. When he had first met her, she was the prettiest thing he'd ever seen in his life—long yellow ponytail, big blue eyes, a smile he liked better than air. Now she wasn't pretty anymore. She was beautiful, the way a goddess is beautiful, the way the moon is beautiful. Perfectly formed, luminous, chilly, and . . . distant. That was the word for it. Distant.

Where've you been, Michelle?

The unexpected quake of emotion pissed him off. He didn't need this, didn't want the memories she stirred up. Turning away from her, he tucked the card back in his pocket. "Look, kid, forget about the trailer."

The boy let out an explosive breath of relief. "Hey, thanks. That's pretty cool of you—"

"He'll be at your place tomorrow." Michelle's voice was flat, neutral. Sam had no idea what he was seeing in her eyes, her face. A stranger. Michelle had become a stranger. The person who had once been the sole keeper of every hope and dream he'd ever had was now a complete mystery to him.

"You don't have to—" he began.

"Yes, he does, and he will."

"Mo-om," the kid said.

What an annoying little shit. Sam got prickly hearing some kid call Michelle "Mom." He felt even more weird thinking that somewhere in the world there was a guy the kid called "Dad." So where was he? Sam wondered. He knew he wouldn't ask.

"Now," she said, "where's your 'place'?"

He reluctantly held out the card. Their hands touched as she took it and stuck it in her pocket. A cold, impersonal brush of the fingers. A stranger's touch. What was he expecting? Fireworks? Electricity? Christ, violin music?

She wore a thick, artsy-looking ring that was more sculpture than jewelry. A wedding band? He couldn't tell. He wouldn't ask.

"I'll have Cody there in the morning," she said. "Is nine o'clock all right?"

"Yeah, okay. Nine o'clock."

"Mom," the kid said. "Do I really have to—"

"Get in the Rover, Cody," she said brusquely. "And *I'll* drive."

Chapter 5

M ichelle shivered against the cold as she walked across the guest compound to the main house at Blue Rock Ranch. The moon was out, dazzling above the peaks of the Swan Range. She could see all the lunar craters as if through the lens of a telescope. Icy silver light poured invasively across the snow-covered meadows.

She experienced a gut reaction she hadn't felt in a very long time. It was a strange, impossible-to-forget combination of pain and ecstasy that always preceded inspiration. Artist's inspiration. Joseph Rain, who had been her teacher that long-ago summer, called it the touch of the damned, because it hurt, it burned, it was beautiful.

When was the last time she'd felt this desire, this ache? This sharp need to create an image, to speak in color and shape when there were no words?

She couldn't remember, because she had learned to squash the feeling as quickly as it came over her. She didn't have time. She was too busy at work, too busy with Cody and Brad.

But here? Would she be too busy here? The thought of actually having time on her hands frightened her, it really did. Back in Seattle she took a certain comfort in having so much to do that she never found time to think.

At the moment she couldn't do anything *but* think. Sam McPhee was here. He had a ranch called, according to the business card he'd given her, Lonepine. It was located up the old logging road between two hanging lakes. A guy who wasn't supposed to amount to anything had a place of his own. And first thing in the morning, she had to take his son to see him.

She hugged herself, staring up at the white winter moon, wondering if he'd guessed yet. Wondering if he would stay up late tonight, thinking about the past.

The garden gazebo rose like an ice sculpture in the middle of the front yard. She had been sitting on the steps of that gazebo, drawing, the first time she met Sam. She remembered the quiet of that afternoon, the scratch of her pencil on the Firebrand tablet she held in her lap. Joseph Rain had called Montana a "place of great breathing," his apt phrase for the expansiveness of the landscape.

"Nice picture," said a voice behind her.

She froze, charcoal pencil in hand, at the sound of that voice. It was nice, a baritone, but youthful, too.

"You think so?" she asked, getting up. And it was him, just as she had suspected—hoped, prayed—it would be. The boy from the training arena. She'd spotted him the day she arrived. Her first glimpse of him had been from a distance.

He'd been working in a round pen with a mare on a

lunge rope. She had been watching from the porch. He wore scuffed boots and blue jeans, a plaid shirt and battered cap with the Big Sky Feed Company logo on it. He was tall and rangy, like Gavin's favorite trail horse. She knew, to the very depths of her eighteen-year-old soul, that no one in the entire universe had ever looked so good in a pair of Levi's.

Up close, she noticed that he had sandy brown hair, a lean, suntanned face, and eyes the color of her birthstone.

"Yeah, I think so," he replied. "Haven't had much call to look at art, but that's a fine picture."

She stuck her pencil behind her ear, suddenly self-conscious in her cutoffs and cropped T-shirt. "I'm Michelle."

"I know. I've seen you around with your sketchbook."

He noticed. Hallelujah, he noticed.

Michelle had been drawing ever since she was old enough to hold a crayon. It was all she ever wanted to do, and she excelled at it, blazing like a comet through high school classes and special courses she took outside of school. Her inspiration and talent had served her well when she went to Montana to spend that precollege year with her father. Montana seemed so huge and limitless that she got into the habit of drawing constantly just to feel a measure of control over something so overwhelmingly vast and wild. She drew everything: the placid bovine face of a cow; a line of trees along the creek with the stars coming out behind them; the silhouette of a mare and her foal on the slope behind the paddock; a common loon nesting in a marsh.

"I never go anywhere without my sketchbook," she said.

"I'm Sam. Sam McPhee. I work for your dad." He

grinned, and her heart began to melt. If she looked down, she figured she'd see it in a puddle like hot fudge at her feet.

"I know." She grinned back, hoping her neck didn't go all splotchy the way it usually did when she blushed.

"So you're an artist?" he asked. Not with the hefty skepticism a lot of people exhibited when she told them her ambition, but with genuine interest.

"I want to be." She gestured at the sketch. "This is practice. I want to paint for real."

"You mean like on an easel with brushes and a palette and a beret and stuff?"

She laughed. "Exactly. Well, maybe not the beret."

"So do it."

"Do what?"

"Paint for real. Don't just say you're going to. You can't be an artist if you don't paint, right?"

"Guess not." She scuffed her foot against the gazebo steps. "You ever heard of Joseph Rain?"

"Sure," Sam said. "He eats at the café where my mom works. I heard he lives out on the Flathead reservation, but he's a recluse."

"Well, he's just about the most famous painter in the West," she explained. "I came here to study with him." Her father had arranged it all. Though the artist rarely accepted students, Gavin had sent him a box of her sketches and attached a very large check. Mr. Rain had kept the sketches, returned the check, and agreed to work with her—for a fee, not a bribe.

"Yeah? I'd heard he was an artist or something."

"He did a series of paintings for the National Trust." In her mind's eye she could picture them—deep burning emotional scenes that haunted her long after she had walked away from them. "I'm lucky he agreed to be my teacher."

"Is that the best offer you've had all summer?"

"So far." She dropped her sketchbook. Klutz, she thought.

Both she and Sam reached for it, their hands touching. He gave an easy laugh, keeping her hand in his.

The sound of Sam McPhee, laughing. The feel of his hand, touching her. These were the first things about him that she had loved. In the years that ensued, they were the things she remembered more vividly and more frequently than she wanted to.

She wished she had never come back. How would she bear the beauty of this place with its pure light, its slashing cold, and now Sam McPhee? Gritting her teeth, she let herself into the main house. When she stepped inside, she remembered her first visit here, how grand and solid everything had looked. Back then, she'd had her own room upstairs. Now she and Cody occupied a guesthouse. Gavin thought Cody would feel more comfortable in his own space.

"I'll be right out," Gavin called from somewhere upstairs. "Make yourself a drink."

She crossed the living room—a Ralph Lauren ad in 3-D—and stepped behind the wet bar. On a polished shelf, she found a heavy crystal highball glass and shook some ice from the undersized freezer. As she perused the bottles of exotic, expensive whiskey and liqueur, she tried to get her thoughts in some sort of order.

She tended to put things into compartments. Here, in this box—worries about Cody. She spent a lot of time sifting through them, never getting to the bottom, because every day he came up with a new challenge, from asking to get his eyebrow pierced to wanting permission to go to an overnight rock concert.

In another box—work. The agency liked her because she did good work and kept her clients happy. This spring, she would make partner and would earn more money than she ever dreamed of. The other partners lived in fear that she would leave them for a bigger, more lucrative firm, taking her clients with her. But why go elsewhere? To draw bigger, more lucrative ads for fertilizer and tampons?

Another box—Brad. After three years together, they hovered in the same spot where they had begun. They'd bought side-by-side units in a tony Seattle town-house complex, their outdoor decks divided by a wall of cedar planks. They were socially compatible. Sexually compatible. Financially compatible. Rough when it came to Cody, because he and Brad didn't get along.

Now she had a couple of other boxes under construction. Her father, whose life depended on her giving him one of her kidneys, took up a lot of space in her thoughts. For most of her life, he had ignored her, and only when his survival hung in the balance did he acknowledge her existence. A psychiatrist would have a field day with the two of them, she reflected wryly. Sharing their flesh, an organ, the mysterious life force—so damned symbolic. And—she kept telling herself not to think this but she couldn't help it—it was *icky*. There, thought Michelle. I'm a terrible person. Acting like Mother Teresa on the outside, while the coward inside trembled in horror at the ordeal to come.

And now Sam. Good God, Sam McPhee.

"I don't need a drink," she muttered under her breath, regarding the array of bottles. "I need a twelve-step program."

"Try the Booker's. Used to be my favorite."

She whirled around, startled. "Daddy. I didn't hear you come down."

He winked, looking spruce in a thick terry-cloth robe and leather slippers. "Light on my feet."

Obediently, she poured a splash of Booker's over some crushed ice. The first sip brought tears to her eyes. "That's lighter fluid, Dad."

"Good, huh?"

She coughed a little, feeling the rich amber liquid burn her throat. "You want something?"

He held up a tumbler. "My trusty cranberry juice. I've been on restriction for a long time."

A long time. When had he first fallen sick? How long had he suffered with no one to talk to about what was happening to him? Michelle didn't know him well enough to ask.

They sat together in the sunken living room. Rustic millionaire, she mentally classified it. Muted evergreen-and-burgundy plaid, peeled lodgepole pine, a massive field-stone fireplace. She stared intently at the flames lapping at a big log and sipped her single-barrel bourbon.

"So here I am," she said, hopelessly inane.

"Here you are. My angel of mercy."

She blinked fast, taken aback by the bitterness in his voice. "You're mad at me?"

"Hell no, honey, I'm mad at the world. Have been ever since the frigging diagnosis. I failed the medical standard for renewing my pilot's license."

"Daddy, I'm sorry." Everyone knew how much flying meant to him. A week seldom went by that he didn't take off, even for a little while, in his beloved airplane. He had brought her to Blue Rock for the first time in his vintage

P-51 Mustang, modified to accommodate two seats, and she used to love flying with him.

"Do you still have your plane?"

"Yep. I keep the Mustang out at the Meridian County Air Park. And a biplane for stunts." He held up his glass. "Can't even have a drink with my long-lost daughter. The kidney specialist has some diet Nazi monitoring me almost twenty-four hours a day."

"Does it help?"

"Yeah, kept me off dialysis longer than it should have. The biggest culprit is protein—damned hard to stay away from. Cheating isn't an option, either. If the kidneys have to work extra hard, it just hastens the breakdown. I guess that's why I'm resentful. And because I wish I was brave enough to just shoot myself rather than take a goddamned *organ* from my own child."

"Stop it." Michelle was starting to worry, trying not to show it. "We already agreed it's the right thing to do."

He fell silent, staring at the fire in the grate. His famous profile was illuminated by kindly soft light. He still had the charisma that made him a beloved icon in the world of film and a stranger to his family. After a while he let out a heavy sigh. "Anyway—" he clinked his glass against hers "—welcome home, long-lost daughter."

"I was never lost, Daddy."

"You stayed away a long time."

"You should have invited me back."

"Didn't think you'd want to come." He rubbed his cheeks, looking no less handsome than ever. Lord, the man was an android. Dorian Gray with bigger shoulders. He never seemed to age. Even sick and white-haired, he appeared tanned and fit, mature yet ageless.

"Dad, you should have asked me to come back. Before it was too late, got too awkward."

"What would you have said?"

She laughed humorlessly into the crystal highball glass. "I'd have told you to piss off."

"That's what I figured."

They finished their drinks, and somewhere in the house a case clock struck eleven. All the things they weren't saying to each other—about Cody, about the transplant, and now about the surprise cameo appearance of Sam McPhee—hung like cobwebs in the air between them. Why hadn't Gavin told her the father of her child was in Crystal City?

The prospect of an explosive, accusatory conversation held no appeal at this late hour. Without even speaking a word, they made a tacit agreement to avoid touchy subjects—for now.

Gavin looked tired. Frighteningly tired. And she could see, hidden in the folds of his robe . . . *something*.

"It's a sac of dialysis fluid," he said.

Her cheeks heated. "I didn't mean to stare."

"Not to worry. I don't have much dignity left since I got sick." He smiled, but there was a hardness in his face that gave away his fury and frustration. "The stuff in the sac flows through an abdominal shunt. Want to see?"

"Dad, please."

"Okay, I apologize. I stare at it too, sometimes, like it belongs to someone else. Can't believe my own body's turned traitor on me."

They sat for long moments, sipping their drinks and watching the fire, not speaking. The silence swelled. Only in the mountains in winter, Michelle reflected, did the quiet have this all-pervasive quality.

Suddenly she realized what she and Gavin were doing. Another battle of wills. Who would admit to being tired first? Who would make the first move?

No more games. She yawned elaborately, stretching her arms behind her head. "The Booker's did the trick."

"Guess I'll hit the hay, too." Gavin got to his feet. He was too good an actor to look relieved, but she figured he was. "You sleep in, now, Michelle. Since I didn't expect you until tomorrow, I didn't make any plans."

"Plans?"

He cleared his throat. "You know . . . appointments."

"Oh." The impending procedure was becoming more grimly real to her with each passing moment. "We can talk about that tomorrow."

"You got everything you need in the guesthouse?"

"It's fine." She stood, feeling awkward. "Thanks for stocking the fridge." She wondered if she should kiss him good night. Self-consciously, she lifted up on tiptoe, gave him a peck on the cheek, and let herself out the front door.

As she crossed the silent, starlit compound, she knew she wouldn't be sleeping in tomorrow. She had to take Cody to work at Sam's place. She had to figure out how to tell her son who Sam was without destroying him, without destroying them all.

Sunday

Chapter 6

At 8:45, Sam heard the growl of a motor and the grind of tires over snow. Out in the yard, Scout, the Border collie who ruled the ranch, launched into a barking frenzy.

Sam had taken Loretta Sweeney home early last night. He'd been up since six, and felt all jumpy in his gut; didn't even want his morning coffee. Damn it, he was a grown man. The last thing in the world he should be doing was getting nervous over seeing an old girlfriend.

Except that the words "old" and "girlfriend" didn't seem to apply to Michelle. Though their love affair had burned like a forest fire half a lifetime ago, she didn't seem old at all. Just . . . different. He remembered a girl with yellow hair and a quicksilver smile. Now she seemed far away and sort of fragile. But still so damned beautiful. And as for the girlfriend part—you didn't call your first grand passion a "girlfriend." The term was too inadequate to cover the delirium, the ecstasy, the sweaty palms and fevered dreams of that lost, intense season.

The sound of car doors slamming made him wince. Shit. He *was* nervous.

Going to the window, he expected to see Michelle's Range Rover. Instead, he spied Ruby and Molly Lightning getting out of their old Apache pickup. Scout's "who-the-hell-are-you" barking changed to "I'm-all-yours" whimpers of ecstatic greeting.

Sam gritted his teeth and tried to smile. Ordinarily he'd be glad to see Ruby and her daughter. But it wasn't an ordinary day. He was expecting Michelle, and he didn't look forward to entertaining her, the kid, and now these two.

He went out onto the porch. Sunlight glinted off the snow in the yard and driveway. A row of icicles dripped from the eaves. The Border collie nuzzled Molly's hand.

"Hey, ladies," he said. "You're out bright and early this morning."

Ruby propped an elbow on the battered hood of the pickup. She had a broad, pleasant face, one gold tooth, and an ease around people that made her a popular teacher at the high school. "Hey, Sam," she said.

"Hiya, Sam." Molly scratched the dog behind the ears. "Nice ride last night."

"You, too," he said.

Ruby opened the door of the truck and started rummaging around. "I heard you wanted to buy a blanket."

"Ma'am, I wanted to buy them all."

Molly rolled her eyes.

"I did," Sam said. "It gets mighty cold up here in the winter."

"Well, I brought you one." She held out a folded blanket.

At that moment, another car turned off the highway and started up the drive. The Range Rover. Scout launched into her watchdog routine.

Sam took the blanket from Ruby. The thick wool felt warm against his hands. Plenty warm. "Hey, thanks." He reached into his back pocket for his wallet.

Ruby reached around behind him and grabbed his wrist, holding it firmly. "Sam McPhee, don't you dare. It's a gift because you never let me pay you for delivering Glenda's babies."

He laughed. "Glenda's an Irish setter. She didn't need much help."

"Whatever. The blanket's to say thanks."

Michelle parked and got out of her car. And there stood Sam with Ruby's arm halfway around him, her hand pressed against his hip pocket.

He stepped back. "Morning, Michelle."

She inclined her head politely. Distantly. "Hello, Sam." The collie hung back, head tilted to one side, waiting to see how friendly this one would turn out to be.

"This here's Ruby Lightning and that's her daughter Molly over there."

"Pleased to meet you." Although Michelle smiled readily, the temperature seemed to drop a few degrees. "Look, if this is a bad time—"

"Not at all. You ladies want to come in for coffee?"

Ruby shook her head, winking at him. "I better get going. We've got church this morning."

Molly walked over from the paddock adjacent to the barn. A few of the horses, their coats thick with inch-long hair, stood at the fence waiting for their morning feed. "I could stay and help out with the horses," she called out.

Then Michelle's son got out of the Range Rover, looking as sulky and undernourished as a Calvin Klein ad. Interest sparked in his eyes when he spotted Molly, but he was quick to hide it with a squint that reminded Sam eerily of Gavin Slade. The kid would probably love having her around all day.

"Not today, Molly, but thanks for the offer," Sam said. He didn't want her to have to put up with the little hoodlum.

"My son's name is Cody," Michelle said, motioning him over.

It occurred to Sam that he didn't know the boy's last name, or if Michelle had a married name now. The kid shook his hair back. Stuck his thumb in the top of his belt. "Hiya."

"Hi," Molly said, transparent in her interest. She regarded the kid with the same fascination Red Riding Hood had for the Big Bad Wolf.

Ruby climbed into her truck. "See you around. Nice meeting you both."

Molly took her time getting in. "'Bye, Sam. 'Bye, Michelle and . . . Cody." The smile she sent him was way more than the kid deserved.

As the truck pulled away, a sense of amazement crept over Sam. Michelle had been dead to him. For seventeen years she had been gone, as permanently and irrevocably as if she had been buried six feet under. Now here she was, back again in all her beauty and all her strangeness, and he found himself vacillating between elation and rage. He found himself with a hard-on that made him glad his jacket was zipped.

"Cody's ready to get to work," Michelle said.

"Is that right?" Sam asked Cody.

The kid shrugged, slouching in the time-honored fashion of teens with attitude. "Guess so."

Sam flicked his gaze over him from head to toe. Shining light-colored hair cut too long in some places, too short in others. A leather jacket that would get him knifed in certain neighborhoods. Black jeans and designer combat boots.

The humane thing to do would be to give the kid one of the Filson coveralls from the stable lockers, but Sam wasn't feeling too humane about this guy.

"Let's go to the barn," he said, putting on his John Deere cap. "I'll introduce you to Edward and he can get you started."

"Started on what?"

Sam thought of the heap of manure Diego had left unshoveled. "Oh, I've got a real treat for you, Cody."

He turned to Michelle, flashing her a grin. She blinked at him as if his smile startled her. "Go on inside, Michelle. Make yourself comfortable. There's coffee in the kitchen."

She opened her mouth to say something, then seemed to think better of it and went toward the house. He stopped for a second and looked at her on his porch, and their gazes caught and held.

Though he made no move, a part of him stepped back, and he caught his breath. Michelle, here at his house. Looking as pure and brittle as the sun-shot icicles that lined the eaves above her, a dripping frame of cold and light. Sam felt as if he was in the middle of a dream. This wasn't real. *She* wasn't real.

Just then, the sun won its battle with the ice, and the row of icicles crackled and fell, coming away in slow motion and then falling all at once, stabbing into the snow-covered hedge in front of the porch. The sudden, glittering tumult seemed to startle her into action. She gave a brief, taut smile and disappeared into the house.

Sam started toward the horse barn, the collie leaping at his side. He didn't look back to see if the kid was following.

Situated inside the barn door was an office with papers, certificates, and permits plastered all over the wall, a cluttered kitchenette and coffee bar, and a refrigerator with a keg tap on the door. A pellet stove heated the room.

Edward Bliss sat with his feet up on a battered metal desk, a phone cradled between his shoulder and his ear, and a beatific smile on his face.

"Morning, Romeo," Sam said.

"I'll call you later, darlin'," Edward crooned into the receiver. He hesitated, listening, and his grin widened as he hung up. "You took the purse last night, boss, but I was the one who celebrated."

"So what else is new?"

"That biff on the back of your trailer. Did you see that? Looks like some idiot nailed you last night."

"As a matter of fact . . ." Sam stepped out of the doorway and motioned the kid into the office. "This is Cody. He's going to be helping out around the place. Cody, this is my partner, Edward Bliss."

Edward glanced up distractedly. Then he did a double take, looking from Sam to Cody and back again, his eyes wide. "Jesus H. Geronimo Christ—"

"Something wrong?" Sam knew Edward didn't care for punks, but he'd never known his partner to make such a snap judgment. So the kid had hit the trailer, so he'd made a mistake. It wasn't the end of the world.

Edward stood up, gathering the papers on the desk into a stack. "Nope, not at all. Cody's going to take Diego's place, then?"

"That's what I figure. For a while, at least." Sam hadn't even had time to ask Michelle how long she'd be visiting.

Scout lost interest in the entire situation and trotted out to the yard. Edward kept staring at the kid as if to drill a hole through him. Cody stared back, eyes narrowed.

"All right." Edward snapped his suspenders and reached for his battered plaid coat, flecked with hayseed and oat grains. "Let's get started."

Most of the stalls were empty, the horses turned out for the day since it promised to be sunny. The barn had the feel of a cathedral. Daylight streamed through high windows under the eaves, and the echo of footsteps sounded loud in the hush.

"So what do I do?" Cody asked, dubiously eyeing the area. Mild suspicion tinged his voice.

Edward opened the door to one of the stalls. "Simple. You move the manure out and the cedar shavings in."

The kid swallowed, staring at the floor of the stall. "Just this one?"

"Nope." Sam gestured down the length of the barn. "What've we got here, twenty jugs?" Sam told himself not to enjoy this, but he couldn't help it.

"Great," said Cody.

"Don't go into this one without Edward or me present." Sam showed him a roomy stall in the middle. "That's Sylvia. She's expecting, and she's getting kind of cranky."

Cody peered over the top of the half door. The roan mare flared her nostrils at him and laid her ears back in warning. Her sides fanned in and out like a set of bellows.

"Yeah?" Cody asked with the first spark of interest he'd exhibited since seeing Molly.

"The foal could come tonight," Sam said. "Sylvia's

showing signs of her labor. We'll be bathing her today and getting the birthing stall ready."

The mare glared white-eyed at the stranger. The boy glared back. Sam added, "Just relax, act a little friendly, and she'll warm up to you." He made a clucking sound in his throat. The mare's ears eased up, and she stuck her head out of the stall. Cody hung back a moment, then put out his hand. The mare sniffed his shoulder. He rubbed her nose and cheek, hesitantly at first and then with more force.

"Don't put any cedar shavings in Sylvia's stall," Sam said. "Sawdust and chips are bad for the foal. Straw only. Edward'll show you, and you can help hose her down, too. But remember—she's cranky."

"Just wait till we give her that phosphate enema," Edward said.

Cody winced. "I can wait."

Edward held out a pair of leather gloves and rubber pac boots. "Put these on and let's get started."

Cody looked askance at the boots, but took them and sat on a plastic milk crate to unlace his faux-biker shoes.

"I'll leave you guys to get after it." Sam started walking back toward the house, then turned.

"Glad you showed up," he called.

"Yeah, right." Cody tossed his hair out of his eyes and rammed his foot into one of the boots.

When Sam reached the doorway, he turned back one more time, intending to tell Cody to help himself to a drink from the barn fridge if he needed one. But the words froze in his throat.

The light from outside slanted down just so, and in the uneven yellow glow, Cody stood out sharply in profile. He straightened up and hitched back his hip, stomping his foot down into the boot, a motion so familiar to Sam it was like looking in a mirror.

He leaned back against the door of a stall, feeling as if he'd just been sucker-punched. He couldn't seem to grab a breath of air.

Slow down, McPhee, he told himself. Take it easy and think for a minute. Think think think. Think of the kid, and of Michelle's cold manner, her nervousness. Think of the look of amazement on Edward's face when he'd seen Sam and Cody standing side by side.

Think of the calendar, the years that had passed. Do the math.

Count the years.

Piece by piece, he put it together. The kid looked younger than sixteen, but Sam's first impression had been wrong. Cody *was* sixteen.

"Holy shit," Sam said under his breath. "Holy goddamned shit." An icy wind blew over him from outside, but he barely felt it. He stood motionless in the doorway of the barn and watched Cody wield the shovel. His slim form bent and straightened; the light from the cracks in the eaves streamed down over him, down over the shining sandy hair and the clean profile and the unsmiling mouth and the eyes that were not quite blue.

"Holy shit," Sam said again. Then he turned on his heel and strode away from the barn.

Chapter 7

S am McPhee's kitchen appeared lived-in but not fussed over. Stainless-steel appliances, tile countertops, a garden window with a few tired-looking potted herbs struggling along. A coffeemaker hissed beneath a set of wall hooks with an array of mismatched mugs bearing imprints of various feed brands and drug names. Drug names? Atarax. Was that a veterinary drug?

Brad would know, thought Michelle. Brad the pharmacy franchise owner. Her "boyfriend," Gavin called him.

Feeling like an intruder, she helped herself to coffee. She had a devilish urge to poke around the rest of the house, but she resisted and sat down at the table. A tabby cat leaped onto the seat of the chair next to her, peering solemnly through crystal eyes.

"Hi there." She offered a finger for the cat to sniff, then rubbed its fur. It turned its head nearly upside down beneath her scratching finger. "I bet you wonder what I'm doing here," she said, and sipped her coffee. "I'm wondering the same thing myself."

Outside, the wind kicked up whirlpools in the snow. The Border collie pounced on the snow dervishes, making a joyous game of it. In her wildest imaginings, Michelle had never dreamed she would find herself sitting in Sam McPhee's kitchen, drinking his coffee and petting his cat. He wasn't the sort she even thought of as *having* a kitchen, much less a cat.

It took all her self-control to stay seated, to keep from running outside, grabbing Cody, and driving away, not stopping until Seattle. She dreaded telling Cody the truth. She wasn't stupid; she knew her kid. Sam represented the sort of dad—the fantasy dad, the Disneyland dad—Cody had been secretly wishing for all his life. The swift ride, the cheap thrill.

What Cody was too young to realize was that the minute he gave himself to a guy like Sam, he was a goner. Sam would break the boy's heart the way he broke Michelle's so long ago.

But she was going to stay in Crystal City no matter what her instincts urged her to do. Because when it came to self-control, Michelle Turner was an expert.

On some level, she might even savor the visit, she told herself, watching the cat curl into a ball on the braided seat cover of the chair next to her. This morning she had awakened early to sunshine and new snow that had come silently in the night, covering every flaw of age and softening all the sharp edges of the world. The landscape looked as clean and stark as an unpainted canvas. The miles of white meadows and the mountains rearing against a tall cerulean sky had a calming effect on her; they always had. Here, she felt a sense of drama and richness she had been missing ever since her adolescence had given way to the brutal chaos of instant adulthood.

Though her mother had raised her in the hushed elegance of Bel Air, Sharon Turner had lived way beyond her means. Her unexpected death had left Michelle a legacy of unpaid taxes and debts. By the time all accounts had been settled, there was nothing left but grief.

Michelle could have prevailed on her father for help even after she'd left Crystal City. Writing checks was what Gavin Slade did best. But she had never asked. All the money in the world couldn't provide what she needed far more than monthly rent—love, support, stability. Money was the least of her problems, and it was the first one she solved.

On her own she built a life she could be proud of— a kid who, until recently, had been great; a waterfront town house filled with furniture from Roche-Bobois, a Lexus, a ski condo in Whistler.

Hers had been a life that hadn't slowed down since she'd fled Montana all those years ago. And now she was back, and she had no idea what to make of it, what to think, how to feel. Slowing down and giving herself time to think was dangerous. Seeing Sam again was even more dangerous. He had broken her heart once. She wanted to believe he had no power to do it again. But when she saw him at the arena last night, she knew a secret, fragile part of her still belonged to him.

All her instincts had rebelled against bringing Cody here this morning. But honor demanded it. Cody had trashed Sam's trailer, and he had to make amends.

Truth to tell, Michelle had been incredibly curious. She had always assumed Sam had never amounted to anything more than a rodeo bum, rambling from show to show until the inevitable injuries of his sport retired him. She used to picture him battered and stiff at age thirty, tending bar in some little Western town. He'd wear his champion's belt buckle, and behind the bar amid the array of beer nuts and whiskey bottles, there would be a few dusty trophies and photographs of him looking like a young Paul Newman.

There wasn't a single photo in sight in this kitchen, not even one taped to the refrigerator. Odd.

She finished her coffee and rinsed the mug, taking a long drink of icy tap water. The window over the sink framed the distant mountain peaks rearing against the sky. As she gazed out across the empty, perfect meadows, a wave of nostalgia had swept over her. She'd spent so little time in Montana, yet it seemed like the place where her soul had always dwelt. What a magnificent sight to greet Sam when he got up in the morning. How different it was from the soulless cocoon of her office at the agency in downtown Seattle.

Sam had managed to confound her expectations. He didn't seem to suffer any permanent injuries from the rodeo. He had a horse ranch with a comfortable house, sturdy outbuildings, covered and open-air arenas and pens. But in a way the place seemed as empty as her own town house.

Had he surrendered his dreams? Had it hurt? Had he simply awakened one morning to discover that the life he'd envisioned for himself didn't match the one he actually had? Did she dare to ask him?

"Of course not." Michelle stroked the cat. "It's none of my business."

As she watched out the window, a stocky dark-haired man on a tractor came out of the barn, towing a load of manure on a stone boat. The Border collie cavorted like a clown through the drifts of snow. Cody followed, wearing oversize boots and hefting a shovel over one shoulder. Amazing. He was actually working. It had been forever since Michelle had been able to make him do anything.

She took another drink, savoring the sweetness of mountain well water. Footsteps thudded on the back porch and a door slammed. She turned to see Sam standing in the kitchen doorway. Faded jeans, fleece-lined denim jacket, battered John Deere cap, gloves protruding from a hip pocket. The Marlboro man without the cigarette.

"I helped myself to coffee," she said uncertainly. "Want some?"

He ignored the question. He flexed his jaw, shifted his weight to one side. Though he barely moved, a subtle threat seemed to emanate from him. It was hard to explain, but Michelle sensed a dangerous turbulence in the air between them. Old intimacy mingled with fresh suspicion.

He took a step toward her. "So when were you planning on telling me I have a son?"

His blunt words pounded at Michelle, but she felt no shock. In the back of her mind she had known since last night that he would figure out the truth based on Cody's age. She folded her arms protectively across her middle. "God, if you said something to Cody—"

"What the hell do you take me for? Of course I didn't say anything. Thanks to you, I don't even know the kid." His gaze flicked over her, measuring her contemptuously from head to toe and back again. "So I guess that means you've never told him, either."

She returned his glare. "I didn't see the point. I didn't think he'd ever meet you."

He grabbed the back of his neck in a distracted gesture. "Jesus Christ. You had my kid, and you never told me."

"And this surprises you?" Too many years had passed for Michelle to feel bitter, but she did. The regrets, the resentment, the frustration, all came bubbling to the surface. "I was eighteen years old and pregnant. You'd run off to be a rodeo champ. Do you think I had the slightest idea how to track you down? And what makes you think I didn't try?"

"Did you?"

"Of course I did, Sam. I was in l—" She broke off, unwilling to continue down that path. "Are you telling me it should have been easy to find you? Did you and your mother leave a forwarding address? Did you stay anywhere long enough to have one?"

"Permanent addresses were never my mother's strong suit." His voice was low and hoarse. "We weren't all brought up in gated communities in Bel Air."

She flinched at the implication. She and Sam came from different worlds, though at eighteen they had sworn it didn't matter.

"I didn't have a whole lot of time to spend trying to figure out where you'd gone. I had a baby to raise. Beyond the twenty-four hours a day that took, I couldn't seem to squeeze in a missing-persons search."

"I deserved to know, damn it."

"Oh, right. So you could do what? Marry me?"

"So I could have a say in what you did with my kid. You never even gave me a chance."

"Tell me an eighteen-year-old cowboy wants a *chance* with a baby."

She was dangerously, humiliatingly close to tears. She refused to shed them. She had wept an ocean for Sam McPhee and he'd never come to find her. Crying now would only prove what Michelle had been trying to deny since seeing him last night. Seventeen years ago he had taken possession of her in ways she was too young to understand. She had never given herself so wholly to another person, nor taken so much from someone else. After Sam left, she had dreamed of meeting someone new, but she'd never found that depth, that completion, with any other person. So she learned to do without.

Michelle forced herself to get a grip, to stand up from the table so she didn't feel at a disadvantage. "This is stupid. We shouldn't argue about the past. We can't change what happened."

"Maybe not." Unhurried yet unrelenting, he walked toward her, stopping only inches from her. The smell of snow and wind clung to his clothes, underlying the unique scent of him. She thought she had forgotten it.

"Sam—"

"We've got a lot of talking to do." His low voice caught at her, mesmerized her. "Problem is, now that you're here, I want to do a hell of a lot more than talk."

"You're crazy." She didn't know this man anymore, but she could feel the anger and passion seething from him. She searched his face, wondering about the lines that fanned out from his eyes.

"Crazy? I've been called worse." He took another step toward her. "I couldn't sleep for thinking about you last night."

She inched back. "You came in here wanting to talk about Cody."

He stuck a thumb into his jeans pocket, his hip propped on the edge of the counter. "So talk. I'm listening."

This can't be happening, Michelle thought. "I don't know where to start."

"You had my child and you never told me." He spoke coldly, the words hard as stones. "How about starting there?"

"The day I found out I was pregnant, I went to see you. And you had left without a trace. I don't believe I owed you a thing."

The heat of his glare was a tangible thing; she could feel it blasting away at her. "I won't discuss this with you if you're hostile," she added.

"Excuse me if I'm a little disoriented by all this. It's not every day a woman I used to sleep with shows up with a kid she had sixteen years ago."

"I didn't know I'd find you here."

"Well, here I am, honey." He spread his arms mockingly. "I'm surprised your daddy didn't warn you."

She was surprised, too, but she wouldn't admit it to Sam. She wondered if he knew she and her father were strangers, and that only Gavin's illness had brought her back.

"We should be talking instead of arguing." She sat back down at the table, took a deep breath. "Maybe I was wrong. I should have searched high and low for you. But everyone said I'd get over you. Said I was better off without you, that I'd go off to college and meet someone who—" She broke off and shrugged.

"—wasn't a born drifter with a hopeless lush for a mother," Sam finished for her.

"I never said that."

"You didn't have to."

"I had to think about Cody, too. I spent my childhood ducking the paparazzi. I'm very protective of him in that way."

His eyes narrowed. "Oh, yeah, the tabloids would've had a field day with us. Gavin Slade's only daughter makes it with a ranch hand."

She flinched, knowing he wasn't far off the mark. As a child, she had shown up occasionally in the scandal sheets—a grainy photo taken through a long lens: *Gavin Slade's Love Child*, the caption always read.

A juicy story like an illicit Romeo and Juliet–style affair would have revived the attention she shunned. That was why she worked so hard to maintain her anonymity. Every once in a while a reporter in search of a scoop came sniffing around. One even snapped her photo when she was pregnant. The incident had scared her so much that she moved to Seattle, where no one knew her.

Sam sat down across from her. His hands were big, not as work-scarred as she would have thought. She caught herself staring at those hands, remembering how she used to rub Bag Balm on them to soothe the calluses.

"None of that old stuff can matter now, Michelle. What matters is that we have a son." He clenched his hand into a fist on the table. "A son. I can't believe it."

She was terrified to ask the next question, but she had to. "Sam, what are you going to do?"

"Do?"

"About . . . learning that Cody's your son." She tasted the burn of resentment in her throat. "Your biological son." Yes, that sounded better. More distant.

He studied her hands, and she wondered if he remembered the Bag Balm, too. On her right one, she wore a Cartier onyx ring. On the left forefinger, a large sapphire.

"Did you raise him alone, or are you in a relationship?"

She guessed that meant he wasn't thinking about the Bag Balm. *In a relationship*. It was such a modern thing to say. Like so many modern things, it had no meaning.

"Alone, more or less."

"Explain more or less."

"I've been with someone for the past three years. But

it's not—he's not—" Damn. How could she explain Brad? "He's not raising Cody."

"I see." Sam got up from the table and poured himself a cup of coffee. He seemed hesitant when he turned. "So did Cody ever ask about me?"

"Of course he asked."

"And you told him what? Obviously my name doesn't ring a bell with him."

"I was worried about the tabloids. So I left the father's name blank on his birth certificate."

"Christ—"

"Sam, I was young. Scared. I grew up with cameras shoved in my face every time I sneezed. I didn't want that for Cody, and I didn't want anyone to go snooping through records—"

"—and finding the name of a mongrel cowboy."

"Quit putting words in my mouth. I didn't know what to do."

"Didn't he want to know, just for him? Jesus, a name wouldn't have sent him off the deep end."

"A name's just . . . a name. And maybe I was afraid—" She stopped, wishing she could reel in the words.

"Of what? What were you afraid of?"

"That maybe he'd get mad at me one day and go off looking for you." The confession rushed out like air escaping a balloon. "Since school started this year, he's been . . . in rebellion."

Sam hesitated, took a sip of coffee. In his face she saw more than she wanted to see—interest, understanding. Compassion. "The kid's mad at the world, Michelle."

Ouch. He had seen that so quickly. "We've had rough times before. We've dealt with trouble. This year . . . is more difficult than most." Damn. She knew she should keep her thoughts to herself, but with Sam, it was hard.

Years ago he'd had that effect on her, and it hadn't changed. He still drew truths from deep inside her, made her say things better left unsaid.

"So what's going on?" he asked. "Is he having trouble in school?"

All right, thought Michelle. You asked for it. The good, the bad, and the ugly. "His last grade report was awful. Up until this year, he's been an A and B student. Now it's Cs and Ds. At first I thought it was a normal, predictable rebellion, but I don't see the end of it."

"Is he hanging out with his regular friends?"

"Not as much as he used to. He's got a girlfriend, and they're pretty exclusive."

"So what are you doing about his problems?"

"I'm working on it, Sam! Do you think this is easy? Do you think you could do better?"

"Is it my turn to take over? You had him the first sixteen years, I get the next sixteen?"

"I didn't bring him here because he's a troubled teen. I brought him here . . . to see my dad." She didn't feel like discussing Gavin's health with Sam. "My father's never met Cody." She got up from the table and went to the door. She was afraid. She was angry. And God help her, she felt an old, old yearning unfold in her heart, a burning ache she thought she had buried forever. "What time should I pick him up?"

Outside, Cody and the dark-haired man were loading bales of hay onto a flatbed truck. It was startling to see her son doing physical labor. It had been ages since he exerted himself doing anything more strenuous than lifting the telephone receiver.

"He'll be done around five, I guess," Sam said. "Edward can give him a lift over to your father's place."

"All right." Taking her jacket from a hook outside the kitchen door in the mudroom, she shrugged into it. "Sam?"

"Yeah?"

"You won't . . . say anything to him, will you?"

"Hell, no, I won't say anything. I don't even know the kid." He held open the door for her. He was as tall as she remembered, and broader in the shoulders and chest. His face was more deeply carved with character. His scent, God, why did she remember it so perfectly? Perversely, she had an urge to touch him, just once, but she resisted.

" 'Bye, Sam."

" 'Bye." He followed her out onto the porch and waited while she got into the Range Rover. "Hey, Michelle?"

She rolled down the window. "What?"

"That doesn't mean we're not telling him."

She leaned back against the headrest, closing her eyes. "Damn. I was hoping for a quick getaway."

"No such luck, Sugar. Tell him. I want him to know exactly who I am."

"But—" She opened her eyes. "All right. I'll tell him."

"When?"

"I'll . . . figure out the right time. Sam, I've got a lot on my mind. My father isn't well, and the next few days might be pretty difficult."

He stared at her for a long time. She couldn't read him. Didn't know him anymore. Yet that stare was as compelling now as it had been the first time she had met him. "All right. But I want him to know, Michelle. Soon."

Chapter 8

C ody felt like a cockroach in his grandfather's house—gross, unwelcome, and out of place. After shoveling horseshit at Lonepine all day, he wanted to shower for about nine hours and then crash facedown in his bed.

Instead, they were having dinner with Legendary Actor Gavin Slade. That was how Gavin was always referred to: Legendary Actor. Elder Statesman of Western Classics. In capital letters, like the guy was a walking headline or something. Lately, instead of showing him with his arm around some bimbo with big tits, the fanzines showed him alone on a horse, his cowboy hat pulled low over his brow. The headlines announced that he'd been in touch with aliens.

Cody liked the bimbo pictures better. It was pretty bizarre, thinking about his grandfather getting laid by women younger than his own mom, but it was even worse thinking about his grandfather dying of kidney failure. Mostly, he tried not to think of Gavin at all. It wasn't like Gavin thought about *him* all the time.

Cody had tried his best to weasel out of dinner, but he hadn't gained much sympathy from his mom. After crunching that cowpoke's trailer last night, he'd used up most of his goodwill points with her. Not that he had many to begin with. Since last summer she'd been driving him nuts, hovering over him, waiting to pounce the second she caught him doing something she disapproved of.

He'd tried a minor whine—*I'm too tired, I worked like a dog today*—but all he'd gained was the Look. That cold jackhammer of a stare still affected him sometimes, although he was getting pretty good at ignoring her lately.

When he was little, he used to be moved by the Look. He used to want to do just about anything to please her. Little by little over the years, he'd figured out that there was no way to please his perfectionist mother. No way to win a smile that wasn't sad at the edges, or to get praise from her that didn't demand things he didn't even know how to give.

So he quit trying, and he wasn't even sure she noticed. She was so lame, she and that loser Brad. All Brad cared about was making the almighty buck and showing off to the world that Cody's mom was his lady, like she was some sort of bowling trophy with boobs.

That was the only good thing about coming here. It gave him a break from Brad the loser.

"Hiya, Cody." Gavin Slade came into the living room. Unlike Cody, he looked exactly right in his surroundings. Jeans and a red corduroy shirt and cowboy boots. Big white hair that made his eyes look bluer than the heated swimming pool on the patio.

"Hi." Cody hadn't decided what to call his grand-father, and it would be too dorky to ask. Jamming his hands into his pockets, he pretended great interest in the objects arranged on a lighted glass shelf by the wet bar. After a couple of seconds, he didn't have to fake it anymore.

Holy shit. He was looking at an Oscar statue.

"That's pretty cool," he said, pointing to it.

"You think?" Gavin hooked a thumb into his back pocket like he was posing for a picture or something. Except he didn't even seem conscious of the pose—it was the natural way he held himself. "I guess so. I liked that movie. *The Face of Battle*. You ever see it?"

Only about a zillion times.

"I think maybe I caught part of it on TV once," he lied.

"It's about a misfit, a real loser. Nobody cared whether he lived or died. After a while, he quit caring, too. And in the end, that's why he was able to save his battalion. He quit looking for guarantees, and he made the sacri-fice."

Cody pictured the scene in his head. It was one of those film sequences the experts always showed when they were going over classic movies—the moment Gavin's char-acter stood alone on a tank-destroyer turret, the only vol-unteer of his battalion, shooting through a deadly hail of sniper fire at a 77mm tank gun. Like the image of Gary Cooper in *High Noon,* Gavin Slade's *Face of Battle* mo-ment had put him on the pages of the film history books. The memorable image showed a close-up of a face filled with nobility, anguish, and the wisdom of a man who knows he is about to die. It had become one of the most famous movie stills ever published.

"How come you stopped making movies?" Cody asked.

"It was always a job to me, to tell you the truth. A job I liked most of the time, and either loved or hated the rest." He had this intent way of speaking, leaning forward and lowering his voice so you had no choice but to listen. "The business is brutal, Cody. You live and die by the box office. Your looks and your image are everything. Sometimes you don't get a minute of privacy, and other times you can't buy attention for yourself. I got sick of the roller coaster. As soon as I could afford to retire, I got out of acting. I still coproduce things here and there, but it's pretty low-key. Haven't seen a film on the big screen in ages."

"Mom said the movie theater in town is closed down."

"That's a fact. They were going to tear the Lynwood down, so I bought it."

A spark of interest flashed in Cody. "Yeah?"

"I'd like to reopen, for old time's sake. One screen, maybe show some independent films."

"That'd be cool." Cody studied the other objects in the case—a baseball autographed by Joe DiMaggio, the stub of a ticket to a Beatles concert, a display of prize rodeo belt buckles, and photos of Gavin posing proudly by his vintage airplane. Pretty radical stuff, he decided.

His perusal drifted to a framed picture of his mom on a horse. "When was that taken?" he asked, to fill the silence.

"First summer after high school," Gavin said. "I invited her to spend a year up here before starting college. She studied painting with a local artist."

"She never finished college," Cody said, hearing contempt in his own voice. He didn't care. All his friends' parents had degrees and stuff. His mom had, well, her job. And him. And lame-ass suspicious Brad who lived in fear that Cody and his friends were going to help themselves to uppers or painkillers from his sample cases.

He looked at the picture, taken in a pasture with the mountains in the background. Slender and suntanned, long legs and bare feet, her head thrown back with laughter, she looked pretty amazing. For the past couple of years, his friends had been giving Cody a hard time about his mom. She was a lot younger than most moms. She looked like a shampoo ad or something. It was kind of cool sometimes, having a mom who was a babe, but mostly it was embarrassing as hell.

"I still have that horse," Gavin said.

"The one in the picture?"

"Yeah, that's Dooley. Your mom learned barrel racing on him."

"He must be pretty old."

"Twenty-something. Do you ride, Cody?"

"Not horses."

Gavin chuckled, showing perfect teeth. And his eyes— they had that crinkly, twinkly look Cody recognized from old movie posters. He didn't trust this guy. How did you know he was being sincere when he was an actor?

"I guess that'll change now that you're here," Gavin said. "Or maybe I'll take you flying once I pass my physical and get my license renewed. You interested?"

"We're only staying until you get through with your recovery period." Even that was too long for Cody. Worse, he had to enroll in the local high school here in Noplace, Montana. He had stormed for weeks in rebellion, but his mom was adamant. He got a minor reprieve this week— it was winter break in Noplace. But pretty soon he was going to have to be the new kid. A fate worse than death. "Mom says a few weeks or so. Then we're out of here."

Gavin's grin stayed fixed in place. But the movie-star

gleam in his eyes dimmed as if Cody's words were a light switch that suddenly turned it off. "Let's go see if supper's ready."

Cody felt kind of shitty as he followed his grandfather into a big dining room with fancy crystal and china laid out. What did the old man expect? Instant bonding, like on those long-distance phone commercials? He and Gavin Slade were complete strangers. After this transplant thing was over, they probably wouldn't ever see each other again.

Grandfathers made friends with grandsons when they were little and cute, not when they were sixteen, wearing a ponytail and combat boots. Not that Cody wanted to cozy up to the old man, anyway. It was gross, thinking about his illness. He had some kind of fluid bag attached to a tube going inside him, doing the work his kidneys were supposed to do. The very idea of it made Cody want to hurl.

His mom joined them in the dining room. She was smiling in a nervous way. Her gaze kept darting from her father to Cody. "Hi, guys," she said.

Gavin held a chair for her. It was corny but kind of nice seeing the old guy do that. Once, Cody had tried holding a chair out for Claudia. "What, like it's going to get away from me?" she'd asked, then cracked up. Cody had laughed, too.

Dinner was about the best thing that had happened since his mom loaded him into the car at the crack of dawn yesterday. Prepared by an Asian nutrition expert named Tadao, it consisted of pasta with fancy sauce, fresh bread, a bunch of grilled veggies, and a big salad of exotic fruit.

After shoveling away about nineteen pounds of food, Cody glanced up to see both his mother and his grandfather watching him. Neither of them had eaten much. Gavin was on some sort of low-protein diet. He couldn't eat things that made his kidneys work hard because they didn't function at all anymore.

"You must've worked up an appetite out at Lonepine today," Gavin commented.

"It's good," he said, and sucked down a whole glass of milk.

"Be sure you tell Tadao you enjoyed it," his mom said.

Shit. She was always doing that. No matter what it was—having a good meal, talking on the phone, whatever, she had to add her own little goody-goody twist on it. Her own little adjustment or correction. This morning he'd expected her to totally humiliate him in front of that girl, Molly. But for once his mom had shown mercy.

She'd seemed kind of flustered around Sam McPhee, like she couldn't quite decide what to make of him. Cody wasn't sure what to make of the guy either. He was okay, but Cody thought it was totally bogus of him to make him pay off the trailer damage with slave labor.

He helped himself to more milk from a cut-glass pitcher, feeling a slight sting from the blisters on his hand. *Blisters,* for chrissakes. He was pretty sure he'd never given himself blisters before. Especially not by shoveling horseshit.

He got the idea from that Bliss guy that Lonepine was some kind of hotshot horse breeding and training ranch. It was cool, working in a barn where a mare was about to give birth any minute. When it was time to go today, Cody had felt a twinge of disappointment. He wouldn't have minded seeing the horse being born. It would have given him a good story to tell Claudia.

Maybe the manure story was funny enough. But honestly, he hadn't felt much like laughing. There had been a moment, when he was alone in the barn, with the smells around him and the light falling between the rafters, that an odd feeling had settled over him. Maybe it was the quiet or the sense that he was totally alone; he didn't know. But it had felt kind of pleasant.

"It's nice to be together with the two of you," Gavin said suddenly, pressing his palms on the table as if he never planned to eat again.

"We let too much time go by," his mom said in a quiet voice.

"I know, Michelle," Gavin said. "I'm sorry. I can't tell you how many times I picked up the phone, but I never knew what I'd say—"

"Let's not do this, Daddy. Let's not drag up all the old regrets. We can't get back the years we lost. We can only go on from here."

Cody did his best not to roll his eyes. This was just what he'd been hoping to avoid—a big emotional scene where they go "I'm sorry I'm sorry" all over each other and then drag him into the middle of everything as The Grandson You Never Knew.

"Can I be excused?" he asked too loudly.

They both looked at him as if he had a booger hanging out of his nose.

"I told Claudia I'd call her."

"Girlfriend?" Gavin asked.

"Yeah." Cody felt about two feet taller just saying it. He loved walking through the halls at school, hearing everybody whisper: *He's going out with Claudia Teller.* . . .

"So can I be excused?" he asked.

His mom nodded. "Go ahead, honey."

"Thanks . . . for dinner," he said, then hurried out into the cold night. When he got to his own room, he collapsed on the bed, clicked on the TV, and realized that working outside in subfreezing temperatures all day had made him more tired than he'd ever been in his life. He was asleep before he even remembered he meant to call Claudia.

Monday

Chapter 9

Y ou're kidding, right?" Cody asked at the breakfast table.

"Don't talk with your mouth full." Cradling a coffee mug between both hands, Michelle regarded her son in the clear light of the mountain morning. His cheeks were stuffed with blueberry muffin. Chewing slowly, he washed it down with a big gulp of black coffee.

When did her son start drinking coffee—black, of all things?

He took a final swallow. "I said, you're kidding, right?"

She'd heard him the first time, but making him repeat himself for the sake of manners was ingrained in her. Funny how he'd never learned that lesson. The second time around, he was supposed to fix his tone of voice, ask his question politely and without food in his mouth. Yet in all his life, he'd never done it.

Maybe he kept thinking she'd get tired of correcting him. He'd worn her down on so many other matters. When he wanted something—ridiculously expensive shoes, a pierced ear, a snowboard—he became like water dripping on a rock: constant, incessant, wearing her away until she caved in.

"No," she said. "I'm not kidding. You're going back to Mr. McPhee's today."

"I'm not going." Cody jutted his chin defiantly and held up his hands, palms facing out. "I have blisters because I spent eight hours shoveling horseshit yesterday. Horseshit, Mom."

Michelle felt her lips twitch. Laughing now would enrage him, so she composed herself. "When Mr. Bliss dropped you off yesterday he said there was lots more work to be done and to be there at nine again."

"That sucks." He shoved back from the table, giving his long two-colored ponytail an insolent toss.

"What sucks is backing the car into a guy's trailer," she reminded him. *What sucks is that the guy's your father, and I have no idea how to explain it to you.*

"So go get ready." She put the mugs in the sink. "I need to phone Brad, and then we'll leave."

"Hey, I was going to call Claudia—"

"Later. When you get home tonight—"

Cody curled his lip. "I'll call her when I damn well please."

Her face felt hot, burning hot, yet the anger was directed at herself. When he spoke to her like this, she had no idea how to make him stop. It was frightening sometimes, knowing how completely out of her control he was. "Let's not argue, Cody. Gavin and I have an appointment in Missoula and we need to get going. In case you've forgotten, we're here for Gavin."

Cody tugged on his jacket, yanking out a pack of Camels, flashing them as he jerked open the door. "Yeah, I almost forgot. You're here to offer spare parts to your long-lost father."

The kid had great timing. He knew just when to pick a fight. She had to call Brad, drop off Cody, and accompany her father to Missoula. She didn't have time to deal with the rage and the hurt that had been ricocheting between her and her son since he turned sixteen.

The kid's mad at the world. Sam had seen that instantly.

She snatched up the phone and punched in Brad's number. He sounded groggy when he picked up.

"Oops," she said. "I forgot you're an hour earlier."

"Hey, babe." A sleepy smile softened his voice.

Michelle tried to relax, but she was too jumpy. "I wanted to call and say hi. I miss you."

"Miss you, too. Is everything okay out there? Do you need me to come out?"

What she needed, she realized suddenly, was for him to come without asking. To understand her well enough to know that of course she needed him. She was facing a terrifying ordeal; he was supposed to support her.

Dumb. If he showed up now, he'd be bored and fretful about missing work, and Michelle knew she'd feel guilty and that would make her cranky, and then she'd have a terrible attitude about the surgery. She shook her head, trying to veer away from that line of thinking. It was enough that he'd promised to fly in the day of the surgery.

"No, we're fine," she said. "Did anyone call?"

"Natalie." Distaste rumbled in his voice; he'd never

liked her best friend. An oft-unemployed cellist, Natalie Plum was the original free spirit. She drove a diehard planner like Brad crazy. "She's bringing her stuff over to your house today."

"Good. I was hoping she'd house-sit while I'm away. So how was your weekend?"

"Excellent. Dinner at Canlis with the Albrights. A round of golf at Port Ludlow. Babe, we should really look into getting a place up there. Mike was saying the lot values for the waterfront area have really shot up . . ."

She tuned out the monologue about real-estate investments. She did that a lot lately. He loved to collect things—resort property, sports equipment, luxury cars—displaying them to the world like hunting trophies. She admired his ambition, the way he was so driven to succeed in his career. In addition to the pharmacy, he had made a killing in the stock market, and money was an obsession with him. Sometimes she wished he'd slow down.

". . . he's a vascular surgeon at Swedish, got into the resort development on the ground floor . . ."

Michelle made the appropriate murmurs as her mind wandered further afield. She remembered the day she'd finally figured Brad out. He'd just put money down on a thirty-six-foot Hunter yacht, and she told him he was crazy. The vacation home, the ski lodge, the golf membership at Lakeside, the ski place at Whistler—he was wearing her out.

"Brad," she'd told him last summer while standing on the dock next to the gleaming new sailboat. "Wouldn't it be easier simply to *become* a doctor?"

His reaction had been unexpected and sharp. "No, goddammit. It wouldn't. What the hell sort of question is that?"

He so rarely spoke in anger that she didn't press. But

she knew she had touched a raw nerve. He used to want to be a doctor the same way she used to want to be an artist. Now he owned a chain of pharmacies and she was a commercial illustrator.

She listened patiently as he finished his recitation. She waited for him to ask how Cody was doing, but he paused in the middle of talking, yawned, and said it was time to get up and into the shower.

"Wish you were here," he said, the suggestion in his voice both sexy and familiar.

"Me too." Out the window she could see Cody puffing away on a cigarette. Dear God. Her kid was smoking, and she had no idea how to stop him. She wanted to tell Brad everything—that her father still had the power to make her cry. That Cody was doing his best to drive her crazy. That she had met Sam McPhee again.

That she couldn't think of anything but Sam—oh, shit. She'd have to tell Brad. How was she going to tell him?

"I'll call you later, Brad."

"Yeah. Take care, babe."

She gathered up her coat and purse, pausing to glance into the mirror over the hall tree. What, exactly, did one wear to meet a transplant team? They sounded so important, so intimidating. Would they think her red wool blazer was too boldly colored? Should she have gone with the black angora instead?

She shoved aside the ridiculous questions. She was nervous about the appointment. She was nervous about being with her father again. She was nervous about Sam. Clothes should be the least of her concerns.

She stepped into boots and went out to find Cody. He tossed his cigarette butt into the snowy yard.

Fixing a glare on him, she groped in her purse for

car keys. "You know, you really should take up bungee-jumping from live power lines. It's a lot less risky than smoking." -

"Very funny." He got in the car.

She didn't want to launch into yet another big lecture about smoking, not this morning. She had to be focused on her father.

When she'd first found out about his illness and bullied Gavin into the transplant, she started some of the tests in Seattle. Once she'd qualified as a donor, she had donated some of her own blood for the surgery ahead of time, and it had been shipped from Seattle and stored. She had more blood and X rays taken, did a lung capacity test, and did the twenty-four-hour urine collection study, a delightful routine she hoped she didn't have to repeat.

She felt as if she had been holding her breath for twelve weeks, and she was about to let it all out soon.

At today's appointment, the team wanted to go over more details, schedule a renal angiogram, and make sure she was mentally prepared for this.

She was not doing so hot on that count.

"So," she said, flexing her hands on the steering wheel. "What did you think of Mr. McPhee?"

"He said to call him Sam. And the other guy said to call him Edward."

"So what do you think of Sam?" She tried to keep her voice light, casual.

"He's okay."

"Just okay?"

"You want me to think he's great for making me work in the freezing cold like a farmhand?"

"Ranch hand."

"Whatever."

"I think, given the circumstances, you're lucky to get off with a few days' work. So you like him?"

"Did I say that, Mom? And why do I have to like anyone around here? We're leaving as soon as you finish this thing with your—with Gavin."

"I'm not leaving him until the critical period is over." She shuddered inwardly, horrified by the possibility that the surgery wouldn't work, that her kidney would be rejected. "It wouldn't hurt to make a few friends."

Trying to push that worry aside, she watched the scenery. The morning sun on the majestic landscape brought out the harsh poetry of the high country. The sight of blanketed fields and soaring mountains filled her with a strange yet familiar yearning. The truth was, she needed the mountains, the air, the clarity of light found only in Montana in order to paint. And maybe she needed to be the person she had been all those years ago, too. A person who dared to love, dared to dream.

But she knew of no way to recapture that young, naive self. The disappointment ate at her, a quiet dull pain, the surrendering of hope. Sometimes she believed her gift was only slumbering or maybe frozen inside, waiting. When she was pregnant with Cody, she had enrolled in a small liberal arts college, and for one glorious semester she had painted. She had a rare talent, and she knew it. Her instructors knew it. The gallery owners who approached her knew it. But making a career as a painter would take years of work and study and time.

After Cody was born, reality intruded. She counted herself lucky to land an entry-level position at an ad agency. Late at night, after Cody was asleep, she'd fall into a dream world that was hers and hers alone. Those hours were precious; the work she did was dark, important, and expressive. She produced dozens of paintings, working from pain rather than joy, producing fast as she was wont to do. Perhaps a part of her understood that the creative burst would fade away.

Time crept on, eating secretly away at her soul. Inch by inch, her imagination and energy deteriorated until she simply stopped painting. She dropped her art classes and changed the direction of her dreams. It was easier to collapse on the sofa, take her precious baby boy in her lap, and read stories to him. Those paintings lay stacked against a wall in a spare closet. She rarely looked at them. Once Cody started school, she had more time to pursue her art, but she never did. The prospect terrified her. It was like standing in front of the door to a dark, forbidding room. She'd be nuts to go there.

At the firm she did good work, got promoted through the ranks, achieved some recognition in her field, and quit thinking about painting.

But sometimes she still wanted to. Oh, how she wanted to.

"I used to know Sam," she said carefully to Cody.

"I figured that out when he called you by name after I hit his trailer."

"He worked at my father's place. I met him when I came here after my mother died."

Before her death, Sharon Turner had advised Michelle to start college straight out of high school. Always chilly, self-absorbed, and distant, Michelle's mother had suggested a practical course of study in design or architecture. Her death had left Michelle adrift, vulnerable. Terrified. And then, like the cavalry riding to the rescue, Gavin had made his offer. "Don't go rushing off to college at a time like this, honey," he'd said, his charm and warm sympathy palpable. "You'll never again get a year of your life to do anything you want. I showed your work to a local teacher, and he agreed to meet you. Come to Montana."

And so she had gone, never asking herself what he expected from the relationship, what he hoped it would become. Perhaps she had wanted to believe he acted out of selfless compassion, opening his home to the grieving daughter who hardly knew her. If there was such a thing as the classic absentee Hollywood dad, Gavin was it. He had sent checks, phoned her, and showed up on significant occasions—her first ballet recital, her Bluebird fly-up, a dressage championship—and she'd been thrilled to stand back and let him be the center of attention. She remembered her first communion at All Saints in Beverly Hills, the girls in stiff white dresses and new gloves. She'd felt like a bride that day, and when her father, incandescent as the Holy Ghost and twice as handsome, came striding across the parking lot toward her, she'd squealed and wrenched her hand out of her mother's grip. Racing to greet him, she flung herself into his arms and he picked her up, swinging her round and round as she laughed with joy. She could hear camera shutters clicking and people whispering *Gavin Slade. It's Gavin Slade. He's even better-looking in person. . . .* The days with her father, few and far between, stood out vividly in her memory. When his visits ended she always experienced a gaping emptiness. The world was duller, flatter, when Gavin wasn't around.

She glanced over at Cody, waiting for him to say something else. Waiting for him to ask more about Sam.

But Cody said nothing, and neither did Michelle. It wasn't the right time to bring up all the events that started here so long ago. They'd need hours for that. You always need hours to recover after a bombshell drops into the middle of your life, thought Michelle. She pictured them buried by the rocks and relics heaved up by her confession. Each bit of rubble would have to be removed with care to avoid damaging the fragile, angry victim beneath it. Hours, yes. Maybe days. Maybe a whole lot longer.

When they arrived at Sam's place, Edward greeted them and set Cody to work loading avalanche fencing onto a stone boat on stout wooden runners. Sam was already gone, Edward explained, pointing at a snowmobile trail leading into the low, distant hills. A mountain lion had been lurking around, and Sam went to check it out.

Her eye wandered along the corrugated track while her knees turned to lime Jell-O. A reprieve, she thought weakly. For now, at least.

Chapter 10

Gavin insisted on driving to Missoula. Michelle couldn't discern his state of mind. He seemed quiet, preoccupied. A crimson rash marred the side of his neck. She wanted to ask him about it, but she didn't. Somehow it seemed too personal.

It was going to get worse before it got better, she knew. He'd told her this morning, a little sheepishly, that his last mistress had left him when she found out how sick he was. She'd recently sold her story to a sleazy magazine. Once it hit the stands, it was sure to bring the paparazzi flocking around like carrion birds.

Michelle felt a peculiar violence when she thought about the mistress. Her name was Carolyn and she was about Michelle's age. *If I ever run into her,* thought Michelle, *I'll set her hair on fire.* It was one thing to sponge off a guy when you're his mistress, but to sell the story after dumping him was disgusting.

The road to Missoula rolled out in front of the chrome-grilled truck, and the land was deep and stark, lit by a sun that shone brighter than anywhere else in the world.

"It's a boring drive to the city. You might want to get some shut-eye," her father said.

A little hitch of disappointment caught in her chest. Part of her wanted to talk with him, to get to know him. But another part kept its distance, circling warily around the whole bizarre situation. It would be noble indeed to insist she was going through this because of the selfless filial love she felt for him, but how much of that love was a sense of obligation?

And was there any way to tell the difference?

She used to know exactly what love felt like. She closed her eyes against the glaring snowscape and let the years roll away until she was back in the past again, the week before Thanksgiving, 1983. A fresh snowfall had blanketed the farm. Flush with excitement, she'd rushed into the guesthouse Gavin had set up as an art studio for her. There, on a sunny morning not much different from today, she had finished the best painting of her life. After laboring over theory and composition with Joseph, she had produced something of merit and value. She couldn't have known back then that she would never again equal that effort.

She had painted for hours, stopping when Sam came in from work, his cheeks chapped and his lips cool until he warmed them by kissing her. She was covered in paint and all awash with the wonder of creating a work that grew from every level of her heart. He'd peeled oranges for her and brewed steaming cups of tea while she worked. And when she took a break, he'd made love to her.

"It's unbelievable, Michelle," he'd said that chill November day, tackling her on the low sofa in front of the woodstove.

"I bet you'd say that if I was painting Elvis on velvet."

"Maybe." With the frank lust only teenage boys exhibit, he lifted her sweatshirt and unhooked her bra.

Michelle still remembered the way he kissed her neck, her breasts, her stomach. Trusting him, she relaxed and let it happen. Since the very first time they'd made love, he had created a world of sensation for her. Colors glowed brighter. Edges appeared sharper. When they struggled out of their clothes and came together, she saw a million glinting stars behind her squeezed-shut eyelids.

Later as they lay spent in each other's arms, she had listened to the beat of his heart, drifting, dreaming. She'd done a lot of pictures in the summer and autumn—landscapes and wildlife, abstracts with bold splashes of color and subtle shadows hiding in the hollows of space.

"I want to be an artist," she said.

"You already are."

"No, I mean I want my paintings to hang in exhibits where anyone who wants to can see them, even buy them."

"So go for it." His belief in her was unshakable and straightforward.

She had loved that about him, how he never doubted her. But what did he believe about himself? It used to worry her sometimes, how quiet he was about his own life, so she asked, "What about you? What do you want?"

He'd chuckled without a great deal of humor. "For my mother to quit fucking up."

Michelle hadn't known what to say. Tammi Lee Gilmer was holding down a waitressing job at the Truxtop, yet she knew Sam was concerned. If Tammi Lee's pattern held true, she'd go on a binge, miss work, lose her job, then collect unemployment until it ran out and she drifted to another town, dragging Sam along with her.

It was the only life he had ever known, and thinking about it made Michelle's heart ache.

"That's not what I meant, Sam. I meant you. What do you want for you?"

"For me?" He hesitated.

"Come on, you can tell me. What, do you think I'd laugh at you? I'm the one who wants to make a living as an artist."

"At least you know what you want."

"So do you. But you have to tell me." She figured he was headed for the rodeo circuit. Already, he'd placed in a lot of the local shows, riding her father's bucking stock, competing in team-roping and bulldogging. "Come on. Truth or dare."

He wiggled his eyebrows comically. "I'll take the dare."

"I want the truth."

Another hesitation. Finally, without looking at her, he said, "Would you believe medical school?"

Michelle had pulled back, studied him. The shaggy light hair, serious eyes, and a mouth that made her melt inside were all so blissfully familiar. But this was a stranger speaking. It was the first she'd heard of medical school. "Since when?"

"Since forever, I guess." He began getting dressed. The ranch hands were riding fence, and he was an hour behind because of their diversion. "I've never told anyone."

"I'm glad you spilled the beans. You should go for it, Sam."

He shook his head, flashing a self-deprecating smile. "I'm a high school dropout."

"You can get a G.E.D."

"I can't afford college."

"My dad could help with—"

"He wouldn't, and I wouldn't ask him."

"Then *I'll* ask him."

"In case you haven't noticed, I'm your dad's best roper. Why would he want to lose that? And why would I beg some rich guy's help? Believe me, I wouldn't be worth a bucket of spoiled oats if your dad ever found out how I've been spending my lunch hour."

"We're consenting adults."

"Right. You think that would make a difference to your old man?"

"He's been a hound dog for years. He's got no call to talk. I don't know why you insist on keeping this a secret. I *love* you, Sam."

He paused, touched her cheek. "Aw, honey. That's why we can't let him catch on. He'd try his damnedest to keep us apart."

"He can't keep us apart. It's a free country."

Sam had laughed at that. "Is that what they taught you in that fancy-ass girls' school in Cal-if-orny?" His smile was tinged with a weary tolerance that made him seem infinitely older and wiser than Michelle. "That's not the way the real world works. In the real world, the daughter of a rich movie star doesn't go out with a waitress's son. Believe me, your dad wants you to fall for some guy with a golf handicap, not a PRCA rating."

"That's dumb. Besides, I've fallen for you. And that's not going to change. Not ever." As they finished dressing, she had considered telling him that she was alarmingly late with her period. But she'd said nothing. If it was a false alarm, there was no need to worry him.

He took her hand. "Honey, I don't want it to change. That's why we're better off keeping this quiet."

His words made her feel hopelessly naive. There were differences between them, class differences she didn't want to see. Looking back, she realized that had been apparent to Sam right from the start. That was probably why he didn't think anything of simply disappearing one November night.

She had walked outside with him, into the dry cold and sunshine, bringing along the finished winter landscape.

"Damn." He squinted in the direction of the training arena.

"What's wrong?"

"Jake Dollarhide. I think he saw us."

The foreman's son. She saw the gangly young man standing in the distance, and he was staring directly at them. "So what?" she'd said with breezy disregard. "Let Jake Dollarhide stare all he wants." She put the finished painting behind the seat of the truck.

"I can't take that, Michelle—"

"Yes you can. I'll paint a hundred more for you."

"Believe me, honey, this is enough."

She hadn't known back then that those would be his last words to her. That his last kiss would be a quick, furtive brush of his lips over hers. But after that moment, she had never seen him again.

"Ms. Turner, we're ready for you in Dr. Kehr's office."

Goose bumps rose on Michelle's arms as she entered a comfortable office with a generic but good-quality Robyn Bloss serigraph print on the wall behind the desk. Michelle studied it for a moment, remembering that she used to paint freely, in intense colors of her choosing, not in hues to match the burgundy wing chairs in doctors' offices where people waited for the bad news.

The Bloss print was supposed to be pacifying. To some it might have been. But to Michelle it was profoundly disturbing. Seeing that print was like looking into a mirror.

She seated herself in a leather armchair beside her father. A large window behind the desk afforded a view of the city, gray and bleak in midwinter, the river a colorless vein through the middle of town. Dr. Kehr, the nephrologist, sat opposite them, her ultraclean hands folded atop a stack of files and charts. She had a bland but pleasant smile, no discernible personality, and somehow meeting her for the first time made the whole situation starkly real.

They were going to cut out one of her kidneys and sew it into her father.

Sucking in a deep breath, Michelle shifted in her chair and waited for the rest of the team to arrive. They met Donna Roberts, the transplant coordinator, who was a registered nurse specializing in organ transplantation. Donna did a lot of touching and hand-holding, which Michelle didn't particularly need at that moment, but she figured she'd be grateful for later. Then there was Willard T. Temple, the psychologist and social worker. He could scuttle the whole thing if he didn't think her father and she were mentally prepared for it.

They would each have their own surgeons. They showed up in scrubs, alike as Tweedledee and Tweedledum but with firmer handshakes. Neither of them could stay long because, after all, they were surgeons and they spent all day cutting people, not talking to fading movie stars and their neurotic daughters.

To Michelle's surprise, one of the surgeons held the door open. "This way, Mr. Slade."

Gavin got up. Briefly, he rested his hand on her shoulder. "I'll be back shortly, okay?"

"You're not staying?" Panic pounded in her chest.

"I think they need to draw lines on me or something."

After the door closed, she scowled at Dr. Kehr. "He should be here."

Temple, who held a clipboard with a yellow legal pad, said, "Your father's been drilled on this procedure for months. We wanted a private meeting with you."

"Why?" *Oh my God. Are they going to tell me he won't make it?*

"Because if you have any uncertainty whatsoever about the transplant, we need to determine that. Living kidney donation is an emotional decision. It's natural to feel anxiety about the procedure, even though you want to help. You can speak freely to us. If you decide against the surgery, your father will be told you're not a good match. Our hope is to maintain the relationship between patient and donor, regardless of donation decision."

"I've made my decision," Michelle snapped, stung because she knew she and Gavin didn't have any relationship to maintain. "I already passed all the tests."

"We still have to do the renal angiogram," Dr. Kehr reminded her. "Chances are, you'll be a near-perfect donor. But there could be other issues that make you less than an ideal candidate."

"I'm here, aren't I?" she said fiercely.

"Sometimes there are emotional issues," Temple said in his low-key voice. "Your father indicated you've been estranged for many years. This decision—"

"Don't you get it?" Her voice rose. "There was never any decision to be made. You're welcome to explore my feelings all you want, but you're not going to get me to change my mind." She forced herself to glare straight into his eyes. "My father is dying. My kidney can save him. *That's* the issue, Dr. Temple."

He nodded briefly, and annoyingly made a note on his legal pad. "You should be aware that this procedure alone won't mend the estrangement between you and your father. Flesh and blood alone can't accomplish that."

"I just want him well again," Michelle said, painfully close to tears. "The rest . . . we'll deal with."

When Dr. Kehr started speaking, she was thorough, encouragingly so. She explained what everyone's role would be. She talked about recovery periods, follow-up care, side effects of the meds, and long-term prognosis. She took out badly drawn charts—medical illustration was not terribly lucrative—to show what would happen in the procedure.

That's what she called it. The Procedure.

"Unless the renal angiogram indicates otherwise, the surgeon will take the left kidney." The doctor pointed to the chart.

"I had no idea there was a difference." A heaviness weighted the atmosphere. Though he had left the room, her father's need pressed at Michelle, smothering her. Her hands in her lap ripped a Kleenex to shreds. Guiltily, she balled up the evidence and tucked it into her palm. Too late. Temple had seen. He made a note on his clipboard.

"Using the left kidney is standard," the doctor continued. "The connecting vessels are longer, so we've got more material to work with."

Michelle's hand, out of control now, stole back to press against her left side.

"You have a couple of options for entry." The chart was propped up again. "Later, we'll discuss whether it'll be the front or the back." Her finger traced incision lines on the chart. "Generally, we advise against the back entry, because although it's a more direct route, the recovery is quite painful due to the splitting of the rib cage."

Michelle wished she hadn't said anything about splitting her rib cage. It was hard to keep from looking terrified when the doctor talked like this.

"Also, an incision scar on the back might be troublesome," Donna added.

"What do you mean, troublesome?"

"In the fashion sense. If you like wearing dresses cut low in the back, the scar might show."

"That's not important."

"It doesn't seem like it now. But it's a consideration. A team in Seattle pioneered a harvesting technique that only requires a four-inch incision in the donor."

Harvesting. "That's good to know," Michelle said wryly.

"The long-term effects of having only one kidney are minimal. But there *are* long-term effects." Donna smiled pleasantly. She had honest eyes; Michelle liked her.

"You mean I should avoid cliff diving and logrolling?"

"That would be advisable, yes."

"Suppose I were to get pregnant." She had no idea where that came from; it just slipped out.

"You'd be at a higher than normal risk, but pregnancy isn't prohibited."

"Just asking." Quickly, to cover up her embarrassment, Michelle said, "Here's the big one. Will I be able to play the violin after the surgery?"

"Of course," the nurse assured her, though Michelle could tell from the smile in her eyes she knew this joke.

"Great," Michelle said. "I never could before."

"Just use good sense. Protect that one kidney."

By the time the meeting ended, Michelle was feeling both exhilarated and frightened. Her father came back as everyone was filing out. Dr. Kehr shook hands with her, and she held on to her longer than she should have. Her life and that of her father would quite literally be in this woman's hands.

"Any more questions?" Dr. Kehr asked.

Her father stood still and upright, looking heart-breakingly stoic. It was one of the things that distinguished him as an actor. He had a way of touching people's hearts without moving a muscle.

"Not at the moment," Michelle said. "You were really thorough. Dad?"

"No questions either. I've been doing my homework on this for months, so I guess I'm as prepared as I'll ever be." He sent the doctor a grin. Michelle could see her visibly falling for him. "Can we call you if any questions come up?"

"Of course." She held out a pale blue business card. "You have my home, office, pager, and cell phone. Call anytime." She walked them to the door. "Until next Saturday, then? If Michelle's final tests check out, Monday's our day."

Michelle held the stack of brochures and paperwork in front of her like a shield as they walked out of the hospital annex. "You want me to drive home?"

"No. I'm fine." Before long, they were heading back down the highway.

"The psychologist kept making notes on me," she remarked.

"Temple? He's got a bunch of notes on me, too."

"What do you suppose he was writing?"

Gavin stared straight ahead at the road. "I imagine he's wondering if we're up for this."

"That's stupid. You need a kidney, I'm a match, end of story."

He cleared his throat, seeming to draw words from a hiding place deep inside him. "You have every right to resent me, Michelle."

"I don't resent you."

"Sure you do. Christ, I don't blame you. I wish I'd been a father to you when you were growing up."

Before she could stop herself, she thought of her childhood, the older split-level home in Bel Air. Though there were plenty of single-parent families in Southern California, Michelle always focused on the unbroken ones. She couldn't help the sharp envy she felt watching her friends with their two doting parents. The terrible ache that would engulf her when she saw a girl playing Frisbee in the park with her father . . .

"Is it too late to be a father now?" she asked, the words surprising even her.

A long, awkward silence. His hand came across the seat, touched her shoulder. "I'm willing to try, Michelle. But remember, I'm new at this. I've got a lousy track record."

"What's that supposed to mean?"

He took his hand away. From the corner of her eye, she noticed a furtive flash of guilt in his expression. "You know, last time. You took off, and I didn't know what the hell to do. So I did nothing."

Michelle shut her eyes, but the memories rushed in. *"I'm pregnant, Daddy."*

"I'm not surprised. Your mother was careless, too."

"I figured that McPhee boy was up to no good," her father had said on that bitter November night.

She hadn't asked him how he knew it was Sam's. Jake

Dollarhide had probably ratted on them, just as Sam had predicted.

"I shouldn't have told you," she had said, scared and hurt by his reaction. "Sam will help me through this."

"Is that what he promised?"

"He will when I tell him."

Gavin had snorted with disbelief. "He's cowboy scum, and his mother is trash. Even if he says he'll stick by you, Tammi Lee will drag you both down. You'll be living in some trailer park trying to hold off the law from her. Don't look for any promises from him."

And—damn him—Gavin had been right. That evening when Michelle went to tell Sam about the baby, he was gone without a trace, the shotgun house he'd shared with his mother an empty shell.

"Michelle?" Her father's voice brought her back to the present. "You got mighty quiet there."

"I guess that's because there's so much to say."

Chapter 11

Sylvia was in labor. The mare had been restless all night, hadn't eaten. She was fully dilated, her sides bellowing in and out in the peculiar manner of laboring mares. She kept looking back at her own flanks as if they didn't belong to her. As Edward had taken such glee in showing Cody the day before, her udder was full, her nipples waxy, the milk veins distended. Now she was covered in sweat, a sure sign that her water would break soon.

Sam walked across the field where Edward Bliss and Cody were uncoiling snow fence, readying the slope for the avalanches the spring thaw would bring. He had to force himself to walk at an even pace, to keep his expression neutral when what he really wanted to do was rush headlong and gawk at his son. His *son*. His own flesh and blood.

How was it that Cody had been born and Sam hadn't realized it? Shouldn't he have felt some upheaval inside himself, some alteration in the most essential part of his being?

Babies were born all the time without their fathers knowing. Maybe Sam was no different from Calyx, the champion stud quarter horse that had sired Sylvia's foal. But he still couldn't understand how a baby boy with half his chromosomes had been born and he hadn't even felt a ripple in the pond water.

At the time of Cody's birth, he'd been running. After he and his mother had left Crystal City only hours ahead of the law, they hadn't made much of a home anywhere for a while. Hot checks, unpaid bills, and collection-agency notices had trailed behind them like kicked-up dust.

On that long-ago night, when everything had fallen apart, he hadn't even had time to button his shirt. In the months that followed, they stayed in motels with weekly rates, lay low in a couple of run-down trailer courts, even slept at a roadside park or two. Nothing lasted—not their jobs, not their money, not their luck.

Until the Lander rodeo. It had been pure dumb luck that the Valiant had broken down in Wyoming, right under the billboard for the annual summer event. Tammi Lee had scrounged up enough cash for a pint of Ripple, and Sam had walked into town, hoping to earn a few bucks helping out as a gate runner.

Instead, he'd encountered a guy lying on a stretcher, his face floury white and his severed thumb in a Dixie cup with a piece of ice. Sam had looked on with more interest than horror as the paramedics whisked the cowboy off to reattach his thumb.

It was a classic injury for a team roper. If he dallied the rope the wrong way, the tug of the fleeing steer could sever a thumb. The guy's roping partner had cast a worried eye at the pay window. He didn't want to disqualify himself, even though without a heeler, he couldn't compete. With nothing left to lose, Sam had stepped up. Everyone was so ball-squeezed by the accident that there hadn't been much discussion. They pinned a number on Sam and off he went.

By the end of the night he and the header had won the regional title and nine thousand dollars. Fired up by good fortune, he'd launched a new career by buying an old beat-up trailer and pickup. Then he'd gone looking for a horse. It took him four months to find Sherlock and several more good purses to acquire him, but the quarter horse was worth the trouble. He became Sam's business partner and best friend.

Sam went solo, specializing in calf roping. He didn't want to split his earnings with half of a team. Leaving his mother in a motel on the outskirts of Cheyenne, he took off in the pickup, entering rodeos from San Angelo to Calgary. At night he slept in the gooseneck of Sherlock's trailer and ate his meals out of fast-food bags. He often went home with a woman—there was no shortage of rodeo groupies, and they loved a winner—but he always felt hollow after those encounters. Always caught himself thinking too much of a soft-limbed girl with soulful eyes. He'd lie awake listening to the crickets and consider calling her, and once he actually picked up the phone.

"You got a lot of damned nerve, boy, calling here," Gavin Slade had roared at him.

Sam had braced his fist on the window of the phone booth, an ovenlike kiosk in Oklahoma City. "I want to talk to Michelle, Mr. Slade."

"Over my dead body. You stole from me, McPhee—"

"That's a damned lie." Over the months of rambling,

Sam had put the puzzle together. The day Jake Dollarhide had seen him and Michelle come out of the art studio, several hundred dollars had turned up missing from the foreman's cashbox. Sam had been set up, plain and simple. He wasn't certain Gavin was in on it directly, but it sure as hell was convenient timing—Sam being run off the day he'd been caught nailing the boss's daughter.

"Don't call here anymore," Gavin had warned him. He'd slammed down the phone.

Sam didn't try again. There was no point. His mom was in trouble, and he had to stay on the circuit. Michelle had to go to college. The impossibility of a rich girl–poor boy romance was finally real to him. Shame and hurt pride burned away the last of his innocence. Did Michelle believe he was a thief, or would she realize he'd been framed? Shoot, it really didn't matter.

By the end of that season, Sam had won enough purses to lease his mother a little clapboard house near Seguin, Texas. A year later, he'd passed his G.E.D. and saved up for college tuition. Between rodeoing and school and his wet-brained mother, he hadn't had time to come up for air, much less realize the only girl he'd ever loved had given birth to his son.

As he approached Cody, Sam told himself not to wonder about him as a baby, a toddler, a little boy. That child was gone now, and in his place was an angry teen. The hell of it was, Sam didn't know what to think. Did he really want to know this kid, learn his rage and his flaws, excavate his virtues from beneath the layers of resentment?

"Hey, guys," he said, scanning the fence. "How's it coming?"

"Okay." Cody stood back and gestured at the long line

of pickets curving under the brow of a hill where the avalanche danger was the worst. "I guess."

Sam held his breath. *Did she tell you, Cody? Did she tell you I'm your dad?*

Clearly not, judging by the kid's offhand manner. He held his shoulders hunched up, and his nose was bright red from the cold.

"See any sign of that cat?" Sam asked.

"You mean the mountain lion?"

"Yeah, Edward spotted a carcass last week."

"Snowshoe hare," Edward said. "How's Sylvia doing?"

"That's why I came to get you," Sam said. "It's time."

"What?" Cody snapped to attention, forgetting to sulk.

"Sylvia, the mare," Sam explained. "Her water's about to break, and the foal will come pretty fast after that."

"Yeah?" The kid's face brightened a hundred watts. He was a damned good-looking kid even with the ponytail and earrings. "Can we see her?"

As Sam returned to the snowmobiles, he concealed a smile. "You're not squeamish, are you, Cody?"

"Me? No, man. I got a stomach of iron."

The icy wind blasted their faces as they drove back to the barn, dismounting fast and running inside to attend the birth.

A low grunting sound issued from the birthing stall. A foaling kit, with OB sleeves, tape, the foaling record, a stopwatch, instruments, and drugs lay on a crate. Sam hurried in to find the mare bobbing her head up and down, pawing the straw and acting skittish.

"Everything okay?" Edward asked.

"Let's have a listen." Sam took a stethoscope from the foaling kit and pressed it to the mare's abdomen. The vigorous hiss and swish of her pulse reassured him. He could detect the faint racing pulse of the fetus as well.

But it was beating too fast and shallow for comfort. "Might be some fetal distress, possible dystocia."

"Should I call the vet?" Edward asked.

"Go ahead and put in a call, but I have a feeling the foal will arrive before the vet does. Let's see what kind of shape the amniotic sac's in when it emerges." He set his jaw against a curse. He loved this mare. He sure as hell didn't want to lose her.

"What's that mean?" Cody peered over the edge of the stall. "Dystocia. Sounds bad."

"It means a bad presentation and stress on the foal. Not great news. Edward," he called down the breezeway, "see if you can get the heat turned up higher in here. Don't want the baby to catch a chill." He indicated a bucket outside the birthing stall. "Cody, do me a favor and wrap her tail with that white tape. Then you can wash her perineum and teats, okay? If we don't get everything clean, we're risking infection."

"Wash her . . ." Cody gaped at him in disbelief.

"Teats. And perineum."

"What's a—"

"It's exactly what you think it is."

"Oh, man."

"You said you had a stomach of iron."

Cody grumbled, but he picked up the wrapping. Gingerly, he lifted the mare's tail, grimacing as Sam palpated the abdomen.

"Gross," Cody commented.

"A mare in labor urinates and defecates a lot," Sam said unapologetically.

"Great."

But the boy did a good enough job of wrapping the

tail; then he brought out the bucket of water and disinfectant. With all the diligence Sam could have hoped for, he scrubbed away at the teats.

"Hey," he said, "something's, um, dripping from her."

Sam examined the teats. "Colostrum."

"What does that mean?"

"It means you might want to hurry and get that perineum disinfected, because things are going to speed up pretty soon." Sam tried not to seem anxious. He and Edward had yanked foals many times before, usually with good results. But God. Sylvia. She was the best mare he'd ever had.

The kid took a deep breath and dipped a clean cloth. He lifted the wrapped tail and dabbed hesitantly at first. Then he blew out his breath in a show of determination, planted himself right behind her, and finished the job.

"You might want to stand a little to one side," Sam advised as Cody was rinsing. "Because if you're directly behind her when her water breaks—"

Too late. It broke before he could finish speaking.

She spewed like a fire hose, directly at Cody. The projectile of warm fluid, probably a couple of gallons of it, completely drenched the boy.

"Holy shit," he yelled, jumping back.

"Sorry." Sam bit the inside of his cheek to keep from laughing. "I tried to warn you."

"Thanks for nothing, man."

"You want to go find some dry clothes?"

Cody made for the door, then hesitated. "Will I miss anything?"

"The foal will come any minute now."

"I'll stay then." He ripped off his coat—the black leather thing Sam hated—and dropped it on the floor in the corner. And it was odd, but it seemed to Sam that the kid shed some of his cynicism along with the coat. He could look at Cody now and see a boy, eager and bright-eyed, his young face ablaze with interest.

"Holy shit," he said again. His eyes grew round.

The silvery-slick balloon of the amnion started to come through. "Lie down, baby," Sam said to Sylvia. "Lie down, there's a girl."

After a few minutes, she complied, lowering herself with a grunt of effort.

"Stay down, baby." Sam knelt by her head, holding it and murmuring in her ear. "Stay—"

With a defiant clearing of her throat, Sylvia lurched to her feet.

"That's bad, right?" Cody asked, his face paler than it had been a minute earlier. "She shouldn't be standing up, right?"

"It's better if she lies down," Sam admitted. "But it's pretty pointless to argue with a fifteen-hundred-pound horse. She—"

He broke off as the mare's sides began to fan violently in and out. "Here she comes," Edward said, returning from the office with a cordless phone in his hand.

Sam gave Sylvia's neck a pat. "Vet?"

"Up in Big Arm. He can't get here for an hour."

"Then we're on our own," Sam said. "Get down again, baby, there you are . . ." He coaxed gently, stroked her, massaged her. "Down, that's a girl." Eventually she obeyed. Sam hoped she'd stay put as he knelt to see how things were progressing. "Cody, give me a hand here."

The boy hesitated just for a beat. "Yeah, okay."

The foal was trying to present with its legs sticking up toward the croup, a dangerous situation. Sylvia rolled and twisted, driven by instinct to correct the position. When that didn't work, Sam nodded at Edward. "She needs some help turning it." He held the mare's head, murmuring mind-less phrases, trying to soothe her. Edward and Cody stripped down to T-shirts to wrestle with the slippery emerging legs, Edward uttering low curses and Cody goggle-eyed with fascination and worry.

"I keep losing hold. Damn, that's narrow," Edward said, his hand caught inside. "Cody, are your hands smaller than mine?"

"I guess. You want me to try?"

Edward hesitated, then eased back when the contraction ended. He passed a tube of lubricant to Cody. "Here's what you do. We want the forelegs first, but turned this way, see?"

"Yeah." Cody smeared on the lubricant and took a deep breath. A few seconds later, his hand disappeared in-side the mare. If the situation hadn't been so dire, Sam would have laughed at the expression on the kid's face. Edward coached him, instructing him to bring the legs down and around, working between contractions.

Sylvia grunted and pushed, expelling Cody's hand and then, pulse by pulse, the foal, hooves first. Cody didn't move out of the way in time but caught it against his knees, rearing back when the hindquarters slipped out.

"Easy there." Sam bent to examine the foal, suction-ing out its mouth and nose. It gave a jerk of its bony body, then a strange cough, and began breathing on its own. Its pale muzzle took on the color of life. Its umbilical cord, still attached, pulsed in time with the mare's heartbeat. She stood with a lumbering effort, twisting to lick at her baby.

"Wow," said Cody, his eyes bugging out, his entire front covered with birth fluid, his mouth wide in a grin. "Wow."

Sam squirted iodine on the umbilical cord. He should have become a vet. Or a teacher.

Instead, he was a father who didn't know his son.

That, he decided, as he looked at Cody's sweat-streaked face, was about to change. Whether Michelle liked it or not.

The sac still hung from the mare, slapping against her hind legs. Sam saw the reflex coming, but before he could speak, she kicked out. In a flash of movement, the hoof caught Cody, right on the temple.

Chapter 12

As they approached Crystal City, Gavin kept his gaze fixed dead ahead, his jaw perfectly square, his hands relaxed on the steering wheel. Yet Michelle could tell—there was some subtle turbulence in his manner—that the hospital appointment had rattled him. Monday: 6:45 A.M. Perhaps knowing the precise day and time of the transplant was disconcerting.

It sure as hell was for Michelle.

"Are you all right?" she asked.

"I'm in end-stage renal failure," he said. "How all right can I be?"

"I'm sorry. I wish I knew what to say to you."

"You don't have to apologize for anything." He flexed his hands on the steering wheel. "I'm a lousy father, have been from the get-go. Being sick only makes me lousier."

"I don't know." She tried to keep her voice light. "A

true believer would say it's the universe's way of bringing us together."

"Are you a true believer, Michelle?"

She stared out the window. Long gray-white smudges of highway and snow. "I used to be."

He trained his eyes on the road. "When your mother told me she was pregnant, I panicked. I was just getting started in my career. I was in the most cutthroat business in the world, and I didn't think I'd make it on my own, much less with a family to care for. Kept seeing myself as a failure, pumping gas for a living, trying to make ends meet, chasing down bit parts and making everyone miserable. Didn't have a pot to piss in, Michelle. I had a rented room in Studio City and a risky role coming up."

His words sounded like lines recited from a script.

"That must have been *Shelter from the Storm.*" The film had made him a star and a household name.

"As excuses go, it's pretty weak, but my career was everything at the time. I thought all a father did was send a monthly check, maybe show up for special occasions. The truth is, I never knew how to be a father, and I was too scared to try. Michelle, I'd give anything to change that, but I can't. It's one of the lessons people never seem to learn—that you can't change the past." He glanced sideways at her. "I just hope it's not too late to fix things."

"Why didn't you even try, Daddy? Didn't you know I needed you?" The anguished question burst from her.

"Michelle—"

The mobile phone chirped, startling them and shattering the tension in the truck. Michelle felt a twinge of annoyance. For once she and her father were actually beginning to talk, and now this. He clicked on the speaker phone. "Gavin here."

"It's Edward Bliss, from over at Lonepine."

"What can I do for you, Edward? You're on the speaker phone."

"Is Michelle with you?"

"I'm here." Like a sudden shadow, a chill swept over her. "Is everything all right?"

"Michelle, I'm at Meridian County Hospital. Your boy, he—"

"Jesus Christ." Gavin's foot pressed to the floor, and the truck shot forward, hurtling down the highway toward town.

"What happened?" Her chest pounded with dread.

"He's going to be okay," Edward said quickly. "He was kicked in the head by a horse."

"Oh my God—"

"It happens sometimes, it—" Static crackled, obliterating Edward's voice. As the peaks of the mountains plunged the road into gloom, the connection died.

"We'll be there in five minutes," Gavin said. "You got your seat belt on?"

Michelle nodded. She couldn't speak, could only hang on as they sped into town. The hardware store, the café, the municipal building and library passed in a blur. She died a thousand deaths, racing to get to her son. She imagined Cody, her beautiful boy, broken and bleeding in some emergency room, his head bashed in. *Please. Please. Please.* She could barely find the words to pray.

The truck screeched to a halt in front of the community hospital. Built of narrow reddish brick and small windows, it had an awning that stretched over the emergency entrance. She jumped out, dragging her purse along. The automatic doors hissed open. Lurching to the admittance desk, she was barely able to catch her breath.

"Cody Turner." The lump of dread in her chest started to hurt. "He's my son. He was kicked in the head—"

"—by Sam McPhee's mare," the attendant said. "Curtain area in the examination room, ma'am." She held up a clipboard. "Now, if we could just get some information—"

"Later." She raced down the hall. Earthtone linoleum, green-tiled walls, extra-wide doors with frosted glass windowpanes—were all hospitals alike? A nurse holding a tray of instruments was in the exam room. "You're the mother?"

The Mother. Spoken that way, it sounded so weighty, so dire. She straightened her shoulders, forced herself to get a grip. "I am."

The nurse, whose name tag read Alice O'Brien, nodded at an aqua-colored half curtain enclosing a wheeled cot. Blue jeans tucked into snowmobile boots showed at the bottom. She could hear a low, masculine voice murmuring something indistinct.

"The doctor's with him right now," Nurse O'Brien said.

Michelle parted the curtain. "Cody?"

"Hey, Mom." His voice was small. A flesh-colored patch covered part of his head. Rusty bloodstains streaked his hair. A bluish cast tinged his complexion. His clothes were wet, smeared with blood and a whitish slime. She wanted to touch him, hold him, scream with relief that he was conscious.

The other person in the cubicle was Sam McPhee. "Sam? Where's the doctor?"

Then she noticed what he was wearing. A green fiber gown and a pair of high-intensity lighted eyeglasses. Surgical gloves.

Michelle blinked fast, confused.

"Mom, Sam *is* the doctor," Cody muttered.

"He's what?" She stared at Sam. "You're what?"

"The doctor." Sam lifted a corner of his mouth. "Why do I feel as if I should apologize for that?"

"My God." She sank to a metal swivel stool beside the gurney. The information was coming at her too fast. "Okay, just tell me about Cody. He's a mess. Is he—"

"It's a head injury, Michelle. And he was lucky—it appears to be mild." Sam's voice was gentle. "The other stuff all over him is from the mare."

The nurse arrived with another tray and set it on a rolling table by Sam. The attending clerk came in, too. "Ma'am, you need to sign this."

"What is it?"

"A consent form."

She took the clipboard and lifted her gaze to Sam. He looked like a stranger in the gown and headgear, tall and slightly mystical, the high priest of some alien nation. "What am I consenting to?"

"Treatment. In this case that means you're authorizing me to debride and stitch this head wound."

"I don't want any stitches, man." Cody's lips were practically blue, stark against the shocked pallor of his face.

"We'll numb the area. Easier than going to the dentist," Sam said.

Michelle scribbled her name across the bottom of the sheet. On the next page, she swiftly answered a series of questions about Cody's health history, allergies, reactions to medication—all negative. The form under that was covered with small print. "What's this one?"

"An admit form," the clerk said.

"I want to keep him overnight," Sam explained. "His GCS scale was fifteen—that means all his neurological responses are fine. The CT scan showed a mild subarachnoid hemorrhage, so observation for a short period is probably the only treatment needed. We'll do a routine follow-up later, but I don't expect any complications."

Her hand trembled wildly as she signed. She heard her father come in. "Hey, Sam," he said.

"Gavin." Sam didn't look up from Cody.

Gavin seated himself in a molded-plastic chair inside the door. For a moment an eerie sense of unreality closed in on her. Here she sat, surrounded by her father, her son, and Cody's father in a situation straight out of a nightmare.

One thing at a time. She needed to force herself to concentrate on one thing at a time. "So tell me what happened."

"Cody was helping with a mare in labor," Sam said. "And doing a damned good job of it. Tweezers," he said to the nurse, and began to pick at the edges of the wound. "He helped Sylvia give birth to a gorgeous little filly. That's the good news. Hold this clamp, will you, Alice?

"The bad news is," Sam continued, "Sylvia got a little antsy during the afterbirth and started kicking." He teased away the patch, revealing an alarming curved gash. The flesh gaped open, showing blood-drenched tissue. "Breathe through your nose, Michelle. This isn't pretty."

She rolled the stool closer to the bed. Cody's hand crept out from beneath the blue-paper sheeting and she grasped it, holding on hard. His fingers were icy cold.

"It's okay, Cody-boy," she whispered, calm now, although she knew that later she would fall to pieces. "Just hold real still."

He swallowed, his cheeks and his neck pale. For once he didn't sneer with disgust when she called him the old pet name.

Sam and the nurse cleansed the wound. Somehow she maintained a measured stoicism even though the large flap of skin and copious flow of blood terrified her. The wound was an upside-down crescent shape. She sat transfixed by Sam's hands, noting with a strange, horrified awe how deftly and delicately they worked, how sensitive they were.

His intense absorption in his work both reassured and frightened her. Like a rock tumbling in a stream, the revelation turned over and over in her mind. Sam had become a doctor. A *doctor*.

An ugly, sinking sensation spiraled downward through Michelle. She didn't want to feel this, didn't want to think this, but she realized she had convinced herself that Sam would never amount to anything more than a rodeo bum. That was how she had rationalized the past seventeen years. That was the excuse she gave herself for not moving heaven and earth to find him. She had convinced herself that he'd be a tumbleweed, a ne'er-do-well, hardly a fit father to Cody.

Yet now she saw that Sam had held on to his dream, pursuing it long after she'd abandoned her own.

Don't let me be this small, this petty, she thought. *Don't let me resent this.*

In the end, it was Cody who saved her from her own thoughts. The nurse turned on a pair of buzzing clippers. Cody squeezed her hand in sudden surprise and terror, and a powerful wave of love washed over her. Sam had become his dream, but she had become Cody's mother, and there could be no comparison.

"Mom," Cody said breathlessly.

She forced a smile. "I've been nagging you for months to get a decent haircut. I guess now's as good a time as any."

She couldn't be certain, but as Nurse O'Brien clipped away at the hair, Sam's mouth twitched, just a bit shy of a smile.

She shouldn't be surprised that he actually became a doctor. It made sense, after the way his mother raised him. He wanted a way to make people better.

The attending clerk brought Gavin a cup of water. Michelle had forgotten he was there. The glaring overhead light magnified the lines of fatigue around his eyes.

"Dad, you should go on home. It's been a long day."

"I'll stay."

"No, really. The last thing I need is for both of you to be laid up. I'd feel a lot better if you waited at home. I'll call."

"I'm staying," he said in his deep actor's voice.

He had known. He had known all along that the father of her son was a doctor, living here in Crystal City, and he had never bothered to tell her.

"Damn it." The coiled tension in her sprang up. "You make me nervous, sitting around and waiting. *Please,* Dad—"

"I'll give Michelle a ride home when we're done," Sam said, an edge of impatience in his voice. And he was right to be impatient. He had to concentrate, not mediate family squabbles.

Gavin hesitated; then he nodded and got to his feet. He came over to the table and gave Cody's shoulder a squeeze. "Take care now, you hear?"

Other than their first handshake, this was the only time she had seen him touch her son.

"Yeah," Cody said. "See you."

"We're going to numb the area now," Sam said. Nurse O'Brien finished clipping, then disinfected and draped the wound.

Because of the draping, she could no longer see his face. A calculated move, she surmised once she saw the needle Sam was using.

"This'll sting," he warned, being honest but not alarming. "You'll feel a pinch, and it'll probably make your eyes water."

Pretty smooth, thought Michelle. Giving the kid an excuse to cry if he needed to.

Cody squeezed again. She squeezed back. Sam injected Xylocaine in a few spots, then set aside the syringe.

"Okay, we have a few minutes to talk," he said. "Need to give the anesthetic time to work."

Michelle swallowed, the lump in her throat still painful. "So talk."

"It's a big laceration." Without touching Cody, he followed the curve of it with a finger. "Cody and that mare were really up close and personal. It could have been worse, but Edward removed the horse's shoes last night, because we knew the birth was imminent. So the damage is slightly less than it could have been."

She thought about the strange yet familiar smell on Cody's damp clothes. It was musky, faintly sweet, yet with an oceanic tang. The birth smell. Her son was drenched in it.

Sam pointed again. "See how this goes down to his temple?"

She nodded, thinking how delicate the tracery of tiny veins looked. How vulnerable. The terror pushed upward from her chest, but true to form she contained it.

"That means I'll be stitching in the region of his face, just here."

There was about an inch between his brow and hairline. The wound was stark there, the flesh amber in color from the disinfectant. "Now, I'm not a plastic surgeon," he said. "I usually refer cases like this to a specialist."

"But this is unusual?"

"Somewhat. I'm inclined to do this myself, here and

now. I can take a lot of tiny stitches—I had practice during a clinical rotation I did with a cleft palate specialist in the Yucatán."

The Yucatán? It was strange to think of all the places Sam had been, all the things he had done in the years they'd been strangers. He had gone to the Yucatán while she had raised his son.

"You're probably going to see a scar," he concluded.

"So is there an alternative?" she asked.

"I could clamp the wound, and then you could take him to Missoula. There's a great face guy there."

"The plastic surgeon wouldn't come here?"

Sam hesitated. "Not this guy."

"So you want me to decide."

Sam regarded her for a long time. She wondered what was going on in his head, what it was like for him to have his wounded son lying here yet to have no say in his treatment. She thought of all the times she'd had to make a decision about Cody, wishing for someone else to talk it over with. She'd felt so alone on those occasions.

"I've given you the options, Michelle."

"I don't want to know the options. I want to know what to *do*."

"Chances are excellent that a trip to Missoula won't do him a bit of harm—"

"Quit being such a . . . a *doctor*. I want you to tell me the right thing—"

"Just stitch the damn thing up." A small, annoyed voice crept out from under the draping.

Both Sam and she looked down at Cody. "Really?" she asked.

"Yeah. I want to get it over with. A drive to Missoula doesn't exactly sound fun."

"How big a scar?" she asked Sam.

"You can see where it'll be. A thin line. Red at first, and eventually it'll fade to white."

A shiver eddied over her. It was an accident, yes, but Cody was going to be marked by this incident, marked for life. He'd never be the same.

"Go for it," Cody said miserably.

"All right." Her voice was soft. "Go ahead and finish, Sam."

He held himself very still for a few moments. He didn't move, though she sensed an odd calm settling over him. It was invisible, yet she could see it happening, like some new sort of medical Zen.

True to his word, he took tiny stitches, working with a needle and silk so fine she had to squint to see it. During the procedure, she sat holding Cody's hand as he lay silent and still.

Despite what Sam said about not being a specialist, she could tell one thing for certain. He was a good doctor. He worked smoothly with the nurse. The two of them had a comfortable rapport as if they'd known each other a long while. From time to time the attending clerk came in, and he answered her questions without so much as glancing up or breaking his concentration. His hands moved with a precise, mesmeric rhythm.

Through it all, Cody lay motionless and admirably calm, his hand in Michelle's.

As Sam was finally finishing up, she decided to say what was on her mind. "So I guess this means you know about my father."

"I'm a family practitioner."

"But you know about his illness."

"My partner, Karl Schenk, is his primary-care physician. Gavin didn't tell you?"

"It's all I can do to keep up with the nephrologists and surgeons."

Sam tied off a stitch. "He's getting good care in Missoula."

"He's getting one of my kidneys."

He hesitated for a beat, then took another stitch. "That's really something, Michelle. I figured they'd eyeball him for a transplant."

"How did you figure that?"

Without even looking up, he seemed to sense her getting defensive. "Now, don't turn all prickly on me. Gavin's general health is excellent. Nonsmoker, nondiabetic. Physiologically, he couldn't be a better candidate. That's all I meant. No doctor I know would use Gavin's fame to make a transplant poster boy of him."

He removed the draping. Cody looked pale but relaxed, his eyelids heavy.

"Okay, cowboy?" Sam asked.

"I guess." He took his hand away from Michelle's. He seemed embarrassed that he'd been clinging to it the whole time.

Sam beamed a pen-sized light in Cody's eyes, first one, then the other. "You're not going to kick me in the head like your last patient did to you?"

"I'll decide after I see the stitches."

Michelle liked Sam's ease with the boy. He'd only known him two days, yet his manner was open and natural. Sometimes she wished Brad would—

Alice, the nurse, held up a hand mirror.

Sam grinned. "Take a look, Frankenstein."

Cody grimaced. "Nice haircut."

"You can have Hazlett fix it. He's the local barber, does house calls at the hospital. Or you could wait until you're discharged," Sam said.

"Hey," said Cody. "Do I have to stay?"

Sam's gaze was level and direct. "Yep. Just overnight, okay?"

Michelle studied Cody's dubious face, then Sam's. Dear God, she thought, they look alike. The similarity was apparent now that Cody's long hair had been cropped. He looked almost exactly like Sam did, back when Sam had been the beginning and end of her world.

She got up quickly. "I'll stay with him."

"Oh, no you don't, Mom," Cody said. "I can handle spending one night in the hospital."

She patted his leg. Again she felt that dark hollow of loss, as if her little boy had disappeared before her eyes. "Tonight's going to be a lot harder on me than on you."

"Don't worry about me, Mom."

"I'll always worry about you." The lump in her throat swelled. "Thanks for holding my hand through that."

He lifted half his mouth in a crooked grin. Sam's grin. "Right, Mom."

Chapter 13

When Sam left the hospital, he found Michelle sitting in the dark outside, cradling a Styrofoam cup of tea and crying.

The sight of her on the concrete bench, looking so small and alone, stopped him in his tracks. "Hey," he said, easing down next to her. "Have a Kleenex."

Nearby, the door opened and Alice O'Brien came out, a duffel bag slung over her shoulder. She had that weary sort of prettiness common to a lot of nurses, and she regarded him with more kindness than he deserved, given their history together. "'Night, Sam," she said.

"See you tomorrow, Alice."

Michelle's gaze followed her until night cloaked her in darkness. "She doesn't call you doctor."

At some point he'd have to explain about Alice. But not now. There were other things to discuss now. "To these folks I'm just Sam McPhee. One of them. One of the tribe." He turned to her, noticing the silvery track of a tear on her cheek. He wanted to touch it. Taste it. Make it go away. *Christ.* He shoved his hands into his jacket pockets. "You okay?"

She wiped her face with the tissue. "A little overwhelmed, I guess. It's been a long day."

"You held together like a champ in there," he said, and he meant it. If she was like other mothers of injured kids he'd treated, her insides were a train wreck. Yet outwardly, like so many of those steel-spined mothers, she had been calm and efficient while helping Cody get settled into his room. She'd bought him a paperback Anne Rice novel and a kit of toiletries from the gift shop, sat with him for a while, then left after dinner was served and a Bruce Willis movie came on.

"I can always hold together for Cody," she said.

"He's never seen you lose it?"

"No." She scrubbed away the last of her tears. "I told myself right from the start that I'd be the Rock of Gibraltar for him."

His heart heard what she would not say. That she had been all alone. That in two-parent families, one had the luxury of the occasional breakdown while the other took over. That during all her parental crises, no one had ever been there to hand her a Kleenex.

He couldn't help wondering what it would be like to be in that picture with her. Couldn't help wondering what this strange grown-up Michelle was like. Did she still cry when she heard a sad song on the radio, still get the hiccups when she laughed too hard? Did she still make that funny sound in the back of her throat when she came?

He stood up, his head spinning with anger, frustration, loss—and a lingering fascination with this woman who, despite years of separation, had never quite left him. "Let me buy you dinner."

"No." Her refusal came swiftly, automatically.

"Wrong answer, ma'am. Remember, I'm your ride home."

"But—"

"No buts. Stay right there. I need to change out of my scrubs, and then I'm taking you out to Trudy's for a steak." He walked toward the automatic doors. "People from Seattle eat steak, right?"

She lifted her face to him, the parking lot light carving graceful shadows on her cheeks. And finally, fleetingly, she smiled. "I guess people from Montana would be insulted if we refused, right?"

Sam tried not to make too much of her acceptance as he headed inside, but the light warmth in his chest was the most pleasurable thing he'd felt all day. He went to his locker in the lounge, thinking how unreal it had been to treat his own son. To know that the fragile flesh and bone beneath his hands belonged, at least biologically, to him.

He thought about the day he'd decided to become a doctor. He'd been eight or nine years old, riding in a beat-up old car along a straight, flat road. It was a Valiant with a fake Navajo rug covering the torn upholstery. A bag of Cheetos and a bottle of something red lay on the seat beside him. His mother was smoking a cigarette and singing with the radio.

His mother knew the words to all the rockabilly songs, because for one amazing year she had been the vocalist for a Denver band called Road Rage. Sam was too young to remember it, but she claimed it was the best year of her life. They'd traveled all over the country, and their hit single, "Dearly Departed," had rocketed to number one on the *Country Billboard* charts.

Finding success even harder to deal with than failure, the band had broken up, its members scattered. Still, his mom sang along with the radio, her voice harsh with the static of drinking and cigarettes.

Sam had sat silent, watching bugs squishing on the windshield. After a while, he told his mother he had to pee, so she pulled off at a rest stop. By the time he finished in the men's room, Tammi Lee was asleep in the car. So he climbed on top of the hood to wait.

There he was, a towheaded little kid sitting alone on the hood of a beat-up old car, watching people pull off the highway to rest. Whenever he saw families, he felt a funny tugging sensation in his gut. A mom, a dad, two or three kids, a dog. Doing stuff as simple as having a game of catch or sitting at a concrete picnic table, eating sandwiches and pouring Kool-Aid from a plastic jug. These things—these simple, unremarkable rituals—were things he wanted so bad he ached inside.

On that particular day, he twisted around on the hood of the car, stared at his mother, and wished for some magic spell to make her wake up, smile at him, ruffle his hair, ask him if he wanted a glass of milk.

Her eyes flickered open and just for a second, he thought the spell was going to work. Then she wiped the back of her hand across her mouth, dug in her pocket, took out some quarters. She held a trembling fist out the car window and said, "Get me a Tab, will you, hon?" in what he thought of as her tired voice. Later he figured out it was her hungover voice.

And even though she wasn't like the mothers pouring Kool-Aid, he loved her. Kids, he found out later when he became a doctor, loved their monster parents, no matter what.

On the way back from the vending machine—cold can of Tab held in both hands—a boy and his dad ran past, tossing a softball back and forth. The kid almost slammed into him, but sidestepped at the last minute. He never looked at Sam. Just sort of moved on by. They drove a nice car with M.D. plates. Sam was on the road so much he knew about M.D. plates.

His mom was acting funny when he got back to the car. Her face was white and shiny with sweat, her eyes glazed and rolled back in her head. She arched her back against the seat of the car and a thin, terrible noise crawled from her throat. Sam dropped the cold can on the ground and raced for the man with the softball. "Hey, mister," he yelled. "Are you a doctor?" When the man nodded, Sam said, "My mom's sick."

The doctor came over to the car and put his hand on her forehead, lifting her eyelid with his thumb. "Ma'am?" he asked. "Ma'am, can you hear me?" His wife came over with a bag. The doctor asked some questions—what had she been drinking, how long had she been like this—and Sam babbled out the answers. Rummaging in the bag, the doctor went to work. A short time later, Tammi Lee lay groggy but calm, acting sheepish as she spoke with the doctor, assuring him she'd seek help in the next town.

Sam decided right then and there he wanted to be a doctor. He wanted to be the kind of guy who drove a nice car and played catch with his son and when someone got sick, fixed her.

That little kid seemed a distant stranger now, and many years passed before Tammi Lee kept her promise to get help. Sam hurried, getting into his street clothes in record time, worried that Michelle might change her mind, disappear like a bursting bubble from his life.

Sort of like he'd disappeared from hers.

He shoved his feet into his boots, combed his hair, and slammed his locker shut. When he got outside, she was gone. He stood there, a curse forming on his mouth.

She came out of the hospital behind him. "I went to check on Cody one last time."

He exhaled, the curse unspoken. "And?"

"He's sleeping."

"Good. Best thing for him."

She bit her lip uncertainly. Sam took her hand, feeling the shape of it through her winter glove. She pulled away, and he didn't try again. "He's going to be fine. I'm on call all night, and Raymond's on duty."

"Raymond?"

"Raymond Bear, the head nurse. We call him the Shaman. He can sense a patient in distress even before the monitors, I swear it. Damnedest thing you've ever seen."

"Is he the guy reading *Soldier of Fortune* magazine at the nurses' station?"

"That's him. If he's reading a magazine, that means he's not worried." His hand flexed, remembering the shape of hers. "Come on. My truck's over here."

Only four of the eighteen tables at Trudy's were occupied, but that wasn't unusual for a cold Monday night. With its red vinyl tablecloths, gold plastic tumblers, and longhorn salt and pepper shakers, the place resembled a garage sale from the seventies. What it lacked in elegance it more than made up for in good, simple food.

"Just stick with the straightforward stuff, and you can't go wrong." Sam opened his menu.

"I see the wine list is a no-brainer." She cracked a

smile that did funny things to his insides. "Red, white . . . I assume Rosy means rosé?"

"Welcome to Crystal City."

Her smile lingered. "Still pretty provincial around here."

She was a stranger to him. She was a vast, uncharted continent. Mysterious, but something he wanted to explore.

"You can find all the glitz and sophistication you want in Kalispell and Bozeman. Your old man was one of the first to move up here from Hollywood, but he sure wasn't the last. In downtown Whitefish you can buy a Tiffany bracelet and millesime cognac."

"You could have made a lot more money setting up your practice in one of those towns." She closed her menu.

"Why do people always assume doctors are in it for the money?"

"All the doctors I know are."

He thought of Karl, and of Dr. Brower in the Yucatán. "Then you know the wrong doctors," he said. "There used to be three of us in the practice here, but one defected to Kalispell." He didn't say so, but the third partner made a fortune writing prescriptions for Valium and Zoloft.

"So why didn't you follow the money?"

"I belong here. Karl and I work for the tribe up at the Flathead reservation. It's not about money, Michelle. If it was about money, I could make fifty grand roping calves for a week in Vegas."

"You're not only a doctor, but you're noble."

"Is that what you think?"

"I think you came back here just to give everyone an inferiority complex."

He laughed. "Right."

"Why *did* you pick this particular town?"

No one had ever asked him that before. His creden-

tials were good enough; he'd gone through a six-year combined degree program, and his training from UT was first-
rate. He could have gone anywhere.

"I started thinking about a small-town practice when
I was working in the Yucatán, mainly with Mexican Indi-
ans. I learned more than medicine there. A child is born
with a cleft palate? You fix it, and the kid has a better
life. A man suffers from hepatitis? You treat him, he sur-
vives, and you immunize his family. That's the beauty of
working in third-world countries."

"So why not stay in a third-world country?"

"Because we have those right here in our own back-
yard. Small towns, Indian reservations, depressed areas
that can't support a lucrative practice." He studied
Michelle, noting the understated elegance of her gold
watch, the French designer earrings. "I know what it's like
to have money—I had that in my rodeo days. Well, some
of the time, at least. I know what money can and can't
do for a man."

"See? You are too noble."

He thought about the early days when he'd slept in
his horse trailer or the back of his pickup truck, and how
he'd lie awake nights on fire and in agony from wanting
what rich folks like Gavin Slade had. It had been a sickness with Sam, that need to feel he could measure up, and
it probably explained why he drove himself so hard, both
in the arena and in the clinic. Only time, and the deep
self-knowledge that came of healing people, had cured him
of the sickness.

"I'm not noble, Michelle," he said. "I'm just a guy."

They ordered steak dinners and a bottle of wine from
a waitress who knew Sam by name. When she departed,
Michelle watched her from the corner of her eye. "Are
we fueling gossip?"

"In a place this size?" he asked. "Are you kidding? You'll probably read about this dinner on the front page of the *Towne Tattler*."

"I didn't know the paparazzi were so vicious here." She smiled with an old mischievous sweetness he remembered well. Too well. He was getting dizzy gawking at her. It should come as no surprise that the daughter of Gavin Slade turned out to be even more of a knockout at thirty-five than she had been at eighteen. But then again, she had always surprised him.

She watched him with an expression that made his gut churn. Dewy eyes and moist lips. Total absorption in what he was saying. "And so you chose Crystal City," she said.

"Yeah. I knew Edward Bliss from the circuit, he needed a partner for Lonepine, the town needed a doctor, so it all worked out." What the hell, Sam thought. He might as well level with her. He wanted to be in the place where he had been with Michelle, where his dreams had been born and where hope had lingered in spite of everything. "And I figured I'd see you again."

She had no reply to that, but contemplated it with a silence he couldn't read.

While they ate, he thought about the night he'd left. The old Valiant had puttered through the quiet streets of Crystal City, passing the Truxtop and the feed store and the Lynwood Theater, the one-screen cinema where he and Michelle had sat holding hands in the dark. He remembered the yellowish beam of the headlights, the cigarette smell of the blanket covering the seat, the tinny sound of the radio playing a cowboy song, the too-quick rasp of his mother's breathing.

She was nervous, even though Sam, full of outrage,

had wanted to stay and fight his accusers. "I didn't steal a thing," he insisted. "Not a damned thing."

"I know that," his mother had said with weary resignation. "Do you think that matters? Gavin Slade doesn't want you hanging around his daughter. This is his way of telling you that."

"Let's not run away, Mama. It's a free country—"

"Gavin Slade owns this town. If he wants us gone, we're gone." She had looked at him sideways, peering through the darkness. "You're not the only one they've decided to pin something on."

He braced himself. "What do you mean?"

"I had a little visit from Deputy O'Shea this evening. Seems he suddenly discovered a couple of hot checks, a couple of parole violations, and at least two outstanding warrants in Colorado. And that *wasn't* a set-up. I'll have to do time, son. Is that what you want?"

"What I want is for us to quit running."

"Well, we sure as hell can't afford a lawyer. And I sure as hell don't want to be a guest of the state for the foreseeable future. So off we go." Tammi Lee had reached out to punch in the cigarette lighter. "I guess it won't help much to tell you I'm sorry," she said. "I screwed up. Again. Just when you were starting to like living around here."

He had a fierce urge to fling himself out of the car. For years he'd been fleeing with her, but now he had someone to fight for. Michelle. And his own innocence. But he knew he had to stick with his mom. Tammi Lee Gilmer would never survive without him.

Michelle would.

"At least let me stop and say good-bye to her," he'd said.

Tammi Lee grabbed his arm. "This is serious, son. It's

the real world. People like us can't take a risk like that. We set foot on that property, and we're toast."

Sam knew what she wanted him to say. *It's okay, Mama. We'll find someplace else. Something will work out for us. . . .* That's what he always said to her, every time they left a town on the lam. Well, not this time. This time, he wasn't going to tell her everything was okay.

The full moon rode high in the cold November night, and he could see Blue Rock Ranch on the way out of town, a snug compound in the distance, lights twinkling from the windows, a twist of smoke coming from the chimney of the main house.

'Bye, Michelle.

Knowing her had taught him something medical school never could—that the human heart could sing. He had vowed that night to come back to her once he and Tammi Lee settled down somewhere. But there was no time to call the next day, or the day after that, and when he finally scrounged up a handful of change to call from that pay phone in Oklahoma City, he was too late.

"I left Blue Rock the day after you disappeared," she said softly, after her long silence. "My father wasn't terribly understanding about my pregnancy."

Now, that didn't surprise him. Gavin Slade was a man devoted to his own image. The perfect acting career, perfect stock to parade at rodeos, perfect daughter . . . until she had turned out to be human and flawed. After that, she couldn't be part of his image. He had excised her swiftly and cleanly from his life.

"I wish I'd known that," he said quietly.

She sipped her water, a droplet gleaming on her lower lip. Sam tried not to stare. "There's probably a gloat factor involved in my coming back, too," he admitted. "Maybe

on some level I wanted to say 'screw you' to guys like—"
He broke off, catching himself.

"Guys like my father."

"Yeah, okay."

"He should have told me you were living here. But I
can't seem to get all worked up over old business like
that. His illness makes everything else seem so petty."
Michelle set down her water glass with a nervous rattle
of ice. "So tell me how you did it," she said. "Tell me
how you became a doctor."

"Rodeo."

"What do you mean?"

"I used rodeo money to put myself through school."

"You're kidding."

"No, ma'am." He took a bite of his steak. "I passed
my G.E.D. and got into a combined degree program, so I
could get my bachelor's and M.D. in six years. It was a
pain in the butt, living on the road, sleeping in a horse
trailer most nights. I lived on autopilot for a lot of years.
Didn't look left or right, didn't let myself falter. I stayed
focused on that one and only goal—to get through school
and residency, and I didn't let up until I made it." He
picked up a breadstick, snapped it in half. "Sometimes I
wonder what I missed in those years." A shadowy wave
washed over him. "The birth of my son, for one thing."
He took one look at her face and said, "Aw, shit. I didn't
mean to—"

"I want to know the rest. What about your mother?"

"She's okay. On the wagon, living over on Aspen
Street." It sounded a hell of a lot simpler than it had been.
With Sam pushing, sometimes bullying her into rehab,
she'd fought every inch of the way. But each time she
stumbled, he picked her up, checked her back in to rehab
or sent her to yet another AA meeting. Sometimes he had

to be harsh with her, because sometimes that was the only thing that worked. The experience had given him an edge of ruthlessness he didn't particularly like.

Finally, after years of battling Tammi Lee's addiction, sobriety stuck. She had been sober for five years.

"Really? That's great, Sam."

"She works at LaNelle's Quilt Shoppe in town." Ah, Christ, he thought. He was going to have to tell Tammi Lee about Cody. He had no idea how she'd take it. She was sober, but she'd always be fragile. You never knew what might set her off. "So what about you? I'll bet you've got paintings hanging in the Met."

She stared down at her salad plate. "Maybe the *rest room* of the Met. I work for an ad agency."

"Functional art, then." He immediately wished he could reel his words back in.

She laughed, but the sound was brittle and forced. "Oh, yeah. Pictures of scrubbing bubbles and industrial extrusions."

He felt a sinking regret. She had been so vibrant, so damned talented that people caught their breath when they saw her paintings. She had loved art the way most folks loved food or air. "So is painting a hobby for you now, or—"

"I don't paint, Sam." She stabbed her fork at her salad. "I never had the time. I was busy with Cody."

Shit.

"You should have found me," he said, an edge in his voice. "Should have made me help."

"Oh, right. In between roping championships? Clinical rotations? Trips to Mexico?"

"I want those years back," he said brusquely. "All those years I didn't know I had a son."

"You weren't there. I couldn't find you."

"How hard did you look, Michelle? It wasn't like I was in hiding."

"Neither was I," she snapped.

"But I wasn't keeping anything from you, goddammit."

"If I'd tracked you down, would it have mattered? Would you have given up rodeo and medical school for us?"

"Why would I have to choose? We could have done it all, Michelle."

"You're dreaming. I tried doing it all, and it's too hard."

He thought of the drawings and paintings she'd turned her back on. Was it because her passion was gone, or because she just didn't have time? "Okay, so I missed my son's childhood. We can't get back the years we lost. But maybe we can go on from here."

Even as he spoke, he wondered why he thought he could succeed with Michelle, who was infinitely more complicated, more demanding, more challenging than any woman he'd known.

"I don't understand."

"Damn it, Michelle, I'm not going to apologize for my goddamned life. You got the kid, I got the career. Which one of us should be gloating?"

She winced. "Sam. Please."

He reminded himself that her son had been injured while in his care, and that she'd been in Missoula all day with a transplant team questioning her, poking at her. "What say we change the subject?"

She relaxed against the back of the red Naugahyde booth. "Think we have anything in common after all these years?"

A son. A boy I never knew. He forced himself not to say it. "Keep talking, and we'll see."

The tension eased up a little. Never in a million years did Sam think he'd be here, with her. Watching her pick at her meal, he wondered what she thought about, what she wished for, these days. When he'd first come back to Crystal City he figured he might see her now and again when she visited Gavin. But local gossip had put that expectation to rest. Everyone in town knew Gavin Slade and his daughter were estranged. But no one knew the reason.

"So where do we start?" he murmured.

She set down her fork. "You mean, telling Cody about us?"

He wasn't sure what he meant. But he nodded, because it made sense. "Yeah. Do you want to tell him yourself or together or what?"

"Um, I guess I thought I'd do it myself. I'm not used to consulting with anyone on decisions that have to do with Cody."

"Whose fault is that?"

"Oh, Sam. I'm not trying to hurt you. I'm trying to be realistic here. I raised Cody alone. I made some good choices and some bad ones for him, just like any parent. I never expected to have to deal with *this*."

"You say *this* like it's a case of VD or something."

"That's not what I mean. Damn it, Sam. You jump on everything I say. Just like—" She shook her head in bewilderment. "Just like Cody does."

"How do you think he'll take the news?"

"After today?" There it was again, that soft smile that drove him crazy, reaching across the years to remind him of how well he used to know her. "He'll be amazed."

"Yeah?"

"He's a complicated kid. Used to be a pretty great

kid, actually. You'd never know it to look at him now, but this is a boy who used to bring me the paper in bed every morning. He'd sit in my lap and fiddle with my hair while I read him the funny pages."

Sam closed his eyes. And he saw the picture so clearly it nearly choked him. *Why couldn't I be there? Goddammit, why couldn't I be in the picture?* He felt a jolt of anger—heated, irrational.

"Anyway, he's not so warm and fuzzy anymore," Michelle said.

Sam opened his eyes. "Hell, I noticed."

"Some days I don't even think I know him. But I believe he'll be . . . glad to learn you're his father."

"Glad. What do you mean by glad?"

"Just . . . glad. Wouldn't you, if you finally met *your* father?"

"Assuming my mother knew for sure who he was. But yeah. Maybe I'd be glad." He cleared his throat. "Once we—once you tell him, what do you think about asking him if he'd like to stay with me for a while?"

She reared back in her seat. *"What?"*

"You heard me, Michelle."

Her hand closed into a fist. She seemed to grow in stature, a lioness defending her cub. "Out of the question."

"Why?"

"We didn't come back here for good. We live in Seattle."

"You said yourself he was giving you a rough time—"

"That doesn't mean I'm willing to give him up. He's not a dog you take back to the pound because he turned out to be a pain in the neck. Jesus, Sam, what can you be thinking?"

"That I have a son you never bothered to tell me about. I want to find out what he's like, what his plans are for college." He hesitated. "I intend to contribute to that and everything else."

She pressed her palms on the table. How clean her hands and fingernails were. They used to always be smeared and spattered with paint. He remembered that about her, remembered her paint-smudged hand touching his cheek, his chest, lower . . . *Damn.*

"Child-support payments? I don't expect it, Sam. And I certainly don't need it."

"Too bad. I intend to contribute anyway."

She stared off into space. "That's the kind of father I had. The one with the checkbook."

He glared at her, but the truth echoed through him. He wasn't sure Cody was something he wanted or needed or was ready for right now, but one thing was certain—if he wanted a place in the boy's heart, in his life, he'd have to earn it. And he sure as hell couldn't do that in a few weeks.

Tuesday

Chapter 14

When the phone rang, Michelle jerked herself out of the restless half sleep that had tormented her all night. Fumbling for the receiver by the bed, she felt a swift revival of every fear and nightmare that had plagued her since leaving her injured son in the hospital.

She clutched the receiver with both hands. "Yes?"

"Mom?"

"Cody!" Her heart shot straight to her throat. "What's the matter? Are you all right? Did something—"

"Hey, Mom, slow down. I'm okay. Sam said I should call and let you know."

Her chest sagged like a deflating balloon. She felt as if she had been holding her breath, bracing herself, for hours. "Wow, Cody. It's good to hear your voice."

"Sam says I'll be discharged today. No sign of concussion."

She glanced at the clock: 6:45 A.M. For all his teenage bravado, Cody probably hadn't had a great night, either.

"I'll come right away." She sat up against the headboard.

"Okay. Sam wants to talk to you for a minute. See you, Mom."

During the pause while she waited for Sam, she let her mouth form a tremulous smile of relief. Nothing, absolutely nothing in the entire universe matched the terror of a mother's fear for her child. When the fear was alleviated, it left in its wake a powerful euphoria, almost a giddiness.

"Hi, Michelle." Sam's voice raised the giddiness to a windstorm in her chest.

Get a grip, she told herself. This is Cody's doctor. *Doctor.*

"Thanks for letting him call. I earned another four hundred new gray hairs last night."

"So wear a hat."

Not even a smart remark could dim her mood. "As soon as I let my dad know what's going on, I'll be there."

A scant ten minutes later, Michelle had put on wool leggings and an oversize Irish sweater, and she was considering the array of hats on the hall tree. She knew she should take the time to call Brad and fill him in on all the drama, not to mention letting him know how the appointment in Missoula had gone.

But she couldn't phone him yet. It was too early in the morning, and Cody was waiting.

There was another reason she was reluctant to phone Brad, but she refused to ponder it right now. Feeling guilty was just something she had learned to do—must be a mother thing. Or a woman thing.

She snatched a heather wool cap from the hall tree, jammed on her boots, and trudged outside. Faint dawn veined the mountaintops in the east, drawing a stark, fiery line over the highest peaks and sending shadows of pink down the ridges and valleys. Snow had dusted the area in the night, and it was cold enough to squeak beneath her boots as she walked across the compound to the main house. Steam wafted gently from the pool on the patio.

A single light burned in the kitchen, sending a fan of gold across the new-fallen snow in the yard. Before mounting the steps to the front porch, she stopped, spying her father inside.

He stood at the counter with the robe half open as he did something with the dialysis apparatus he'd been so reluctant to discuss. It was a private moment, and she couldn't intrude; she knew she mustn't. She took a step back. Gavin turned his head slightly, and she saw him in profile.

Just for a second or two he fell still, bringing his hand to his forehead and leaning the other hand on the counter.

Her throat constricted as she forced her gaze away. For the first time since learning of his illness, she felt the thudding reality of the disease, and it was strange to feel the truth while standing out in the cold fire of dawn, looking in at a scene so painful and private that she nearly choked on her own breath.

Her father was sick, dying, desperately in need of the operation. Urgency pumped through her like adrenaline. She wanted to have the surgery *now,* not next week. Dear God, if she could pluck out the organ with her own hand and give it to him right this moment, she'd do it.

Hurrying back to the guesthouse, she scribbled a note

of explanation to her father and left it at the front door.
On the porch she hesitated. Maybe she should go in, say
good morning, ask him if he needed anything. What if he
wanted Michelle, her company, the comfort she could
offer?

But she couldn't go do it. Couldn't go in there, intrude. Couldn't be the daughter he needed. They were
strangers in too many ways.

As she drove into town, she grabbed the cell phone
and punched in the renal specialist's number. The doctor's
answering service asked if there was an emergency. When
she admitted there was not, she was advised to call during regular office hours.

"I need to speak to her now," she said.

"Ma'am, I'd be happy to take your number—"

"My father is sick now, not during office hours."

"The emergency number is—"

"I know the emergency number." She dragged in a
long breath. "What about Donna Roberts, the transplant
nurse. Is she in?"

"She's on duty at nine o'clock."

"Temple, then. Damn it, is he taking calls?"

"I'll forward the call, ma'am."

Simple as that. Temple, the psychologist, knew people didn't get neurotic on a schedule.

"This is Dr. Temple." He sounded crisp and alert, considering the hour.

"It's Michelle Turner, remember?"

"Of course. What can I do for you?"

The words came out in a rush. "Look, I want the transplant to happen sooner. I'm not willing to work around
the surgeon's ski trip or whatever's holding it up. This
morning my father—I saw—" She broke off, picturing
Willard Temple at a Corian breakfast counter in his sub-

urban tract mansion, drinking coffee and looking out over the golf course that backed up to his yard.

"Anyway, I can't stand seeing him like this. Why can't I do the rest of the tests today and the surgery tomorrow?"

A pause. An ominous, doctorlike pause. "Actually, Ms. Turner, I was going to recommend that your surgery be postponed until you and your father could go through some more counseling about the procedure."

A silent scream echoed through Michelle. Her knuckles whitened as she gripped the receiver. "Um, wait a minute. Run that by me again?"

"I don't have your records in front of me at the moment, but there's some concern that there are issues that need to be explored and resolved before we proceed."

Devastation and rage had a taste, she realized. They tasted rusty and bitter, like blood.

"Just a goddamned minute." She tried not to shout, but it wasn't working. She didn't care if her voice blasted him out of his brick McMansion onto his ass in the snow. "After all these weeks of testing, after meeting all those difficult physical criteria, you're telling me we have 'issues'?"

"Ms. Turner, your relationship with your father is unusual. You've spent very little time together—"

"What the hell do you want from me?" she raged. "Do you want me to have some big confrontation with him? Do you want me to accuse him of never being a daddy to me, for chrissakes? Should I accuse him of not seeing me as a daughter, but a donor? Not wanting anything from me except to harvest a few more years? Are those the sort of fucking 'issues' you're getting at?"

His next silence was so long she started to get embarrassed.

"Very impressive, Ms. Turner."

"I'm trying to impress you," she forced out through her teeth. "I'm trying to impress you with the fact that we've waited too long already. I want the surgery now—"

"There is nothing simple about this surgery. It's not a rare procedure, but it's a serious one."

"You're damned right it is. Because—" She shut her mouth, realizing that she was about to threaten Willard T. Temple with death. Not a wise way to dazzle him with her sanity. "Listen. I'm calm now, Doctor. But I don't want any further delays."

As she turned off the phone, she checked the speedometer. Her speed had climbed way out of control. Easing her tense foot off the accelerator, she tried to force the rest of her to slow down, too. It was hard, though. She felt as if she was running from one crisis to another.

Natalie, her best friend, often told her the benefits of slowing down, of being "in the moment." Easy for Natalie to say. She could live "in the moment" as much as she pleased. She flitted from one day to the next with nary a care in the world. She was Michelle's polar opposite, yet they had been best friends for years.

"Okay, Nat. I'm trying to be in the moment." Her breath fogged the air of the still-cold Range Rover. "I'm going to pick up Cody. I've got nothing else going on today, so I can bring him home and make him soup and mother him all day long. I'll see if Sam can figure out a way to get the transplant done sooner. How does that sound?"

Like she was losing it, talking to herself while driving along the highway. But somehow, taking the day step by step calmed her. By the time she walked into the hospital, she had most of her sanity back.

She stopped at the desk, manned this morning by a

different clerk. "I'm Cody Turner's mother. He's being discharged today."

The clerk tamped a stack of file folders together and set them in a metal tray on the counter. "So he is. I think he's getting dressed now. Here are a few forms for you to sign."

"I'd like to see the bill, please."

The clerk opened a folder and handed her a pen, then clicked at a keyboard. A long sheet drifted out of the printer. She studied the itemized bill and pointed to a line. "Does this mean the doctor waived his fee?"

The clerk nodded. "Appears so."

For some reason, this made her mad. She turned the page, spotting the financial liability sheet. Another unwelcome bit of charity leaped out at her.

"It says here the balance has been paid in full."

"That's right, ma'am."

"By Gavin Slade."

"I understand he's the boy's grandfather." The clerk smiled with the dreamy admiration Michelle remembered from Gavin's fans years ago. "Must be something, having him for a father."

She scrawled her signature beside all the Xs. "Oh, it's something, all right." Be in the moment, she reminded herself. She would confront Gavin about the bill later. And Sam waiving his fee. Damn them both. She had a good job with benefits. She didn't need either of them to come blasting into her life, taking over.

"Morning, Mrs. Turner." Nurse O'Brien looked crisp and pretty in pink slacks and tunic, a cardigan draped over her shoulders. "Your son's looking good."

Michelle summoned a smile. "I didn't have a chance to thank you yesterday. I appreciate everything you and Sam did for Cody."

"You're more than welcome."

She didn't seem to be in a hurry to go anywhere. To make conversation, Michelle asked, "Have you worked with Sam long?"

She hesitated, giving Michelle the strangest look. The desk clerk stopped typing, and from the corner of her eye Michelle saw her lean forward. "Nearly five years, since he came on at County," Alice O'Brien said.

Michelle sensed there was a lot more the nurse could tell her about those five years, but not now. Hiking her handbag strap securely on her shoulder, she hurried down the hallway. The door to Cody's room stood slightly ajar. She knocked. "Cody? It's Mom."

"Yeah, I'm ready."

She was unprepared for the sight of him. The ponytail was gone. A thick white bandage covered the stitches. There was an actual, recognizable style to his hair. She remembered the way it used to grow when he was tiny, in gorgeous swirly waves as if his head had been licked all over by a friendly golden retriever.

He looked at her and his cheeks colored up, and all she could think was *thank God*. The pallor was gone. He actually had blood flowing to his face. A good sign.

And even though she felt like crying, she forced her mouth into a momlike smile.

"Love the haircut, son."

"Some guy came in at the crack of dawn and said he'd just even it out, and look what he did."

"It's fine, Cody. Really."

"It sucks."

It was creeping back over him, she saw. The attitude. After an injury or a bad sickness, a kid usually had a period of perfect sweetness. Cody had been that way yesterday while Sam was stitching him up. He'd been that way on the phone with her. But now things were getting back to normal.

Did he do that on purpose? she wondered.

He held up a white plastic bag with MERIDIAN COUNTY HOSPITAL printed on the side. "Here's all my stuff. Can we go now?"

"I have to see Sam first," she said, her mouth tasting the name, tasting wonder. "I've got some questions for him."

Cody handed her a pink slip. "He already gave me this prescription."

"Watch two hours of MTV and call me in the morning," said a voice from the doorway.

Michelle turned, and there he was, leaning with one shoulder propped against the doorframe. Sam McPhee in scrubs. Yesterday she'd been too worried about Cody to appreciate the sight. It was so different from the way she remembered him, the way she'd always imagined him.

This was the man who wanted to barge his way into Cody's life, she reminded herself.

"Take that prescription for the pain." Sam came into the room. The photo ID tag hanging from his pocket—not to mention the stethoscope and drug-company pocket protector—gave him an air of authority that made her feel strange. "Use as directed, and he should be all right." He propped some films in a lighted display box on the wall. "He checked out fine this morning." With a pencil, he pointed out some areas that reminded her of Rorschach figures, symmetrical paint blobs that shrinks used to see how the mind works.

"This one's from yesterday, and here it is this morning. Head trauma was minimal."

For some reason, she felt like crying. She studied the film. Did it show where the sweetness was hiding? Did it tell you why Cody was so hateful all the time? She bit her tongue against asking.

Sam grinned at Cody. "You've got a thick skull, kid."

"You've got a lame barber," Cody grumbled.

"Hazlett? We're lucky we've got someone who makes house calls."

Cody shuffled toward the door, his jeans dragging at the heels. "I'll be in the car, Mom."

"All right." She waited, biting down on her lower lip, because she knew what she wanted him to do, but she didn't want to tell him to do it, because it wouldn't be the same. *Turn around, you little shit. Turn around and tell Dr. McPhee thank you.*

He didn't. She was not surprised. She didn't think Sam was, either. After only a couple of days, Sam knew good and well that Cody was a surly kid, dancing on the edge, too cool for his oversize jeans.

"Anything else I should know?" she asked.

"The usual. Take it easy for the next couple of days. Stitches come out on Friday or Saturday."

She nodded, looking down at her hands. She was suddenly and unpleasantly conscious that she'd barely slept all night, and here she was unshowered, no makeup, in clothes she threw on in five minutes.

"You waived your fee," she blurted out.

"The kid was in my care when he got kicked in the head. You've got a dandy lawsuit here if you care to pursue it."

Oh, that would be fun, thought Michelle. She could see the tabloids now. *Celeb Mom Sues Dad for Injury to Love Child.* "Don't even think about a lawsuit, Sam."

"I wish everyone had that attitude."

"I have another question."

"Shoot."

"It's about Gavin and the transplant." Her insides twisted into knots. "Um, there might be a glitch."

"A glitch?"

"A postponement."

His face didn't change, but something about the quality of the light in his eyes did.

"Is Gavin having trouble?"

She shifted from foot to foot. The room felt overly warm. "Well, not specifically. It's just that . . . I got up this morning and saw . . . I realized this has gone on too long already, the stuff with the dialysis and all the meds. So I spoke with Dr. Temple, the psychologist from the transplant team. I told him that every single moment of waiting is cruelty." She took a deep breath, feeling tears of exhaustion and frustration pressing to get out. She willed them away. "And the son of a bitch said he's not sure we're ready."

"Ready. You mean they need to order more tests, or—"

"No, the renal angiogram's the only thing left. He's playing head games, Sam. He doesn't think Gavin and I are ready *psychologically*."

"And you think you are?"

"I know I am, goddammit. My life has stopped, and nothing can start again until this is done. And he wants me to determine whether I'm acting out of guilt or loyalty or God-knows-what? How can that matter, Sam?"

He was quiet for a long time. Too long. She was starting to think it was a doctor thing. A conspiracy. Torture the patient until she's over the edge, then collect your fee.

Finally he said, "I'll offer a personal reference."

The bones in her legs turned to water. "Oh, Sam. Would you? Please?"

"I'll do what I can. I've met Maggie Kehr. I could

give her a call." Her business card said "Dr. Margaret Kehr," but Sam called her Maggie. "She's the best," he added.

"That's good to hear." *So what's this about you and Maggie?*

"Anyway, I'm sure she told you how complicated this procedure is. It's got to be orchestrated down to the last second. Everything's got to come together at the right moment. The scheduling can be a nightmare."

"I'm trying to be patient. But it's so damned hard."

"A few more days aren't going to matter, not with Gavin. Like I told you before, he's in great shape. That's not likely to change."

Michelle caught herself putting her hands on her hips. No, not on her hips. At the back of her waist, in the vicinity of the kidneys. She had been doing that a lot lately.

"All right," she said, suddenly self-conscious. "I'll take the reference. Just tell them I'm not a psycho trying to earn cosmic brownie points by giving my dad a kidney."

His eyes twinkled. "I can do that."

"Thanks."

"And Michelle, I meant what I said last night. About Cody."

He couldn't have planned his stealth attack better. He'd waived his fee, offered to intervene on her behalf with the transplant team—and now this. "Are you blackmailing me?" she asked. "A personal reference if I say it's okay for you to steal my son?"

"I don't aim to steal a damned thing from you, Michelle. Do you think it'll damage him to hear the truth? That knowing who I am could harm him?"

She slumped against the doorframe. "I don't know

what I think. I haven't even had my first cup of coffee yet."

Eerily lit by the glow from the light boxes behind the films, he was both strange and painfully familiar to her. The white of the light accentuated his features—the fine nose and high cheekbones and Val Kilmer mouth she remembered from so long ago. Yet she also saw the lost years imprinted on his brow, the maturity put there by Lord-knew-what, and somehow he looked totally alone.

"Sam, I'm going to tell him."

"When?" His response was instantaneous, as if it had been balanced on the tip of his tongue during the entire conversation.

She made herself hide the fear. "I'll do it today."

"How do you think he'll take it?"

Lord, but she wanted to touch him, right now. Take his hand and give it a squeeze. Because for the first time, she finally realized that he was scared, too. Knowing the vulnerability that lay at the heart of this mysterious, familiar man made him so much more to her than a memory.

"I couldn't say, Sam. Really. Cody is . . . unpredictable lately. I never know if something's going to please him, annoy him, anger him."

"Doesn't he still ask?"

Michelle felt as if she was balanced on the blade of a knife. Did it matter what she told this man? Sam was not in their lives now. But . . . how could she lie? What would it serve?

"He used to every once in a while after he started school." Before that he had no idea a two-parent family was the norm.

"And . . . ?" Sam held himself stiffly. She could see the taut cords in his neck and part of her exulted in his suffering, because she had struggled, too, raising her son alone. But another, softer part of her still wanted to touch him.

"I said you were someone I met when I was too young to make good decisions. I told him you were a cowboy, following the PRCA. I explained that I never heard from you again after a brief . . . affair." She almost said love affair.

A muscle tensed in his jaw. "Made me out to be a real prince, did you?"

"There was no point in telling him more. It was dangerous because of the press. Because I'll always be Gavin's daughter. I didn't want them writing things . . . about us, about Cody. If I'd told him your name, given him details, some snoopy reporter would have found out. That's not fair to a kid."

She wished Sam would say something, but he just kept looking at her, and suddenly she was remembering how it used to be between them. His silences, her ramblings. How he'd pretend to be mad at little things, like when she wore his chambray work shirts, but she could tell he was secretly pleased. How those shirts smelled exactly like him.

She had taken one with her the day she'd left Blue Rock Ranch in disgrace. When she was pregnant, she used to take it out and hold it wadded up against her chest, letting the texture of soft faded cotton soothe her skin as she inhaled the scent of him. She had never laundered that shirt, because she was terrified the smell would wear off and it would just be a shirt. When that happened, she told herself, Sam would be gone from her life, finally and irrevocably.

Something very unexpected happened with that old blue shirt. She might tell him about it some time, but not now.

"All Cody knows about the past," she said, "is that I was a statistic, an unwed mother who had to grow up too fast." A shadow crossed his face, and she hurried on. "I didn't tell him in those words. I'd never make Cody feel guilty simply for being born. He is the greatest blessing in my life." There was a little hitch in her throat, because that part was true. "I would lie down and die for that child, and he knows it. I've loved him more than I ever thought possible. I've given him the best life I could. Kept him out of the camera's eye and kept him in school. And . . . that's about it." She was running out of steam, and the thought teased a wry smile from her.

His beeper went off, startling her. He checked the number. "We'll talk later. I'll see Cody later in the week about the stitches."

"All right."

As he walked away, long tails of his surgical coat belling out behind him like a cape, she thought about the task ahead, and she shivered. Not with cold, but with fear. Some small, icebound part of her lived in terror that Cody—her angry, beautiful, troubled boy—would leave her if he had a place to run.

Chapter 15

S am and his partner, Karl, each spent one day a
week at the reservation about twenty miles from
Crystal City. They served as medical advisors for
the Confederated Salish-Kootenai tribes. There, in a trailer
adjacent to the tribal elementary school, he practiced the
type of medicine he was best at—direct, hands-on care.
The doctoring was frustrating, often sad, sometimes infu-
riating, and every once in a while, rewarding.

For his troubles, he received a minuscule stipend from
the BIA and, if circumstances permitted, an hour of athletic, no-strings-attached sex with a woman named Candy
who lived at the north end of the settlement in a Pan-
Abode cabin.

Today at the free clinic he'd done a four-month well-
baby checkup and booster shots on a perfect baby boy.
Moments later he'd seen a diabetic seventy-year-old who

wouldn't stop drinking. He had delivered the usual warnings and produced the usual pamphlets and brochures, he'd written a prescription and sent the old guy, who moved with a curious dignity, on his way. If the man lasted the winter, it'd be a miracle.

He treated a shame-faced teenage girl for chlamydia, and extracted a pinto bean from the nostril of an inquisitive three-year-old. He'd seen Linda Wolf, not for the first time and certainly not for the last. She claimed to have a problem with clumsiness. Sam could tell she was too weary and in too much pain to work hard making up a lie. She'd mumbled vaguely that she'd fallen; then she'd wept silently as Sam taped her up and prescribed something for the pain. It was torn elbow cartilage this time, but over the years he had treated the funny, caustic, and ultimately pathetic woman for cracked ribs, lacerations, a detached retina, countless contusions.

When he questioned her, she always gave her usual reply. "I'm a big girl, Dr. McPhee. I know what I'm doing."

And there it ended. Her husband would abuse her until he stepped over the line and committed murder, or until she wised up and left him.

Each time he saw Linda, Sam did everything short of kidnapping the woman to convince her to leave her husband. He talked to Social Services, urged the tribal police to pick up the scumbag on another charge—running a red light, illegal waste disposal, expired tags. But Randy Wolf was, oddly enough, a model citizen, working in the timber industry. His only crimes were against Linda, and she refused to press charges. Once, a few years back, Sam had confronted him. And Randy had gone home and beaten the crap out of his wife.

At the end of the day, Sam parked at the back of a cabin north of the village. Candy opened the door, letting out a herd of cats as Sam stepped inside. She wore a smile and a hand-painted silk kimono. "Hey, Doc," she said. "Long time no see."

He grinned, nodding his thanks as she handed him a cold beer. "Ditto," he said, taking a swig and then setting down the bottle. He kissed her hard, walking her back to the bedroom without lifting his mouth from hers. In a matter of minutes they were naked, straining together, twisting the bedclothes every which way. He liked her softness, the beer-and-perfume taste of her, and the way she used her hands and mouth.

But afterward, he never wanted to stay for long. He got dressed in a hurry, handed Candy her kimono, and went out to his truck. Wrapped in a wool coat, she stood watching him, her face thoughtful. "You're in a hurry today, Doc."

"Uh-huh. I've been busy."

"You want to stay for supper? I got a pot of beans on."

"Not tonight, Sugar-Candy. I'd best be going."

"You take care now," she said, shivering as he got into his truck. Her cats darted in from the woods, swirling around her ankles as she stood watching him.

Sam waved and pulled away, vaguely disgusted with himself for being able to dismiss her so casually, vaguely annoyed at her for letting him. He came away from the encounter with a hollow sense of futility. Sam knew he was deliberately shying away from commitment, even though a part of him ached for it. He snapped on the radio for the drive home. He thought about the four-month-old. Even now he could feel the creamy texture of the baby's skin, the downy fluff of his black hair. He could picture the crooked toothless wet grin when the baby focused on his face.

His gloved hands tightened convulsively on the steering wheel. What had Cody been like as a baby?

Just start where you are, common sense told him.

Start with an angry teen who was probably more at risk than his mother dared to believe. Start with a kid who was well past the age of giving a rat's ass who his father was. Start with a kid Sam knew he'd have to work at liking.

Christ. What sort of father had to work to like his own kid?

Sam stopped his truck in front of the yellow-trimmed bungalow at the edge of town. Late-afternoon sunlight spilled across the ripples of snow in the small yard. He knew she'd be waiting for him inside. She always was on Tuesday afternoons, her half day off. Ever since he'd moved to Crystal City, he'd saved Tuesdays for her.

He sat at the steering wheel, unloading the invisible burdens, mentally leaving all the baggage from the long, trying day inside the truck. Then he slammed the door behind him and walked across the yard to the front porch.

He knocked lightly and let himself in. The familiar smells of vanilla-scented candles and cigarette smoke greeted him.

"Hey, Mama," he said, stomping the snow from his boots onto the doormat.

"Hiya, son." Tammi Lee Gilmer tucked a bookmark into the paperback novel in her lap. Late in life, she had discovered something she enjoyed almost as much as she used to enjoy drinking and partying. She read voraciously: detective novels, romance novels, thrillers, memoirs, and her beloved *National Enquirer* and *Country Billboard*. Sam had no memory of books among their possessions. It was as if Tammi Lee was making up for lost time.

She got up from her lounger and crossed the room,

giving him a brief hug and a kiss on the cheek. Her scent of cigarettes and Charlie perfume clung to the sweater she wore. She was a thin, angular woman whose body had miraculously survived years of self-abuse. Though attractive in an old-fashioned Patsy Cline way, her face bore a delicate webbing of lines and creases, a busy road map of her past.

"You doing all right, Mama?" Sam asked her.

"Sure." She went to the kitchen and poured two cups of coffee, handing him one. "Just made it fresh."

"Thanks." He had a seat at the table as she rummaged in the refrigerator for something to feed him. Though he wasn't hungry, he knew better than to stop her.

This was the woman who had raised him in a beat-up Plymouth Valiant, who had parked him in a playpen while her band laid down the tracks of her one whiskey-voiced hit, who had taught him to buy cigarettes from a machine before he was old enough to count, who had used him to wrest suspended sentences from disapproving judges, who had made him leave the only girl he'd ever loved. She had taken from him any chance of a normal upbringing.

Yet when Sam looked at his mother, he felt only one emotion, a feeling that radiated out from the middle of him and reverberated through his soul. And that emotion was love.

Because in the middle of all the travels, the running, the ducking, the hiding, the arrests, the arraignments, the shouting and the pain when he'd grown old enough to force her into treatment, she had loved him with all that was in her.

Sometimes that wasn't much. Sometimes looking for love from her was like going to the auto-parts store for milk. But during her brighter periods, she'd managed to give him enough to get by on. She used to touch his cheek, tell him she was sorry for missing a parent-teacher conference or forgetting to buy groceries or running out of money when he outgrew his clothes. Without really intending to, she had taught him to dream.

These days, at LaNelle's shop, she listened to the local gossip and snipped fabric for curtains and quilts. It was a quiet life compared to her raucous past, but she didn't complain. She did a lot of serenity work with her AA sponsor, and it seemed to sustain her.

She set down a plate of processed cheese and crackers. "So how are things with you? How's my son the doctor?"

"I'm having an interesting week. Started off by winning a rodeo purse Saturday night."

Tammi Lee wrinkled her nose. "I don't understand why you keep on with that, hon. You're going to hurt yourself."

"Going to? Mama, I've hurt myself in so many places, there's nothing left to hurt." He spread his arms. "Rodeo's my sport."

"Doctors are supposed to be into golf and skiing."

He laughed. "Now, where did you read that?"

"Some magazine I found in your office."

"I reckon I'm not that kind of doctor." With his practice, his service in a public hospital, and the indigent patients he treated, he'd never get rich.

His mind flashed on Cody. The kid's leather jacket alone was probably worth a week of malpractice insurance. Everything he wore was expensive. Was it just his age, or was he the sort of kid to whom status symbols mattered?

Tammi Lee drummed her fingers on the table. He knew she wanted a cigarette, but she tried not to smoke too much around him. As a kid, he'd probably inhaled enough secondhand smoke to choke a moose. He ate a cracker, sipped his coffee. "I ran into someone at the rodeo," he said carefully. He'd learned early to insulate his fragile mother whenever he could, but this wasn't something to hide from her.

Tammi Lee's hands fell still, and she regarded him with a sharp-edged, penetrating look. "Yeah? Who?"

"Michelle Turner, Gavin Slade's daughter."

His mother leaned back in her vinyl-covered chair and let out a low whistle. "Theda Duckworth was in the shop this morning, and she mentioned something about that. She here because Gavin's sick?"

Sam nodded. He didn't want to discuss details with his mother. In a town the size of Crystal City, Gavin's illness could hardly be kept a secret, but it wasn't Sam's place to divulge the progress and treatment of the disease.

"So . . . how'd your old girlfriend turn out?" Tammi Lee asked. She'd known Michelle only vaguely as the blond actor's spoiled daughter Sam had been seeing as a teenager. He suspected his mother knew how far the relationship had gone, but Tammi Lee had never said much. Once, he recalled, she'd tried to warn him about Michelle.

"That girl's going to be nothing but heartache for you, son," Tammi Lee had said.

He remembered the day she'd said it. She'd come home from waitressing all afternoon at the Truxtop Café. In her white polyester uniform, she'd sat in a stained easy chair and unlaced her white leather Reeboks, massaging her aching feet as Sam got ready to meet Michelle at the boathouse. He'd been in a great mood.

"You hear me, son?" Tammi Lee had repeated. "Nothing but heartache."

"Give me a break, Mama," he'd said, toweling his hair after his shower. "We have a great time together."

"You do now. But you can't let yourself forget who she is, and who you are."

Sam's patience had worn thin. "I'll see you later." He'd left her sitting in the rickety rental house, an old wood-frame dwelling on the wrong side of the tracks, with a caved-in garage attached by a shotgun corridor to the main house. It was all they could afford on Tammi Lee's tips and Sam's paycheck from the ranch.

When Sam had first returned to Crystal City to start up his practice, he'd driven past the house, finding it abandoned. The windows had been blown out, probably by kids with BB guns. The roofline sagged like the back of an ancient horse, and the siding had weathered until it was the color of the dusty, sage-choked yard. He'd battled an urge to set fire to the place and watch it burn to the ground.

"Well?" his mother prompted. "How'd she turn out?"

"She's a commercial artist in Seattle."

"I recall she was some kind of artistic prodigy."

"And . . . a single mother."

Her tweezed eyebrows lifted. "Guess she and I have something in common after all."

Sam thought about that for a moment. Like Cody, he too had rarely asked about the man who'd fathered him. "Some old guy," Tammi Lee had always replied, pulling a name out of thin air. "Some old guy, name of . . . McPhee."

Sam had made no attempt to learn more. Because when he'd grown old enough to know how to track someone down, he'd also been old enough to understand just how little it took for a man to father a child. And because, in Sam's mind, no man could equal the fantasy dad he'd created for himself.

He wondered if Cody had done that. Lacking a father in his life, had he fashioned the perfect dad out of wishes and whimsy? Had he imagined someone big and strong, someone who laughed and tossed a football to him and took him fishing? Someone who turned on the hall light at night and checked on him?

The elusive father had been a powerful figure in Sam's life, and he had been wholly imaginary. Sam tried to decide how he'd feel if he had the chance to know the actual guy.

He was bound to be disappointed.

"Michelle's son is sixteen, Mama. She was pregnant with him when she left Crystal City that winter."

Tammi held herself very still, though her pale gray eyes filled with amazement. Finally, she said, "He's your son, then."

"Yes."

"And you never knew about him?"

"No. We left town before Michelle told me."

"She never tried to contact you?"

"No." Sam didn't want to get into it with Tammi Lee. Didn't want her to feel guilty for dragging him along her rocky road. Her sobriety had been hard won. She had gone off a few times before; an emotional upset could push her unmercifully toward that next drink.

"So what do you make of all this?" she asked.

"I'm still getting used to the idea. The kid's name is Cody, he's sixteen, and pissed at the world."

"Sounds like a typical sixteen-year-old."

"When I was sixteen, I don't remember being pissed at the world."

She stared down at her lap. "You were too busy trying to hold down a job and stay in school, son. And you had to give up school when we kept moving. I'm sorry for—"

"Don't be sorry, Mama," he cut in. "You kept me from being a rebellious little shit, so I ought to thank you for it."

"So this guy's a rebellious little shit?"

"Pretty much, yeah."

"What's he think of you?"

"Michelle never told him I fathered him. But she said she'd tell him soon, maybe today. And then . . . we'll see."

"Any boy'd be proud to call you his dad," Tammi Lee said. She credited him for saving her life, dragging her kicking and screaming into rehab again and again. No matter how many times he explained it was her strength, not his, she insisted on giving him credit.

"He might want to meet you," Sam suggested, and he couldn't resist adding, "Grandma."

Tammi Lee froze for a moment. Then she stood up. "I need a cigarette." With quick, jerky movements she grabbed a pack of Virginia Slims from a cupboard and lit one, turning on the exhaust fan over the stove and leaning against the counter.

"He'll hate me." She blew out a stream of smoke.

"If he does, it won't be your fault. I told you, the kid's trouble. Michelle's dealing with it the best she can."

Tammi Lee eyed him through a thin veil of bluish smoke. "Any chance the two of you will start seeing each other again?"

Even though the possibility was as remote as the moon, Sam had been seared by it from the moment he'd seen her in the arena parking lot.

"No way," he said quickly. "She lives in Seattle, and she's . . . involved, I guess. My life is set, Mama. I don't gamble. I tried marriage once, and you know what happened. I'm not about to screw around with an old flame."

Tammi Lee nodded. "Nobody ever ends up with their childhood sweetheart. Or if they do, they wind up dead, like Romeo and Juliet."

Sam laughed. "I guess you're right, Mama."

"So what happens next?"

"I suppose, next time I see Cody, he's going to know I'm his father."

She ground out her cigarette in a fluted aluminum ashtray on the stove. "You scared, son?"

"Hell, yeah, I'm scared, Mama."

Chapter 16

*I*t was insane, thought Michelle, mooning over Sam
McPhee like a lovestruck schoolgirl. But she couldn't
seem to stop herself from thinking of him, picturing
his big hands, and how delicately they had handled Cody's
stitches. She couldn't keep from remembering the color of
his eyes or the look on his face when he was watching
her from the hospital-room doorway. She had an almost-
grown son, a sick father, a significant other in Seattle. She
had no business speculating, even to herself, what it would
be like to know Sam again.

"So you never did tell me about the foaling," she said
to Cody on the ride home, as much to distract herself as
to get him to talk.

"It was way cool. There was a dys—dyst—um, a difficult presentation, and the vet couldn't make it on time,
so we all pitched in. Sam, me, and Edward. The mare kept

getting up when she wasn't supposed to, so that was kind of bad. I had to get my hand right up inside her to bring the foal around."

"I'm getting this incredible mental picture. So you didn't gross out?"

"Nope. Like I said, it was kind of cool."

Maybe it was the blow to the head. That had to be it, Michelle thought, because no son of hers would think sticking his hand up a mare's birth canal was cool. But on the other hand, horses had once filled her life and made it beautiful. She wondered if a horse could do that for Cody.

Dooley had been four years old the summer she'd moved to Montana. A trim quarter horse with a splash of white on his forehead, he had snagged her interest when she'd seen him kicking up his heels in the paddock. Her father, eager to spoil her during the year she'd given him, had offered the gelding to her.

Everyone at Blue Rock Ranch must have thought she was a snooty city girl, with her tight buff-colored riding pants and tall English-style boots, an array of dressage ribbons and trophies spread out on her bedroom bureau.

Dooley had no patience for a dressage rider who wanted him to skip over little ivy-covered jumps and arch his neck and trot prettily around a ring. It took a lot of spills—and a lot of coaching from Sam—for her to figure that out.

They rolled up to the house and she cut the engine, turning to Cody. That haircut! She tried not to smile, looking at it, but it made her ridiculously happy to see the last of that obnoxious dual-colored ponytail hanging down his back.

"How do you feel?" she asked him. "Can I fix you something to eat?"

"I'm thrashed, Mom. I think I'll zone out for a while."

She resisted helping him out of the car. When he shrugged off his jacket and flopped down on the sofa, flipping on the TV, she resisted grabbing the afghan and tucking it around him. He used to be hers to tuck and touch and mother as much as she pleased. Now when she did it, she felt as if she was trespassing.

Okay, so tell him, she urged herself. Tell him about Sam.

But as soon as she opened her mouth to speak, he picked up the phone on the end table and punched in a long string of numbers. "Is Claudia there?" he asked. "Hey, Claudia. It's me. You won't believe what happened . . ."

Feeling like an intruder, she left the guesthouse with her coat still on, and crossed to the huge barn at the end of the main drive. It resembled the set for a sentimental movie, the sunlight on the snow, the weathered cranberry-colored structure too perfect to be real.

In the barn, she ran into Jake Dollarhide. The sight of him startled her; she never expected that he'd still be around.

"Jake? It's me, Michelle Turner. Gavin's daughter."

"Welcome back, Michelle. Good to see you." He was only a couple of years older than Michelle. His father used to be ranch foreman, an important and lucrative position on a spread the size of Blue Rock. Jake looked a lot like he did seventeen years ago. Thicker, more weather-beaten. He had the big, callused hands of an experienced horseman, the limp of a longtime cowboy, and the reserved manner of a man who felt more at home with animals than with people.

"Is there a gelding called Dooley here?" A long shot, but she had to ask him.

"Oh yeah. The old man's still one of the boss's favorites."

She didn't want Dooley to be an old man. She wanted him to be as young and quick as she remembered.

Jake led her down the middle aisle of the barn. She wondered if he remembered what happened all those years ago and what part he played, but she knew she wouldn't ask him. They stopped at one of the stalls. A long, paint-splashed chestnut head came out over the half door.

Dooley. Her best guy. She didn't ever remember loving a horse the way she had loved Dooley, and now he stood there in front of her, chewing indolently on a mouthful of alfalfa, the steam puffing gently from his damp nostrils.

Dooley.

They said horses, like elephants, never forgot. She believed that. She believed it with all her heart, because the minute she said his name aloud and hugged herself up against his long, hard skull, he whickered and blew gently into the quiet of the barn.

And Michelle, for no reason she cared to name, burst into tears. She supposed it was because this moment was the culmination of everything that had been building up inside her. In a world that had gone crazy while her back was turned, Dooley lived his life and chewed his alfalfa and stood patiently in this stall. Now he was old, and he was glad to see her.

Jake stepped back, probably embarrassed by her display. Eventually she looked up, wiped her face on her sleeve. "Sorry, Jake. This is my favorite horse in the world, and it's overwhelming to see him again."

He stared at her intently. He used to do that when they were young. It always gave her the creeps, because there was a quiet hunger in his look. "You ought to take the old man for a ride," he said, making her feel foolish for her suspicions.

Michelle knew she should protest, object, think of a bunch of reasons she shouldn't be out riding Dooley for an hour when there was so much else going on, but when she opened her mouth, the only word that came out was "Yes."

In the tack room they took down reins, a curb chain, a Twickenham bit, and a Flores saddle she remembered from years ago. Her father might be one of the Hollywood upstarts Montana loved to hate, but he was a serious upstart. Blue Rock Ranch gave every attention to the animals. The success of a rodeo stock contractor depended on the quality of his livestock. Each piece of tack and saddle was perfectly scrubbed down and oiled. She thought someone must vacuum the blankets; they were that clean.

Dooley stood patiently—she fancied willingly—in the crossties while they saddled him.

"He's fat," she said, grinning as she pulled up on the girth.

"Doesn't get much exercise. This'll be good for him."

"Is he okay, then? No lameness?"

"He's just slow. Lazy. But he'll do what you ask him to do."

She walked him out into the yard where the snow was deep and feathery light. The sunshine and sharp cold nailed her, and Dooley arched his neck in exactly the way she remembered. He knew the route to the vast, covered arena. Her leg cues were superfluous. She started him off slowly, an easy walk around the arena. As he loosened up, he naturally rolled into an easy canter, a smooth-as-wind gait that matched her own heartbeat.

Out of respect for his age, she didn't ask him to extend into a gallop. She just listened to the thud of his nimble hooves against the soft earth, the rhythmic huff of the horse's breath, and the steady creak of leather.

Like windblown leaves, bits and pieces of the past tumbled through her mind. The first time she ever rode Dooley, she'd put an English-style saddle on him and tried to coax him over jumps. He'd balked mulishly, and in the battle of wills that followed, neither horse nor rider won. Then one day Sam came along. She had been bashful and defensive when he came to the fence, wedged a foot up on the rail, and said, "You ought to try barrel racing that horse. That's what he's been drilled on."

She told him she knew how to ride, thank you very much, but he just laughed and waited her out. When she was about to quit in frustration, he gave the horse a break, then set a Western saddle on him and put him through his paces around the barrels.

From that moment on, she was hooked. To hell with prissy ribbons and plastic bouquets bordering fake fences. She gloried in the speed and agility of barrel racing—never in competition, just for the joy of it. Dooley must have been born with the pattern imprinted on his memory, because he did it perfectly, with all the heart she could wish for. A lightning gallop out of the alley, clockwise around the first barrel, counterclockwise around the second, and then finishing with a gallop so swift she felt as if part of her got left behind each time.

And always, flowing with the bits of memory, Sam was there, his loose and long frame a friendly presence at the edge of the arena.

She had thought, that summer, when Dooley and Sam filled her days and nights, that she had found a perfect happiness.

She had thought it would last forever.

Dooley wasn't stupid, he felt her mood slump, and he

took advantage, slowing his pace to a rocking-horse gait. It soothed her; she wondered if he sensed that. He sweated so much that steam rose from every inch of him, so she slowed him to a walk, letting him cool out.

"You both look great," said Gavin. He was no longer the vulnerable invalid she saw in the kitchen early that morning. Looking deceptively hardy and vigorous, he wore a sheepskin jacket and wide-brimmed hat, the tips of his ears and nose red with the cold.

How long had he been there? She'd been so absorbed in riding that she couldn't say.

"I hope you don't mind." She dismounted and led Dooley in a long oval a couple of times around the ring.

"Hell, no, I don't mind. It's good to see him getting some exercise."

"I think he remembers me."

"Wouldn't surprise me. That's one of the smartest horses I've ever had."

Things were quiet and easy between Michelle and Gavin as she put Dooley up, taking the time to grain him, curry him out, paint a bit of red disinfectant on his hock, where she had noticed a small cut. She cleaned the tack while Gavin looked on approvingly.

They checked on Cody to find that he had fallen fast asleep, so they went for a drive out to the small local air park. Gavin greeted people by name there, and showed her into the hangar where he kept his two planes—the vintage biplane, and the P-51 Mustang, his prized possession. The Mustang still had its original D day invasion stripes. It was one of the few surviving WWII planes. Most were in museums these days.

"As soon as your license is reinstated," she said, "I'm going to expect the ride of my life, Daddy."

"You're on," he promised her.

It was early twilight when they returned and walked over to the guest quarters to see Cody. He was curled up, still asleep on the sofa, the TV on but the volume down. Seizing the opportunity to do what he wouldn't let her do when he was awake, Michelle covered him with a knitted striped afghan and brushed a curl of hair off his forehead.

"He all right?" Gavin whispered as they left.

They started across to the big house. "He's doing fine."

"I can't say I'm sorry to see some of that hair disappear."

They stomped the snow off their boots, leaving them in the mudroom. Inside, they sat staring at the fire. Tadao brought cocktails—Dry Sack for her, watered-down cranberry juice for Gavin, a bowl of salt-free pretzels neither of them touched.

"I had a chat with Dr. Temple this morning." She sipped her sherry. "He said he might advise postponing the surgery."

"Yeah?"

"I told him he was full of shit, that I wanted to go ahead right now."

Gavin shook his head. "I've been living with this for a long time. Another week or so isn't going to kill me."

She stiffened against the back of the leather sofa. "I wish you wouldn't talk like that." When she looked at his face, she wanted to think that she was seeing what all daughters saw when they looked at their fathers. But the memories simply weren't there. Maybe that was what she was seeking now. If not history, then at least something dear, something precious. They didn't have that. Maybe there was still time. Would having the transplant bring a new intimacy?

It seemed a fanciful notion. A kidney was just an organ. A spare part, as Cody liked to call it. There wasn't any sort of mystical power in a kidney. And yet she kept thinking, because of what she gave him, he'd be healed.

He clearly had no inkling of her thoughts, because out of the clear blue he asked, "So what does Sam think of the boy?"

"Of Cody?" she asked stupidly.

"That would be the one." Gavin spoke with exaggerated patience and humor.

"He thinks Cody is angry and rebellious."

"So is this a phase the boy is going through, or is there a problem?"

She gazed at her father incredulously. "You really don't know, do you?"

"About raising a teenager? I don't have any experience at it, Michelle."

And she felt it again—the anger, the resentment. "It's both a phase and a problem."

"Maybe getting him together with Sam wouldn't be such a bad idea," Gavin suggested.

"Um, I haven't told Cody that Sam's his father." She swirled the ice in her tumbler. "Why didn't you ever tell me Sam moved back to Crystal City?"

"I didn't think you were interested in hearing that or anything else from me."

She sensed something more beneath his words, some judgment or evasion. She couldn't quite put her finger on it. "I could have done with a word of warning," she said.

He combed a splayed hand through his white hair. "Hell, honey, I guess I was afraid you wouldn't come if you knew Sam was here."

"I would have come anyway," she insisted. "I'm going to let Cody know about Sam this evening." Helplessly she watched the flames leaping in the grate, reflecting against the iron fireback. "I have no idea what he's going to think when I tell him."

"So how's Sam taking all this?" he asked.

"He says he wants to get to know Cody, but that's what's making me so insane. You can't know a kid in a few weeks. You have to raise a child from birth to truly know him."

"You believe that?"

"Yes."

"Then I don't know you? I can't know you?"

She gulped the rest of her drink. "We're talking about Cody."

"Fine, so talk."

"I just . . . don't understand what Sam expects. What if he wants something I can't give? Like more time with Cody?"

"Are you willing to allow that?"

"Of course not." The refusal flew from her, surprising her with its swiftness. Was she that settled in her ways? Certain that nothing unexpected could ever happen to her? Like a middle-aged matron, was she so inflexible that she couldn't imagine straying from a path she'd mapped out long ago?

"Brad and I have goals." She tried to convince herself as much as her father. "We've made commitments. We're building a life together, and I'm not about to change that just so Sam McPhee can get used to the novelty of having a son."

"Honey, believe me, it's not a novelty."

Something in the tone of his voice tugged at her, and she set down her glass. The mica lamps overhead cast radiant heat down into the gathering shadows of the room, and she couldn't help but think they resembled stage lights, showering over his broad shoulders, his magnificent hair, his face craggy with living and troubles. Was she looking at Gavin Slade the actor, or Gavin Slade the man?

"What do you mean, Daddy?"

"Knowing you've got a child somewhere in the world is like carrying a tube of nitroglycerine around. You're scared stiff all the time, scared you're going to drop it, or someone's going to jostle you and the world's going to explode."

"I'm not sure what this has to do with Sam."

"Maybe you should cut him some slack. Let him spend some time with Cody while you're here and see what happens."

"I was sort of hoping you'd spend time with Cody, too."

He wouldn't look at her. "He's not interested. What do I have in common with a sixteen-year-old kid?"

"You never know. Your airplanes?" She remembered the problem with Gavin's license and quickly changed the subject. "He likes the movies. You ought to give him a tour of the Lynwood."

"Okay, maybe I could screen an old movie or two for him."

The whole idea was, her dad should sit in there with him. But she stopped short of suggesting it.

"Always thought it'd be nice to renovate and reopen the place," he went on, surprising her. "I own the adjacent retail space, too. Seems a shame to let it all just sit there."

"It sounds like quite a project," she said. "But first things first," she said. "We'd better concentrate on getting both you guys well in this next week."

They were silent with their thoughts during dinner, perfectly prepared and served by Tadao. Eyeing the young man as she helped him clear the table, she wondered if he was good company for her dad, if he was more than an employee. As a teenager, Michelle had enjoyed the folksiness of the ranch help. Though it was always clear her father was the boss, there was a casual ease at Blue Rock she'd never known at her mother's house in Bel Air. At the ranch, they were like a big family. Though she had only lived a short time at the ranch, it was the only place she had ever really fit in. Despite being born in Southern California, she had never quite belonged there, never quite lived up to her mother's high style and standards. Once, long ago, she had asked her father why he had moved away from California, and he had said simply, "For the breathing room." One of the few things they had in common, she thought. There might have been more if Gavin hadn't—

She stopped herself. Vowed she would not dredge up all bitterness, old regrets.

After dinner, Tadao gave her a covered tureen of soup and a turkey sandwich for Cody. She thought she had done a pretty good job playing it cool in front of her father, but when she said good night, the last thing he said to her nearly made her drop the soup.

"Don't put it off any longer. Tell the boy tonight, okay?"

Chapter 17

Cody's mouth tasted rank when he woke up to find the evening news flickering in his face. He stared unseeing at the TV for a few minutes, trying to decide if his head hurt. Barely. When he held perfectly still, not stirring except to breathe, he didn't feel any pain at all.

Sam McPhee had given him some pills. The little brown bottle was on the counter. Maybe he'd take a couple tonight.

No, he told himself. Those were for Claudia. When he'd told her about his injury, her first question had been to ask what kind of pain pills the doctor had given him. She liked getting high on pills. Cody had done it with her once or twice, stealing some Darvons from Brad's sample kit. Brad was so lame, with his designer clothes and big plans, he never even noticed. Clueless, too, but that worked in Cody's favor. He could get away with a lot when Brad was around.

Last Friday, right before a school dance, he and Claudia had swallowed a couple of pills with mouthfuls of beer. The world had turned blurry and bright, and everything he said made Claudia laugh. He loved the way she laughed, shaking back her head with all those red curls and her voice going up and up with each syllable. She had a sexy laugh. He'd walked her home after the dance—his mom was a pain in the butt about not letting him drive unaccompanied at night.

On a storage bench in the darkened mudroom of Claudia's house, she had let him go almost all the way. Cody got a hard-on just thinking about those soft curves and soft lips. She had this amazing way of sucking his tongue that made him nuts. Her spicy-smelling perfume and her taste of Zima and Lifesavers got him higher than any pills could.

Inside the house, someone had flicked on a light, interrupting the magic. He knew Claudia would let him go all the way the next time. They just needed a little more privacy.

But he never got the chance. The very next day, Cody's mom had dragged him all the way out here to the middle of nowhere so he could work his butt off on some guy's ranch and get kicked in the head by a horse.

By the time his mom came in from the main house, he'd worked himself into a lousy mood. And she, of course, put on that chirpy smile of hers. "Tadao sent you soup and sandwiches. You hungry?"

He was starving after that nap. "I guess."

"Stay there. I'll bring your dinner on a tray."

"Okay."

"How's your head?"

"Hurts when I move it."

She banged around in the kitchenette for a few minutes, then walked into the den with a tray of soup in a mug, a sandwich, and a glass of milk.

"Thanks." For some reason, it annoyed him that there was a sprig of parsley floating on top of the soup and that she'd cut the sandwich into triangular halves. His mom was always doing stuff like that, trying to make a nice thing nicer.

Maybe it was because she was an artist. Once, when they'd moved to the new town house next door to Brad, Cody had taken a look at some of her old paintings and drawings. Incredible, wild stuff, tons of it, nothing like the ad layouts she did for work. He couldn't believe his own mother used to paint stuff like that. It was almost scary.

While he ate, his mom had the news on, but she didn't seem to be paying much attention. In fact, she seemed jumpy. Scared about the transplant thing, he figured. It was too gross to think about, but from the second she'd heard about her dad's sickness, she'd insisted on going through with it.

"I have to do this. I *want* to," she'd told him and Brad. "The transplant works best from a living, related donor—a blood relative."

Deep inside Cody lay the knowledge that his mom wasn't Gavin Slade's only blood relative. But when he thought about surgeons cutting him open, taking out a whole organ, for chrissakes, he couldn't even speak, much less volunteer as a donor. So he kept his mouth shut and let his mom be the martyr.

"You want seconds?" she asked.

"Nope, I'm full."

"Dessert? There's ice cream in the freezer, and a bag of cookies—"

"No *thanks*." His voice had a rude inflection, and she flinched, but he didn't care. After telling him to save her some of his pain pills, Claudia hadn't found much to talk about, and their long, awkward silence echoed in Cody's ears now.

His mom took the tray away and returned to the living room. Cody reached for the remote to turn the channel to MTV, but she intercepted him, grabbing the device and killing the power.

He glared at her, surprised and affronted. "What gives, Mom?"

"I need to talk to you about something."

"Yeah?" He was starting to feel bored already. Maybe she was feeling nervous about the surgery, and she wanted to say how much she loved him and all that shit in case something went wrong during the transplant. It was the last thing Cody wanted to discuss.

"Yes." She tucked one foot up under her in the chair and picked up a throw pillow, her right index finger fiddling with the tassels. "This is serious, Cody. I need you to pay attention."

He lifted both hands in an exaggerated shrug, even though it hurt his head. "Do I look like I'm going anywhere?"

"I, um, I need to talk to you about the man who fathered you."

Holy crap. Cody felt himself come to full alert. He forced himself to stay still on the sofa, his face expressionless and his voice bland when he said, "Yeah? You said he was just some cowboy, and you'd never seen him again."

"That's true. I mean, I thought it was true. But he's living here, Cody. In Crystal City. I had no idea where he was until I saw him Saturday night."

Oh, man. He didn't know what to do with himself, with his hands, with his eyes, with his mind. So his mouth said a lazy, "No kidding."

But his brain went into overdrive. He tried to picture the crowd at the rodeo arena. All he remembered from Saturday night was the girl named Molly Lightning. And a mass of people who looked like hicks and hillbillies.

"I wouldn't kid about this, Cody."

"So who's the guy?"

Her finger kept twirling the tassel, faster now. "It's . . . Sam. Sam McPhee."

"Whoa." The exclamation escaped him before he could stop it. His heartbeat sped up. A father. He had a father. Sam McPhee was his goddamned father.

It was too weird, knowing now, after all the years of imagining, who he was. Stranger still knowing Sam and his mom had been bonking each other as teenagers.

"Thanks a lot for never telling me, Mom."

"I didn't know how to tell you. It was a shock, seeing him so unexpectedly." She hugged the pillow up against her chest. "And really, we've been so busy, this is the first chance I've had."

Suddenly, in the place in his life where there had been a blank picture frame, a face showed up. A cowboy's face, tan and lean, some guy dressed in a plaid flannel shirt and Levi's. A guy with big hands and a screw-you attitude. A guy who made his voice go all serious while he was sewing Cody up with the same big hands he'd used to heft a wheelbarrow full of manure.

Christ. Sam McPhee. His father. There was an earthquake heaving up inside Cody. The world was rearranging itself, and he had no idea what it would look like when things settled.

"Cody?" His mother's voice was light, quavery. He

hoped like hell she wouldn't start bawling or trying to get him to talk about his feelings. "Is there anything . . . you want to say?" Her voice kept wobbling.

He wanted to say everything, and nothing. He wanted to yell at her for keeping this huge secret from him. He wanted to ask what was so goddamned wrong with him that he didn't deserve to know his father. He wanted to hide behind a wall and wait for the world to return to normal.

But most of all, he wanted to know the answer to one big burning question.

"So does he know . . . who I am?"

"Yes."

"Shit, you told him before you told me? Thanks a l—"

"I didn't tell him. He figured it out based on your age. Or, I guess it was your age. Might have been something else."

"What else?"

"You're alike in . . . subtle ways. The way you hold yourself sometimes, I suppose. Certain movements. It's hard to say." She started picking at the tassel. It was driving him crazy, the way she kept fidgeting. "But I imagine it was your age. He realized you were born just a few months after we . . . after I—"

"After he fucked you," Cody exploded.

He heard his mom draw in a breath, but he didn't look at her. Gripping the arm of the couch, he pushed himself up. Battling a wave of dizziness, he stalked down the hall to his room and slammed the door as hard as he could.

Damn it. Goddamn it to hell. *Now* what was he going to do?

Chapter 18

O h, *that* went well, thought Michelle. With a savage tug, she jerked the stupid tassel off the stupid pillow. Then she tossed both pillow and tassel aside.

Her cheeks were on fire. Her insides—stomach, heart, throat—were all on fire.

After he fucked you.

Cody's words hung in the room. She couldn't hide from them. She couldn't make them not be true. She couldn't make them not hurt. Sure, he had much worse problems than using foul language, but the moment seemed to crystallize all their issues into a single, sharp hammer blow of a syllable.

She wanted to go to him, sit at the side of his bed, tell him she knew, she understood what a shock this must be, yet it didn't change anything between them—

But it did. It already had. She couldn't put things back the way they were.

Pulling her knees up to her chest, she stared at the blank screen of the TV, then at the wall shelves filled with old novels and knickknacks. She wondered if the knickknacks had any meaning, or if Martha Stewart had been a guest here, putting dried flowers in rusty horseshoes and making an umbrella stand out of an old cowboy boot.

Cody's furious reaction had thrown the universe out of whack for her. He'd been rebellious lately, but in a strange way it had seemed like a manageable anger, not some out-of-control dark substance that hardened, like coal into diamond, into indestructible hate.

Dry-eyed, she forced herself to assess the situation. Minimize the problem. He was in shock over finding out about Sam, but the shock would fade, and he'd be back to his old self again. She and Cody would be here only a short time. After that, there would be no need to come back.

I just stopped by to drop off a kidney and save my dad's life. Then I'm out of here.

Sam claimed he wanted to know his son, to get involved, but his involvement ended the day he skipped town seventeen years ago. The only reason she had told Cody was that it felt deceptive not to. She didn't owe Sam a thing. He didn't owe her a thing.

And really, she had no business thinking about him.

She picked up the phone and dialed Brad's number. He needed to hear this, too. Would he worry? Feel threatened?

Early on in their relationship, he had asked about Cody's father, and she'd told him exactly what she always told Cody—a youthful mistake, they'd never been in contact, she had no idea where he was.

That had all changed now.

Sam McPhee was real and rock solid. He had a career and a ranch and a business partner and the respect of a town that had once kicked him in the teeth.

He had large gentle hands and a way of watching her that brought warmth to forbidden places inside her.

She hung up the phone when Brad's answering service picked up. He'd always hated answering machines, so he paid strangers to take his messages for him. She couldn't imagine telling a stranger what had just happened. What would she say? "Tell Brad to call me, because I just told my son who his real father is, and now he hates me."

The phone rang, startling her. She grabbed it, praying it would be Brad. He'd never been the sort of guy who popped up just when she needed him, but she kept thinking he would be one day.

"Hello?"

"Michelle, it's Sam."

God. Oh, God. "I don't want to talk to you right now."

"Is this a bad time?"

"The worst." Her heart pounded. Her throat ached with the things she wanted to tell him.

"Cody's all right, isn't he?"

"Of course he's not all right—" She broke off. Sam meant the injury. "His head's fine. He had a nap, and a pretty good dinner, and he's in his room right now."

"Then why did you say he's not all right?"

She swallowed hard, and it hurt, as if something enormous was stuck halfway down. "I told him about us. I told him you're his biological father."

Silence. In the background on his end, a dog barked. The Border collie. The morning she'd gone out there, she had noticed that Sam had an unconscious, affectionate way with the dog, idly stroking her head and ears without even seeming to know he was petting her. He was probably doing that right now.

"How'd he take it?" Sam finally asked, his voice low.

"He's not a happy camper. After he said the word 'fuck' to his mother, he walked out and closed himself in his room."

"I'm coming over."

"No, Sam, you can't—"

His end of the line went dead. She couldn't stop him now. She felt helpless. Should she tell Cody that Sam was coming over? No; then he might barricade the door, or worse, run off somewhere.

She settled for straightening up the bungalow, doing the most mundane of chores. A fresh hand towel in the bathroom. A light on over the front door. Minutes dragged by, and she ran out of things to do. Restless, she took out her sketchbook and favorite pencil—a Primacarb Number One. Accustomed to bringing her work with her from the office, she never went anywhere without a sketchbook. Even though she had given up painting, she still thought in pictures, and she never knew when an idea for an ad design or concept would hit her.

Her pencil swirled and danced over the page, and she felt a tug of sensation, something she hadn't felt in a long time. Nerves, she told herself. That's what it was. And when she saw what had emerged onto the paper, she knew it was nothing more. The image she had outlined was icy cold, a vineyard everyone had seen before on a dozen wine labels. It came from her mind's eye but not from her heart. Perfect for one of their big winery accounts.

She shut the book and put it back on the table. A few minutes later, a knock sounded at the door. She went to Cody's room and said, "Sam's here."

No response. He probably had his Discman on, fitting the headphones over the dressing on his head.

Sam took his boots off at the door. He didn't smile when he greeted her. He just sort of stared, those eyes probing, seeing her in a way she didn't think anyone else ever had. Finally, he said, "You look awful."

"Thanks. I'm having a swell evening." She gestured at the fridge. "Can I get you something to drink?"

"Not right now, thanks. Where's Cody?"

"In his room." She indicated the door.

Sam didn't hesitate; that was the first thing she noticed. She had always hesitated when it came to dealing with Cody. She tended to stop, weigh the options, rehearse the scenario in her head, and proceed with caution. Sam plunged right in. Of course, he had a lot less to lose than Michelle did. Sam couldn't lose what he'd never had.

He knocked on the door and said, "Cody, it's Sam. Your mother and I want to talk to you."

Your mother and I.

Michelle had never thought she'd hear those words, not in the context of her own life. There had never been a unit known as "your mother and I." The phrase conjured up images and yearnings Michelle didn't want—a partnership, a union . . . a dream she once had.

Cody's reply put the sentimental thought into perspective: "I got nothing to say to either of you."

At this point, she generally let him be, let him chill out. But Sam didn't know Cody's implacable moods. He put his hand on the knob. "I don't recall giving you that option. Now, you can either come out here or I'll come in there. Either way, it happens in the next five seconds."

"Or what? You'll spank me?"

Sam twisted the doorknob, and Michelle was surprised it didn't come off in his hand. He looked perfectly calm as he strode into Cody's room. The bedroom was done in muted plaids and stripes, like an upscale resort hotel. Cody lay on the bed, his hands clenched into fists, his eyes full of hate as he watched Sam.

Michelle stood in the doorway and held her breath.

"I'd never hit you." Sam kept his voice soft and low, the way he always did when he was angry. That was one of the things Michelle remembered about him. The madder he got, the quieter he got. "I'd never hit anyone. But I also don't take no for an answer. So why not get up off your butt and get into the living room?"

"Maybe I don't feel like it."

A small, evil part of Michelle took pernicious delight in this exchange. In the past she had been the one on the receiving end of Cody's defiance. Finally, someone else had to hear it. Sam stood like a shield between Cody and Michelle, absorbing the boy's contempt as if it were nothing.

"So you want us to camp out in here?" He moved Cody's suitcase off the luggage bench and had a seat. "Fine with me."

Cody didn't say a word, but levered himself up from the bed, marched out of the room, and plunked himself down in an armchair in the living room. He didn't look at either Sam or Michelle. She was amazed that Sam got him to come out.

"I guess I'll start, then." Sam lowered himself to the sofa, and she did the same, folding her arms, unconsciously protecting herself.

"First of all, you've got to know this, Cody. Finding out about you is the biggest thing that's ever happened to me."

This was a man who had been a six-time national rodeo champion. A man who had saved lives, delivered babies, told people a loved one had died. And yet he could still say this was a bigger deal.

Cody stared straight ahead, stone-faced. And Lord, even now, startlingly good-looking, a fallen angel with a mended head.

"Second thing," Sam continued, "is that if you ever talk to your mother like that again, you'll be sorry you ever found me."

Cody turned to her, contempt written in hard lines around his mouth. "Great, Mom. Already running to him and telling him private stuff."

"I don't blame you for wanting to keep it private. I'd be ashamed, too, if I said stuff like that to the woman who raised me." Though Sam's voice was mild, there was an edge to his words, an edge that was sharp with warning.

Watching Cody, she could see that he sensed the sharpness, too. He was out of his league here. Sam had grown up fighting his way through the rodeo, through school, through seventeen years of battles she could only imagine. Cody's attitude might have the power to hurt her, but to a man like Sam it was nothing.

"So what are you doing here, anyway?" Cody asked.

"Same thing as you are. Trying to figure out what to do next." Sam crossed one foot over his knee. He wore flecked gray thermal socks. Bits of snow still clung to the cuffs of his jeans. "I have figured out what not to do. And that's mouth off to your mother. I won't tolerate it, Cody. Do you understand?"

Their gazes locked. From the very start, there was no question who was going to win. Within a few seconds, Cody shrugged and looked away. "Whatever."

"Your last outburst was just that," Sam said. "Your last. Believe me, I know what you're thinking. You're thinking I'm just some old guy. I have no authority over you."

"You don't," Cody pointed out.

"You know what?" Sam leaned back congenially. "You're absolutely right. I won't take you over my knee. But I can tell you this. Don't be such a little shit to the person who's put in sixteen years and nine months raising you."

Cody did his best to look bored, but she could tell he was fascinated by all this. "Why not?"

Still maintaining a relaxed pose, Sam nailed him with a stare that would wither grass, and he spoke softly, with deadly control. "Don't ask me that again."

Michelle unfolded her arms and studied them both, and in a flash, she saw an uncanny resemblance. They looked so much alike she was surprised the whole town hadn't figured it out by now.

"All right," Cody said at last, keeping his chin up despite his capitulation. "Whatever."

"Well," Michelle said, trying to dissipate the tension. "I suppose we have to decide what's going to happen next."

"You're going to finish this operation thing and then we're going back home," Cody said.

"It could happen that way," she conceded. "Is that what you want?"

"Why would I want anything else?"

"No reason, maybe," Sam said, and she was glad he spoke up, because she couldn't think of anything more to say. "But then again, maybe there is a reason."

Silence. And sadness. Sam's words filled Michelle with a huge ache. Because in her heart she knew they had both made cocoons of themselves. And somehow, it had diminished them. No strings, no connections. *Safe from love, safe from hurt.*

"So what are you talking about? You think I want you to take me to baseball games and buy me stuff and all that crap?" Cody demanded. "I'm a little old for that."

"Good. I can't stand baseball. Hate shopping." Sam drilled him again. That stare was powerful. Where did he learn to do that? Michelle wondered.

"So here's the deal," Sam continued. "If you feel okay in the morning, and it's all right with your mom, you come out to my place. See how that foal's doing. Maybe we'll talk some, maybe we won't. We'll just see."

Cody sat stiff and silent for a while. "What if I don't feel like it?"

"Then you don't come." But Michelle and Sam had both seen it. The spark in the boy's face when Sam mentioned the horse. "You stay here and . . . do whatever it is you do."

More silence. Cody was as still as a stone, but she knew a battle raged inside him. Finally, he said, "Can I go to my room now?"

Sam's face turned hard with a silent demand.

Finally, reluctantly, Cody added, "Um, please?"

Wonders never cease, thought Michelle. He asked permission.

Sam looked at her. "Michelle?"

"See you in the morning, Cody," she said. "You can let me know then if you need a ride to Sam's place."

Chapter 19

Sam watched Cody leave the room, noting the studied slouch, the hands jammed in his pockets. Despite the attitude, he was still a good-looking kid, and Sam had thought so even before he'd figured out who fathered him.

He wanted to ask Michelle what Cody had been like as a baby, a toddler, a little boy, but each time he thought of all those lost years, he nearly choked on rage and frustration. Those years were gone and there was no way to get them back. But that didn't stop the hunger in him to know.

"What's going through his head right now?" he asked softly.

"In a minute, probably Marilyn Manson on his Discman. I hate his music. And I hate it that I hate his music, because I love music."

"Believe it or not, I understand what you're saying."

That coaxed a fleeting, weary smile from her. Sam knew he should go, but he didn't want to. Leaning forward, he picked up a sketchbook off the table. "May I?"

"Sure. It's work, though. I doubt you'll find it very interesting."

He'd always liked looking at her drawings. When they were young, she'd had the sort of talent that made people do a double take. They'd look, then look again, and then the low-voiced comments would start.

But when he opened the sketchbook, he didn't see the wild, emotional abstractions he'd been expecting. These were studies, mostly of inanimate objects—furniture and running shoes and grapes and shower nozzles—and a chilly, anatomical study of a winter merganser in flight. Each was rendered with remarkable control and perfection, as if a computer had done it.

Michelle shifted on the couch, tucking her feet up under her. "I told you, it's work. I'm a graphic designer."

"You're damned good," he said with total honesty. "I can't believe you quit painting. You were so passionate about it."

"Sam, I was eighteen years old. I was passionate about everything—about my art, about horses . . . about you. The trouble was, life outlasted passion. Some people call it growing up."

Her statement thumped into him like a dull blow. The firelight flickered off her cheek, illuminating a haunting sadness in her face. He didn't like seeing this wistful melancholy in her. But he sure as hell didn't know how to make it go away.

"Aw, damn it, Michelle." He moved closer to her on the sofa. "I didn't mean to upset you." And because it was late and he was on autopilot, he did the next thing quite naturally. His arm extended across the back of the seat and went around her.

In the space of a second, she softened against him, and he couldn't believe the rush it gave him to feel her like this, pliant and giving. But only a heartbeat later, she seemed to realize what she'd done and pulled away. He let out his breath in relief. His life was finally on track, and getting involved with Michelle Turner could cause a train wreck. Nobody in his right mind wanted a train wreck.

"I'm all right, really," she said with a quaver in her voice. "Things've been difficult lately."

"That's putting it mildly. But you and your dad are strong. You'll do great with this procedure. I had a talk with Maggie Kehr today, and she accepted my personal reference. The surgery's going forward as scheduled."

She shut her eyes for a long moment. "Thanks, Sam." Then she opened her eyes and looked at him. "And . . . thank you for coming over tonight."

"So is Cody what parents like to call a 'handful'?"

"Oh, yeah. Year Sixteen has been a real picnic."

"I got that idea."

"Let's see. He came home the first week of school with a pierced navel and a cigarette habit. He didn't even try hiding either one from me. I think he liked seeing the effect self-mutilation had on me."

"I imagine he did. What's the point of piercing something if no one notices?"

"And your suggestion would be?"

"I guess I'd ignore it until he injures himself zipping his pants. Then let the wound heal over."

"And the smoking?"

"That's tougher. Maybe the smell will gross out some girl and he'll quit."

"Cigarettes are one of his girlfriend's major food groups."

"He needs a new girlfriend, then."

"Oh, and my telling him so is going to work? Sam, you're not that naive."

He *had* been once, long ago. He'd believed in a love so strong no outside force, certainly no parental disapproval, could interfere. It had taken Gavin Slade precisely one evening to lay waste to that belief.

Sam pushed away the thought and concentrated on Cody. "Does he play any sports?"

"Skateboarding and snowboarding. Even a smoker's lungs can handle both. Here's the deal, Sam. I haven't been the most perfect parent in the universe, but I haven't been awful, either. Something happens to a kid who's growing up, something the Dr. Spock books don't mention. The kid becomes his own person. And sometimes that might be a person who does things that drive you nuts, and nothing you can do will stop him."

"Is it possible he *wants* to be stopped?"

"You mean is he looking for limits? Of course. Do I draw the line? Of course." She stood up, went to the window, stuck her hands in her back pockets. "Does he step over the line, of course."

Clearly this was familiar territory to Michelle. But there were hidden facets she wasn't seeing.

"You know, I reckon it's none of my business, but it appears to me that you're so concerned with making the kid happy, giving him some kind of life that looks good on paper, that you're forgetting something."

She turned to face him, defenses going up like an invisible wall. "And you've figured this out based on knowing us three days?"

He sent her a lopsided grin. "Hey, it's a gift."

She rolled her eyes.

"Seriously, Michelle, it's my job to figure out some-body's problem based on a fifteen-minute office visit. Sometimes that's all I get—it happens a lot around here, where most people don't pay regular visits to the doctor and don't follow up. I have fifteen minutes to work on a patient's trouble. In the past five years I've had a lot of practice."

She folded her arms beneath her breasts and eyed him warily. "All right, you have my attention. Tell me your expert opinion, Doctor."

Shit. Why was he doing this?

He planted his elbows on his knees. "My opinion as a doctor is this—Cody's like a lot of kids I see. The more rope you give him, the more ways he finds to tangle himself up. He needs a shorter rein."

"He didn't come with a how-to manual," she said. "That's the thing about raising a kid, Sam. You have to figure it out as you go along."

He felt himself teetering on a precipice. Common sense told him to pull back. His heart made him dive in. "You know as well as any doctor that kids who have unhappy parents wind up a lot more troubled than kids whose parents are relatively content. It doesn't have anything to do with how much money they earn or the sort of house they live in. It has to do with their perception of their place in the world."

"Oh, you're good, Sam. Let's make it my fault."

"Damn it, Michelle—" He was talking himself into deep shit, so he stopped and studied her, petite and slim, unsmiling and coldly beautiful as she stared at the black squares of the window. Then he glanced at the sketchbook on the table. And finally, he stood, taking a wad of keys from his pocket.

"Michelle, get your coat. I want to show you something."

"But Cody—"

"We won't go far."

She pulled on a jacket and boots while he did the same. The night wind slashed at them as they stepped outside. A high three-quarter moon spread a frozen blue glow over the area, and lights from the main house fanned across the yard. Sam led the way along the darkened drive past the cluster of bunkhouses. At the last one, he turned and waded over the unshoveled walk to the front door.

Angling his wad of keys toward the light, he selected one, old and worn, nearly lost in the mass of other keys. "Wonder if it still fits."

Michelle stood silently by as he inserted the key. It stuck, but that was mainly from the cold. Then it turned, and he opened the door, stepping into a room he hadn't seen in seventeen years.

Ghosts haunted this moonlit place. The presence of sheet-draped furniture heightened the eerie effect. He flicked a switch, and the light came on. "Remember this?"

"What would you do if I said no?"

"Call you a liar." He plucked a sheet off a threadbare chair, and one off a nearby table.

"Sam, I don't see the point—Oh."

He watched her take in the scene, wishing he knew her better, wishing he knew what she was feeling. He'd counted on Gavin Slade having a hidden streak of sentimentality, and he'd been right. The old man had left this place alone, a shrine to the daughter who had walked out of his life.

"It's exactly the way it was when I used to work here." Michelle's words made little frozen puffs in the air.

Gavin had equipped the bungalow especially for her.

It had a drafting table, easels and clipboards, tons of canvas and jars of brushes, tubes of paint. Everything was still there, left to atrophy with time and neglect. Sam removed another sheet to reveal an old-fashioned sofa, covered in flea-bitten velveteen.

The sight of it gave him a flash of memory so hot that he nearly shoved Michelle down on the musty cushions. He remembered the feel of her beneath him, the way her legs went around him, the sound of her breath in his ear. He remembered what it felt like to be buried to the hilt inside her. He remembered what it was like to feel a love so pure and strong that it burned like a flame that would never go out.

Jesus. It was eighteen degrees in here, and he was starting to sweat. He cast a furtive glance at Michelle to see if she noticed.

She was blushing red to the tips of her ears.

"I wonder if it happened there," he said softly, recklessly. "I wonder if that's where we made Cody."

She caught her breath with a little hiccup. "No. It was the boathouse. It . . . happened at the boathouse."

The place by the river had been their secret retreat, where they could steal away and find privacy together. Suddenly Sam was inundated with memories of that summer. It was the one time in his life when he saw everything with perfect clarity, when he felt absolutely certain he was going in the right direction, absolutely certain he knew what the outcome would be.

Funny thing about life. It had a way of spinning you around, shooting you off in a totally different direction, like a wild ride on a greenbroke horse. You had no idea where you were heading until you landed ass-first in the dirt.

"Sam, why did you bring me here?"

I keep remembering what it was like to be with you. He gritted his teeth to keep from saying it. Instead, he said, "There's a lot of waiting around involved in transplantation and recovery. You could be painting while you're here."

"No." She spoke swiftly, decisively. Almost defensively.

"Why not?"

"I draw and paint for work. As long as I have this enforced sabbatical, why would I do anything that resembles work?"

He wanted to say that the paintings she used to do were so different from the sketches in her book that they didn't resemble work at all, but a gifted mind and eye and hand creating something extraordinary.

He didn't say anything. She was hard to read, this grown-up Michelle. One thing was certain—she was in a skittish state, and he didn't seem to be helping matters.

He could feel himself moving fast toward a conviction that there were things he and Michelle should explore. What would it be like to get to know her again, to look at her through adult eyes? He could see the yearning in her eyes, the shadows of unfulfilled dreams, and he knew he couldn't dismiss her from his life when the transplant was over.

"Besides," she said, picking up a frozen paint tube, "the supplies are spoiled."

"You could replace them easily enough. Next trip to Missoula, you could lay in a bunch of paint and brushes."

"I'm really not interested, Sam."

He let her words sink in. "We'd better get out of here before we freeze to death."

He walked her back to her door and stood there for a moment, studying her in the glow from the porch light.

Suddenly he felt like a trespasser. "I've got to go, Michelle."

"'Night, Sam."

"'Night." His hand, without consulting his head, came up and cupped her cheek.

She didn't move. "Your hand is cold."

"Your cheek is warm." He leaned down and kissed it, soft skin and a subtle fragrance of perfume and snow. "I guess I'll be seeing you around . . . or not," he added. Then he walked to his truck, resisting the urge to whistle.

Chapter 20

When Michelle rushed back inside the house, she pushed aside the kitchen curtain to catch a last glimpse of Sam. The moon, a cold white smile, threw a stream of light over him, and he held up one hand in farewell. Embarrassed to be caught, she dropped the curtain and leaned against the counter. She was shaking all over. Shaking with memories and wanting and, most of all, with fear. Sam McPhee was part of her past, part of a past she had traveled far, far away from, and she shouldn't be having this explosive chemical reaction to him. But he was so bound up in things that were important—Cody and her art and Montana and Gavin—that she felt both wildly attracted to him and terrified of him.

She checked on Cody, finding the door to his room firmly closed. Then she brewed a cup of tea, using two bags to make it stronger, and when she sat down on the sofa, her hand went to the phone.

After two rings, she was tapping her foot with impatience. He picked up on the fourth ring. "Brad Lovell."

"It's me."

"Hiya, babe." He sounded warm and comfortable.

She smiled, her insides watery with relief. "What are you doing? Are you busy?"

"Going over some papers. Looks like we'll be able to afford a condo on Kauai after all—"

"Brad?"

"Yeah, babe?"

"I have to tell you something."

"What, you'd rather find a place on Maui?"

"No, nothing like that." God. When did he get the impression she wanted a condo in Hawaii in the first place?

"What is it, Michelle?"

She blew on her tea, took a sip. "It's about Cody."

"Shit. Is he in trouble already?"

It bugged her no end that Brad's first assumption was that Cody got in trouble. It bugged her even more that, basically, he was right.

"Well, there's trouble . . . and there's trouble."

"So you want to tell me, or are we going to play twenty questions?"

She took another sip, then set her cup down. "It's about his . . . about the man who fathered him."

"The cowboy."

"Yes. Um, he lives in Crystal City now. The other night I . . . ran into him." She made a swift decision not to explain the details.

"So did he recognize you?"

She was a little insulted by the implication. "Yes. And

it didn't take him long to put two and two together and figure out about Cody."

"Silence."

"Brad?"

"I keep waiting to hear you say you're going on *Oprah* with all this."

She smiled in spite of herself. "Right. Anyway, we— I told Cody tonight. He wasn't thrilled, but I think he's still getting used to the idea."

"What about you, Michelle? Are you thrilled?"

She felt a sting of guilt, because she wanted to be able to say that seeing Sam again meant nothing to her. That she felt nothing.

"I was shocked, I guess. Surprised. I never thought I'd see him again. But it turns out he did all right for himself, became a doctor, and he's a partner in a horse ranch about ten miles from here. His name is Sam McPhee."

"Do you think he wants something from you?"

She thought about the way Sam had touched her, the way he'd said good night. A shiver passed over her. "Like . . . what?"

"Like visitation rights or something."

A terrible chill touched the base of her neck. "I have no idea. It all came about so fast. He hasn't asked for a thing." *Yet.* But tonight she had seen the questions in his eyes.

"Well, if he gets some idea that playing the dad is all fun and games, remind him of what college tuition costs these days."

"It's not a matter of finance."

"Sweetheart, everything is a matter of finance."

"Not this. I'm going to let Cody get used to the idea and . . . see what happens. Oh, God, Brad, what if he wants

to be with his father more than he wants to be with me?"
She poured her fears into the receiver.

"Why would he want that?" Brad sounded genuinely
baffled. "Look, don't worry. You're good to Cody. He loves
you. He's just having a tough time right now, like any
kid." Brad changed the subject easily enough, and she let
him, grateful for once to hear him ponder the merits of
Kauai over Maui. After making the appropriate murmurs,
she said good-bye and hung up.

The conversation left her with a vague, ineffable sense
of dissatisfaction. Why can't Brad be as decisive about us
as he is about vacation property? she wondered.

Restless, she finished her tea and made a second cup,
knowing the caffeine would keep her up, but she was past
caring. For a long time, she gazed at the small framed picture of her mother, which she carried in her briefcase
everywhere she went. Sharon Turner stood swathed in a
Dior gown, her hair and makeup perfect as she blew a
kiss to someone behind the camera. "Miss you, Mom,"
Michelle whispered. "I sure as heck would like to hear
your voice right now." She drummed her hands on the
phone. She knew who she was going to call. She knew
she'd probably regret it, but she was going to do it anyway. She punched in the number and waited.

On the third ring, a voice said, "Hello?"

"Natalie, sorry to call so late. It's me."

"Michelle!" she squealed in unfeigned delight.

"Are you busy?" Michelle asked, though she knew
that whatever Natalie was doing would come to a halt, because she was that sort of friend.

"I've been practicing arpeggios on my cello. Very exciting. But I love house-sitting at your place. Awesome
hot tub. Now *you*, sweetie! What's happened? How's it
going?"

Aside from Cody and Brad, Natalie was the only one Michelle had told about the transplant. It wasn't the sort of thing to be discussed with casual work acquaintances. And with Gavin Slade for a father, Michelle had learned to keep quiet lest the media sense a story.

"I'm all set to go into the hospital Saturday for one more procedure. If that checks out, we'll get a thumbs-up for surgery on Monday."

"When's Brad going over? Will he meet you at the hospital in Missoula?"

Soft leather creaked as she shifted position on the sofa. "Brad and I had a long talk about this before I left. I can't decide what I need from him. Maybe I don't even need him to come at all."

"Oh, for Pete's sake. You're taking this I-can-cope-on-my-own crap too far. Of course he needs to come."

"If Brad's around, I'll worry about what he's doing and thinking, pacing the halls of a hospital in a strange city. I'll go nuts wondering if he and Cody are getting along. It might be better to let him stay in Seattle, keep him posted by phone. Anyway, he's on standby. He promised that if I decide I want him with me, he'll drop everything and come."

"Brad's never dropped a thing in his life. Except maybe hints that I should take a hike."

There was a grain of truth in that. Brad and Natalie drove each other insane. "My dad and I are prepared. Everything will be fine."

"You're going to save your father's life. I'm getting a rush thinking about this."

"Don't knock yourself out, Natalie. It's just a surgical procedure."

"Just? *Just?* Not hardly, sweetie. I know you don't believe in this stuff, Michelle, but it's real. You've got to think about the spiritual aspect of it. You're giving life to the father who gave you life."

"I'm giving a kidney to the father who gave me a monthly check."

"No, listen, you have to listen." Michelle could picture Natalie sitting forward in that in-your-face way of hers. She wondered what color her friend's hair was tonight. Natalie had discovered hair mascara and hadn't been the same since. "There is a deeper meaning to this. It's not just plumbing."

"Natalie, it *is*. And thank God that it is, because that means it can be done at all. If it required magic and miracles, we'd be in big trouble."

"Okay, at least think about this. Physiologically, it *is* just plumbing. But you have to stay open to the possibility that something more is going to happen to you. Something amazing. You're going to connect with your father on a *cellular* level."

Michelle laughed, trying not to spray tea. "Yeah, Nat, that's the part I'm really looking forward to."

"You wait and see. How are you and your dad getting along?"

"I hate to disappoint you, but we're like a couple of cordial strangers. He's embarrassed and apologetic about the whole thing. Like he committed a faux pas by getting sick. And now that we're together again, it's . . ." She paused, feeling a sting of regret. "Let's just say there's been no cellular connection."

"There will be. I bet he went bananas over Cody."

This time she almost choked. "Natalie," she gasped into the phone, "you're killing me."

"What? Your dad's never seen Cody. It must be wonderful, bringing them together."

"It's like bringing together Johnny Depp and Charlton Heston. Cody's being horrible, my dad doesn't know what to make of him, and they're both inches from exploding."

"Oh, Michelle. I'm sorry. Let me talk to the Cody-boy." She had known him since the day he was born—literally. As Michelle's birthing coach, Natalie was the one who, sobbing as hard as Michelle was, had cut the umbilical cord. She decided then and there that she loved him, and her love hadn't wavered since.

"He's asleep. He had a little accident."

"*Accident?* You bitch, why didn't you call me?"

"It was minor. He cut his head."

"How?"

"On . . . a horse's hoof."

"Hold the goddamned phone, Michelle. You're telling me he got kicked in the head by one of your father's horses?"

"Actually, he got kicked in the head by one of *his* father's horses."

"Michelle!" She could picture Natalie now, totally agitated, pacing up and down in her designer living room, shrieking into the phone. "Do you mean to tell me the cowboy's there?"

She had never told her any more than she told Brad or Cody. "He lives in the area now."

"*Get out.* Did you know he was there?"

"No, it was a complete surprise. He's actually a physician now."

Silence. Complete and utter stunned silence. It was rare, a totally quiet Natalie, and Michelle grinned, enjoying the novelty of it.

"Holy goddamned horseshit," she said at last. "So let me get this straight. The no-account cowpoke who knocked you up came back to town and is now a respected citizen and doctor?"

"That's about it."

"And your dad never thought to tell you?"

"We never spoke, Natalie."

"Okay, get to the good part. Is the cowboy doctor married?"

"No."

"Involved?"

"I don't know."

"If he was, you'd know. What did he and Cody say when you told them?"

"It's . . . complicated."

"Fine. I'm coming."

"What?"

"Probably take me a day and a half in the Volkswagen."

"Natalie, you can't—"

"I said, I'm *coming*." She slammed down the phone.

Though she knew it was fruitless, Michelle hit redial a couple of times, but she got the expected voice-mail pickup.

"Nat, I've got enough going on without you showing up," she said, knowing her friend was ignoring her as she flew around the town house, flinging mismatched, inappropriate clothes into a woven Costa Rican shoulder bag. "I think," Michelle said, speaking to the tape, "there's such a thing as being *too* good a friend." She went on in this vein, trying to dissuade Natalie, but she knew it was useless.

When she hung up the phone, she felt strange and sort of disoriented. She was happy Natalie was coming. She was dismayed that Natalie was coming. She couldn't make up her mind how she felt. But one thing was certain. Natalie was the sort of person who got everything out in the open. And she knew Michelle better than anyone else in the universe.

Natalie would take one look at Michelle when Sam was around, and she'd *know*. Natalie would know that Michelle couldn't stop thinking about him, and that she had no idea what to do about him.

Michelle kept reminding herself that she had a life. She had Cody and Brad and her career. That was what she needed to focus on. That, and getting through the surgery.

She lay down on the sofa, shut her eyes, and suddenly the ideas started coming. There was a part of her, a wild, out-of-control part, that had some very explicit ideas of what to do about Sam McPhee, and if she knew what was good for her, she'd ignore them.

Wednesday

Chapter 21

Cody was glad his mom didn't demand some big explanation when he said he wanted to go to Sam's in the morning. All he had to tell her was that his head felt fine, he'd wear a hat, and he wanted to see the foal he'd helped deliver.

Her face took on that tight, nervous expression she got when she suspected he was up to something, but she drank her coffee in thoughtful silence. He wondered what she was thinking. Then he decided he didn't really want to know.

Cody waited, stiff and apprehensive, while she called Lonepine. But she didn't talk to Sam. She talked to that Indian guy, Edward Bliss. Edward was okay, kind of goofy but not too bad. He said it was fine to come, so by nine o'clock Cody was jumping out of the Range Rover and heading for the barn. The dog—Sprout? No, Scout—came churning across the snow to accompany him.

He heard his mom calling stuff after him—keep his hat on, call if he started to feel bad, all that crap—but he simply waved without turning. It was rude to blow her off, but if he didn't walk away, she'd sit there for an hour telling him be careful of this, watch out for that, and he wasn't up for maternal lectures this morning.

"Hello," he called as he stepped into the barn. Scout trotted around, sniffing loudly, acting important. The central breezeway was dim and a little warmer than outside thanks to some heat lamps hanging from the rafters.

He poked his head into the cluttered office. "Anyone here?"

No one in sight. He figured Sam was probably at work, and Edward was either out on the range somewhere or still in his cabin across the way. The Border collie found a heap of old blankets by the wood-burning stove and curled into a ball for a nap.

"Excellent," Cody said under his breath. It felt good to be alone, away from everybody. He didn't like people hovering over him.

Outside the office, he put on the boots he'd worn the other day. He picked up a set of tan coveralls and stepped into them. Stomping his feet to warm them, he was glad there wasn't a mirror around, because he was sure he looked like a complete dork. As he pulled on a pair of gloves, he quit thinking about how he looked. He wanted to see the mare and her foal.

The birthing stall had its own set of heat lamps in all four corners. The light from them fell at an angle over the mare and the baby, and for a second Cody gawked at them with a hitch in his throat. Sylvia stood calmly in the middle of the stall. She made a noise, like someone clearing her throat, when she spotted Cody. It was a friendly sound. At least, he was pretty sure it was friendly. Then she used her big muzzle to nudge at the foal, which was sleeping curled up like a kitten near her feet. The little one lifted its head, then staggered up, all wobbly. First it splayed out its front legs, then its hind legs, and after a minute it figured out how to get up on all fours. Cody was tempted to help, but Sam had said it was best to let the baby get up on its own.

It lurched against its mother, lips nibbling comically at her belly. She nuzzled it some more, twisting back to guide it to her udder. After a while, the foal stuck its head in the right place. Cody had never expected the sound of nursing to be audible, but it was—sucking, swallowing, gurgling. He'd probably be embarrassed if anyone else was around, but he had the moment all to himself, so he leaned on the stall door and grinned.

The soft morning light, the little drift of steam from the mare's nostrils, the funny sucking sound made by the foal and the way its skinny legs splayed out. Aunt Natalie—she wasn't his real aunt but his mom's best friend— would get all gushy at this point. But hell, Natalie got gushy over Hallmark commercials on TV.

When he'd talked to Claudia last night, he'd tried to describe what it was like seeing a foal being born, but she'd just said "Gross" and started nagging him about the pain pills. He sort of wanted to tell her about finding his father, but he couldn't figure out a way to bring up the topic. Sometimes he wished Claudia was the kind of friend he could tell this stuff to, but the fact was, she never really seemed interested in heavy personal stuff. She was too into having a good time, and when Cody was with her, that's what he wanted, too. But sometimes he wondered what it would be like to have someone he trusted, some-

one he could really talk to, because some days, like today,
he had news burning a hole in him.

Maybe he couldn't unload about Sam, but he'd try to
find a camera somewhere, take some pictures of the horses
to show Claudia. The filly was so goddamned cute, how
could anyone not want to see it?

His mom used to draw awesome pictures of horses.
He thought of the paintings stacked in the closet of her
study at home. The large, flat folder was filled with old
sketches and watercolor and acrylic studies. When he was
little, he had asked her about them, paging reverently
through the stack and regarding the horse drawings with
astonished admiration. "What are these, Mom? Did you
do these?"

"Years ago, baby." She always used to called him baby,
sometimes even slipped and did so now. "I don't have time
for that kind of drawing anymore. I'm too busy drawing
for work."

"I like these better than work."

She'd looked at him with big, sad eyes and tousled
his hair. "So did I, baby. So did I."

She had never said much more about those pictures,
but Cody used to look at them in secret sometimes. Now
that he'd seen his grandfather's ranch, he knew where those
drawings came from. Horses and mountains and a rushing river. A tall fir tree next to a salt lick. A nest of loons
in a marsh, the still water mirroring a snow-peaked mountain. They were all pictures made while she was at Blue
Rock Ranch.

Sam's mare and foal would have fit right in with those
pictures. His mom could have made a hell of a drawing
of those two. But she had given up painting when he was
a baby, and he had no memory of her doing anything but
agency work. Still, she kept her old pictures.

One Fourth of July when he was about ten, Cody had been awakened by the boom of fireworks over Elliott Bay. He'd gone looking for his mom, and he'd found her in her home office, the drawings spread out on the floor. She was drinking a glass of wine and silently crying. Disconcerted, Cody had crept back to his room.

Now he knew the source of her memories and her sadness. When she had lived at Blue Rock Ranch all those years ago, she'd met Sam McPhee.

His father. His goddamned father.

Cody scowled the thought away. He actually did some work, cleaning the lines and pans of the watering device. The contraption served all the stalls, filling with fresh water when one of the horses pressed its tongue against a bar in the center. He filled the wheelbarrow with manure from empty stalls and hauled it outside. He kept stopping to check on the mare and foal.

After a while, the filly quit nursing. The mare started doing motherly things, like sniffing it all over, giving it a lick here and there. Cody wondered if he'd be welcome in the stall. The kick in the head had been an accident. A reflex. Even with his limited experience, he knew that.

When he lifted the latch of the stall door, his hand trembled a little, surprising him. He didn't think he'd be afraid. That was stupid. He made himself open the half door and step inside, boots sinking into the soft layer of straw. He made a smooching sound with his mouth, the way he'd heard Edward and Sam do.

The filly shied, but the mare looked up, nodding her head in a funny way that made him smile. "Hey, Sylvia," he said softly. "How you doing, girl?"

She grunted, then stretched out her neck so her big soft muzzle nudged his shoulder. And Cody, the most self-conscious kid ever born, forgot to be self-conscious. He rubbed her nose, and her bristly chin, and her neck, murmuring soft nonsense. She sighed with contentment when he scratched her between the ears.

The foal kept watching them, tail flicking, ears pricked forward. Cody held out his hand, low with the palm open. "C'mere, little one. I won't hurt you. C'mere . . ."

The foal lurched to its feet. Cody went down on one knee, moving slowly so he wouldn't startle her. She sniffed his hand, nose twitching, and jerked her head back. He held his hand steady, keeping up a low-voiced monologue. The foal sniffed and pulled back a couple more times. Finally, she allowed Cody to give her a rub between the eyes. She pressed forward in clear acceptance, letting him rub her muzzle and head. He laughed out loud when her small pink tongue came out and licked his hand. She latched on to his finger, sucking away. She was so damned cute, shiny as a new penny, cuddling up to him like a regular pet. Completely lost in the moment, he looped his arms around the foal's neck and pressed his cheek to her warm, smooth face.

He heard a noise behind him. The mare, thumping her foot on the floor, he told himself. Please let it be that.

He stood up and turned, knowing goddamned good and well it wasn't the mare that he'd heard. Someone had just caught him red-handed at his most ridiculous.

"Hi, Cody," she said. "I came to see the new foal."

"Um, Molly, yeah." He could feel his face filling up with a blush like a thermometer rising. "That's your name, right? Molly?" As if he'd forgotten. As if she'd be fooled.

She grinned at him, and the sun through the skylights seemed to get brighter for a second. She was amazing, her long straight black hair so shiny it was like water. Her face was the type of face you never wanted to look away from.

"That's my name."

His ears were on fire. He could feel the flames rising from them. "I was, um, making friends with her myself."

She let herself into the stall, expertly stroking Sylvia to put the mare at her ease. But her eyes never left the foal. "Ooh, she's such a little beauty." She dug in her pocket and pulled out a treat for Sylvia. "It's okay that I saw you doing that," she said as the mare crunched down the carrot.

Cody nearly choked with embarrassment. "I was just—"

"I usually kiss 'em on the lips," she stated, then squatted and held out a hand to the foal.

He stood back, feeling a tad superior that the filly wouldn't have a thing to do with the girl. He didn't care how long she spent trying to coax it. He'd be happy to stand here all day staring at Molly. Barn clothes looked just right on her. At his school in Seattle, the tight leggings and paddock boots, oversize sweater and puffy down vest would draw comments of dork and dweeb. But here in Sam's barn, she looked natural and comfortable. He found himself wondering what it would feel like to hold her slender form close to him. He wondered what her hair smelled like, and if her cheek was as soft as it looked, and if her lips—

Whoa. His thoughts were way out of control. He owed Claudia his loyalty, not this skinny backwater stranger. Claudia was the one who had pulled him out of obscure mediocrity at school. Because Claudia was his girl, he was suddenly someone, suddenly important. People knew his name when he walked down the halls at school.

The trouble was, when Molly Lightning looked up at him with shining eyes, she made it real easy to forget all that stuff.

"She's a perfect filly," Molly said. "Just perfect. I knew she would be."

"How'd you know that?"

"She's by Calyx, out of Sylvia. The perfect combination."

"By Calyx. You mean that's the father?"

"Uh-huh. Or the stud, you could say. Breeder talk, I guess."

"Whatever." Awkwardness stole over Cody. "Um, do you want to get a Coke or something?"

She stood. "Sure. We should leave the baby alone, anyway."

It turned out she was right. Practically the second they left the stall, the foal curled up and fell asleep. They raided the beat-up old refrigerator, filled with shots and wormer and soft drinks. The Border collie thumped her tail, then went back to sleep. They stood in the barn office, sipping from the cans as unease settled over them again.

"So my mom heard you got kicked in the head." Molly eyed the knitted gray cap Cody had pulled on that morning.

He felt a little swell of pride as he touched his forehead where the edge of the bandage showed. "Yeah. I got in the way of Sylvia's hoof at the wrong time."

She regarded him with such admiration that he felt inches taller. "I'm glad you're all right."

He liked the way she sipped her Coke from the can. He liked the way her fingernails were cut, short and plain. Claudia painted hers a different color practically every day, and on special occasions she painted tiny designs on each one. He had never seen the point of it, but it was a girl thing, he supposed.

"So how'd your mom hear about the accident?" he asked.

Molly rolled her eyes comically. "My mom hears everything. She teaches English at the high school. I bet Edward Bliss told her."

"Did he tell her the other stuff?" Cody felt a strange lightness in his chest, as if he'd inhaled cigarette smoke and was holding his breath.

"What other stuff?"

"About . . . Sam McPhee."

"What about Sam?"

"That he's my dad." He made sure he sounded totally blasé. "My biological dad." He didn't look at her, but he felt her stillness, her dawning amazement.

"Wow," she said at last.

"So I guess your mom doesn't hear *everything*."

"Guess not. Did Sam know about you?"

Something that felt uncomfortably like shame touched Cody. It pissed him off that he had been conceived so carelessly and then dismissed, no more important than a foal to a stud. "Nope. He and my mom lost track of each other."

"Do you have a stepdad?"

He thought of Brad, with those clean hands and that fat wallet. And those eyes that didn't trust him. "Nope." He poked the toe of his boot at a coil of rope on the floor.

"So are you happy about it or what?"

"He's just some guy my mom used to know. It doesn't change anything."

Molly put her empty can in the recycle bin. "Are you sure?"

"What, you think they're going to pick up where they left off and fall into each other's arms?"

"What if they do?"

"They won't," he said quickly, fiercely. "We live in a different state. We're here temporarily."

"I really like Sam. Everybody does."

"I don't even know the guy."

She paused. "He was seeing my mom last summer."

Cody's head jerked up; he narrowed his eyes. "Yeah? Are they still together?"

"Nope. They're good friends and all, but they don't really go out. I heard he sees a lot of different women." Her cheeks glowed pink. "That's what I heard, anyway."

"What about your dad?"

She shrugged. "Ditched us when I was little. I barely even remember him."

"I guess you know Sam a lot better."

"I guess."

Cody waited, wishing she'd say more. Since learning about Sam, he'd been on fire with curiosity. There was so much to wonder about. Where was Sam from? How had he grown up? Did he have any brothers or sisters? What did he eat for breakfast?

Why didn't he come looking for me?

He slammed his can into the recycle bin and stalked out of the barn office. "I better get to work," he said, growing short-tempered with all the thoughts swirling through his head.

"Want some help?" Molly asked.

"Nope."

"I could—"

"No." He turned and faced her. She stood in the doorway, backlit by sunlight. He wished she'd leave in a huff, but she stood her ground. "There's not much to be done," he said lamely.

"See you around, then." She walked out of the barn. A tall Appaloosa with a shaggy winter coat stood tethered to the paddock rail. She untied the horse and swung up into the saddle, turning him and walking him away with unhurried dignity.

Chapter 22

The illness was the enemy. The moment he had been diagnosed, Gavin had envisioned it as a living thing, a monster stalking him through the dark. Initially, he'd wasted a lot of time in denial and rage. Humiliated by the disintegration of his body, he had cursed the universe, embraced a death wish. A binge of drinking and tomcatting had nearly brought him to his knees. He had awakened one morning in an emergency clinic in Kalispell to find that they'd dragged him back from the edge of a coma—temporarily. The rest was up to him.

He went home and got down to the business of survival. He waged a battle against his disease, planning strategy with the precision of a film director blocking out a scene.

Yet he was losing ground. Hiring a special nutritionist, participating in special therapies had only postponed the inevitable. His kidneys were useless. Dialysis wasn't getting the job done. He was slowly poisoning himself. If the transplant didn't work, he'd be dead in a matter of months.

Driving down the highway away from town, he flexed his hands on the steering wheel. Part of his strategy for dealing with this was to act as if everything was fine, as if he didn't carry around a bag of dialysis fluid connected by a tube sticking out of his side. He still went to the feed store, still placed his stock orders and gossiped with the cow buyers and rodeo directors who came through town. Still stopped in at the diner for a cup of tea—coffee had been banned long ago.

He was a fixture in Crystal City. Even now, years after his last film, he was regarded as the town celebrity. People liked coming up to him and saying hi. They liked telling their kids he was the guy on all those tapes at the video store.

They kept his movies in the Classics section.

He drove along the empty road, thinking about Michelle and wishing like hell for some alternative to the surgery. Christ, she didn't owe him a thing, least of all a frigging *kidney*.

But the minute she'd figured out the score, she'd latched on like a tick, and she wasn't about to let go.

Why was that? Filial love and devotion didn't explain it. A sense of duty—maybe. The trouble was, they were doing this ass-backward. Forgiveness should come first. *Then* the transplant. Sad to think it took a crisis to bring them both to the table.

He pondered the long gap in their relationship, a gap that spanned the years of Cody's life.

I'm pregnant, Daddy.

I'm not surprised. Your mother was careless, too.

Christ. What the hell had he been thinking, speaking to his young, frightened daughter that way? Worse, Gavin had made sure she didn't have Sam McPhee to turn to. No wonder she had left, erecting a wall of silence that had endured for years. He didn't blame her.

He had responded to her departure by finding a mistress nearly as young as Michelle and becoming the resident playboy of Crystal City. He threw himself into work, producing a few small-studio independent films and giving the rest of his attention to the rodeo stock breeding program on his farm. There had barely been time to come up for air. And he sure as hell hadn't been inclined to let her know her old boyfriend had made good and moved back to town.

He'd salved his guilt about Michelle in equally typical fashion—by setting up a massive college fund for her child. He knew better than to suppose he could buy her forgiveness, but at least the boy would never have to worry about paying for his education.

Many times since his diagnosis, Gavin had picked up the phone, even dialed the number. It was a terrible thing, a pathetic thing, to use pity and compassion to bridge the gap. He'd held off telling her as long as he could. Michelle caught on when Gavin had set up a new trust fund in Cody's name. Within hours of receiving the papers to sign, she had called.

On some insane level, he was grateful for the illness that had brought her to him so swiftly and unquestioningly. If the transplant didn't work, he'd feel like a failure. But that was asking for a guarantee, and for once in his life, he knew better than that.

The sight of a breakdown at the side of the road startled Gavin from his musings. He recognized the beige Chevy Celebrity parked on the shoulder with its hood propped up. He eased off the road and parked behind the car.

"Car trouble?" he asked the woman bent over the engine.

She straightened up. Instant recognition froze her face. Tammi Lee Gilmer was in her fifties and looked it, with tired skin and overtreated hair teased high. She was slender and pale-eyed, a wary smile playing about her mouth. In the years since she'd moved back to Crystal City, she had lived a quiet life, never showing any signs of the out-of-control partying that had once made her the talk of the town.

She worked in a fabric shop—Gavin had never set foot inside it. On the rare occasions that he saw her, they dismissed each other with a nod and a murmured hello. Now he was trapped.

"It just died on me," she said. "I can't think what happened." Her voice was husky. As far as Gavin could tell, she'd given up drinking, but the habit still haunted her voice.

He opened the passenger door of his truck. "I'll give you a lift."

She slammed down the hood and grabbed her purse off the seat. "Thanks, Gavin. I was on my way out to Sam's. I can call McEvoy's Garage from there."

It was a tall step up into his truck, and he held out a hand to steady her as she climbed in. Her arm felt small and bony, but she was spry enough as she settled into the passenger seat. She smelled of cigarettes and drugstore perfume, and he found the fragrance unpretentious and therefore slightly welcome. He came from a world where women donned formal dress to go to the mailbox. He didn't miss that world at all.

He walked around the truck and got in, easing back onto the highway.

"You know the way to Sam's?" she asked.

"Yeah, I know where Lonepine is. I've been out there once or twice." Gavin had bought a couple of horses from Sam. Beyond that, they hadn't spoken.

Tammi Lee crossed one leg over the other, adjusting the wool cuff of her snow boot. Gavin kept his eyes on the road, but he found himself remembering, almost against his will, one of the meetings he'd had with his transplant team. The psychologist had pretty much guaranteed him he'd have no interest in sex for a good long while—maybe never again. The antirejection meds had a motherlode of side effects.

"But it's life," Dr. Temple had said, his painfully earnest face animated by optimism. "Preferable to the alternative."

Gavin hadn't smiled. "Shoot me now," he'd grumbled, and the psychologist had scribbled something on his clipboard.

Gavin missed Carolyn, who had lived with him until he'd been diagnosed. A former first-runner-up Miss California, her favorite things were riding horses, watching movies, shopping, and having imaginative, recreational sex.

When he told her about his illness, she had looked at him in horror, left that same day, sued him for eight thousand a month in palimony, and sold her story to a magazine.

His attorney had negotiated a much cheaper settlement, and Gavin had set up the second trust fund for Cody.

"I guess you know why I was headed out to Sam's," Tammi Lee said, bringing his thoughts around full circle.

"To see the boy, I imagine."

"I've been told the boy's name is Cody." Her voice held a gentle censure. "Cody Jackson Turner. So it's lucky I ran into you. Now you can tell me all about him, sort of prepare me."

"I haven't seen much of my grandson, Tammi Lee."

"Yeah, well, he's my grandson, too, and I've *never* seen him."

"A word to the wise. Don't expect a bunch of hugs and kisses."

"From a sixteen-year-old boy who doesn't know me from Reba McIntyre? Don't worry, Gavin, I'm not that stupid." She was pensive for a few moments. "When Sam was that age, he acted more grown up than me. Quit school and went to work for you. I took that boy's childhood away from him. No. I never let him have a childhood in the first place."

The frank regret in her voice made him wince. "Hey, take it easy on yourself. Sam's fine. Not every mother raises a boy to become a doctor."

"He did it all on his own. I never forget that. Never."

"You have a right to be pretty proud of Sam," Gavin remarked.

She laughed briefly, shaking her head. "I keep thinking he was left with me by mistake, that he was actually meant for some couple with a nice house full of books and a piano and supper hot on the table every night."

"I bet that would have made him too soft to do everything he's done." Gavin wished she'd drop the subject. He knew what she'd been like when Sam was coming up. Though she'd been his full-time mother, in a way she had been as absent from Sam as Gavin was from Michelle. Because when you were a drunk, you weren't there. Simple as that.

"Okay, here we are." He turned down the drive to

Sam's place. It wasn't a showy spread, not like Blue Rock was. A battered mailbox was the only indication that it had a name; LONEPINE was stenciled on the side and the flag was up. In the middle of the front pasture, the huge old lodgepole pine tree that had given the place its name stood draped in snow.

A slim girl on a tall Appaloosa rode in the opposite direction, leaving the ranch. Gavin recognized her as Ruby Lightning's girl.

"Wonder if she was keeping Cody company," Tammi Lee murmured. "If the youngster's anywhere near as good-looking as his dad, he'll have no trouble in the girl department. How about that daughter of yours?" she asked suddenly. "I hear she's some big-shot ad executive in Seattle."

"Uh-huh. But I didn't have anything to do with that."

"Nice she came back after all these years."

He pulled up to the barn and parked. A Border collie scampered out, barking and leaping in the snow.

Turning to Tammi Lee, Gavin forced himself to level with her. "Michelle didn't come back to be nice."

"Oh . . . ?"

"I've been sick." He hated saying it, nearly gagged on the words. "You probably heard that."

"There was talk of it in the shop."

"I've been on dialysis, but it isn't doing it for me. I could go toxic anytime. I need a kidney transplant. Michelle's going to be the donor."

"My God—"

"I'll never be able to thank her."

"Just get yourself healthy, Gavin. That'll be thanks enough. I know that for sure."

Sam's partner, Edward Bliss, came out hefting an extra

large Havahart wildlife trap. Gavin opened Tammi Lee's door for her.

"Hey, folks," Bliss said, his greeting light, his stare heavy with curiosity.

"Hey yourself, Eddie." Tammi Lee tucked her knitted hat down over her ears. "My car broke down. I'll use the phone in the barn office."

"Sure. Sam's at work today."

"I know. I came to see Cody."

Bliss's interest was so intense it was almost comical. "He's in the barn."

Gavin said, "You want some help with that trap?"

"No, thanks." Bliss shuffled away on reluctant feet. "I've got it." He deposited the trap on a flatbed sled hitched to a snowmobile. "Better be going. We've had a cat prowling around lately."

"Let me know if that thing works. I've had trouble with mountain lions myself the past couple of years," Gavin said as Bliss started the engine and rode off. Gavin stood between the truck and the barn, undecided. There was no need for him to stay, but he didn't feel like going just now either.

Tammi Lee hesitated at the barn door. "Hey, Gavin?"

"Yeah?"

"Maybe you could, um, introduce us."

For the first time since finding her on the side of the road, he smiled. He didn't blame her, feeling nervous about meeting a sixteen-year-old grandkid she never knew about. Cody was enough to make anybody nervous. "Sure," he said. "Of course."

They went into the barn together. The fecund smells of hay and molasses oats and manure filled the air and, somewhere, a radio played terrible music designed to drive people crazy.

"I'm no square in the music department," Tammi Lee whispered to Gavin. "Does this count as music?"

He made an exaggerated show of covering his ears. "Welcome to Cody's world."

They spotted him cleaning a stall. Oblivious to the visitors, he had a pretty good rhythm going with the shovel, bending to load, then swinging up to deposit the load in a wheelbarrow.

"Too bad Sam got to the kid first," Gavin commented, surprised to see him working so industriously. "He would be pretty useful around Blue Rock."

"You should give him some chores," said Tammi Lee, her stare devouring Cody. "I bet he'd work for both of you."

"When I first laid eyes on the boy, I didn't think he'd turn out to be good for much of anything. To me, he looked like every reason I never watch MTV."

Tammi Lee crossed her arms in front of her, leaning against a post. "Then you forgot the cardinal rule of kids."

"What's that?"

"Underneath the most terrible attitude and the most terrible clothes, he's just a kid."

"I don't have much experience with kids."

"Me neither." Apprehensive as a nervous filly, she took a step toward Cody.

"You okay?" he asked, surprised by her hesitation.

"Look, I didn't do so hot with Sam," she said. "I don't want to blow it with Sam's son."

Gavin's heart took an unexpected lurch. Suddenly it struck him that getting off the bottle had been a struggle for her, a battle, a war. And that she was never really safe from a relapse.

Without thinking, he took her hand. "Come on. I'll introduce you."

Reaching for the radio, he switched it off.

Cody's uncertain tenor voice kept singing, then broke off. "Hey, what the—" He stopped himself again when he saw Gavin and Tammi Lee.

"Sorry about that." Gavin grinned in a friendly fashion. But he'd screwed up already, embarrassing the kid.

"You shouldn't sneak up on people like that." Cody set aside his shovel and peeled off one glove, inserting his finger up under his cap where the edge of his bandage showed.

"Your head all right?" Gavin asked.

"It itches."

"I brought someone for you to meet. This is Sam's mother, Tammi Lee Gilmer."

He felt her give his hand a squeeze before she took the final step toward Cody. For someone Gavin barely knew, she was easy to read. The woman was petrified. And moved—he could see that in the tremor at the edge of her smile, in the extra sparkle in the corner of her eye.

"Hey, Cody," she said in her cigarette voice. "This is such a surprise. I couldn't wait to meet you."

He quit scratching. After a second, he held out his hand. She took it briefly.

"Hi," he said.

"I guess you'd better call me Tammi, or Tammi Lee," she said.

"Not Granny or Grandma?" Gavin asked in a teasing voice, trying to lighten the moment.

"I sure wouldn't mind," she said in a rush of honesty that left her flushed. "But 'Grandma' is a name that has to be earned, don't you think? Cody and I have only just met."

She folded her hands in front of her and studied his face. "You're probably going to get sick of hearing this, but you look exactly like Sam did when he was young. Sam was just about the best-looking kid in town."

The boy shrugged. He was a little lacking in the poise department, Gavin observed. Too much time plugged into Nintendo? He didn't know. There was too much he didn't know about this boy.

"Cody," Tammi Lee said, "I don't want to embarrass you. I don't want to push myself on you. But if you don't mind, maybe we could spend a little time together sometime."

"I have to work," he said bluntly.

"Oh," she said. Her fingers knit together. "I make a mean homemade pizza," she added.

He nodded noncommittally and pulled on his glove. "I'd better get after it then."

"See you around, maybe," Tammi Lee said.

"Maybe."

Gavin walked away with her. The music came back on. They stopped to look in on the mare with the new baby, leaning against the half door and admiring the little one. Gavin chanced a look at her, and wasn't surprised to see a tear tracking down her cheek.

"Hey, he's just a jerky little kid," he said, handing her a bandanna from his pocket.

"I didn't expect him to fall into my arms. But Jesus Christ, I wanted to hold him." Her hands shook as she grasped the top of the stall door. "How I wanted to hold him."

Her stark, honest yearning touched Gavin. "I think we both missed out on that stage with Cody."

She blotted her cheeks and handed back the bandanna. "I guess what makes me so sad is that I missed out on a lot of that with Sam, too. Some things you just learn too late."

An old twinge nagged at Gavin. Seventeen years ago, he'd made up his mind about Tammi Lee and Sam—and he'd been wrong.

"I better go call about my car," she said.

As they reached the barn door, the loud music cut off. Tammi Lee and Gavin turned back. Cody stepped out into the breezeway.

"Hey . . . Tammi Lee." He sounded uncertain as he spoke her name.

"Yeah?"

"What kind of pizza?"

A smile broke across her face. "Whatever you like, hon. Whatever you like."

Chapter 23

Sam's snow tires crackled on the drive as he turned into his farm. He was surprised to see Gavin Slade's Ford 350 parked outside the barn. Damn, what was Gavin doing here?

Sam pulled up to the house and spotted a light on in the kitchen. He stopped on the back porch, amazed to see his mother offering a steaming mug to Gavin Slade.

Sam paused to collect himself. His first meeting with Gavin Slade had set in motion events no one could have predicted. When Sam was seventeen, his mom's car had died in the parking lot of the Truxtop Café in Crystal City. The owner, above average in the decency department, had arranged a tow to McEvoy's Garage and had given Tammi Lee a job. A few inquiries steered Sam to Blue Rock. Good reputation, rodeo stock contractor. The kind of operation a cowboy dreamed of.

Gavin's foreman had taken one look at Sam in the saddle and summoned the boss. Sam's physique had always worked in his favor. He was tall and rangy with long hands and a relaxed way that gave people—and horses—confidence.

"Well, you look like a cowboy. Can you ride like one?" Gavin had wanted to know.

Digging in his heels, Sam had demonstrated on the borrowed quarter horse.

"How'd you get here?" Gavin had asked.

"Walked."

"From town? That's six miles."

Sam made no comment. Gavin hired him on the spot.

Sam had been quietly fascinated by the parade of glitterati that came to call on the famous actor. He recognized faces from old movies, late-night talk shows, celebrity game shows. Beautiful women and well-dressed men came seeking favor, for after retiring from movies, Gavin Slade became a respected producer, picking and choosing his projects with care.

Gavin had entered Sam in a few local roping events. The purses at the small shows didn't amount to much, but Sam had a taste of something he hadn't sampled before—possibility.

Fate had worn a yellow ponytail, expensive riding clothes, and a soft-eyed, dreamy look that made him forget his place in the world.

Damn. The boss's daughter.

Could he have been more stupid?

Sam yanked open the kitchen door. Gavin was a charmer, a ladies' man. What the hell did he want with Tammi Lee?

"Hey, Mama." Sam took off his hat, holding out his hand. "Gavin."

"Good to see you." Gavin flashed a smile, but his eyes stayed cool, wary.

"I had car trouble," Tammi Lee explained. "Gavin gave me a lift out here."

Sam relaxed a little. That seemed innocent enough. But he didn't kid himself about Gavin Slade. The old man had considered him ranch-hand scum, not good enough for his daughter. That in itself might have been forgivable, but Gavin had played hardball. Even the ruse with the missing money had been understandable, if not forgivable. What Sam couldn't ever forget, though, was that Gavin's schemes had knocked Tammi Lee in the dirt when she was already down.

"I wanted to meet Cody," Tammi Lee continued.

"He was feeling well enough to come to work." Pride touched Gavin's voice. "Frankly, I was glad to see it. A little work sure can't hurt the kid."

"So you met him, Ma?" Sam studied the lined and faded face, and he sensed the sadness that always seemed to linger at the edge of her mood. For as long as he could remember, he had felt responsible for that sadness. He knew it wasn't his fault, but he'd give anything to banish it.

"Gavin introduced us," she said. "I won't bullshit you, Sam. We're not the Waltons."

"I hope he was civil, at least."

She waved her hand. "I don't think we'll find much in common, but I'm glad we met. He's a good-looking boy, Sam. Reminds me of you at that age."

Sam wondered if he'd had that same screw-you attitude. Maybe he had. Maybe bonking the boss's daughter had as much to do with his attitude as his hormones.

"Speaking of Cody, we'd better head out." Gavin picked up his hat from the rack behind the door. "It's getting dark."

Sam shot his mother a look. Had she been hanging out with Gavin Slade all afternoon? Telling himself it was none of his business, he went out to the barn. While Gavin warmed up his truck, Sam found Cody standing at the far end of the row of stables, his shoulder propped against the door. Sam was pleased to see all the equipment had been washed down and put up. He was a lot less pleased when he saw that Cody was smoking a cigarette.

He tried to sound casual as he remarked, "Those things'll kill you."

Cody turned quickly. A rebellious look shadowed his face. "It's just something I do sometimes. I can quit anytime."

"How about now?"

"I'll choose the time."

"Well." Grabbing a water hose, Sam twisted the spray nozzle and doused both Cody's gloved hand and the cigarette. "I choose now."

"Hey!" Cody jumped back, shaking water from his hand. "That's cold as hell."

"So don't smoke around here anymore."

"I'll do what I—"

Sam held up the hose. "Don't push me. I'm armed."

Cody flung off his glove in disgust. "You could have just asked me to put it out."

"I'm *telling* you to quit."

"And I'm *telling* you to get off my case."

They faced off, glaring like a pair of rival dogs. Sam refused to flinch, but so did Cody.

"How's your head?"

"Itches. I better get going. 'Bye." He stalked away, muttering under his breath.

Welcome to parenthood, Sam thought. Christ, how did Michelle do it?

Thursday

Chapter 24

Waking up was hard for Michelle at home. She had done her bedroom in soft aquas and golds, spent an absurd amount on bedding from Nordstrom's, and invested in an imported eiderdown, the kind you sink into like a cloud. Her bedroom exuded comfort and luxury, and she responded by sleeping too long and too hard there.

In Montana, she woke up at the crack of dawn and hurried like a child to the window to look out at the long fields and pastures of her father's ranch. The sides of the mountains corrugated by the blue ripples of glaciers. The fall of light from the rising sun.

And God knew what was going to happen each day.

She got a clue when the early light glinted off a car parked in the circular drive in front of Gavin's house.

There was probably only one lime green Volkswagen bug in the Northwest.

Michelle paused to check on Cody—dead asleep, a benefit of hard physical labor—then pulled on her old gray sweats, stuffed her feet into boots, and hurried across the compound to the main house. She entered through the kitchen, greeting Tadao in passing. The aromas of coffee and kidney-friendly roasted green tea wafted over her, but she was not hungry, just on fire to know what the hell was going on.

Gavin and Natalie sat in the sunken living room before a roaring blaze. Gavin spotted Michelle first; he was in the middle of laughing, and the smile on his face lifted her heart. He stood up. "Hey, Michelle. Morning."

"Hi, Daddy. I see you've met Natalie."

"I certainly have."

"At about five o'clock this morning." Natalie's bangle bracelets and hoop earrings, silken head scarf and tie-dyed leggings, and especially her warm smile, were familiar and dear to Michelle.

"Hey, you," she said, holding out her arms.

"Hey, you," Natalie said back, standing up to give her a hug. "I tried to get here last night, but the old Volkswagen wouldn't cooperate. I had to take a breather in Coeur d'Alene."

"You should have called, Nat."

"We talked, remember? You knew I was coming."

"Yes, but—" Normal logic didn't work with Natalie Plum. Michelle sat down on the big leather sectional with them.

Natalie's eyes twinkled. "I acted as though I'd never seen a movie star before—"

"You haven't," Michelle reminded her.

"Well, that explains why I kept staring and stammering." She sipped from her mug of coffee. "Your dad got all squirmy on me. You'd think he's never been awakened at five in the morning by a crazed fan before."

Her father leaned back, crossing his booted feet at the ankles. "I admit it's been a while."

He was loving this, loving every minute of it. His need to put his face in front of millions of people was nearly as strong now as it had been at the height of his career in the movie business. There were those who hungered for recognition, even though it didn't necessarily mean anything to them except recognition. She thought it was true in her father's case. Anyway, he was far from annoyed by Natalie's breathless admiration.

"So we've been up talking for a couple of hours." Natalie sent him a look of melting sympathy. "You should go back to bed now. I feel so guilty getting you up."

"I'm an early riser. And this visit was worth it." He patted his hand on a stack of fat photo albums on the coffee table.

"You brought those from Seattle," Michelle said, sounding slightly accusing.

"You bet I did, girlfriend." Natalie sent her a smile. "I can't believe you forgot them."

Guilt stained her cheeks. To be honest, Michelle had never even thought of bringing the photo albums to show her father. Never even thought he'd be interested in snapshots of Cody's first birthday, or the bike Santa brought him one year, or his first day of school.

"I loved the pictures, Michelle," her father said quietly. "More than you can know. I'm proud of you for the life you've built for yourself and Cody."

She blinked, startled. Since she arrived at Blue Rock, they had avoided talking about certain topics. Dr. Temple and the social worker on the transplant team had been saying how important it was to discuss personal stuff, family stuff. They gave Michelle and Gavin some little blank books for writing down thoughts and feelings. Michelle's was still blank. She bet Gavin's was, too. So his statement about being proud of her took her by surprise.

Putting his hands on his knees, he got up, his thick heather gray sweater looking warm and comfortable on his big, lean frame. The bulkiness of the knit camouflaged the dialysis bag. "Chores," he explained. "I've got a meeting with the arena director."

"See you around, pardner," Natalie said in an exaggerated, corny drawl.

"Jake turned on the heat in the bungalow next to Michelle's. If you need anything, holler."

"It's all perfect, Gavin. Thank you for welcoming me."

"My pleasure, ma'am." He went out through the kitchen, and Michelle drummed her fingers on the arm of the couch, trying to figure out if he was flirting with her best friend or not.

Natalie and Michelle sat alone in the living room, watching morning sunlight steal across the hand-painted tile floor. Michelle picked up a plaid pillow, tossed it at her, saying, "You bitch."

She caught the pillow, laughing. "You have no idea."

Suspicion stole into Michelle's radar range. "I don't?"

Natalie propped her sock feet on the leather-bound albums. "I figured your dad would want to see the old family photos. But I really brought them for you to show Sam McPhee."

"God, you really are a bitch."

"You have to show him. You have to let him in on Cody's whole history."

"I don't have to do squat."

"Legally, probably not, unless he sues for visitation."

A chill skittered down Michelle's spine. "He wouldn't dare."

"Who knows? But he'll want to see the pictures."

"You know what makes you such a bitch?"

"What?"

"It's that you're right."

She grinned. "I know. So when are you going to show him?"

"I guess I could today, when I drop Cody off to work at his ranch. Sam's on split shift." It was amazing how quickly Michelle had memorized his schedule. He'd explained how he split the clinic duties with his partner, how his on-call situation worked. He'd only told her once, yet she had absorbed it like a sponge. Funny.

"You don't have any more . . . appointments and stuff with your father?"

"It all starts Saturday." She took a shaky breath, silently blessing Sam for intervening with Dr. Temple.

Natalie held Michelle's cheeks between her hands. "Do you know how special this is?"

Michelle swallowed a sudden painful lump in her throat. "I can't seem to look at it as anything more than a fairly complicated surgical procedure."

"It's so much more than that." She stood up, tossing a glance outside at her car. "I've been naughty."

Michelle picked up the heavy leather albums. "True."

"I mean, not just the photos. For once in your life, you've got time to get back into painting."

Not you, too. Michelle got the feeling Natalie had colluded with Sam about this. Or maybe her secret wish was absurdly obvious. "Give me a break," she said flatly.

"As if." Outside, Natalie lifted the front hood of the Volkswagen, revealing the trunk. In addition to her luggage, there were shopping bags from Madrona Bay Art Supply in Seattle.

Michelle's heart lurched. Madrona Bay was a Mecca for fine artists all over the West. The store was one of the first things she had discovered when, newly pregnant, she'd moved to Seattle. She used to save every last scraped-together dime to buy art supplies. It was a magical place, filled with all the things she needed to give life to the images burning inside her.

She hadn't been there in years, though.

"You bitch," she whispered, her eyes glazing over with yearning and frustration. "I don't need any of this."

"Oh, honey." Natalie grabbed her flowered bag and hefted it over her shoulder. "You do. You absolutely do. What else are you going to do while Gavin recovers?"

"I—" Well, really, thought Michelle. Natalie had a point. The studio was still there, untouched, as Sam had showed her the other night. "I guess I could mess around in my spare time."

"Good girl. So let's get a move on. We've got to bring poor Camille in out of the cold."

Camille was her cello, a 1968 Juzak concert instrument from Hungary. She never went anywhere without it. She kept it in a hard shell case plastered with stickers from all the places she'd visited—places like Sri Lanka and Lake Lucerne and Montreal and Rio de Janeiro.

They walked across to the bungalows, and Michelle stowed the photo albums in the Rover. She wondered if she would dare to show them to Sam. Natalie was right, Michelle conceded reluctantly. He needed and deserved to see what Cody's first sixteen years had been like.

They toted the paints, brushes, and Belgian linen canvases into the studio. Then Michelle helped Natalie carry her stuff into the guesthouse. It was already warm and cozy inside, and Natalie sighed with satisfaction. "Let me freshen up a little, and we'll go together."

"Go where, Nat?"

"To Sam McPhee's. Didn't you say Cody's working there? He needs a ride, right?"

"Yes, but—"

"Do you think I could stay away?" Natalie rummaged in her bag and found a brush, which she used to draw upward through her spiked hair. "I'm dying here, Michelle. You're my best friend, and you've got a scarlet past I know nothing about. Do you have any idea how crazy that makes me?"

In spite of herself, Michelle grinned. "I sort of like this."

"Bitch," Natalie said, and gave her a hug.

Chapter 25

S am walked out onto the front porch with Edward
Bliss as the Range Rover pulled into the yard.
Sam felt a now-familiar lurch in his chest when
Cody got out of the car.

My son. I have a son.

Yet other than stitching his wound, Sam had never
touched him.

"He's doing a little better in the wardrobe department."
Edward sipped from a mug of coffee. "Starting to dress
for the weather and the job, eh?"

Cody still appeared a little ragged, though he had abandoned the studied slouchiness of his city garb in favor of
old jeans, work boots, a fleece-lined denim jacket. A warm
hat covered the new haircut and the bandage.

"Who's that in the car with Michelle?" Edward asked.

Sam squinted, but the glare of the sun off the windshield blinded him. "Not sure. Gavin again?"

The passenger door of the car opened and out stepped the strangest woman Sam had ever seen. She resembled a butterfly, wearing a long multicolored shawl, crazy purple boots, and a Sherpa mountain guide's alpaca hat. With her skirt and shawl flowing, she skimmed over the snow toward the house, gabbing with Cody the whole time. Michelle went around to the back of the car, lifting the rear cargo door.

"Ai caramba," Edward said under his breath. "Who's the babe?"

". . . so unbelievably cool of your mom," she was saying to Cody as they reached the porch. Barely pausing for breath, she tilted her head back, revealing earrings in unexpected places, and said, "Okay, Cody, shall we play *What's My Line?* Which one's your dad?"

She took off her hat to reveal spiked hair with purple and green streaks. She had slightly uptilted eyes and the face of a pixie—impish, animated, and sly. Tinkerbell on acid.

Red-cheeked but clearly enjoying himself, Cody said, "Sam and Edward, this is—"

"Wait, wait!" The imp held up a hand, impractically covered in fingerless black lace gloves. "Don't tell me. Let me guess." She grew very serious, looking from Cody to Sam to Edward to Cody. "No contest," she said. "It's the tall one. So introduce us, numb-nuts." She elbowed Cody in the side.

"This is my mom's friend."

"Not your friend?" Tinkerbell looked wounded.

"Yeah, mine too." Cody stuffed his hands in his pockets. "Natalie Plum."

"Actually, I'm his fairy godmother." She stepped up onto the porch. "He didn't tell you about me?"

"I better get to work," Cody said, hurrying toward the barn.

Sam was gratified by his haste to check on the mare and foal. He wanted to believe the kid could get interested in the horses. Maybe that way they'd find some common ground.

Natalie stepped up onto the porch and shook hands with Edward, then Sam. "You'll have to excuse me," she said. "I've had about nine gallons of coffee. You might find me a tad talkative. Hope you don't mind."

"We don't mind a bit," Sam said.

Edward put the full force of his charm into a comical bow. "Welcome to Montana."

Natalie's face lit up. "Thank you."

Michelle arrived, lugging an armload of large, thick books.

"Here." Sam jumped down from the porch. "Let me help you with those."

"Michelle, you bitch," Natalie burst out, turning on her friend. "You didn't tell me he was George Clooney!"

Sam took the top two books from Michelle. "I'm not George Clooney."

Natalie Plum raked him with a frankly assessing glance. "Close enough."

"But I'm friendlier," Edward cut in. "And I have better work hours."

"Perfect," she said with a dazzling smile. "Then you can show me around the place. Cody wouldn't shut up about the new baby."

Edward took her hand and led her toward the barn. "My pleasure."

As they walked off, Sam heard her say, ". . . every last thing, do you hear? I want to know absolutely *everything*."

Michelle watched them go. The morning light was soft on her face, nose and cheeks tinged by the cold. She held two of the books against her like a shield. "And does Edward know everything?" she asked.

"If he doesn't, he'll make it up."

"I'm serious, Sam."

"Okay, he figured out about Cody even before I did. The second he saw him. But he didn't say anything until I told him. Edward doesn't lie, and he doesn't hurt people. Ever." He indicated the books. "So what's all this? Photo albums?"

"Uh-huh. You got a minute?"

"I'm guessing this will take more than a minute. But as a matter of fact, I've got all morning." He glanced down at the pager clipped to his belt. "So long as the beeper stays quiet. Come on in."

In the living room, he added a couple of golden larch logs to the fire crackling in the woodstove and cleared a spot on the coffee table. "Can I get you something to drink?"

She didn't answer. He glanced at her to find her staring at the painting over the mantel.

"My God," she said. "I had no idea what happened to this."

The picture had occupied a place of honor over the mantel ever since he had settled in Crystal City. It was the only gift Michelle had ever given him. The painting had a life of its own; it glowed with the sheer wonder expressed in every brushstroke, echoing the underlying tenderness of a very young, very talented artist.

"I'm glad you kept it," she said, her voice soft, husky. "It's a good picture."

"I've always thought so. Everyone who sees it says so."

She shivered, though it wasn't cold. "I thought I had so many more pictures in me."

"I still can't believe you don't paint anymore."

"Painting took more out of me than I had to give. Life comes first, then art."

"I bet your pal Natalie doesn't agree."

"Natalie's different."

"I noticed."

Her manner became brisk, almost businesslike as she seated herself, as if her show of vulnerability had embarrassed her.

"You should still be painting, Michelle."

Her chin came up. "What, in all my spare time?"

"You make time for what's important."

The anger that flashed in her eyes was new to him. The Michelle he'd known years ago had a temper, sure. But her anger had never been cold like this. Or strangely directed at herself.

"What's with the books?" he asked, changing the subject.

"Natalie brought these from home."

Sam lowered himself next to her. His heart thumped; until now he wouldn't have thought a moment like this was important, critical. "Pictures of Cody growing up?"

"Yes. You interested?"

Here it was, then. The past, staring him in the face. Here in these four fat books lived the history that had left him out. The years he had lost with his son.

"Hell, yeah, I'm interested."

She picked up the top one. "I haven't had time to go through these and edit them, so what you see is what you get."

"What would you want to edit?"

"You'll see when we get there." She took off her shoes and tucked her feet up under her on the sofa. Sam, who had seduced a decent number of women on this very sofa, found the gesture almost unbearably sexy. He forced himself to focus on the photo album.

She flipped open the front cover. "My first apartment in Seattle. Natalie and I shared a place on Capitol Hill when I first moved there." Unremarkable, a snapshot of a sunny room with sliding glass doors and overstuffed furniture. Neat, nicer-than-average student housing.

"I studied painting while I was pregnant," she said. "I tried to keep it up after the baby was born, but life just got too hectic."

His gaze dropped down the page to a picture of Michelle. It wasn't a very good shot, but it moved him. She stood at the rail of a ferry boat painted white and green. Blue water and forested islands and a distant mountain range in the background. She wore her hair in a silky blond ponytail, and she had on a denim jumper.

A breeze plastered the blue dress against her round, ripe abdomen. She was the picture of a healthy young woman in the last trimester of pregnancy. Sam stared, fascinated by the knowledge that only months before the shot was taken, he had held her in his arms. He had planted that baby in her.

He lightly rubbed his thumb over the girl in the photo. "I hate it that I missed this."

"Right." She seemed to be working to keep her voice in control. "I was fat and cranky all the time. I think this is the only picture of me pregnant."

"Who took it? Natalie?"

"Yes." She turned the page. "Ah. Here we go."

The next photo showed a black-haired imp with thickly mascaraed eyes peering over a surgical mask.

"Natalie again?" Sam asked.

"She was my birth coach."

He set his teeth. Then, when he could trust himself, he said, "Should've been me."

Michelle shook her head. With the motion, a light drift of her fragrance hit him, and his body heated with the need to touch her.

"Sam," she said, "you were eighteen. You weren't ready to go through childbirth—"

"You were only eighteen, too. Were you ready?"

"I didn't have a choice."

"I wasn't *allowed* a choice. I would've stuck with you, Michelle. You know damned well I would have."

"I didn't know a thing. You were gone so fast, I didn't even have a chance to tell you I was pregnant." She pointed to a poorly focused photograph. "And there he is, hot off the press."

There was nothing unique about the picture. As a physician, Sam had seen his share of moments-after-birth shots, and this one wasn't particularly well done. But because it was Michelle, holding his son, his mouth dried. He couldn't speak; he couldn't even swallow.

Cody's wet red face lay against her chest, clad in a dotted hospital gown. The baby's tiny foot flailed, and Michelle wore a look of complete, exhausted relief.

"You had the glow," he remarked.

"The glow?"

"The new-mom glow. Some people deny its existence, but it's a very real thing." Gently he outlined the shape of her face and the baby's.

"Very scientific, Dr. McPhee," she said, though a soft edge diluted her sarcasm.

And then, step by step, page by page, she took him through the lost years. It was like opening a door and stepping into a world whose existence he hadn't even suspected. A parallel universe, hidden from him for seventeen years.

He saw Cody as a round-faced baby, doted on by Natalie. A toddler in overalls and a Seattle Mariners cap waved at him from a wrenching distance of years.

"See that blue thing in his hand?" Michelle rubbed her finger over the photo. "He never went anywhere without that thing. It's one of your old work shirts."

Sam felt a powerful jolt of emotion at the sight of his shirt, clutched in that chubby little hand. "Yeah?"

"When I left here, it was one of the few things I brought with me. Your—" She broke off and bit her lip.

"Your what? What were you going to say?"

"Your smell. It had your smell on it."

He put his arm around her. This was why things never worked out with him and women. He couldn't handle their softness, their fragility, the way his heart twisted in a knot when sentiment struck. "Aw, Michelle, damn it—"

For a moment she leaned into his shoulder. Then she seemed to get a grip and turned her attention back to the album. A first-day-of-kindergarten shot revealed a kid who was becoming his own person as he stood by a redwood fence with a Power Rangers lunch kit and a Looney Tunes backpack. Sam viewed school portraits, Little League team photos, excursions to the zoo, the aquarium, ski trips, summers at remote beaches.

What struck him about Cody was the kid's smile. It was the kind of smile that made the sun look dim—it covered his whole face and lit his eyes. Joy radiated from every photo of him.

Cody didn't seem to smile much anymore.

Natalie Plum appeared in a lot of the pictures. Every so often, there would be a picture of Cody with a guy.

"So who's this?" Sam indicated a man in a Hawaiian shirt, roller-blading with a six-year-old Cody.

"Someone I used to date. I haven't seen him in years."

Sam hoped she didn't hear him let out his breath. He found a couple more interlopers—Cody's third-grade teacher: "He was the gentlest man. Cody really loved him."

"And you? Did you love him?"

"He wanted a full-time wife. I had no idea how to be that, so we stopped seeing each other."

"And this other guy?"

"Someone else I used to see. We met at a commercial-art convention."

"Did he want a full-time wife, too?"

She gave a humorless chuckle. "As it turned out, he preferred several part-time lovers. What a jerk."

"So did you date a lot?"

"Did you?" she shot back. "You're digging for dirt, Sam. And trust me." She drummed her fingers on the photo album. "You won't find it here."

Sam spotted a good shot of Cody at about twelve, frozen in the midst of executing a perfect soccer kick. His face was intent, his gaze focused like a laser on the ball.

"He scored a goal with that kick," Michelle said.

Sam would have traded anything—*anything*—to have seen that kick in person. "Looks like he was a good little athlete."

"He was, but he lost interest in team sports."

"Do you know why?"

"Because he turned sixteen?"

"Plenty of sixteen-year-olds go out for sports."

She drew a quick breath. "I told myself I wouldn't get defensive. I'm working really hard not to."

"Sorry." He touched the photo. It was a five-by-seven, covered with the gluey cellophane of the album page. "This is a good shot."

She hesitated. "Brad took it."

"Ah. Brad."

"The year I met him. He was a community sponsor for the soccer club. His pharmacy franchise was, actually. Med-Plan Pharmacies." She flipped ahead a couple of pages. "Here we are at our ski place in Whistler."

It showed the three of them in front of a modern condo. Cody smiled his winner's smile. Michelle's gaze seemed curiously off focus, as if she was searching for something beyond the camera. The guy called Brad was tall, probably six-two, and thick-set, with a tanned face and a white-toothed grin, designer logos splashed across his ski outfit.

Sam had no doubt this was a decent guy, well-heeled, caring.

But as he regarded the picture, he felt such a stab of complete hatred that he had to look away.

As Cody grew older, the pictures of him were sparser, taken at infrequent intervals. "I think that's always the way," Michelle confessed. "When they're little, you want a picture of them every time they sneeze. But by the time they're in high school, a Christmas picture is about all you remember to take. Here he is with his girlfriend," she said. "Claudia Teller. They didn't want me to take their picture, but they figured it was the only way I'd get out of their hair."

"What are they dressed for, Halloween?"

She laughed. "A school dance. This is formal attire."

The girl was somberly pretty, with anorexic shadows under her eyes and cheekbones. Her hair was too red to be natural, her smile too sly to be genuine. Standing next to her, Cody looked tall and fiercely proud.

"Is she still his girlfriend?"

"As far as I know. Her parents are upper management at Microsoft, and she's supposedly the most popular girl in the school."

"She looks like a barrel of laughs."

Michelle grinned. "I'm glad it's not just me, then. But—" She looked away.

"What, Michelle?"

"It's awful."

"So be awful. I won't tell anyone."

"I'm hoping our stay here will cause his relationship with Claudia to chill. Is that awful?"

"Cody would think so."

She pressed her hand down on the picture. "I want him to have a girlfriend. Just not *this* girlfriend."

Sam studied the pale girl in the photo. From the perspective of years, could he still blame Gavin?

"Face it, Michelle," he said, "the days of arranging your kid's social life are past."

"But I *know* she's bad for him. He's completely blind to that. He thinks they're totally in love. Just like—" She stood up quickly. "We'd better see what Natalie's up to. She's a bit unpredictable."

"Finish what you were saying."

She went to the front window and stared out at the long white fields and mountains. He stood behind her. He wanted to clamp his hands around her shoulders, draw her back against him.

What did her hair smell like? What would her hips feel like, cradled against his?

"Were we wrong, too, way back then?" she asked softly. "Were we blind?"

"Your father thought so."

She turned to him, worrying her lower lip with her teeth. "My father never knew about us. At least, not until I told him I was pregnant." She moved past him. "You were gone by then."

"He knew, Michelle." Sam couldn't believe she thought otherwise.

"He never knew, not until I—that last day. We were careful," she insisted.

"You ought to ask him sometime."

Something like panic flickered in her eyes. Her relationship with her father was complex, unfathomable to Sam. He sensed that she was afraid it might crumble under scrutiny.

"It's lunchtime already," she said in a rush. "I'd better get Natalie out of Edward's hair." She went to the door and got her jacket from a hook. "I'll leave those albums here in case you want to look at them some more."

The moment had twisted, turned, changed. He had connected with her briefly, but she was slipping away again, eluding him. She seemed agitated as she stuck her arm in her jacket and fumbled with the zipper. "Damn," she swore between her teeth.

Sam took hold of the zipper and pulled it up. "Easy, Michelle." When the zipper reached the top, he didn't step away, but placed two fingers under her chin, holding her gaze to his. Her skin was as soft as it looked. Maybe softer. "Thanks," he said, his entire awareness fixating on her lips. "Thanks for bringing those pictures. It meant a lot to me."

"Thank Natalie." She ducked away, bending to put on her boots. "Why are you looking at me like that?"

"Maybe I still carry a torch for you, even after all these years."

"Men like you don't carry anything that long."

"You don't know me, Michelle."

"No, I don't." She went out onto the porch. "I guess that's my point."

"We can fix that," he said.

"If something in my life needs fixing, I'll take care of it myself." She seemed flustered, disconcerted by his attention.

It made him mad, the way she held him at a distance. "Oh yeah? From what I can tell by looking through those photo albums, you sure as hell haven't found what you want with . . . what's his name? Brad."

"How would you know that?"

"It's obvious. You're like this picture-perfect icon—a lover he doesn't really have to love, a partner who carries more than her share of the weight, a Barbie doll that looks good on the arm of his Armani tux."

"You don't know anything about me and Brad."

"Tell me I'm wrong."

"You're trivializing us. Trivializing a relationship that's been building—"

"Building toward what, Michelle? A marriage, or a business merger?"

"Oh, and you're the expert on relationships, right?" She marched outside without waiting for him to reply.

He felt a stab of guilt because maybe she had pegged him right. Certainly his track record bore it out, more than she could possibly know. *Tell her. Tell her now about the marriage.* But the moment passed, and he followed her outside.

Against the unrelieved white of the snow-draped paddock, Natalie Plum's tie-dyed skirts and leggings made a wild splash of color. She and Edward stood at the loading gate. She was talking a mile a minute, making fluttery gestures with her hands. When Cody came out of the barn leading the mare, even Natalie fell still. Sam and Michelle hurried over, stopping at the opposite side of the paddock. "What's going on?" Michelle asked.

"Edward and I decided the mare and filly could come out today," Cody answered.

"That's the one that kicked Cody in the head," Michelle told Natalie.

"She's dangerous," Natalie said, aghast.

"All females in labor are. But she's fine now. Watch."

Edward must have been giving Cody pointers. The bridle was buckled on correctly. Cody walked the horse with the proper amount of lead, her steam-puffing nose at his shoulder. She followed him like a big docile dog. Across the paddock, Natalie's coos of admiration carried on a light, cold wind.

The foal stood on stick legs in the open breezeway, whickering nervously as Cody led its mother slowly away. Unwilling to let its mother out of its sight, the baby took a tentative step into the snowy yard, then another. Its front legs splayed apart and it stumbled, then righted itself. Its muzzle came up covered in snow. It sneezed, shaking its head. Cody looked back and laughed, a ringing sound that made Sam think of the pictures he'd just seen, of a younger Cody. A happier Cody.

It made Sam's heart hurt to watch them. His son and his favorite horse, and the foal they'd helped bring into the world. There was something special and right about the fact that they were all here together.

"She's a beauty, Sam," Michelle said. "A perfect little filly. No wonder I can't keep Cody away."

Cody unhooked the bridle lead to let the mare walk around at will. The foal stuck close by her side, though it veered over to inspect Natalie, probably drawn to her flowing garments.

"I hope he doesn't get too attached," Michelle said softly.

"Would that be so bad?"

She lifted her face to his in a way he remembered from many years before. No other face, no other eyes had that particular softness, that vulnerability. "He'd never get to see the filly."

"Never?"

She blinked, long lashes sweeping down with a tragic knowing that chilled Sam to the bone. "After the transplant, I don't see us coming back here too often. Before long, Cody'll be off to college, and I'll—" She broke off and her gaze slid away from his.

"What'll you be doing, Michelle?"

She was quiet for a long time. The only sounds came from Natalie and Edward's chattering and the occasional blowing of the mare.

"When I first came out here," she said, "I had some wild notion that my father and I would finally connect. That we'd finally get to know each other the way a father and daughter should know each other. Maybe I bought into some of that cellular memory stuff, thinking that if we shared our own flesh and blood, a perfect relationship would surely follow." She loosed a small, bitter laugh. "Instead, I think we're proof that there's nothing particularly special about a living related donor except maybe a few antigens in common."

"You're making up your mind about a lot of things in a short period of time," Sam pointed out. "Slow down, Michelle. You—" A snowball exploded square in the middle of his chest. "Hey!"

Edward and Natalie were both armed, hurling snowballs as fast as they could make them. Cody jumped the rail of the paddock and joined the attack. "Be careful of your head," Michelle called.

Cody barely acknowledged the warning. Sam aimed low with a snowball, missing. The kid was quick, a hard target.

Michelle took one in the shoulder before ducking to make some snowballs of her own.

The war drove off all thoughts of lunch. Natalie's wild squeals filled the air. Sam got in a few good shots, glad to ease the tension. Michelle, complaining of snow down her neck, grabbed his shoulders and held him in front of her like a shield.

"Wait a minute," he said, though her grip on him felt eerily right. "What's wrong with this picture?"

Cody took advantage, pelting him in the face and laughing so hard that Sam laughed, too.

Sam scooped up another handful of snow. The pager clipped to his belt went off.

"What's that?" Michelle held up her hand to signal a truce. Her face was wet from snow and beautifully flushed. Sam felt a strong surge of desire. If they were alone, he knew just where he'd kiss her, taste her. . . .

He checked the digital readout on the pager. His skin chilled at the code. "Michelle, your father's gone to the hospital."

Chapter 26

I hate it that I know the way to the hospital," Michelle said as the landscape whizzed past. She ran a finger around her collar, feeling the damp spots from the snowball fight. "It's sort of ghoulish, knowing the way to the hospital."

"Not if you work there." Sam's voice was calm, doctorly.

She pressed her knuckles to her mouth to keep the questions in. *What happened? Why? Does this mean the transplant has to be postponed?*

She didn't want to ask those questions yet. She was not ready to hear the answers. She wanted to see her father. Wanted to hear his voice again, take his hand in hers. Wanted to let him know she loved him.

I love you, Daddy.

How hard was that to say? Why hadn't she said it before? Because she wasn't sure she meant it, or was she afraid it would be one-sided?

"Almost there," Sam said, his truck veering around the snow-covered Salish statue in the middle of the town square. They arrived at the hospital, and under the awning she jammed her shoulder against the car door and opened it, feet racing as they hit the ground. The electronic doors hissed open.

"Gavin Slade," she told the clerk, the same one who was there for Cody's accident. "I'm his daughter, Michelle."

"In the exam room."

She rushed in to find her father with a stocky, gray-haired physician. Gavin looked haggard, a yellowish cast to his skin and the whites of his eyes.

"I'm Michelle Turner," she told the doctor, not taking her eyes off Gavin.

I love you, Daddy.

"Hey, Michelle. This is my doctor, Karl Schenk." His voice was gravelly, tired, thin.

"What happened?"

"Toxemia. The dialyzing fluid failed."

"But it's going to be fixed, right? He's going to be fine?"

Schenk stayed busy with the monitoring equipment.

Sam walked in, bringing the smell of snow and wind with him. She thought about what he'd said to her earlier, that her father had known about them as kids.

Is it true, Daddy? Are you the reason Sam disappeared?

She cast away the thought. This was hardly the time or place. She wanted to touch her father, but she didn't know where. He had an IV stuck in the top of one hand and another in the crook of the opposite arm. Tubes snaked from his midsection. She settled for laying her hand on his leg, covered in a thin aqua-colored sheet.

Time for the questions. She took a deep breath. "Will this have any effect on the transplant?"

Schenk regarded her with a level look. "I've got a call in to his nephrologist."

"And?"

"If Gavin stabilizes, he can proceed."

She looked her father severely in the eye. "So stabilize."

He tried to smile. She could tell he felt crummy, but the attempt encouraged her. "I'm trying."

Then Sam took charge. It didn't surprise her. In the past few days she had come to realize that the attractive, serious boy she'd once known had turned into a calm, decisive—still-attractive—man. So when he started going over the tests Schenk ordered, then switched to making sure someone called Edward to tell him to send Natalie and Cody home in the Rover, and then called her father's nutritionist, Tadao, she just stood back and let him work.

It felt good. Sinfully good. To have someone else in charge for a while. To have someone else say, "This is how it's going to be," was a luxury.

She watched Sam with a phone cradled on his shoulder and a metal clipboard in hand. Why did it feel so good when he took charge?

She felt vaguely disloyal, having such thoughts. Brad was a take-charge guy, too. But the things he took charge of were . . . different. The vacation plans, his next real-estate investment, country-club dues. He never burdened her with that sort of thing, because he knew it wasn't that important to her.

But there were burdens she had never asked him to share.

The sorts of things Sam was helping with, and she hadn't even asked.

As the afternoon headed on toward evening, she stood back in a daze of dissipating worry. Gavin's tests came back, indicating that he was stabilizing. Orderlies arrived to take him to a private room, and she stood by his bed while attendants checked all the monitoring equipment.

"Don't scare me like this again, Daddy." She tried to sound stern.

"Go on home to supper. I'll call for Jake when they decide to release me."

"I'd rather stay—"

"Michelle, I'm trying to tell you politely that I'm tired as hell, and as soon as you leave, I'm going to sleep. Okay?"

She peered at his thin face. It was a wonderful face, full of character and experience. He had such a stunning aura of charisma that even lying sick in bed, he still qualified for *People* magazine's "most beautiful" issue.

"Okay." It was awkward to kiss his cheek because of all the tubes and monitors. The cool, medicinal smell hung thick in the air. "'Bye, Daddy. See you tomorrow."

"First thing in the morning, I'm out of here."

"I hope so."

Sam was waiting in the corridor as she came out, quietly closing the door behind her.

"Never a dull moment," she said, trying to lighten the mood.

"That's Crystal City, all right."

They walked outside to find that it was sunset already. A glaze of orange tinted the mountains, and the temperature had dropped a few degrees. A gleaming black sport-utility vehicle drove by, slowing down as it passed the hospital. "Someone you know?" she asked Sam.

"Nope. Car's too new. Probably a rental." He opened the truck door for her. "You'd be a great candidate for primal-scream therapy."

"Why do you say that?"

"The tension. You're so damned tense even I can feel it. I think it's contagious."

"Sorry. You think it'll affect my kidney tests if I drink myself into oblivion tonight?"

"Most definitely."

"That's what I was afraid of."

"I'm not a big fan of drinking to oblivion on any night."

She climbed into the truck, shivering against the chill vinyl seat. "Sorry, Sam. I know it was awful for you, dealing with your mother's problem."

The streetlights blinked on, just a few along Main and Aspen. There was a certain coziness to this town that tugged at her. Some people thought it would be oppressive to live in a place where everyone knew everyone else's name. But after years in the big city, she understood the appeal.

"Cody mentioned meeting your mom," she said, uncomfortable with Sam's silence.

"Yeah?"

"He's curious. I think he wouldn't mind getting to know her."

"She'd like that. No idea what they have in common, though."

They passed the movie house. When they were teenagers, they had gone to the movies there. She remembered sitting in the popcorn-flavored darkness with Sam, holding hands and watching *An Officer and a Gentleman.*

"Too bad the Lynwood folded," she said, bothered by

the sight of the unlit marquee. The movable letters gaped like rotting teeth, spelling out the imperfect message, "CL SED."

"I think it had its last season about three years ago."

"My father wants to reopen it, but everything's on hold until after the surgery."

Sam pulled around to the side of the old building. "Want to go in?"

"Can we? It's not locked?"

In the lowering light she could see his smile as he rummaged in the glove box for a flashlight. "I've sneaked into a few picture shows in my day. Come on."

She felt a little furtive as they headed for the back of the building. She saw the gleam of headlights on Main Street, but no one was likely to notice the truck parked in the alley by the theater. As Sam had predicted, the rear fire exit wasn't locked. They went in, and he switched on the flashlight.

The shifting beam illuminated an eerie scene straight out of *Phantom of the Opera*. Michelle gazed at the old-fashioned chandeliers draped in cobwebs, peeling fleur-de-lis wallpaper, the shirred-velvet curtain over the screen in shreds.

"Creepy," she said, her breath making frozen puffs.

"You want to leave?"

"No, let's look around."

Floorboards creaked as they walked up the aisle. The box office and concession stand were dusty and deserted, the lobby empty, lined with vintage movie posters. The ones featuring her father bore his autograph. Sam beamed the flashlight on *Act of God,* a disaster epic that set box-office records and blasted her father into the ranks of the highest-paid stars of his day.

In the thirty-odd years since the poster had been printed,

Gavin Slade had changed very little. He had a classic, time-less bone structure that weathered well despite the years.

"I've always been ambivalent about his career," she confessed to Sam. "On the one hand, how could I look at something like this, or watch his performance in *The Face of Battle* and *not* be proud? On the other hand, he put his career before me—at least, until he needed something only I can give him. How can I not resent that?"

He was silent, and she hugged herself against a chill. "I'm a terrible person. I shouldn't think things like that."

Sam touched her shoulder. "You're not a terrible person. I figure it's pretty normal to feel that way, given the circumstances."

"Now you're sounding like Temple. The one who thought we had too many 'issues' to sort out."

An electric heater hung over the concession stand. Sam plugged it in, and Michelle was gratified when the coils took on a comforting red-orange glow. Evidently her father still kept up the utilities on the old place. Within a few minutes, the overhead heater bathed the lobby in faint light and a pleasant heat. She remembered the funky old furnishings from long ago: a musty club chair and chaise, marble ashtrays yellowed by the years. She took a seat on the old velvet-covered chaise lounge with rolled ends and fringe. Its springs creaked as she settled in.

"The way I figure," Sam said, turning to her, "your 'issues' will work out a lot better after the surgery's behind you."

So simple. She felt as if someone had taken a fork-lift and moved the weight that had been pressing on her chest. Why hadn't she thought of that? Why hadn't she made herself look beyond the surgery and understand that the real healing would take place if she simply let it happen?

"Thank you," she whispered as he sat beside her on the chaise. "Thank you for saying that."

"Feel better?"

She sensed the warmth from the heater and the comfort of Sam's presence and the dry odor of the abandoned building, and a strange and unaccountable feeling of peace and safety came over her.

"Much better."

"Good." He grinned. "It's what I live for."

Michelle drew her knees up to her chest, watching him. "I can't get over that you're a doctor."

He lifted his hand, skimmed his thumb over the ridge of her cheekbone, and everything inside her fell still, waiting, totally focused on the spot he was touching.

"I can't get over that you're a mother," he said.

He reached a place inside her no one had ever reached before—except the boy he had been so long ago. How could she have known, when they were eighteen, that he would be the only one? How could she have known that when he left her life, he'd leave a gulf of emptiness and loneliness no one else would ever fill?

"Damn it, Michelle," he said, dropping his hand, "I wish you'd told me."

She heard his anger, too, echoing her own, and the problem with this sort of anger was that it was fueled by regret—for what they didn't do, for the road they didn't take. And the problem with regret was that it had no place to *go*. It just stayed inside, turning dark and bitter.

"I tried to tell you," she said softly, picturing herself that day, frightened and excited and oh, so very young. It was November, the sunset dull in the sky, and she was wearing her riding clothes—buff-colored leggings and a big cable-knit Aran sweater. "You didn't show up for work that day."

He held himself very stiff, as though every cell in his body had come to attention. She could tell he knew which day she was talking about. She borrowed a Jeep from the ranch, and she drove slowly, terrified because of what the home pregnancy test had just revealed and nervous because she had never gone to Sam's home before.

It was a weathered, wood-frame shotgun house on the east side of town, one of a row of dwellings built for migrant cherry pickers to use in the summer. She had not missed the symbolism of having to drive over the railroad tracks to reach his house.

No lights burned in the windows, and the driveway was empty. On some gut level she could already sense the desertion, could already predict the silence that would greet her knocks upon the door. But she knocked anyway, at the front door and the back, ducking under a clothesline with a single forgotten sock hanging frozen from it. She called out, and then tried the back door, not surprised when it opened. Crystal City was a small town where people left their doors unlocked—particularly if there was nothing in the house to steal.

She had shivered, walking through the four rooms, picturing Sam there with his mother. Sagging furniture with holes in the upholstery, a dinette set from the fifties, swaybacked beds in the tiny bedrooms. No wonder he'd never invited her over.

"You were gone," she said after a long silence. "Your house was empty. I drove up to the café to see if your mom was still working there. Earl Meecham said she took off, hadn't even left a forwarding address for her last paycheck."

"Forwarding addresses are always a problem," he said, "when you don't know where you're going."

She stared into the ripening glow of the heater. "What would it have cost you to tell me good-bye?"

He was quiet for a long time, so long that she got suspicious and studied his face in the light from the heater. She didn't know him anymore, couldn't read that lean, serious face. He seemed tense, his eyes turbulent as if he was at war with himself.

"Sam?"

"I don't know why I didn't say good-bye," he said at last, his voice quiet and controlled. "It was a long time ago."

"Everything was a long time ago."

The anger drained away and brutally soft memories crept up to seize her. There was a time when they stood at the center of the world, and everything seemed possible. She remembered the laughter, the passion, and the utter belief that all their dreams would come true. She remembered the love everyone thought they were too young to feel.

He rubbed his thumb over her cheek. "I've never been good at good-byes."

She knew he was going to kiss her. He had his hand in the right place, cradling her cheek, and he had their eyes in the right place—they were both staring at each other's lips—and, most of all, he had the moment in the right place. She was not thinking of anything beyond the here and now, and how badly she wanted him to kiss her, hold her.

He leaned forward and she moved her knees out of the way, and neither of them hurried, because every heartbeat, every breath, every second was important. Their lips touched, and the taste of him rushed through her with a powerful force, memories exploding across the years, and the passion between them was fresh, alive, yet as old and familiar as something they had carried around for decades.

They didn't speak. They knew better than that. Because if one of them spoke, they'd start to rationalize, and if they rationalized, they would know this was insane, and in a tacit agreement they decided to explore the insanity. Their coats came off, then boots and sweaters and jeans, and his hands were everywhere, and so were hers, sensations tumbling faster than thought. Hard muscle, soft flesh, his mouth mapping the topography of her body until instinct and remembrance converged and they knew each other again. Finally, the hurrying started, because there was an urgency, a need that wouldn't wait. She leaned back against the curve of the chaise and he braced his arms on either side of her, and he came down and she came up, and there was a moment of union so perfect that she saw stars.

Afterward he stayed on top of her, and she wanted to keep him there forever, because as soon as one of them moved or spoke, life had to start up again. She felt his back warm beneath her palms, listened to his heightened breathing, touched her lips to the pulse in his neck.

"What are you thinking?" he asked, and he remembered that thing with her ear, the way it made her tingle all over when she felt the heat of his intimate whisper.

No one but him had ever discovered that about her.

"That we shouldn't move or talk," she whispered back.

"Good idea."

But after a while, she couldn't help it, and she asked, "What are *you* thinking?"

"Oh, honey. Dirty thoughts. Really dirty thoughts." And he told her in explicit detail, shoving her back against the chaise, whispering into her ear in the way only he knew how to do, and all of a sudden they were making love again, his kisses and the strokes of his body harsh the way she needed them to be, bringing her to a soaring climax that had her crying out, her voice echoing through the gloom of the empty building.

"*Now* what are you thinking?" he asked, long afterward.

"That I'm glad for the dark." She kissed him briefly— that inventive mouth that had just done such unspeakably exquisite things to her—and forced herself to sit up, pull on her sweater.

"Why?"

"Because—" she stood up, hurriedly pulling on panties and jeans "—I'm not an eighteen-year-old girl anymore. I'm thirty-five, and I look it."

He laughed in disbelief, zipping his jeans. "You're worried I'll be disappointed in how you *look?*"

She fumbled with the buttons of her fly. "Well, maybe not worried, but—"

"Listen." He took her busy hands and put them against his bare chest, his unbelievably muscular, sexy bare chest.

"I'm listening."

"Of course I remember the way you looked back then. How could I not? I was eighteen, too. Your body used to drive me nuts. Yeah, I remember that." He traced his finger down her throat, over her breasts, waking them up again. "But what I was thinking about when I was holding you just now was how I used to love you."

She felt dizzy, suddenly, sick and dizzy with guilt and confusion. "We'd better go."

He hesitated, as if he was going to say something else. But then he buttoned his shirt, turned and unplugged the heater, and flicked on the flashlight.

They left through the door they had come in. It had started to snow, big thick flakes, the kind pictured on

Christmas cards. In the sodium vapor glow of the corner streetlamp, the swirling snow looked glorious, magical.

Halfway between the door and the truck, a shadow fell across the alley.

Sam put his arms around her, catching her against his chest. "What the—"

A flash exploded in their faces, and although Sam didn't realize it, she knew exactly what had happened.

They'd found her. The dirt diggers. The paparazzi. The kidney-patient stalkers. The princess-murderers.

Tires spun on the salted and sanded road, and then the sport-utility vehicle sped away, leaving Michelle and Sam frozen like a pair of coyotes caught in a bounty hunter's searchlights. The familiar glowing ache from the flash filled her head. She should have recognized them. She had seen their Explorer pass the hospital earlier this evening. She should have known the buzzards were circling.

"What the hell was that all about?" Sam asked.

"You'll read it in the papers," she said dully, feeling her insides coil up with dread. "Could be as early as tomorrow." Digital file transfers had made the process as swift as a phone call.

"I don't read that kind of paper."

"You'll be amazed when you see who does."

Friday

Chapter 27

*M*ichelle stood in the hall of the hospital feeling weak with relief. Her father had stabilized and he was back on the pre-op meds he'd been taking in preparation for the transplant. Barring any other crisis, they were back on track for the procedure. In a few minutes, he'd be discharged.

But she felt as if all the other parts of her life had careened off in different directions. Last night, in the mysterious darkness of a half-forgotten place, she and Sam had made love. She'd wanted him with a wildness and a hunger so uncharacteristic of her that she had begun to think she was becoming someone else entirely. A stranger to herself. A traitor to the life she had built so far from here. She should be feeling shame, regret, guilt . . . but she couldn't.

Restless with her thoughts, she wandered to the small

waiting lounge by the reception area. No one was around, so she helped herself to coffee. Nurse O'Brien came in, smiling a greeting.

"Michelle, right?" she asked.

"Michelle Turner. I'm spending way too much time at this hospital."

The nurse sat down on a vinyl-covered sofa and gave a weary sigh. "Tell me about it. There's a flu going around, so I've been working overtime for the past week. Your boy doing all right?"

"He's fine. But that head wound was a big scare." She paused, wondering how much the nurse knew about them. Everything, probably. This was a hospital, after all. "Did you happen to notice a reporter or photographer snooping around last night?"

"Uh-huh. I'm afraid your father was seen checking in yesterday." She sent Michelle an apologetic look. "We didn't let anyone in to see him."

"Good. It's a constant worry," she admitted. "I've tried to keep Cody anonymous for years." She took a deep breath. "Um, so are people here talking about it? About Sam and Cody?"

"That they're father and son?" she said easily. "Oh, yeah."

"I was afraid so." Michelle was dying to ask what they were saying, but she was not sure she wanted to know.

"I never could picture Sam with a kid of his own."

Something in Alice O'Brien's tone, in the deep knowing of her observation, caught Michelle's attention. "Have you worked with Sam long?"

Alice O'Brien lifted her eyebrows in surprise. "He didn't tell you?"

Michelle felt a strange shift in the atmosphere and instinctively braced herself. "Tell me what?"

The nurse waited, clearly weighing her options. Then she said, "Sam and I used to be married."

The atmosphere silently exploded. "Oh." *God.*

"It appears you and Sam must have a lot of catching up to do."

"He should have told me," Michelle said, mortified by the situation he had put her in.

"It's all old history, but it's no secret." Alice O'Brien spoke straightforwardly. "When he came here five years ago, I took one look at him and fell like a ton of bricks." She grinned. "Most of the staff did. Sam and I got along great, decided to get married. I think Sam just drifted into the relationship, and I was fool enough to mistake it for love." Tugging her pink sweater close around her shoulders, she added, "I have the classic nurse personality—nurturing, caretaking—and he wanted love and sex and a woman."

"Alice," Michelle said, "you don't have to explain this." *Sam should have.*

"I don't mind. You're bound to hear the story from somebody or other. It wasn't too dramatic. I fell hard, and Sam—well, he sort of came along for the ride, I suppose. When I said I wanted to start a family, that was my wake-up call." She pushed back the sleeve of her sweater, checked her watch. "He had a bad reaction to that. Said he saw enough unwanted kids in his practice. And I realized he was never going to give me what I needed. Hell, what I *deserved.* So we split up." A tolerant smile tilted her mouth. "He felt bad about it, but I stuck to my guns. It's better this way. We're still friends, colleagues."

Michelle leaned back in her chair, her thoughts spinning. Though younger than Michelle, Alice spoke with the wisdom of a much older woman, and her words reverberated in the silence. *He was never going to give me what I needed.*

"In his way, I think he loved me for a while. Just wasn't meant to last," she concluded, standing up and checking her watch again. "He's a complicated guy, had a rough life. He learned to love fast, he learned to love hard, and he learned to let go. No one ever taught him how to hold on."

Mounted on a line-backed dun mare named Daisy, Michelle rode along a track that wound to the south and west of Lonepine. She felt the cold slice of air in her lungs, the numbing lash of the wind on her face. The afternoon sky was overcast and tinged bronze by a stingy leak of sunlight.

After Alice's revelation, Michelle had taken her father home; then she drove straight to Lonepine. Sam had gone off on horseback to check a wildlife trap. "He'll probably stop at the hot springs on the way back," Edward had informed her. "He generally likes to do that when he's in a mood."

In a mood. She didn't ask Edward what he meant by that. She'd find out for herself soon enough.

The trail was easy to follow, just as Edward had said it would be. She rode up past an abandoned slash pile from an old logging operation, then angled down toward a low field where the snow had melted away to reveal steaming mudflats. A herd of elk shied away as she approached. At a rock-bound natural pool, a tall roan horse was tethered, but she couldn't see Sam. Dismounting, she wound the reins around a low alder branch and climbed up to the pool. Thermal springs abounded in the area, and the wispy steam softened and obscured everything, adding a faint tinge of salt and sulphur to the air.

"Fancy meeting you here," said a disembodied voice.

Michelle peered through the steam, and there he was, sitting chest-deep in the pool, wearing nothing but a smile. She tried not to think about that smile, or the way the dampness curled his hair, or the beads of water on his shoulders. "I had a little talk with Alice at the hospital today," she said.

His smile disappeared. "Then I guess you'd better have a seat."

"Maybe you could get dressed, Sam—"

"Or you could join me." The smile sneaked back across his lips.

She sank down on a flat rock, covering her face with her hands. "I can't believe you didn't tell me you were married."

She heard a trickle of water, and suddenly he was gliding toward her, taking her hands away from her face. She should leave now, just get up and ride away, but she felt stuck here, unable to move.

"I would have told you, Michelle, but we haven't had that much time to talk."

"We've had time to do a lot more than talk."

"Yeah." His hands—damp, warm, insistent—peeled off her gloves and unzipped her jacket. "Yeah, we have."

The rising steam and the heat and his touch filled her with a strange and helpless lassitude, and everything she'd planned to say simply evaporated. With slow and deliberate care he removed her boots and socks.

"It's my fault my marriage to Alice didn't work out." His whisper rasped in her ear, and then he kissed her in a leisurely way, imprisoning her by her own desire. It was a powerful drug, the taste of him, the taste of passion.

"She claims her needs . . . weren't met." She forced the words out even as she surrendered, peeling off sweater and jeans, letting the delicious shock of cold air and hot water race over her bare skin.

"She's right. I couldn't give her what she needed." Long slow slide of his hands down over her body as he drew her deep into the silky water, secretly heated in the heart of the earth. "Because I gave it all to you."

Sam had always been one to think on a matter before deciding what to do. But the thing was, all the thinking in the world never seemed to do a damned bit of good. He always came around to what his gut told him to do in the first place. The second he had figured out the truth about Cody, he had been consumed by fascination. He wanted to know the boy, be near him, be with him. Circumstances had handed him a way to do that—if he could get Michelle to agree to it.

Still sitting in the thermal pool and squinting through the thick wisps of steam, he watched her getting dressed. His body reacted as fast as it had when he was eighteen—maybe faster. Because now he knew from experience that sex like they'd just had didn't come along every day.

He figured he ought to be dressed when he broached the topic of Cody, so he made himself chill out, waded to the shore, and dried off before the numbing cold hit him. Yanking on jeans, socks, and boots, he kept stealing glances at Michelle. She was beyond beautiful, always had been, but now that he was coming to know her again, he saw something more in this woman. Years ago, he had seen the promise. Now he saw the way time and caring and motherhood had molded her, softened her. Though she was slender, her breasts and belly had the sweet roundness common to any woman who had ever given birth and nursed a baby. It didn't seem to matter how much time passed. The mother-shape was always there.

"What are you smiling about?" she asked, slightly suspicious, still flushed from the hot springs and from their lovemaking.

He tugged a gray UT Athletic Department sweatshirt over his head. "Do you have to ask?"

She sniffed, but not before he caught a flash of amusement in her eyes. "I didn't come out here looking for sex. I came looking for answers."

"So the sex was just sort of a bonus, I guess," he said.

"Very funny." She put on her boots and started walking toward the horses.

"Michelle, wait." He followed her, jumping from stone to stone to keep clear of the steaming mud. A few elk, only slightly perturbed by the presence of humans, sidled off toward the woods. "There's something I need to ask you."

His tone must have touched off her suspicions, for she turned to him with her eyes narrowed and her arms folded across her chest, unconsciously protecting herself. "What is it?"

He figured he'd best just get it said. "When you and Gavin go in for the surgery, I want Cody to stay with me."

He knew she was going to object before she even said a word. It was there in her narrow-eyed, guarded expression. He didn't wait for her to speak, but went on, "I've been thinking about it for days, and it's a good plan. He can—"

"I already have a plan for Cody," she said. "He's staying at Blue Rock. Tadao and Jake are there, and now Natalie. They—"

"They are not his family." Sam tried to keep his temper, his desperation, in check. "His flesh and blood. He's got me and my mother. He needs a chance to know us. The timing's right, Michelle."

She took a step back. "No."

"What are you worried about?" he asked. "I want to spend some time with my son. How can you object to that?"

"Because I don't think you know what you're asking." She spread her arms. "You just dismissed your marriage to Alice with a shrug, more or less. You split up with her after a year. And now you want to take on a son?"

The barb dug deep, but Sam wouldn't let his pain show. He knew what she was doing. She was trying to make him mad, hurt him, so he'd back off. Suddenly, he saw her so clearly that he wanted to hug her. "Aw, Michelle, you don't need to be afraid."

Her chin came up. "I'm not afraid."

"You are. You're scared Cody and I will become best friends and he'll forget the person who walked the floors at night with him, and fixed him birthday cake, and stood in the rain at all his soccer games." Sam walked over to her, took her hand, pressed his lips to it, and kept hold. She tasted of the mineral springs. "You don't need to worry. A kid will always choose his mother. Trust me on this."

He stepped away and jammed on his hat. He hadn't meant to say something so revealing. "Come on, Michelle. You've had sixteen years. I'm asking for a week."

She unlooped the lead rein of her mare, then raked her fingers through the horse's thick winter coat. "Where are we, Sam?" she asked him. "I need to know that before I decide."

He knew she wasn't asking for directions home. They had come to a place where there were no more secrets, no hesitation. But with their new closeness came vulnerability on both their parts. He didn't know for certain he could become a family man overnight. His experience with his mother had taught him the tender hurts of commitment and responsibility. But he wanted to try. They were opening themselves to trouble—but also to joy, if they could make this work. Sam was sure of it.

"Well?" she asked, waiting. "Where are we?"

He held her horse's head while she mounted and stood looking up at her. "At the beginning, I guess."

The restaurant called Trudy's was one of the few good things about Crystal City, Cody decided. His meal of a giant cheeseburger and fries, followed by chocolate cream pie, had been a welcome change from the macrobiotic stuff his grandfather's nutrition specialist served.

Too bad his parents had ruined it by dropping a bomb on him right after dessert.

He scowled into the darkened display window of the Northern Lights Feed Store. He had asked to be excused after dinner, and for the past fifteen minutes had been wandering down Main Street, which was basically the only street in town. At one end lay city hall and the library, which appeared to be the only place other than Trudy's that stayed open after dark. At the other end was an old movie house with an abandoned shop adjacent to it, the glossy windows practically begging for someone to throw a rock through them.

His mom said Gavin owned the Lynwood and might do something with it one of these days, but for now it was as empty as a Sunday afternoon. A few kids came and went from the library, and the sight of them—guys pushing and jostling each other, girls with schoolbooks hugged to their chests—only lowered Cody's mood. Day after tomorrow he would be starting school, which added insult to injury.

Hunching his shoulders up, he moved along, passing the shop where Tammi Lee Gilmer worked. His mom and Sam were probably wondering where he'd gone. He pictured them sitting across the table from each other at the restaurant, maybe holding hands and looking worried. Hell, let them worry. He had promised to stick around, said he just wanted to get out for some air. Fat chance—the Greyhound bus was idling across the street, puffing diesel fumes into the night. The lighted header over the bus bore enticing destinations: MISSOULA-SPOKANE-SEATTLE.

Man, what he wouldn't give to hop on that sucker right now. Digging in his pocket, he found a flattened pack of Camels. Two left. When those were gone, he didn't know what he'd do. How did kids get their smokes in a town where everyone knew everyone else? He lit up, letting the match burn for a minute while reading the matchbook cover: "Alone? Scared? Broke? Dial 1-800-RUNAWAY . . ."

"I should be so lucky," he muttered under his breath, then took a deep drag of the cigarette. Around the first of the school year, he had taken up smoking in order to hang out with Claudia, and it had worked. She'd noticed him, bummed a cigarette, and within a few weeks they were going out. He wondered what she was up to now. They'd only been apart for a week, but he was already worried she wouldn't wait around for him. The thought pissed him off so much that he nearly plowed down a couple of kids coming out of the library. He said a brusque, "Excuse me" and propped his hip on a cold steel bike rack in front of the building. There were only a couple of bikes chained to the rack. Must be hard to ride on these pitted, icy streets. Why did people live in Montana anyway? he wondered, blowing out a stream of smoke.

"Hey, Cody," said a familiar voice.

He looked up to see Molly Lightning, her arms laden with books. He held his pose at the bike rack. "Hey."

Her gaze fell to the orange-tipped cigarette in his hand, and he felt stupid all of a sudden. Stupid and self-conscious, the way he had when he'd first learned to smoke. Trying to act nonchalant, he dug for the nearly empty pack. "You want a smoke?"

"No."

He'd known without asking that she didn't smoke. Ah, well. At least she wasn't going to be all sanctimonious about it.

She seemed ill at ease as she glanced up and down the street.

"You waiting for someone?" he asked, trying to be discreet as he dropped the cigarette and ground it out in the damp snow. Good move, he thought peevishly. Half of a perfectly good smoke, and now it was gone.

"My mom's supposed to pick me up at eight." She gazed at him with unmistakable interest. She might have a crush on him, he thought, and the idea pleased him.

At the other end of the block, three guys in baggy pants and big parkas made a racket, laughing and shoving each other. One of them picked up a rock or a chunk of ice and hurled it at the marquee over the awning of the Lynwood, punching the air in victory at the sound of shattering lightbulbs.

"Jerks," Molly said softly.

Cody felt a little better to hear her echo his own thoughts. "Who are they?"

"Guys from school. Billy Ho, Ethan Lindvig, Jason Kittredge." The threesome crammed themselves into the cab of an old El Camino and roared off into the dark. "Everyone thinks Billy is so cool, but I think he's a jerk.

He was on juvey probation last year for stealing, but that only made kids think he's even more cool. He didn't even get kicked off the football team." She fell silent, looking worried, as if she had said too much. She shifted uncomfortably from one foot to the other.

"Um, can I take those books from you?" Cody asked, hoping he didn't sound too dorky.

She smiled the way she had the first day they'd met. Sort of shy, but also a little bit sexy. "Thanks," she said, transferring the stack of library books to him. "I didn't want to put them down in the snow." She smelled really good, like soap and fresh air. Cody hoped the cigarette smell didn't cling in his jacket. "So what are you doing out here?" she asked.

He nodded toward Trudy's in the middle of the block. "My mom and . . . Sam McPhee took me to dinner. I just wanted to walk around a little." She didn't say anything, but listened with an expectant quality. "My mom's going into the hospital to donate a kidney to my grandfather," he blurted out.

He braced himself for her shock and disgust, but she surprised him. She simply smiled again, and said, "Cool."

"I guess." For the first time, Cody started to think maybe it *was* kind of cool. "But," he added, his rush of candor continuing, "while they're in the hospital next week, they want me to stay at Sam's. They sort of left the decision up to me."

"So what are your choices?" she asked.

He liked it that she seemed genuinely interested. He had planned to call Claudia tonight and get her take on all this, but she didn't know the people involved. It was easier standing around talking to Molly, face-to-face. "I can stay at Blue Rock with Jake and Tadao—they work for Gavin." He rested his chin on the top book. "Or I can go to Lonepine."

She grinned and put her hands on her hips. "Are you kidding? Like there's a decision to be made? Sam's your dad, and he's got a horse farm. It's a no-brainer."

Saturday

Chapter 28

Tammi Lee Gilmer didn't usually get Saturdays off work, but she had arranged to be off in order to pick up her car at McEvoy's Garage. Setting a freshly lit cigarette on the cluttered bathroom counter, she took a round brush and teased some loft into her hair. No one teased their hair anymore; she knew that. Hell, no one smoked anymore. But that sure didn't stop her.

She knew Sam didn't like her smoking, but he never said a word. He had stood by her, helping her break so many other habits that the cigarettes probably seemed minor in comparison. She picked up the cigarette and took a drag, scowling at the amber burn mark it had made on the edge of the faux marble countertop. It was disgusting, really. She should quit.

Tomorrow.

Today, she wasn't going to beat herself up over it. This

was something it had taken her years of AA to learn. She had to forgive herself, to avoid sinking into regrets about the past. It was an everyday battle for her.

She did her makeup and put on a pair of jeans and a loose sweatshirt. She still fit into her size-eight Wranglers, and she was proud of that. Yet deep inside her dwelt a strange longing that seized her at the oddest of times. It was a longing to be soft and doughy, maybe like LaNelle Jacobs, who owned the quilt shop. She secretly dreamed of being like LaNelle: plump and bespectacled, with forearms that jiggled and a double chin, wearing a housedress and a bib apron and sensible shoes. Smelling of talcum powder and Jergens lotion and freshly baked bread.

Tammi Lee walked outside, lifting her face to an overcast sky and feeling the tingle of the nineteen-degree temperature on her face. Yeah, it was insane, but she wanted to be one of those plus-size blue-haired women. Because when you looked like that, it told folks you knew your place in the world. It meant you'd raised a family, making pancakes for them on the weekends and reading bedtime stories to the kids. It meant you'd made a house into a home, putting up curtains and picking out the right color for the walls and buying flats of petunias for the garden every spring. It meant you had grandkids who came running up the walk to the front door because they couldn't wait to see you. It meant you had a husband who had several annoying habits, but you loved him anyway because he was your whole world.

God, what she wouldn't give to fit into a life like that, instead of into her size-eight Wranglers.

She felt a familiar buzzing heat inside her and started walking down the street toward the center of town. The buzz was a warning; it was the craving, the dark desire that had consumed her for so many years. One drink, that was all it would take. One drink, and the buzzing would quiet and she'd feel normal again.

She quickened her pace, clenching her hands into fists inside her jacket pockets. Maybe she'd better give her sponsor a call. This was a weak moment; it had come out of nowhere. They always did.

Yet as she walked, the cold had a calming effect on her, and the sick, thirsty moment passed. She had the life she had. God knew it was more than she deserved. By the time she got to the garage, the craving had settled to a dull roar. "Hey, Tom," she said, stepping into the overheated, grease-scented office. "Am I all set?"

"New water pump did the trick," he said.

She paid him in cash. She used cash for almost everything these days, because writing checks had never brought her anything but trouble. Sam had given her a debit card drawing on his own account, but she avoided using that. Giving her her life back was enough; she didn't want to take more from him than she already had.

A block from the garage, she pulled into Ray's Quik Chek to get a cup of coffee and the latest *Enquirer,* hot off the press. Sam gave her grief about all the gossip rags and movie magazines she bought, but she loved them.

The new *Enquirer*s were still wrapped in plastic binding. As she poured herself a cup of coffee, Ray opened them up and sold her one, along with *People* and her own reserved copy of *Country Billboard.* She went to her car and sat there sipping the coffee, waiting for the blower to heat up and paging through the magazines.

A giant picture of a 108-year-old *Titanic* survivor occupied the front page of the *Enquirer,* but a small inset at the top caught her eye.

"Ho-ly shit," she muttered, nearly dropping her coffee. Her hand shook as she set the cup in a holder and opened the paper to page two. A file photo of Gavin Slade and Michelle, looking as golden and fit as Peter and Bridget Fonda, caught her eye. Next to that was a blurry shot of someone on a stretcher being wheeled into County Hospital. On the same page, a grainy black-and-white picture showed Michelle Turner and Sam, caught in an embrace in the middle of a snowy street. The headline read: *Daughter of Dying Movie Idol Seeks Solace with Lonesome Cowboy.*

The Chevy fishtailed out of the parking lot. One of the few good things about her rambling lifestyle was that she had probably driven more miles than a long-distance trucker, and she was good at it. Negotiating the icy patches on the highway, she raced home and picked up the phone.

Sam was on duty today, but his service took the message. "No emergency," Tammi Lee said, "but it's important."

Next, she tried Blue Rock Ranch. The guy who answered the phone said Mr. Slade was "unavailable." Tammi Lee had no choice but to try the hospital. Maybe the *Enquirer* was right about something for a change.

She reached the hospital in five minutes, and the first thing she saw was Cody Turner sitting hunched on a concrete bench outside the attached professional building where Sam's office was. He wore a knitted black cap and little wiry headphones. His foot jiggled in time to the music only he could hear.

My grandson. That's my goddamned grandson, she thought wonderingly.

He looked cold, sitting there, restless and sulky. And a bit like Sam.

She got out, boots crunching on the sand-and-salt surface of the parking lot. "Hey, Cody. Remember me? Tammi Lee Gilmer."

He took off the headphones. "Hi."

"So what's up?" She kept her voice casual.

"My grandfather drove me over to get my stitches out. And he had some kind of checkup."

"So how's the cut?"

He took off his black knit cap. "Okay, I guess."

She studied the curved wound. "Some week, huh?" she said. "All this hospital stuff."

"Yeah, it sucks."

She indicated his Discman. "What kind of music do you like?"

"Alternative, some heavy metal. And some older stuff," he said vaguely.

"Ever heard of rockabilly?"

"Sure." He put his hat back on.

"I know something about rockabilly. Used to sing in a band."

"Nuh-uh," he said, regarding her with dubious interest.

"I did. A group called Road Rage. Had a big hit single called 'Dearly Departed.' " She hummed the melody line.

His eyes grew wide. "No way. I've heard that song."

"A lot of folks have. It was on a Dodge truck commercial." She steadied herself. "Listen, maybe you could come over for a while today."

He was quiet, scuffing his toe against a lump of ice on the sidewalk.

"If you get bored, you can go right home, promise."

He looked her straight in the eye, and she realized he had a great face, a beautiful face, the face of a boy who was turning downright handsome. But in addition to handsomeness, Tammi Lee could see insolence, difficulty. Michelle Turner must be having quite a time, raising this kid.

"I saw that thing in the paper," he said.

She forced herself not to drop her gaze. "I was hoping you hadn't."

"Sam saw it, too. All the nurses were waiting to show it to him when he got to work this morning."

"The paper's a rag. They print lies and innuendo." She took a deep breath, wishing for a cigarette. "That picture doesn't mean a thing. Your mom probably slipped on the ice and Sam grabbed her so she wouldn't fall."

"Maybe," he said. "I hate those damned tabloids."

"Me, too," she lied.

"When I was little, my mom was always worried they'd come after us because of Gavin."

"And did they?"

"No, but she'd always say, 'Look at Lisa Marie Presley. You want to end up like that?'" His mouth hinted at a grin.

"So what do you say? Want to come see where your old grandma lives?"

He hesitated. "I guess."

"Wait here, then. I need to make sure it's okay."

He replaced the headphones and Tammi Lee went to the clinic entrance of the brick building. She usually got a big kick out of seeing Sam in his long white coat, but today she was worried. "Got a minute, Sam?" she asked him quietly.

He held open the door to the staff lounge. It was empty, a clutter of coffee mugs and well-thumbed medical manuals and clipboards on the table.

"So how much truth was there in that tabloid story?" she asked. No point in beating around the bush. "Are you taking up with a girl you went nuts over seventeen years ago?"

It was hard to read her son's mood. He had always been a stoic. In one of her many recovery sessions, she had admitted to taking shameless advantage of his calmness, his willingness to forgive her, no matter what. When she'd said so to his face, he had given her a sweet-sad smile and said, "You are who you are, Mama. You don't forgive the clouds for raining."

The memory touched her, and she took Sam's hand. "So is this just a fling," she asked, "or—"

"It's not a fling," he said.

She wished she could be the kind of mother you saw on TV, the one who could pat his arm, say a few wise words, and make everything work out fine before the next commercial. "Well, I'm no expert, but you'd better be sure you know what you want out of this. Because there are three of you involved, and one's just a kid."

"I realize that. Cody's going to stay with me while Michelle and Gavin go in for surgery."

"Yeah?" She rinsed a coffee mug at the sink and poured herself a cup, trying to picture her son being someone's father. "So are you excited?"

"Sure. Nervous, too. He's got to start school on Monday. I never heard of a sixteen-year-old starting mid-year in a new place and actually liking it."

She sipped the slightly stale coffee. "Builds character." She set down the mug and glanced at the door, making sure they were alone. "What are you going to do about the tabloid story?"

"Ignore it."

"Is Michelle ignoring it?"

"We haven't had a chance to talk." His face looked taut with frustration. "She and Gavin just left for Missoula to prep for the surgery."

"Maybe you'd better get on down to Missoula and talk things over with her." Something—fate, destiny, pure chance—had brought Sam and Michelle together again. Lord knew, they'd never had much of a chance as kids. "Don't second-guess her, Sam. You know, this morning I was having regrets, wishing I'd done things differently, made better choices. I don't want you to do that. I don't ever want you to have regrets."

"I can't get away until tomorrow morning."

"Then go tomorrow morning," she said. "I swear, for a doctor, you're pretty dense sometimes."

He sent her a fleeting grin. "Okay. I'll offer to drive Cody down in the morning."

Cody was quiet on the way to her house. As she let him in the front door, she wished she had put out some potpourri. The house smelled of stale cigarette smoke and yesterday's coffee. She wouldn't blame the kid if he turned and walked out.

He stepped inside hesitantly, looking around.

Tammi Lee couldn't stand it anymore. She grabbed a cigarette from a pack on the counter and lit up. Belatedly she asked, "You don't smoke, do you?"

He shrugged. "Sure."

"Well, I'm not offering you one. Your dad would kill me. How about a Coke?" She went to the fridge. "I understand Monday is the big day. For the transplant."

He popped open the can. "Yep." He drank his Coke while a long, awkward silence spun out. Tammi Lee finished her cigarette and lit another one. Cody's gaze wandered around the room like that of a trapped animal looking for escape. And suddenly his expression changed from wary to wondering.

"Wow," he said under his breath. "Is that a Stratocaster?"

"Yeah. Just like Dick Dale used to play." She took the vintage electric guitar from its stand in the corner. The old instrument was a classic. She'd pawned and rescued the thing countless times, and in the end she still had it. She rarely played these days, but she knew she'd kept it for a reason.

As she looked at Cody's face, she finally figured out what that reason was.

"Do you play?"

"A little," he said. "Do you?"

She took the guitar, adjusted the tuning, strummed a few riffs, her fingers surprisingly nimble. Glancing at Cody, she laughed at his expression. "What, you didn't believe me?" She stuck a cassette tape into the console. "This is a demo tape called 'Hand-Me-Down Dreams.'"

She hadn't heard it in ages, and the sound of her own playing and singing startled her. She remembered laying down the tracks in a Reno studio they'd rented by the hour. She'd left Sam wailing in a playpen in the control room. After the final cut, they'd all gone out to get wasted, Sam sleeping in his carseat under a table in the dim, smoke-filled club.

"It's a good song," Cody said when it was over.

"You think so?"

"Sure."

"Feel like making pizza?"

"I could eat, I guess."

Amazing. A teenage grandson who actually wanted to spend time with her.

And she didn't even have to wear a housedress and sensible shoes.

Sunday

Chapter 29

S am had no privileges at St. Brendan Hospital in Missoula, but he used his credentials to inquire about Michelle's procedure, and learned that everything was still on schedule. She was staying at an old Arts and Crafts–era hotel built for timber barons early in the century. Now, because of its proximity to the hospital, it was always occupied by families of patients and visiting doctors. Early in the morning, he stood outside her door, trying to collect his thoughts, but they refused to be collected so he knocked.

"Who is it?" Her voice was small, but not sleepy.

"It's Sam."

"Come on in," she said, opening the door. Bathrobe. Bare feet. A look of apprehension on her face. On the bed lay a paperback novel and several newspapers spread across the rumpled covers.

"Hi." He bent and kissed her, aiming badly, his lips grazing her temple. She smelled of toothpaste and pHiso-derm disinfectant.

"Is Cody all right? Did he drive down with you?"

"He's fine. I left him downstairs in the coffee shop with Gavin, eating pancakes."

"So you think this arrangement—him staying with you—is going to be all right?"

"Sure, Michelle. We agreed."

"If he gets to be too much for you, I want to know right away."

"Your confidence in me is so gratifying."

She sent him a fleeting smile. "I think you believe it's easier than it is."

So far, it *had* been easy, but he and Cody had only been together one night. Cody had been quiet, probably thinking about the surgery and school. Sam almost felt sorry for the kid. "How did your angiogram go?" he asked, deliberately changing the subject. The procedure was the last and most physically invasive of all the testing done on a living donor. He knew it to be a fairly scary and un-comfortable procedure. She had been treated to a mild sedative. Through a small incision, a tube was inserted into a vein and a dye injected so the transplant team could study her kidneys and all the related connections.

"It was great. A barrel of fun. Natalie and I laughed for hours."

"Ah, a sense of humor. That's always a good sign."

"That's what the nurse who shaved my groin said."

"You feeling all right now?"

She sat down on the bed, leaning back against a bank of pillows. "I felt all right five minutes after the proce-dure, but they made me lie motionless for six full hours. They picked out a lovely kidney for my father, so I guess everything worked out. They're going to take the one from my left side."

She paled a little as she spoke, and Sam's heart constricted. Who did she tell her fears to? Her hopes and her dreams? Natalie? The elusive Brad? Was Cody old enough to understand?

"So do you want to talk about it?" Unable to ignore the issue any longer, he indicated the paper on the bed.

She picked it up by her thumb and forefinger. "I've seen worse. When I was twelve, they printed a photo of me dancing with one of the Kennedy cousins at a wedding, with a caption about a child bride."

The paper was folded open to the story. The headline and text were filled with blatant suggestions and outright lies, but the camera had caught . . . something. The falling snow softened the focus, and there was a suggestion of movement in the way Sam's arm went around her and her head was tucked against his chest. It was a picture of two alone, absorbed in each other. The invasion of privacy made him sick.

"When I saw this rag," he said, "I wanted to hurt somebody."

"Welcome to Gavin's world." She gave an unapologetic shrug. "You get used to it by learning to ignore it."

He didn't want to get used to this. Didn't want to ignore it. But he felt himself being drawn to her, just as he'd drawn her into the hot springs. The first time he'd lost Michelle, he had built a hard wall around his heart, and that wall had protected him from the very things he was starting to feel now.

She worried her lower lip with her teeth. "So did Cody see the story?"

"Yeah."

"Did he say anything?"

"Not much. Just that you made out better than Lisa Marie Presley."

"So you don't think . . . he's reading anything into it?"

"I don't know. He didn't say much about it to me or my mother."

Her eyes widened. "He was with Tammi Lee? By choice?"

Sam felt a twinge of annoyance. "What, you don't approve of my white-trash mother?"

"Oh, Sam. Damn it, you know that's not what I meant. I have trouble picturing Cody hanging out with anyone over sixteen. I hope he was civil to your mother."

"They seemed to get along okay. Talked about music, I think."

She drew her knees to her chest. "I guess I don't really know her myself."

"She's changed a lot," Sam said.

"We've all changed a lot."

"Some things don't change at all." He took a deep breath. "After all these years, I still want you."

"Sam—"

He gestured at the papers. "There's something going on between us."

"Don't believe everything you read," she shot back, her pale cheeks turning red.

He stepped closer to the bed, touched her shoulder. "I didn't have to read it in the paper. But you know, I'm kind of glad it's out in the open."

She shifted away from him. "Do you know how incredibly bad your timing is?"

"What, because I didn't show up at a soccer game when you were feeling lonely?"

"Screw you." She glared at him. "I never thought I'd

see you again, Sam. Ever. And now I'm just supposed to make room in my life for you?"

"Why are you so testy?" he asked.

She took a deep breath, closed her eyes briefly. When she opened them she appeared more composed. "It's nerves," she admitted. "I've never been much good at dealing with . . . unforeseen circumstances. I'm letting Cody stay with you this week. What more do you want? What?"

He paused. Put away his frustration. "It's not just Cody. I want to know you again. I want . . . what we had Thursday night, and Friday at the hot springs."

"We got carried away. It's not like me to lose my . . . perspective like that." Her hands twisted into a knot of nerves in her lap. "I have a good job, I'm up for partner, I have a perfectly fine life in Seattle. Shall I chuck all that because you've got those great eyes?"

"I never knew you thought I had great eyes."

"There's a lot you never knew about me. If you knew me, you'd understand that I can't have a fling with you for old time's sake."

"What makes you think it's a fling?" He watched the agitated pulse leaping in her neck, and he traced it with his finger. Soft. So soft, like dry silk.

"We have no business getting involved no matter what our hormones are telling us."

He threaded his fingers up into her satiny hair. The years swept away, and everything he had felt for her, everything he had kept inside him all his life, rose up, seeming to push the air from his lungs. "Michelle, I'm not listening to my hormones. I'm listening to my heart."

Her lower lip trembled, and she caught it in her teeth, looking away. "What on earth," she asked with tears in her voice, "makes you think this could work?"

He drew her around to face him. "What makes you think it can't?"

A sharp knock on the door interrupted them.

"Michelle," a voice called. "It's me."

"Oh, God," she whispered. "Brad."

Chapter 30

*D*on't get up." Sam walked over to the door, cool and calm, as if he had not just turned Michelle's world inside out. He opened the door, and in walked Brad.

He was good-looking in a clean-cut J. Crew way. He had a "yachty" air about him. One of the things that first attracted her to him was that settled refinement. There could be no chaos in the life of such a man.

"Brad." She tried to compose herself. "I wasn't expecting you." She was dying to know why he was here. Earlier they had agreed he wouldn't come unless she asked him to. But he was here. Was it because of the tabloid, or had he decided she needed him?

Her voice deserted her as he and Sam regarded each other like a pair of rival stags about to tangle their antlers. Then he brushed past Sam and came over to the bed, bending to kiss her forehead. Expensive aftershave and a shirt that crackled with starch. Altoid mints. *Brad.*

"Hi, babe." He stood back, regarding her critically.

She shifted nervously on the bed. Was she blushing? Could he see where Sam had been touching her cheek, her hair—

"So how'd it go? You okay?" Brad asked.

"Great. We're all set for tomorrow. Brad, I want you to meet Sam McPhee. Sam, this is Bradley Lovell."

"You're the guy," Brad said, his voice controlled. "The guy in the paper." He patted the side of his Louis Vuitton flight bag, stuffed with folded newspapers. "Michelle told me all about you."

"Yeah?" Sam looked over at her, lifting an eyebrow. "She didn't tell me squat about you." There was nothing— *nothing*—J. Crew about his looks. It was obvious he hadn't shaved today. He had on time-worn jeans that had custom-tailored themselves to his long, lean body. A gray athletic sweatshirt and a baseball cap. And he was asking her with his eyes: *What did you tell him, Michelle? Did you tell him we made love? Did you tell him you saw stars? Did you tell him you cried yourself to sleep that night?*

"Michelle said you used to be . . . what, some sort of hired hand at her dad's place?" Brad spoke nonchalantly, as if it really didn't matter to him. A small muscle tensed in Sam's jaw.

"That was years ago, Brad," she said, breaking in. "Sam's a physician now. I told you that, too."

"So what are you doing here?" Brad's gaze was blunt and challenging as he glared at Sam.

"Wondering why a guy would let Michelle go through this alone."

The testosterone was getting thick, she thought wryly. "I'll tell you what he's *not* doing. He's not getting into a pissing contest with you." She scowled at Sam, then at Brad, daring them to defy her. "In case you've forgotten, this is about my father."

Sam went to the door. She knew he was not retreating. It was clear on his face that he wasn't through with her yet. "I have to get back. I'm on call this afternoon. So I guess . . . I'll see Cody after school tomorrow." He stared at her for a moment, and she felt strange soft echoes of the way he had touched her when they made love. He adjusted the bill of his baseball cap. "Your transplant team's the best. Everything will be fine."

Michelle felt compelled to explain to Brad, "Cody's going to stay with Sam this week."

Brad let out a low whistle. "More power to you. Don't let him pull the wool over your eyes. The kid's bad news."

Sam's eyes narrowed. "My son is the best news I've ever had. See you around, Michelle."

Brad turned to her before Sam was even out the door. "Hey, I didn't expect a three-ring circus," he said. His easy grin relaxed her. This was the Brad she knew, the one who charmed her clients at office parties, the one who took her out to dinner every Friday night, the one who attended swing-dancing lessons just because she asked him to.

Even as she welcomed his familiar presence, she felt Sam's absence, a dark and gaping hole in the day. A sense of unfinished business. And the terrible, wonderful words echoing through her: *I'm listening to my heart.* She should have let him go on, but she hadn't dared.

"God, what a week it's been." She deposited the papers and magazines on the floor.

One week. In that short span of time, the world had been transformed. Everything she used to believe was being challenged, pushed, reshaped. Everything she thought she had planned out was starting to unravel.

Even the idea of family. When she was growing up, "family" was something she and her mother lacked. When she was bringing up Cody, it was something she insisted they define for themselves. "Family" included Natalie, who was the sort of aunt every kid wanted, the sort of sister every woman should have, related by something much more potent than blood. And it was Brad, who tried to get along with Cody because of her, an effort she knew not many men would make. Cody hadn't been making it easy for him.

Now the circle widened to encompass her father, and Sam, and even Tammi Lee, who—wonder of wonders—had spent the day with Cody yesterday. She had to fit them into her life now. She *needed* to.

"So did he spend the night here, or what?" Brad asked bluntly.

For a second, she was too stunned to answer. "I can't believe you asked me that."

"I can't believe I showed up at your hotel room at ten in the morning and found some guy with you."

"He's not some guy. He's Cody's father."

"Then he should be with Cody."

"He was worried about the bullshit story in that tabloid. He wanted to talk to me about it."

"Yeah, he looked real worried to me." Brad took a tin of Altoids out of his shirt pocket and offered her one. She shook her head, and he said, "You didn't answer me, Michelle."

"Answer what?"

"Did you sleep with him or not?"

Sleep? She could safely deny that. No sleeping had taken place. "I had a surgical procedure yesterday. I ordered a tuna sandwich from room service and watched

HBO last night." She folded her arms defensively in front of her. "Why did you show up without calling first?"

"I wanted to surprise you. Wanted to do something spontaneous."

"You've never done a spontaneous thing in your life."

"Okay, so maybe that tabloid thing made me curious."

As he lowered himself to the bed and put his arms around her, she realized she had a lot of things to explain to Brad. A huge confusion swirled through her. She knew she should confess, but she had no idea how to begin.

"Have you had breakfast yet?" she asked him, chickening out.

"A cold bagel and weak coffee on the early flight."

"We could join Cody and my father downstairs, or maybe call for room service."

"Room service sounds good." He went over to the desk, picked up the hotel guide with the menus in it.

While he was reading off the selections, the divider door to the adjoining room opened. Natalie, who had driven down to be with Michelle during yesterday's procedure, waltzed in. Her bright hair was damp from a shower, her skirts and shawl shimmering around her. "Beat you to it, buddy." She crossed the room to give Brad a kiss on the cheek. "I already ordered breakfast." Her smile was full of mischief as she winked at him. "But I'll let you buy it, okay?"

"God, it *is* a circus," he said, standing back to look at Natalie. "We've got the tattooed lady and everything."

She touched a spot just above her left breast. "You're not supposed to know about my tattoo."

"You weren't supposed to go topless in my hot tub, either," he reminded her, laughing.

Michelle laughed, too, remembering that night last summer. Natalie had come over, weeping because she'd just dumped her current boyfriend, a timpani player named Stan. A few tequila slammers later, they had stripped down and jumped, giggling, into the hot tub on Brad's deck. Michelle hadn't realized back then that he'd noticed the tattoo.

Natalie stuck her tongue out at him and came bounding over to the bed, sitting on the end. "Okay, so give me a report."

"I'm fine. Had a great night," Michelle told her.

"Really?"

"Really. I'm dying for a shower."

"I thought you weren't supposed to get that incision wet."

Brad rifled around in his bag. "I'm way ahead of you, babe." He brought out a packet of DermaSeal, something from the pharmacy to keep wounds dry during bathing.

"You're a lifesaver." She hiked up the hem of her nightgown. "Have at it."

"This is too kinky for me," Natalie declared, hurrying to the window and looking out.

In the shower, Michelle took longer than she should, standing in the steamy tub, feeling the water needle down on her neck, shoulders, back. After a long time and plenty of soap, she got out of the shower and put on leggings and a loose sweater, wrapped a towel around her head. When she walked out to the bedroom, there was Natalie in the lotus position on the floor, her eyes closed and her lips moving soundlessly. It was a bizarre start to a day that promised only to get more bizarre.

Beginning with the breakfast Natalie had ordered— cheese blintzes, fruit compote, scrambled eggs, smoked salmon, and a pot of herb tea. Michelle sat on the edge of the bed, nibbling a croissant, and it hit her. Brad had barely mentioned Cody. The kid had just found the father he never knew, and Brad hadn't even asked about what the experience had been like for Cody.

She wondered why. Was it because he felt threatened?

"So I was talking to the concierge, and he gave me a list of recommendations for tonight." Natalie passed her a folder with the hotel logo on it.

"What's tonight?" Brad asked.

"The night before the big event, numb-nuts." She sampled a spiced apple from the fruit compote. "I decided we need a party."

"A party? You can't just have a party—"

"Watch me." She rolled her eyes. "God, Mr. Wet Blanket, can't you for once in your life be spontaneous? I bet you schedule your bowel movements."

"You're a real charmer, Natalie. You really are."

"Just listen, okay? Tomorrow, Michelle and her dad are going to make a miracle. Don't you think it would be good karma to mark the occasion in some way?"

Michelle expected him to argue, but instead he softened. "A kidney party. It would be a first for me."

"Wait till you see the menu," Michelle warned him, giving Natalie a hug.

Monday

Chapter 31

Michelle stared at the glowing red digits of the hotel-room clock: 4:45 A.M. She was supposed to be asleep, resting up for the big event that loomed only hours away.

The truth was, she had barely slept at all. Natalie's party had been as strange and wonderful as Natalie herself. The group, consisting of Gavin, Brad, Cody, Natalie, and Michelle, had occupied a corner of the restaurant. Somehow, Natalie had managed to get Dr. Kehr, Donna Roberts, both surgeons, and Dr. Temple to show up. Natalie and Cody hung up balloon people with incisions drawn on them. Some of the balloons bore terse instructions: *Please close carefully after opening. Did you leave anything behind? Please check in the overhead compartment for personal belongings.* Lave los manos.

The laughter and toasts ranged from silly to sentimental. Her family, Michelle had thought, regarding them with a powerful surge of affection. They were not exactly a Norman Rockwell painting, but they were hers, and her love for them burned strong and steady. The doctors, acting officious, broke up the party by eight o'clock, sending Gavin to sterile isolation and advising everyone to get a good night's sleep. Michelle wanted to feel grateful for Brad's closeness, for the familiar feel of his arms around her as they lay in the dark of the hotel room. But it felt awkward being with Brad again. In Seattle, she had become accustomed to a predictable schedule, making plans together, letting herself in and out of his house at will, confident of her place in his life. Now she didn't know anything at all.

She moved restlessly in the bed. Brad awakened, squinting at the clock. "Hey, stranger."

"I didn't mean to wake you," she said.

"I sure wouldn't mind making love to you," he whispered.

She froze, her throat locking shut. Dear God.

"But we need to watch that incision." Brad's pronouncement rescued her from having to answer. "Besides, I bet that's the last thing on your mind."

Had he always done that? Made up her mind for her? Idiot, she told herself. He was a stable, responsible man who knew her well. Most women would kill to have that.

He turned over, mumbling, "Go back to sleep, Michelle."

Sleep. He was telling her to sleep when she needed him to listen. Really listen—to her fears and apprehensions about the surgery, her guilt and confusion about Sam. She sat up in bed, looped her arms around her drawn-up knees, moving gingerly to protect the incision. "Brad?"

A long-suffering sigh. "Yeah?"

"If something goes wrong with this surgery—"

"Hold on," he said, reaching over and snapping on the lamp. "We've discussed this. As a donor, your risk is completely within reasonable limits."

"Of course," she agreed. "But I thought you should know. If anything happens to me, I'm leaving Cody in the custody of Sam. I had the papers redrafted yesterday."

"Makes sense, since he's the kid's father. But it's a moot point. You're not in any danger. You'll be home before you know it, and all this will be behind you."

"No." She barely spoke above a whisper. "I don't think it's going to turn out like that."

"So do you want me to stay?" he asked.

She knew he'd wait through the surgery if she asked him to. But was that what she had been doing with Brad the past couple of years?

Making him stick around?

"No," she said. "Everything is going to be fine. You don't need to stay."

He was quiet for a long time. Then, with a small, curious smile on his lips, he got out of bed and slowly, deliberately got dressed.

She got up, feeling ill at ease. "Do you want to talk about it?"

"Michelle." His voice was quiet, firm. "I know what you're going to say."

It had been a long, strange week, she was an emotional wreck and a ball of anxiety, but she got it. She finally got it. They'd had a good run, she and Brad, three years of a relationship that went no deeper than the epidermis. And they didn't even have to discuss this. Just by watching his face, she could see that they had come to the same conclusion independently. But it was time to move on. He deserved more. She deserved more. Sam hadn't made her any promises yesterday, but she didn't need promises. She simply needed to be free.

"I feel like crying," she admitted.

"I hate when you cry."

"I know." A very slow smile formed on her lips. "That's why I never do it around you." She sat quietly on the bed while he finished packing and phoned to check on the early commuter flight to Seattle. A brief, awkward peck on the cheek, a wish for luck, and then he was gone.

After Brad left, she crossed to the glass doors that led out onto a second-story balcony. The heavy drapes were shut, but she could hear the sounds of the road outside, trucks' air brakes hissing, the scrape of snowplow and sander.

There was a table in front of the window, and on the table was a telephone. She could take it outside, sit in the cold predawn, and call Sam on the pretext of last-minute instructions about Cody.

She hated it that she wanted to call him.

Fighting the impulse, she stared at a narrow gap in the curtains. The sky was getting lighter. And something started to happen in her head. She couldn't look away from that space. Almond-shaped, it framed nothing but the sky, yet her mind transformed what she was seeing. The slender gap in the drapes became a round, ripe, pregnant shape. Or an eye. Or a raindrop. Or the space between two praying hands.

It was a space that she suddenly wanted—*needed*—to fill.

On the table lay the flat folio box with the art supplies Natalie had brought from Seattle. Almost without thinking, Michelle grabbed a pencil and began drawing in the half-light, her heart guiding her hand. Something inside her had come unstopped, and it gushed over the paper, and she filled page after page, her hand barely able to match the speed with which the images and emotions overtook her.

By the time the sun tinged the sky with a pink blush, she sat at the table with tears streaming down her cheeks. Maybe it was only for a moment, maybe it wouldn't last, but for the past hour she had glowed with an inner light she thought had burned out. She didn't know what had sparked the change; it was probably a combination of everything that was happening: being back in Montana, saying good-bye to Brad, facing the surgery, finding Sam again.

With shaking hands, she looked at what she had done. She had no judgment. Trash or treasure, she couldn't tell. But the work was hers. She knew where it came from, and it was a place more honest, more deep, than anything she had recognized in herself in more years than she could count.

She felt a certain quiet reverence as she gathered up the drawings and slipped them into the zipper compartment of her suitcase. And for the first time as she faced the surgery, she thought, I can do this. *I can do this.*

When the radio clicked on at precisely 6:00 A.M., she was ready.

As ready as anyone could be for an organ transplant.

The final preparations felt almost surreal. Forms being checked and double-checked. Signatures in triplicate. Meetings, IV drips, paper gowns and caps. Cody and Natalie hovering, chattering nervously. Michelle looked in on her father and found him waiting with a patience and a stillness that broke her heart. When an orderly came to take her away to her private room, Gavin turned to her.

Neither of them said anything. Gavin put his hand on

his heart. She did the same, afraid to speak, afraid she might cry. *What do I do?* she wondered. If she said her good-byes, did that mean she was afraid something would go wrong, that she'd never see him again? If she said nothing, what would they have to hang on to if something *did* go wrong?

In silence, with all the unsaid things screaming inside her, she walked away, following the orderly to her room.

She hovered wildly between acting like this was the most mundane of procedures and feeling convinced, as Natalie was, that it was a spiritual event. Natalie and Cody came in. Each bent to kiss her, to murmur "I love you," and to hear her whispered echo of the phrase. Cody looked pale, unable for once to cover his apprehension with attitude. She hadn't said much about Brad—just that he'd taken the early flight to Seattle. Explanations would come later.

She was glad Cody was starting school. He needed the distraction. Rather than pacing the halls during the procedure, Natalie would be driving him back to Crystal City in time for first bell.

"It's going to be all right, Cody," she said from her hospital bed.

"What if it's not?" he asked, his voice breaking as it sometimes still did.

"You have to believe it'll be all right." Michelle watched his face, loving him with all the fullness of her heart. "For months the doctors have been telling us that attitude is everything. That includes your attitude."

"You didn't answer my question. What if something goes wrong?"

"Nothing will—"

"Mom, cut it out."

She took his hand, noticing with mild surprise that he

had calluses from working at Sam's. "All right. Yes, there is a risk that something could go wrong. But it is a tiny, calculated risk that's hardly worth considering when you think of how this is going to help my father live again."

"Why wasn't I tested?" he demanded suddenly, anger pushing through his fear, redness rising in the pallor of his face.

"What?"

"When you started in on all these tests to find a donor, why wasn't I tested?"

"Right from the start, it looked as if I was the best match, Cody. There was no need."

"You didn't even bother testing me."

She was stunned. He actually resented her for overlooking him as a donor.

"Hey, sport." She forced herself to sound calm. "I did you a favor. How'd you like to be in my position right now?" She gestured at the thin, printed gown, the wheeled bed, the cold tile walls.

Natalie came hustling in. "We'd best get going, kiddo. School today."

"Aw, man," he said, genuine distress in his face. "Why can't I go back to Seattle with Aunt Natalie—"

"Hey," Natalie cut in, her voice uncharacteristically sharp. "We went over this last night. You're going to school today. You'll knock 'em dead."

"Yeah, right."

Michelle's heart sank at the misery in his voice. She had never felt more helpless in her life. Cody had to go to a new school, and she was too out of it to be of any use at all.

He glared at her. "You should have tested me for the kidney."

"I love you for saying so, Cody. Remember that. I love you."

A pair of orderlies came in. "Time to go to pre-op," one of them said.

"One more kiss, for luck," she said to Cody.

He kissed her cheek and squeezed her hand, and she closed the sweetness of the moment into her heart. "I'll see you soon," she whispered.

"'Bye, Mom." His eyes flooded with brightness, and then she lost sight of him as they wheeled her around a corner of the corridor.

"You got a nice kid, ma'am," an orderly said.

A gentle cottony calm, augmented by the sedative she was given, washed over her. Doing the sketches this morning had been cathartic, and the last moments with Cody had set a seal of serenity upon her. The orderly had called her kid "nice." What a concept.

They reached the pre-op area, and she was amazed to see a second gurney there.

"We've got to stop meeting like this." Gavin winked at her.

Reaching out, they could touch hands. "I didn't know I'd see you here, Daddy."

"Me neither."

Their respective anesthesiologists came in and chatted with them, telling them what to expect.

Then the oddest thing happened. The orderlies and the anesthesiologists left. Gavin and Michelle found themselves alone for long, quiet minutes.

"They gave me a pre-op sedative," she said. "You?"

"I'm not sure. They've been prepping me all night." He rubbed his finger over hers. "So here we are, just the two of us."

"Here we are." She didn't know what to say. They'd

had plenty of time to express their regrets, proclaim their commitment, acknowledge the love that lay at the center of everything. But had they said it? *Had they?*

Michelle's mother had died during surgery. She tried to keep her mind from going there, but she couldn't help herself.

"Daddy?" The word came out on a high note, sounding juvenile, but she didn't care.

"Yeah, honey?"

"I'm scared."

She could feel him smile, could feel it somewhere in the region of her heart. He squeezed her hand. She had forgotten they were still touching.

"Me too, Michelle. I'm scared, too."

"I don't think it's something we're going to get over, do you?"

"Not likely. But we'd better not let Temple hear us. He'd put the brakes on this whole thing."

"He was a pain in the ass, wasn't he?"

"Yeah. Listen, I know I only showed up in your life every once in a while." He took his hand from hers and touched his chest. "But you've always been here, right here in my heart."

She wanted it to be true so badly that she held her breath.

"Michelle?"

"What?"

"You're giving me my life back. I wish I could tell you what that means to me."

Emotion came in a warm rush, driving away the chill of the tiled pre-op. They lay side by side, helpless in their hope and love and fear. She swallowed hard and tried to keep from crying.

"Don't cry, sweetheart. I don't ever want to make you cry."

She felt it flowing, the smooth warm river of light that she had felt earlier, and she finally believed that maybe there was some merit in what Natalie had said about this bond, this invisible connection between father and daughter, between mother and son.

"I don't mind crying for you, Daddy."

"Everything's done, Michelle. I fixed my life as best I can. I played my hand the best I know how. I don't know what more I can do."

The doors swished open. "Showtime, folks," someone said. "Ladies first."

Michelle kept thinking she should say one more thing to her father, something hopeful and profound, but the only words that came out were, "See you around, Dad." Then they were both wheeled away, passing the glass-enclosed scrub area where surgeons and nurses readied themselves like postulants in some strange cleansing rite.

The operating room looked smaller than she had pictured it in her mind. Too many doctor shows on TV. In the real world, operating rooms were chilly and crammed with monitoring equipment. Blue-green tile and stainless steel. Glare from the observation dome overhead—dear God, she thought, someone might be watching this?—and the transplant team assembled in a semicircle around her. Masked and capped, miner's headlamps strapped to their heads, plundering hands in skintight gloves. The nurse stood on a stool to tower over the rest.

Their questions came fast, floating disembodied from behind the anonymous masks: Did she remember them from the meetings? Did she feel all right? Did she know each person's role and what was happening? Did she have any more questions?

Michelle shook her head, mute with terror. Now it was real. Now it was happening. No turning back.

The mask came down, the sharp lemony taste of the drug invaded her air passages, and images swam and stuttered before her eyes—the blue-green tile, the monitors and masked team, and then all that was gone and she saw faces tumbling through her mind: Cody and Gavin and Sam and finally the slender space formed by a gap in the draperies, a hole in the world, a shape she had to fill in, had to fill and fill with everything that was in her.

Chapter 32

"Quit driving yourself nuts, son, and go on down to Missoula."

Sam kept shoveling. It had snowed last night, and he was clearing his mother's front walk and driveway. "I'm not driving myself nuts."

Tammi Lee sat down on the porch step and regarded him with a knowing sympathy. "Well, you're driving the hospital down there batty by calling every fifteen minutes."

"I'm not calling every fifteen minutes."

"Yes you are. And Karl's on call, Cody's at school, and if you shovel any more snow, you'll end up having a coronary right here in my front yard. So get your butt in the truck."

"I should be around when Cody gets out of school. See how his day went." It felt strange thinking about a kid's school schedule. He had never imagined himself in such a role. The thought led to a flash of memory. When he was a kid, riding the school bus home, he used to observe kids getting off at their stops, eagerly awaited by their smiling mothers. Watching them used to make Sam sick with envy.

"You can get to Missoula and back before school's out," his mother said.

"I'm not needed in Missoula," he said after a long, ponderous silence. He kept telling himself that. Maggie Kehr had promised she'd page him the minute each surgery was over.

"How do you know that?"

He sliced the blade of the shovel into the new-fallen snow and thought about Brad Lovell. Serious, sure-of-himself Brad Lovell, who had a 401(k) plan, who had seen Cody play soccer before Sam even knew his son existed. Lovell was the perfect example of someone a woman *needed,* pure and simple. He was steady and clean-cut, practical and predictable. A regular bachelor of the month.

How did a guy get like that? Sam wondered, deliberately ignoring his mother's question. He wished he knew, because he ought to try it himself. Try listening to common sense. After surviving a chaotic childhood, struggling through school, and failing at marriage, he'd finally put his life in order. His mother was sober. He had his practice, his horses, a respected place in the community. Did he really want more than he had? He was wary of taking on more. He didn't know if he had what it took.

Michelle Turner had only been back for a week, and already people were starting to talk.

He shoveled at a furious rate, scraping the driveway down to bare concrete. He was fighting to stop the knowledge building inside him, but he couldn't run from it, couldn't hide from the truth.

In all the years he'd lived and all the miles he'd traveled, he'd never loved anyone the way he loved Michelle.

When he had taken her into the empty theater, he'd felt a harsh desperation to possess her, even if it hurt them both. At the hot springs the harshness had softened, reminding him that he still had tender places deep inside him, places only she could touch. In that moment, he'd known with a certainty he hadn't felt in years that they needed a second chance. They needed to get to know one another, to look at one another through adult eyes and see if the passion they shared as teenagers really meant something.

At least, that was what he'd thought.

Now he had no idea what to think.

When his pager went off, he stabbed the shovel into the snow and pressed the readout button.

His mother stood up on the porch step. "Any news?"

"The surgery's over."

Chapter 33

Michelle. Michelle, wake up." A woman's voice reached like ghostly fingers through a fog.

"Mmm." Her mouth felt welded shut. Taste of rust and clay. She supposed what she was feeling was pain, but it was so huge, so overwhelming, that she couldn't call it pain. It was a vast red cloud, pulsating in the middle, holding her in a grip of such power she couldn't think.

She moved her jaw from side to side. "'S'it over?" No saliva in her mouth. Completely dry. The crimson fog throbbed, intensified, punishing her for her effort.

"You're all done. You did great, just perfect." Donna. That was the woman's name. Donna Roberts, the nurse.

Michelle didn't feel perfect. She felt inches from death. The pounding in her head blotted out all sound. She forced her eyes to focus on the nurse's mouth, made herself listen carefully.

Donna checked a green-and-black monitor. "We'll be transferring you to your room pretty soo—"

"My father. I want to see my father."

"He's all right, Michelle. He's in post-op, too."

I want to see him. But she couldn't get the words out. The pain surrounded her, clouding her brain, lifting her up and swirling her far, far away, and she couldn't see anything except that tiny slit of space opening up to the paintings she hadn't done. Two hands, parting a curtain. Giving her a glimpse of something she hadn't created yet. Now it was clear to her. She had to learn to do it anyway, even though it hurt.

She sank deeper and deeper into the formless red morass of pain, and she let herself go, a victim of slow drowning, too weak to fight her way back to the surface.

Chapter 34

There was something wrong with the clocks in this frigging school, Cody decided.

They didn't move like normal clocks. They must be from another dimension where a minute equaled an hour and a day lasted forever.

Because that was how long his first day at Crystal City High School had lasted—forever.

And it was only lunchtime.

Feeling like a complete dork, he had shown up in homeroom with a "New Student" folder under his arm and this enormous zit on his forehead. He hadn't had a zit since September, and he'd woken up that morning looking like he was about to sprout a unicorn horn.

No sympathy from Aunt Natalie, who had driven him up from Missoula. "Nobody will notice. It just feels obvious to you. Act like it's not there."

"Oh, right, like no one's going to notice Mount Vesuvius in the middle of my face."

"Sweetie, if this is the worst thing that ever happens to you, consider yourself blessed." In his mom's absence, Aunt Natalie played the part of the expert on all things.

At least Brad had gone back to Seattle. Cody had been worried that he'd hang around asking a bunch of questions. Brad liked to act all buddy-buddy, and Cody didn't feel like answering stuff like how did it feel to meet his father and all that crap.

Coming in new mid-year was a special torture that should be reserved for convicted felons. First there had been the homeroom teacher's "Class, we have a new student" routine. Then the issuing of books and supplies. The stack of forms to be signed.

The Assignment of the Seat.

The teachers all thought they were doing him this big favor, putting him right up front in the middle so he wouldn't miss a second of their fascinating lectures on the Voting Rights Act or phytoplankton. What they were actually doing was making him vulnerable to the whispers. This was the equivalent of blindfolded torture, because he could hear bits and pieces of the conversation, but couldn't see the speakers.

". . . like some skater from the inner city . . ."

". . . he's got a pierced *what?*"

"Well, *I* think he's cute . . ."

". . . acts like hot shit because his grandfather's a movie star . . ."

". . . wait till you hear who his *father* is . . ."

The hissed speculation, through civics, trigonometry, and science, had hit him like spitballs to the back of the neck. When he'd try to get a look at the speakers, dropping a pencil or something and twisting around, he was met by mute, blank stares.

Losers. Everyone in this frigging school was a loser.

After third period, he had trouble with his locker—of course—and once he got it open, couldn't cram all his books in along with his coat, so he kept the coat on even though he was sweating like a hog in the overheated building.

Lunchtime. In his regular school it was his favorite period of the day, because he sat at the table where everyone was cool and where everyone else only *wished* they could sit. Claudia would be at his side, eating like one potato chip and then saying she was full, and talking and laughing the whole time.

He was a long way from that lunchtime, a long way from Claudia.

Shit. Shit. Shit.

He went through the fast-food line and ordered a burger and a Coke. Safe choices. Picking something different for lunch was risky, even at his school in Seattle. If you had something like tofu or Thai noodles, you were in danger of being Different. There was a guy named Sujit at his other school who brought the weirdest stuff because of his religion. During certain times of the year, he couldn't eat meat or dairy products or anything normal. The kids had made a big deal of it, holding their noses and gagging when he walked by, sometimes playing keep-away with his falafel burger or hummus. One time, Sujit had lost it totally, calling them all pig-eating infidels, which had only made them laugh harder.

Cody wasn't laughing now. He wished he hadn't teased Sujit. Because now *he* was the one surrounded by pig-eating infidels.

He took a long time getting his napkin and straw, lingering at the counter while letting his gaze dart frantically around the busy, noisy cafeteria. Where to sit? *Where to sit?*

Though fewer in number, the tables were segregated exactly as they had been at his old school. The popular kids occupied the middle. Just as in Seattle, these kids were uniformly good-looking, relaxed, laughing while the whole school revolved around them. Nearby sat the football players and cheerleaders. The jocks were like jocks everywhere—food fights erupting, body noises followed by a chorus of "eeeeuw . . ."

Around the busy inner sanctum tables, there was a neutral buffer zone of regular kids with no distinguishing status. And of course, on the fringes of all the activity were the dweebs, geeks, and losers.

They had plenty of room at their tables. Some hid behind comic books or thick-lensed glasses. The fat ones ate furtively, pretending they didn't eat but were just fat because they had unlucky glandular activity. The totally clueless ones acted as if they had no idea they were dweebs. They just gabbed away and had lunch—lots of nerdy thermoses and Tupperware kits. These kids didn't give a rat's ass that they were the scum-sucking bottom-dwellers of the school population.

Maybe he could just hunker down at the end of a geek table, scarf his burger, and slip out to the Commons, an outdoor spot for hanging out during break.

But man, a *geek* table.

If he didn't do better than that, he'd be a goner for sure.

He sucked in a deep breath and went to one of the neutral zone tables. Like all of them, it was crammed. He spotted one possibility. A gap at the end of a table of mostly boys who were talking loudly about snowboarding. Hey, he could talk snowboarding. Keeping his eyes focused on the empty spot, he moved in, trying not to hurry, determined to make it look as if he'd arrived there almost by accident.

"Sorry, that's my spot." A kid scooted in fast, grabbing the seat.

Cody felt his face redden, though he shrugged nonchalantly. But now he was trapped, standing like an idiot with his tray in the middle of the lunchroom.

Somebody jostled him from behind, sloshing his Coke on the tray.

"Hey, look out," he muttered, but not loud enough to be heard.

The bun of the burger was soggy with Coke. If he didn't find a place to sit in a minute, people were going to notice. But the only seats he could see now were at the geek table. Sweat trickled down his back. Damn, he wished he'd taken his coat off. A feeling of impending doom pressed at him, and he felt as if he was about to lose it. The geek table. The goddamned geek table.

"Hey, Cody!"

At the sound of his name, he looked up, and there was Molly Lightning.

It was like seeing an angel, watching her stand up with one knee propped on a bench, waving her slender arm at him.

"Hey, come have a seat." She was at a neutral table where the kids weren't particularly geeky or particularly cool. Just regular.

He nodded, nonchalant as you please, but inside he was exulting. She'd saved his butt, no doubt about it.

*   *   *

Feeling like an ex-P.O.W., Cody exited the loud, gym-bag-smelling school bus and stood at the side of the highway. Breathing. A survivor after a disaster. Man, he felt as though he'd been holding his breath all day, expecting an ambush. They'd promised to get him out of class if anything bad happened at the hospital, but there had been no interruption of the slow torture of school. He had to feel grateful for that, at least.

Swinging his backpack over his shoulder, he trudged up the frozen gravel drive toward Sam's house. Another bonus, he thought sourly. On top of everything else, he had to stay here all week.

In spite of his thoughts, his heart lifted when the Border collie came careening down from the field and leaped at him, long pink tongue reaching for his face. For a minute, Cody couldn't help himself, and he laughed aloud. Then he saw Sam coming out of the house.

If he asks me how school was, I'm going to hurl, I swear it.

"Hey, Cody." Sam swung a canvas bag into the back of his old pickup truck. He put a cooler of drinks and a bag of tortilla chips in the cab. "I guess you want to get on down to the hospital right away."

The guy had read his mind.

They were both quiet as Sam pulled out onto the highway and headed south. The old Dodge truck smelled of timothy hay and motor oil, and the column shift rattled with the bumps. Sam McPhee sure wasn't like any of the doctors Brad played golf with, Cody reflected. But then again, he pretty much wasn't like any other doctor, *period*. Or maybe Cody just thought he was weird because he was his dad.

"My mom taught me to ride a bike when I was five,"

he said suddenly, for no particular reason. His breath fogged the window.

Sam flexed his hands on the worn, shiny steering wheel and kept his eyes straight ahead on the road. "Yeah?" Another long silence. And then, "We're a little short on bikes around here. Plenty of horses, though. You could do some riding."

Cody felt a spark of interest, but forced himself not to show it. The truth was, he really did want to ride a horse, but he thought he'd feel stupid. Most of the kids at Crystal City High had been born knowing how. They were all goat ropers and cutters and stuff. "Maybe," he said guardedly.

"You could fool around on a snowmobile, too."

"That'd be cool, I guess."

"Can you drive a standard shift?" Sam asked. "A car, not a horse, that is."

Cody's mouth twitched. "Sure. I learned on one."

"There's an old Jeep in the pole barn I could let you use for getting to and from school. That way, you wouldn't waste time waiting around for the school bus. You'd have more time for chores in the morning."

Cody carefully weighed the merits of the offer. It was really no contest. The bus that smelled like a locker room or chores and his own wheels. "That'd be good," he said. Then, reaching through reluctance, he said, "Thanks."

Sam acted like it was no big deal. He opened the chips and passed the bag to Cody. They were silent again until Cody spoke up without even thinking. "This morning really sucked," he said, feeling stupid but unable to keep quiet.

"The transplant, or school?"

"The transplant. School—well, that sucked all day. At the hospital, everybody was like, really nervous." He made a face in the side mirror. "I kept thinking how totally gross the whole thing was."

"Gross, huh?"

He stared out the window at the scrubby landscape swishing past. "You must think I'm really selfish." He immediately wished he hadn't said that. It was none of this guy's business what was going on in his head. But it was so strange. Cody just kept wanting to *talk*.

"Why would I think that?"

"Because I didn't make them test me to see if I could be the kidney donor."

"I suspect they would have tested you if your mom hadn't turned out to be a near-perfect match."

"Nobody even asked me."

"And that's a problem?"

Cody scrubbed the side of his hand at the fogged-up window. "They should have checked me out instead of treating me like I didn't exist."

"Did you say you wanted to be tested?"

"My mom didn't even tell me what was going on until a few weeks ago. And then it was like, 'Well, we're moving to Montana so I can give this guy a kidney.'"

Sam cleared his throat. Cody thought he might be grinning. For some reason, Sam was pretty easy to talk to. He didn't push, didn't try too hard. He was just . . . there. Quiet. Cody's mom was always nagging him about "opening up." She didn't seem to understand that he was not going to open up if she kept talking all the time.

"So anyway," he said, "it was like, really intense. They had my mom in this room with one of those paper hair things on her head and a bunch of tubes and wires all hooked up to her, and I had to go in and say good-bye, like she was going to another planet and I wouldn't ever see her again. And all that was *before* I had to go to Hicksville High."

"I can see how that would suck."

Though Sam didn't take his eyes off the road, Cody could feel the full force of his attention, his fascination. It was a new experience, having an adult be this interested in what he had to say. Why? Because Sam was a doctor? Or his father, or just a guy? Or because he'd been hanging out with Cody's mom and they put that stupid picture in the *Enquirer*?

"Since nobody called from the hospital while I was at school, I guess everything went okay. But I was wicked nervous all day."

"Uh-huh," said Sam in that lazy way of his. "So was I."

Chapter 35

"Mom. Hey, Mom." *Cody*. More powerful than any drug, her child's voice drew Michelle out of the fog.

"Cody . . ." She could feel her lips move, but only a whisper of sound came out. She had the sense that time had passed; she remembered hearing that her father was all right. The pain-cloud still surrounded her, but this time she wanted to fight her way out of the fog.

"Where . . . am . . ."

"In your room, Michelle." A deeper voice. A man's voice.

"Brad—" No. Sam. *Sam.* "Hurts," she said.

"She's miserable." Sam spoke to someone in a clipped voice. "I want her to have a self-administered morphine pump."

Bless you, Sam.

"Yes, we've ordered one—"

"Now, okay? Not in a minute, but now."

Typical doctor. That aggressiveness, that obnoxious, abrasive personality. His staccato order worked. She couldn't open her eyes or count the minutes, but in a short while she felt the drip, and someone guided her thumb to the button that would deliver the gentle, numbing surge of narcotics to her system. She pushed the button, and almost instantly felt the wavelike swish of morphine curling in, then rolling back out, taking some of pain's fury with it.

" 'S' working," she said. Dry. Mouth was so dry.

"That's good, Michelle," Sam said. "You rest now."

She couldn't remember if he'd touched her or not since she awakened. Probably not. Doctors didn't do that so much, not anymore. She tried to recall what had passed between them the last time they'd been together. Hotel room. Something big, important, interrupted. She couldn't think.

"School." She formed the word carefully with her lips. "Cody. How was school?"

"I survived," he said simply.

She wanted to hear it all, every detail, but she couldn't stay focused on one subject. "You've seen . . . my father?"

"I'll take Cody in a minute," Sam said. "Gavin's on this floor, different wing. He has to be quarantined in ICU for a while, but we'll look in on him."

Michelle drifted in and out of pain and consciousness. Heard the TV news, and smiled when she felt Cody come over to the bed and awkwardly, hesitantly, touch her head.

Floating in the morphine fog, she listened to them getting ready to go back to Crystal City. She mouthed *I love you* and when they left she turned her face to the wall and wept for no reason she could name.

When she woke up again, the room was empty except

for the drips and equipment. The space between the drapes showed a night sky.

She pressed the button on the morphine pump. Gentle swish of drugs.

The sky grew red around the edges as if it had caught fire.

Later, someone put something around her ankles. Helpless but resentful, she mumbled, "What's that?"

"Air cuffs. You'll hear the electric pump come on about every twenty minutes."

"Too loud. Won't get any sleep at all."

"You have to keep these on until you can get out of bed."

With that powerful motivation, she was up at sunup, clinging to the arm of a nurse's aide as she took one step, then lowered herself gingerly to the chair by the bed.

"Okay," she said. "Off with the cuffs already."

The aide touched a buzzer. "You win. Your husband warned us that you were a fighter."

Husband. Sam. No way. He wasn't her husband. He was . . . too damned complicated to explain to the nurse's aide.

Later she forced herself to get up again and wait patiently, staying in the chair, even eating something. Rice pudding. Too sweet, not enough nutmeg. Then it was back to bed, feeling as if she'd run a marathon. At one point Donna checked in on her, face wreathed in smiles.

"Just wanted to be sure you heard—your kidney is working great."

Michelle squeezed her eyes shut and felt a powerful rush of gratitude.

We did it, Daddy. We did it.

Tuesday

Chapter 36

G od, these are incredible. When did you do these?" Natalie's voice pried into a strange dream Michelle was having. In the dream, she floated through the wisps of steam that curled off the surface of the hot springs where she and Sam had made love. Only she was alone in the fog, searching, calling out, but no one could hear her.

"Michelle?" Natalie was insistent. "I was asking about these drawings."

She gave up on the dream and dragged her eyes open. "What . . . drawings?"

"Here." Cody held a plastic bottle with a flexible straw to her lips.

Michelle drank gratefully. "Thanks. What drawings?"

"I found them in your suitcase." Natalie held up one

of the sketches Michelle had done before the surgery. "These are wonderful."

"They're pretty cool, Mom."

She took another drink. Didn't want to think about the drawings and what had happened the morning of the transplant. Truthfully, she had no idea if the experience meant anything at all. "I feel as if I've been away forever," she said. "What day is it?"

"Tuesday."

She studied Cody. He seemed . . . different. She supposed that working outside a lot added color to his usually pale face. He might be eating better, too. He looked bigger. Filled out. When had that happened? she wondered with a clutch of apprehension. Changes don't happen overnight. Why hadn't she noticed?

"Is school going all right?" she asked.

"Yeah."

She didn't believe him. Someone had probably coached him not to say anything to upset her. "Are you and Sam getting along okay?"

He shrugged. "I guess."

"I've been keeping tabs on the situation," Natalie reminded her. "They're getting along fine."

"He doesn't know me," Cody pointed out. "He's just some guy. Ow! Quit kicking me, Aunt Natalie."

"Now the big question," Michelle said. "How's school going?"

"Sucks," he said predictably, then winced as Natalie kicked him again. "I'll survive, Mom. But I really want to get back to Seattle."

"Speaking of getting back, I have to leave, sweetie," Natalie said. "That is, if you'll be okay without me."

Michelle smiled, feeling her lower lip crack with the

effort. "I'll be okay without you. Just not nearly as entertained."

"Call me, all right? Anytime, night or day."

"Sure, Nat. You've been a peach."

"Take care of yourself. I'll keep the home fires burning."

After visiting hours were over, the nurses let Michelle walk in the hallway, wheeling her IVs. She made them take out the catheter at the first opportunity. Pain flamed through her, but she kept walking, concentrating on the scuffing sound of her slippers on the linoleum tile floor. She found her way to Gavin's room.

Her father was asleep, zippered in a sterile cocoon of clear plastic. He looked terrible, a waxen corpse. *No.* She wanted to scream it. *Daddy. Oh, Daddy.* We're not finished, she thought frantically. We just found each other again. The very air around her suddenly felt unnatural, noxious. Everything was broken.

But his coloring was remarkable—a healthy flush to his cheeks, hands and fingernails pink. Everyone assured her that the transplant was a success, the kidney was working.

Please let it be true. Please please please let it be true.

She lifted her hand, pressed her fingertips lightly to the plastic bubble, and said, "I love you, Daddy." Her words sounded muffled and small in the machine-snarled room. His chest gently rose and fell, rose and fell.

As she shuffled slowly back to her bed, she wondered if she'd ever told him that when he was awake.

She hadn't.

But if he didn't know it after this, he'd never catch on.

Chapter 37

Sam cleared away the Styrofoam remnants of Trudy's takeout. Never much of a cook, he felt lucky Cody had taken a shine to Trudy's burgers and pizza. Cody picked up his backpack and headed for the stairs. The two of them had been circling each other like a pair of wary dogs, giving a little here, taking a little there. In some moments, Sam felt a connection, but usually they were strangers. He kept telling himself to be patient. Most fathers had years to get to know their kids. He had only days.

"There's a Sonics game on tonight," he said. "You a Sonics fan?"

Cody paused at the bottom of the stairs. "Sort of."

Sam went into the den and flicked on the TV, filling the room with bluish light and the rapid-fire monologue of a basketball commentator. Without looking at Cody, Sam took a seat and gave his attention to the game. Cody sat on the end of the couch, poised to spring up and flee any minute. When a beer commercial came on, his attention wandered, touching on the stack of journals Sam didn't have time to read, the beige drapes, the photos of horses. Alice had tried to spiff the place up when they were married, but Sam had never put much effort into it. He didn't know diddly about fixing up a house to resemble a home.

Then Cody's gaze fixed on the large painting that hung over the fireplace. "Did my mom do that?" he asked.

"Uh-huh." Sam reached up and turned on the mantel light. "Have a look."

Cody stood with his hands dug into his back pockets, studying the winter scene. Sam kept his face neutral, remembering the day Michelle had given him the painting. They had done everything teenagers are lectured *not* to do. They had unprotected sex, they believed love would be enough, they dared to cross the invisible-but-rock-solid barrier of class and privilege. The result had been a pair of broken hearts . . . and this boy.

"It's pretty awesome," Cody said, staring at the signature and date in the bottom corner.

Sam tried to imagine what was going through the kid's head just then as he stood looking at something his mother had done before he was born. He wondered if Cody was able to picture the girl she had been, to think of her as someone other than his mother. Probably not. That just wasn't the way a kid's mind worked. "Your mom says she doesn't paint anymore."

"She does stuff for work, mostly on the computer." He sat back down on the sofa. His expression gave no clue to his thoughts.

The game came on again, and Sam couldn't think of

anything else to say. But he wanted to fill the silence, so he asked, "Did that Jeep run okay?"

"Yeah, it ran fine." Cody hesitated. "I gave Molly Lightning a ride home after school today."

Sam wasn't sure how to respond to that. Should he commend the boy for giving a ride to a friend? Admonish him to drive carefully and wear seat belts? Chastise him because he hadn't asked permission to give rides to passengers?

He said, "You should have checked with me before offering rides to people."

Cody stared him straight in the eye. "Why?"

"Because I'm responsible for you."

Cody snorted. "Right."

"This week I am, damn it—" Sam stopped, amazed to find that his pulse had sped up. This kid had a killer instinct when it came to pushing buttons. "Okay, look," Sam said, pressing the mute button on the remote control. "I should have told you not to take on passengers unless you check with me first."

"So why didn't you?"

"Because I'm new to this, that's why. I'm making it up as I go along."

"That's obvious."

"You're not making it easy, Cody."

"Why should I?"

Sam clenched his teeth until he brought his temper back in check. In a slow drawl, he asked, "Are you enjoying this?"

"What, being here? Hell no," Cody said bluntly. "You're not having any fun, either, so maybe you should just send me back to Seattle to stay with Natalie." He patted his shirt pocket. "I have a copy of the bus schedule."

"Not an option," Sam said, his gaze flashing to the painting over the mantel. "I said I'd look after you this week, and that's what I'm going to do. We could probably have an okay time together if we could get past the bickering stage. What do you say?"

Cody picked up a thread on the arm of the sofa. "I don't see the point."

"Maybe there doesn't need to be a point. Look, you're a teenager. It's your job to question every rule and push at every boundary. It's my job to tell you the rules and boundaries. By not telling you about passengers in the Jeep, I fell down on the job. So here's the rule—number of passengers cannot exceed the number of seat belts. Got it?"

"Yeah. Whatever."

"It's your job to tell me where you're going when you leave and what time you'll be back."

"I don't see why—"

"So if you don't show up, they'll know where to look for the body," Sam snapped.

Cody got to his feet. "Jeez, I didn't mean to start World War III. I just mentioned I gave a girl a ride home. She likes me. Is it so hard for you to believe someone likes me?"

"Christ, no, Cody. *I* like you. I want you to be safe. I want us to get along, okay?"

"Whatever," he muttered one last time, stooping to pick up his heavy backpack and heading for the stairs. "I've got some homework to do."

Crossing his arms across his chest, Sam scowled at the TV screen without really seeing it. The conversation had exposed glaring inadequacies he never knew he had, and it bugged the hell out of him. As a parent, you had to figure out when to say yes and when to say no. When to praise and when to upbraid. And getting it right was harder than it seemed.

Wednesday

I t wasn't until he pulled up to the barn at Lonepine after school the next day that Cody realized he'd forgotten to call Claudia—again. If he didn't keep in touch with her better, she was going to think he'd died or fallen off the planet or something.

But the days kept rolling along, the distance between here and Seattle seemed endless, and time got away from him.

Still, he should have phoned her. But he'd been so eager to get away from that frigging school that he'd roared off in the old Jeep without even remembering he'd meant to stop at Blue Rock and call Claudia. He didn't want to use Sam's phone for long-distance. Sam would probably let him, but Cody didn't want to ask.

He just didn't know where he stood with Sam. It was so weird being in his house, knowing the brand of shaving cream he used and what magazines he subscribed to, learning personal stuff about a stranger. Sometimes they had normal conversations and everything seemed fine, and then they'd rub each other the wrong way and argue. Cody kept trying to tell himself it didn't matter. He kept telling himself he didn't want to know this guy. He'd done fine without a father and he didn't need one now.

Sam McPhee was a hard guy to know. He sure as hell wasn't a guy Cody wanted to ask favors from, like phone permission.

Ah, well, he thought, swinging down from the driver's seat, he'd call Claudia tomorrow.

The Border collie came racing across the yard, barking her foolish face off. She knew Cody by now, having slept at the foot of his bed the past few nights. She launched herself like a missile at him. He caught her in his arms, staggering back a little with the motion, and laughed as she licked his face. It felt good, having someone greet you with this level of enthusiasm.

When they got back to Seattle, he'd talk his mom into getting a dog or a cat, maybe.

"That's loyalty for you," Sam said, ambling across from the house. "The minute I turn my back, I find my best girl in the arms of another man."

Cody tried not to grin as he set down the dog. "How's the new horse doing today?"

"Come on back and see for yourself." Sam didn't spend a long time looking at Cody, studying him. He just turned, totally casual, and ambled away.

Cody wondered if Sam was just naturally cool, or if he didn't care, or if he didn't want to get involved with a kid he didn't know. Maybe Cody was trying to read too much into Sam's attitude. It was hard as hell not to ask a bunch of questions, but he'd be damned if he'd make the first move.

Seeing the filly wiped out all his worries for a while. She acted as if she was happy to see him, frisking around the stall and thumping the walls, butting up against the mare. When the mare tried to eat, the filly kept trotting back and forth in front of her. With a quick, exasperated motion, the mare shoved the filly bodily away.

"Hey, why'd she do that?" Cody asked.

"The filly got in the way of what the mare wanted. She didn't hurt it." Sam drummed his fingers on the stall door, catching the filly's attention to distract it while Sylvia ate. "I was thinking she'll need a name one of these days. I have to register her papers."

"Yeah?"

"What do you think we ought to call her?"

Cody looked at the horse, and everything that crossed his mind was hokey and cute. Brownie. Blaze. Socks. He shrugged. "I don't know. Whatever."

Sam crossed his feet and propped his shoulder on the side of the stall. "A good horse might be around for twenty, thirty years. You have to make sure you pick the right name."

"So pick one."

"How about you pick it?"

"Why me?"

"You brought this animal into the world. I thought you might like to be the one to name her."

Cody shrugged again. Shit. He didn't know how to act. How did kids act around their fathers, anyway? "I can't think of anything."

"Maybe something will come to you. You let me know, okay?"

"Yeah. Okay."

The foal got tired and curled up in the straw for a nap. The mare fussed and licked at it for a while. It was amazing how she seemed to know exactly what to do.

"Do you have homework?" Sam asked. Then he shook his head. "Feels strange asking that."

You think you *feel strange,* thought Cody. "I did it in study hall."

"Okay, then you can get started on chores." Before Cody could reply, Sam held out a shovel and said, "It's good having you around."

Cody glanced at him sharply. What was good? His company? Or his manure-shoveling skills? Sam didn't say, and Cody didn't ask. They went to the tack room, put on quilted coveralls and gloves. Cody was mildly pleased to see Sam pick up a shovel, too. After the usual stall duties, today's task was to clean out the oat bins, getting rid of the moldy stuff on the bottom, scouring the galvanized metal bins, and replacing the oats.

"Ever given any thought to what you want to do after high school?" Sam asked.

"Some. I haven't made up my mind, though."

"You interested in college?"

"Sure. Most people go to UW. That's probably where I'll end up."

It helped that they were working as they talked. For some reason, it felt more natural to talk during the rhythm of the shovels. This week had to be the strangest time of Cody's life, starting a new school while his mom and grandfather did the kidney transplant. Talking didn't make things any better, but it didn't make things worse, either.

"You'll probably like college," Sam remarked. "I liked it a lot."

Cody wondered what it had been like for Sam and his mom, years ago, making a baby together and then never seeing each other again. He pushed away the thought and got back to work. Even though the chores were a drag, Cody sort of liked being out here, messing around with the horses and going all over on a snowmobile.

"What do you think of horse ranching?" Sam asked, reaching for a hose.

Cody snorted, chagrined that he even *looked* as if he might be enjoying himself. "It's a barrel of laughs." He stabbed his shovel into a mound of manure. The strange dance of uncertainty between him and Sam McPhee made him nervous.

At sunset, Sam and Edward were in the pole barn, replacing the spark plugs in a snowmobile. Two car doors slammed. Sam walked out to the drive to see Cody and Tammi Lee going toward the house.

"Almost suppertime," Tammi Lee called. She gestured at the two pizza boxes Cody balanced in his hands.

"We'll be in shortly." Sam grinned with the fine pleasure of seeing his mother and his son together. Family had always been in short supply for him. This was a new sensation for him. Did he like it, or was it something a guy like him was better off without?

"I think he likes it here," Sam said. "I think he even likes my mother."

Rummaging in a tool box, Edward regarded him sharply. "So you getting attached to the kid?"

"He's my kid." The wonder of it still swept through Sam each time he said the words. "What, I'm not supposed to get attached?"

"I didn't say that. But what happens when they leave?"

A blunt question, one that had been nagging at Sam. "It's not like they live on another planet," he said.

A faint yelp echoed down from the hill beyond the paddock. Edward shaded his eyes. "Hey, check this out."

Sam followed his gaze and felt a cold churn of fear in his gut. It was Scout, hurrying toward them—but not with her usual swift and joyous abandon. "She's hurt," he said, breaking into a run. He reached the collie halfway down the hill. A smear of blood marked her trail. It came from a long slash down her foreleg. Four scratches furrowed her muzzle.

"Hey, what's the matter with Scout?" Cody asked, jumping down off the porch and hurrying toward Sam.

Scooping up the dog, Sam hurried to the tack room. In one corner was a stainless-steel table and a couple of exam lights. He set her down, eyes and hands scanning her injuries.

"She need the vet?" Edward asked.

"Let's have a look." While Sam took off his gloves, Cody went around the other side of the table and murmured the dog's name, stroking her. Sam met the boy's eyes. "Keep her calm. I need to check out this cut." Edward opened the large first-aid wall station, stocked with instruments and supplies, and Sam used the clippers to trim away the long white-and-black hair, exposing a wicked gash.

"What happened?" Cody asked. "Is that from barbed wire?"

"Cat, more likely," Sam said. "A mountain lion. See the scratches across her nose? Scout's been known to tangle with a big cat if it wanders too close."

"Is she going to be okay?"

"Yeah, we'll fix her up."

Cody looked at the indigo sky through the small square window. "Are there a lot of mountain lions around here?"

"A fair number," Edward said, bringing some medicine from the office fridge. "We put out a trap, but they're street-smart. Last season we caught three, sent them down to Yellowstone to be turned out in the wild." Muffled thumps came from the stalls, the horses settling in for the night.

Sam snapped on a pair of surgical gloves. He and Cody worked together, Cody soothing the dog while Sam disinfected the superficial scratches. Edward stood back watching them thoughtfully.

"Hand me that syringe of lidocaine," Sam said to Cody. "Don't break the seal until I tell you." He cleansed the site and injected the topical anesthetic. The dog whimpered, and Cody hushed her. While he waited for the lido to work, Sam caught himself studying his son's hands, gently splayed across the collie's silky fur.

Wow, he thought, the kid's got my hands.

"You okay?" he asked Cody. "This is on the gory side."

"I can handle anything after pulling that foal," Cody assured him.

Sam used a double-ended needle and surgical thread to stitch the gash. At one point he glanced up and caught the boy looking at him, and the expression on Cody's face nearly bowled him over. Having a son was a fine thing. Having a son who admired you made you feel like a god.

"Go ahead and spray her with the Furex," he said, nodding at the plastic bottle. "That's right, up and down the wound." With intense concentration, Cody applied the yellowish antiseptic.

"Ever give an injection?" Sam asked.

"No."

"Want to learn?"

"I guess."

Sam prepared a dose of anti-inflammatory and penicillin, then coached Cody through the injection. As he worked, Cody's face wore an expression of complete absorption. Scout whimpered and took advantage of the extra attention she was getting. Walking tall with a sense of accomplishment, Cody carried her across the yard to the main house, putting her down gently in the kitchen.

"You guys make a pretty good team," Edward said, as they washed up at the sink in the mudroom. A certain quiet ease pervaded the atmosphere, and it felt good to Sam. A hell of a lot better than coming home to an empty house.

That evening after supper, Tammi Lee hung on Cody's every word as he described the treatment. She made a good listener, and he responded to that. Absently, he kept his hand on the dog's head as he spoke, and the sight evoked echoes of that rare warm feeling that had come over Sam earlier. Then Tammi Lee glanced at the clock.

"Better go," she said. "I've got some videos to return before closing time. You know what folks say." She winked. "Crime doesn't pay."

Sam was pleased to see that Cody stood up when she did, out of courtesy. She turned to him. "You looking forward to your mom and granddad getting home?" she asked.

"Yeah." Yet the reminder seemed to agitate him. He lifted a shoulder, just this side of insolent. "The sooner they get better, the sooner we go back to Seattle."

"You miss your friends?"

"Sure."

"I figured you'd make new ones here," said Tammi Lee, heading for the door. "Nice kid like you."

Cody looked startled. He was probably trying to recall the last time someone had called him a nice kid.

Thursday

Chapter 39

With a weary motion, Cody shrugged his backpack over one shoulder and made his way to the main door of the school. Somehow, another endless day had ended.

Somehow, he had survived another day at this armpit of an institution.

He was sort of glad to be going to Sam's rather than the hospital this afternoon. His mom was lots better, but that meant she'd ask the usual questions about how his day went, and what were his teachers like, and did he make some more friends, and all that crap, and he didn't want to talk about it.

The only bright spot in this godforsaken place was Molly Lightning. She was great, not making a big deal of him but making sure she introduced him to a couple of her friends each day. They were way different from his friends in Seattle. Who would have thought he'd be sitting around at lunchtime talking about goat roping and 4-H Club?

At least it wasn't the geek table.

Maybe he'd call Molly tonight, pretend he needed a homework page or something.

"Cody?"

A voice behind him. Female, but not Molly.

He stopped at a heavy door with wire mesh through the glass. He recognized the girl from homeroom, the one he was already thinking of as the Blond Bombshell. Shiny yellow hair, huge tits.

He smiled. "Yeah?"

"It's Cody, right? Cody Slade?"

"Turner."

"Oh." She stuck her thumb in the top of her jeans pocket, tugging the waistband down to show a little of her bare stomach. "Someone said you were related to Gavin Slade."

"I am, but I've got a different last name." He pushed the heavy door open, stood to one side to let her pass. She smelled like bubble gum and shampoo. Her sweater was tight. Really tight. "He's my grandfather. I'm staying at his place."

Her face lit up, pretty and bright. "I think that's so cool." She ducked her head and looked up at him through long eyelashes. "I'm Iris York. We're in homeroom together."

"And English." Color flooded his face. "I noticed you in English class last period." He'd noticed her in the lunchroom, too, at the inner sanctum table, but she hadn't called out to him.

She made a face. "I can't stand the teacher, Mrs. Lightning. She's picky, picky, picky. I can't wait until the term's over and I can take drama instead."

Cody had actually thought Mrs. Lightning—Molly's mom—wasn't too bad. She was the only one who hadn't made him sit in the front, and she didn't act all chummy with him just because she was friends with Sam McPhee.

"Can I give you a ride somewhere?" he asked boldly, gesturing at the Jeep.

"Um . . ." She looked from side to side, then shrugged. "I don't see my usual ride, so I guess I'll take you up on that. I live up in Windemere Hills, on the golf course."

"Great." They headed across the parking lot.

"So tell me about your grandfather. I think his old movies are sooo bitchen—"

A Bondo-colored El Camino came around a corner and lurched to a stop in front of them. Cody jumped back, flinging out his arm in an instinctively protective gesture. Slush from a filthy puddle sluiced over his feet. Ice-cold water trickled into his shoes.

"Hey, Iris." The driver got out and came around the car, opening the passenger door. "I thought I'd missed you, but here I am."

Iris bit her lip. "Hi, Billy. This is Cody Turner. Cody, this is Billy Ho. The guys in the back are Ethan Lindvig and Jason Kittredge." Gangsterlike, they nodded at him from the rusty bed of the truck.

Billy was one of the coolest guys in school; Cody could tell. Good-looking in a Native American way. Outside the library Molly had pointed him out, said he was big trouble. But he was just cool. Molly probably couldn't see that.

"Cody offered me a ride home," Iris explained. "I thought you'd left without me," she hastened to add, pushing out her lower lip.

"Today's your lucky day." Billy opened the door wider.

When she hesitated, Cody knew it was now or never. Speak up now and get the cutest girl in the school on his side, or forever hold his peace . . . and sit at the dweeb table.

"The offer's still open," he said.

Billy didn't speak, but his glittering black eyes and go-to-hell expression said it all. Cody was trespassing, and Billy didn't like it one bit.

"Maybe another time," Iris said.

"Maybe never," Billy snapped.

Billy grabbed for Iris's arm. Cody didn't think, he just stepped between them.

"Maybe she can make up her own mind," he said.

"Out of my way." Billy shoved him. Hard. Cody stumbled back, putting out a hand behind him, but there was nothing to catch him, so he plopped, ass-first, into a puddle of muddy, half-frozen slush.

He came up swearing, ready to fight, but it was a stupid move. He wasn't cut out for fighting, and Billy Ho was built like a dump truck. Cody laughed and hoped he sounded convincing. "Hey," he said, trying not to let his teeth chatter. "No big deal, right?"

At that moment the El Camino coughed and died.

"Balls." Billy reached in and tried the ignition. "This has been giving me trouble all day." He tried several more times, but the heap wouldn't start. "We better push it out of the way."

Iris got behind the wheel. The guys went around to the rear. Billy tossed his long black hair out of his eyes. "Yo, Cody. You gonna stand there, or you gonna help?"

Cody threw off his backpack and his anger. Here was his chance to get in good with these guys. Being one of their crowd might even make school bearable.

Once they'd moved the car to a parking spot, Iris pouted at Billy. "*Now* where's my ride home?"

Just for a second, Cody recalled his conversation with Sam about passengers in the Jeep. Only if there were enough seat belts to go around. They were one short, but Cody didn't even hesitate. Screw Sam. He'd never find out. "I'll give all of you a lift,"

"Excellent, man. I need to get to the auto-parts store." They all piled into the Jeep. Cody's jeans felt squishy, making him wish for a hot shower and clean towels. As he pulled out of the parking lot, he heard a faint "Hey, Cody!"

"Who's that?" Billy asked.

"Ugh, Molly Lightning." Iris wrinkled her nose. "The *cowgirl*."

Molly emerged from a knot of students. "Can you drop me by the arena?"

"No!" Billy said, putting his hand on Cody's shoulder. "Jeez, the teacher's kid. Her mom's flunking me."

Cody had a split second to decide. He made eye contact with Molly as she approached the Jeep. Taking a deep breath, he said, "Sorry, kid. Car's full." At least he didn't have to lie. He punched the gas pedal too hard, sending up a plume of mud and slush.

"Good move, man!" Ethan thumped him on the back.

Cody glanced in the rearview mirror to see Molly standing on the curb, shaking out her book bag. He felt something icier than the parking lot slush. Something that wouldn't come off with a shower and a stack of towels.

Friday

A n old El Camino, pockmarked by rust, came fast up the drive to Lonepine, spitting a rooster tail of gravel and ice in its wake. Favoring her wounded leg, Scout had to dart to the side of the road to avoid getting hit. Annoyed, Sam walked out onto the porch. He was still in his office clothes, having just got home after a long day of clinic visits.

Behind the El Camino came Cody in the Jeep. Patience, Sam told himself as he crossed the yard to the horse barn. No one ever said this fatherhood gig was going to be easy.

But as four disreputable-looking kids tumbled out of the vehicles—the most disreputable of all being his son— he gritted his teeth into a forced smile for the introductions. With a decided lack of grace, Cody gestured at each boy in turn—Billy, Ethan, and Jason. He recognized Billy from providing his school sports physical every year. The kid was wearing a jacket that looked brand-new and unaffordable. Sam grew annoyed at himself for having the thought. He was turning into a pretty judgmental s.o.b. lately.

A throaty screech, far off but distinct, echoed down from the veil of trees above the meadow. Scout growled and crouched in close to Sam, too smart to run off after the predator a second time. Sam shaded his eyes, studying the blue-shadowed distance, but he saw no movement in the field.

"Hey, guys," Sam said to the boys. "How was school?"

They rolled their eyes in unison. "Sucked," Cody said.

"Yeah?" Sam asked, tugging his tie loose. "You might consider the alternative."

"What, no school? That'd be awesome."

Sam shook his head. "When I was sixteen, I was working ten hours a day unrolling frozen bales of hay. Trust me, it's not awesome."

They didn't trust him, of course. Kids never fell for that "in my day" stuff. He ought to know better.

"I brought the guys over to show them the filly," Cody said.

"Fine. Take it easy around the mare. Don't get between her and—"

"I know, I know," Cody waved a hand. "Always face and acknowledge the mare, blah blah blah."

"You got it."

"Can we use the snowmobiles?"

Sam hesitated. "All right. But they're working vehicles, not toys. So don't screw around—" He stopped. Christ, he was talking to them like an old schoolmarm. "Okay, so you're going to screw around. But be careful. Use the helmets."

"We will," Cody said.

Sam nodded to Cody's friends. "Nice to meet you, but I can't stick around. I need to shower and shave." He rubbed his jaw.

"Big date tonight?" Billy Ho asked with a sly wink.

"I guess you could say that." If you counted a hospital visit as a date.

Cody regarded him with narrow-eyed suspicion. He'd made it clear he didn't favor Sam and Michelle getting to know each other again. Probably a natural reaction—kids raised by single mothers tended to feel threatened by any interloper—but it annoyed the hell out of Sam.

"C'mon." Suddenly in a hurry, Cody headed into the barn. His friends trailed after him, and Sam went back to the house.

He had no idea how to judge what kind of job he'd done with Cody this week. He was a difficult kid. They weren't all like that, Sam thought as he got into the shower and raised his face to the hot needles of the spray. Take Molly Lightning, who lived down the road. Bright, athletic, good student. She had prospects. You could look at her and picture her in a good place in ten years. As for Cody, it was hard to imagine where he was headed. Sam sensed that he'd never been tested. Never been forced to the wall, because Michelle had been so concerned about insulating him—from photographers, from hurt, from want. It wasn't her fault, but everything had come so easy to Cody that he had never learned to work for what he wanted. He maintained a sense of entitlement that bugged Sam. It was a hell of a thing.

So far, the father-and-son bond had eluded them both. There had been moments, here and there, when something, some connection, could be felt. Sam supposed that was all he could hope for at first. Deep down, he still wondered if he wanted more, and his own hesitation bothered him. Above the hiss of the shower, he could hear the nasal whine of snowmobiles being ridden fast. Too fast. He had to force himself not to go yell at them to take it easy. They'd just blow him off anyway, he knew. These kids were like creatures from another planet. He felt awkward around them, as if he had never been that young himself.

He scrubbed himself hard and efficiently, cleaning off the remnants of a rough day. Too many patients, too much red tape, not enough time. At least when he went to see Michelle at the hospital, it would be as a visitor, not a doctor. He was just drying off when he heard someone pounding at the door.

Pulling on a pair of jeans, he hurried downstairs.

Billy Ho stood on the back porch, his eyes wide, looking different from the go-to-hell kid who'd climbed out of the El Camino. "Um, Cody had sort of a . . . problem. With the horses."

Sam was already stuffing his feet into a pair of snow boots by the door. He grabbed a parka from the mudroom and put it on over his bare, damp chest. "What kind of problem?"

"Well, the little horse—the foal—got out."

"No big deal," he said, relaxing. "She'll come back in once we put the mare up. A filly that young won't stray far from her mom."

"No, man. I mean *out*. Like outside the paddock. Then it kind of panicked and took off."

Sam broke into a run. Billy trotted alongside him, breathless, trying to choke out an explanation. "We were just goofing around. No one knew the horse would take off. Cody went after her."

"Where's the mare?"

"She tried to follow the foal out, but Cody put her up. She's pissed, man—"

Sam could hear her. Frantic whinnies and stomping hooves echoed down the breezeway of the barn. He could see the snowmobile trails slashing and crisscrossing the broad slope of the meadow leading up to the woods. Shit. A filly that young would never leave her mother or the familiar terrain of the paddock unless she was truly terror-stricken. The boys had probably herded her uphill on the snowmobiles. As he put on a pair of gloves, he tried to remember what Cody was wearing. School clothes. If he got lost, he'd freeze to death in no time flat.

Sam harnessed a utility sled to one of the snowmobiles. He shot out of the yard, following a crooked line of footprints up the rise behind the barn. The panicked foal had traveled fast; he could see the stretch of its stride in the snow. Despite its young age, it could outrun Cody, especially if it was scared and lost without its mother.

The footprints disappeared into a cover of larch and fir trees. Sam drove into the woods, feeling a shower of golden larch needles rain down on him. He had to slow down to dodge the trees. Before long the density of the trees stopped him altogether. The sled behind the machine was too wide to negotiate the forest. Turning off the snowmobile and cursing through clenched teeth, he continued on foot.

In the silence after the engine's rumble, he heard a sound midway between a cough and a snarl. His blood ran cold. It was the distinctive call of a mountain lion. A big cat didn't usually bother things it couldn't easily kill, but if it felt cornered or hungry enough, it might take a swipe at a young horse. Or a kid. The eerie screeching escalated, a deadly rasp that echoed through the winter woods.

Sam climbed to the top of the ridge. There, he spied

a bitten-off section of snow that had crumbled down the opposite face in a small avalanche. Pressed against the curve of the scarp was Cody, waist-deep in snow, the horse floundering, its skinny legs sunk uselessly into the bank.

A livid smear of blood stained the snow.

Crouched on a bare rock above the boy and the foal was the cat. This one was big, maybe ninety pounds.

Its paw slashed out, claws extended, lips peeled back in a snarl. Cody had grabbed a branch and held it out, trying to fend off the reaching paw.

"Yah!" Sam yelled, waving his arms. "Yah, beat it, you old bitch!"

The cat froze and faced him with glittering eyes.

"Stay calm, Cody, and don't crouch down or turn your back, okay?" Sam called.

The boy's face was gray with terror.

"These cats like small prey," Sam said, praying the kid wouldn't panic. "Don't run, or you might trigger her instinct to attack. Keep waving the branch. You have to act aggressive."

He walked steadily toward the cougar, and his gut twisted as she swung her tawny gaze back to the boy and the horse. "Don't look it in the eye," he yelled, cupping his hands around his mouth.

The long tail switched slowly, rhythmically, nervous as a rattlesnake. The horse fell still, its stamina gone.

"If she attacks, you fight back, Cody," Sam hollered, hurrying as fast as he dared. "You hear me, son? Fight back!"

"O-okay," Cody said, his voice thin, snow-muffled. He brandished the branch like a sword.

The mountain lion coiled like a spring. For a sickening moment, Sam feared it would attack. A cougar always went for the head and neck. He reached the top of the bank and waved his arms, kicked up snow. The mountain lion retreated a few steps, turned, snarled. He yelled and waved his arms again, close enough now to see a string of drool drip from her mouth. Sam grabbed a chunk of ice and hurled it as hard as he could. Grumbling low in her throat, she slunk into the woods.

"Cody!" Sam half ran, half tumbled down the bank. "You okay? What's all this blood?"

The kid's bare hand kept its hold on the mane of the horse. "I'm okay. Let's get her up. She's stuck, see?" His face was dull white, his voice shaking.

"What's bleeding?" Sam demanded.

Cody held up his free hand. "Hit it on something on my way down." His chin trembled; maybe it was a shiver; Sam didn't know. "Help me, Dad."

It just seemed to slip out, the *Dad* part. Probably didn't mean a thing, but it had an incredibly powerful effect on Sam. "Okay, keep hold of the mane, you've got it. She's in a panic because she can't get her footing. We'll help her up the bank." Inch by inch, they pulled the foal upward. She was terrified, her eyes rolling, her hooves kicking out every which way.

"Watch the feet," Sam said through his teeth. They had no bridle, no way to control the horse except by brute strength. The minutes seemed to crawl as they struggled up to the top of the escarpment. The snow crumbled beneath them, sending them back a foot for every few feet they gained. Cody was panting, almost sobbing, when they reached the top, then staggered, pushing and pulling the horse to the snowmobile. She flailed every step of the way, twisting and snapping, hooves slashing out, impossible to contain.

"I'll hold her on the sled and you drive," Sam instructed. Using his teeth, he peeled off his gloves and tossed them to Cody. "Put those on. You'll get frostbite." He wrestled the foal onto the sled and Cody held her in place. Off they went, a smooth ride down the mountain, then into the paddock. The El Camino was gone. He wasn't surprised the kids had hightailed it at the first sign of trouble.

Sylvia had practically torn a hole in the stable door. The little one trotted inside and Sylvia was on her immediately, sniffing and licking her from stem to stern. Cody stood in the breezeway, teeth chattering, his nose bright red.

"Thanks," he said in a quiet voice.

"I'm just glad I found you."

The boy hesitated, then looked him in the eye. "I'm glad I found you, too."

And then without even thinking about it, Sam hugged him. It could have been awkward, but it wasn't. It was the most natural thing in the world to let a sudden wave of love for this boy spill out and over, to gather him in his arms in a hug that tried hard to make up for all the years of hugs he'd missed. Sam's throat felt tight as he stepped back. He didn't know if he was cut out for this. He'd never felt anything like the icy burn of terror that had ripped through him when he'd seen Cody in danger. His nerves were shot.

Cody was shuddering violently now. "Are you going to tell my mom?"

"Your mother's got enough to worry about." Sam grabbed his arm, pulling him toward the house. "We need to warm you up, have a look at that hand," he said.

A minute later they sat at the kitchen table, Cody's arm propped on a towel while Sam used tweezers to clean the grit out of the cut.

"When was the last time you had a tetanus shot?" Sam asked.

"Not sure." Cody winced as the tweezers dug deeper. "I had a bunch of shots before going to camp two summers ago. Ow!"

"Sorry. Don't watch. It's making you tense up."

Cody turned his head away. "Who's Alice McPhee?" he asked, focusing on the stack of junk mail on the table. The top item was a lingerie catalog with a label bearing Alice's name.

Sam hesitated. "My ex-wife."

Cody drew breath with a hiss. "Man, I didn't know you had a wife."

"I don't."

"It's bogus not to tell me you were married before."

"I was married before."

"I mean it's bogus that you didn't tell me right off."

"Cody—"

"Does my mom know?"

"She knows." Sam tweezed a sliver of dirt from the wound. "Hey, cut me some slack. I'm new at this."

"Yeah, well, so am I," Cody muttered.

Sam wanted to take the focus off him and Alice. She represented a failure he didn't like to talk about, so he changed the subject. "So what happened?" he asked, concentrating on the deep gash.

Cody shrugged, some of that old screw-you attitude slipping back into place.

"Hold still," Sam said through his teeth. "What happened?"

"We were just goofing around, man. We let the mare and the foal out into the paddock. Then we started riding snowmobiles and . . . the filly got out and took off. The noise confused her, and she went up the hill."

"Because you left the paddock gate open."

"Somebody did. I don't know who."

"Do you think that matters? You were in charge, Cody."

"Everything worked out okay, no harm done. Back off, man."

Sam's hand didn't falter, his gaze didn't waver as he cleaned the cut. But inside, he froze. "Everything *didn't* work out. A valuable filly almost died or broke a leg. Sylvia could've injured herself going ballistic in her stall. You almost got killed. What if I hadn't been around to come after you?"

"Man, you haven't been around for sixteen years, and I survived." Contempt dripped from his voice.

Sam stopped working. He set down the tweezers and regarded the sullen, defiant face so like his own—and yet so strange to him. "Well, I'm back now. And the bullshit is over. I figured putting you in charge of the filly would be good for you. Don't prove me wrong, Cody."

"Yeah, well, maybe you *are* wrong about me."

Sam got out a bottle of disinfectant. "This'll sting."

"Ouch. Hey, man." Cody tensed the muscles in his arm.

"Maybe you'd better choose your friends more carefully. You could use a few more responsibilities—"

"Hey—"

"—don't interrupt. You screwed up, and there are consequences. If you thought the work around here was hard before, you—"

Cody snatched his hand away before Sam was finished. "You're not my frigging jailer." He stood up fast, his chair legs scraping the floor. "What do you want with me?" he demanded.

Sam didn't have an answer for that. *Did* he want a

kid, or was it a concept he liked better in the abstract? No matter, he told himself. The reality was, he had a kid— and a difficult one at that. He had no idea if he knew how to be a good father. He picked up a length of gauze. "Let me wrap that wound."

Cody grabbed it from him. "I'll take care of it my- self." He backed away, pausing in the kitchen doorway. "I know what you want with my mom, and I can't do any- thing about that, but stay the hell away from me."

Saturday

Chapter 41

It seemed like half the population of Missoula found some reason to stop by Gavin's room. They were timid at first, asking if he needed anything, making small talk. As the week wore on and he was moved from the SICU to a private room, their numbers increased. Nurses, aides, orderlies, residents, volunteers. The timidity fell away and then finally, on a rush of hard-won courage, they started asking for his autograph.

The mistake had been in giving out that first one, to a brown-eyed aide who looked a little like Carolyn.

"You remind me of the last woman who dumped me," he said, scrawling his signature on the back of a work-order pad. "No, on second thought, you're prettier."

She must have alerted the whole ward, maybe the whole floor, because all through the week he had to deal with furtive fans. He'd given the hospital strict instructions that the transplant was to be kept private, but strict instructions only went so far.

"They're wearing me out, Doc," he said to Maggie Kehr when she stopped in. She wore a shamrock in her lapel and a little leprechaun clinging to her scope. "You've got to let me go home and get some rest."

She smiled down at the chart she'd been writing on. "I want to keep you at least a week."

"It's St. Paddy's Day, fer chrissake," he said in an ex- aggerated brogue. "I've been lying around on my poor arse long enough."

"A week, Gavin."

"Aren't you the one who said it's the best kidney trans- plant you've ever seen?"

"Yes, but—"

"Didn't you say we set some sort of record, getting the kidney to work? Didn't you remove the catheter forty- eight hours sooner than you thought you could?"

"I did, Gavin—"

"Didn't I just take the healthiest piss you ever saw a man take?"

"Now *that*," she said, "is debatable."

"Only because guys piss for you all the time."

"One of the great perks of my specialty."

"I'm going home, Doc. With or without your bless- ing, I'm checking out when Michelle leaves here." She was being discharged today, and he was bound and de- termined to go with her. There was something vaguely horrifying about being left behind while his daughter went back to Crystal City. If he stayed, he'd feel like the loser in some battle or race.

"Never say whining doesn't work," Dr. Kehr said, signing a sheaf of forms.

"What do you mean?"

"You're a free man, Gavin. You've got the luck of the Irish on your side."

"I love you, Maggie, I really do."

"You're an old coot. Take care of that kidney now. They're a little hard to come by."

"My body is now Fort Knox."

"Just make sure that body doesn't miss a single follow-up appointment or a single pill. A pharmaceutical therapist will stop in to go over your meds and your daily log with you."

"Again, huh?" He didn't argue. From the very start, they'd impressed on him the importance of taking the antirejection medications. With a decided lack of sympathy, Maggie had warned him that the drugs would make him itch and sweat and suffer from impotence. He'd probably gain weight, and it would show in the cheeks and gut.

Not a pretty picture. Still, given the alternative, he'd settle for night sweats and chipmunk cheeks. But if this didn't work and he died, what the hell. It had brought him and Michelle together. It was up to them to find the things that mattered. Maybe they hadn't quite found that just yet, but they would. He knew they would.

The discharge was nicely choreographed so that he and Michelle were both wheeled into the main lobby at the same time from opposite wings. Smiling volunteers gave them green carnations for St. Patrick's Day. Gavin looked around suspiciously, thinking maybe the media had managed to barge in. He'd hate having this moment captured by some shutterbug who'd get five grand for the photo.

But what a moment it was.

Michelle. His daughter. She had always been incredibly beautiful, blond and luminous, with a way of looking at the world that was completely original, completely unique. It was something he had seen even in the cray-oned Father's Day cards she'd dutifully sent him as a small child. Seated in the wheelchair, smiling at him, she touched his heart.

He felt his throat fill with thick emotion, and the act-ing skill that usually came so naturally deserted him. He held out his hand. "Thank you, honey," he said, suddenly reaching forward to touch her cheek. "You know, you're the best thing I ever did."

For a moment she just blinked at him, almost comi-cally speechless. They'd seen each other now and then through the week, visiting, talking quietly, but this was different. They had done what they'd set out to do. They were going home now.

She took his hand and pressed it against her cheek. "All set, Daddy?"

"Yes. I want to tell you, I haven't felt this good in two years. I'm not sick anymore. No matter what I'm doing or thinking, I just stop in the middle of it and say to my-self, 'I'm not sick anymore.'"

"That's the point." Her smiled widened. "Ready?"

"Past ready." He signaled to the orderly pushing the chair and put on an English accent. "Driver, to the eleva-tors."

"Feels good to be going home."

Gavin wondered what she meant. "Home" as in Blue Rock, or "home" as in Seattle? He didn't know much about her life there, had only met two of her friends. Natalie was great. Brad Lovell was . . . adequate. The sort of solid guy you'd want for your daughter. Except that you wanted a guy to look at your daughter with worship, pure and simple. Not pride of ownership, which was what Gavin had detected in Brad's manner.

Gavin's burgundy Cadillac pulled up beneath the

awning. He expected his foreman, Jake, to get out, but instead, it was Cody. He sent Michelle a questioning look, narrowing his gaze suspiciously. "Did you know about this?"

She laughed. "Uh-huh."

He gave a low whistle. "I think I'd rather wheel this chair home."

"Be nice, Dad. The drive's nothing. A straight shot up the highway. It hasn't snowed, so the roads are clear. And he's worked really hard. Sam said he was practicing all week."

Gavin saw her knuckles tighten on the arms of her chair. "So how did the week go, him staying with Sam?"

She watched the suitcases being loaded into the trunk. "I don't know. He hasn't said much." Finally, she turned to him. "Daddy, what if he does better with Sam than he did with me?"

Gavin wished he was close enough to touch her. "It's not a competition." It was all he had time to say, when she needed so much more from him. She needed the years he couldn't give back to her, when pride and anger had kept them apart. "We'll be all right," he said, and vowed to make it so even if it killed him. "We're going to be fine."

The doors swished open, and out they went. Cody looked a little out of place, but very determined behind the wheel. Probably gave the kid a charge, driving Gavin's Caddy. Something about driving two people who were full of stitches and drugs probably made him feel particularly important.

"Here goes nothing," Gavin pushed himself up out of the chair.

The electric doors opened, and he stepped out into the bracing cold air. He wore a shirt and slacks that hadn't been cut to fit over a dialysis bag, and his blood sang. He wasn't nervous about the kid's driving. How could he be? Something magical had happened to him in the hospital, and now he was going home.

"I do love the occasional miracle," he said.

Sunday

ody was pretending he wasn't nervous about school in the morning, Michelle observed that evening. It made her nuts that she'd been so out of it the past week, unable to be there for him every second, helping him through the ordeal of starting a new school. She had been there for every moment of his life, big and small, but last week, he'd been on his own.

And—wonder of wonders—the world had not come to an end. She was thankful he'd survived that first week, but she could tell he was anxious about the days to come. She knew that look, the shifting of his eyes, the jiggling of his foot against the chair as he ate dinner—a feast prepared by a beaming Tadao. They had eaten in the huge den of the main house, with Gavin and Michelle reclining like Romans on sofas. She had asked Cody if he liked his classes, if he'd made any friends, how he'd liked staying with Sam, but he'd only given her one-syllable answers. That was all she'd heard all week. She'd questioned him about the bandage on his hand, but all he'd said was he'd cut himself working at Sam's.

Gavin drank a glass of wine, his first since he was diagnosed, and he got almost teary-eyed as he tasted the Jordan Cabernet. With both Tadao and Michelle supervising, he took his evening meds and noted them in his daily log. Though he didn't whisper a word of fatigue, Gavin excused himself to go to bed early.

After an extralong shower, Cody went to his room, leaving Michelle lying on the sofa, fiddling with the TV remote. She was oddly manic and restless on her first night away from the hospital. She felt fragile and vulnerable from the lingering pain of an invasive procedure. She worried about bumping into things, worried about sleeping, worried about her father, worried about how she'd feel seeing Sam again.

But when she looked out and saw the snow begin to fall, her worries seemed to have no more substance than the weightless snowflakes settling over the yard. That was the gift that had been given back to her the morning of the surgery. She hadn't recognized her old friend at first, but it was just as Joseph Rain had said, so many years ago. *The gift comes to you in secret. If your heart and your mind are not open to inspiration, then it passes you by.*

Now, finally, in the midwinter of her life, she understood. It was the space she had glimpsed between the two parting curtains. That was the offer. What she did with it was up to her.

She didn't allow herself to think. Ignoring her doctor's orders, she bundled up and walked through the blowing snow to the small dwelling at the end of the compound, the studio she had abandoned seventeen years before. There, she turned on the heat, rubbed her hands together, and took a deep, steadying breath. Physically, she felt dead tired. But she couldn't quell the restless need inside her. Time enough later for sleep, she decided.

Natalie—bless her—had set up stretched and gessoed Belgian linen canvases and laid out new paints and brushes. But even if these had been the crudest of supplies, it wouldn't have mattered, because at last she was ready. She lowered the legs of the easel and positioned it in front of the old red couch so she didn't have to stand up. Then she rolled up her sleeves and began.

She worked at a fever pitch from a vision that had been hidden inside her for years. It was a painful emergence, a birthing of sorts. For someone so conditioned to look outside herself, to emulate the hard lines and precise angles of that which could be seen and quickly grasped by someone paging through a magazine, it was a difficult transition. But for once that didn't stop her. After enduring what she had endured this past week, nothing could seem hard.

The transplant, confronting mortality, and coming face-to-face with her past had forced her hand. From her slumbering subconscious emerged the inspiration, the sense of awe and wonder, that had once meant everything to her.

The shapes and colors of her soul exploded onto the canvas. She didn't think, didn't evaluate. She just worked. And inside her, something happened. Something magical and true and luminous. She felt free, racing above the earth, elation pouring over her, out through her hands and her heart, becoming something wholly original, wholly her own.

She had no sense of time passing. She simply sank

into a strange beta state where nothing mattered except the painting, where the colors and emotions came from, and what the images were. The urge was sensual, predatory, dangerous, seductive, and in a leap of faith, she gave herself to it utterly.

When Sam McPhee walked into the studio, she should have been surprised, but she was not. It made a terrible, wonderful sense that he would come here alone, searching for her.

He stood in the dim foyer, his shoulders dusted with new snow, his face unsmiling, his eyes filled with a look she recognized from long, long ago.

"I saw the light on," he said.

Suddenly nervous, she grabbed a linseed rag and wiped her hands. "I . . . couldn't sleep."

"You sure as hell ought to be. You're recovering from surgery—"

"I'm all right, Sam. Don't doctor me. I've had enough doctors hovering over me, okay? I'm on the couch, see?"

"You're supposed to be flat on your back."

"That would make it hard to paint."

"Worked for Michelangelo." He studied her, and she braced herself for further argument, but he didn't pursue it. Taking off his coat, he hung it on a hook behind the door. He wore jeans and a thick flannel shirt.

"You're staring," he said.

"Am I?" One Christmas, she had bought Brad a shirt exactly like that. It was still in his closet, still folded with the pins in it.

"Michelle. Are you feeling okay?"

It was a question from Sam the doctor. Not Sam the ex-boyfriend. Not Sam the father of her child.

"Yes." She settled back on the old sofa. "I'm fine, really. My father and I are fine. We had a nice dinner to celebrate coming home. And I'm glad you came over. I want to thank you for keeping Cody last week."

He lifted the corner of his mouth in a half grin. "He's a barrel of laughs. We're going to have to do something about him being so accident-prone."

We. Did he really mean that? "He never did explain how he hurt his hand."

He tucked his thumbs in his back pockets. "Barn chores," he said dismissively.

"It was sweet of you to take care of him, Sam."

"I didn't do it to be sweet." He crossed the room and sat down beside her, very close, and the unique smell of him was achingly familiar. He touched her chin. "So you're fine."

"Uh-huh."

"Been painting."

"Yes." She held her breath while he regarded the tall, spattered easel with the halogen lights shining down. "It's not finished."

She watched him, still not daring to breathe. She saw the impact of the painting go through him as if he'd touched an electrified fence. His arms, legs, shoulders, neck stiffened; then he turned to her quickly.

"Wow," he said.

"Is that good wow or bad wow?"

"You mean you don't know?"

"Sam, the paint's still wet. I barely know my own name."

He held out his hand. She hesitated, then took it, studying the broad canvas. She saw an abstraction of pure emotion. It was no use. She had no objectivity.

"It's the first time in years I've done a painting that wasn't for work," she admitted.

"It's about damned time, Michelle."

"But what do you *think*, Sam?"

"Hell, I'm no art expert. To me, it's amazing. I look at this, and it makes me think differently. Makes me want to stare, fall into it, I don't know. I don't have the vocabulary or the expertise."

She tried to see the picture as he saw it. The composition was classical, straight out of Art 101. But so were van Gogh's compositions. The principal motif in the middle came from her vision—the mysterious space between the parted curtains. Within that space dwelled an abstract study of color, light and shadow. She saw pain and passion and depth, and realized she was looking at a painting that expressed precisely what she wanted it to express. Whether or not that had any particular value didn't matter.

"You know what?" she said suddenly. "You don't have to tell me if it's good or not. It's the painting that came out of me."

"I think it's incredible."

"Do you think it could be the drugs? I'm on Percocet."

"It's not the drugs, Michelle."

They sat together for long, silent moments, staring at the painting. She felt drained in a good way—the tension had flowed through her. She was the crucible. All the feelings, emotions, good and bad, had melted down inside her and then emerged in a new form, a thing of power and beauty, this painting.

She looked out the window, weighing her thoughts. What if she asked him about Cody's week? Then Sam would know Cody had barely spoken to her. But then she remembered her father's words: *It's not a competition.*

"What?" Sam asked, regarding her reflection in the blackened window. "Are you all right?"

"Just . . . thinking. I'd like to hear how last week went from your perspective. With you and Cody."

"It was fine, Michelle. Not every second, but we got along all right." Lord, just like Cody. He wasn't telling her a thing.

"What does he think of school?"

"Sucks," Sam said, emulating Cody's sullen manner. "But what else is he going to say?"

"Has he made any friends?"

"Hard to say. He was hanging with some guys. I don't know if you'd call them friends. He spent some time with Molly Lightning, too."

It felt . . . normal, talking over her son with Sam. Maybe this was what married couples did. She recoiled from the thought. "I feel so bad, making him go to a strange school."

"You ought to try to get over feeling bad on the kid's behalf."

"I'm a mother. It's what I *do*." She fell silent.

After a while, Sam said, "I was surprised Brad didn't stick around for the surgery."

Michelle felt a stab of defensiveness. She didn't know how to tell him about Brad. It was too . . . embarrassing. And he might read something into Brad's departure that wasn't there. *Would* she have broken off with Brad if Sam hadn't been in the picture? She wanted to believe she would have, but the truth was, she didn't know for certain.

"His job is incredibly demanding," she said evasively. Color heated her cheeks. She had let Sam make love to her. Did he understand that she hadn't given herself to him lightly? Did he understand she had never done anything remotely like that before? Did he understand that she'd been swept away by yearning and nostalgia and a passion that she needed more than air?

Or were those just excuses?

"If you're so committed to some other guy, then why is he in Seattle while I'm sitting here doing this?"

"Doing what?"

"This."

He cupped his hands over her shoulders and kissed her long and searchingly just then. His embrace caught her, supported her, and imprinted the texture and taste of his mouth on her, and when it was over, she felt stupid and dazed.

She wanted to speak out, to stop him, but she held a hush in her throat, trusting the knowing tenderness of his hands as he caressed her. He drew from her a shameless and powerful wanting.

"We can't do this, Sam." Guilt shuddered through her. If she let him make love to her again, she was a goner.

He pulled back and gave her a look. "Only because you're still recovering. Otherwise, we'd make friends with this old couch again."

Laughing at her blush, he helped her turn off the lights in the studio and walked her back to the guesthouse. At the front door, he kissed her again, like a suitor dropping her off after a pleasant date. She went inside and stood at the window in the darkened living room, watching his headlights illuminate the snowy night and letting the tears come, feeling her heart shatter. What sort of life would she have had if they had stayed together?

If only.

The big burning issue in her life.

If only she had believed in Sam, if only she had worked harder to find him and tell him about the baby, her life would have been so different. They might have supported each other through the hard years, and now they'd be a family.

No. If Sam had known about Cody, there would have been no rodeo circuit for him, no medical school, no Yucatán. Burdened with a family, he might not have become a doctor at all, and all the lives he had saved would be lost, all the wounds that he'd healed and all the illnesses he'd cured might have gone untreated. Perhaps everything happened for a reason. Perhaps their estrangement was some sort of preordained event, designed to make their lives work out the way they had.

The thought nagged at her. She was back in Crystal City, wasn't she? Beyond the obvious, what could be the reason for that?

It was idiotic to speculate. Gavin's illness wasn't part of some cosmic plan. It was something that had just . . . happened. Meeting Sam again was pure coincidence. She shouldn't make any more of it than that. Certainly she shouldn't be having these thoughts just because Sam McPhee had a way of kissing her until she couldn't see straight, because he made love like a form of worship.

She had failed with Brad. Sam had failed with Alice. Maybe the two of them just weren't cut out for the long haul.

The thought followed her to the edge of sleep.

Monday

M ichelle spent the day lost in thoughts of Sam. Her father was in bed, on the phone trying to arrange the renewal of his pilot's license, and Cody was at school. Michelle tried reading, watching television, sketching a plan for a painting, but after a while she simply gave in to memories of Sam. She felt herself being sucked back into the past, dredging her heart through memories that burned. He was the first boy she had ever loved, and that one long-ago summer stood out vividly as a magical time. Each sunset burned brighter, more beautiful than the last. Each moonrise glowed with a promise she had felt certain was meant for her, only for her. She had been so naively young back then. She thought her love was like a river, ever flowing, never ceasing; nothing and no one could stop it—not even the granite boulders that divided the stream. She used to tell Sam her wildest dreams, and he would confess his deepest secrets. They were so open with each other, so trusting. She had thought she would remain in that dream-state of bliss all the rest of her life. She hadn't understood that those golden days were rare, never to be lived again.

The hours passed so quickly that she felt startled when she heard someone drive up. Getting out of bed, she saw Cody getting out of the Jeep Sam had lent him. It was a cranky old thing, one that would have caused Cody acute embarrassment to be seen driving in Seattle. But here it was different. Her son was different, she thought, observing his assurance as he hefted his backpack over one shoulder and headed for the barn complex.

She put on a jacket and went outside, finding him with the farrier and a bright sorrel horse in the crossties. The hot smell of the blowtorch pervaded the air.

"Howdy, ma'am." The farrier spoke past the wad of snoose that bulged in his lower lip.

"Hey, Mom." Cody sat with a box of shoeing nails in his lap.

She couldn't help smiling. "I guess this is something you don't see every day."

The farrier aimed a stream of tobacco juice into the waste trough. "Hand me one of those sixes," he said, all business.

Michelle was surprised that Cody could distinguish a six-nail from a five or an eight. When the horse shied, she was even more surprised to see her son help out while the farrier worked.

"Let's see what's going on in the arena," Michelle suggested when the shoeing was finished.

They stood at the rail, watching some of the hands work with the broncs. The horses wore flank straps to irritate them so they'd kick up their back legs, the higher the better. Raising rodeo stock was serious business. A good bronc or bull could become famous in its own right, and many Blue Rock animals had, but it required constant care and training.

"Until we came here, I never even knew they trained bucking broncs," Cody said, lapping his elbows over the top rail. "I just thought they were wild horses."

"Some cowboys have been known to ride their broncs home after a show. They just take off the flank strap and the horse turns into a kitten."

They watched for a while, and Michelle took in the clear bright air, the sound of hoofbeats and equine snorts, the sharp profile of white mountains against blue sky. The ranch hands and horses worked together with a rhythm that seemed ancient, timeless. And in some way, crucial.

"You were a bit late getting home from school," she said to Cody. "Did you stay after?"

"I gave some kids a ride."

"I'm glad you've been making friends." She took a long, slow breath and stared straight ahead at the jagged line of mountains. She didn't want her expression to sway her son's response in any way. "Hey, Cody?"

"Yeah?"

"Uh, Brad and I aren't going to be seeing each other anymore."

From the corner of her eye, she saw him stiffen. "Yeah?" he said again, this time with a different inflection.

"He's a good guy, but we weren't really going anywhere." She hesitated. Cody didn't seem to have any comment. Michelle asked, "Do you ever wonder what it would be like if we lived here instead of Seattle?"

"Hell, no, Mom," he said, almost panicking as he jumped down from the fence and backed away. He touched the healing wound on his head where the stitches had been. "There's *nothing* here. Nothing! We live in Seattle. It's where we belong." He paced up and down in the snow. "No one moves in the middle of high school. It sucks here." Eventually he slowed down, then stopped, leaning against a fence post. "You're not really thinking about moving here, are you?"

"I've been thinking about a lot of things, Cody."

He picked at the gauze bandage on his hand.

"I wish you'd tell me how it really went last week, with you and Sam," she said, frustrated.

He stuck the bandaged hand in his pocket. "It didn't *go* any particular way. He's just some guy to me. We got thrown together because of you, that's all."

Could it be? No chemistry, no magic, just circumstance between them?

"It's too early to tell."

"There's no point. We're going back soon. Right, Mom? Right?"

She didn't answer him.

Tuesday

Chapter 44

S ome days, it was the emptiness that hit Sam hardest. It didn't happen often; long ago he had taught himself to survive without support from another person. Yet every once in a while, it caught him, that emptiness. Especially after having Cody around the week before.

To make things worse, today had been one of those days in doctoring that made him wonder why he thought he could help anyone. First there was the forty-year smoker who had decided to hold Sam personally responsible for his inoperable lung cancer. Followed by a harried mother whose HMO benefits had just been cut—she could no longer bring her asthmatic son in for therapy. She had to lie awake at night, crying helplessly while he wheezed for breath. Then there was a guy with a broken hand—claimed he'd done it on a hay baler, but when, shortly afterward,

Deputy O'Shea showed up, Sam knew the cowboy had done it on some other guy's face. He had seen Mrs. Duckworth for imaginary aches and pains, turned away a drifter who came looking for a prescription for narcotics, and listened as a teenage girl wrestled over whether or not to terminate her six-week pregnancy. Given the recent changes in Sam's life, her dilemma took on a painful, personal edge.

As he drove home, he felt tension building in his neck and shoulders, and he knew it was one of those days when the empty house would echo with the void that existed, usually hidden, in his life. He used to visit Candy on the rez for some uncomplicated sex, but that wasn't what he needed. He had to quit fooling himself. What would it be like, he wondered, to walk into a house that was warm and glowing with evening lights? That smelled of dinner and the presence of another human being?

What would it be like to talk about his day, really talk, not just complain or vent his frustration but to explain what went on in his heart, in his soul, when he had to look a good man in the eye and tell him he had cancer or when he lost a patient to the absurd vagaries of the health-insurance system?

He had attempted, long ago, to create that sort of life. It hadn't worked. He and Alice had both tried, but their marriage had felt wrong, artificial. The end-of-work conversations were strained. The affection felt both false and forced. He was always pulling back when he should forge ahead.

The thing about it was, Sam knew how to take care of a needy person. He'd done it all his life, and never knew any other way. But he didn't know how to love a woman who didn't *need* him. A woman who could stand strong without support. Life had taught him that relationships were hard work, not a quest for joy and completion.

Ordinarily there was nothing Sam couldn't get over by sitting down and having a beer with Edward, tossing a rope at a dummy steer, or taking one of the horses on a long, solitary ride up to the hot springs. But now that Michelle was back, he wanted more.

More than talk.

He wanted a connection, and he wanted it with Michelle. God knew, he'd seen enough other women over the years to understand that it only worked with a certain person.

Christ, she must think he was a maniac, coming on to her while she still had a healing incision. He wondered if she was pissed about that.

He swore between his teeth, and when he reached the turnoff for Lonepine he drove right on by. Kept going until he got to Blue Rock Ranch, its imposing gates and the dark boulders at the entrance as ostentatious as a castle drawbridge.

A glare of lights burning in the window of the studio beckoned him. He didn't pause to think, just parked the truck and walked to the door. Through the sidelight he could see her on the sofa, and he paused, waiting for the nervous energy churning through him to calm down.

She was in another world; he could tell by the look on her face. He knew that look. It was the expression she had worn as a girl, totally absorbed by the images on the big canvas in front of her. Michelle was a beautiful woman, there was no doubt about that. But Michelle in the act of creation was beyond beautiful. As she painted, there was an incandescent quality about her that made him believe in her with all that he was.

He knocked at the door, but didn't wait for her to answer it. "It's me," he called, letting himself in. "Don't get up."

"Sam." She sounded pleased. But cautious.

"Where's Cody?"

"He's over at the main house, doing homework. He needed to do an assignment on a computer, so he's working in my dad's study."

"How's Gavin doing?"

She squirted something on her hands and scrubbed them with a rag. "He's amazing. Stronger and healthier every day. He complains about the medications he has to take, all the side effects, but he's faithful about it. We had a checkup today, and my staples are gone." Drying her hands, she pulled her knees up to her chest. "I'm so glad it's over." She caught his expression. "The doctor in you probably feels compelled to point out that we're not out of the woods yet. The transplant team warned us about rejection episodes, but I've already put my father on notice. He wouldn't dare reject my kidney."

She smiled and spoke lightly, though he could tell she worried. Rejection episodes were always devastating. Between Michelle and her father, more than the kidney was at risk.

"These days, the episodes are treatable," he said. "I recommend you quit worrying about something that hasn't happened and might not."

"Okay. Thanks, Sam."

"Michelle, about the other night—I was damned pushy."

Her face darkened with a blush. "Was that an apology?"

"Well, I'm not sorry I kissed you like that."

She ducked her head and fell silent.

"Can I see what you're working on?" He hung his coat on a hook behind the door.

"Um, sure." She angled the easel toward him. "I'm in advertising, remember? I'm used to people looking over my shoulder. Breathing down my neck, even."

He walked over to the easel. It was the abstract painting she had been working on before. The big, violently emotional images hit him on a visceral level. Maybe he was reading a lot into it, yet he thought he could see the rage and the melancholy, but more than that, the sense of hope radiating through a distorted, two-sided structure near the center. It was a strange and moving work, startling and possibly disturbing.

"Michelle, this is no advertising art."

"I thought I'd work on some things for the firm, but I keep wanting to paint." She shrugged apologetically.

Her attitude bothered him. "Don't apologize for doing work like this."

"I'm not apologizing. I'm just—"

"Don't explain this or rationalize it, either. Not to me."

She glared at him. "I wasn't."

"And don't get defensive on me. It's a bad start, especially when you consider what I came to say."

She eyed him warily. "And what's that?"

He took a deep, steadying breath. Held her gaze with his. "For seventeen years you were dead to me," he said. "I had to live my life as if you'd never existed. Then, out of the blue, you come back here."

Her hands twisted in the hem of her painting smock. "I didn't come to torture you."

"True. But your coming here made something happen. Something new and good."

"Sam, that's all in the past."

"Look, if it was just a youthful fling, we would have

forgotten, would have moved on. I know, because in seventeen years, I never forgot you, and believe me, it's not for lack of trying. It's because I never stopped loving you, Michelle."

She tore her gaze from his, shaking her head. "How do I know I didn't just catch you between 'tryings'? How do I know your sudden interest in me isn't because of Cody?"

"He's a part of this, too. And you know better than I do that he's not an easy kid. But he makes me want to try like hell to work this out."

She went to the long worktable by the easel and started cleaning up, her hands moving nervously as she put the caps back on tubes and swirled paintbrushes in jars of cleaner.

"What is it you want from me?" she asked.

"For starters, I want you to sit back down. You're supposed to be resting."

"I'm sick of resting." She worked faster, finishing her cleanup with an air of defiance. That was her way. Finish one thing before starting another. Finish cleaning up the paints before you give your attention to a man baring his soul.

He waited for her to finish. When she finally did, he said, "I've been thinking about you a lot, Michelle. You don't seem happy, and your happiness matters to me."

She wadded up her smock between her hands. "Don't pretend this is about me and my happiness, Sam. It's about you—"

"Let me finish, damn it." He knew he was stepping out on thin ice, but he'd already decided to take the risk. "You asked what I want from you. Why didn't you ask what I want to *give* you?"

"Why should I think you have anything to give me?"

"You've trained yourself not to expect anything from anyone. You're the giver, Michelle, not the taker. You give Cody every last thing he needs and expect nothing in return."

"It's called parenting."

He ignored that. "You give your friend Natalie a roof over her head when she needs it, a shoulder to cry on. You give your father complete forgiveness for anything in the past, and just in case the world needs a symbol of your daughterly devotion, you give him a damned kidney."

"I think you'd better go. Before we both say things we regret."

He shook his head. This wasn't coming out right at all. "I'll regret the things we *haven't* said, Michelle."

"What hasn't been said?" She stood there, beautiful, challenging, vulnerable.

And he thought back over his life, and the years that had gone by, the path he had taken, and where everything had brought him. In all the places he'd been and people he'd met, he had learned and moved on. But there was one person in his past from whom there was no moving on. Someone he was destined to carry around in his heart for the rest of his days. The truth of it stood out like a scar on pale flesh.

"I love you." The words sounded so inadequate for the size of what he was feeling. "I never stopped."

She sat down and hugged her knees up to her chest as if she'd felt a sudden chill.

His gut churned, and he realized he was scared, scared in a way he hadn't been in a long time. He'd been doing fine, his life had been set, and suddenly she had him walking off the edge of a cliff. "I mean it, Michelle. It's not hard to love you. It's one of the only things that came easy when I was young. And it's still easy."

She looked terrified. "But it can't mean anything. It can't change anything."

He put out his hand, cradled her cheek in his palm. "It already has."

"No, not in the way you're saying. That night at the theater—"

"What, you're saying that didn't change anything? The hot springs didn't mean anything?" He took his hand away. "Does that mean you're in the habit of cheating on your boyfriend?"

"I believe that's my cue to smack you across the face."

He raked his hand through his hair. "It was a shitty thing to say. But you've got to do better than tell me 'it can't work' or 'it hasn't changed anything.' Because we both know it can. And it has."

She sat silent, pale and tight-lipped with anger. And fear, too. He saw that in her eyes, and he hated being the reason for it.

"Just what do you expect from me?" she asked at length.

"I want you to be completely honest. Do you have the life you want back in Seattle? Or is it just something you settled for?"

"I worked damned hard to get my act together in Seattle—"

"That's not what I asked." He gestured at the canvas. "Do you do that in Seattle?"

She waved a hand dismissively. "When I'm home, I *work*. This time I'm spending here, Sam, it's not real. I'm not on a sabbatical from work. I'm on a sabbatical from my life. But that's the thing about sabbaticals. They're temporary. And you still haven't been straight with me. What do you expect? You want me to ditch everything

I've built for fifteen years and move out here? Be your 'woman'?"

"Now you're talking."

"How about the other way around? How about you drop everything here and move to the city?"

"Is that what I should do, then? Sell my place, set up practice in Bellevue or some nice suburb?"

"You'd do that?" Her voice was small, disbelieving.

"Haven't you been listening? This kind of love doesn't just happen every day. Believe me, I know that. Took me a while to figure it out, but now I know. I loved you when we were young, and I lost you. After all these years, we've found each other. I'm not about to lose you again without a fight."

"This is not a fight." Panic flashed in her eyes. "You haven't thought this through. Say Cody and I decided to live out here. I'd turn into some beatnik studio artist selling my paintings at county fairs. Cody would never forgive me for ripping him away from his school and his friends in the middle of high school. The difference is, he'd have two of us to blame for his misery. Two of us to torture."

"I'm not about to let the kid torture either of us, Michelle. Or dictate my life for me."

"Oh, Sam. It's what kids *do*. It's what they're about. Until you're a parent, day in and day out, facing every crisis and triumph and dealing with him moment by moment, you won't get it."

"Then give me a chance. Give me a chance to 'get it.'"

"What if you decide it's not for you? Then you just move on? Send us back to Seattle?"

"You aren't listening. I'm not saying let's give this a try. I'm saying let's do it. Let's be a family, Michelle."

She shut her eyes. "Don't you think we should give this a little more time?"

"Time's not going to change my mind."

"*I* need the time. It's late, Sam. You'd better go."

He stood, forcing himself to walk away from her. "See you, Michelle." He left before she could answer, and stepped out into the cold, clear night. "By the way," he said, turning to see her framed in the warm light of the doorway, "what I said earlier about us being a family— that was a marriage proposal."

Wednesday

Chapter 45

A marriage proposal. Michelle kept her eyes straight ahead, watching the vanishing point of the trail framed between low bramble and bunchgrass trying to push up through the snow. She had gone AWOL. Her surgeon wouldn't approve of her taking a walk so soon, but she couldn't help herself, and she'd picked a day when spring felt like a certainty instead of an empty promise. Physically, she felt fine. Emotionally, she was roadkill.

A marriage proposal. With those three words, Sam had taken her world, her life, and turned it upside down, and then he'd gone home, leaving her stricken by doubts . . . and aching with hope.

After a restless night, she needed to get out into the wild spaces of Montana, to watch spring arrive on a sudden gust of warm chinook wind. Moving slowly and gingerly, she walked a short way to a ridge top. A timberline of towering Douglas firs skirted the mountains. Layer upon layer of snowy peaks stretched out against the endless bowl of the sky. An eagle circled, then dived, and she watched the silent fury of its descent. The mystery and magnificence of the place gripped her. She felt infinitely small and insignificant, yet at the same time a sense of vastness and possibility expanded her soul.

The silence gave way to the sound of a stream. Rounding a bend, she came to a snowbound creek. Awakened by the chinook, the sun beat strongly on the south face of the mountain, and chunks of melting snow and ice littered the trail. Even as she watched, the thaw escalated. The irrepressible power of the flowing water and the relentless glare of the midday sun worked at the stingy trickle. She stooped to drink the icy, numbing water from her cupped hands. The constant, steady swish of the current echoed the flow of blood in her veins.

In the corner of her eye something glittered and instinctively she turned to look. As a trio of hawks spiraled against the blue sky, a ledge of snow gave way above the stream. The avalanche boiled down a natural couloir that curved away from the trail. In its wake, the stream was unleashed. A whitewater cataract sprang from the heart of the mountain, shooting out and down over the rocks, making the sound of someone exhaling after holding a long breath. A rainbow, thrown up by the sun-shot water, dazzled her eyes.

Inside her, something rose up like the rise of the hawks, kettling and then moving off in a different direction.

It was the artist—Michelle recognized her exuberance and her darkness. For years she had kept this creature imprisoned, icebound, but she was free now. She was home.

All her life, Michelle had tended to hide from things

that scared her. Losing her mother and being estranged from her father taught her to avoid facing the rocks and relics of emotional entanglements. But now she had changed; the hurt was still there but not the fear. She let all the feelings in like the cataract tumbling over the rocks, and the exultant pain cleansed her, reminded her that she was alive. Awakened her to old dreams that had never really died. Like the icebound stream, she had been silent, but the current never stopped coursing through her.

Sam's words had hung over her head all night long, and now they nagged at her, unanswered, impossible to ignore. She had been haunted by their last conversation. *A marriage proposal.* He'd left her stunned, speechless, her tongue numb with the inability to reply to him.

No one had ever proposed to her before. She had tried to savor the novelty, but instead it scared her. Brad had never proposed, even though they had been together, neighbors and lovers, for three years. They had both been extremely adept at avoiding that level of intimacy.

But Sam didn't know the rules. He didn't know how she operated. He didn't know she tended to hide from things that scared her, surrendering her dreams in order to keep herself safe.

As marriage proposals went, his was a doozy. It had done everything it was supposed to do. Gave her chills, made her blush, kept her awake at night, stopped her from thinking about anything but him.

His schedule gave her the gift of this new spring day all to herself, to gather her thoughts and steady her nerves. He was working at the clinic and then at the Flathead reservation, so she wouldn't be seeing him until tomorrow night at the earliest. Maybe by then she would know what to say.

Perhaps the reason she hadn't given Sam an immediate answer to his proposal was that on some level she didn't really trust that he'd meant to ask her. It could be a way of saying he wanted to spend more time with Cody.

As for herself, she had to figure out the secrets of her own heart. Watching the spring thaw, she thought she was beginning to hear what her heart was telling her. Sam McPhee made her feel as starry-eyed as a girl again. Yet in the end she had to acknowledge that she was a big girl now. The grown-up part of her knew the truth—that asking was the easy part.

It was what came after that was so hard.

That was why she was still resisting him. She could look beyond the dizzying whirl of passion and see that there was work to be done—and it wasn't the sort of work she and Sam had proven themselves to be good at. After the passion, there was struggle, sometimes disappointment, the daily grind of living—could they survive that, year after year?

She tipped her face up to the dazzling brightness of the sun. In that moment she realized that she knew the answer. She'd always known.

Chapter 46

*T*ammi Lee Gilmer's car reeked of cigarettes, but Cody didn't mind, because she was letting him drive it. He'd pretty much slacked off smoking because cigarettes were too hard to get in this one-horse burg. The clerks at Ray's Quik Chek knew all the kids by name—and by age. They were anal about not selling to minors.

Cody probably could have sneaked a pack or two from Tammi Lee, but he would have felt too shitty, stealing from her. She was pretty cool, and he didn't mind hanging out with her now and then. If anyone would have told him he'd actually *like* having a recovering alcoholic rockabilly grandmother, he would have snorted in disbelief. But the fact was, he and Tammi Lee got along more like friends than relatives, and that was fine with him.

He'd had supper with her tonight because the ranch

Jeep was in the shop and wouldn't be ready until McEvoy's Garage closed at eight. It was a gas, driving around here. Cody didn't have to worry about traffic and winos and one-way streets like in Seattle.

Tammi Lee had made fried chicken for dinner, with chocolate mud pie for dessert. After dinner, Cody had to go to the library to get a book on Montana state history for some bogus assignment, and his grandmother had offered her car. She also asked him to return a rented videotape she'd left at the shop. She hated being late. It wasn't just the fines, she'd explained, but the whole idea of being forgetful.

It was kind of spooky, thinking about her lonely existence, and how she stayed up late watching movies and reading paperback novels to keep from wanting to drink again. She'd told him that some days, it wouldn't take much to set her off, make her take another drink.

"While I'm out, I'll get the tape from the shop and return it for you," Cody had offered.

She hadn't hesitated a single second. "Here's the key to my car, and this one's to the shop. I left the tape in the storeroom in the back. Little cubby with my name on it."

Cody was getting too used to this small town. He realized, as he drove along Main Street past the Indian statue in the square, that it was becoming as familiar to him as the palm of his hand. He passed the darkened Lynwood Theater, thinking that a movie house would be a huge improvement around here.

In the library, he found the book he needed and applied for a card, the whole transaction only taking a few minutes. Under "Home Address" he had written Blue Rock Ranch, wincing as he did so. When his mom had asked him what he thought of moving here permanently, he'd instantly hated the idea. If she was just checking, she had her answer.

In the parking lot, he spotted some kids coming out of the library, backpacks on their shoulders, shoving each other as they skidded along the icy sidewalk. One student walked alone, slim and straight. Cody leaned across the seat and cranked down the window.

"Hey, Molly," he said.

She tensed, reminding him of Sam's filly. He didn't blame her. They hadn't spoken since the ride incident because he couldn't figure out a way to apologize. He'd never been big on explaining his behavior or apologizing.

She came to the car, tucking a silky black lock of hair behind her ear as she bent to peer into the passenger-side window. "What's up, Cody?" She didn't look at him the way she had when they'd first met—the sideways, kind of shy-but-interested way he liked. She was neutral now. Guarded.

"I'm running an errand for my grandmother," he said. A ride, yeah, that would do it. He'd offer her a ride home. That would give them a chance to talk. "Hey, you want a lift—"

"Yo, Cody!" a familiar voice called. "Where'd you get the wheels?" Without waiting for an answer, Billy Ho and his sidekick, Ethan Lindvig, jumped in, one in front, one in back. "My El Camino's wasted again. Couldn't get it to start." Billy sent an "aw-shucks" grin to Molly. "You want to come along, cowgirl?"

She shook her head and stepped away from the car. Her face went all hard, her eyes flat and glossy. "See you, Cody," she said, her tone dismissive.

He couldn't very well call her back with Billy and Ethan breathing down his neck. "Where to?" he asked them.

"My house," Ethan said.

"I've got to make a quick stop." Cody eased away from the curb. "Then I'll give you a lift." He glanced in the rearview mirror. Molly stood on the sidewalk, slender and straight as a young tree. She watched the car for a moment, then turned and walked away.

Damn.

He didn't listen to Billy and Ethan yakking away as he drove a few blocks and stopped at the quilt shop. "Be right back. I need to grab something for my grandmother," he said.

He used the key to let himself in. The shop smelled of dry goods and old ladies. A dim light over the counter cast its glow on an old-fashioned brass cash register.

"Cool," Billy said. "I've never been in here before. What *is* all this shit?" He took a bolt of fabric and draped the loose end around him, strutting in the aisle and singing the wedding march off-key.

"Hey, you shouldn't be in here," Cody called. "I just need to get something from the back room."

"Chill out," Ethan said, honking the breast of a mannequin. "We're having a little fun."

Losers, Cody thought as he went to the back room. He didn't know why he put up with them. It wasn't like they liked *him,* they liked who he was—Gavin Slade's grandson, the one with the big allowance and the reliable wheels. He couldn't believe he'd left Molly Lightning freezing on the sidewalk for these two clowns. He'd make it up to her, he decided. He'd ask her out, maybe invite her over to Sam's to ride some of his horses. She'd like that.

He could hear the guys goofing around in the shop while he retrieved the rented video from a cubby with Tammi Lee's name cross-stitched over it. Then, closing the storeroom door behind him, he said, "Okay, let's go. Did you put back whatever it is you were messing around with?"

Ethan and Billy exchanged a glance. "We didn't mess with anything, man," Billy said.

Cody didn't like the furtive glee on their faces, but he was in a hurry. He wanted to get them out of the shop before they wrecked anything.

Thursday

Chapter 47

The way the morning light cut down through the skylight of the big kitchen of Blue Rock reminded Michelle of those old murals in church, the ones she used to stare at when she was little. They went to All Saints on Camden Drive in Beverly Hills, her mother wearing white gloves and Michelle in lace-edged socks, gleaming Mary Janes, and an outfit bought on her father's I. Magnin account. She used to sit beside her mother, studying the little girls seated securely between two parents, swinging their legs and bumping their toes against the soft foam-covered kneelers. Mom on one side, Dad on the other, a pair of bookends to prop her up no matter which way she leaned. Michelle used to lift her eyes to the back wall where a pair of gigantic pre-Raphaelite angels soared, the sun pouring over them like melted butter, and when mass was over, she would go home and draw what she had seen.

Fixing herself a bowl of raisin bran, Michelle realized she hadn't thought about those moments in church for a very long time. Something about the angle of light and the quiet of the house brought back the memory.

And of course, it was easier to think about the past than the future.

She owed Sam an answer, but they hadn't had any time alone together. Yesterday he'd worked out of town, and last night he was on call. He had office hours today, and she had to go to Missoula with her father for another checkup. She supposed they could discuss it on the phone, but this was the sort of thing to talk about face-to-face.

Her confidence faltered. It was fun playing two-crazy-kids-in-love, but when real life intruded, it intruded with a vengeance. Already, outside events were conspiring to keep them apart.

Her father came into the kitchen just as the alarms on both of his wristwatches beeped. Medicine time.

"Hey, Daddy." She got up from the stool at the counter and poured him a glass of water.

"How's my girl?" He grinned, and the flush of health on his face was so welcome it made her want to weep.

But she felt compelled to ask, "You feeling okay?"

"Fine."

"Really? I'm not making idle chitchat here."

"Okay, the side effects of the medicine can get annoying." He held out his hand, and for a second she noticed a tiny, brief tremor. "Cyclosporin does that. Prednisone and immunosuppressants are their own kind of fun." He grinned again. "Enough whining. All I have to do is consider the alternative, and it shuts me right up."

She handed him the water and waited while he took

out a massive plastic pill box with dividers for each day. He swallowed his meds, the radical cocktail of stabilizers and antirejection pills that were so critical after the transplant. So far so good. The transplant team had declared that their speed of recovery was one for the record books.

Gavin set a stack of mail on the breakfast bar and slowly picked up a thick envelope. Michelle saw his hesitation and the slight shaking of his hand as he broke the seal and took out a packet of official-looking papers. He studied them for a minute, then shut his eyes and kissed the certificate with beatific reverence. "My pilot's license has been renewed," he said. "I'm back in the game, honey."

"Daddy, no kidding?"

"No kidding." His legendary blue eyes shone. He poured himself a bowl of raisin bran and then methodically proceeded to pick out all the raisins. Michelle watched for a second, hiding a grin. She and her father were alike in ways that startled her. An occasional gesture, a look, a quirk of taste. She didn't eat the raisins in raisin bran, either.

Her father seemed unaware of his thoughts. He ate some cereal, then drummed his hand on the stack of papers. "This is the second-best thing that's happened since I got sick."

"What's the first best?" She held her breath.

"Finding you and Cody again, honey. Didn't you know that?"

She couldn't speak for a moment. This, she thought as her heart soared. This was the essence of life. A moment of joy and triumph so sweet that her entire being filled up with happiness. How long had it been since she'd allowed herself to feel this much, this deeply? "Ah, Daddy," she said, and something in her inflection made him look up. "I did know."

Simple little words. An ordinary conversation. But she had waited a lifetime to share a moment like this with her father. They finished their breakfast; then he helped himself to coffee, shutting his eyes and smiling as if he had just seen God. "I've missed drinking coffee."

They sat in companionable silence for a while, sipping their morning coffee and watching the play of sunlight over the polished-granite countertops and gleaming copper cookware hanging from the range hood.

"You going to work on your painting today?" her father asked.

"Yep. I have no idea what I'm doing over there, but I'm loving it."

"That painting you've been doing. It makes me damned proud of you."

His words filled her with warmth. Just for a second, she wanted to ask him where that belief in her came from, why he had never expressed it until she gave him a kidney. But the second passed, and she knew there was no answer, and no point trying to get one.

"Thanks." She indicated his clipboard, covered with pink phone message slips. "You've been busy."

"As a matter of fact, I have."

"What is all that?"

He paged through the notes. "Here's one from Carolyn." He winked, though buried in his cynicism was an almost-hidden hurt. "She's ready to kiss and make up now that I don't have a dialysis bag hanging out of me."

"So are *you* ready?"

"I told her to piss off." He crumpled the note. "Pun intended. Here's one from a contractor in Polson. I'm going to reopen the Lynwood on Memorial Day."

"Really?" She felt a rush of excitement. The old theater was filled with memories for her, memories of that long-ago summer, but even more important, memories of a snowy night not so very long ago. "I'm glad. This town's more than ready."

He pushed a fax across the counter to her. "This is what we really need to talk about."

It took her a minute to assimilate what he was showing her. "Daddy?"

"It was on the fax machine when I got up this morning. It's from the same contractor who's going to be renovating the Lynwood."

Michelle swallowed, but she couldn't banish the dryness from her mouth. "Daddy," she whispered, "what the hell's going on?"

He beamed at her. "Keep reading."

It was a bid for restoring the vacant retail space in the shop next door to the old theater. At Gavin's request, the space would be converted into an art gallery. Picturing the vintage storefront, the old plank floors, the hammered tin ceilings, Michelle felt a giddy light-headedness. A buoyant sense of wonder.

"A gallery," she said.

"Might bring some culture to Crystal City." He touched her hand. "You've never had a showing, Michelle, and God knows, you deserve one. That is, if you think this is something you want."

It was something she hadn't even dared to want—until now. Maybe that was what the whole ordeal of Gavin's illness had been about. It was a kick in the pants. A way to jolt her out of the comfortable monotony her life had become. She got up slowly, walked around the counter, and put her arms around him. "Dad—"

The phone rang, and he grabbed it. "This might be the contractor." But then he handed her the receiver. "It's Sam."

"Sam!"

"Did I catch you at a bad time?"

"Um, no."

"I've missed you." His voice was low and sexy.

A shiver ran through her. She could feel her whole body start to smile. "Same here." She stared at the fax on the counter. She thought about what he had said the last time they were together, and all the things they had to talk about. What would it mean if she decided to marry Sam? So many questions. They had so much to discuss. It was too much, too big to explain to him right here, right now. "Have dinner with me tonight, Sam," she managed to say. "I have something to tell you."

A pause. Then she could hear the grin in his voice as he said, "Honey, wild horses couldn't stop me from seeing you tonight."

Chapter 48

*I*t's okay to grab the apple," Molly said.

Cody looked down at her from the dizzying height of the horse's back. This was a terrible idea. It was the worst idea he'd ever had, inviting Molly over to ride horses at Sam's after school.

"What apple?" he asked, mortified when his voice broke on the last syllable.

She didn't seem to notice. "The saddle horn," she explained. "If you feel a little unsteady, you can always grab hold of the saddle horn, pull a little leather."

"Oh." He clutched it, two-handed, white-knuckled. "I thought that was against the rules."

"Are you competing?"

He liked the laughter in her eyes. It almost made him forget he sat atop fifteen hundred pounds of bone and muscle and hoof, a sorrel gelding called Ace. "No," he said.

"Just try to relax, okay? If you're tense, he can feel it." It was pretty great, the way she instructed him. She had lots of patience and didn't make him feel inferior just because he'd hardly ever ridden a horse. She started him out really slow, and before long he actually began liking the rocking motion of the horse, going round and round the fenced arena, listening to the creak of the saddle and the heartbeat of hooves. Thanks to Molly, he was feeling pretty good, all things considered.

This afternoon during study hall, he'd gone right up to her, looked her in the eye, and apologized for being a jerk. Instead of making him squirm like a bug on a pin, she had forgiven him with more generosity than he deserved. He would always remember her words: "I like you, Cody, no matter what." No one had ever said such a thing to him. When he'd said he'd like to try his luck riding a horse, her smile had lit up the day.

After about an hour, Ace had worked up a sweat, so Cody got off and put him up, carefully hanging the saddle and pad and all the gear. They went into the barn office, where he washed his hands at the sink and got some soft drinks from the fridge. They sat together on an old couch with lumps in the seat, and it felt perfectly natural to put his arm around her. She made it clear that she liked it, setting her head easily on his shoulder. For a while, they just listened to the whistle of the wind through the barn, the flutter of swallows high in the eaves, and the occasional low-throated sound of a horse stomping and muttering. They had the whole place to themselves. Sam was at work, and Edward was doing errands in the city.

He turned on the radio and couldn't find anything but country western. But he didn't mind.

Molly didn't say a word, just took his can and set it on the floor next to him. When she turned her face up, he kissed her, softly at first, then longer and harder. She tasted like Dr Pepper, chilly and sweet, and everything about her was perfect. She pressed close, clearly liking the kiss as much as he did, and when he eased back on the sofa so he was half-lying down, she came with him. He put his tongue in her mouth. His hand strayed. He really, *really* wanted to touch her.

She lifted her mouth from his just a little. "It's okay," she whispered, and undid the top two buttons of her denim shirt. "I've been thinking about this a lot, Cody. I don't mind."

She spoke as if she'd read his thoughts, and her honest desire touched off a forest fire inside him. Yet despite her words and the excitement shining in her eyes, he realized that she probably hadn't done much fooling around at all. But she wanted it, he could tell, and she took his breath away. Her kisses were open and searching and inviting, her hands like a pair of inquisitive kittens crawling over him. Quickly enough, things got away from them—shirts undone, and then the top button of his jeans, and she held him and made a nervous, excited sound in her throat. It struck him then that she was not going to tell him to stop. What happened next was totally up to him. He pulled back and looked down into her face. "Girl, you're driving me crazy."

Her eyes shone. "Really? I wasn't sure you wanted me."

"Hell, yes, I wanted you."

"I'm glad, Cody. I'm real glad about that." She lifted herself toward him, and he couldn't help himself. He kissed her again, opening his mouth over those soda-sweet lips.

She was soft and willing, her touch honest and warm. For the first time since he'd started dating girls, he'd found one who made him feel something tender and new, something that had more to do with feelings than with sex. Amazing.

And so, at the crucial moment, Cody astonished himself. "You're a nice girl, Molly," he said. "But I think we'd better stop."

"I don't want to stop," she said quietly, pressing her open hand to his chest.

"I don't either," he admitted. "I like you, and maybe one day it'll be right for us. Just not now. We should wait. Okay?" Man. It *hurt*. He couldn't believe he managed to get the words out.

"I'm not a baby. I know what I want."

"Then waiting a while won't change that." He ground the words out through gritted teeth. Faintly he heard a car or truck, but it sounded very far away, and he had more immediate concerns. He had Molly right where every guy dreamed of getting a girl—ready and willing—and he was blowing his chance. How stupid was that? Still, it was the right thing to do, and by some miracle, Cody still knew what the right thing was.

As he drove home from work, Sam caught himself pushing hard on the accelerator. Unlike most days, he was eager to get home, to get cleaned up, and go see Michelle. Tonight it would begin. The love that had started more than seventeen years before kept growing stronger every day. It was a scary thing, to love someone like that. But scarier still to think of life without her.

He drummed his fingers on the steering wheel and tried to shrug the day off his aching shoulders and back. He had set a bone this morning—a sheep rancher's tibia. He'd seen four flu patients, an infant in respiratory distress, treated a dog bite, and had gone over a special diet with Earl Meecham, who had an ulcer. The last appointment was with a mentally handicapped ranch hand. Sam had to show him how to use a rubber and he wasn't sure the lesson would stick. The kid was slow, but his body was that of a man. Bad combination. Sam still had some of the rubbers in his back pocket.

The day just wouldn't go away until he filled his mind with Michelle. That was the magic of her. Before she'd come back to him, his bad days and hard thoughts had no place to go. He tried to picture her in this house, in his bed, in his life. And the worrisome thing was, the picture wouldn't form. She was so damned sophisticated. Could she really be happy here, a ranch wife, of all things?

It was almost as ludicrous as picturing himself living in some suburban sprawl outside of Seattle. Then there was Cody, who needed things Sam didn't know how to give.

Details, he told himself, loosening his tie. That's all they were. Details. They'd work things out. He saw a shadow in the sky over the highway and looked up. He thought it might be Gavin Slade's little P-51 Mustang, banking through the breaks and draws of the valley over the country air park. Sam grinned in spite of his complicated feelings about Michelle's father. So Gavin was flying again. He was truly on the mend now.

When Sam pulled up at Lonepine, he noticed the Jeep parked outside the barn, and country music wailing from within. Curious, he went over to the barn and saw a horse from the Lightning place tethered to a loop. Good, he thought. He'd rather see Cody making friends with Ruby's daughter than those punks who had spooked the horse. Sam decided to go in and say hello, let them know he was home.

When he walked into the office, Cody and Molly Lightning were as stunned and embarrassed as he was.

They both jumped up from the sofa, brushing hastily at their rumpled clothes. Molly's hair was mussed, her face red as a beet. She clutched the front of her unbuttoned shirt.

"I, um, I was just leaving," she said in a strained voice. She was gone before Sam could think of a single thing to say.

He swung around to glare at Cody. Still no words. His earlier thoughts mocked him. He was totally unprepared for this situation.

Cody tried to brush past him. "I'd better get over to Blue Rock," he muttered.

"The hell you will," Sam burst out, planting himself in front of him.

"Hey, man—"

"Don't you hey-man me," Sam said, flexing his hand. "What the hell were you thinking, groping her like that?"

"We're both sixteen," Cody pointed out. "And you might not believe this, but I wasn't going to do anything."

"Yeah, sure," Sam said. "I *don't* believe you."

"I wasn't." Cody jutted his chin out. "But that's between me and Molly, not me and you."

"Under my roof, it's my business."

"Hey, I didn't ask to come here. I'll go back to Seattle anytime, just say the word. But if I'm stuck here, the least I can do is try to make friends."

"Looks like you were trying to make more than that. You've grown up thinking you're entitled to every goddamned thing in the world." Sam's anger wasn't rational, the way a wildfire wasn't rational. It flared and flamed with a life of its own. "Smart-ass like you ought to know better than to have unprotected sex."

"We were just fooling around," Cody snapped. "Not having sex."

"Only because I happened to show up before things got out of hand."

"You don't know that. You always want to think the worst of me."

Something inside him snapped, and he blew up with anger. "Did you even think for one second what you're risking? Bringing another unwanted baby into the world—"

Sam stopped himself. Too late, he realized what he'd just said. Too late, he recognized the source of his anger. And the deep red flush on Cody's face meant he recognized it, too. Neither of them said a word, but a silent storm howled between them.

And Sam knew in that moment that he loved his son. He knew, because it hurt so bad to hurt him.

The phone rang, shrilling into the tense quiet of the office. Holding Cody with a raised hand, Sam grabbed the receiver from the wall. "Sam McPhee." He frowned as an automated message instructed him to press 1 to accept the collect charges from the incoming call. With a shrug, he pushed the button.

"Hiya, hon. It's your mama."

He didn't move, but at the unmistakable slur in her voice, he could feel everything inside him curling up, burning down to nothing. "Mama. Where are you? What've you been drinking?"

Cody's pale face sharpened, but Sam couldn't think about the boy now. "Mama? Talk to me."

"Lessee. Made it to Kalispell. They got a honky-tonk here, the Roadkill Grill. Think they'll lemme be in the band? I used to sing real good. 'Member when we cut that album in Reno? You were in your playpen still . . ."

He could hear the lazy slide of liquor through her

voice. Jesus, five years. She'd been sober five years, and now this. "Mama, slow down. What happened?"

"That old cow LaNelle fired me from the shop."

"LaNelle Jacobs fired you? Why?" From the corner of his eye, Sam could see Cody edging toward the door. He pinned him in place with a fierce stare. The boy flattened his lips and squinted defiantly, but he didn't leave.

"They said I stole all the money from the cash register. All forty-two bucks of it. A staggering fortune. Jussst . . . staggering."

"That's absurd, Mama. LaNelle knows you wouldn't steal from her shop."

"Someone saw my car parked there last night. 'S'morning, the cash was gone. 'Course she's gotta blame me. Who else could it be, son? Who the hell else could it be?"

"Mama—"

"You never really outgrow what you are, do you son? Folks' opinions of you never really change."

"I'm coming to get you," he said. "Don't move. Get a cup of coffee and sit tight."

She wasn't listening now. He could hear someone asking her if she wanted another tequila sunrise, could hear her cackle with harsh glee. *Oh, Mama. Not again, Mama.* He slammed down the phone.

"What's going on?" Cody asked, his face strangely still. "Someone's saying she stole from the shop?"

"When I find the son of a bitch who did, I'll kill him, swear to God I will."

Cody paled. "Hey, it's not the end of the world, man."

"I don't have time to deal with you now," Sam snapped. "I have to go." He grabbed his parka and his keys. "Tell your mom I can't make it tonight. Tell her—" He broke off. "Ah, hell. Tell her I'm sorry."

Chapter 49

How was school today?" Michelle's hairbrush hit the carpet with a *thunk*. Klutz, she thought. She was a bundle of nerves.

"Okay," Cody mumbled into the refrigerator. He stood in the white glow of the interior light, scanning the contents.

Michelle picked up the brush and studied her son. He wore his black jeans and leather jacket, and she felt a frisson of unease. For some reason, it struck her that he looked exactly as he had when they'd first come to Crystal City. He wore gloves, concealing his bandaged hand. A knitted hat covered the scar on his head, so there was no evidence of the wound Sam had mended.

She walked toward him. "Is something wrong?" she asked.

He twisted away from her, ducking his head as if to

avoid getting an unwanted kiss. "Just the usual." He dropped his backpack on the floor and took out a carton of milk.

"Uh-uh," she said automatically as he put it to his lips. "Use a glass."

He eyed her over his shoulder as he got a tumbler from the cupboard. "Can I ask you something?"

"Sure, Cody."

He sloshed some of the milk on the counter. Without thinking, she grabbed a paper towel. Annoyed, he took it from her and wiped up his own spill. "I was wondering. Did you . . . want me? I mean, did you ever think of getting rid of me?"

He had never, ever asked her before. Michelle wondered how long he'd held the question inside him, unasked, festering. Tears gathered thickly in her throat, and she touched his cheek. "Oh, Cody. Not for a single second. You were so wanted. You were my life." She swallowed and hoped she wouldn't cry. He had almost never seen her cry. She remembered, with startling clarity, every sensation of being pregnant, and pain was no part of that sensation, no part at all. She had gone for natural childbirth, and she had felt his entire journey from her womb into the world, and seeing his tiny face for the first time had filled her with a fierce sense of purpose. "Having you saved me," she said. "You were the best part of my life, and you still are."

He seemed a little embarrassed by the display his question had incited. "Cool," he said, and took a deep gulp of milk. "What're you all dressed up for?"

She laughed, wanting to hug herself with glee. "Well, I've got some news."

He narrowed his eyes in distrust. When had he learned to do that? To conclude that her good news meant bad news for him? He leaned against the counter, drinking his milk, waiting.

"You know I've been painting lately." It felt good to voice the notion that had been at the back of her mind for days. Saying it aloud made her heart soar. It was impractical, impulsive, but she was determined to reclaim herself. "Like I used to, years ago. I've been thinking about making some changes. Gavin and I are looking into opening an art gallery in Crystal City." She felt almost fearful about how badly she wanted this. How much it meant to her.

His gaze flicked over her—black cashmere trousers, black angora sweater, her good pearls. "So what's with the outfit?"

"Sam's coming over for dinner." She tried to keep the tremor from her voice as she told him the *real* news. The one thing she wanted more than the next breath of air. "Sam asked me to marry him. I haven't said yes yet, but I'm going to. Tonight."

"Shit." He set down his glass and brushed past her, flopping down on the sofa.

She tasted lipstick as she bit her lip. "I was sort of hoping for a more supportive reaction from you." Don't do it, she wanted to beg him. Don't take this happiness from me. But on the heels of that thought came the thoughts any mother was conditioned to think: How can I do this to my child? How can I rip him out of the middle of his life and plunk him down amid strangers? Isn't there some compromise? Can I have what I want and keep him happy, too?

He was quiet for long, long moments. She was dying to know what was going on in that head of his. Finally, he took a deep breath, looked her square in the eye, and said, "Don't bother waiting for Sam to show up. He took off."

"What do you mean, he took off?"

"He's gone, scram, vamoose."

A chill of disbelief snaked through her. "Gone where?"

"Out of town. He said to tell you . . ." Cody hung his head.

"What? What did he say? What happened?" Disbelief hardened into a horrible dread. She had to know. She needed a reason. She was inches from shaking this kid's teeth right out of his head.

"I guess he didn't want to be my father after all."

"Oh, for Pete's sake, that's ridiculous. Sam loves me. He wants to love you, Cody—"

"Not anymore." His head hung lower. "Something, um, happened."

She pressed herself against the counter until she felt her surgical scar. What occupied the space where the kidney used to be? she wondered irrationally.

"Talk, Cody," she said, fixing her attention on him with a will. "Start at the beginning."

"Molly and I were hanging out at his place this afternoon, and he . . . he acted like I was molesting her or something. We weren't doing anything much, Mom, we weren't."

Michelle took a deep breath, trying to assimilate everything he'd just told her. "Let me get this straight. You and Molly were at Sam's."

"Yeah." He glowered at the toes of his shoes. "I was riding a horse, and it was great, and then we went into the barn office. We were like, fooling around a little bit, no big deal—"

"Fooling around." Her stomach knotted.

"No big deal," he repeated sullenly. "We're not babies. We know the score. We were fully clothed, Mom, every second. But Sam scared Molly off and started yelling at me."

Overnight, she thought. Overnight her son had changed from a little boy with grass stains on his knees to practically a grown man . . . with a man's desires. "Look at it from his perspective. She's a neighbor. The daughter of a friend. Can you blame him?"

"I should've known you'd take his side."

"I'm not taking sides—"

"But you don't believe me. You didn't hear the things he said, Mom. He went into this big insane lecture about safe sex and unwanted babies." Cody folded his arms across his chest. "Then he said he . . . he doesn't want me for a son."

The pain was sharp, hot. "He can't have said that."

"Call him. Just try it. He won't answer. Swear to God, he doesn't want me, and good riddance, I say. I don't want him either."

She studied his pale, worried face. And deep in the center of her, a core of ice formed, grew bigger, colder. "Why would you say a thing like that?"

"Because I mean it, Mom. Sam has the hots for you, but that doesn't mean he gives a shit about me."

Michelle went through the motions even though her horrified certainty hardened with each creeping moment. She called Edward, who had been in the city all day and had seen neither hide nor hair of Sam. She called Sam's service only to be told Dr. McPhee would return calls when he checked in for his messages. No answer at his mother's. His partner Karl was brusque, telling her to try the service or, if it was an emergency, to go to County.

Her hand was ice-cold and shaking as she hung up

the phone for the last time. A terrible sense of déjà vu broke over her. She remembered exactly how she had felt that long-ago night, sick and exhilarated with the knowledge of her pregnancy, rushing over to Sam's house only to discover that he'd left without a word.

He took off. He took off. He took off. Disappeared into the night just like before.

Friday

Chapter 50

Almost dizzy from lack of sleep, Michelle dressed in the gray quiet of the dawn. Cody's bedroom door was firmly shut, and not a sound came from within. She wondered how well she knew her son anymore. She could only guess at what was going through his head. The emotional roller coaster of finding his father so unexpectedly, then having the big quarrel with Sam, was a lot for a kid to handle. A lot for *anyone* to handle. Yet beneath the hurt and anger, she had detected something a little harder to put her finger on. Evasiveness. Shame, perhaps.

Resolving to talk to Cody about it when he got up, she put on a pair of boots and went over to the main house. She walked into the great room, stood before the fire, and thought of that first night when she and Gavin had sat together in this room. It seemed long ago that they had been so awkward with one another. She'd gone to him because, at long last, he needed her. The irony was that she had needed him just as much.

She pressed a wadded Kleenex to her cheeks. Her father came in, took one look at her, and opened his arms. It felt so right to collapse against him, and the tears spilled again. She knew her father now, and she needed him in a way she never had before. "Sam's gone, Daddy. He and Cody had a fight last night," she said. "It was bad. Cody thinks Sam doesn't want him."

"Cody's wrong. Sam wants his kid. Trust me," Gavin said, bringing her to the sofa and sitting down.

"How do you know?"

Lines deepened in his craggy face. "I did a stupid thing years ago, letting you leave. Before you came to me when your mother died, I didn't think I wanted a kid. I didn't know how to be a father. I sure as hell wasn't much good at it. When you left, I convinced myself it was for the best. But I was wrong. I wanted my daughter. I just didn't know how to bring you back. Anyway, that's how I know Sam wants his son. Whatever went on between them won't change that."

"But if Cody doesn't believe Sam wants him, then we've got problems. And something tells me they won't just blow over."

"If he's gone, there's bound to be an explanation. He's not some no-account drifter. He'll be back this time."

"True. But how can I get Sam's side of the story if he simply takes off at the first sign of trouble? He should have called me."

"Don't jump to any conclusions."

"I'm trying not to. But I just feel so . . . stood up. Maybe I'm not cut out to be with a guy like Sam. People don't really change, Daddy. He took off seventeen years ago, and he's done it again." She felt the chilly ghost of the old feelings of abandonment. In different ways and for different reasons, she had lost her mother, her father, Sam . . . and now she felt Cody slipping away from her. "Maybe," she admitted, "I don't have it in me to love them both in the way they need."

Gavin turned to her on the sofa. "You know better than that. You have the most generous heart of anyone I've ever known, Michelle. You came to me in spite of my failings. You came even though you knew it would be hard for you. Things turned out to be even harder than you imagined, and you stayed, honey."

A long silence stretched out, and the sun broke over the mountains. Michelle turned to her father. "The first time Sam took off, I never even tried to find him." She took a deep breath and finally admitted something about herself, something she wasn't proud of. "There was probably a part of me that saw him as a delinquent, no good, a guy who would never amount to anything. I was wrong back then. The failing was mine, not his. That's what I don't know, Daddy. I don't know if I'm better than that now."

"About the first time." Gavin put his hand on her arm.

His touch made her pause. She looked up into his face, a little puffy now from the meds, but still so expressive, so anguished.

"He and his mother left town because I arranged it," Gavin said quietly.

Michelle stared at him. Her fist tightened around the Kleenex. "I don't understand."

"There was money missing from the foreman's office. Maybe Sam took it, maybe he didn't. I wasn't really thinking about that. I was thinking about you, Michelle. I'd just found out you were seeing Sam, and I wasn't thrilled with the idea. I thought the boy and his mother were trouble, and I didn't want you hurt. So Deputy O'Shea and I confronted him with the missing cash. He denied taking it, of course. For good measure, O'Shea also reminded Tammi Lee of her rubber-check habit and several outstanding warrants. She was given a choice. Disappear, or do time. Sam really didn't have a choice."

"My God." She drew away from her father.

"He never told you about that, did he?" Gavin asked in a pained voice.

"He never said a word."

"I'm sorry as hell, honey. I didn't know what to do. I was afraid you'd go running off with him."

"And I did run off. Only not with him." She pulled her knees up to her chest.

"I wish I could undo what I did. But I acted out of desperation because I loved you, and I was so damned scared."

Her throat stung. "Why—" she said, and had to pause. "Why didn't you just say so? Why didn't you tell me you loved me? You never said it."

"I thought you knew." He was silent for a long time, staring down at his hands. "You're a parent yourself now. The love happens whether you talk about it or not. You've made choices for Cody—some good, and some bad. But you always acted out of love for him."

The stark truth struck hard. He was right. She didn't approve of Cody hanging out with Claudia Teller. Every once in a while, Michelle would "forget" to pass on a message that Claudia had called. Or manage to schedule Cody for a dental appointment when she knew he and Claudia had plans. Michelle was uncomfortably certain she would resort to devious means if she thought she could keep them apart.

"Sometimes a parent does the wrong thing for the right reasons," Gavin pointed out. "I'm so damned sorry, Michelle. I should have trusted your judgment."

"Are you saying I should trust Cody's?"

"Maybe. Yeah, I am. Look, I failed with you. But you have a chance to succeed with Cody."

"Right now it's Cody's judgment that he doesn't want Sam in his life."

"I suspect he'll come around. He's a kid, thinking about himself first and foremost. He doesn't want to move in the middle of high school—what kid would? But he's also your son. He wants you to be happy, Michelle. Do what's right for you. He'll come around."

"I can't do it, Daddy. I can't force the two of them together and pretend it will be fine."

"You don't know how it will be. Maybe it won't be fine, maybe not all the time. But what is? What the hell is in this life?"

Restless, she got up and opened the doors to the front porch, feeling the harsh chill of the morning air on her face and hearing the sounds of the ranch coming to life—diesel vehicles firing up, the foreman's whistle, the hydraulic hiss of a dump truck. Horses blowing and stamping, the tinny sound of the farm and ranch report on someone's radio. She needed to clear her head, had to think about what it would really be like to marry Sam—a man who had just taken off without a word of explanation.

It scared her when she considered how hurt she was by that. How vulnerable she was when it came to Sam. "I'd better go wake Cody for school," she said.

Returning to the guesthouse, she knocked lightly on Cody's door. No response. "Cody?" she said, and pushed the door open.

Reality registered slowly. The bed that hadn't been

slept in. Closet door carelessly open to empty space. The big duffel bag gone.

Terror broke over her in a dizzying wave. Gone.

Her son was gone.

It was every mother's nightmare. She tore out of the room, screaming for her father, her mind filled with visions of Cody broken, bruised, abused by someone who had picked him up hitchhiking.

Gavin met her halfway across the yard, holding out the cordless phone. "It's okay," he said.

His words barely penetrated her icy, heart-freezing terror.

Her father closed her hand firmly around the phone. "It's okay. He's in Seattle. Here, let Natalie tell you."

Standing in the blanketed yard, her hand shaking, she put the phone to her ear. Natalie was calm, uncharacteristically subdued, as she explained that Cody had taken the all-night bus from Missoula. Dear God. Her son had run away from home last night. No, he'd run away *to* home. He had run away from *her*.

"Let me talk to him," Michelle said. Tears threatened to melt the ice of terror, but she held them in, afraid that if she started to cry, she'd never stop.

"He's on his way to school. He wanted to get there early to re-enroll."

"You let him go to school without calling me?" She wanted to jump through the phone line and throttle Natalie.

"I told him he should call you. He said he would. Later." Natalie hesitated. "Michelle, he didn't explain why he showed up here alone, but I can guess. He's safe. Let him cool off, okay? If you don't give him time to realize on his own how much he loves you and misses you, he might never figure it out."

She was still trembling when she hung up. Her first impulse was to phone Garfield High School, demand that they find him, bring him to the phone. Then she looked across the white mystery of the fields of Blue Rock, and a small, surprising voice inside said No and then louder: *No.* She handed the phone to her father.

"You want me to fly you to Seattle?" he asked.

"No." The word formed of its own accord. "Natalie just said something to me that makes perfect sense. He's got to fix this on his own, Daddy. It's time he made his own decisions and figured out how to deal with the consequences."

Gavin looked at her for a long time. "When you were young, you went away, too. And like a fool I just let you go. I was too stubborn. Are you being stubborn or is this the right thing to do?"

She spread her arms. "Who knows what the right thing is? I just know that what I've been doing lately isn't working. Maybe I was too much of a perfectionist, too demanding. That's probably what made him turn into a rebel in the first place."

Now, with a lurch of her heart, she suddenly understood. It was only natural to distance himself from her expectations. And it was her job to let him find his own way.

"I was smothering him with love, getting him out of scrapes when I should have let him fall and pick himself up again." The decision hurt, but it felt right. She realized that what she really had to do was make the painful choice of letting Cody go. He might discover the answers on his own, or he might not. It was no longer up to her.

At six-thirty at night, Cody stood on the rain-slick sidewalk in front of the town-house complex in Seattle. It was weird, but he missed the dark of Montana, the inky purity of the night in the mountains. Here in Seattle it was never all the way dark, not with the yellow shore lights, the busy ferry docks, and the ribbons of reflected neon snaking along the wet streets. The high bluff framed a view of Elliott Bay, a glittering necklace of lights along the shore.

Today had definitely been one of the strangest days of his life. He had gone to school, handing a re-enrollment slip to the clerk in the office. After the initial paperwork it had been like a regular day. Same classes, same kids.

Same Claudia.

He'd found her at the usual place, a wooded area everyone called the smoke spot. Unobserved, he had stood at the fringe of the woods and looked at her, expecting a theme song to start up or something. He'd watched her throw back her head and blow out a cloud of cigarette smoke, and he'd felt . . . nothing. Not the rush of excitement that used to keep him awake at night, not the heady pride that made him walk tall through the school halls. No theme song, just the boring hiss and spatter of the incessant Seattle rain through the alder and cedar trees.

When she'd seen him, she had squealed and flung herself at him, but her questions had all been about Gavin, and what it was like to have a celebrity grandfather, and why hadn't he ever *told* her that his grandfather had played Lucas McQuaid, and had he saved any of his prescription painkillers . . .

He had tried hanging out with his old crowd after school, but nothing felt right. There was nothing different about them, but it *was* different. The energy had gone flat, like a Coke left out too long. Their jokes sounded stale, their laughter rang hollow. He couldn't share their reminiscences of the Phish concert last weekend. It was as if he had been away for years rather than weeks.

He planned to call Claudia tonight and break up with her. Then, if he could get up the nerve, he'd call Molly Lightning. It was shitty, the way he'd left without explaining anything to her. She probably thought he'd been shipped off to reform school. It wouldn't be the toughest call he had to make, though. He had to figure out what to do about his mom and, tougher still, Tammi Lee. It was his stupid fault she'd lost her job. His stupid fault for chickening out and not telling the truth about what had happened. His stupid fault she'd gone out drinking.

Through the window of the gated entrance, he spotted a movement. A shadow. His heart thumped. Behind him, a wino shuffled along the sidewalk, muttering to himself. Noticing Cody, he said, "Hey, gotta smoke?"

"Nope," Cody said. "I gave it up."

Slowly, his backpack feeling like a load of bricks, he trudged up the walk toward his house. For a few more minutes, he stood listening to the low hum of the hot-tub pump and feeling the moist chill of the Seattle evening on his hair. Then he took a deep breath, punched the security code into the keypad, and let himself in.

The place smelled vaguely of patchouli oil and Natalie's experimental Middle Eastern cooking. She had a performance tonight, and so she'd left dinner in the fridge and a note in fat pink magic marker—*Call your mother.*

"I know, I know," Cody murmured under his breath. He set down his backpack with a thunk and went to put on some music. It was too quiet in the house. He found himself wandering around, feeling more alone than he'd ever felt before. Without really planning to, he found himself in the study, a neat-as-a-pin room with a glass-topped desk, a big angled drafting table, and two computers, their black faces gathering dust. He went to the closet and folded the louvered door aside, and then he realized what he was looking for.

His mom's paintings.

They were stored in the very back of the closet in a large, flat portfolio with three clasps. Working carefully, he took out the canvases and sketches and leaned them against the walls. There weren't very many of them, and he'd only seen them a few times.

He supposed he'd always known the pictures were good—great, even—filled with color and life and movement. They seemed to say something important. Like the painting that hung in Sam's house. But up until today he had always regarded these pictures as something created by a stranger, someone he never knew.

For the first time, he managed to connect the paintings to his mom. He pictured her in the studio at Blue Rock, lost in her work, not harried and tense like she was at the agency. Pacing in agitation, he thought about how she had looked yesterday when he'd told her he and Sam would never get along. In his heart, Cody didn't believe he was wrong. Sam *didn't* want him.

But maybe Cody had twisted the truth . . . a bit. It was pretty obvious Sam was pissed at him, but he'd never actually said he didn't want a son. It was a fine distinction. But if Sam was pissed about Molly, he'd go ballistic when he learned who the real culprit was in the quilt-shop incident.

Cody felt a rank lump of guilt in his throat. He didn't blame Sam for not wanting him.

The reason Sam had left Crystal City didn't have a thing to do with Cody or his mom. That phone call Sam had received . . . In his mind's eye, Cody could still see rage and fear on his face. And something worse—the hurt.

Sam had to take off in order to save his mother, and Cody had done the only thing he could think of. He'd fled.

Now he knew how the filly had felt, driven up to the woods in terror of the snowmobiles. He'd run away, but maybe he'd wound up in a place of greater danger. Hell, he didn't know. He should just stay away from Montana, where he didn't fit in. He'd never fit in.

Feeling restless and unsettled, he grabbed a yogurt from the fridge and scarfed it down, then drank half a quart of orange juice. Then he picked up the phone and jabbed in Claudia's number. Might as well get the easy call out of the way before he decided what to do about the rest.

In the middle of the third and fourth ring, the sound of the buzzer from the security office nearly made him jump out of his skin. Frowning, he hung up the phone. He wasn't expecting anyone.

He was amazed when the guard announced the name of his visitor. *Gavin Slade.* Switching on the lights over the entranceway, he opened the door.

"Hey," he said tentatively.

"Hey yourself." With a jangle of flying-ace buckles and straps, an unsmiling Gavin Slade strode into the house.

Cody followed him inside. "Um, how did you get here?"

"Flew the Mustang to Boeing Airfield. I wasn't planning on taking her out for a long haul so soon, but here I am." The bluewater eyes inspected Cody. "I expect you know why I came in such a hurry."

Cody eyed him warily. The angry energy of defiance coursed through him. "If you came out to lecture me because I blew it with my mom, you wasted a trip. My mind's made up. I don't fit in there."

Gavin scanned the room and Cody realized he was

seeing where his daughter lived for the first time. "Actually," he said, "it's more than that. I guess I came because, a long time ago, *I* blew it with your mom. She needed me, and I wasn't there for her, and she took off." His eyes looked deep and sad. "For seventeen years," he added. "I'm here because this is what I should have done for my daughter all those years ago. I should have come after her."

"This is different. Sam can't stand me, and the feeling's mutual."

Peeling off his leather jacket to reveal several more layers of clothing, Gavin studied a big studio photograph of Cody and his mom, done about five years before. He walked right up to the framed picture and pressed his palm to it. "How old were you in this picture?"

"Maybe ten or eleven." Cody remembered the red Izod shirt, and the feel of his mom's open hand on his shoulder, and the way the photographer had tried to flirt with her.

"I wish I'd known you then," Gavin said. "I feel lucky to have met you at all, Cody. Look at all the time we lost, with us being so stubborn." He turned to face Cody. "I don't know what went on between you and Sam, but the one who's getting hurt is your mom."

Cody's throat felt dry as sandpaper. Gavin was right. She had been happy and flushed and calm up until last night. Up until Cody's big lie.

"It took a kidney failure to get us back together," Gavin said. "What's it going to take this time? A heart attack?"

"You don't understand," Cody said. "You don't understand how bad I am." He felt too miserable to be embarrassed when his voice broke.

"Then make me understand, Cody."

The genuine caring in Gavin's quiet voice reached out to Cody. "You're not going to like it," he said. And then his voice steadied, and he told the truth. He told his grandfather what he had done.

Gavin gave a low whistle. "That's pretty damned bad."

"See? Sam'll never forgive me, and who can blame him?"

Gavin was quiet for a long time. Cody's stomach knotted. He hated what he'd done. Hated what a jerk he'd been. Finally, Gavin spoke. "I think I get the picture. You know, Michelle doesn't have the sort of troubles your grandmother does, but that doesn't meant she doesn't need you."

"What does she need with a screwup like me?" Cody demanded.

"You're only a screwup if you don't know how to straighten out the mess you've made," Gavin pointed out. "Nothing'll ever feel right again until you do. You know that, don't you, son?"

"You're right," said Cody, filling up with elation and terror.

Sam stood in the shower, letting the too-hot water pound down on his head. There was nothing, he thought, *nothing* worse than dropping your mother off at rehab. He felt as if a bomb had gone off in the middle of his life, and pieces lay scattered about, unrecognizable.

He'd had to pry her away from the dim, smoky cocoon of the honky-tonk; he'd listened to the familiar protests and promises; he'd hardened his will to her desperate pledges. Then he'd spent most of the day getting her checked in at the facility in Missoula.

"We did it again, di'n' we?" she had said, staring woozily out the truck window. "Stepped over the line.

Tried to fit in with respectable folks, where we don't belong. We're still on the wrong side of the tracks, Sammy. We always will be."

During the drive home, the rage had struck Sam hard, as it always did. What the fuck had LaNelle Jacobs been thinking, blaming the robbery on Tammi Lee? All the slights and slurs of years past had suddenly come back on a wave of resentment. Five years of peace and quiet in Crystal City had lulled him into thinking the past didn't matter.

Sam turned off the shower. Slinging a towel around his waist, he picked up the phone and stabbed his fingers impatiently at the numbers.

"Blue Rock," said a familiar and unwelcome voice. Jake Dollarhide.

"Sam McPhee here. I'm looking for Michelle."

"I'll see if I can get her on the intercom." Sam heard an unpleasant sneer in Dollarhide's slow drawl, and suddenly the years peeled back to expose the gaping wounds of the past. He remembered all the times he had tried to call her long ago, all the times Gavin and his staff had put him off.

"On second thought," Sam said brusquely, "never mind." Without further explanation he hung up and got dressed.

Screaming gusts of wind kicked up a ground blizzard, and everyone with a lick of sense stayed indoors. Not Sam. Not tonight. He was exhausted to the last inch of his shadow, but he had to see Michelle.

He wasn't sure what he'd say to her. He'd never had anyone to talk to in the middle of a crisis; he was used to going it alone. Still, he owed her an explanation. After all, he'd stood her up.

Have dinner with me tonight. She had sounded so excited. Fresh and alive, the Michelle he had known as a young man. But a lot had happened since her breathless invitation. He had lost his cool with Cody, and the incident made him wonder just what sort of father he would be. His mother's fragile sobriety had been shattered, reminding him that loving someone carried hazards that could crush even the stoutest of hearts.

It did not escape him that the other time he had disappeared from Michelle's life had been on his mother's behalf. The reason had not changed. Michelle was strong. She knew how to keep herself safe and secure. No matter how much Sam loved her, he also loved his mother, who could not survive without him. Michelle's very strength was her Achilles' heel. She had trained herself not to need, want, desire. And perhaps the habit was so ingrained that now she no longer remembered how to want something.

But when he saw her through the window of the studio, standing and staring at her canvas, he knew there were mysteries inside her he could not guess at. They would reveal themselves to him gradually—but only if he knew the right way to unlock them.

When he knocked at the door and stepped inside, she folded her hands in front of her. "Sam."

"I had an emergency," he said. "This was my first chance to call."

She stood quietly in the warm glow of the studio lights. He told himself to explain the rest, yet the words wouldn't form. When it came to his mother, he was private and intensely protective. And even a little ashamed, as if his mother's disease were due to some weakness in him. The silence opened a gulf between him and Michelle.

Last time they were together, he had proposed to her. Now he couldn't even make small talk.

The ground blizzard pounded at the windows and doors. Michelle shivered, and he saw that the fire in the woodstove had dwindled to embers. To occupy himself, Sam wrenched open the iron doors and added a quartered log.

"Cody told me what happened when you found him and Molly in the barn," Michelle said.

He crushed up a wad of old newspaper and stuck it under the log. "He told you his version. Molly's the daughter of a good friend. A nice girl."

"According to Cody, they weren't doing anything that risky. Sam, they're sixteen. It's what teenagers do. We can't stop them. We can just hope they don't do anything rash."

He grabbed a bellows and pumped at the banked embers. "The trouble is, sometimes hope isn't enough to stop them, and the consequences are pretty far-reaching." The air wheezing from the bellows sparked the yellow edge of a flame under the new, raw log.

"You made that clear to Cody. You made it clear he was an accident, an unwanted child. When he came home, he asked me if I'd ever considered having an abortion or giving him up for adoption. That's the first time he's asked me that, Sam. Ever."

Sam shut the stove door and stood to face her. A cold chill hardened in his gut. Doubts buzzed through his mind. He *had* lost it, overreacted. How was it that he'd been so sure of himself only two days ago?

Now he didn't know a damned thing, except that loving someone carried a commitment that could crush you. All his life, he had borne the responsibility for his mother.

The price of that had been that he'd had no parental guidance of his own.

"Well, what should I have said, finding him like that?" he asked.

"There's no oracle that lays it all out for you. You just have to pray you get it right most of the time. When it comes to sex, Cody knows the decision is his to make, and all I can do is hope that whatever he decides, it will keep him on course with who he is and what he wants to become."

"You didn't answer my question, Michelle."

She held out her hands to the stove, warming them. "I suppose I would have told him to wait, to be careful. I would have reminded him that he has all the time in the world." She fixed her gaze on Sam. "I would have told him I know it's damned hard to wait when you're sixteen."

"That's naive as hell. The kid is a bundle of raging hormones—"

"He knows when to stop, Sam. I have to trust that. If I can't, what sort of a mother am I?"

Sam envied Michelle her conviction. He realized now that he doubted his own ability to be a good father. God knew, he wanted to be, but he was afraid he'd screw up.

"I'm sorry I made that remark to Cody," he said. "Maybe I just don't have enough patience and understanding to handle him—I guess I proved that by blowing up at him." He gestured toward the door. "I should stop in and talk to him."

She was quiet for a long time. Shadows sculpted her face, and he couldn't read her thoughts.

"Michelle?"

"You'd better go, Sam. This isn't a good time for a discussion with Cody."

His heart lurched. "He's taking it that hard?"

More silence strained between them. Michelle bit her lip, hesitant to speak, and pushed her hair out of her eyes with a weary motion. "This just isn't a good time," she repeated. "I don't know what to think, except that you and I don't work until you and Cody figure out a way to get along." She opened the door to the howling night. "I won't let myself be torn to pieces by the two of you." Her good-bye was as brief and painful as the cauterizing of a wound.

He drove home, the chill inside him expanding. Damn it. Last time he'd seen Michelle, he'd asked her to marry him. Two days later, she was practically throwing him out. Sam squinted at the dry, blowing snow. He was tempted to turn back, but the doubts—and the remembered words of his mother—held him back.

"Don't go chasing after her again." Only yesterday, his mother had admonished him in a tequila-harsh voice. "Don't go getting your heart stomped into the ground."

He told himself not to jump to conclusions. They'd work out their problems. But no matter what he told himself, he still remembered that Michelle hadn't tried to find him years ago.

Saturday

Chapter 51

*T*he next morning, Michelle was still wearing the sterling-silver earrings she had put on for her big night with Sam. The night that never happened. It seemed like ages ago. Miles ago. A lifetime ago. With Sam, she had known a love so deep that it left her gasping and haunted her still. Watching him leave last night had crushed her, and it was far worse now than it had been years ago, because now she understood exactly what she had lost.

She took off the earrings and made a fist around them. Something had broken down between her and Cody and Sam, and she didn't know how to make it right. She didn't know if it could be made right. Maybe she should have told him Cody had disappeared. The fact that she hadn't was revealing in and of itself. Regular couples would discuss the issue right off, up front, and confront it together.

Instead, she had resisted telling Sam that after his quarrel with Cody, their son had taken an all-night bus to Seattle.

That was important, overwhelming. She should have told him. Yet she hadn't. Why?

Because it would make her look like a failure. A mother who lacked control of her own son. She was tired of feeling like that. She was embarrassed. She imagined people saying, "Her son took off on her." People's opinions shouldn't matter, but to Michelle they always had.

She hadn't seen her father since breakfast the day before. He'd gone to the air park. She had spent the day painting and worrying and waiting for Cody to call.

He hadn't.

It was all she could do to keep from jumping in the Rover and racing across three states to him. But she forced herself to stick by her decision. The old Michelle would have done that, and the old Cody would have expected it. But things were going to be different now. Different and new. Until Thursday night, she had thought Sam would be a part of it, but now she wasn't so sure. The child they had made together should be a part of their love. Instead, he had become a symbol of their doubts and differences.

It was just as well that she had come to see those differences now rather than sinking even deeper in love with Sam. The thing to remember was the hurt. The sense that, when all was said and done, the past few weeks had been an interlude. By nature, an interlude had to end.

Sam McPhee was all her heart wanted. But she was so scared. Was she to spend her life with this ache of yearning in her chest, the walking wounded of failed love?

She had made a studious effort not to try to second-guess Sam. Who knew what he was thinking, blowing up at Cody and then disappearing like that? Maybe everything got a little too real for him. Maybe he started thinking about what it would be like actually to be married, to be the father of a difficult teen. Maybe it was not what he wanted after all.

And so she couldn't look to him for comfort. Her wounds had to stay private. The pain was too raw, too sharp to show anyone yet.

The past weeks must have happened to someone else, she thought. Her giddy happiness with Sam felt surreal, a fairy tale made of myth and spun sugar. No one's life could actually turn out like that, she realized. But her hopeful, foolish heart reminded her that at the center of every fairy tale lay a truth that gave the story its power.

Lord. Even now. Even after last night, she was still dumb enough to hope. It was a shock to realize that even though she loved Sam with everything that was in her, it wasn't enough. Her throat filled up, and her eyes swam, and she blinked frantically. She decided to go riding, work on her painting, try to feel normal for a while.

And maybe, please God, maybe, wait for the phone to ring.

The crisp edge of winter kept its hold on the ranch even though a dazzling sun kept trying to warm things up. On her way to the barn, Michelle passed the calving shed, hearing sounds of bovine distress and a few well-chosen swear words. In the lot adjacent to the stockyard, protesting steers were being loaded for shipping to some rodeo or other. A dark-skinned young man, carrying a bucket of oats for the horses, tipped his hat in greeting. She remembered how enchanting she had found all of this when she had come to her father, eager and shy, to live as his daughter for the first time. They couldn't have known then the turns their lives would take, and she had never dreamed she'd be back here again, loving this place even more, if that was possible.

On a day like this, Blue Rock was the idyllic place in the imagination of everyone who had ever dreamed of the West. The rim of mountains, the fields of snow with bunchgrass showing through, the clusters of buildings and ranch vehicles spoke both poetry and permanence.

She heard a grinding of tires and saw a car turn in from the main road. Sunlight glared off the windshield of her father's Cadillac as it parked in front of the old building she used as a studio. Shading her eyes, she watched two people get out of the car. Her heart seemed to drop to her knees.

Cody and her father didn't see her as they went around back to the trunk. They were both wearing leather flight jackets and weary grins. She couldn't believe it. Couldn't believe her father had gone after Cody, and that Cody had come back to Blue Rock. Yet it made perfect sense. Gavin had done for Cody what he should have done for Michelle—brought him back to the place he belonged, whether he knew it yet or not.

Her throat stung as she watched her father and her son facing each other—Gavin tall and white-haired and distinguished, Cody slender and intense. They spoke for a moment, then Gavin clasped Cody's shoulder in a way that was so awkwardly male that she couldn't help smiling through her tears.

For so long, she had thought Gavin had been no father at all to her. But last night, she had sat down with the blank book the transplant team had given her months ago, when she had first agreed to the transplant. The pages had stayed blank, as empty as she had been before coming to Montana. Then last night, she had lain in bed and written in the book, and by the time she finished, she understood that Gavin had been her father in the only way he knew how. She had written of the precious time she and Gavin had spent together seventeen years ago. An early-morning ride on horseback. Lazy afternoons on the porch, watching the mountain wind ripple through the fields of avalanche lilies. Evenings by the fire, sketching while he read his mail. That was what he had given her. And it was, she suddenly knew, enough. Enough. *Thank you, Daddy.*

She blotted her cheeks while Cody lifted the lid of the trunk. He took out something she hadn't seen in a very long time—her portfolio case.

The tears threatened again, and Michelle pressed a hand to her mouth. Cody went into the studio, and she was dying to know what he was up to, but she had something to do first. She went and got the journal and took it to her father.

Gavin's expression indicated that he recognized the book.

"Read it," she said, kissing him on the cheek. "I think you'll like it."

"I love you, honey," he said, taking the gift. "Now go see your boy. He's got a lot to say for himself."

"Thanks, Daddy. Thanks for bringing him home." She kissed him again, then hurried to the studio to find Cody. "Hey, stranger," she said from the doorway.

His shoulders stiffened, and the reaction stung her. Lately it was automatic, the way he braced himself for the worst. He turned to face her. "Mom," he said. "Mom, I'm really sorry I took off."

She tried to say something, but no words came out. She stepped into the main room of the studio, and her heart soared.

Cody had taken out the paintings and lined them up against a wall. The light flowed over bold splashes of color, and she thought about how long it had been since she had looked, really looked at her own work. The paintings were honest and painfully beautiful, filled with truth and emotion. She could see the evolution of frustration, grief, joy. When she regarded the paintings now, they seemed to have been done by someone else. Someone more emotional. More tender. With more of her soul to give. It seemed a miracle to Michelle that these images had come from her. There was one significant painting missing, she realized. It was the snow scene—the one that hung over the mantel in Sam's house.

Sam.

Pushing away the ache of regret, she opened her arms. Cody hugged her, and she marveled at how tall he was, tall and wiry and stronger than she remembered.

"Hey, Mom—"

"Cody—"

They both spoke at once. She gave a little laugh and stepped back. "I'm so glad you came back," she said.

He picked at the bandage on his hand. "I never should have left like that, Mom. It was so stupid."

"We'll get over it," she said, and was pleased to feel actual conviction behind the words. "Cody, I owe you an apology."

His face paled. "Mom, no. I'm the one who—"

"I do." She held up a hand to quiet him. She felt a sting of regret for the way things had been between them lately. She'd always thought it was her job to protect him from being hurt, but she'd wound up teaching him to shy away from emotion. "I was awful to you sometimes, Cody, and it was my own frustration making me pick at you and fuss at you. That was wrong, and—"

"Mom, there's some stuff I need to tell you."

Struck by his tone, she went over to the cushioned

window seat. Cody was somber and tense as he sat beside her. In Gavin's bulky flight jacket, he looked strange and poignantly familiar. His hair was combed, there were no headphones in sight, and when he looked up at her, she saw both Gavin and Sam in his face. "I screwed up, Mom," he said. "I screwed up big-time."

"What do you mean?"

He rubbed his hands on his thighs. "Um, I don't blame you if you get mad at me."

"So just say it, Cody. I can't read your mind."

He picked at the fraying gauze bandage on his hand. "I didn't tell you the whole truth about Sam taking off Thursday night." His voice was low but steady. "His, um, mother—Tammi Lee—got in trouble. Sam didn't say, but I think she was drinking. So he had to drop everything and go help her."

Michelle's stomach lurched. Sam hadn't said a word about this. He had kept it from her, just as she had kept Cody's disappearance from him. She had never known much about Sam's life with his troubled mother. How hard it must be for him, for them both, every day. And her son had held his silence. Her son . . .

"Why didn't you tell me?" she asked Cody, more baffled than angry.

"I didn't know what to do. Everything happened so quick—Sam was yelling at me about Molly and he made me feel so bad, and then he had to go help his mother. She got fired from her job, see? And I'm the only one who knows the real reason why." His cheeks flamed, and Michelle was shocked to see tears in his eyes. "Some guys from school took money from the shop, and Tammi Lee got the blame. Instead of speaking up, I just let Sam go running off to help her, and then I started thinking how much he'd hate me when he got back, so I didn't tell anyone . . . it just got away from me."

She detected a hint of his old sullenness. But she wouldn't stand for evasion, not anymore. "Those are excuses, Cody. What's the real reason?"

He didn't speak for a moment, and she felt a little shock of disorientation as she watched him fighting tears. "I got scared, Mom," he said.

"Scared of what? Cody, tell me."

"I got scared, thinking about what it would be like to have Sam for a father." The admission was squeezed out of him along with the tears he had been struggling to hold back.

Scared. Michelle's heart skipped a beat. She knew then what Sam had tried to tell her the last time they were together—that Cody was in danger of becoming like her. Holding back and hiding from love because it was frightening. Overwhelming. All her life she tried to buy emotional safety at the risk of feeling only half alive.

"I saw how happy he makes you," Cody added, "and I guess I was afraid you'd love him more than me."

"Oh, son." She touched his face. "It's totally different. You have my heart, all of it, and that will never change."

"I'm sorry, Mom. I'm sorry. I'm sorry." His arms went around her. He still smelled like a boy, of soap and outdoor air, and he still needed his mother. As much as she needed *him*.

"I'll make everything right with Sam and Tammi Lee," he said. "I swear I will. I just hope they forgive me." Cody straightened up and scrubbed at his face with the back of his hand. Then he put his arm around her, and the universe came back into balance.

She gazed at him, and in his eyes, she saw Gavin's

eyes. Her father and her son. It took both of them to make her understand that life was short; who knew how long anyone had? When she got to wherever she was going, she wanted to have painted her paintings. She wanted to have loved with a passion beyond reason. She wanted to know that Cody was not just her son, but her friend.

She used to look at him and wonder where her little boy had gone. Now she realized she'd found him. She'd found him in this hurting, confused, and ultimately good kid who was becoming a good man. She paused, drew a breath, tried to think of the right thing to say.

"You know what's even more scary?" she asked. "It's that I almost lost you, Cody. But I think we're going to be okay." She realized that she'd almost lost Sam because she hadn't trusted herself with him. What she should have done was fling herself into the relationship the way she had flung herself into painting. Because it wasn't just the painting that came back to her after its long sleep in the frozen tundra, but life. And Sam had awakened her to that.

She thought about the transplant. Fear and love were sometimes the same thing, both necessary, unavoidable. Now she understood that it was okay to bleed if you know how to heal.

"So we'll call Sam, right?" Cody said. "He'll give me another chance, won't he?"

She put her hands on his shoulders. Lord, but it felt good to hold him again. She had never felt closer to her son. At sixteen, Cody was learning what she wished she had known long ago—that you have to love even though it hurts, even though there are no guarantees. You have to spend it all even though you never know what you'll get in return.

"Oh, Cody." She wanted to reassure him that of course

Sam would forgive him. But how did she know that? She'd had sixteen years to love and understand Cody, to learn who he was. Without all that groundwork, Sam's forgiveness would have to be a leap of faith.

Chapter 52

*I*t snowed later that day. An oppressive quiet shrouded the land, and flying snowflakes pocked the colorless sky. Michelle rode beside Cody in the Range Rover with headlights shining in the bleak day. The heartbeat rhythm of the windshield wipers, batting at the snow, punctuated the silence.

This was nuts, she thought. This was asking for heartache. When Cody had phoned Lonepine, he'd spoken to Edward Bliss, and the news was not good. Sam had taken his mother to detox, then brought her back to the house for a day or two while she found her footing. No, Edward wasn't any too sure they wanted company. And yet here she was, driving her son over to Lonepine, just as they had that first day—Lord, was it only three weeks ago?—before Sam and Cody had any idea they were father and son.

Why did she ever think this was a good idea? Barging back into Sam's life, hoping and praying he would let her back in.

Self-doubt and sheer terror pounded in her gut. In the past, the fear would have stopped her from taking this step. She would have chosen emptiness over pain and joy. Now she knew better. For a short and glorious time she had found the essence of all she desired in the arms of Sam McPhee. It was something she wouldn't get another chance at, something most people didn't even experience in a lifetime.

Parking at Lonepine, she stared out the window at the white-quilted landscape that was starving for spring to come again. Tammi Lee stood out on the porch wearing a big jacket with the collar up and smoking a cigarette.

"You want me to come with you?" Michelle asked Cody.

"Nope. I'm on my own."

He got out of the car and walked toward the house. She realized he didn't need her to prop him up as she had so often in the past, even when it would have been better to leave him be.

Tammi Lee tossed out her cigarette and sat very still, waiting for Cody to come to her. She felt drained, wrung out, as if she had just run a marathon. She hated having her grandson see her like this, but this was who she was—someone who had flown high and crashed-landed more times than she could count. She hovered in a low gully, wondering if she'd rise or fall this time.

"Can I talk to you?" Cody asked. His face looked pale and tight, hands jammed hard into his pockets.

"Sure," she said, her breath freezing in the air. She could listen. Yeah, she could do that.

"It's about . . . what happened with the shop and stuff."
He stepped up onto the porch. "That night I borrowed your
car, something happened."

Tammi Lee's head began to buzz, craving her meds.
She focused sharply on the nervous young boy. He was
so good-looking. And right now, he looked as wrung out
as she felt.

"It's my fault the money in the cash register went
missing," he blurted out. "I didn't know—I—it's my fault."

Tammi Lee sat very still. She was so used to getting
kicked in the teeth that she braced herself.

"The cash disappeared when I went into the shop after
hours," he said. "It's all my fault."

"Did you take the money?" she asked quietly.

His hands dug even deeper into his pockets. "That
doesn't matter. I was responsible. And I blew it. I went to
see Mrs. Jacobs today, and I explained it all to her, paid
her what was missing. She feels real bad, and she's going
to ask you to come back to work. That is, if you want
to." He scuffed his foot at a frozen lump of snow on the
edge of the porch. "I'm real sorry," he added. "I'll do
whatever I have to do to make it right. I just—I'd like to
have a second chance."

Tammi Lee felt herself rising a little, hovering above
the abyss. Her head pounded, but the pain meant nothing.
This was it, she realized. She could forgive this boy and
go on from here, or she could let anger and resentment
drag her down.

When she looked into his eyes, she saw Sam's eyes.
Sam, who'd given her more second chances than anyone
had a right to expect. Sam, who deserved a chance of his
own. There was really no choice to be made. She stood
up and opened her arms. A tentative smile started in Cody's
eyes as he hugged her. Over his shoulder she saw Michelle

Turner standing by her car, watching them, one hand pressed to her mouth.

"I think we're going to be all right," Tammi Lee whispered, and she started to soar, lifted by hope. "I think we're going to be just fine."

Sam came out of the main barn and started walking toward Michelle. Her knees felt liquid, threatening to buckle. She was aware of the bruising cold, the snow coming over the tops of her boots, her incision aching.

She used to think healing meant stitching up, scarring over, turning a mess to neatness. Now she understood that she had to let things melt down, unravel, and then come back together in the way they were meant to be.

She had to quit looking for a reason that things happened. This was life, it was messy, and now she knew better than to expect a guarantee. Her heart pounded, she had never felt more alive. She had no idea what the expression on her face was, but she didn't care. When she looked up at Sam, she saw everything she wanted her future to be.

And no matter what that was, it was bigger and brighter than her dreams had ever been.

Hope and fear were locked, unspoken, in her throat. She and Sam walked to the edge of the snow-covered driveway and stood beneath the twisted skeleton of a crabapple tree.

"Cody blames himself for everything that happened," she said at last. "He wants to make things right with you and your mother."

He looked over at the house, where Cody and Tammi Lee stood very close, talking. "I guess I'm glad to see that."

"Can he?" she forced herself to ask. "Can he make

things right? Can *we*?" She twisted her gloved fingers into knots.

"I've been asking myself the same thing."

"Last night, we were both still hiding things. You didn't tell me about your mother, and—" she swallowed hard "—I didn't explain to you that Cody had run away." She forced herself to meet his disbelieving gaze. "He took the bus to Seattle. I wanted to tell you, Sam, but I didn't know how. My father brought him back this morning."

"I guess I'll just let Cody do the explaining, then." Sam held her gaze for an endless moment. "We'll give it our best shot, honey. Okay?"

She managed to choke out his name, and the dam inside her broke like the thawing mountain streams. The sobs of relief came from the deepest part of her, a part she couldn't discipline or control. Sam was a wall of warmth, silent and steady as he absorbed the brunt of her tears. She found a sanctuary, not a threat, in loving him.

"I was so afraid." Her hands clutched at his jacket. "I was so afraid you'd decided Cody and I were too much for you."

His arms slid around her. "Ah, Michelle. Everything's not going to be perfect all the time. But we can survive the mistakes. You know that. You *know*."

"Sometimes I think I'm just not good enough at this," she whispered.

He held her away from him, and dear God, he had the most magnificent face, so full of hardness and soul, weathered by life's joys and sorrows. Snowflakes landed and disappeared on his cheeks, his shoulders. "We'll work it out. You and me and our son."

"*Our* son. It sounds just right." There was a catch in her throat, and she swallowed hard. "I love you, Sam." It was time to say it, long past time. It was so easy. It had turned from impossible to effortless. "I always have, and I always will."

He pulled her against him, pressed his lips to her hair. In that moment, the last of her doubts slid away, and Sam said, "I know, honey. I know."

"You do?"

"Oh yeah."

Michelle closed her eyes as joy settled over them, as silently powerful as new-fallen snow. And like the snow over a stubbled field, it covered everything else—all the flaws and ruts and bruises of the past—with its perfection and purity.

Reading Group Guide

1. The novel begins with a quote by Mignon McLaughlin that reads: "Most of us become parents long before we have stopped being children." What do you think this means? And why do you think the author has chosen this quote to begin her novel?

2. Cody is clearly going through a rebellious phase—Sam describes him as being "mad at the world" after only spending a few hours with him. Why has Cody suddenly become hostile and sullen at age sixteen? Is his attitude due to adolescence or is something else going on?

3. Why do you think Michelle never told Cody who his father was? Should she have worked harder to find Sam for Cody's sake or do you understand why she made the decisions she did? Similarly, was it wrong of Michelle not to tell Sam that she was pregnant with his son, even though she believed he had left her?

4. Was Sam was wrong to leave town the way he did in 1983? Should he have been in touch with Michelle despite his circumstances?

5. Sam and Michelle had a passionate love affair when they were teenagers, but then fell out of touch for sixteen years. Yet when they reunite their attraction is as strong as ever. Do you believe that love can sustain itself even after a relationship dissolves? Do you think it's possible to ever forget your first love?

6. What do you think of Michelle's decision to come back to Montana in order to help her father? Not only does her decision have emotional consequences, but it also has physical ones. If you were in her position, would you have done the same thing?

7. Michelle and Brad have been together for three years, but they aren't married. Why is Michelle with Brad? How is he different from Sam? Have you ever stayed in a relationship that didn't make you entirely happy or that lacked a certain degree of passion?

8. This novel is in large part about parenting and the complicated and imperfect relationships

between parents and children. Discuss the different parental relationships in this novel. How are the various parental figures (Michelle, Sam, Gavin, Tammi Lee) alike? How are they different?

9. Michelle is a painter, but she hasn't painted in years until she returns to Crystal City. Why is painting so important to Michelle and why hasn't she been able to paint since leaving Montana sixteen years ago? What role does "creation" play in this novel?

10. What role does class play in this novel? How do class differences, real or perceived, affect the actions of Sam, Michelle, Gavin, and Tammi Lee?

11. When Gavin admits the truth of his actions to Michelle at the end of the book, he says, "Sometimes a parent does the wrong thing for the right reasons." What does he mean by this? Why is Michelle able to forgive him so easily?

12. How do you interpret the book's title? Who is the "you" the title refers to?